D1631336

THE VERSATILE DEFOE

To the Memory of Paula
1912–1955
"And death shall have no dominion"

DANIEL DE FOE.

THE VERSATILE DEFOE

An Anthology of Uncollected Writings by Daniel Defoe

Edited and Introduced
by
LAURA ANN CURTIS

1979
GEORGE PRIOR PUBLISHERS
London . England

Published in the United Kingdom by
George Prior Publishers
37–41 Bedford Row
London WC1R 4JH

British Library Cataloguing in Publication Data

Defoe, Daniel
The versatile Defoe.
I. Title II. Curtis, Laura Ann
828'.4'08 PR3401

ISBN 0–86043–210–6

Printed in Great Britain by
Biddles Ltd, Guildford, Surrey

CONTENTS

(Reproduced by kind permission of the Mansell Collection and the Mary Evans Picture Library)

ACKNOWLEDGEMENTS

The studies culminating in this book have claimed a good part of ten years of hard and frequently lonely work. But the scholar's retreat is the road to a lost world of fascinating personalities and issues; in addition, it leads to the satisfaction of becoming part of a cherished and permanent community. It is to a few of the members of this community that I should like to express my thanks.

I am very grateful to Professor Karl Hardach of Rutgers University for guiding me through the economic history of Defoe's age. Professor Gerald Straka of the department of history, University of Delaware, by an almost uncanny instinct, found his way to the heart of several matters about Defoe and his times that required greater clarification. Dean Henry Snyder of the University of Kansas kindly imparted to me that portion of his encyclopedic knowledge pertaining to Arthur Maynwaring and the Whig press; after his scrutiny, any error of bibliographical reasoning I may have committed about the pamphlet *A Letter from a Gentleman at the Court of St. Germains* is entirely my own. Dr. Frank O'Gorman of the department of history, University of Manchester, has been very generous about sharing with me the preliminary findings of his research on the middle classes in the eighteenth century; Professor Herbert Rowen of the department of history, Rutgers University, has directed me to sources of historical details arcane to literary scholars; and Professor Geoffrey Holmes of the department of history, University of Lancaster, has graciously taken time to answer questions about Robert Harley and to send me an elusive article of his own.

Professional colleagues and writer friends who have read and offered valuable criticisms of the manuscript include, first and foremost, my husband, Professor Michael Curtis of the department of political science, Rutgers University; Mr. Stephen Dobell, my helpful, considerate, and efficient editor and collaborator in modernizing Defoe's texts; Professor George Dorris of the department of English, York College, City University of New York; Ms. Claire Paisner, Mrs. Ruth Rarback, and Mr. Kenneth Frost of New York City; Mr. Stanley Yaker, assistant general attorney, Office of Legal Counsel, of New York University; Professor Eloise Goreau of the department of English, Rider College; and Professor Manuel Schonhorn of the department of English, Southern Illinois University at Carbondale. I have been continuously sustained in an arduous undertaking by the enthusiasm of Professor Sidney Ratner of the department of history, Rutgers University.

I must also thank Professor C. F. Main, Associate Director of the Research Council of Rutgers University, for the inspired suggestion that I concern myself with the uncollected writings of Defoe. Professors Daniel Howard and Bridget Lyons of the department of English of Rutgers University made constructive editorial comments on my original manuscript. But my particular debt is to Professor Paul Fussell of the department of English, Rutgers University, whose 1961–62 seminar on Swift, Burke, Johnson, and Gibbon first opened my eyes to the power of the written word and attuned my ears to "the other harmony of prose".

New York, 1978 *Laura Ann Curtis*

A NOTE ON THE TEXTS

With the exception of *The Complete English Tradesman,* all the texts are based on first editions. The aim of the conservative modernization has been to make Defoe's texts easily accessible to present-day readers, while retaining the flavour of original spellings and punctuation. Since neither Defoe nor his printers were as precise about consistency in spelling or punctuation as is now customary in journalism, decisions about accidentals or printing errors have not always been easy to make.

Typography has been normalized to modern usage: capitals and italics have frequently been eliminated, spaces between two words now written as one have been closed up, and ſ has been replaced by s. Punctuation has been altered where necessary for clarity: colons, in particular, frequently used by Defoe where a modern writer would use a full stop, have usually been replaced by periods.

Spelling has generally been left in its original form, with certain exceptions. Contractions have been spelt out in full. As consistently as possible for the modernizers' fallible eyes, distracting variants of words which Defoe spells in their twentieth-century form elsewhere in the texts, have been normalized.

INTRODUCTION

Few who have read *Robinson Crusoe* are aware that its author, Daniel Defoe (1660–1731), was the most prolific writer in English literary history. Even those familiar with *Moll Flanders*, which has risen in critical esteem in the twentieth century and is often studied as the first English novel, are unlikely to have more than a nodding acquaintance with the titles of Defoe's other major fictions: *Captain Singleton*, *Colonel Jack*, *A Journal of the Plague Year*, *Memoirs of a Cavalier*, *Roxana*. And literary critics who have read little of the non-fiction in which Defoe served his apprenticeship continue to make many erroneous inferences about the sensibility displayed in his fictions, because they do not know the whole man.

This general ignorance about one of the most important of English writers is not surprising, since collected editions of Defoe's writing contain only a small fraction of the entire corpus (557 items, according to the final calculations of his best-known twentieth-century bibliographer,[1] and one of the items, Defoe's *Review*, runs to over twenty volumes), and it is difficult to obtain copies of the uncollected works. In addition, Defoe's ideas were so complex and so intimately enmeshed with the events of their age that modern readers find him difficult to understand, embracing with relief those of his works that seem simple in conception and plain and forceful in style. The following anthology, therefore, is intended as a partial remedy for the lack of texts, of explication of individual works, and of recognition of Defoe's versatility in interests and in style. It does not propose to substitute lesser for greater works in the familiar Defoe canon; rather, it aims to promote a more nuanced understanding of Defoe's masterpieces in his readers.

Few aspects of the life of Defoe's times escaped his alert and sympathetic eye; grasping Defoe's protean consciousness is tantamount to grasping the entire early eighteenth century. But readers who wish to know more about him could do no better than to begin with politics, for the politics of his age played a greater part in shaping Defoe's mind and art than it did for contemporary writers also active in politics, Joseph Addison, Richard Steele, and Jonathan Swift. The experience of political writing taught Defoe which of his many styles was most eagerly read, accustomed him to writing quickly and with apparent spontaneity, trained him to express only one part of his mind at any one time, through one point of view or one character, and gave him practice in shaping facts to his own design. Above all, it seems to have fixed his novelistic perspective on the quintessential political issue of power. All of his fictions concern the efforts of a protagonist, usually like Defoe an outsider, to control an initially chaotic environment, either natural or social.

Defoe came to the attention of leading Whig statesmen in the 1690s, but his spectacular rise to national prominence took place with the immediate success of his *True-Born Englishman* of 1701, a vigorous poem defending the Dutch-born William III against the xenophobia of Defoe's countrymen, and continued with his provocative *Legion's Memorial*, also of 1701, calling a recalcitrant House of Commons to task for its refusal to vote war supplies to King William, reminding the M.P.s that they were accountable to the freeholders of England, and concluding with the ominous words, "For Englishmen are no more to be slaves to Parliaments than to a King. Our name is LEGION, and we are many." But the first stage of his public political life ended in personal disaster in 1703. The pillory and jail were the Nonconformist Defoe's reward for the 1702 pamphlet, *The Shortest Way with the Dissenters*, in which he had mimicked the fulminations of the High-Church priest, Dr. Henry Sacheverell, against Protestant Dissenters from the Church of England. Defoe was released from jail as a result of behind-the-scenes activity by Robert Harley, later Earl of Oxford, who as Speaker of the House of Commons, according to one report, had received *Legion's Memorial* from the hands of Defoe himself. Harley was particularly interested in the power of public opinion in politics and the ability of a good writer to mould this opinion. He had perhaps also been impressed by the effect of Defoe's *Hymn to the Pillory*, distributed while its writer stood exposed to public view; it had contributed to converting a potentially garbage-hurling pro-Church of England mob into a flower-strewing audience. In 1704, with backing from Harley, Defoe began his long-lived journal, the *Review*, and from 1703 until 1714, with an intermission between 1708 and 1710, served Harley in many political capacities.

The heat and turbulence of the political world in which Defoe moved during the reigns of William III and Anne come as a shock to a twentieth-century reader taking a first plunge into the polemical literature of the period. Far more acrimonious than the journalism of our age of the Fourth Estate, political writing of the late seventeenth and early eighteenth centuries occupied a remarkably large number of brilliant, talented, and above all, contentious partisans. Many who remained on the sidelines were acute observers, addressing penetrating comments to friends in private letters. And as a foreign commentator, describing Londoners' avidity for news, reported in 1726, the very shoeblacks "club together to purchase a farthing paper", and working-men refused to begin the day before they had devoured the latest newspapers.[2] The political arena, then, was a brightly-lit stage where the slightest gesture of a principal player, statesman or writer, was immediately interpreted in a thousand different ways in the whispers of an audience of sharp-eyed connoisseurs.

The reasons for this intense activity and excitement were complex. First of all, the reigns of William, Anne, and George I occurred before the post-Tudor emergence of a period of political stability, defined by J. H. Plumb as "the acceptance by society of its political institutions, and of those classes of men or officials who control them".[3] Parties and factions were engaged in a fierce war for political power, a war complicated by the fluid and unsettled relationship between Crown and Parliament. Second, the English were bitterly divided over major political issues, most basic of which was the very legitimacy of the national agreement to bypass the male heir of James II in favour first of his daughters, then of a more distant Protestant line of cousins. While Mary, wife of William III, then her younger sister, Anne Stuart, occupied the throne, misgivings could temporarily be repressed; but when, in 1701, after the death of the last of Anne's many children, the Hanover line was designated successor to the Stuart, and when, after her accession in 1702, Anne's uncertain health compelled attention to the imminent end of her reign, a painful facing up to the question of the Succession could no longer be postponed. Complicating the disagreement over the Hanover succession were the unsettled questions of the extent of toleration to be accorded to Protestant Dissenters from the Church of England and the degree to which England would accept the continental responsibilities accompanying her rise as a major European power. English men and women could and did take different stands on each of these issues, a propensity that makes their classification as Whig or Tory difficult for modern readers and complicated extraordinarily the day-to-day decisions of both parties trying to accommodate the claims of each issue.

To the splintered power centres concomitant with so fierce a struggle over power and principles fuel was supplied by a large and combustible electorate that had entered the political arena during the course of the seventeenth century. According to the calculations of W. A. Speck, "The electoral system was more representative in Anne's reign than it had ever been before, or was to be well into Victoria's". And this excitable electorate, with its crucial weather-vane seats in the House of Commons "dictating the fate of Whigs and Tories throughout virtually the whole period from 1679 to 1722", was exercised in seventeen elections in forty-three years, "or one on average every two and a half years".[4] Twelve general elections, more in so short a period than at any time in English history, took place between 1689 and 1715.

For the capture of voters in the fierce struggle over power and principles during what Geoffrey Holmes calls the first age of party, the press was quickly pre-empted by parties and factions as a crucial tool. The lapsing of the Licensing Act in 1695 and Parliament's inability to frame a viable new law despite general agreement that some pre-publication censorship was advisable, resulted in an explosion of polemical literature in the form of newspapers, newsletters, journals, pamphlets, broadsides, lampoons, and so forth. Paper wars were waged as various issues of the period forced their way to the forefront of the general controversy: the highpoint was reached in 1711–13 during the ministry of Robert Harley, when the question of whether or not to end the War of the Spanish Succession by making peace with France at the expense of England's allies was decided in the affirmative. Many of the writers of newspapers and pamphlets were humble Grub Street hacks, but some of the journalists were talented, many of the pamphleteers counted among the most distinguished minds in public life, and a few of the writers—Daniel Defoe, Jonathan Swift, Richard Steele—were giants of literature. The London coffee-house was the place where men of "a remarkably wide social gamut",[5] from peer to porter, rubbed shoulders as they perused or picked up the latest news in discussion; ale-houses and inns served as news centres outside London. Henchmen of politicians gathered or spread rumours, going as far as to send "runners" to guide the conversations or to stir up the coffee-house groups.

The struggle for power, the struggle over basic issues, and the attempt to capture a large electorate (or at least its crucial volatile element) by influencing public opinion, explain why there was so much political writing in the early eighteenth century and why it was of so feverish a nature. Another reason for its heat was the temperament both of the writers themselves and of the audiences to which they were appealing. Very far from what we think of today as the typical Englishman, restrained, tolerant, moderate, was the character of John Bull as described by John Arbuthnot in 1712: "Bull, in the main, was an honest plain-dealing fellow, choleric, bold, and of a very unconstant temper. ... John's temper depended very much upon the air; his spirits rose and fell with the weather-glass".

The immediate success with the English public of Richard Steele's periodical, the *Tatler*, like the even greater success of Joseph Addison's *Spectator*, both of them designed to improve the manners of the age by the example of a correct, restrained, and gently humorous style, can largely be attributed to a general longing for relative peace and quiet. As Addison had hoped, his *Spectator* made a rapid escape from the stormy surroundings of the coffee-house into the more congenial intimacy of the family tea-table. Universal admiration for Addison's essays in the eighteenth and nineteenth centuries, contrasted with increasing reservations among literary connoisseurs of the twentieth century, suggests that the turbulent English spirit required a taming process of more than two hundred years before jaded tastes began to call for the vigour of a Swift or a Defoe.

If Addison's and Steele's principal contribution to the emergence of stability in eighteenth-century England was the lowering of emotional temperatures through the refining of manners, part of Defoe's principal contribution was to hasten the eventual settlement of the major political issues themselves. He was an enthusiastic supporter of the Revolution: of the hereditary Protestant monarchy it prescribed, of the fundamental rights of Parliament and people it recognised, not to be dispensed with by royal prerogative, and of the legal toleration it entailed for Protestant Dissenters. He also campaigned vigorously for an active foreign policy in continental affairs for an England that was now a major European power, no longer under the tutelage of France. He advocated, was even an influential participant in, negotiations for the union of England and Scotland. An outspoken opponent of the theories of divine right and of passive obedience professed by adherents of the Stuart dynasty, a ridiculer of Jacobites (supporters of James II and of his son, the Pretender), Defoe contributed to turning England away from its Stuart past to the present of its revolution settlement.

In economics, where even his opponents admitted that "he was generally looked on as a man who thoroughly understood the theory of trade and the true interest of this Nation", his sympathies were with the dynamic element in English economic life: business in its various aspects of finance, overseas commerce, domestic trade, and manufacture. His writings helped to establish this element as respectable at a time when the landed gentry was generally accorded a monopoly on virtue.

Defoe was a mercantilist, concerned first about the wealth of the nation as a whole and only second with that of individual members. He was one of a very small minority, however, who advocated high wages for workers, believing that their prosperity would advance the prosperity of the nation. Sympathetic to the financial revolution occurring in his time with the 1694 founding of the Bank of England, Defoe may have had some new insights into the area of public finance. Nevertheless, he cannot be considered an original economic theorist. Possibly he possessed the requisite talent, but his interests were always too diverse to permit him to concentrate even upon the whore he "really doated upon", as he admitted on 11 June 1713, in the final issue of his *Review*. He was an excellent statistician, economic mediator, and financial administrator. As an intelligent economic observer, his name is greatly respected by economic historians of our time; his descriptions of contemporary conditions appear unfailingly in modern economic histories dealing with special problems of the early eighteenth century.

Perhaps even more important than Defoe's contribution to the emergence of political stability in eighteenth-century England through his political and economic writings was his contribution to social and literary history through his popularization of the notion of modernity itself. As defined by J. H. Plumb, modernity is the systematic effort to improve upon nature for the purpose of ameliorating man's living conditions.[6] During the eighteenth century, this new world view spread from a social and intellectual elite down through the entire social hierarchy, permeating all social classes, highest to lowest, oldest to youngest, and eventually displaced the traditional world view of a static providential order. The instantaneous popularity of *Robinson Crusoe*, published in 1719, and its enduring appeal to all classes and all nations, attest to Defoe's crystallization of the modern spirit in his first work of fiction.

Alone on his island, Crusoe learns slowly and arduously to control his own wayward impulses while co-operating with nature for the purpose of harnessing its force to improve his living conditions. Single-handed he constructs a substitute civilization to replace the one he has lost as the result of his restless inability to settle down in a fixed social niche or occupation. The social impact of *Robinson Crusoe* must have been tremendous; a contemporary writer envious of Defoe's success reported, "There is not an old Woman that can go to the Price of it, but buys thy *Life and Adventures*, and leaves it as a Legacy, with the *Pilgrims Progress*, the *Practice of Piety*, and *God's Revenge against Murther*, to her Posterity ...". Even the fastidious, who rarely acknowledged good writing unless it bore the cachet of a strict training in classics, were impressed by *Robinson Crusoe*, Alexander Pope remarking that it was excellent.

Crusoe's paean to control is reiterated throughout Defoe's writings, where a recurring motif is the triumph of moderation and cool-headedness over emotion, anger, or violence. As an Irishman, James Joyce testified with some acerbity to this quality in Defoe, one of his favourite writers, when he characterized it as the English colonizing spirit, and Defoe as the quintessential Englishman. This direct confrontation between primitive forces, human passions or energies of nature, and civilizing forces, dramatized repeatedly in Defoe's popular instruction manuals such as *The Complete English Tradesman*, *Religious Courtship*, and *The Family Instructor*, must have contributed to the dissemination of the new world view throughout the middle and lower ranks of society.

Although many of Defoe's works contributing to the emergence of political stability in England, and to the dissemination of the new world view that characterizes the modern period, were couched in a plain style comprehensible to the semi-literate, his role as political writer required his mastery of a variety of styles. Members of the Houses of Commons and of Lords were avid readers of the pamphlets, periodicals, and newspapers poured out by the presses on all the major issues of the period. The possibility of influencing votes on specific legislative measures in this audience of educated, information-seeking readers probably accounts for the high level of political writing in Defoe's day and for the participation of important literary figures in its production. Printed material was designed also for particular segments of the general electorate, for non-voters who nevertheless counted in the moulding of public opinion, and even for the mob, and the versatile Defoe tried his hand at most genres and at most audiences. Recognized by his contemporaries as the foremost of journalists, with some of his pamphlets best-sellers, many of them influential, and his best-known periodical, the *Review*, quoted in governmental and business circles, Defoe played an important role in shaping public opinion among many different sectors of the nation, and in modernizing the political, religious, economic, and social ideas of his time. In addition, as the most clear-sighted observer of his age, Defoe contributed to posterity's understanding of that period. His first-hand accounts of contemporary conditions and events serve so frequently as primary sources for historians of our day that the chapter heading "Defoe's England" has become a cliché.

Nevertheless, Defoe's direct and straightforward advocacy of modernizing ideas is apparent only to the superficial eye: his contemporaries distrusted him, regarding him as shady and somewhat disreputable; twentieth-century scholars acquainted with more than a few of his works have difficulty in deciding precisely what this Proteus believed. Addison allegorized him in the *Trial and Conviction of Count Tariff* of 1713 as follows:

> When the Count had finished his speech, he desired leave to call in his witnesses, which was granted: when immediately there came to the bar a man with a hat drawn over his eyes in such a manner that it was impossible to see his face. He spoke in the spirit, nay, in the very language,

of the Count, repeated his arguments, and confirmed his assertions. Being asked his name, he said the world called him Mercator [the name of a journal Defoe was writing in favour of the commercial articles of the Treaty of Utrecht, opposed by Whigs like Addison]: but as for his true name, his age, his lineage, his religion, his place of abode, they were particulars, which for certain reasons, he was obliged to conceal. The court found him such a false, shuffling, prevaricating rascal, that they set him aside, as a person unqualified to give his testimony in a court of justice. ...

Much of the contemporary distrust of Defoe was the product of circumstances over which he had little control: the violence of partisanship, his close relationship with the controversial Robert Harley, and his occupation as ministerial writer justifying deviations from opposition purity of principle inevitable in the day-to-day execution of policy. In addition, Defoe's political and economic ideas, idiosyncratic amalgams of conservatism and modernity, were complex; and the moderation he claimed to espouse and to which he usually adhered is the political stance most difficult to define and most liable to misunderstanding. Finally, Defoe's own history, behaviour, and style, partly his own choice, contributed to his contemporary reputation for duplicity.

Although many counted themselves as either Whig or Tory, several of the most influential statesmen of the period fell into neither category, becoming aligned with one or the other party only because of irresistible political pressure that prevented them from executing the duties of their office without eventual capitulation to extremists of one side or the other. King William, the Duke of Marlborough, the Earl of Godolphin, and Robert Harley were a few of the most eminent of these "trimmers", the pejorative defended by the great Marquis of Halifax as a compliment in his famous essay, "Character of a Trimmer". Defoe, who admired Halifax, wrote for all three of these moderate statesmen; like Swift, he was bitterly reviled as a turncoat when he deserted the Whigs serving Godolphin to enroll under Harley's Tory ministry in 1710.

Harley himself was a complex figure. In an age of bribery and licentiousness, he was an incorruptible official, frugal with public money, a faithful family man, a pious Christian, loved by numerous friends and followers. His exemplary private life was probably an important factor in Queen Anne's warm affection for him. The most illustrious member of a close-knit family active in political life, he shared with his kinsmen an abiding concern for integrity in political behaviour. Nevertheless, the sobriquet accorded him by his many political rivals and enemies was "Robin the Trickster". He deserted his first political partners, Whigs, to join with Tories opposing King William's policies, and he was regarded as a quasi-Whig by partisan Tories, especially after 1710. His biographer describes "the cloak and dagger aura that always clung to Harley—spies planted everywhere, constantly intriguing".[7]

Because of his shifting from Whigs to Tories, his attacks on the members of the Whig Junto under William III, his disagreements with his moderate, non-partisan fellow managers under Queen Anne, the Earl of Godolphin and the Duke of Marlborough, and his engineering of the ministerial revolution of 1710 that swept Godolphin and the Whigs out of power and substituted his own initially moderate but eventually extremist Tory ministry, Harley is still a controversial figure to twentieth-century historians. The central debate is on whether he was an unprincipled opportunist, primarily interested in advancing the power of his family and himself by attacking the Junto, Godolphin, Marlborough, and Tory High-Churchmen and partisans; or whether he was a moderate, committed above all to the principle of constitutional balance between Crown and Parliament and therefore opposed to the control of the ministry by the party dominant in Parliament. A second controversy is whether or not his insistence upon separation of executive from legislative power with its corollary of a ministry above parties was quixotic.

Because of the close relationship between the puzzling Harley and his mouthpiece Defoe, one's judgment of Defoe's political morality and realism is almost inseparable from one's judgment of Harley's. The connection between Defoe and Harley was a curious one, partly because both men were highly secretive, and partly because Defoe acted almost as alter ego to his employer, performing many services in addition to writing: he was a secret service agent, organizer of a news and public information network, personal agent in the negotiations leading to the 1707 union between England and Scotland, and contributor of advice on political tactics, constitutional issues, foreign commercial and colonial ventures, and political issues. Defoe's letters to his superior, an eminent bibliophile who was a compulsive collector of papers, advising him even about personal morality in the matter of lying, are almost intimate in tone, in spite of the social barrier between the two men never transgressed by Defoe. Defoe later claimed that he had always written according to his own conscience and that Harley had never dictated to him. Since from 1703 to 1714 (except for the 1708–10 intermission when Harley had been edged out of office and the services of his personal propagandist transferred to Godolphin) he tacked and veered in the wake of his master, contemporary observers and later commentators have been sceptical about his claim, especially because, like Leslie Stephen, most have approached Defoe with the prejudice that his chief talent was for telling lies convincingly.

Harley was a consummate politician, hypersensitive to the motives and impulses of others, alert and responsive to the current of public opinion. His observation to Swift that it is an easier and safer rule in politics "to watch Incidents as they come, and then turn them to the Advantage of what [one] pursues, than pretend to foresee them at a great Distance",[8] was based upon his early experience of attempting to organize the anarchic backbench country gentlemen to "follow a concerted policy of opposition".[9] According to Angus McInnes, he preferred appeals to the mind over the use of patronage: "The essence of Harley's programme was of course the appeal to conscience".[10] In addition to his political experience and predilection, his personal manner—he was a turgid public speaker, a dilatory conveyor of instructions, a man who rarely finished a sentence or made his meaning clear verbally—suggests that he gave Defoe a great deal of freedom in executing his duties.

Defoe, who possessed to an uncanny degree the gift of empathy, presumably initiated many of his projects on his own (on one occasion he even composed a list of instructions to himself on behalf of his dilatory employer), guided by his sense of Harley's political direction and the feeling of the nation; and his instinctive understanding of the former was aided by similarities in temperament as well as in principle between the two men. Even their writing styles resembled each other in some ways: biblical references, concrete, homely expressions, appreciation of the difference in verisimilitude between circumstantial and generalized narrative.[11] When Defoe insisted so loudly that he had always written according to his own mind, he probably felt partially justified in claiming that the policies he had supported were as much his own as they were his employer's.

The contrast between Defoe's relationship with Harley and Swift's furnishes a striking example of the difference between tacit and overt direction—yet Swift too claimed that he had always been independent. Temperamentally more akin to Bolingbroke, Harley's extremist Tory colleague, Swift never really understood Harley in spite of being entertained by him almost as a social equal. Their relationship began in 1710, when Harley sought Swift out, knowing that, like the Defoe of 1701–3, Swift was capable of arousing public opinion by his writing. His pen brought rapid success to the new periodical, the *Examiner*, the official organ of the Tory ministry. In addition to writing and directing other writers working on the journal, Swift produced semi-official pamphlets like the best-selling *Conduct of the Allies* (1711). Chief press adviser to the ministry, he directed a corps of government writers and offered advice on politics, on propaganda (himself taking a leading role in the Tory vilification of the military hero, the Duke of Marlborough), and on press relations (including the dispensing of patronage and the stepping up of prosecutions of opposition political writers instigated by the hot-headed Bolingbroke). All these activities were conducted with such a fanfare as to offend his former Whig friends, to whom his offers of patronage seemed insufferably condescending.

Whereas Swift was revelling at convivial dinners with Oxford and Bolingbroke, Defoe was conversing with his employer by night. The services Swift was performing with such careful direction from Harley and Bolingbroke were being quietly duplicated behind the scenes by the self-sufficient Defoe. While Defoe knew Swift was employed by the ministry (indeed, he probably kept tabs on everyone writing for it), Swift expressed contempt for Defoe, whose name he professed to have forgotten, and was quite unaware of his connection with Harley. While the *Examiner* took an increasingly ferocious partisan tone in appealing to High-Church and landed interests, the *Review* continued speaking in a moderate voice to anti-clerical and business interests. Sophisticated in politics, Defoe accepted as a matter of course Harley's desire to appeal to as many interests as possible, concentrating his efforts on defending and on retaining support for the ministry among moderate Whigs and the London business community. His highly effective *Essay on Public Credit* of 1710 was popularly assumed at the time to have been written by Harley himself, and his new journal, *Mercator*, supported the unpopular articles of commerce between

England and France negotiated by Bolingbroke as part of the peace treaty. Defoe was circumspect in the ministry's campaign to discredit the Duke of Marlborough, who had to be removed from office if the Tory peace of Utrecht was to be effected; Swift was ruthless in his persecution, reflecting the relatively simple partisanship of Bolingbroke. Finally Swift, who ceased writing for the ministry after being frightened by the danger of prosecution for his *Publick Spirit of the Whigs* of 1714, "lay low and failed to acknowledge until the danger had passed that he had been close to Oxford;"[12] while Defoe took the more practical measure of writing anonymously and effectively on Harley's behalf, in spite of Harley's public disavowal of that writing, after the ex-minister had been charged with treason by a new Whig ministry under George I.

For his support of Harley Defoe gained the opprobrium of Whigs and the loss of respect of the readers of his *Review*, whose decline in popularity during its last years resulted from the repercussions of violent partisanship engendered by the ministerial revolution of 1710, in which Harley had ousted Godolphin and the Whigs. Defoe was called a turncoat because he advocated the conclusion of peace with France after having for so many years warmly supported the war, and because he argued in favour of the articles of commerce with France after having previously regarded France as England's economic rival.

The violence of partisanship thus exaggerated tactical shifts required by Defoe's symbiotic relationship with Harley into betrayal of basic political and economic principles. The decision that it was time to make peace could charitably be interpreted as a tactical one, reached as much because Defoe was sensitive to public opinion—war weariness had swept the Tories into power in 1710—as because Defoe was working for Harley; his advocacy of the Peace of Utrecht did not necessarily imply that Defoe had abandoned his interventionist principles in foreign policy. Similarly, Defoe's advocacy of Bolingbroke's articles of commerce with France could also have been a matter of tactics. His basic arguments, economists have discovered, were not based upon new free trade principles reflecting those of the near contemporary Sir Dudley North or anticipating those of Adam Smith. Instead, they consistently rested upon familiar mercantilist principles; Defoe simply interpreted the detailed statistics, to which as government spokesman he had access, as indicating advantage to England from the proposed trade agreement.

Inevitably Defoe's role as defender of successive ministries, non-partisan, Whig, and Tory, exposed him to the criticisms of the political opposition, which can always afford to be purer in principle than an acting government. Regarding himself as a civil servant, he seems to have conceived it his paramount duty to help keep the ministry running and to have reasoned that as long as the Protestant Succession and the fundamental liberties of the nation were being protected, no betrayal of principle was involved. In a period not long after James II had challenged these fundamentals, when a substantial threat of a Stuart restoration still hung over England, Defoe's pragmatism need not be dismissed as mere mercenary opportunism.

In addition, a moderate position in politics is in itself most difficult to define and easiest to attack. Defoe's moderation, according to a careful student of his *Review*, was synonymous with Whiggery,[13] whereas Harley's meant keeping the reins of government out of the control of either party's extremist faction by coalition between moderates of both sides. The two varieties of moderation overlap, but they are not synonymous. Although both men were concerned above all with threats to liberty, Defoe regarded the enemy as High-Churchmen and Jacobites; Harley's "greater hatred for the Junto, whom he often castigated for their rapacity and doctrinal laxity (real or supposed), was to force him always into the Tory camp, except for brief interludes".[14] During the 1705 election campaign, High-Church advocates, attacked by Harley and Defoe as extremists for wishing to eliminate the practice of occasional conformity among Dissenters, interpreted the "moderation" professed by their opponents as an excuse to eject High-Churchmen from office, an excuse, moreover, particularly appropriate for those who were lukewarm in their religion. With its high content of pragmatism providing a source of rationalization for sheer opportunism, moderation can easily intoxicate its professors into self-deception. Finally, a moderate position in politics, rarely a clear-cut yes or no, irritates those who are impatient with intellectual nuances.

The complexity of moderation, as well as Harley's influence on the not always so moderate Defoe, is illustrated by Defoe's position on Protestant Dissenters. While Defoe wholeheartedly supported the Toleration, even advocated its extension into the political sphere, he had an ambivalent attitude toward occasional conformity. As a pious

Presbyterian, he could not countenance the Dissenters' practice of taking communion occasionally in an Anglican church in order to qualify themselves to hold public office; as a political theorist, he regarded High-Church efforts to forbid the practice in order to keep Dissenters out of public office as tyrannical. As a supporter of the underdog and an occasional political incendiary, he could suggest that Dissenters parry High-Church bullying by organizing an economic boycott to force Whigs into extending the religious toleration to civil life; but as a contributor of practical advice on politics to Harley, constrained by occupation to consider the nation as a whole, he could admit that the Dissenters were a potentially obstreperous group, best kept at a distance from political power by mollifying them with guarantees that their religious liberty was safe. Complex as this moderate and balanced attitude toward the application of the principle of religious toleration may be, it is not inconsistent: Defoe preferred civil toleration for Dissenters, but was willing to settle for religious toleration alone if the public were not ready to be generous.[15]

An example of the complexity of Defoe's ideas themselves can be found in a more abstract issue of political theory. Where it was once assumed that Defoe, a modernist, popularized the social contract theory of John Locke, scholars have recently begun to examine his writings more closely to see how much he owed to the earlier Sir Robert Filmer's patriarchal theory of monarchy.[16] Although Defoe defended the notion of contract in his writings before 1701 and insisted during the Sacheverell trial of 1709 that the Revolution had resulted from resistance, justifiably based on the rights of Parliament and the people of England, not from the abdication of James II, he fervently admired the authoritarian King William and seems to have taken for granted in his fiction the analogy between royal and paternal authority. Definition of the final position of this ardent opponent of High-Church doctrines of passive obedience, divine right, and non-resistance to royal authority, is therefore long overdue. But such definition of his balancing of earlier and later theories of sovereignty will be complicated by consideration of how far Defoe was influenced by Harley, an intellectual descendant of James Harrington in his theory of constitutional balance between Crown and Parliament.

Distrust of Defoe stemmed mainly from contemporary partisanship, his connection with Robert Harley, the tactical shifts required by his role as spokesmen for several different ministries, the complexity of his political and economic ideas, usually an idiosyncratic amalgam of seventeenth-century and modernizing tendencies, and his particular brand of moderation. In addition, however, Defoe's personal behaviour in some ways invited accusations of shiftiness. He had a penchant for writing on different sides of the same issue, an idiosyncrasy for which there are a number of explanations: his mind was so inquisitive and active that he could rarely rest content with any final answer, and thus frequently devoted separate works to different points of view on the same issues; he seems to have enjoyed exercising his fertile imagination by devising as many arguments as he could; indeed he advocated writing for both sides at the same time in order to develop one's scope as a writer; at times he felt obliged to register his disagreement with his employers, especially on issues where he felt more Whiggish than the ministry he was serving, even if he had to do so anonymously; finally, of course, Defoe wrote for money.

Defoe himself seems to have harboured doubts about his moral rectitude: he suffered from a guilty conscience for his decision not to enter the ministry for which he had been trained, and his feeling that he was being justly punished must have grown as a result of repeated failures in his chosen career of business, one of them involving the shabby treatment of his own mother-in-law, and probably all of them involving the use of subterfuge to keep creditors at bay. His guilty conscience must have been exacerbated by the secret impulses that had originally impelled him to a Crusoe-like rejection of his calling: the irresistible attraction to a lively yet sinful world of economic and political activity; the secret knowledge of his own superior gifts; the half-conscious contempt for his excellent but stodgy fellow Dissenters; the religious faith and moral rectitude that would not free him, as it had others like Harley, to make the easy transition from non-conforming Presbyterianism to the Low-Church Anglicanism required for full admission into English political and social life; the irrepressible energy that drove him to over-confident business gambles which led to lawsuits, bankruptcy, and prison; and the sense of humour that drove him to imprudent political hoaxes. Defoe's critics must have been responding in part to a sense of guilt he himself projected; Steele, after all, was criticized, not for dishonesty in incurring debts he had no intention of paying, but for the profligacy of which he himself was ashamed, and the self-assured Addison was usually regarded, except by Pope, as modest rather than cold.

Defoe's general sense of unworthiness engendered by his status as a Dissenter in a Church of England society, must have been greatly exacerbated by the searing humiliation of having plunged in the space of one year from the height of a king's favour, via the pillory, to the depth of a jail.

Finally, Defoe's contemporary reputation for duplicity was the result of a blatant contrast, perceived by his enemies as well as by himself, between his popular, homely writing style and public persona, the forthright Mr. Review, and his own subtlety of mind. Repeatedly accused of hypocrisy, Defoe himself was aware of one reason. In 1705, while Mr. Review addressed country gentlemen to persuade them to support Harley's policy of uniting moderate Whigs and Tories against High-Church extremists, Defoe secretly wrote a column called "Truth and Honesty" for the *London Post.* As Mr. Truth and Honesty, he lumped all Tories together as enemies of religious toleration, attacking Mr. Review for drawing over-subtle distinctions between good and bad Tories: "Truth and Honesty is plain and square, and values none of your nice distinctions ... *he that is not for us is against us*".[17] The intellectual limitations of the plain-speaking, plain-dealing person to whom so much of the political writing of Defoe's period was addressed and whose voice was so frequently imitated by contemporary writers, but most successfully by Defoe, were always clear to him. As a high-flying parson says on 21 May 1705 to Truth and Honesty, "You pretend to Truth and Honesty, but not to much sense I find, and so you count all that know more than you hypocrites". Truth and Honesty replies in character: "I pretend to know everything that belongs to Truth and Honesty, and I know enough of you, and your High-Church principles, as to know, you don't belong to me, and I'll have nothing to do with you".

When Truth and Honesty asserts, on 28 and 30 May 1705, that Mr. Review is "damnably sly and cutting by the way of innuendo, or retort",[18] he is attesting to the subtlety with which Defoe manipulated his seemingly forthright Mr. Review to address different messages, sometimes at the same time, to different audiences. When the Earl of Godolphin, unaware that the *Review* was a ministerial journal, protested to Robert Harley that its emphasis on the power of France was odious, Defoe answered the complaint in his journal, explaining to Harley that his apology had been expressed in the voice of Mr. Review, "not as if the objectors were of such quality as to whom the stile should be unsuitable".[19] Mr. Review's comment on the Duke of Marlborough's victory at Blenheim was designed to elicit support from Tories for the war against France by exploiting Tory prejudice against war-profiteering Whigs: "Let not our war jobbers, or men of arms, who live by the ruin of their friends ... let them not be afraid the war will be over too soon, I am of the opinion there is no danger of it. ... They won't find France so easily reduced". As J. A. Downie observes, "By satirising those who were enthusiastic about the war for its own sake, yet persistently urging the dire necessity of it at the same time, Defoe was hoping to demonstrate the true position that a disinterested patriot should adopt. He was parading the Government view without revealing it as such".[20] And Defoe was correct in assuming that the most important people in England were reading his *Review* over the shoulders of his ostensibly humble reader: during the Sacheverell trial of 1710, Sir Simon Harcourt, speaking for the defendant before the House of Lords, made use of an expression from the *Review* that was apparently proverbial to the distinguished assembly.[21]

From the time of his release from prison in 1703, Defoe seems not only to have accepted the subterranean life offered him by Harley—after all, he had a large family to support—but actually to have embraced it. His services were largely secret, he adopted a variety of pseudonyms in those services and in his writings, and he used the disguise motif frequently in his writing. One of the few self-revealing passages in his letters to Harley was written in 1706 when Defoe was in Scotland working to forward the negotiations then in progress toward the Union. In it he displays his exuberance about his assignment:

> Though I will not answer for success, yet I trust in management you shall not be uneasy at your trusting me here. I have compassed my first and main step happily enough, in that I am perfectly unsuspected as corresponding with anybody in England. I converse with Presbyterian, Episcopal-Dissenter, Papist and Non-Juror, and I hope with equal circumspection. I flatter myself you will have no complaints of my conduct. I have faithful emissaries in every company, and I talk to everybody in their own way. To the merchants I am about to settle here in trade, building ships, &c. With the lawyers I want to purchase a house and land to bring my family and live upon it (God knows where the money is to pay for it). Today I am going into partnership with a Member of Parliament in a glass-house, tomorrow with another in a salt work. With the Glasgow mutineers I am to be a fish merchant, with the Aberdeen men

a woollen and with the Perth and Western men a linen manufacturer, and still at the end of all discourse the Union is the essential, and I am all to everyone that I may gain some.

After the passage of the Union, Defoe attempted to gain the office of commissioner of customs in Scotland as public recognition of his service to the Crown, but permitted himself to be dissuaded by Godolphin and Harley, who believed he would be "more serviceable in a private capacity"; by 1711 he even derived private satisfaction from seeing Harley, now Earl of Oxford, secretly:

I have one humble request to subjoin to this relating to my attending Your Lordship in the morning, as by Your Lordship's appointment for tomorrow. It is my honour and a privilege no man values more, that Your Lordship admits me to wait on you at any time, and if Your Lordship commands my attendance in public I shall thankfully obey. But as my being able to serve Your Lordship and Her Majesty's interest consists much on my being concealed, I humbly submit it to Your Lordship whether I should not rather attend in an evening. I say no more, leaving the rest entirely to Your Lordship's wisdom and direction, only begging leave to attend this evening, rather than tomorrow morning, till I have your farther commands.

After the death of Queen Anne and the accession of George I of Hanover, Defoe's path seems to have reached vertiginous heights of duplicity. He became a triple agent, accepting employment from the new Whig ministry for the purpose of infiltrating rabid Tory journals and moderating their anti-ministerial and anti-Hanoverian rhetoric. As a writer stamped with the imprint of Harley's now discredited Tory ministry, Defoe's access to Tory journals was an asset he could and did exploit with Whigs. Yet while he worked secretly to draw the teeth of extremist Tory writers, he also published anonymously a series of effective pamphlets and a whole book written from the different view-points of various fictionalized "inside" observers in order to defend Harley against the charge of treason.

Through all this shifting and tacking, nevertheless, it is possible to discern a consistent course. As a civil servant, he could, without incapacitating qualms, serve a Whig ministry after having served a Tory one; he was still the servant of a law-abiding Protestant monarch. To extreme partisanship he was always opposed; he had never lent his pen to the excesses of Bolingbroke's campaign to discredit the Whig-backed Duke of Marlborough; he would never have relished the persecution of Harley by triumphant Whigs. Indeed in Harley's case, Defoe had an enduring loyalty to the ex-minister under attack.

The Defoe who was devious underneath his ostensible directness, consistent underneath his ostensible deviousness, was *sui generis* among contemporary writers of his calibre. Addison was a prudent and temperate Whig who charted a steady course in the diplomatic and political career to which his literary efforts were secondary. Steele was a passionate, generous, and often unreflective partisan, an Anglican who applauded unreservedly the attacks on Church authority launched by the Whig apologist Benjamin Hoadly, Bishop of Bangor, while the Dissenting Defoe expressed reservations about Hoadly's onslaught against all Church authority. Swift was a Whig attracted to Oxford's Tory ministry by the prospect of patronage defaulted upon by his Whig friends, dazzled by Harley and Bolingbroke's recognition of his genius, and enthusiastic about Tory High-Church and anti-Dissenter policy. He was the most violent and unabashed partisan of them all, but his politics were dictated more by personal loyalties than by reasoned principles.

Separated from writers of secondary rank by his superior talents, Defoe could expect no welcome from his natural peers, partly because loyalty to his religious and social origins and stubbornness about his unorthodox ideas prevented him from "passing" in a higher social rank like Prior, son of a carpenter, Pope, son of a linen merchant, or even Swift, son of an attorney (attorneys were frequently regarded as disreputable in that period). And partly, of course, the eductional result of his Nonconformity disqualified him from their conversation. All except Addison, the son of a country clergyman, came from the lower and middle ranks of the urban middle classes; more important, except for Pope, a Roman Catholic invalid who educated himself at home in the classics, all but Defoe were members of the Church of England and therefore eligible for admission to the universities that monopolized the training in classics regarded as indispensable to gentlemen. Although Defoe had received an excellent education at the Stoke Newington Academy run by the Reverend Charles Morton, future vice-president of Harvard College, his training was stronger in subjects like history and modern languages than it was in the classics, and his formal education ended before university. Accordingly, he was considered unpolished, even when at best recognized by leading statesmen and writers as "ingenious" (the contemporary adjective for "brilliant"). At worst, he could be lumped with Grub Street hacks and dismissed by people like Swift as "a stupid, illiterate scribbler, a fanatick by profession", out of whose "*rough*, as well as ... *dirty* Hands" Swift resolved to remove the work of spreading the gospel of moderation.[22]

Because his Latin was rudimentary, Defoe wrote without most of the customary allusions to classical literature, either through quotation or through imitation of Latin literary forms. In addition, he concentrated upon subjects other than polite literature, never venturing to present himself as a connoisseur of letters. He admired the writing of Steele, subscribing in his own name and that of his son to a collected edition of the latter's works, but he seems to have decided after a brief fling in the 1690s to abandon polite literature to those who had been trained for it. Accordingly, his writing is remarkably deficient in allusions even to English writers, with the exception of Milton and of Rochester, a significant pair when we consider Defoe's curious combination of moral fervour and sophistication tending toward cynicism, of directness and duplicity.

In the scope of his interests outside literature, and in the depth of his understanding of many of these fields, Defoe had no peer. As Peter Earle observes, "He clearly had some sort of three-dimensional matrix in his head whose axes were time, space and ideas. From this matrix he could draw at random, immediately relating the effects in Virginia of something happening in the empire of the Grand Mogul, while at the same time retaining a very strong temporal, that is chronological, sense of why the thing had happened in the first place".[23] He wrote on politics, economics, religion, history, geography, military art, social welfare, psychology, travel, crime, the occult, and the techniques of many crafts and occupations. The number of Defoe's interests distinguishes him even in a period when versatility was common among the gifted, and most writers tried their hand at political writing; the quickness and even the depth of his understanding of many of these subjects further distinguishes him from his peers. Never single-minded enough to pursue one interest far enough to compete for the laurels awarded to important thinkers, always attempting to balance the claims of the past with those of the present, and always distracted from the pursuit of pure theory by consideration of actual practice, Defoe possessed sufficient gifts of mind, observation and intuition to rank in several fields among the first of contemporary experts, for whose productions his unsigned works were occasionally mistaken. (Someone as perceptive as Arthur Maynwaring wondered if Defoe were not the author of Swift's anonymous *Conduct of the Allies*, on the basis of "the strength of the reasoning, and the exactness of the political calculations".)[24] His political ideas have been and are still being examined to determine how original they were, his economic ideas were complex enough to warrant the attention of Joseph Schumpeter before he dismissed Defoe from his history of economic thought, while his ideas about social reform were far enough in advance of his age and too infrequently expressed by anyone else to fall on fertile ground.

Defoe's extra-literary activities and accomplishments had an important effect on the fiction that immortalized his name. Although *Robinson Crusoe* has a mythic quality that makes it seem spontaneous, the product of no individual author and of no arduous apprenticeship in literary craftsmanship, in fact, like Defoe's other fictions, it was written after the age of fifty-nine, when Defoe had already spent more than thirty-five years producing over four hundred works of astonishing variety. It was not by inspiration or intuition alone that this seasoned political journalist, accustomed from his early years at Morton's academy to addressing many different audiences in many different voices, articulated in his first work of fiction the new spirit of modernity in the plain-dealing voice so popular with his contemporaries. During the troubled days of August 1714, between the death of Queen Anne and the setting up of a new ministry under King George I, when no one could tell what position the new king would take toward leading Tories and especially the members of Harley's now discredited ministry, Defoe described his life-long habit of listening for the sense of the nation. In the latter part of August, the "juncture" was still "so nice" that he could hardly tell "which way to direct words so to suit the fluctuating tempers of the people as not to do harm instead of good". He decided the most prudent course for the time being would be to write in generalities.[25]

Not only had Defoe spent a lifetime listening to public opinion; he had acquired his training by writing about politics at a time when a careless expression could and did send writers to prison. Sensitivity to words, their specificity, their generality, and their connotations, was second nature to him. His daily experience as editor as well as writer included tuning rhetoric up or down for political purposes. The unfortunate outcome of his *Shortest Way* resulted from the effect on his readers of his exaggeration of the actual words of the fiery Dr. Sacheverell against Dissenters; Defoe's 1716 redaction of the journal of the Stuart rebel, the Earl of Mar, a redaction that pushed the original right out of the market, consisted of changing a few strategic words to make the Jacobite cause seem ridiculous.[26] In his *London Post* column of 6 June 1705, "Truth and Honesty" supplies an example of Defoe tuning up words for his own purpose, exaggerating and simplifying. Truth and Honesty is discussing Charles Leslie, a nonjuring journalist rival, with a parson:

"Well, Sir," said T. and H., "in what (pray) does he dissent from the government?"

Parson "Why, he cannot take the oaths."

T. & H. "That is, he does not acknowledge the Queen to be his rightful sovereign. Don't you mean so?"

P. "Yes, yes."

T. & H. "That is, in English, he looks upon the late King James and his Perkinite race to be the true line."

P. "And that he is bound by his oath to them."

T. & H. "Or in truth and honesty, that the Q——n is an usurper, and sits in a throne she has not right to."

P. "You are always for putting things in the worst terms you can, softer words would do it as well."

T. & H. "I am always for speaking truth, according to my name, my faculty and practice ..."

Another example of Defoe's subtlety with words dates from 1709, when he deliberately exaggerated the sneer of Dyer, an anti-Marlborough journalist, to get him into trouble. Dyer's original gibe about the bloody victory of Malplaquet had been couched in these words: "This great success (as the Duke of Marlborough calls it)". Defoe's misquotation was: "This happy parenthesis, victory, as Marlborough calls it". Not only did Defoe exaggerate Dyer's sneer; he also implied that Dyer had been so insolently familiar as to omit the Duke's full title. The point was that Dyer's original criticism of the Malplaquet battle had deliberately been expressed in terms he could legally defend at their innocent face value before a jury; if he had really expressed himself as Defoe reported, Dyer might have been fined or imprisoned.[27]

Defoe's experiments in writing fiction took place at the point in his career when he had lost his position as a favourite writer of the ministry. Harley was by now irrevocably out of power, and Defoe had to struggle to maintain tenuous connections with a new generation of statesmen. Far from being "Walpole's laureate", as one hostile commentator has designated him,[28] and critics unfettered by concern for historical accuracy have parrotted, Defoe had a long-standing acquaintance with Sunderland, who, with Stanhope, eventually lost the battle for power to the Whig faction of Walpole and Townshend. The uncertainty of his future prospects perhaps provided an immediate incentive to try his hand at a new genre, and the overwhelming success of his first major venture in 1719 must have encouraged him to continue working the vein of fiction. When he discovered that didactic works were more profitable, or when his inspiration for fiction began to wane after the remarkable year of 1722, which produced, among other full-length books, *Moll Flanders*, *A Journal of the Plague Year*, and *Colonel Jack*, Defoe concentrated his efforts upon popular self-instruction manuals like his *New Family Instructor* and *Complete English Tradesman* and books on the occult, directed at the same lower- and lower-middle-class audience he had reached with his fiction; he aimed at an upper-middle-class audience, however, in *A Plan of the English Commerce* and *A Tour thro' the Whole Island of Great Britain*, and his 1718 *Family Instructor*, and at the middling ranks of the middle class in such pamphlets as *Every-Body's Business, Is No-Body's Business*, the *Protestant Monastery* and *Parochial Tyranny*. With these last works he returned to an interest of his early days of the *Essay upon Projects* (1697), that of social reform, adopting the name and voice of a somewhat querulous old man, Andrew Moreton.

The nature of the audience for which Defoe wrote the best-known of his fictions (except *Roxana*) dictated the popular style for which he is known today. Although this vigorous and relatively unpolished style was already distinguishable in the short works that catapulted Defoe to national attention in the early years of his writing career, it is neither his only style during that period, nor is it the only style Defoe used in the voluminous political and economic writing in which he acquired most of his training. Perhaps most significant, it is not the style in which he conducted his correspondence of 1704–14 with Robert Harley. Although the letters to Harley include elements of Defoe's vigorous plain style, they are not strikingly different from letters by other educated and intelligent men of his period; readers are unlikely to recognize in the writer of the letters the characteristic style of the author of *Robinson Crusoe*.

A long professional career that had accustomed Defoe to writing quickly with little revision was as important in creating the spontaneity, even carelessness, of his fiction, as was his much decried lack of artistic concern for a polished literary product. Critics who condescend to Defoe, denying him the intelligence or self-awareness to recognize contradictory ironies in his fiction, are simply demonstrating their ignorance of the bulk of his writing and of his mastery of innuendo, acknowledged by his contemporaries, and testifying to Defoe's success in achieving the effect of artlessness he considered appropriate to his chosen audience. Ironically, they are permitting themselves to be tricked as completely as the simple readers Defoe had in mind, for whom, as for his classmates at the Stoke Newington Academy, he harboured ambivalent feelings of affection and contempt.

As well as the mythic quality, the spontaneity, and the unresolved ironies in Defoe's fiction, the curious resonance of many brief passages in these works results from the fact that his fictions are distillations of a lifetime of writing, thinking, and feeling. Virginia Woolf was only one of a number of sensitive readers whose ears have picked up unspoken meanings in passages of Defoe's fiction, almost as if the writer's unique powers of observation had outstripped those of his conscious understanding and his pen had recorded more than his mind had analyzed. Mrs. Woolf recognized that "he seems to have taken his characters so deeply into his mind that he lived them without exactly knowing how; and, like all unconscious artists, he leaves more gold in his work than his own generation was able to bring to the surface. ..."

But Defoe has fared badly among critics tone-deaf to his idiosyncratic melodies, in spite of the instantaneous popularity of *Robinson Crusoe*, admiration for *A Journal of the Plague Year*, and the gradual acceptance of *Moll Flanders*, once regarded as too coarse for polite tastes. Respected for his intelligence by outstanding statesmen of his time, he was looked down upon by important writers for his supposed lack of learning. Later on in the century, when prose had grown more balanced and formal, even Swift's writing was regarded by the discerning Samuel Johnson as inferior to Addison's. Although Johnson wolfed down in one sitting the *Memoirs of Captain Carleton*, now usually attributed to Defoe, in the mistaken belief that the memoirs were authentic, it is unlikely that knowledge of the real authorship would have suggested to Johnson that Defoe ought to be included among the ranks of important writers. His scope could not be appreciated, for most of his works were anonymous, and contemporary standards of literary elegance eliminated popular writers from serious consideration.

In the nineteenth and twentieth centuries, the charge of artlessness, no longer regarded as an insuperable barrier to literary credit, was replaced by charges suggested by sentimentality, social snobbery, and political bias. Dickens, a popular writer himself, was disgusted by Defoe's heartlessness; Leslie Stephen, father of the appreciative Virginia Woolf, found Defoe repulsive, ostensibly because of his lack of imagination and insensitivity to psychology, but probably because of his lack of gentility. Whatever the excuse for underrating Defoe, the real motive seems to lie in the deplorable human tendency to despise anyone who has failed to gain admittance to the fashionable circle of his period.

Some twentieth-century historians, respectful of Defoe's intellect, seem intimidated by the clamour of a literary establishment that assures them his writing is not really first-rate. Defoe specialists, whose increasing number bears silent witness to the truth, find themselves trapped between the polite contempt of genteel Tories, whose judgment of early eighteenth century people and events is identical with the social prejudices of Swift or Pope (although Pope recognized that Defoe was a gifted writer), and the active animosity of those influenced by Weber and Tawney, whose numbers have recently been augmented by the adherence of armchair anarchists. Tawneyites and anarchists, convinced that some vague entity they call the middle class is responsible for everything they deplore about both the human condition in general and the twentieth century in particular, knowing little in detail about the early eighteenth century, have elevated Defoe, regarded by contemporaries as an unpolished but vigorous writer to porters and oyster girls, to the Addisonian ranks of spokesman for the bourgeoisie or upper middle class.

The brandishing of the philosopher's stone, the rise of the middle class, before the complexities of the early eighteenth century, has had a deadening impact upon Defoe criticism. The concept itself is vague; as a description of British society, it is historically false. By 1722 the middle and lower middle classes had been forced out of the political arena along with the small landowning gentry: the expanding electorate of the seventeenth and early eighteenth centuries was being systematically contracted by a series of parliamentary decisions in favour of narrow franchises under the Whig leaders of Hanover.[29] The emergence of political stability under Walpole saw the consolidation in control of an oligarchy of landed magnates, Tories as well as Whigs, for most of the leading Tory families joined their Whig counterparts once they realized where the highway to power lay.[30] As J. H. Plumb writes, "Politics was power ... for the class which had come to dominate British life—commercially minded landowners with a sharp eye for profit".[31]

In addition, what we now think of as the middle class had no clear existence in Defoe's period at the beginning of the eighteenth century. Even later it was "minutely divided and sub-divided at the level of occupational groups".[32] The ubiquitous rise to economic power of an entity clearly identifiable as the middle class took place, not at the beginning, but toward the end of the eighteenth century, along with the Industrial Revolution. Finally, as Peter Earle has observed, far from being the prophet of this entity, Defoe "had no premonition of the Industrial Revolution and ... if he had he would almost certainly have disliked what he foresaw".[33]

In so far as the contradictory Defoe, "difficult to regard ... as representative of any class, sect, or opinion",[34] was a class spokesman, his vigorous voice expressed that "sense of the nation" hearkened to by his contemporaries with respect, with enthusiasm, or with fear, the voice of the sturdy yeoman, independent craftsman and small shopkeeper silenced by the terms of the Walpolean settlement that brought stability to early eighteenth-century England. In so far as Defoe is the spokesman of modernity itself, he is classless. The essence of the rational *Robinson Crusoe* is the triumph of the ego, or of civilization-building man; the essence of the comical and paradoxical *Moll Flanders* is the triumph of the id, or of the spirit of anarchic man; the essence of the nightmarish *Roxana* is the revenge of the super-ego, of the spirit of guilt-ridden man.

A fresh appreciation and understanding of the protean Defoe requires clearing away the rubble of preconceptions about him and his age. This can best be accomplished by first-hand acquaintance with a range of his writing, especially the writing that preceded the fiction and so served to train the Defoe known to most of us today. But collected editions of his work, as I have mentioned, cover only a small fraction of the entire corpus, and it is difficult to obtain copies of the uncollected works. Anthologies in print duplicate material already available in collected editions and contain excerpts selected more or less for their familiarity from Defoe's voluminous output. Thus they contribute inadvertently to the misconception that Defoe's best-known style, that of the plain dealer, sums up the sensibility of Defoe himself.

The following anthology is based on a different principle of selection from other collections of texts that are generally available. The choice of excerpts was dictated by three major considerations: firstly, that the work is rare, relatively inaccessible to non-specialists; secondly, that it is interesting for its style; thirdly, that it is important for an understanding of one or more of Defoe's major ideas in politics, economics, history, or sociology. Additional considerations, when choice was possible, were that the works were relatively well known in Defoe's own time or afterwards, and that they illustrated some of his many styles and were addressed to different audiences. The excerpts are organized, for the first time, into categories: politics and religion, economics and commerce, history and memoirs, and sociology and psychology.

An essay including an analysis of literary technique and historical background introduces each excerpt. The discussion of background is essential because Defoe's practice of basing his writing on contemporary events has the disadvantage of making that writing inaccessible to modern readers. Moreover, his ideas require clarification, for ideas are essential in his writing. Defoe played with points of view on ideas as Swift played with images.

In addition to the analysis of literary technique in each introductory essay, literary rather than chronological considerations dictate the arrangement of the selections in each category. The politics and history sections are arranged to make audible an undertone in Defoe's works set in a different key from that of the plain-dealing, plain-speaking voice usually associated with his name, no matter what age, sex, or class he is mimicking. The *sotto voce* is polished and devious. It rings out clearly in a minor satanic key as the voice of a disguised Jacobite gentleman in the section on politics; in the history section it emerges by inference in a major comical key as the voice of Harley, who in behind-the-scenes activity outwits the apparent protagonist, the sinister manipulator, M. Mesnager.

The politics section includes a work of extended irony, significant because it reveals at some length the mechanics of Defoe's irony, which in his fiction appears in so fleeting or allusive a manner that readers are never sure whether the protagonist or Defoe is speaking, and whether or not the author was conscious of his irony.

The audibility of two voices, plain speaker and devious manipulator, and the two attitudes about the devious manipulator, disapproving when he is a satanical Jacobite, approving when he is the clever Harley, are relevant to a reconsideration of the fictions, especially *Moll Flanders* and *Roxana*. So is the discovery of extended works of irony based on a conflict between principle and practice, theory and fact. In *Moll Flanders* the unreconciled juxaposition of ethical principle and moral conduct is, in the final analysis, funny; *Roxana*, with its sombre pronouncement of sin on practices unreconciled with principles, is frightening. Defoe's abiding concern in his non-fiction with questions of ethics and his frequent indication of inability to reconcile the irreconcilable, suggest why his morally contradictory fictions are imbued with such deep moral earnestness, and why the expectations aroused in readers are so invariably disappointed. Familiarity with the patterns of his non-fiction can provide a key to understanding the elusive Defoe whose occasional sallies from behind his protagonists unsettle the imaginative worlds of his fictions.

The sections on history and economics are both arranged to emphasize the idiosyncratic combination of fact and fiction that has so exercised scholars and bibliographers attempting to distinguish constructions by Defoe from authentic memoirs and accounts. Beginning with works of an essentially factual nature, both sections end with works very close to the pole of fiction. Defoe's fictional imagination appears to have developed as he shaped historical, geographical, and economic facts to his own design and imbued his narrators with imagined emotions. The reluctance to relax his grasp on the facts is not surprising in a writer so gifted with empathy that he could easily enter other situations and psyches, yet so plagued by guilt that he had to invent a fictional medium allowing him to conceal his unstable sense of self, fluctuating between plain man and devious manipulator because rejected by his contemporaries as the educated, intelligent and sophisticated man revealed in his letter to Robert Harley.

The economics section begins with excerpts demonstrating

Defoe's ability to select, simplify, and arrange details of complicated processes in an interesting way. It ends with excerpts on finance, a more abstract area of economics that permitted Defoe greater freedom to introduce fictional techniques. Defoe's affection for economics, which he described in terms suggesting sinful and immoderate love, even idolatry, was apparently aroused not only by his innate ability with figures, but also by his relief at finding a subject suited to his undoubted bent for explanation, but free of the quagmire of desirable goals and undesirable means that so plagued him in the political world. Economic analysis must have relieved him in some degree from the strain of dealing with what he sometimes regarded as a comical, sometimes a satanical, strain in his own sensibility; the stock-jobbers who serve in his economic world as the equivalent of Jacobites in his political one, are clearly not shadowy doubles of Defoe.

Defoe's descriptions of manufacturing and distributing processes will remind readers of Crusoe's production of bread and of pottery; in *Robinson Crusoe* mechanical processes take the place of historical facts or political ideas. In that work Defoe's intense concentration upon the conquering of self and of nature by the protagonist, whom most readers identify with the writer himself, is possible only because of the unusual absence of ethical complications introduced by interaction with other human beings. It is a reflection of the peculiar circumstances of Defoe's own life, not of the history of capitalism in general,[35] that his imagination seized on the notion of a man isolated from society in order to depict his ideal of a civilization-building activity.

The history section begins with excerpts from works like the *Storm*, which Defoe regarded as pure history, and in which he therefore took scrupulous care about the accuracy of his facts; moves through the semi-fictional genre of the military memoir, and ends with an excerpt from the *Minutes of the Negotiation of Monsr. Mesnager*, a work in which historical facts are deliberately distorted and obscured in order to create a fictional scenario in which Robert Harley can star. The fictional masterpiece *A Journal of the Plague Year* arose from *The Storm*; *Memoirs of a Cavalier* from semi-fictional memoirs of an officer engaged in the wars of Charles XII of Sweden; *Roxana* was obliquely refracted from the *Mesnager Minutes*.

The excerpts in the section on sociology and psychology, on the eduction of tradesmen, on family governance, and on social reform, were chosen to clarify the different tones and styles assumed by a Defoe ambitious to be a "universal writer" as he spoke for the lower, middle, and upper middle classes, for city dwellers and country gentlemen, for men and women, for the young, the middle-aged, and the old. The excerpts are arranged in an order demonstrating Defoe's tendency to transform sociological into psychological writing, or to subordinate non-fictional elements to fictional ones; the last two excerpts might easily be confused with the darker parts of *Moll Flanders*, or with any part of *Roxana*.

The stress upon Defoe's versatility in this anthology, and the explanations of his ideas and stylistic techniques, are designed to correct the common misconception of him among those familiar with few of his works. Defoe was a brilliant and subtle man who posed as a crackerbarrel philosopher, both because of the curious circumstances of his own life and temperament and because of a public that was calling for plain dealers and speakers. So solitary a sensibility that communication was most complete for him with the ultra-subtle Harley, he first sought a substitute companionship with readers in the bonhomie of Mr. Review, contenting himself with the intellectual limitations of this companionship by setting his own literary personae to dialogues with each other. Then he resorted to companionship with the narrators of his great fictions, so fusing his own perception of the external world with each of theirs that readers of all countries and of all periods have sought the elusive author in vain.

The reader of *Robinson Crusoe*, *Moll Flanders*, and *Roxana*, no longer simply the friend of the gregarious Mr. Review, is cast by Defoe in the role of God-like judge: respected in *Robinson Crusoe*, mocked in *Moll Flanders*, feared in *Roxana*. Like Robert Harley's appeal to conscience in politics, Defoe's appeal to the readers of his fiction arises from the strain of puritanism in his sensibility concomitant with respect for human complexity. The frequent, always scornful, use of terms like "shortest way", "make oneself easy", "a parcel of folks", in Defoe's writing suggests that this man who prided himself on his equanimity found nothing so irritating as the common assumption that individuals are interchangeable and short cuts will suffice to deal with them. Defoe's puritanism, like Harley's, was indelible, in spite of repeated accommodations with practicality necessitated by the circumstances of politics and of life itself.

If modern readers are to honour fairly the trust reposed in

us by Defoe, we must remove the distorting spectacles of disrespect inherited from generations of biased commentators, spectacles that impair the reading not only of Defoe, but of realistic writing in general. It is our responsibility to look afresh at the writing of the man who had faith that "a constant, steady adhering to personal virtue and to public peace" would "at last restore [him] to the opinion of sober and impartial men", for his posthumous reputation has been like his life, described by an eminent modern historian as one long kick.

Contemporary masters of prose style have for some years now been contributing to the long-overdue revaluation of Defoe. James Joyce included him in his literary pantheon among the craftsmen Jonson, Flaubert, and Ibsen, presumably because of the vigour of his prose, even though Joyce was probably unaware that one of the secrets of its vigour was a compression acquired through simplification. Increasingly, one finds among personal reminiscences of and about writers, Saul Bellow and Kenneth Rexroth for example, expressions of partiality for Defoe. For our own age, one seeking a vigorous, precise, graceful, yet colloquial language, a study of Defoe's various styles is invaluable. In every one of them, impeccably chosen words fall into seemingly inevitable cadences. Of particular interest in his plain-dealer style are his concrete and vigorous diction and imagery; in his educated style, the clarity and power of his reasoning; in his devious manipulator style, the insidiousness of his innuendos and the calculated ambivalence of his diction. It is hoped that this anthology will contribute to making him better known to literary specialists and to historians, but above all, to general readers of good prose.

Notes

1 John Robert Moore, *A Checklist of the Writings of Daniel Defoe*, 2nd ed. (Hamden, Conn.: Archon Books, 1971).

2 *A Foreign View of England in the Reigns of George I and George II: The Letters of Monsieur César de Saussure to His Family*, trans. and ed. Madame van Mayden (London: John Murray, 1902), p. 162.

3 J. H. Plumb, *The Origins of Political Stability: England 1675–1725* (Boston: Houghton Mifflin Co., 1967), p. xvi.

4 Geoffrey Holmes, "The Electorate and the National Will in the First Age of Party", an inaugural lecture delivered on 26 November, 1975, at the University of Lancaster, pp. 2, 7, 14–15. Speck's calculations are cited in this lecture.

5 W. A. Speck, "Political Propaganda in Augustan England", *Transactions of the Royal Historical Society*, 5th Series, 22 (1972), p. 27.

6 J. H. Plumb, "The Acceptance of Modernity", a speech delivered 6 May 1977, at the eighth annual meeting of the American Society for Eighteenth-Century Studies, at the University of Victoria, in Victoria, B.C.

7 Angus McInnes, "The Political Ideas of Robert Harley", *History*, 50 (Oct. 1965), 312.

8 Jonathan Swift, *Prose Works*, vii, *The History of the Four Last Years of the Queen*, ed. Herbert Davis (Oxford: Basil Blackwell, 1951), p. 73.

9 J. A. Downie, "Robert Harley and the Press", unpublished Ph.D. dissertation, University of Newcastle, 1976, p. 12.

10 Angus McInnes, p. 317.

11 Harley's *Taunton-Dean Letter* of 1701 is reproduced in Downie's appendix. It contains Defoean expressions like "Flesh and blood cannot bear to see half the House go out to make water when I rise up to begin my speech", and "I will lay this new ministry as flat as a flounder when once I begin to brandish my pen", although it was written before the period of collaboration between Harley and Defoe. It is, however, an answer to the Kentish petition, and seems to refer to *Legion's Memorial* by Defoe.

12 Downie, p. 355.

13 J. A. Downie, "Daniel Defoe's *Review* and Other Political Writings in the Reign of Queen Anne", unpublished Master of Letters thesis, University of Newcastle upon Tyne, 1973, p. iii.

14 B. W. Hill, *The Growth of Parliamentary Parties 1689–1742* (London: George Allen & Unwin Ltd., 1976), p. 79.

15 See pages 13–14 of Donald Davies, *A Gathered Church: The Literature of the English Dissenting Interest, 1700–1930* (New York: Oxford Univ. Press, 1978), for a generalization about the effect on eighteenth-century Dissenters of the Revolutionary Settlement insuring the Protestant Succession. What Davies points out applies very well to Defoe: "Politically disabled they Dissenters might be, and would growl and protest about it, but mostly it seems they tolerated it readily enough as a price to be paid for getting protection from Papists, Jacobites, and high-flying Tories."

16 The most careful and up-to-date study of this question is Manuel Schonhorn's essay, "Defoe: The Literature of Politics and the Politics of Some Fictions", in *English Literature in the Age of Disguise*, ed. Maximillian E. Novak (Berkeley: Univ. of California Press, 1978).

17 Quoted in Downie, "Daniel Defoe's *Review*", p. 85.

18 *Ibid.*, p. 86.

19 Quoted by Downie, "Robert Harley and the Press", p. 130.

20 J. A. Downie, "Daniel Defoe's *Review*", pp. 72–73.

21 See Geoffrey Holmes, *The Trial of Doctor Sacheverell* (London: Eyre Methuen, 1973). p. 187 and note.

22 Jonathan Swift, *Examiner*, No. 15, 16 Nov. 1710 in *The Prose Works of Jonathan Swift*, III, *The Examiner* ..., ed. Herbert Davis (Oxford: Basil Blackwell, 1940), pp. 13–14.

23 Peter Earle, *The World of Defoe* (London: Weidenfeld and Nicolson, 1976), p. 44.

24 [?Arthur Maynwaring] *Remarks on a False, Scandalous, and Seditious Libel Intituled The Conduct of the Allies*, London, 1711, p. 2.

25 Quoted by W. T. Laprade in *Public Opinion and Politics in Eighteenth Century England* (New York: The Macmillan Company, 1936), p. 158.

26 John Robert Moore, "Defoe's Hand in *A Journal of the Earl of Marr's Proceedings*", *Huntington Library Quarterly*, 17 (1954), 209–28.

27 Quoted by Frances Marjorie Harris in "A Study of the Paper War Relating to the Career of the 1st Duke of Marlborough, 1710–1712", unpublished Ph.D. dissertation, University of London, 1975, p. 19.

28 Isaac Kramnick, *Bolingbroke and His Circle* (Cambridge, Mass.: Harvard University Press, 1968), p. 188.

29 J. H. Plumb, "The Growth of the Electorate in England from 1600 to 1715", *Past and Present*, 45 (Nov. 1969), 116.

30 J. H. Plumb, *Sir Robert Walpole: The Making of a Statesman* (London: The Cresset Press, 1956) and volume II: *The King's Minister* (Boston: Houghton Mifflin Company, 1961), *passim.*

31 J. H. Plumb, "Political Man", in *Man Versus Society in Eighteenth-Century Britain*, ed. James L. Clifford (Cambridge: Univ. Press, 1968), p. 9.

32 Frank O'Gorman, Department of History, University of Manchester, letter of 3 Feb. 1978.

33 Peter Earle, p. 108.

34 Diana Spearman, *The Novel and Society* (New York: Barnes and Noble, 1966), p. 172.

35 Ian Watt developed most persuasively the influential theory of Robinson Crusoe as the individualistic economic man of modern capitalism in his 1957 *Rise of the Novel.* Watt's sway over Defoe criticism is attested to by George Starr, who himself influenced a whole school of critics with his 1965 *Defoe and Spiritual Autobiography*, a study of the sin and salvation pattern of spiritual autobiography in Defoe's fiction ("Defoe's Prose Style", *MP*, 71, Feb. 1974).

CHAPTER ONE

POLITICS AND RELIGION

Engraved by W. T. Mote.

ROBERT HARLEY, EARL OF OXFORD.

OB. 1724.

FROM THE ORIGINAL OF SIR GODFREY KNELLER, IN

THE BRITISH MUSEUM.

London, Published [illegible] by Harding & Lepard, Pall Mall East.

1. King William's Affection to the Church of England Examined

King William's Affection to the Church of England Examined was first published on 25 March 1703, during the period when Defoe was in hiding, a warrant having been issued for his arrest as the author of the "seditious libel", *The Shortest Way with the Dissenters* (December 1702). *The Shortest Way* had dealt with the position of the Dissenters in England; *King William's Affection* deals with the other half of the religious question agitating the English in 1702 and 1703: the position of the Church of England as a favoured institution within the state. In his *Shortest Way*, Defoe had so successfully mimicked the notorious sermon of a High Church zealot, Dr. Henry Sacheverell, that at first the pamphlet was acclaimed by the High Church party. In *King William's Affection*, Defoe uses a persona, the device so often employed by Swift in his ironic writings. Defoe's persona attacks the Church policy of the lately deceased King William. By the weakness of logic in his argument the persona reveals himself to be an ill-tempered and ungrateful bigot, with a very short memory of the dangerous condition of the Church under the attacks of James II.

King James II, a devout Roman Catholic and a fatally obstinate statesman, ascended the throne in 1685 to the enthusiastic acclaim of the Church of England and a new Tory Parliament.[1] His three-year reign was marked by a series of foolish acts that alienated most of his original supporters. Desertion of his throne in a secret flight to France cost him the support of even the few die-hard adherents among Tories and High-Churchmen still left in his camp in December 1688. Both Whigs and Tories joined to welcome William of Orange.

The history of James's brief reign is the story of his unsuccessful attempts to restore to the Crown powers that had passed irrevocably during the seventeenth century into the hands of Parliament and to return England gradually to Roman Catholicism. As G. M. Trevelyan writes, at first James planned to conduct the return to Rome "with the half-unconscious consent of the Church of England and with the active help of a Tory Parliament. It was only their refusal to oblige that led him to adopt another line to the same end, to break the laws, to attack the Church and the party that had placed him on the throne, and to court instead a chimerical alliance with the Puritan Dissenters, who bitterly hated both him and his religion."[2]

Having discovered that Parliament, Tories, and the established Church opposed his Romanizing policy, James attempted to extend the powers of his royal prerogative and to use it to alter laws as he chose. In this attempt, he sought to ally himself with the Nonconformists in order to oust representatives of the established Church from seats of power in the state. He issued on 18 April 1687 a Declaration of Indulgence, suspending by virtue of his royal prerogative all laws injurious either to Catholic or Protestant Dissenters. Some Dissenters consented to become James's allies, but most of them refused to buy religious toleration and political equality at the expense of increasing the powers of a monarch inclined to despotism. In this decision they were influenced by the 1688 promise of High-Church bishops and Tory leaders to support an Act of Tolerance for religious worship of Dissenters, as soon as a free Parliament should meet.

It was not until William III assumed the throne that such a Parliament was convened. The Earl of Nottingham himself, the recognized representative of the Church in Parliament, drew up and presented the bill to the House of Lords, and the Toleration Act of May 1689, granting the right of free public worship to Protestant Dissenters, was accepted by Whigs and Tories without hesitation.

Although the Act brought religious persecution of Dissenters to an end, their civil disabilities were not removed, and the established Church retained its monopoly in public offices. "In short", writes Trevelyan, "the Ecclesiastical Settlement of 1689 was a compromise inclining to the Church and Tory side of things, whereas the Dynastic Settlement had inclined to the Whig side."[3] As their initial enthusiasm at being rescued from anarchy by William III began to subside, High-Churchmen and Tories cooled in their feelings of friendship for Dissenters and began to resent the compromise settlement. This resentment took the form of a series of attempts to limit the scope of the Toleration Act through measures like the Occasional Conformity Bill and the Schism Act.

High-Church dignitaries who believed in the divine right of James were troubled by the dynastic settlement of 1689, and the most scrupulous of them became Nonjurors, refusing to take an oath of allegiance to William and Mary. The church offices they thereby relinquished were naturally bestowed by the new monarchs upon supporters of their regime. Since William himself was in favour of toleration for all Protestants, going so far as to advocate the abolition of laws excluding Dissenters from civil office and to call a Convocation of the clergy in 1689 to consider a scheme for Comprehension (admitting the more orthodox Dissenters into the Church of England), it is not surprising that ecclesiastical promotions during his reign went to men of latitudinarian principles. Nevertheless, the quality of the new prelates was high. Promotions, writes Sir George Clark, "were much influenced by Queen Mary, who did nothing unworthy of a granddaughter of Clarendon [author of harsh laws against Dissenters, passed from 1662–1665], and the new bishops included a number of robust and notable men",[4] including Gilbert Burnet and John Tillotson, new Archbishop of Canterbury.

Understandably, a gap in sympathy grew between the new, more liberal Crown appointees, most of them Whigs, holding a balance in the House of Lords, and the lower clergy, less inclined to admire William III or to tolerate Dissenters. It is as a spokesman for this more conservative group that the persona of Defoe's pamphlet writes, emboldened by Queen Anne's opening speech from the throne (March 1702). In that speech the

Queen had promised to maintain the Toleration, but had added indiscreetly, "My own principles must always keep me entirely firm to the interests and religion of the Church of England, and will encline me to countenance those who have the truest zeal to support it." Here at last was a truly English queen, thought the zealots, no more of that Dutchman, soft on Dissenters. High Church partisans went wild over Anne's words; Dr. Sacheverell preached the infamous sermon mimicked by Defoe in his *Shortest Way*, recommending hanging out the bloody flag of defiance to Dissenters; and Parliament became engrossed in an effort to pass a bill prohibiting the Occasional Conformity to Anglican rites, practised under King William by Dissenters who wished to hold public office.

The speaker in *King William's Affection* is a rarity among Defoe's personae: malicious, bigoted, ungrateful, hypocritical and illogical, he is the opposite of Defoe's customarily moderate, reasonable, and even-tempered spokesmen. Defoe's manipulation of this persona is relatively simple: we are expected to condemn when the persona excuses or admires, and to admire when he condemns. His judgment that James's infringements of the law were only trifling mistakes is thus to be rejected: we are to understand that they were, on the contrary, serious crimes; while William's measures favouring the established Church are not to be taken for granted and dismissed as the perfunctory performance of duty to be expected from any monarch, as the person suggests: they are to be acknowledged with gratitude.

The speaker demonstrates his spitefulness and lack of generosity by accusing William of hypocrisy even in the personal piety he exhibited on his deathbed: "By thus speciously assuming religion, he might even (to the last) hope to secure an interest in the clergy" (in the parenthesis we hear Defoe's own voice). The speaker's contemptible hypocrisy is demonstrated by his laying claim to "the honest freedom of an historian", who must set aside, in the search for truth, inhibitions about treading softly on the late king's ashes. His appeal to "the decent liberty ... of an English historiographer" is an excuse to interpret maliciously every one of William's actions. During the course of his illogical argument that William merited no thanks for signing over to certain bishops Crown rights to dispose of Church preferments, the speaker unguardedly reveals how his own lack of generosity blinds him to this merit in others. He adduces as proof of William's folly the fact that "he had made himself more friends in the Church, and stopped the mouths of a majority, had he kept these preferments in his own disposal". The true source of the speaker's animosity toward King William is revealed as sheer bigotry when he implies that even if the late king had been truly religious and affectionately concerned for the welfare of the Church, all that would have been cancelled out by one fact: "*That in his time the Toleration Act passed.*"

As the speaker recapitulates the arguments of latitudinarian appointees of William in favour of toleration of Dissenters, Defoe's mask begins to slip. First the latitudinarians make a moving plea for moderation which the speaker, a poor judge of logic, dismisses as "too thin and trifling for any serious answer". The last pages of the tract are in Defoe's own voice, as he observes that many of William's own appointees are now busy vilifying King William and his government, branding him as an enemy of the Church, and insulting his ashes "with a virulence and barbarity equal to that of the most rancorous Papist or Jacobite". The last part of the pamphlet, where Defoe says that if men like these are the only true sons of the established Church, then he is willing to be called a heretic, a fanatic, or anything else, rather than an ingrate, is a moving peroration. The last two paragraphs, in particular, contain echoes of Psalm CXXXVII and are Miltonic in their rhythm of periodic sentences.

Defoe's allusions to events of James's and William's reigns are accurate historically, and his judgements about the Act of Toleration and the attitudes of King James II and King William III toward the established Church are echoed by the major twentieth-century historians of the period. His indignation at ingratitude to King William is genuine. In spite of the critical and independent bent of his mind, Defoe had a tendency to hero-worship; William III, who seemed so cold and aloof to his contemporaries, was the most prominent member in the small personal Pantheon of the loyal Defoe.

King William's Affection is by no means a simple work, although Defoe's manipulation of his persona is simple when compared with Swift's. In many of Swift's works the reader must make repeated decisions about where to stop agreeing or disagreeing with the persona, who can at times be plausible or even likeable, at other times ridiculous or contemptible. With Defoe, in this work, the reader must make repeated evaluations of the arguments themselves. As the persona keeps failing to prove his case against King William, he keeps inadvertently proving a case against himself.

The logical dynamics of *King William's Affection* are outlined in the first paragraph, where the speaker suggests he will demonstrate how wrong "every Whiggish cabal" is to tax "friends of the Church, and the present government" with ingratitude to King William. At the same time, he points out that if these friends *were* ungrateful, they would be "like giddy weathercocks" and "base time-servers". This double operation is repeated in the second paragraph and at the start of the new argument beginning "Let us now view him mounted on the throne".

Henceforth in *King William's Affection*, cynical reservations about the speaker's own party appear as passing remarks rather than as announcements about how the argument will turn against the speaker. One such example is the observation that King William was foolish to have relinquished control over Church promotions, offending "those worthy churchmen, who seeing themselves neglected, have ever since been troubled with the spleen". When a bigoted persona condemns himself with this kind of remark, the irony of his author is clear. But the cynical reservation, frequent in Defoe's writing, is usually an unexpected one. His lively and critical mind, which could not be restrained from adverse judgements even of his own party or his own fictional protagonists, frightened the groups he served as spokesman in his nonfiction and disconcerts modern readers of his fiction.[5]

In addition to the logical complexity of *King William's Affection*, the verbal complexity is striking. The first few pages display a richness of invention rare in Defoe's writing. "King William" becomes "K. W.", then is demoted to the "P. of O." (Prince of Orange, William's title before he became King of England); "K. J." becomes "King James", then is promoted to "James the Just". Pairs of alternatives in which one term undercuts the other are offered to the reader: the Church of England was not in a forlorn condition when William arrived in England, and he did not, therefore, have "the good luck, or the honour to save it"; churchmen are to be praised for living peaceably under William, who "deserved so very ill, or so very little of them". James's illegal actions are enumerated in such detail that their description as "mistakes or miscarriages" by the persona is demonstrated to be ludicrously vague and euphemistic.

The homely practical illustration of ideas associated with Defoe's plain style in his *Review* and in his fictions appears relatively infrequently in *King William's Affection*. One example is in reply to the question, why William should be called a deliverer, when he needed the support of the English people for his success: "He that's fallen into a pit, may chuse whether he will be helped out, or no; and if he stretches out his hands, and strains his lungs in begging for help, 'tis hard that all this fatigue must pass for nothing, but that he who only lends his hand, should set up for his sole rescuer." Another of the verbal devices associated with Defoe's plain style appears in his exceptionally forceful adjectives, nouns, and verbs: the Church was in a flourishing state when William arrived in England with his "tattered regiments"; a false idea is "crammed down" the "throats" of the multitude; churchmen loyal to William are "mongrel Churchmen", or "Dutch Churchmen".

The last few pages of the excerpt are entirely in Defoe's plain style. But this plain style is not identical with that of the *Review*, for it lacks the homely illustrations just exemplified, and its diction contains a higher proportion of latinate derivatives than usual. Furthermore, its rhythm is in the long measures characteristic of the formal speech or sermon, not the short measures of idiomatic dialogue that characterize the *Review*. Nevertheless, the peroration of the last two paragraphs reveals Defoe's usual vigour, with its highly active verbs ("cursing"), few but forceful adjectives ("insufferable"), and highly cadenced series of parallel clauses with loose articulation between the individual sets of members.

King William's Affection is not only an extremely well-written piece of satire; its contemporaneity with the better-known *Shortest Way* makes it significant in the long-standing critical controversy over the latter work, indeed in the controversy over irony in Defoe's work in general.[6] Some have maintained that *The Shortest Way* is clearly a work of irony, while others have insisted that it is primarily a work of mimicry. Mimicry, which presupposes authorial identification with fictional characters, is the opposite of irony, which presupposes authorial distancing from characters. Accordingly, Defoe, who wished to do both at once, is frequently accused of being a poor ironist.[7] The argument appears to have been settled in the case of *The Shortest Way* by Miriam Leranbaum's discovery of a recent antecedent, proving that the genre of Defoe's pamphlet is not satire; it is political hoax or banter.[8] Its primary characteristic, therefore, is mimicry. *King William's Affection* demonstrates that Defoe was also perfectly capable during the same period of handling irony successfully in the complex literary form of satire.[9]

The backfiring of Defoe's mimicry in *The Shortest Way* does not indicate that he lacked the technical ability to ridicule Sacheverell's sermon through irony. It indicates, instead, that he was really trying to do exactly what he later professed (in *Present State of the Parties in Great Britain*, 1712) had been his aim: to trap the High-Fliers either into condemning the pamphlet, and thus condemning religious persecution, or into approving of it, thus discrediting and exposing themselves to the disgust of those moderate Englishmen Defoe believed to be the majority. The pillory soon taught him that truth does not necessarily triumph immediately in the free market-place of ideas, but he never lost his skill at touching up and exaggerating a ridiculous argument.[10]

Notes

1 "The new House of Commons was more carefully packed in the royal interest than any other with which any Stuart King had to deal", writes G. M. Trevelyan in *The English Revolution 1688–1689* (New York, 1965), p. 25.

2 *Ibid.*, p. 25.

3 *Ibid.*, p. 81.

4 Sir George Clark, *The Later Stuarts 1660–1714* (Oxford, 1955), p. 156. G. V. Bennett writes that the vacancies in bishoprics and deaneries "were filled by moderate Tories, men of real distinction and learning. It is often said that King William packed the episcopal bench with 'Whig Latitudinarians', but the evidence is quite otherwise." ("Conflict in the Church", in *Britain after the Glorious Revolution*, ed. Geoffrey Holmes, London: Macmillan and Co., 1969, p. 161.)

5 When fellow Dissenters failed in 1703 to stand by the imprisoned Defoe, one good reason may have been the following gibe at the practice of occasional conformity: "If the Gallows instead of the Counter, and the Gallies instead of the Fines, were the Reward of going to a Conventicle, to preach or hear, there wou'd not be so many Sufferers, the Spirit of Martyrdom is over; they that will go to Church to be chosen Sheriffs and Mayors, would go to forty Churches rather than be Hang'd" (*The Shortest Way with the Dissenters*). Defoe had previously engaged in public controversy with Dissenters who practised occasional conformity; his own opinion, placed in the mouth of a High-Church bigot calling for the extermination of Dissenters, could only have infuriated his co-religionists, who at first had been terrified by *The Shortest Way*.

6 For a convenient bibliography, see Paul K. Alkon's "Defoe's Argument in *The Shortest Way with the Dissenters*", MP, 73 (May 1976), S13.

7 Even his distinguished biographer, James Sutherland, takes for granted Defoe's clumsiness with irony. Discussing one of the 1713 pamphlets that got Defoe into legal difficulties, Professor Sutherland, imagines a scene in which Defoe's "beloved daughter Sophy" pleads with him: "No more irony, dear papa! You *know* you aren't good at it". (*Daniel Defoe: A Critical Study* Cambridge, Mass.: Harvard University Press, 1971, p. 64).

8 Miriam Leranbaum, "An 'Irony Not Unusual': Defoe's *Shortest Way with the Dissenters*", *HLQ*, 37 (May 1974), 227–50.

9 Maximillian E. Novak has called attention several times to the importance of *King William's Affection* in the controversy over irony in *The Shortest Way*. See, for instance, "Defoe's *Shortest Way with the Dissenters*, Hoax, Parody, Paradox, Fiction, Irony, and Satire", *MLQ*, 27 (December 1966), 407.

10 See page 23.

King William's Affection to the Church of England Examined, &c.
(1703)

There is not a more common, nor more credited reflection upon the friends of the Church, and the present government, than that of ingratitude to King William. Every Whiggish cabal is full of it; and a man can scarce come into the company of one of these new grumblers, without being deafened with their fulsome cant of forgetting the late king and all his mighty magnified actions for the Church of England. How do the coffeehouses, taverns, nay and their silly pamphlets, abound in this calumny? As if the sons of the Church were like giddy weathercocks constant to no corner, but variously whirled to and fro, as the wind of interest or authority blows, as if they were a company of base time-servers, and apt to revile their best friends, when misfortunes, or death, have put it out of their power any longer to oblige them.

What a perpetual noise have we of deliverances, freeing the kingdom from slavery, and the Church from popery, and being rescued from galleys and gibbets? as if dragooning had been in fashion in K. J.'s reign, or that K. W. could have delivered us without our own help and concurrence. 'Tis owned there were some infringements of the law, in the reign of that unfortunate monarch: but I presume the abused nation is by this time convinced, that those were but trifling bugbears, and that we might have rectified those magnified mistakes, without paying so dear for Dutch assistance, or idolizing a prince, who though he freed us from supposed dangers, did afterwards bring our Church into real ones; and perhaps the State has not escaped without its scars. Now I confess that ingratitude to our true benefactors is such a crime, that it has justly been esteemed a reproach to human nature; and is so much worse in churchmen, as it contradicts all their pulpit eloquence, and renders them most scandalous confutations of their own doctrines. Their ill examples shall infect more, than all their harangues can antidote. And 'tis still more aggravated in them, if they prove ungrateful for the highest services done to the Church, and to that man who rescued it, when it was in the utmost peril of sinking.

But that the Church was in so forlorn a condition when the P. of O. came to England; or that he with his tattered regiments had the good luck, or the honour to save it; or that he afterwards used the power put into his hands for the service of the Church, or that he ever was a true friend to it: these are paradoxes which the multitude seem to swallow by wholesale, and are crammed down their throats by a sort of mongrel churchmen, who indeed made their own advantage of K. W.'s reign by engrossing the best preferments. But by such as these, the poor Church of England has ever been betrayed; and I wish the danger of these false friends, these Dutch churchmen, be yet over. But alas, we have daily experiences of these men's friendship to the Church, in their constant opposition to those good bills which are designed to settle it, on the foot it stood in good King Charles's reign.

I shall therefore endeavour to disabuse those sons of the Church, whom their new fathers have led into these errors, and vindicate the honour and gratitude of all true churchmen, from those base malicious aspersions which the blind admirers of the late government have so freely thrown in their faces; and I hope to prove that the Church of England was in no great or apparent danger from the mistakes of King James's government, nor so mightily delivered by K. W.'s, but rather put into the utmost hazard of ruin, from the favour then shewed to fanaticks, and the partiality of preferring only such as were underhand friends to schism and Nonconformity; and that therefore the true sons of the Church are groundlessly branded for ingratitude, as having none of those obligations to K. W. so loudly talked of in all publick places; and that if churchmen were blameable, it is in the other extreme, of living so easily and quietly under the government of a foreigner, who deserved so very ill, or so very little of them.

We will then first consider, what those terrible things were, which the Church suffered in the reign of James the Just. I have already called them mistakes or miscarriages, and that is the most that can be made of them. It was indeed a mistake to introduce so many priests, Jesuits and friars in their habits into England; it was the same mistake to build them mass-houses and convents, and give them authority to preach and say mass, and make all the converts here they could. So it was, to bring a Jesuit into the Privy Council, and to turn out so many Fellows of colleges, to make room for his scandalous priests and converts. It was the same mistakes which made him set up the High Commission Court for the destruction of all the faithful clergy, as the members of that court have since owned. It was the same to impose a Declaration on churchmen against their consciences, to be read by them in favour of popery; and a gross mistake to imprison and suspend those who refused to read it. So it was in that deluded monarch, to promise so fair at first to the Church, and then to do his utmost to destroy it; and he found his mistakes in the project he had of making the Dissenters his tools for that purpose. He was out too in claiming a right to dispense with all laws, and pursuing that right to the putting out all honest men, and putting none but knaves and desperate beggars into the best offices. The same mistake it was to keep up here a standing army against law, though I dare say he meant to do no more with them, than barely to establish liberty of conscience. He was a little out too, in so violently prosecuting the bishops for doing their duty; and then in sending them to the Tower at such an unlucky juncture; when he knew that the young prince was to be born, and that those bishops might have been as creditable witnesses of his birth as Jefferies, or Wilks, or Delabadie. In short, it was all mistake, to overturn the constitution so very fast, which had he used slower methods he might have done most effectually; and which he brought to such perfection in Ireland, as justified his triumphal embassy to Rome, and all the holy emblems there made of destroying the Northern heresy, and restoring the harmless hind to the kingdoms once her own. These are the formidable miscarriages of that reign, against which we have had so many outcries; and what do they all amount to, but a few slips in politicks? Are there not many worthy men now in high offices, who bore a great part in that exploded government? They are living witnesses of the innocent designs of that unhappy king, and that whatever the Whigs call his plots to bring in popery, slavery, and arbitrary power, were barely some mistaken measures, which common heads fancied to lean a little that way; but that the true design of that unhappy prince was the establishment of the true Protestant Church of

England, and old liberty and property to all his subjects.

And for a demonstration, that these pretended bloody designs of K. J. were pure mistakes, such as may happen in the best governments; what can be more plain, than to see the same good mistaken patriots, now the ministers and favourites of a government, where we are sure nothing is nearer their hearts than the Church of England, the destruction of France, and the exclusion of a pretended king, who inherits a double portion of his father's virtues? And for a further irrefragable proof of the same mistake; let anyone, or all these patriots be asked, whether if the same game were to be played over again, they would do the same thing that they have done in that reign? Whether they would again act as High Commissioners against the Church? Whether they would be tools in the same civil offices? Whether a certain bishop would threaten all his honest clergy, and go again to meet the Pope's Nuncio?* Whether others of them would temporize, and sacrifice their function and consciences and their brethren too, and all for the establishment of popery? Whether lawyers would declare the dispensing power to be good law?

In a word, whether any of them would move a step towards the advancement of those pretended wicked designs against the Church and kingdom? Undoubtedly they would all answer, 'No'; they would rather be martyred than do such base things any more. Does not this therefore prove that all was a plain mistake, that they were only a little deceived in politicks, which is owned to be a difficult attainment? And what a man has once done, and professes he would not for the world do again, 'tis certain he was mistaken in the doing of it. That (as the case yet stands) these gentlemen would not mistake again, is I hope past denial; and what they may do, if such another turn should happen, no man is prophet enough to tell. I believe they are so sensible of the deceitfulness of their own hearts, that few of them would venture to promise or prophesy anything certain for themselves.

Thus it is evident, that all the measures of K. J.'s

* *Nuncio*: The papal ambassador, Ferdinand, Count d'Adda, who had been invited to England in 1685 by James II, but not officially recognised. Wishing to publicize the return of the nation to its Roman Catholic allegiance, James held a splendid ceremony at Windsor in July 1687, after the dissolution of Parliament, to celebrate d'Adda's public reception. Defoe is apparently referring to the Bishop of London, Samuel Parker (1640–88), a favourite of James, who was resented for, among other things, ordering his clerical subordinates to make declarations thanking the King for his kindness to the Church. I can find no confirmation, however, of Defoe's allegation that this "certain bishop" also consented to take part in the ceremony for d'Adda. [Ed.]

government were mere harmless mistakes; for if the same were to be once more acted, and the success as well known, 'tis most sure they would not split twice on the same rock. Where then is the mighty merit of a deliverance from downright mistakes? Mistakes which the good King himself saw, and endeavoured to mend, had not the P. of O.'s fleet fallen into that confounded storm that happened, and which (as ill luck would have it) it had the fortune to escape.

But at length K. W. came, and no doubt had a weighty errand, to deliver us from *hard words, jealousies and fears*, and no more. Had he spared his pains, a little time would have done all this without him. We should have seen what these extraordinary motions would end in, and then could have supplied proper remedies of our own. An English Parliament would have ended all, in spite of armies, Jesuits, priests, High Commissions, closetings, and all the engines of Rome, or Hell, or France. And this might have been assembled without the Prince of Orange or his armies. But the nation was so frighted, that they would not stay for the regular redress of grievances, though they knew the King designed to do all by a parliament. So that nothing but the people's impatience brought about the late Revolution. They would not attend to the final events of affairs, and to see what the good King himself would do; but must needs invite a deliverer to rescue them from armies and arbitrary power, which a parliament with a few votes could have conquered. But however it was, you see that K. W. without the concurrence of the people could have been but half a deliverer; and why should he engross all the honour and merit of it, since the nation had so great share in it? He that's fallen into a pit, may chuse whether he will be helped out, or no; and if he stretches out his hands, and strains his lungs in begging for help, 'tis hard that all this fatigue must pass for nothing, but that he who only lends his hand, should set up for his sole rescuer. Yet thus stupid were all the parliaments in K. W.'s reign, and gave him the only honour of a redeemer, when 'tis notorious, that the whole kingdom was as fond of being redeemed, as he was of coming to their rescue.

Thus I hope, 'tis plain to the meanest capacity, that neither Church nor State were in that hazard, as is pretended, in K. J.'s reign; nor that K. W. deserved all those flattering panegyricks, as if he were our preserver from popery and slavery, and a thousand bugbears besides, which we could not else have escaped. And for the confirmation of what I say, I appeal to daily experience, whether all this be not effectually forgotten, and K. W. and his redemptions turned into a common ridicule? Which 'tis impossible should so soon come to pass, had either the dangers we escaped, or his pretended deliverance been half so great as 'tis some men's interest to represent them.

Thus you have a large account of the P. of O.'s merits before his grasping the crown; and if the mob must needs look upon them with magnifying glasses, I hope the better sort will not borrow their false spectacles.

Let us now view him mounted on the throne, and see how much more the Church was obliged to him in the execution of his power, than they were in his obtaining it; which I hope will disabuse the world effectually, as to that odious imputation of ingratitude so lavishly bestowed on churchmen.

Now the best way to examine this fairly is to set all his actions, which may concern the Church, in their proper light, and then to consider particularly what sort of men he made choice of to fill up the best Church preferments. And if he was blameable in these two points, and managed them both in favour of popery, or fanaticism, what obligation can any real churchman have to value his memory, or tread softly on his ashes? The greatest monarch laid in his grave, must not, cannot escape the honest freedom of an historian; and let K. W. be as high as flattery could make him, whilst he lived and governed these kingdoms, he is now as dead as Alexander, or Oliver Cromwel, and 'tis fit posterity should know what they owe to him, and what they do not. With all the decent liberty then of an English historiographer:

I do not find that his actions in favour of the Church deserve that fulsome applause, which the spurious brood of churchmen (as they are justly called) are pleased to daub them with. And to make this point as clear as the sun, I shall recount most celebrated performances both in England and Ireland; for as to Scotland, Her Majesty having promised to maintain their church, as they have modelled it, I shall not venture to burn my fingers with it at all. For it is plain, her gracious promise is a justification of what her predecessor did, or at least was forced to comply with, at a juncture, when that, or a civil war, was the only choice left him.

In England then, his so much celebrated actions were only the restoring all the honest clergy to their livings, who had been unjustly suspended or deprived; and also to the liberty of preaching, instructing and disputing for the Protestant Church, without the hazard of falling into those hard circumstances purely for doing their duty. And what wonderful merit was there in this? That a Protestant prince, who set up for liberty and justice, should restore men to their rights, when invaded? Indeed had a popish or tyrannical prince done this, it had been wonderful; but why all this thanks to a Protestant, who knows 'tis his duty to do it?

The next thing was, his establishing them so by law, that no future tyrant may possibly hurt them by High Commissions, or any other lawless traps to ensnare them: and therefore he took care to have all the tricks with which they were hampered in the former reign, to be declared illegal, arbitrary, and a subversion of the constitution, and this in full Parliament; and that no pretended power of dispensing should hereafter harm them. It's owned, this is a good law, but what then? Did K. W. do any more towards it than another king might have done? He gave the royal assent to it; and so he did to abundance of good laws besides, which yet he could not have enacted without Parliament. Next he summoned a Convocation, that they should do all that lay in them, to make the best constitutions for the good government of the Church; and whatever they did for this end, was to be ratified, and confirmed in Parliament. But no thanks to him for that favour: it was their right to be summoned to parliament; witness the *Praemunientes*.* And did not that Convocation fall together by the ears, and do much more harm than good? And did not K. W. occasion those feuds by proposing peace and moderation to them? And did he not drop the following one, that should have been assembled to the same purposes with the other? So that his intentions were plain enough by the success of the one, and the not meeting of the next Convocation, which I must tell you is such a slur, as shall blot his memory to the end of the world; but other pens have done wonders, and displayed the horror of the tragedy, thereby designed to be acted, if Providence had not sent the most accurate A. and learned B. to quench the flame, then kindling for the poor Church of England. After this K. W. passed many acts of Parliament, by which the inferior clergy were made easy in acquiring their dues; and it must be owned that he never obstructed any one Act for the good of the

* *Praemunientes*: A clause of the 1295 writ of Edward I, summoning bishops of the Church of England, together with their lesser clerical attendants, to Parliament. This became a tradition by which the spiritual estate was summoned to the opening of Parliament. [Ed.]

Church. But this he knew was for his own interest, or he had never done it; which they who knew his heart intimately are most sure of.

Another great instance of K. W.'s friendship to the Church so much insisted upon, is that impartial justice which churchmen are said to have found in all the courts of justice during his reign. Their causes always met the best countenance from the judges; and I have heard it affirmed, that since the Restoration, there have not so many advantages accrued to the rights of the Church, as in the fourteen years of K. W.'s government. I will not say that the clergy found any favour from the courts, more than the equity of their causes entitled them to; for that is not to be imagined of the best set of judges, that ever adorned Westminster Hall; but I must confess that no point was ever strained against them; and wherever the law could be interpreted to favour their title, it was ever made to speak all that could be said in defence of the Church's rights. Now as to this, it is easily answered, that the judges held their places without dependence on the favour of the Court; and since they did so, no influences of the higher powers could prevail with them to discountenance the clergy, whatever secret orders they might have received to do so; and this being matter of fact, that the judges held their offices during good behaviour, it cannot be imagined, that any Court threats or promises would make them hazard their freeholds, to run down the clergy. So that the advantages which the clergy reaped in that reign are owing to the good judges, and not to the favour of K. W. or his ministry; though it must be confessed, that he took care to fill the benches with those good men who afterwards proved such real friends to the Church.

But of all the evidences of K. W.'s esteem and favour for the Church, that of putting the Archbishop of Canterbury so often at the head of Church and State, is most insisted upon. This (they pretend) is a thing before unheard of, and unprecedented since the Reformation, that during the King's absence abroad, the first in commission, power and trust, should be a churchman. And this not only once done, as might be for some exigency, or to honour a particular man, but (to shew it done out of pure esteem for the Church) the same was yearly continued, as long as His Majesty's affairs required his presence beyond sea. And this they urge, as an instance of honouring the Church and clergy, not to be found before in all our history, since the darkest times of popery, when the clergy usurped all power to themselves, and domineered equally in Church and State. But since churchmen had lost so much of that ancient authority, 'tis plain that K. W. might have left them out if he pleased; and therefore his appointing the Archbishop the chief of them, is a plain argument of the value he had for the function, no less than the person.

But to solve this mysterious riddle, it is to be considered that the clergy and university had long been insinuating themselves into K. W.'s favour, and by the best arts of civility, affection, and complaisance, had so far won upon his temper, that he did this in pure return for the innumerable obligations which the majority of the clergy had heaped upon him. I am loth to tax those complements of the clergy, with the odious name of flattery; but all the world knows, how the university in all their elections, and the clergy in their votes, and their conversation, still studied the honour and interest of K. W. and preferred a foolish admiration of him, to their own safety, property, and security. This I speak, as to a well known majority of the clergy; which I hope is sufficient to explain the secret motive of K. W.'s putting a churchman at the head of his kingdoms in his absence; that it was out of a politick gratitude, and no affection either to their office, or to the persons who bore it.

'Tis urged moreover, that K. W. took the utmost care for suppressing profaneness and immorality, by making some new laws, and enforcing the execution of all the laws made to that purpose; which is looked upon by some to be a good service to the Church. But by their leave, what thanks can K. W. claim on that score? I am sure the Church and State were happier in other reigns, when the people were not put to half that trouble for a few innocent liberties. And where was the equity of making men pay so dear for 'em when taxes run so very high?

But of all the actions of that king, in favour of the Church, not one is so much magnified and admired, as the commission which he gave to a certain number of bishops to dispose of all the Church preferments, which were in his own immediate presentation. This (say they) is such an instance of his love to and care of the Church, as is not to be paralleled in our history; not the best of our kings or queens, but have preserved this as a jewel of their crown; and it had been reckoned a sacred maxim of state, to provide for friends and favourites, with these choice morsels of the ecclesiastical revenues. Yet so strictly did K. W. comply with this unprecedented commission, that I must needs say, I have reason to believe he never was once prevailed with to interpose, or overrule in it: and certainly the delegating this power to so many bishops, was the wisest way imaginable to make it a real service to the Church. Yet even for this, I cannot see how the Church was so mightily obliged to that king. Some say it was done in his own defence, to prevent the many importunities of courtiers to prefer their friends. But the truth of the matter is, K. W. was a stranger to the personal characters and qualifications of most of the clergy; and therefore contrived this method, that he might not bestow his favours blindfold: and what a man cannot so well execute by himself, is he to be admired for trusting it to others more capable? And to my knowledge he had made himself more friends in the Church, and stopped the mouths of a majority, had he kept these preferments in his own disposal: so that in my opinion, this famed commission is rather to be numbered among the follies and weaknesses of his reign, than a token of his love to the Church, its true sons not being in the least advantaged, by putting it into such partial hands. Indeed they who reaped the benefit of that unpolitick commission, may raise the merit of it to the stars; but what is all this to those worthy churchmen, who seeing themselves neglected, have ever since been troubled with the spleen?

* * *

I shall conclude this head of K. W.'s actions for the Church, by confessing with his friends, that he was a constant frequenter of the service of the Church; a devout and frequent communicant; one who never scandalised the profession of the gospel by a wicked and profligate life; that he always freely hazarded his own person in the field of battle, which in any other king had been esteemed a real service and friendship for the Church, its security under God depending entirely at several times on his particular safety: and after so much done both in peace and war, for the establishment of the Church, to shew his steddy affection to it to the very last, he desires, and has the assistance of its bishops in his last hours; receives the sacrament from their hands, and with the most firm, sedate, exemplary piety, dies in the communion of it.

All this ('tis true) looks as if a man were in earnest a friend to the Church. But when you have thoroughly considered K. W.'s character, what deep designs and fetches he always had in all his actions; how little he discovered of his inward or real sentiments, even to his most familiar friends; that ambition or interest was ever at the bottom, whatever face his outside politicks wore; and that by thus speciously assuming religion, he might even (to the last) hope to secure an interest in the clergy: I say, he that duly weighs all this, must own, that the Church is not indebted to him for such hypocrisies; since every true churchman must confess, that in spite of all that has been urged, he was no real friend to the Church. For to all this, it is objected,

That in his time the Toleration Act passed.

* * *

... It may be needless to characterize the reverend gentlemen here set down [church prelates appointed during the reign of King William], nor would I be guilty of so great a presumption: 'tis sufficient to have recourse to our own knowledge and remembrance for the most eminent of them, and there to consider, which of them have been favourers of popery or fanaticism; which of them have betrayed the cause of the Church to its open enemies; which of them have deserted it in times of danger or persecution; which of them have maintained the Church's doctrine and worship against all opposers; which of them have been constant eminent preachers in their respective cures and parishes; which of them had gained any reputation by their labours or writings for the Church; which of them had been guilty of compliances, to the dishonour or disservice of the Church: in a word, which of them had given any just suspicion, that in their principles or practices, they were enemies to our ecclesiastical constitution. And if upon a diligent search, we find the most of them, or any number of them, criminal in the particulars here specified, then 'tis plain that he who promoted 'em had a design to injure the established Church; and by such rotten members to destroy and subvert the whole hierarchy, and to introduce a confused Babel of sects, nations and languages. But if the generality of these reverend divines were men who by preaching, writing, disputing, by their constant labours and blameless lives, had always defended the Church's cause, and supported it in the worst of times, then I confess there is not much to be laid to K. W.'s charge, as if his promotions were designed for the ruin of the Church established; whether they were or were not, I must leave to every man's conscience, that knows their persons and characters.

Yet it cannot be denied, but that many of them are men of latitudinarian principles, that are for widening the entrance into the Church, for complying too far with the Dissenters, and for giving up the decent ceremonies and settled discipline, in exchange for a slovenly, rude way of worship: but they have the confidence to deny this, and to challenge all their enemies to shew what they have said or written or done for the service of the Dissenters, or to countenance their schism. But this they own, that at a time when popery is making its utmost efforts to extirpate the common name of Protestant, it is at least unseasonable to increase, stir up, or widen that division, which has already sufficiently weakened the common cause: and having had the most bitter experience, how in former reigns the politicians have played one party against the other, and made them mutual tools to gratify the humour, or serve the interest of the prevailing faction at court; they think it absurd to run into the same fatal errors with their eyes open, and therefore are for tolerating Dissenters, since the Church is sufficiently secured by so many wholesome laws; and are not for new experiments of effecting that by force, which they have seen before was to no purpose; being assured that the established Church has gained great numbers by the Toleration, and that it lost more by persecution (besides falling under the foul imputation of an unchristian spirit) than ever they are able to retrieve; unless by persisting in that gentle, peaceable temper which in K. W.'s reign procured them so much love and esteem.

And as to compliances with the Dissenters, they owned themselves tied and obliged by their promises made in times of adversity; and are for coming to that temper with them, which the suffering bishops promised in K. James's tyranny, as 'tis called; a scheme of which is now remaining under the hand of Archbishop Sancroft, and the rest of them; and which they are ready to perfect, when the whole Convocation shall approve of, and freely consent to it.

But for any change, to the dishonour or detriment of the established Church, they all affirm they abhor the thoughts of it, and resolve they say (with God's assistance) rather to suffer the greatest hardships here, than either to endeavour, or to consent to so wicked a project. And if for this temper they must bear the name of Low-Churchmen, they are content to bear it, or any other reflection, rather than be tools for introducing popery, or clearing the way for a popish successor. But they desire the world to do impartial justice between them and those who are pleased with the distinction of High-Churchmen; that if their moderation and temper towards Dissenters must pass for betraying the Church, the others' continual caressing, herding with, defending and courting of Nonjurors, Papists and Jacobites may pass for the measure of their thoughts of such men's principles; and how far they love the Protestant religion established in the Church, or the Protestant succession in the State.

Such apologies these gentlemen make for themselves, which are too thin and trifling for any serious answer. But in the list here given, I find many who owe their greatness, their livings and all their elevation to K. W. or those placed in authority by him; and were the list complete, we should see many more. Yet we see to our astonishment, numbers of these running in with those men who use the basest arts to asperse and vilify K. W. and his government, to brand him as an enemy of the Church; and to insult his ashes with a virulence and barbarity equal to that of the most rancorous Papist or Jacobite. That some such are to be discovered in the world, their own daily practice puts it out of all dispute; and I hope the world pays too great a deference to the parts and learning of those worthy gentlemen, to let any of their memorable expressions ever be forgotten, or unrewarded. Yet with their leave I would ask, whether the abusing their master, their patron, their deliverer and best benefactor, be not a base, horrid ingratitude? and if it be, what Church or what religion encourages that abominable sin? Or what real service can such men's preaching and haranguing do to the souls of a people, who generally reckon themselves highly obliged to honour the memory of K. W.? And their spiritual guides, under far stricter obligations to this, than they can be, and yet dare prevaricate with their God, in their most solemn thanksgivings for what K. W. did as his instrument? and in their clubs, cabals and conversations, run him down as a scourge sent from heaven to afflict and betray God's true Church?

If men of these principles and practices are the only genuine sons of the Church established; if the vilest ingratitude must pass for the characteristick of a true churchman; if an insufferable insolence to the memory of the best of princes must be a mark of affection and sincerity to the Church of England; if thanking God for K. W. in the offices of the Church, and cursing his very ashes upon all other occasions, must be the distinction of the Church's real friends, and they who do such things must be the only men of true, undissembled religion: why then,

Sit Anima Mea cum Philosophis; let heresy, let schism, let Low Church, fanaticism or any other controverted reproach asperse me; but let not base ingratitude, owned by all the world to be the vilest, horridest wickedness, and inconsistent with any degree of good, and the sure mark of a soul disposed for all sorts of villainy; let not this monster be laid at my door. Let it never be said that I owe my religion, estate and liberty (under God's Providence) to a generous prince, and when he is laid in the dust, that I dare openly call that great benefactor a tyrant, or knave: or though such a wickedness may be charged on a few private wretches, let the sons of the Church of England never suffer by such an unnatural distinction; nor any of its fathers be ever so infamously dignified or distinguished.

2. A Declaration of Truth to Benjamin Hoadly

A Declaration of Truth to Benjamin Hoadly, published on 29 June 1717, is one of some nine pamphlets in which Defoe impersonated a Quaker. Dealing primarily with the problem of ecclesiastical authority over individuals, it voices with calculated irony radical views about the position of the Church of England as a favoured institution within the State.

The Bangorian Controversy, a fierce intellectual and journalistic dispute in which over fifty writers produced some 200 pamphlets, and to which Defoe contributed with his *Declaration of Truth* and several other pamphlets, was occasioned by a sermon preached before the King on 31 March 1717 by Benjamin Hoadly (1676–1761), Bishop of Bangor. Hoadly was a leading controversialist, appointed royal chaplain on the accession of George I as a reward for his services to the Whigs in the previous reign, and made Bishop of Bangor in 1715.[1] His sermon, "The Nature of the Kingdom of the Church of Christ", was designed to herald the repeal of the Occasional Conformity and Schism Acts (1718) passed against Dissenters as the result of extremist pressure on Robert Harley's Tory ministry.[2] Hoadly disavowed the principle of ecclesiastical authority over individual consciences and asserted the principle of voluntary consent as the basis of church organization. His view of religion, resting upon the conscience of the individual aided only by the words of the New Testament, bore more resemblance "to the new fashionable Deism than to the historic tradition of any Christian Church".[3]

Hoadly's sermon, as well as a controversial work he had written in 1716,[4] emphasized the supreme power of the State, ridiculed the authority of the Church, and consequently aroused fears about the position of the Establishment under the Whig regime. High-Church advocates were worried that acceptance of the right of the civil power to adopt any measures against popery would lead to the sacrifice, in the interest of a united Protestant front against Jacobitism, of the distinctive characteristics of each Protestant sect, on which Hoadly set little store.[5] The Lower House of the Canterbury Convocation attacked the sermon, whereupon the Crown intervened to prorogue the Synod.[6]

Christian laymen, as well as Church officials, were disturbed by Hoadly's conclusions, especially since they came from a bishop of the established Church. As Gibbon later observed, Hoadly became "the object of Whig idolatry and Tory abhorrence".[7]

Relishing almost nothing better than a lively dispute about ecclesiastical polity as deduced from Christian doctrine, Defoe entered the lists from all sides with great enthusiasm, writing against the Convocation that had censured Hoadly, reproaching one of Hoadly's antagonists, Andrew Snape, for his violent language, and attacking Hoadly himself for his arguments. Defoe wrote seven pamphlets on the Bangorian controversy in 1717 alone, and a few more in 1718 and 1719.[8]

A Declaration of Truth, one of the seven pamphlets of 1717, is a brilliant example of argument based upon sheer impudence. The very notion of a pack of obscure Quakers, their fanaticism indicated by ludicrous names like Aminadab and Ebenezer,[9] condescending to treat "respectfully" an eminent bishop of the Church of England, addressing him as "Benjamin", and congratulating him on his sermon, must have shocked or delighted eighteenth-century moderates, united in their contempt for "enthusiasm", but diversified in their sense of humour and literary sophistication.

"Benjamin" could hardly have welcomed the Quaker Ebenezer's demonstration by parallel texts taken from his own and Quaker publications, that their doctrines of religious conscience were identical. Nor could he have appreciated Ebenezer's observation that the bishop's argument has justified Nonconformists, convinced that they are guided by heavenly light, in separating and withdrawing from the "usurpations" of the established Church. Least of all could Hoadly have relished the conclusion drawn from his own denial of power and authority to ministers by the relentlessly logical Quaker, who assumes that, like the Quakers, Hoadly will henceforth recognize only those ministers who have "freely received perfect gifts from God for perfecting of the saints". Men who have received special training for the ministry in schools or colleges or who receive payment for their religious services are scorned as mere "ministers by the will of man" by the intransigent Quaker, who is convinced that Hoadly, having been enlightened by God, will next be "assisted by the spirit of truth to pull down and overthrow the whole power, hierarchy and constitution of that people who call themselves the Church".

His deduction that Hoadly's next logical step should be to demolish the entire structure of the Church of England, gives no pause to the imperturbable Quaker, who is so intent upon the logic of his argument that its practical consequences are irrelevant to him. With the greatest of composure he proceeds to invite Hoadly to join the Society of Friends. The entire argument has been leading up to this impudent invitation: "For why shouldst thou not cause thy life and thy doctrine to conform unto each other?", the ironic climax of the pamphlet which, like most of Defoe's irony, rests upon the contrast between principle and practice. The apparently ingenuous invitation carries a malicious little sting which indicates that the Quaker is not, after all, as unaware of worldly considerations as his argument has thus far suggested. The Quaker observes that the humble station of ministers of his sect may at first seem unappealing to the eminent bishop, but he reminds Hoadly that "the Kingdom of Jesus is not of this world, and that likewise his rewards are not of this world, as thou hast most worthily taught".

Eager to ensure that Hoadly join the Quakers, rather than any other sect of Dissenters, the Quaker concludes his argument by disparaging his most dangerous competitors. These are the Presbyterians, whose doctrines, having many similarities to those of the Church of England, might well appear attractive to potential apostates from the established Church. Pretending to remind Hoadly that Presbyterian doctrines are not as radical as those professed by the Bishop himself, the Quaker lists these doctrines. Like many skilful ironists, Defoe thus reminds his readers of the norm, or accepted standard, against which the deviations he has been describing should be measured.

Defoe's moderate Presbyterian position underlies the pamphlets he wrote on the Bangorian controversy, despite the particular point of view he appears to be espousing in each instance. In his *Report Reported* (1717), a rebuke to the Convention that censured Hoadly, he protests against extreme positions on ecclesiastical authority: "I know not what to say to men, who in so absolute a manner take upon them to lay down positions, as if they were mathematically demonstrated, when at the same time they admit many doubts and exceptions". He insists that in spite of limitations on the authority of the Christian Church suggested by New Testament passages, some authority is necessary and permitted, according to these passages.

While Defoe favours, in these pamphlets, the removal of the Test and Schism Acts heralded by Hoadly's sermon, he disagrees with Hoadly's theoretical justification for such removal, disapproves of the unseasonableness of his sermon, which he fears has aroused such rancour that repeal might well be endangered, and considers a public figure like Hoadly to be a completely inappropriate spokesman for such a theory.[10]

The Quaker idiom Defoe employs in a number of his pamphlets, as well as his use of Quaker characters in several of his fictions, attest to his particular interest in this religious sect. It is possible that his interest in Quakers was originally aroused by William Penn's unsuccessful intervention with Queen Anne to save him from the pillory in 1703,[11] but the Quakers who begin appearing frequently after 1714 in Defoe's writings were of a humbler social class, more typical of Quakers, than Penn's.[12]

Defoe's fascination with Quakers appears to have centered principally on the discrepancy between Quaker profession and the practices necessitated by life in an imperfect world. According to the *Encyclopaedia Britannica*, Quakers originally understood the Sermon on the Mount as a series of principles to be construed "not as counsels of perfection, but as practical guides to life". Yet by the early eighteenth century, Quakers were generally regarded as very shrewd businessmen who made use of their religious connections to establish links with other Quaker businessmen across the nation.

The simple and sombre clothing worn by Quakers was appropriate to the plain dealers to whom much of the popular and polite writing of the early eighteenth century was ostensibly addressed. Defoe seems to have visualized Quakers in this role: in *Roxana* he stresses the efficacy of the Quaker uniform as disguise and in *The Shortest Way to Peace and Union* (1703), he refers to the Quaker as "a plain dealing professor". In *The Complete English Tradesman* (1725), he observes that, in spite of their advocacy of fixed prices, custom has forced even Quakers to concur in the practice of bargaining with purchasers. Although she has strong scruples against lying, the good-hearted Quaker who befriends Roxana is gradually compelled by the latter's unsavoury past into equivocating with her friend's daughter. William Walters, the Quaker who becomes adviser to the pirate Captain Singleton, is an outright rogue, whose equivocal use of the Quaker idiom is the comic high point of the fiction, *Captain Singleton*.

Defoe's use of the Quaker idiom is consistently humorous; obviously considering it an affectation, he was amused by it. His repeated use of phrases like "heavenly light" and "light of the spirit" in his *Declaration of Truth*, is mischievously conceived to arouse all the contemporary prejudices of educated readers against "enthusiasm", and to remind them that Quakers, like other Dissenters, were still considered fanatics by many Englishmen.

Ezra Kempton Maxfield asserts that Defoe's Quaker idiom is inauthentic, resembling "the jargon of stage Quakers". Yet he admits that it must have sounded authentic to those who were not Friends.[13] Its circumlocutory diction differentiates it strikingly from Defoe's habitually concrete and pungent vocabulary. Stylistic indications of Defoe's authorship of the *Declaration of Truth* are the long and loosely articulated sentences growing out of the association of smaller units containing strong parallelism and the idiosyncratic "I say," introduced to remind the reader about the main clause of the sentence: "And wouldst thou, Benjamin, faithfully pursue the light which I perceive is in thee, and which shineth abroad far and nigh; I say, wouldst thou act according to the light which I plainly see is in thee, thou shouldst have praise ...".

Most characteristic of Defoe's sensibility, however, is his dissimulation of a radical, clever, and relentlessly logical argument under the bland, repetitive, and vague diction of a pseudo-Quaker idiom. *A Declaration of Truth* plays relatively little upon the contrast between generalized and concrete diction, in spite of occasional references to mouth and ear. But *A Friendly Epistle by Way of Reproof from One of the People Called Quakers, to Thomas Bradbury* (1715) is full of such play, containing many amusing individual sentences like "I must lead thee by the hand, not by the nose, Thomas, others have done thee that office already ...". *A Friendly Epistle* appears to have been the most successful of Defoe's Quaker pamphlets, for it ran to six editions in one year. *A Declaration of Truth*, however, is superior to Defoe's other Quaker pamphlets by virtue of Defoe's inspired choice of a Quaker perspective from which to measure the distance between Hoadly's profession and practice, and of his amusing disguise of impudence by pious diction.

The Quakers themselves, nevertheless, seem to have been more upset by the less subtle *Friendly Epistle*, which had dangerous political implications, calling upon Whigs to modify their violence against the recently dismissed Tory ministry. Alarmed by Defoe's call for peace, they placed a notice in the London *Gazette* of 5 March and the *Daily Courant* of 7 March 1715, in which they disclaimed authorship of the pamphlet, "believing it to have been a contrivance of some adversary of ours, whereby to vent his own invectives against the government in our name, and to expose us to the displeasure thereof, and the censure of sober people."[14] Defoe hastened to insert his own advertisement on 24 March, insisting that the "said book was written by a friend in unity with the people called Quakers; and that he is moved to reprove them also in publick for their back-slidings."[15] The master equivocator was playing with the word *Friend*, at the time a more polite name for the sect than the pejorative *Quaker*.

If the Presbyterian Defoe was not literally a "Friend", then does his declaration that he was "a friend in unity with the people called Quakers" contain any truth whatsoever? Defoe appears in his fictions genuinely to have admired the Quakers for their good intentions, their common sense, and their peaceable spirit. Yet he was himself a curious combination of moderate and fighter. When he felt himself "moved" to reprove the Quakers publicly "for their back-slidings", he was of course being humorous about their idiom and about their emphasis upon the "light of the spirit". Since Quakers did not in this period engage in political pamphleteering,[16] Defoe could not seriously have expected them to speak up for their principle of peace, even at a time of crisis, when Whigs were roaring for treason proceedings against the deposed Tory ministry, including Defoe's patron, the Earl of Oxford. It is more probable that he was simply using Quakers to personify the principle of peace and thus to comment upon partisan violence from a position most dramatically opposed to such violence. With characteristic mischievousness, Defoe called for the qualities of straightforwardness and equanimity professed by Quakers in such a way as to provoke fear in the Friends and anger in his adversaries.

NOTES

1 Basil Williams, *The Whig Supremacy, 1714–1760* (Oxford, 1939), p. 83.

2 The Occasional Conformity Act of 1711 declared that it was "a penal offence to attend a dissenting chapel after receiving the sacrament in an Anglican church for the purpose of qualifying for office" in local or national government. The fruit of an unprincipled political bargain between High-Church Tories and pro-war Whigs, it marked the success of a long series of attempts by High-Church forces to prevent Dissenters from circumventing the requirements of the Test and Corporation Acts for holding public office.

The Schism Act of 1714 "laid down stringent penalties for anyone who taught in a school or academy without subscription to the articles [of the Anglican Church] and licence from the bishop". It was designed to close down all Dissenting schools and academies. (See G. V. Bennett, "Conflict in the Church", in *Britain after the Glorious Revolution*, ed. Geoffrey Holmes, London: Macmillan and Co., 1969, p.173.)

Some members of the Whig ministry of George I, like Earl Stanhope, would have liked to admit Dissenters fully into the civil life of the nation, repealing the Test and Corporation Acts, but most believed, especially after their experience with the national hysteria aroused by the government's 1710 prosecution of Dr. Sacheverell (see pages 118–120 below), that public opinion would not have countenanced such repeal.

3 Norman Sykes, "Benjamin Hoadly, Bishop of Bangor", in *Social and Political Ideas of the Augustan Age*, ed. F. J. C. Hearnshaw (London, 1928), p. 148.

4 *Preservative against the Principles and Practices of the Non-Jurors Both in Church and State.*

5 Sykes, p. 148

6 Basil Williams explains in *The Whig Supremacy, 1714–1760* (p. 79), that Convocation was a general meeting of the clergy of the Church of England to discuss doctrine and discipline. After the Revolution there was continuous tension between the conservative lower house, consisting of poorly-paid parish clergy, and the more liberal upper house, consisting of Crown-appointed bishops. The bitter disputes between the houses arose from the desire of the lower clergy to return to the conditions of the past, "when Church and State had conjoined in a single authoritarian regime", and the desire of the bishops to "accept the place in English society of a basically voluntary body working within the legal conditions of the establishment" (G. V. Bennett, "Conflict in the Church", p. 165.)

7 Quoted by Sykes, p. 118.

8 It is possible that Defoe's Bangorian activity in 1717 may have been partly motivated by the desire to distract attention from the Earl of Oxford, who was supposed to be tried that year for treason. W. T. Laprade mentions that amidst the excitement caused by the Bangorian controversy, "The Earl ... in the Tower wondered whether strife among his former opponents might not bring to him release." W. T. Laprade, *Public Opinion and Politics in Eighteenth Century England to the Fall of Walpole* (New York: The Macmillan Co., 1936), p. 209.

9 "Aminadab" was "a very common derisive nickname for Quakers in comic literature of the period", explains Ezra Kempton Maxfield in "Daniel Defoe and the Quakers", *PMLA*, 47 (1932), 187.

10 Defoe's excellent sense of dramatic propriety is illustrated by his choice of personae as authors of his anonymous works and his choice of the tone appropriate to their relationship to their particular audiences. (This point is discussed in many of the preceding essays.) He may

first have developed this sense in the writing class he so admired at Morton's Stoke Newington Academy, where the students wrote letters twice a week upon subjects prescribed to them by Morton or chosen by themselves. As John Robert Moore writes in *Daniel Defoe, Citizen of the Modern World* (Chicago, 1958), p. 37: "Sometimes they were ambassadors and agents abroad ... and wrote accounts of their negotiations and reception in foreign courts directed to the Secretary of State and sometimes to the Sovereign himself. Sometimes they were Ministers of the State, Secretaries and Commissioners at home, and wrote orders and instructions to the ministers abroad, as by order of the King in Council and the like."

11 There is some confusion about this intervention. Penn was successful in gaining a brief deferment of Defoe's sentence, but he was unable finally to avert it. It appears from Defoe's letter to Penn of 12 July 1703, that William Penn, Jr. was involved in some way as a messenger and that he made promises to the government, unauthorized by Defoe, that the latter would disclose the names of supposed accomplices to his pamphlet *The Shortest Way*.

It is possible, as Sutherland remarks (see George Harris Healey, ed. *The Letters of Daniel Defoe*, Oxford: Clarendon Press, 1955, p. 8), that Defoe "was firm and weak by turns in those trying weeks of July". It also seems possible that the younger Penn, who was something of a scoundrel, acted in Defoe's opinion as an agent-provocateur.

12 Maxfield, p. 188, discussing the possible occupations of Quakers in the early eighteenth century, mentions nothing characteristic of the aristocracy or even of gentry.

13 *Ibid.*, p. 184.

14 William Lee, *Daniel Defoe: His Life, and Recently Discovered Writings* (London, 1869), I, 245.

15 John Robert Moore, *A Checklist of the Writings of Daniel Defoe* (Bloomington, Indiana, 1960) p. 248. Maxfield believes this notice to have been composed by S. Keimer, a printer and disaffiliated Friend (p. 185), but I do not find his argument convincing.

16 Maxfield reports that in the early eighteenth century, Friends did "not attack the wrongs about them", although they would "occasionally write in self-defence, or go quietly about the work of reform by personal ministrations" (p. 184).

A Declaration of Truth to Benjamin Hoadly (1717)

Be it known unto thee, Friend Benjamin, that albeit we, who are the people of the Lord, own thee not in thy proud titles, neither in thy office, as thou exercisest the same; neither can we treat thee with that distinction wherewith men distinguish thee, forasmuch as we do not acknowledge the same (as thou dost) to be of God: nevertheless I shall treat thee respectfully in this thing, whereof I am now to commune with thee, seeing thou hast uttered much truth with thy mouth, and therefore hast moved much wrath of wicked men against thee.

And wouldst thou, Benjamin, faithfully pursue the light which I perceive is in thee, and which shineth abroad far and nigh; I say, wouldst thou act according to the light which I plainly see is in thee, thou shouldst have praise; for thou hast verily done worthily, in that thou hast restored the kingdom to them to whom it solely appertaineth, and hast dethroned the usurpations of wicked men, who have unrighteously set themselves up in the throne of Jesus.

Verily, Benjamin, thou hast done worthily, in that thou hast appeared for the cause of our God against the unrighteousness of men; and hast not been afraid, neither discouraged, when they have risen up against thee with great wrath. And I am sent unto thee to declare in words of seriousness, that thou shouldst not faint, neither be dismayed, for that many of the faithful servants of God are with thee in this thing, and do say unto thee "God speed", which thou knowest we are forbidden to say to the ungodly, and unto men who are not led in the right way.

Having thus given my testimony to thy good works, I communicated my intentions to Friends. Among these, Aminadab, a righteous man, fearing not the face of men, but fearing God only, saith unto thee, that his heart is likewise with thee in the thing which thou hast said; to wit, that the power of men, or the laws of men, have no authority to interfere with, or to join their power with the right hand of Jesus, who allows no partners in the throne of his glorious kingdom on earth, any more than he will admit partners in the throne of his glorified kingdom in heaven. Moreover, he hath sent messengers unto me, saying, "Speak thou Ebenezer in the ears of Benjamin Hoadly, and say unto him, 'Fear not the face of men, though many rise up against thee, saying "Thou lyest, thou lyest"; for verily thou lyest not Benjamin, but hast spoken the truth, and it shall prevail' ".

Aaron, a man filled with knowledge, and a teacher of wisdom, sent also unto me, saying, "Ebenezer, the things which Aminadab our friend hath communicated unto thee concerning Benjamin Hoadly, are things which favour of truth; and thou wilt do well to speak unto the said Benjamin, saying, 'Fear not Benjamin, for wise men are with thee, and good men are with thee, and verily they be better men, and more in number, that are with thee than those against thee' ".

I might name unto thee many Friends, endowed with wisdom and knowledge, who speak well of thee, for that thou hast spoken the truth with great boldness, and hast not feared to utter it, even in the hearing of the king, and we may not doubt but that our lord the king will be thy strong helper against all thine enemies, and will assist thee to silence the gain-sayers of thy doctrine; for verily, the king is an unfeigned friend unto the truth, and would be willing that all men should walk in the path to heaven, howbeit he may not be enlightened equal to our Friends, which nevertheless we hope he may hereafter be, if God seeth it good to bring his heart over to us.

And albeit Friend Benjamin, thou art not yet joined unto the faithful servants of God, our Friends, but that thou for a little remainest, as to some things, in the darkness of the world; yet, forasmuch as thou joinest with us in the truth, we embrace thee willingly, nothing doubting but that the heavenly light which has shone out in thy word, will hereafter shine in thy heart, and thou will come over more perfectly unto us Friends, who are already established in the truth.

And I am the farther confirmed in the truth hereof, in that thou hast so boldly acknowledged the truths of God, being the same professed by us, and for the sake whereof we are inclined to think well of thee; and seeing I have informed thee that thou hast so exactly taught what we in principle believe, and closely adhere to in practice, I shall let thee know, Benjamin, how exactly thou agreest with us who have received the truth, and that we hold and believe all the truths that thou hast taught, and that also even in the same words in which thou hast declared them, or but with small variation thereof, as thou wilt farther be informed, when thou shalt read the following heads, which are a part of the principles of truth, or of those things about doctrine, which we Friends do most surely believe and receive; to wit,

"Concerning religion, we believe, that it is only the spirit of the Lord that makes men truly religious; and no man ought to be compelled to or from any exercise or practice in religion, by any outward law or power, but every man ought to be left free, as the Lord shall persuade his own mind, in doing, or leaving undone this or the other practice in religion; and every man of what profession in religion so ever, ought to be protected in peace; provided himself be a man of peace, not seeking the wrong of any man's person or estate.

"And we believe, that to reprove false opinions and unsound doctrines and principles seeking to convince them that oppose themselves, by exhortation or sharp reproof, by word or writing, ought not to be counted a breach of the peace; or to strive about the things of the Kingdom of God, by men of contrary minds or judgements, this ought not to be punished by the magistrates and their laws: for we believe that the outward laws and powers of the earth are only to preserve men's persons and estates, and not to preserve men in opinions: neither ought the laws of the nation to be laid upon men's consciences, to bind them to or from such a judgement or practice in religion.

"And we believe, that Christ is, and ought only to be Lord and exerciser of men's consciences, and His spirit must only lead into all truth.

"And we believe, that obedience and subjection in the Lord belongs to superiors, and that subjects ought to obey them (in the Lord) that have rule over them: and that children ought to obey their parents, and wives their husbands, and servants their masters in all things, which is according to God, which stand in the exercise of a pure conscience towards God. But where rulers, parents or masters, or any other, command or require subjection in anything which is contrary to God, or not according to Him, in such cases all people are free, and ought to obey God rather than man; and we believe, that herein God will justify them, being guided and led by his spirit in all that which is good, and out of all that which is evil."

Herein, Friend Benjamin, thou mayest see, as in a vision of clear light, that thou art in the same way of truth with us, and I have freedom to own thee therein; for verily thou hast clearly testified unto *the truth which we believe*, in that thou hast likewise said, even in our words, *that every man ought to be left free as the Lord shall persuade his own mind.*

Now Benjamin let it not seem strange unto thee, that I say unto thee, that these are our own words; for I speak therein with truth and soberness, referring thee for testimony thereof unto a little book published more than forty and five years since, by a body of our Friends, and signed by John Crook, a man endowed with a spirit of a sound mind, and also by three other ancients, who were likewise men of true wisdom. This book is entitled, "Truth's Principles, &c.", in which book the words which I have written unto thee above, are to be found.

Searching likewise thy book, Benjamin, which thou hast made publick, by the command of the king, I find these words, which I hope thou hast learned from our Friends above written; to wit, "That the language of the Word is, *that knowing the terrors of the Lord, we should persuade men*; but that the language of the men's conduct, who profess to succeed Him that taught the other, is, that having the terrors of this world in their power, they do not persuade men, *but force their outward profession against their inward persuasion*".

Verily thou hast spoken, Benjamin, as one having the light of the spirit; and this is a truth which the men of the world cannot be able to resist. Verily, Friend Benjamin, we agree with thee, that the Kingdom of Jesus is not of this world, and that the laws of His Kingdom likewise, and the rewards and punishments of those laws, are suited to the end of those laws, and to the nature of His Kingdom. Nay, Benjamin, I will use thy words as thou hast used the words of wise men, who went before thee; to wit,

"The laws of this Kingdom, therefore, as Christ left them, have nothing of this world in their view; no tendency, either to the exaltation of some, in worldly pomp and dignity; or to their absolute dominion over the faith and religious conduct of others of His subjects; or to the erecting of any sort of temporal kingdom, under the covert or name of a spiritual one.

"The sanctions of Christ's law are rewards and

punishments. But of what sort? Not the rewards of this world; not the offices, or glories, of this state; not the pains of prisons, banishments, fines, or any lesser and more moderate penalties; nay, not the much lesser negative discouragements that belong to humane society. He was far from thinking that these could be the instruments of such a persuasion, as He thought acceptable to God. But, as the great end of His Kingdom was to guide men to happiness, after the short images of it were over here below; so, He took His motives from that place where His Kingdom first began, and where it was at last to end; from those rewards and punishments in a future state, which had no relation to this world: and to shew that His Kingdom was not of this world, all the sanctions which He thought fit to give to His laws, were not of this world at all."

I confirm these thy positions and doctrines, Benjamin, with my voice, and give thee praise therefore, for verily thou art worthy of praise, not only that thou hast spoken boldly the truth, but for that thou hast done it in the face of the adversary, and hast not been afraid. And blessed be the king, into whose heart God hath put it to frown upon the gainsayers; and albeit they were gathered together against thee, he hath scattered them, and hath sent them away discouraged.

Neither do I flatter thee with my lips; for Friends are not guilty of such things, and it would be in me a great iniquity; but I speak to thee in sincerity and in truth, and my thoughts are moved to utter the words of my mouth; for verily thou hast dethroned and pulled down that man of sin, the son of perdition, which has exalted himself; thou hast valiantly encountered the tribe of ungodly priests, who have by an injurious usage of the Lord's people, for many years usurped the authority of King Jesus, and have exercised dominion over the souls who they have had committed by men unto their charge; these they have tyrannized over, and have cruelly persecuted under pretence of authority from Jesus; albeit Jesus the true King and only head of all true believers, as thou hast well said, hath given no such authority unto them.

Now concerning ministers I will tell thee what Friends do surely receive and believe, and I will not give thee my own words, but the words of the said Declaration of 'Truth's Principles' mentioned before; to wit,

"Such ministers as are made by God, who are sanctified by His Word and power, who have freely received perfect gifts from God, and so by the spirit and power of God are sent forth into the world, to turn the people from darkness to light, and from the power of Satan to the power of God; who freely minister unto others, without coveting any man's gold, or silver, or apparel; not seeking theirs, but them; warning every man and teaching every man in all wisdom, that they might present every man perfect in Christ Jesus; such as minister from the spirit, and have the Word of God abiding in them; who are never unprovided, but at all times and seasons, and in all places, do speak and declare the truth, as they are moved and instructed, and as the spirit of truth doth give them utterance: such ministers we own, and have in great esteem."

This we surely do believe, Benjamin, and thou hast done worthily in concurring with us, and in that thou hast taken away from those who call themselves ministers, all that power and pretended authority which they assume, and which we say they usurp contrary to the nature of the office of a minister, which we also declare to be only to teach and instruct, not to terrify and affright the people of the Lord; and herein we know, that although thou wilt offend them, and they will shew great wrath against thee therefore; yet, I say, we know thou hast spoken the truth against them, and I concur with thee therein; nay I acknowledge thee and own thee therein, because thou hast concurred with us in the truth, not doubting but thou wilt be farther enlightened, in the Lord's due time, to join with Friends in all the words of truth which we profess.

I must farther say in thy behalf, Friend Benjamin, that thou hast spoken excellent words of wisdom in defiance of the men of high notions, who are of the tribe who thou didst belong to in former time; for thou hast taken the people out of their hands, and hast set them free from the mock terrors of vain men, such as they call the artillery of the Church; which we that know the ways of truth are acquainted with the deceitfulness of; and as I glory in thy words thereupon, I shall repeat them in thy praise as followeth, to wit,

"Not the least tittle of salvation or damnation depends upon the will of weak men, but all upon God and yourselves; humane benedictions, humane absolutions, humane denunciations, humane excommunications, have nothing to do with the favour or anger of God: but are humane engins, permitted to work (like other evils) by Providence."

These are excellent things spoken with wisdom, and thou

shalt have due praise of the same. Likewise hast thou battered down the strongholds of Satan, in thy words on the same subject.

"In all your religious concerns, that effect your eternal salvation, and your title to God's favour, your rule is plain and evident: Christ is your sole law-giver, and your sole judge, as to those points. The Papists may excommunicate the Protestant Nonjurors; the Nonjurors may excommunicate the High-Churchmen, as well as all other British Protestants, who pray for King George; these again may excommunicate, unchurch, unchristian, those whose church-government, or worship, differ from their own; and these again may exercise the same spiritual discipline, wherever their terrors can extend themselves. They may thus scatter damnation about, playing, one would think, as the man in the proverbs, with firebrands and death, and saying, 'Are we not in sport?' and they may every one flatter themselves, that this power of the keys shuts out from the Catholick Church here, and from the Kingdom of Heaven hereafter: but it is in truth only from *themselves* that they can excommunicate. And this is very often their own crime, and their own loss. But Christ himself and His apostles have plainly told you what it is, and what alone that shall cut you off from Him; and declared a curse upon all who preach any other gospel; and consequently, who add anything as absolutely necessary to His favour, which He hath not made so."

To these truths of thine, such I call them, as thou hast been honoured to speak them first among men, I bear my testimony, and the good people, the people of the Lord, despised by men, of whom I am the meanest, have borne their testimony many years ago: I say, with thee, that the boasted terms which those men make wicked use of, such as *regular and uninterrupted successions*, *authoritative benedictions*, *excommunications*, *absolutions*, &c. are vain words, mere terrors of men, not the terrors of the Lord, niceties and trifles. And therefore it is that we disown the whole tenor and substance of the canons and institutions of that which they prophane, as I doubt not thou wilt in time be led by these lights to do also. I despise and contemn all the pretended authority of that which they weakly and impertinently call a power derived from Christ and His apostles: I know no ministers but such as is before described; as for such as are brought up at schools and colleges, and so made ministers by the will of man, who have not freely received perfect gifts from God for perfecting of the saints, but denies perfection, and so denies the minister's work, neither do minister freely, but seek for gain from their quarters, and will not preach without a price; who are not sanctified by the Word of God, but plead for a continuance in sin while people walk upon the earth; such as minister from the letter, and not from the spirit; who cannot preach except they have time to study, and so by their industry provide themselves, and are not provided of the Lord (such a ministry is of works, and not the free gift from God), such cannot profit people, but lead them captive in an empty and dead form, always hearing, but never able to come to the true knowledge of God: such called ministers we do deny, and turn from them, and testify against them, as the holy men of God formerly did.

I doubt not, Friend Benjamin, but thy words tend to bring thee to the same just contempt, that I have entertained, and that Friends most righteously do entertain of these uncalled priests, and that in the meantime thou wilt, by thy sober and weighty speeches, bring all that wicked hierarchy, which those priests so violently contend for, into contempt among the people.

I am therefore moved to bear my testimony with thee against them; forasmuch as they, usurping high dignity and authority, have erected a kingdom which they say is the Kingdom of Jesus; howbeit, as I verily think, it is a kingdom of this world; forasmuch as they exercise jurisdictions which be of this world therein, and have taken to themselves powers which be of themselves; which nevertheless they take upon them to say are descended to them, and by the notions and pretences of a succession of those powers, they assume a right to exercise those powers over the consciences of men, which Friends say they have no right to do; and furthermore we say and believe that whereas they exercise the power and authority which alone belongs to King Jesus, the King and sole Chief of His faithful followers: they therefore erect their own kingdom, not the Kingdom of King Jesus, and exercise the authority and power, which is His only, as their own.

I rejoice, Benjamin, that thou hast published true doctrine, and hast given thy testimony with us to the truth, which we on so good and solid foundations have received; and I question not but thou wilt be assisted by the spirit of truth to pull down and overthrow the whole power, hierarchy and constitution of that people who call themselves the Church; verily, they are usurpers of the Kingdom and throne of King Jesus; and thou shalt be a champion of the truth, in that thou shalt overthrow those ecclesiastick principalities and powers, which are not of God, and shalt establish true religion in that mighty principle of heavenly light, in which it is only to be found.

This is that inward revelation which thou hast been obliged to bear thy testimony unto, (viz) that light which persuades the minds of men, and whereby every step of reformation which hath been made in the world hath been justified, and which, as thou sayest well, is all the account which Protestants can give for their being reformed from the people called Papists.

And doubtless thou hast by the same arguments justified all those, the people of the Lord, who being persuaded in themselves of their being guided by heavenly light, have separated and withdrawn from these usurpations, of which thou hast spoken so worthily.

And what remains, beloved Friend Benjamin, but that thou shouldst, according as thou hast worthily begun, and according to the light which shineth in thy mind, separate thyself from these usurpers of unrighteous authority, and joining thyself with the friends to truth, shouldst bear thy testimony against all ungodliness; for verily Benjamin, thou canst not but see and abhor the doctrine which these men teach, saying, "We are the Church, and power is with us"; which thou knowest is false, and is not of God, and that the power which they use is not of God, but is the power of men, tending to ungodly dominion and usurpation; such as is that of the Pope of Rome, which nevertheless they have disowned while they yet practise.

For verily, Benjamin, it seemeth to me that thou who hast received such light, and hast acknowledged the truths which are directly contrary to these men, canst not any longer continue among them, or wear those prophane ensigns of idolatry, whereby thou art distinguished from other men, even in a manner which thou thyself knowest is not appointed by King Jesus. For verily, Benjamin, the robes of distinction which thou wearest, and wherewith thou art honoured among men, are the ensigns of that usurped power which thou hast so worthily condemned, and thou canst not longer abide among those who thou knowest are the enemies to the light which thou hast received, and who walk contrary to the doctrine which thou hast taught, and which we, the Lord's people, have so many years ago received.

Wherefore I am moved to advertise thee, in behalf of the truth, that thou shouldst not delay any longer joining thyself unto the Lord's people, whose cause thou hast already so worthily pleaded. For why shouldst thou not cause thy life and thy doctrine to conform unto each other? And why shouldst thou decline to profess openly thy adherence to the Lord's people, whilst thou dost not decline to teach the principles which they believe, and which they have received from the beginning?

It is true, Benjamin, the mean and humble station of those who be teachers and ministers of the Lord among us may not be agreeable to thy present temper, who art exalted to be great among men; but whereas thou knowest that the Kingdom of Jesus is not of this world, and that likewise His rewards are not of this world, as thou hast most worthily taught; so, Benjamin, how shouldst thou not reject the honours given by men, which are the rewards issuing from that usurped power which is not according to the laws of His Kingdom! These sincerely, according to thy own rules, are not of God; neither canst thou, who art now enlightened from a higher spirit, submit to be decked with their ornaments, but shouldst cast them off, like as Christians in primitive times refused to be decked with the garlands and vestments of idolatrous priests; and like as those people who are called Protestants refuse and detest the habiliments and vestments, titles, dignities and distinctions of the Popish priests, choosing to be called by the truly venerable name of Ministers of Christ, rather than by the titles of popes, cardinals, abbots, monks, friars and the like.

* * *

Neither canst thou, Friend Benjamin, be in danger of joining with any other people than those whose profession I have here invited thee to; since there are not any who have received the truths which thou hast preached in their full degrees, so as the people who in contempt are called Quakers; with whom, as I have shewed, thou hast perfectly conformed thyself to the honour of thy judgement, and of the divine light shewing forth in thee.

As for those people called Presbyterians, thou canst by no means join thyself unto them, seeing they have declared themselves in terms greatly opposite to thy doctrines, saying that men have power to make laws binding the consciences of others; and that rewards and punishments of this world appertain to humane authority, exercised by such as they call a succession of officers: these their opinions are not according to truth, as Friends have received it; neither are they like unto those truths which thou hast preached. And therefore we see that questionless thou wilt avoid also the erroneous opinions of persecuting Presbyterians, and wilt join thyself unto us; and this I speak unto thee with the more certainty, forasmuch as, blessed be the Lord, thou art already come beyond the corrupt tenets of those people. Moreover, beloved Friend Benjamin, I make known unto thee that the said Presbyterians are equally guilty of those things which the people of the Lord abhor; to wit, the pretences to a power which, as thou saidst well, Jesus, the King of all those who are led by the light of the truth, never delegated to them; and this they not only give to their followers, but make laws of their own; I say, humane laws, and sanctions of laws such as rewards and punishments, for enforcing others to comply therewith; to wit, that they admit none to be teachers among them, or to preach and prophesy unto the people, unless they profess to believe and to receive certain points which they call, prophanely, articles of faith; wherein these wicked usurpations of power are openly declared by them, saying,

1. "That the Lord Jesus, as King and Head of His Church, hath therein appointed a government in the hand of Church-officers distinct from the civil magistrate.

2. "That to these officers the keys of the Kingdom of Heaven are committed; by virtue whereof they have power respectively to retain and remit sins, to shut that Kingdom against the impenitent, both by the word and censures, and to open it unto penitent sinners, by the ministry of the gospel and by absolution from censures, as occasion shall require.

3. "That these Church censures are necessary, &c. for preventing the wrath of God, which might fall upon the Church, if they should suffer the Seal of the Covenant to be prophaned by notorious and obstinate offenders."

These things thou knowest, Benjamin, are contrary to the doctrines and positions which thou hast so openly avowed, being no less than invasions and manifest usurpations of the Kingdom and authority of King Jesus, and in themselves nullities and trifles.

Yet these things, and in these words, thou wilt find in those heads of belief, which these ungodly Presbyterians call the confession of their faith, Article the XXX. Howbeit, blessed art thou, O Benjamin, in that thou hast borne thy testimony against these also. Wherefore I know, that leaving behind thee all these wicked and erroneous opinions, and bearing witness to the truth, thou wilt at length join thyself unto us; and I rejoice over thee in this, that thou art enlightened to know the truth; testifying that I embrace thee with affection in the Lord.

Friend Timothy greeteth thee in like manner; as also James the aged, a lover of those who forsake the errors of the wicked: in a word, all Friends greet, and speak well of thee.

Fare thee well.

3. An Answer to a Question that Nobody Thinks of, viz. But What If the Queen Should Die?

An Answer to a Question that Nobody Thinks of, viz. But What If the Queen Should Die?, published April 1713, was one of three celebrated pamphlets Defoe wrote in the same year on the question of who should succeed to the throne of Queen Anne. The other two, *Reasons against the Succession of the House of Hanover* (21 February), and *And What If the Pretender Should Come?* (26 March), ran to more editions than *But What If the Queen Should Die?*, and, unlike this pamphlet, were ironical in their arguments as well as in their titles. Though written in the interest of the House of Hanover, they gave some of Defoe's tenacious Whig enemies the chance they had long awaited, and he was arrested in April for writing treasonable libel against the Protestant Succession.

In 1713 Queen Anne's obviously deteriorating health (confirmed in December by her near demise), and her lack of heirs (she had borne and buried some eighteen children),[1] raised the excitement over the succession to a fever pitch. Despite the Act of Settlement of 1701, which had provided that the succession must go to the House of Hanover if William and Mary had no descendants and if Anne, the next in line to the throne, also failed to produce an heir, the issue had still not been settled in England. "William and Mary and Anne had no doubt reigned by parliamentary authority out of the regular order of succession", writes Basil Williams, "but Mary and Anne were both of British stock and daughters of an undeniably legitimate king",[2] whereas the Elector of Hanover, the future George I, not only was merely a cousin, but was not even a Stuart.

Some Tories sincerely believed in divine right and were opposed to the Lockean doctrine of the Revolution later accepted as orthodox in the eighteenth century, the doctrine that government is a contract between governor and governed, forfeited when the executive violates the terms of his trust, and that revolution is the ultimate safeguard of this fundamental law. Unfortunately, those Tories who believed in the dynastic principle were unable to reconcile this belief with their unwillingness to tolerate a Roman Catholic on the throne of England. When the Pretender ("James III") obdurately refused to renounce his religion, they had no real alternative to accepting the Elector of Hanover as George I.

Their position was further complicated by party politics relating to the ending of the War of the Spanish Succession. Sir George Clark summarizes the situation succinctly: "The story of the war and peace in the last four years of Queen Anne is the story of how the Tories became entangled in Jacobitism".[3] The ending of the War of the Spanish Succession, although desirable in itself, was conducted by Oxford's ministry in such a way as to desert and betray England's allies. Anxious to continue the war, the Whigs ill-advisedly encouraged meddling by Dutch and German envoys in English domestic politics. Oxford, and especially Bolingbroke, were forced by this interference to scheme with French and Jacobite interests. The Tories realized that the Whigs would lose no chance of injuring them with the Elector of Hanover and that if George became King of England he would at the very least exclude them from office. By the time that the Treaty of Utrecht was signed, the Tory ministers realized that they might be impeached for high treason if George succeeded Anne on the throne.[4]

In such a situation, Defoe's pamphlets burst into print. *But What If the Queen Should Die?*, the least ironic of the three, is actually the most inflammatory. Conceding, for purposes of debate, that each of the potentially powerful sources of danger to the Protestant Succession (the ministry of Oxford and Bolingbroke, suspected by many of Jacobite leanings, the Jacobites themselves, the French King, and the Pretender), is immobilized by the obligations it owes to Queen Anne, Defoe warns that the death of the Queen must destroy what is only a momentary state of suspended animation.

Turning to the state of the nation, he reminds the English at length (not reproduced) of all the benefits they enjoy under Queen Anne's reign, which rests upon the Revolution and the Act of Settlement: civil peace, religious toleration, Union with Scotland, safety of the Church of England, sanctity of public credit, limitation of the royal prerogative over Parliament, and property rights. The tenuousness of English enjoyment of these benefits is hammered home again and again by Defoe's linking them to the continued life of the Queen, whose physical frailty is so notorious that he has only to generalize that all humans are mortal to send a tremor down his readers' spine.

Toward the end of his tract, Defoe returns to a discussion of the forces that threaten the Protestant Succession. The slender thread upon which the Queen's life depends becomes precariously fragile when he points out that assassination can easily appear attractive as a shortcut to Papists and Jacobites impatient to see the Pretender mount the throne of England. By this point in the pamphlet Death stands at the elbow of the Queen, poised to release from their trance all the enemies of the Protestant Succession.

Challenging this spectre is the pamphleteer-prophet, whose urgent question, "But what if the Queen should die?", has by force of repetition now become a clarion call, awakening the English nation to the "dreadful calamities they will fall into at Her Majesty's death, if something be not done to settle them before her death". Prudently declining to advocate openly the public demonstrations in favour of the House of Hanover that his pamphlet seems designed to incite, Defoe asserts that the English people, once awakened, will have no difficulty deciding what measures are necessary to secure the succession to Hanover.

The inflammatory tone of this pamphlet, written by a man who habitually speaks in the voice of moderation,[5] is only one of the reasons for which *But What If the Queen Should Die?* is an interesting piece of writing. The other reason is that it illustrates again Defoe's talent for adopting different perspectives on an issue, a talent already referred to in the discussion of the pamphlet on the Bishop of Bangor. *But What If the Queen Should Die?* begins with a survey of the points of view of major groups potentially inimical to the Protestant Succession. Every one of Defoe's discussions of these groups demonstrates his ability and interest in considering from every angle what their attitude is. The English ministry, for instance, plays with two-edged tools in employing Jacobites, because "the Pretender's interest is the magnet which draws them by its secret influence, to point to him as their pole". Yet "every ministry will, and must, employ men sometimes, not as they always join with them in their political principles; but as either the men are found useful in their several employments, or as the ministry may be under other circumstances, which makes it necessary to them to employ them". Nevertheless, it does not follow that there is no danger in employing such people, if the Queen should die. Another potential enemy, King Louis XIV, has signed treaties acknowledging the House of Hanover as the legitimate successor to the Stuart Anne. On the other hand his past actions have demonstrated that the honour and sincerity of the King of France are not to be depended upon. The condition Louis has been reduced to by his recent war with England is a more reliable foundation for his keeping faith. The King's conduct, however, may become completely unpredictable in the event of Queen Anne's death.

The compass metaphor underlying Defoe's recapitulation of Jacobite reasoning in this pamphlet is concerned with perspective or point of view. I have already quoted Defoe's description of Jacobites in the Oxford ministry as the needle of a compass, drawn by the Pretender's magnetic influence to point to him as their pole. When Defoe concludes the first section of his pamphlet and turns to the state of the English nation to remind his readers how precious and how precarious are the benefits they enjoy under Queen Anne, "Having then viewed the several points of the nation's compass, whence our danger of Jacobite plots, and projects against the Protestant Succession may be expected to come", he uses his compass metaphor to indicate his change of direction.

Despite Defoe's practice of presenting forcefully different points of view on an issue, a practice that has often earned him the reputation of being completely unprincipled, it is my firm conviction that this reputation is unmerited. As we have seen in the case of the Bangorian controversy, his versatility and his delight in arguing on all sides did not preclude his consistent adherence to Presbyterian principles. In *But What If the Queen Should Die?* his passionate attachment to the Revolution Settlement is indisputable. His debating skill and his talent for close and intricate reasoning are demonstrated by his clever linking of all the benefits of peace and civil and religious liberty to Queen Anne's tenure of life. The inspiration of suggesting his attachment to the Revolution and to the Act of Settlement by means of a simple refrain, "And what if the Queen should die?" repeated with cumulative emphasis in the minor variations at the end of each closely-argued topic, is the secret of the power of this tract.[6] It is also a fascinating example of one of the sources of Defoe's effectiveness as a political writer: the combination of close and intricate argumentation with strong and simple basic premises.

The syntax of *But What If the Queen Should Die?* dramatizes the operation of Defoe's thought. Running through the pamphlet is a tension between the amplifying, circular tendency of a mind fertile in ideas, and the constricting, linear tendency of a mind direct in logic. An example of the logical impulse is the statement: "As there is no objection, which is material enough to make, but is material enough to answer; so this, although there is nothing of substance in it, may introduce something in its answer of substance enough to consider". An example of the amplifying impulse appears in the passage where Defoe explains why the War of the Spanish Succession was so onerous to Louis XIV: it threatened to destroy France, it was becoming more and more difficult for Louis to wage, so much so that he tried by all means to end it, and it could have resulted in the confusion of all Christendom. A short example of the tendency for amplification (suggested by the logic of association) to interfere with a direct line of reasoning, appears in this sentence: "But let the ministry employ these men [Jacobites] by what necessity or upon what Occasion they will, though it may not follow that the ministry are therefore for the Pretender, yet it does not also follow that there is no danger of the Protestant Succession from the employing those sort of people." In the example, the parallel between "necessity" and "occasion", although logical, distracts the reader from following the whole sentence. The omission of "or upon what occasion" would have made the sentence easier to understand. But elsewhere in *But What If the Queen Should Die?*, for instance on page 83 below Defoe's amplifying tendency almost obscures the logic of his explanation why the Pretender cannot rely upon help from Louis XIV.

In spite of some sloppy writing in individual sentences, however, *But What If the Queen Shoud Die?* is a compelling work, well designed as a whole, generally well executed in detail, its imperfections concealed by the power of its refrain. The secret of its effectiveness does not lie in the concrete diction that characterizes Defoe's plain style. Here the diction is precise, educated, but not individualized. The pamphlet achieves its success instead through its play of ideas and of perspectives on ideas, and through its balance between the amplification of ideas and the contraction of a taut logic.

Arrested in April 1713 for writing treasonable libel against the Protestant Succession, Defoe made the error of complaining about this treatment in his *Review*, while the case was *sub judice*.[7] The malice of his judges, condemning him to prison for treason even before the indictment had been drawn (for a trial that was never to be held), boded ill for Defoe's future. Sir Thomas Powis, one of his judges who had denied that the pamphlets were ironical, told him that "he might come to be hanged, drawn, and quartered for these books".[8]

But What If the Queen Should Die? relies very little on irony for its effect. The other two pamphlets, *Reasons against the Succession of the House of Hanover*, and *And What If the Pretender Should Come?* can be classified as ironical tracts, but their irony is transparent, and Defoe does not even bother to sustain it throughout his arguments. It required no great literary acumen, therefore, for Queen Anne, who examined Defoe's petition and the pamphlets in the Privy Council, to perceive "nothing but private pique in the ... prosecution",[9] and to order a full pardon.

Notes

1 J. P. Kenyon writes, "... and a body never more than graceful had been battered into shapelessness by an unrelenting series of pregnancies—one a year from 1683 to 1700—and by the dropsical infection that had brought them all to frustrating, heart-tearing failure. She had twelve miscarriages; of her six children one was still-born and the other five, like the Duke of Gloucester, died at an early age of hydrocephalus." (*The Stuarts*, New York: Macmillan, 1959, p. 206.)

2 Basil Williams *The Whig Supremacy 1714–1760* (Oxford, 1939), p. 15.
3 Sir George Clark, *The Later Stuarts, 1660–1714* (Oxford, 1955), p. 229.
4 *Ibid.*, pp. 242, 243.
5 Defoe was not, however, entirely unschooled in the technique of rabble-rousing. See pages 2–3 above for *Legion's Memorial* and for *A Hymn to the Pillory*. Paul K. Alkon describes why Defoe's rhetoric in *The Shortest Way* is so dangerous, pointing out that twentieth-century analogues "are not far to seek". ("Defoe's Argument in *The Shortest Way with the Dissenters*", *MP*, 73, May 1976, S23.)
6 In the 4 January 1711 issue of the *Review*, Defoe plays with a similar technique, repeating at the end of each paragraph the refrain, "Be not afraid, only believe", and varying the refrain to "Believe", midway through the essay, as the argument turns.
7 Defoe's error was particularly serious, because one of the reasons his enemies wished to prosecute him was to embarrass the Oxford ministry, by forcing it to come to Defoe's aid and thus to acknowledge publicly that he was working for Robert Harley. His complaint gave another cause of offense to the Lord Chief Justice, an ardent Whig, thus making it impossible for the ministry to permit the accusers to run out of steam by allowing them to proceed with a legally dubious prosecution.
8 William Lee, *Daniel Defoe: His Life, and Recently Discovered Writings* (London, 1869), I, 212.
9 *Ibid.*, I, 210.

An Answer to a Question that Nobody Thinks of, viz. But What If the Queen Should Die?

(1713)

* * *

It is far from any reflection on the ministry to say that, however they may act upon a right sincere principle for the Protestant Succession in all they do, which, as above, we profess to believe; yet that many of the tools they make use of are of another make, and have no edge to cut any other way; no thoughts to move them towards any other end; no other centre, which they can have any tendency to; that the Pretender's interest is the magnet which draws them by its secret influence, to point to him as their pole; that they have their aim at his establishment here, and own it to be their aim. And as they are not shy to profess it among themselves, so their conduct in many things makes it sufficiently publick. This is not meant as any reflection upon the ministry, for making use of such men: the late ministry did the same, and every ministry will, and must, employ men sometimes, not as they always join with them in their politic principles; but as either the men are found useful in their several employments, or as the ministry may be under other circumstances, which makes it necessary to them to employ them. Nor, as the *Review* well enough observed, does it follow that *because the ministry have employed, or joined with Jacobites in the publick affairs, that therefore they must have done it with a Jacobite principle*. But let the ministry employ these men by what necessity or upon what occasion they will, though it may not follow that the ministry are therefore for the Pretender, yet it does not also follow that there is no danger of the Protestant Succession from the employing those sort of people: *For what if the Queen should die?*

The ministry, it is hoped, are established in the interest of their Queen and country; and therefore it has been argued, that supposing the ministry had the Pretender in their eye, yet that it is irrational to suggest that they can have any such view during the life of Her present Majesty. Nay, even those professed Jacobites, who we spoke of just now, cannot be so ungrateful to think of deposing the Queen, who has been so bountiful, so kind, so exceeding good to them, as in several cases to suffer them to be brought into the management of her own affairs, when by their character they might have been thought dangerous, even to her person; thus winning and engaging them by her bounty, and the confidence that has been placed in them, not to attempt anything to her prejudice, without the most monstrous ingratitude, without flying in the face of all that sense of honour and obligation which it is possible for men of common sense to entertain. And it can hardly be thought that even Papists themselves under the highest possessions of their religious zeal, can conquer the native aversions they must have to such abominable ingratitude, or to think of bringing in the Pretender upon this Protestant nation, even while the Queen shall be on the throne. But though this may, *and some doubt that also*, tie up their hands during the Queen's life, yet they themselves give us but small reason to expect anything from them afterward; and it will be hard to find anybody to vouch for them then. These very Jacobites, Papists, and professed enemies to the Revolution may be supposed upon these pretensions to be quiet, and offer no violence to the present establishment while Her Majesty has the possession, and while that life lasts to which they are so much indebted for her royal goodness and clemency. *But what would they do, if the Queen should die?*

Come we next to the *French King*. We are told that not the French king only, but even the whole French nation are wonderfully forward to acknowledge the obligation they are under to the justice and favour which they have received from Her Majesty, in the putting an end to the war; a war which lay heavy upon them, and threatened the very name of the French nation with ruin, and much more threatened the glory of the French Court, and of their great monarch, with an entire overthrow, a total eclipse; a war which, by their own confession, it was impossible for them long to have supported the expenses of, and which by the great superiority of the Allies became dreadful to them, and that every campaign more than other; a war which they were in such pain to see the end of, that they tried all the powers and courts in Christendom, who were the least neutral, to engage a mediation in order to a treaty, and all in vain; and a war which if Her Majesty had not inclined to put an end to, must have ended perhaps to the disadvantage and confusion of both France and Spain, if not of all Christendom. The obligations the French are under for the bringing this war to so just and honourable a conclusion, are not at all concealed. Nay, the French themselves have not been backward to make them publick. The declarations made by the French king of his sincerity in the overtures made for a general peace; the protestations of his being resolved to enter into an entire confidence, and a league, offensive and defensive, with the Queen's Majesty, for the preservation of the peace of Christendom; his recognition of Her Majesty's just right to the crown; his entering into articles to preserve the Union, acknowledging the Ninth Electorate in favour of the House of Hanover, and joining in the great affair of the Protestant Succession: as these all convince the world of the necessity his affairs were reduced to, and the great advantages accruing to him by a peace; so they seem to be so many arguments against our fears of the French entering into any engagements against the crown of Britain, much less any against the possession of the Queen during her life. Not that the honour and sincerity of the King of France is a foundation fit for Her Majesty or her people to have any dependence upon; and the fraction of former treaties by that Court when the glory of that monarch, or his particular views of things has dictated such opportunity to him as he thought fit to close with, are due cautions to us all not to have any dependence of that kind. But the state of his affairs, and the condition the war has reduced him to, may give us some ground to think ourselves safe on that side. He knows what power he has taken off from his enemies in making peace with Her Majesty; he knows very well with what loss he sits down, how his affairs are weakened, and what need he has to take breath after so terrible a war; besides the flame such an action would kindle again in Europe; how it would animate this whole British nation against him, in such a manner, and endanger bringing in a new war, and perhaps a new confederacy upon him so violently, and that before he would be in a condition to match them; that no one can reasonably suppose the French king will run the hazard of it. And these things may tend to make some people easier than ordinary in the affair of the Succession; believing that the French king stands in too much need of the favour of the Queen of Great Britain, whose power it well behoves him to keep in friendship with him, and whose nation he will be very cautious of provoking a third time, as he has already done twice to his fatal experience. All these things, we say, may seem pretty well to assure us that nothing is to be feared on that side so long as Her Majesty lives to sit upon the British throne. But all leaves our grand question unanswered; and though we may argue strongly for the French king's conduct while the present reign continues, yet few will say, *What he will do if the Queen should die?*

Nay, we may even mention the *Pretender* himself, if he has any about him whose councils are fit to be depended upon, and can direct him to make a wise and prudent judgement of his own affairs; if he acts by any scope of policy, and can take his measures with any foresight; most easy it is for them to see that it must be in vain for him to think of making any attempt in Britain during the life of the Queen, or to expect to depose Her Majesty, and set himself up, the French power, upon which he has already in vain depended, as it has not hitherto been able to serve him, or his father, but that their exile has continued now above twenty-four years. So much less can he be able to assist him now while he has been brought as it were to kneel to the British Court, to put an end for him to this cruel destructive war. The reason is just spoken to, (viz.) that this would be to rekindle that flame which he has gotten so lately quenched, and which cost him so much art, so much management, so much submission to the Allies to endeavour the quenching of before. To attack the Queen of Great Britain now in behalf of the Pretender, would not only be in the highest degree ungrateful, perfidious and dishonourable; but would forever make the British Court, as well as the whole nation, his violent and implacable enemies; but would also involve him again in a new war with all Europe, who would very gladly fall in again with Britain to pull down more effectually the French power, which has so long been a terror to its neighbours. So that the Pretender can expect no help from the King of France. As to what the Pope, the Spaniard, and a few petty popish powers, who might pretend upon a religious prospect to assist him, and with whose aid, and the assistance of his party here, he may think fit to hazard an attempt here for the crown; it is evident, and his own friends will agree in it, that while the Queen lives it is nonsense and ridiculous for them to attempt it; that it would immediately arm the whole nation against them, as one man; and in humane probability it would, like as his supposed father was served at the Revolution, be the ruin of his whole interest, and blow him at once quite out of the nation. I believe that there are very few who alarm themselves much with the fears of the Pretender, from the apprehension of his own strength from abroad, or from his own party and friends at home here, were they once sure that he should receive no assistance from the King of France. If then the King of France cannot be reasonably supposed either to be inclined, or be in a condition to appear for him, or act in his behalf during the life of the Queen; neither can the Pretender, *say some*, unless he is resolved to ruin all his friends, and at last to ruin himself, make any attempt of that kind during Her Majesty's life. *But what if the Queen should die?*

Having then viewed the several points of the nation's compass, whence our danger of Jacobite plots and projects against the Protestant Succession may be expected to come; let us now enquire a little of the state of the nation, that we make a right estimate of our condition, and may know what to trust to in cases of difficulty, as they lie before us.

* * *

Possibly cavils may rise in the mouths of those whose conduct this nice question may seem to affect, that this is a question unfit to be asked, and questionless such people will have much to say upon that subject; as that it is a factious question, a question needless to be answered, and impertinent therefore to be asked; that it is a question which respects things remote, and serves only to fill the heads of the people with fears and jealousies; that it is a question to which no direct answer can be given, and which suggests strange surmises, and amuses people about they know not what, and is of no use but to make people uneasy without cause.

As there is no objection, which is material enough to make, but is material enough to answer; so this, though there is nothing of substance in it, may introduce something in its answer of substance enough to consider. It is therefore most necessary to convince the considering reader of the usefulness and necessity of putting this question; and then likewise the usefulness and necessity of putting this question NOW at this time; and if it appear to be both a needful question itself, and a seasonable question as to time, the rest of the cavils against it will deserve the less regard. That it is a needful question seems justified more abundantly from a very great example, to wit, the practise of the whole nation, in settling the Succession to the crown. This I take to be nothing else, but this: the Queen having no issue of her body, and the Pretender to the crown being expelled by law, included in his father's disastrous flight and abdication; when the Parliament came to consider of the state of the nation, as to government as it now stands, that King William being lately dead, and Her Majesty with universal joy of her people being received as Queen; the safety and the lasting happiness of the nation is so far secured. *BUT what if the Queen should die?*

The introduction to all the Acts of Parliaments for settling the crown, implies thus much, and speaks directly this language, (viz.) to make the nation safe and easy, in case the Queen should die. Nor are any of those Acts of Parliament impeached of faction, or impertinencies; much less of needless blaming the people, and filling their heads with fears and jealousies. If this example of the Parliament is not enough, justifying to this enquiry, the well known truth upon which that example of Parliament is grounded, is sufficient to justify it, (viz.) that we all know the Queen *MUST die*. None say this with more concern and regret than those who are forwardest to put this question, as being of the opinion abovesaid, that we are effectually secured against the Pretender, and against all the terrifying consequences of the frenchified governors during Her Majesty's life. But this is evident, *the Queen is mortal*, though crowned with all that flattering courtiers can bring together, to make her appear great, glorious, famous, or what you please; yet the Queen, yea, the Queen herself is *mortal*, and *MUST die*. It is true, kings and queens are called gods, but this respects their sacred power; nothing supposing an immortality attending their persons, for they all *die* like other men, and their dust knows no distinction in the grave. Since then it is most certain that the Queen *MUST die*, and our safety and happiness in this nation depends so much upon the stability of our liberties, religion, and aforesaid dependencies after Her Majesty's life shall end, it cannot be a question offensive to any who has any concern in the publick good, to enquire into what shall be the state of our condition, or the posture of our affairs, when the Queen shall die. *But this is not all neither*. As the Queen is mortal, and we are assured she must die; so we are none of us certain, as to be able to know when or how soon that disaster may happen, at what time, or in what manner. This then, as it may be remote, and not [for] a long time; *God of His infinite mercy grant it may be long first, and not before this difficult question we are upon be effectually and satisfactorily answered to the nation.* So on the other side, it may be near. None of us know how near the fatal blow may befall us soon, and sooner far than we may be ready; for today it may come, while the cavilling reader is objecting against our putting this question, and calling it unreasonable and needless; while the word is in thy very mouth, mayest thou hear the fatal melancholy news, "the Queen's dead". News that must one time or other be heard; the word will certainly come some time or other to be spoken in the present sense, and to be sure in the time they are spoken in. How can anyone then say that it is improper to ask what shall be our case, what shall we do, or what shall be done with us *if the Queen should die?*

But we have another melancholy incident, which attends the Queen's mortality, and which makes this question more than ordinarily seasonable to be asked at this time; and that is, that not only the Queen is mortal, and she *MUST die*, and the time uncertain; so that she *may die* even today before tomorrow, or in a very little space of time: but her life is under God's Providence, at the mercy of Papists' and Jacobites' people; who the one by their principles, and the other by the circumstances of their party are more than ordinarily to be apprehended for their bloody designs against Her Majesty, and against the whole nation. Nay, there seems more reason to be apprehensive of the dangerous attempts of these desperate people at this time, than ever, even from the very reasons which are given all along in this work, for our being safe in our privileges, our religious and civil rights during Her Majesty's life; it would be mispending your time to prove that the Papists and Jacobite parties in this nation, however they may, as we have said, be under ties and obligations of honour, interest, and gratitude, &c. not to make attempt upon us during the Queen's life; yet that they are more encouraged at this time than ever they were to hope and believe, that when the Queen shall die, their turn stands next. This we say, we believe is lost labour to speak of: the said people, the popish and Tory party will freely own and oppose it. They all take their obligations to the Queen, to end with Her Majesty's life. The French King, however in honour and gratitude he may think himself bound [not] to encourage the Pretender to insult Her Majesty's dominions, while the Queen with whom he personally is engaged by treaty, shall remain alive, will think himself fully at liberty from those obligations when the Queen shall die. If we are misinformed of the French affairs, and of the notions they have in France of these things: they are generally no otherwise understood than that the King of France is engaged by the peace now in view, not to disturb Her Majesty's possession during her reign and life; but that then the Pretender's right is to be received everywhere. The Pretender himself, howsoever, as abovesaid, he may despair of his success in attempting to take possession during the Queen's life, will not fail to assume new hopes at Her Majesty's death. So much then of the hopes of popery and French power; so much of the interest of the Pretender depending upon the single thread of life of a mortal person; and we being well assured that they look upon Her Majesty only as the incumbent in a living, or tenant for life in an estate: what is more natural than in this case for us to apprehend danger to the life of the Queen; especially to such people who are known not to make much consciencies of murthering princes, with whom the king-killing doctrine is so universally received, and who were so often detected of villainous practices and plots against the life of Queen Elizabeth, Her Majesty's famous predecessor, and that upon the same foundation, (viz.) the Queen of Scots being the popish Pretender to the crown; what can we expect from the same party, and men acting from the same principles, but the same practices? It is known that the Queen by course of nature may live many years, and these people have many reasons to be impatient of so much delay. They know that many accidents may intervene to make the circumstances of the nation at the time of the Queen's death less favourable to their interests than they are now; they may have fewer friends, as well in power as out of power, by length of time, and the like. These, and such as these considerations may excite villainous and murtherous practices against the precious life of our sovereign (God protect Her Majesty from them); but while all these considerations so naturally offer themselves to us, it seems most rational, needful, seasonable and just, that we should be asking and answering this great question: *What if the Queen should die?*

Thus far we have only asked the question itself, and shewed our reasons or endeavoured to justify the reasonableness of the enquiry. It follows that we make some brief essay as an answer to the question. This may be done many ways, but the design of this tract is rather to put the question into your thought, than to put an answer into your mouths. The several answers which may be given to this important question may not be proper for a publick print; and some may not be fit so much as to be spoken. The question is not without its uses, whether it be answered or no, if the nation be sufficiently awakened; but to ask the question among themselves, they will be brought by thinking of the thing to answer it one to another in a short space. The people of Britain want only to be shewed what imminent danger they are in, in case of the Queen's decease: how much their safety and felicity depends upon the life of Her Majesty, and what a state of confusion, distress and all sorts of dreadful calamities they will fall into at Her Majesty's death, if something be not done to settle them before her death; and if they are not, during Her Majesty's life, secured from the power of France, and the danger of the Pretender.

4. Reasons Why This Nation Ought to Put a Speedy End to This Expensive War

Reasons Why This Nation Ought to Put a Speedy End to This Expensive War was published on 6 October 1711 and went into a third edition by 18 October.[1] It was the first and most successful of Defoe's many contributions to the pamphlet war about the peace negotiations that in 1713 culminated in the signing of the Treaty of Utrecht. The popularity of *Reasons Why*, like that of Swift's even more successful *Conduct of the Allies* (November 1711), was attributable less to its literary merit than to its reception by an avid, information-seeking public as a semi-official declaration of ministerial intent about the War of the Spanish Succession. To the modern student of style, *Reasons Why* is of particular interest because in it Defoe, who had pressing reasons for concealing his authorship, speaks in an unctuous voice strikingly different from that of the forthright Mr. Review.

When the court revolution that brought Robert Harley, Henry St. John, and the Duke of Shrewsbury to power, was completed in August 1710, most political observers believed that "a radical revision of wartime policies" was inevitable.[2] The Whigs, ardent supporters of the war, had lost the confidence of Queen Anne, and the Tories, now led by Harley, opposed the interventionist policies in Europe initiated by William III and continued by the Queen. Expectations of imminent change in foreign policy were further aroused by the election of 1710, which strengthened the hand of non-interventionists, sweeping Tories into Parliament on a national wave of High-Church and anti-war sentiment.

But English domestic politics ensured that the path to the peace of Utrecht would be tortuous. The moderate Robert Harley had no desire for abrupt changes; while believing that continuation of the war was counter-productive, he wished to end it without head-on collisions between allies or domestic forces. For that reason, he did not relish the landslide electoral victory of Tory extremism in 1710. Convinced that government could work only on a broad basis of national agreement, he was determined to control, not to be controlled by, zealous and xenophonic Tory followers. Secondly, abrupt disengagement from the war would have been dangerous for England in 1710, entailing the loss of confidence of England's allies, Austria and Holland, and the possible collapse of credit at home as domestic and foreign investors rushed to withdraw their loans from England's "over-extended war economy".[3]

The complex policy pursued by Harley was designed to take account of all these considerations. In order to obtain support from Tory moneyed men, City interests, and foreign investors, Harley disavowed irresponsible pacifism while hinting that the ministry was negotiating for important trade concessions in Spanish America. His South Sea scheme of May 1711, in which Defoe played an important role, was bait for these economic and social groups, as essential to the strength of the Tory party as the country gentlemen eulogized by St. John and by Swift. But commercial advantages for the English in South America spelt commercial disadvantages for the Dutch, whom Harley considered "the essential prop of English foreign policy".[4] His own view of the importance of the Dutch as junior partners of the English and his understanding that betrayal of them would enrage the Whigs and the Allies, meant that he had to try to find a balance somewhere between keeping the Dutch subservient and sacrificing them completely to English interests. His solution to these contradictory positions was "to frame a 'double policy' which had something for everyone and which left maximum room for opportunism and for manoeuvre".[5]

The aspect of this double policy most pertinent to understanding Defoe's *Reasons Why* was the exertion of pressure secretly on the Allies and on the French in order to secure commercial concessions from the partition of the Spanish empire along with the maintenance of a public facade of unanimity among the Allies. St. John had to be kept out of these delicate negotiations, for his anti-Dutch proclivities would have led to

> an energetic public attack on the Dutch or on the Austrians, which could break up the confederacy and lead to a competing downward spiral of separate offers to the enemy. To Harley and to Shrewsbury it was vital that public anger against the allies and ministerial co-operation with them should remain, as it were, on different levels. Tory xenophobia should be bottled up as much as possible, to be released only when the pressure became dangerous or allied obstinacy too glaring.[6]

Disposition of the Spanish empire, source of the commercial concessions coveted by the English, was the knottiest problem facing the ministry. The Allies and the Whigs were determined to wrest Spain away from its king and to present it to Charles of Austria, and they almost succeeded in gaining the assent of an exhausted France at the finally abortive peace negotiations at Gertrydenberg in 1710. The Tories were inclined to leave Spain in the hands of King Philip, grandson of the Bourbon Louis XIV. The death of the Emperor Joseph of Austria in April 1711 provided them with a rationale for this inclination: it was unwise for England to pursue the attempt to place Charles, now the Hapsburg successor, on the Spanish throne, thus uniting two empires in his person. The European balance of power could be endangered as much by Hapsburgs as by Bourbons.

The fruit of the ministry's secret negotiations with the French was the signing in London with the special envoy, Mesnager, of the Preliminary Articles of October 8, 1711. The articles consisted of two documents: the first was a detailed statement of special advantages to England; the second was a generalized statement about issues to be brought before a peace conference. It was the second document, later referred to contemptuously by St. John as "the paper for Holland",[7] that was designed for publication. "Defoe had evidently been commissioned to prepare the way for the simultaneous revelation of the second Mesnager convention and of the expected Dutch acceptance of it", writes Douglas Coombs.[8]

In *Reasons Why* Defoe argues that the war effort has so weakened England that peace is an urgent necessity, that the war has in fact already been won, and that partition is the answer to the disposition of the Spanish empire. He offers two plans for such partition, both awarding the Spanish Netherlands to Holland, alternatives regarded by his avid readers as ministry-inspired. Defoe anticipates objections to his argument by insisting that no betrayal of England's allies is intended; Dutch failure to protest about England's peace-making efforts, he reasons, is proof of the good faith of Harley's ministry. In addition, Defoe counters possible replies with *ad hominem* attacks couched in innuendos: the Dutch are domineering, the Duke of Marlborough (Commander-in-Chief of the allied forces) or his supporters arrogant, the Whigs war-mongering and envious of the Tory ministry's power to initiate a peace offensive.

The reason Defoe goes to some pains in this tract to differentiate his speaker from Mr. Review is that as late as 13 September he had ridiculed in the *Review* the suggestion that the ministry was considering giving up Spain to the House of Bourbon. "No minister England ever had, could, without distraction, think of venturing, and suggesting it at this time," he had asserted confidently. But by 13 October he was drawing a distinction between the kingdom and the empire of Spain, insisting that he had meant the larger entity.

Because he had not been kept closely enough informed about the ministry's peace plans to bring the *Review* into line by the time he was commissioned to write *Reasons Why*, Defoe had to be careful not to arouse Whig suspicion about the authorship of his semi-official tract. In the course of his argument, therefore, the supposed author of *Reasons Why* offers to "expostulate with the *Review*, or his party", about the statement, "No minister of state dares sign a treaty of peace for the delivery of Spain"; in addition, when discussing economic ills occasioned by the war, he remarks, "Discourses of trade are not the particular talent of the author of this ...". He also agrees with his own tracts of 1710 on national credit, referring to himself as "one of their [the Whigs'] own writers".

His tone is most distinct from that of Mr. Review in the lugubrious introductory pages describing the miseries of war-afflicted England:[9] "A mind possessed with any tenderness for the miseries, sufferings and distresses of its native land, ... cannot look upon the present condition of this nation without being in the highest degree affected". The mournful tone of the author is conveyed by vocabulary that is unusually emotional for Defoe: "tenderness", "love", "affected", "groaned", "languish". In addition, the defeatist author of *Reasons Why* emphasizes depressing contrasts between England's tremendous war efforts and small rewards:

> When we look upon our victorious army, and our generals crowned with lawrels, and garlands of victory; how do those very victories ruin us? And how many such battles, as that near Mons, could we bear? There we conquered the Mareschal de Villars, and gained the honour of the field of

battle? But how lie the bones of 22,000 of the best and bravest soldiers in Christendom sacrificed meerly to the pique of glory between the haughty generals, and to decide the mighty contest between us and the French, who should possess the hedges of Taniers, or be masters of the little coppice of Blareignes?

Defoe relies upon his acute ear for the prose rhythm appropriate for conveying a particular mood. In a group of questions like the following, additional phrases contribute little to the logical development of the argument, but varied repetition is necessary for rhetorical effect:

Who ever said of Britain, that she could never be weakened? that her strength was invincible, her wealth inexhaustible? that she could hold out the war forever; that she would never languish for peace, or need respite from a perpetual war? that she could never bleed to death; and that her body was invulnerable?

Finally, he makes effective use of adage to drive home a generalization he has been suggesting through examples:

Now we see our treasure lost, our funds exhausted, all our publick revenues sold, mortgaged, and anticipated; vast and endless interests entailed upon our posterity, the whole kingdom sold to usury, and an immense treasure turned into an immense debt to pay; *we went out full, but are returned empty.* (my italics)

The author of *Reasons Why* is a country gentleman. His first anxiety about the state of the economy is the decay of the wool industry, because that is certain to affect landed men. Much of his description of England's financial plight, as in the above selection, echoes the contemporary anxieties of that class about the national debt: how it would ever be paid, how investment in national securities was enriching the landless and impoverishing the landed.

The contrast in tone between Mr. Review and the speaker of *Reasons Why* can be heard clearly on one page of the tract, where the author points out in Mr. Review's voice that the ministry could carry on the war easily if it wanted to resort to general excise taxes:

It is confessed as aforesaid, that the war might still be continued if the government would so far abandon all concern for the miseries and diseases of the poor, as to load them with the insupportable taxes which are practised in foreign countries; and such as other governments do tax their people with, such as gabels upon cows, as in Italy and Switzerland; polls upon their sheep and black cattle, as in

> Prussia and Brandenburgh, tailles upon their shops and trades, as in France, or general excise upon their eatables to the very turnips, carrets and cabbage, as in Holland.

A few lines further on, Defoe returns to the sentimentally mournful voice in which he began the pamphlet when he mentions how much the tax burden on the poor distresses Queen Anne, "a Queen filled with compassion and moved with the pressures of her subjects, who as a true nursing mother is affected with the sufferings and distresses of her people".

Defoe's repeated use of innuendo in this tract is uncharacteristic of the forthright Mr. Review; the innuendo, indeed, unwittingly transposes in the reader's ears the mournfulness of the country gentleman into an unctuousness attributable to Defoe himself. Examples of innuendo include a reference to English treatment of the French at the abortive 1710 peace meeting: "We treated them as if the King of Spain had been prisoner of war, and the King of France fled from Versailles; or rather, as if a certain general [Marlborough] had put them both into his coach"; a reference to Whig avarice: "By degrees this title [reducing France's exorbitant power] to the war was dropped, perhaps by some that found the end obtained sooner than they desired it should be"; and a reference to Whig war-mongering: "Nor do we find that the Dutch themselves are in the least manner jealous or uneasy at our measures, though the endeavours of some people to make them so, may not have been wanting".

The innuendo most interesting for suggesting the complexities of dupery conceivable by Defoe refers to a rumoured moratorium on the ministry's payment of interest to security holders: "We will not say, the stopping the payment of the funds has been projected by either the present [Harley] or past ministry [Godolphin], though it has been reported of both; but especially was it thrown upon one [Harley], perhaps to conceal its being the real design of the other" [Godolphin]. This innuendo should be borne in mind when reading the next selection, *A Letter from a Gentleman at the Court of St. Germains,* and Defoe's Mesnager *Minutes*, both products of a devious double-dealer.

Mr. Review's voice rings out clearly in the second part of *Reasons Why*, where the proposed partition of Spain and the manner of obtaining it are discussed. In the heart of his tract, Defoe wastes little time on arousing emotion by variation and repetition of phrases. Here his illustrative imagery is concrete and familiar, yet fresh and striking:

> As if no method of treating can be found out but that which was then entered upon, no expedient for this or that difficulty be voted safe for us, but just what was then thought of ... And that the Dutch were the mint in which every article of peace must be coined, or that it could not be current in the Confederacy ...

For all its popular success, *Reasons Why* misfired in two ways. First of all, its argument that the Dutch were not averse to England's negotiating separately was immediately vitiated. The Dutch had not yet concurred in the Preliminaries when, on 13 October, the general document was released to a newspaper by one of the allied ambassadors, to whom the ministry had privately circulated the text a few days before. "After all the South Sea euphoria", writes Angus MacLachlan, "and the inspired leaks of the commercial banquet about to be spread before English merchants, the public articles signed by Mesnager ... could only appear as a bad joke".[10] The ministry, risking "the wrath of its allies in an attempt to retain its support at home",[11] was thus forced to release the first document, which detailed the special advantages promised to England at the expense of its allies by the French.

The second way in which *Reasons Why* misfired was that moderates were not yet ready to accept partition of Spain or separate treating for peace by England.[12] Whig propagandists replied furiously to Defoe's trial balloon, pointing out that the death of the Emperor was only an excuse to cover a partition previously decided upon by the ministry, and that "because of the Austrian weakness in trade and its non-existent naval power, Austria could not be as dangerous as France".[13] Frances Harris summarizes the Whig response in this way: "The choice ... was not between an immediate peace and an indefinite prolongation of the war, but between an unstable settlement, which would break down into further burdensome hostilities within a few years, and the short continuation of the war necessary to secure a safe and permanent peace."[14]

Defoe wrote to Harley on 16 October, complaining that in the absence of instructions from his busy employer, he felt uncertain of his ground. Harley's own uncertainty was indicated by a later remark of Defoe's about the minister's honest judgment at that time "that the war would last another year".[15]

By November Defoe admitted that Whig propaganda against the peace had been all too effective: it was being repeated even by "the poor and ignorant plough-men and servants in the countries most remote ..." As Harris observes, "This was in effect an admission of defeat, for in a series of pamphlets, published immediately after his *Reasons Why* and restating its arguments, Defoe had done all he could, single-handed, to prevent these Whig doctrines from spreading. The Whigs themselves were well aware by this time that they had little to fear from him".[16]

The result of the Whig propaganda triumph was that extremist elements of the ministry captured the lead from Harley's spokesmen, mounting an attack on the credibility of opponents of the projected peace instead of concentrating on defending the peace itself.[17] The best-known contribution to this new stage of the pamphlet war was Swift's *Conduct of the Allies*, issued late in November. In it Swift roundly denounced the principle of European intervention by England, advancing a devil theory of a war concocted by moneyed classes with vested interests in a parliamentary funded debt and by the Marlborough family. He viciously attacked the Duke of Marlborough at length and the Duchess and Godolphin in passing. Like Defoe in most of his pamphlets, Swift claimed to be appealing to a moderate public ignorant of the facts, but his contemptuous tone of voice ("I cannot sufficiently admire the industry of a sort of men wholly out of favour with the prince and people, and openly professing a separate interest from the bulk of the landed men, who yet are able to raise at this juncture so great a clamour against a peace, without offering one single reason, but what we find in their ballads"), rapidly modulating into anger, belied that claim. And his revelation of sordid details about behind-the-scene wrangling among the Allies, with special attention to the Dutch he so detested, was deliberately incendiary. The force and drive of his syntax, unclogged by the qualifying clauses and innuendos of Defoe's *Reasons Why* ... and other pamphlets appealing for moderation, was due less to his superiority as a writer than to his simplification of the complex issues involved and to his extremist design. (A contrast between the incendiary styles of Swift and Defoe can be observed by referring to pages 76–78 above, in which Defoe's complex method of rabble-rousing is described.) "Far from Swift's being the tool of the chief minister [Harley]", declares MacLachlan, "the chief minister was forced to trim his sails to the hurricane produced by Swift's—and St. John's—propaganda".[18]

Defoe's trimming of sails led him to develop a clear anti-Austrian line in his contributions to the peace campaign during 1711 and 1712. In the opinion of Lawrence Poston, a careful student of Defoe's peace writings, this line was basically consistent with his earlier position on the danger of upsetting the balance of power in Europe by permitting any of the Allies to engross power lost by France in the War of the Spanish Succession.[19] Defoe's major service to the ministry in addition to the anti-Austrian propaganda was his advocacy of economic aspects of the peace settlement.

On other issues of the peace debate Defoe wavered. Like Harley, he was generally pro-Dutch except when threats seemed necessary to force them to accept a role as England's subsidiaries.[20] In the despicable character assassination campaign waged against the Duke of Marlborough,[21] Defoe was circumspect, recognizing that the Commander-in-Chief had to be removed from office if a peace treaty were to be concluded by the Tory ministry, but not lending his pen to excessive personal abuse. On the complex question of whether or not the moment for peace had arrived, Defoe, like Harley, sometimes changed his mind. His reservations are stated clearly in his *Review* of 14 March 1713:

> As for my opinion of the peace ... I do not like it at all ... but ... I do not dislike it *for the same reasons that some do* ... nor *did I like the peace* you were making before ... I aimed at another kind of peace ... A peace that should have parted this bone of contention among all the contenders, and particularly should have allotted such an interest, such a strength, and such a commerce to Britain and Holland, as should have made the Protestant interest superior to all Europe ...

Lawrence Poston concludes, "He sometimes swerved in his course, but perhaps this was often part of a search for honourable accommodation".[22]

His own uncertainty about the proper balance of the complex issues involved in termination of the war must have contributed to his occasional forays in defence of the Whigs. Wishing to capitalize on the public interest in the peace debate, Defoe seems also to have desired to elicit a clear mandate from moderates by highlighting the clash of conflicting points of view. His tendency to rush into battle, and his idiosyncratic sense of humour, projected his personal anxieties into opposing Whig and Tory arguments. A good pair of examples are his tracts *Reasons Why a Party among Us Are Obstinately Bent against a Treaty of Peace with the French at This Time* (second edition, 9 October 1711) and *Armageddon: Or, the Necessity of Carrying on the War, If Such a Peace Cannot Be Obtained As May Render Europe Safe, and Trade Secure* (30 October 1711). In the first tract, advertised as "By the Author of Reasons for Putting an End to This Expensive War", Defoe, no longer a mournful, but now a highly partisan Tory, removes his gloves and reveals the inside story of Whig opposition to the peace measures of Harley's ministry. Behind all their professions of principle lies personal animosity toward the present administration: it is not peace to which they are opposed, but a peace which they do not themselves negotiate. In *Armageddon*, speaking for the Whigs, he makes an impassioned plea for the right of free expression of unpopular views, the right of the Whigs to explain their reservations about the negotiations: "We are for peace as well as anyone, we have paid for it as much as anybody, fought for it as much as anybody, prayed for it as much as anybody, and the more we have done so, the more reason there is for us to desire, that when we have it, it may be a good one ..." (p. 7). Later on in the same pamphlet he writes:

> I have heard loud clamours and railing at the Whigs upon this head, yet I could never find they had any worse reasons than such as are here hinted at, why they were for carrying on the war. And suppose these reasons not good, yet are they far from being criminal reasons. Nor are they such as need drive us to extremities with the Whigs, or occasion a general clamour at them. They are not disloyal reasons, undutiful reasons, or contentious reasons, but founded on the good of the whole body of the nation; at least, as far as they apprehend them; and if the intention is good, whether in those that wish for peace without any more war, or those that wish for more war in order to better peace, neither part ought to be blamed for want of penetration. (p. 40).

Defoe's *Defence of the Allies and the Late Ministry: Or, Remarks on the Tories New Idol* (January 1712), a reply to Swift's *Conduct of the Allies*, was motivated in part by indignation at Swift's violent attack on the Dutch and disapproval of his extremism:

> Our author calls his book *The Conduct of the Allies and of the Ministry*; which is (being interpreted) a design to blacken the Confederates, in order to prepare our people to swallow down a notion, which we thank God Her Majesty has declared against, (viz.) of making a peace whether they will consent or no, or in brief, to make a *separate peace*. (p. 3).

Despite the fact that Defoe's principles of foreign policy remained constant and that his wavering was confined to tactics, his service in the peace campaign of the Tory ministry was regarded by contemporaries as evidence of his lack of principle. The contempt that he and his *Review* inspired after 1710 in such ardent Whigs as Arthur Maynwaring[23] had its origin in Defoe's transfer of allegiance from the Godolphin to the Harley ministry. Yet both Godolphin and Harley were moderates. Like the Duke of Marlborough, they were driven into the arms of extremists by the furious struggle for power between Whigs and Tories. A writer, Defoe suffered a different kind of fate: because he never became the spokesman for extremists, his contemporaries misunderstood him, over-simplified his positions, and labelled him an unsavoury turncoat. His reputation is a sobering demonstration to twentieth-century readers of the power of extremist exaggeration to distort the complexities of a moderate and pragmatic approach to political problems.

Notes

1 John Robert Moore, *A Checklist of the Writings of Daniel Defoe* (Bloomington: Indiana University Press, 1960), p. 88.

2 Angus MacLachlan, "The Road to Peace, 1710–13", in *Britain after the Glorious Revolution 1689–1714*, ed. Geoffrey Holmes (London: Macmillan and Co., 1969), p. 198. Much of my historical discussion is based upon MacLachlan's masterly analysis.

3 *Ibid.*, p. 203.

4 *Ibid.*, p. 205.

5 *Ibid.*, p. 204.

6 *Ibid.*, p. 207.

7 Douglas Coombs, *The Conduct of the Dutch: British Opinion and the Dutch Alliance during the War of the Spanish Succession* (The Hague and Achimota, 1958), p. 257.

8 *Ibid.*, p. 258.

9 Perhaps it was Defoe's description of England's weakness that inspired Mesnager to convey 100 pistoles to the author for *Reasons Why*. Defoe accepted the money but declined Mesnager's service, letting him know that he was employed by the ministry and reporting the attempted bribe to Queen Anne. All our knowledge about this incident comes from Defoe's account in his Mesnager *Minutes* of 1717.

10 MacLachlan, p. 209.

11 Coombs, p. 261.

12 W. T. Laprade, *Public Opinion and Politics in Eighteenth Century England* (New York: The Macmillan Company, 1936), p. 97.

13 Lawrence Poston III, "Defoe and the Peace Campaign, 1710–1713: A Reconsideration," *HLQ*, 26 (1963), 9.

14 Frances Marjorie Harris, "A Study of the Paper War Relating to the Career of the First Duke of Marlborough, 1710–1712", unpublished Ph.D. thesis, University of London, 1975, p. 271.

15 Paraphrased by Laprade, p. 98.

16 Harris, pp. 271, 272.

17 St. John also took direct action against Whig writers, summoning fourteen booksellers, printers, and writers before the Queen's Bench to answer the charge of libel (Laprade, p. 98).

18 MacLachlan, p. 211.

19 Poston, p. 19. With certain exceptions in 1707, 1709, and especially in 1710, when Defoe had been carried away momentarily in the wave of euphoria occasioned by the English general Stanhope's dazzling and temporarily successful campaign into the heart of the Spanish Peninsula, Defoe spoke in favour of a partition of the Spanish empire, following the spirit of William III's policy of a balance of power in Europe. (See Poston, pp. 3–4.)

20 On June 5, 1712, when Defoe was more critical of the Dutch than at any other time, he wrote to Robert Harley, then Earl of Oxford:

> I am farr from Exciting the people against The Dutch, and believ it is not the Governments View to Injure or to Break with the Dutch; but it Seems Necessary, and I believ it is your Ldpps Aim, to have the Dutch Friends and Not Masters; Confederates not Governours; and to keep us from a Dutch as well as a French Mannagement.

The contrast between Defoe's and Swift's emotions is plain from the latter's comment to Stella on September 28, 1711, when the English were trying privately to get Dutch agreement to the Preliminaries, long before the height of the anti-Dutch campaign:

> The Earl of Strafford is to go soon to Holland and let them know what we have been doing: and then there will be the devil and all to pay; but we'll make them swallow it with a pox.
>
> *Journal to Stella*, ed. Harold Williams (Oxford, 1948), II, 372.

21 The unpublished dissertation by Harris, cited above, traces this campaign in fascinating detail.

22 Poston, p. 20.

23 Maynwaring's biographer, John Oldmixon, reports in his *Life and Posthumous Works* (London, 1715), the violent contempt that Maynwaring felt toward Defoe for his desertion of Godolphin's for Harley's service (p. 169). Maynwaring described Defoe as "the most ignorant rogue that ever scribled".

Reasons Why This Nation Ought to Put a Speedy End to This Expensive War, &c. (1711)

A mind possessed with any tenderness for the miseries, sufferings, and distresses of its native land, that has the happiness of any generous principles, and shares something of that sublime quality, called by the Ancients "love of our country", cannot look upon the present condition of this nation without being in the highest degree affected. Our Saviour's most affectionate view of the Holy City, expressed in that most emphatical text, "O Jerusalem, Jerusalem!" may be with the greatest justice and propriety applied to this island. We seem to have the things which belong unto our peace entirely hidden from our eyes. How have we above twenty years groaned under a long and a bloody war? How often [have] our most remote views of peace gladdened our souls, and cheared up our spirits? Our stocks have always risen or fallen, as the prospects we had of that amiable object were near or remote.

We have seldom seen any of our publick Acts, whether of Parliament or of Council, but they are prefaced with something or other relating to the war. The word WAR is not expressed in them without the adjunct of some epithet, such as "bloody war", "heavy war", "chargeable war", "dangerous war", &c. Our politicians have promised themselves every year that the enemy will be reduced, that the war cannot hold long, that surely this year, and that year, and the other year, will be the last of the war. Thus have we kept up our spirits with the hopes of coming to the desired port, viz. the haven of peace; and every effort which the nation has made for the raising money to carry on this war, has been encouraged both from prince and people, with the putting us in hopes that all shall at last be crowned with peace; that this, 'tis hoped, may be the last year of the war. Thus once more, and once more, &c. and still we hoped the work will be over; and in all this I do not see, that a nation plunged so deep, whose weights and pressures have been so many, can in any wise be reflected on; neither her courage, her patience, her strength, her wealth, or any part of those things whereof her sons so boast in the behalf of her their mother, can be reproached. Who ever said of Britain, that she could never be weakened? that her strength was invincible, her wealth inexhaustible? that she could hold out the war forever; that she would never languish for peace, or need respite from a perpetual war? that she could never bleed to death; and that her body was invulnerable? These are things no wise man will pretend to; nor would such a way of arguing please the most sanguine among us at this time. At the beginning of the war such excursions might be borne with, when our youth first felt their own strength, and our national riches were so immense, that we persuaded ourselves they had no bottom. But *the case is altered now*. Now we see our treasure lost, our funds exhausted, all our publick revenues sold, mortgaged, and anticipated; vast and endless interests entailed upon our posterity, the whole kingdom sold to usury, and an immense treasure turned into an immense debt to pay; we went out full, but are returned empty. We find our great navy spread the seas to the expense of above three millions yearly, which yet our enemies regard so little, that they carry on the war as it were without a navy, and think it not worth the expense, to fit out their fleet to prevent us; but they gain from us every year by their privateering, as much as they would lose by fitting out their navy.

In our land armies, we expend mighty sums to perform trifling exploits, and please ourselves with a few inches of the enemy's ground, bought too dear, and paid for with a double price of money and blood. How do we flatter ourselves in the war, and call it a glorious campaign (!) when we have taken a little fort, ten of which have scarce sufficed our enemy, the King of France, for the triumphs of a summer's service.

When we look upon our victorious army, and our generals crowned with lawrels, and garlands of victory; how do those very victories ruin us? And how many such battles, as that near Mons, could we bear? There we conquered the Mareschal de Villars, and gained the honour of the field of battle? But how lie the bones of 22,000 of the best and bravest soldiers in Christendom sacrificed meerly to the pique of glory between the haughty generals, and to decide the mighty contest between us and the French, who should possess the hedges of Taniers, or be masters of the little coppice of Blareignes? Where was the necessity of this trial of skill at so great an expense? What enterprise was made easy by it? Mons was taken afterwards, and Mons might have been taken before; the enemy possessed again the very same spot of ground in less than 10 days, and bid you come on again at the same price, experience teaching us (*bloody experience is war indeed!*) that this was not the way, that such victories would vanquish the conqueror, that this was the only way to ruin the troops, and give the enemy at length the superiority. We fall next to besieging towns, Douay, Bethune, St. Venant, and Air, finish another glorious campaign, as we call it, and 35,000 of our boldest and forwardest troops lie buried in the ditches of those paltry places. The execution is so terrible, that it becomes the aversion of the very army itself. And whereas at the beginning of this present campaign, it was given out that the General would begin the operations, &c. with the siege of Ypres, or of St. Omer, 10,000 of your men ran away and deserted to the enemy in a very few weeks. This is confirmed by, as it was the occasion of, that cruel proclamation of the King of Prussia, appointing all that should desert and be retaken, among his troops, to have their noses cut off, and be kept in perpetual slavery at hard work, with a chain about their necks. Notwithstanding this, we attack Bouchain, and with small loss obtain that conquest, having not above 6,000 men killed and wounded in that glorious conquest. His Grace the Duke of Marlborough, resolving to make what advantage he possibly could of the present consternation of the French, makes preparations for another siege, which, as was given out, should be that of Cambray, or of Valenciennes, Le Quesnoy, or Maubeuge; but the season being advanced, and the siege of Aire being fresh in the memory of our men, the apprehensions of another autumn siege has so intimidated our people, that the desertion is as great as ever among our troops; so that our advices from the army tell us, the resolutions of a siege are laid by, and the troops will be put into quarters of refreshment, and this glorious campaign, which has cost the Allies so many millions, must end on that side *avec le prise de Bouchain*.

This brief recapitulation of the state of the affair in Flanders is thus laid down here, not in the least to lessen the esteem we ought to have for our generals and great officers employed in this war, of whose conduct and bravery the world speaks such glorious things; no, this does not detract from their characters, but rather confesses that they have done all that it was possible for men to do. That notwithstanding the superiority of the enemy, they have offered them battle in the field, have entered their lines, which they gave out were impenetrable; attacked and taken a town in their view, after all their efforts to prevent it; and a thousand gasconades* of Monsieur Villars to his master, that it was impossible the Duke of Marlborough could invest it. But this is not the subject of the present treatise; the question before us is of another kind. It is not to enquire whether we are able to fight and conquer, able to push Monsieur Villars out of his fastnesses, and take towns with an hundred thousand witnesses; but the main hinge whereon all the affair now turns, is this: what is this to ending the war? How long may the King of France keep us thus at bay? How many towns have we yet to take from him, before he can effectually be humbled and reduced to such terms of peace as we pretend to desire? Whether to resolve to carry on the war till France is reduced, after the rate of one town every summer, will not eternize and entail the war to us and to our heirs forever, or to issue a few more such glorious campaigns in an inglorious peace at last? It may be therefore a most needful enquiry for the curious heads of this age to reflect back a little upon our own circumstances, and enquire what reasons we have, which are drawn from within ourselves, and turn upon the great hinge of our own affairs only, and which move, and press, and call upon us to put an end to this war upon the best conditions we can.

Before we come to this enquiry, it may be also very needful to suggest or premise, that by putting an end to the war, is not meant that we should sue to the King of France for peace, and take such conditions as he shall impose upon us, as if he was conquerour, and we were subdued. But by putting an end to the war, is here to be understood, listening to a treaty with a sincere desire and resolution: if the enemy may be brought to make just, reasonable, and fair proposals, to close with them, and not insist upon one thing after another, and grow, and encroach in demand from one thing to another, till at last we come to insist upon impossibilities, and make such demands as, we know, the enemy cannot grant; or which, if they should have granted, we knew they could not execute. It is not needful that we enter here into a dissertation concerning the

* *gasconades*: boasts. Natives of Gascony were regarded as notorious boasters. [Ed.]

reasonableness of our last method of treating with the French; or whether it was sincere on either side. On our part we were daily told, the French ministers hovered about the thing itself, kept at a distance from the substance of the treaty, which was the security of the performance, and trifled with Confederates. On the other side, the French alledged, that the Conferates treated haughtily, as if they were with their armies at the gates of Paris; that they kept the French commissioners like prisoners in a garrison, permitting them to speak with nobody but the Dutch deputies, who came and went like meer messengers of an errand; that they were not allowed to see any of the ministers of the other allies, though they were concerned in the war as well as they, as if the Dutch were afraid that their proposals were so reasonable, the rest of the Allies should think them sufficient, and be enclined to close with them; that the Dutch acted by the pensionary, and the Lord T—— in concert with the D—— of M——, and the English Court would never come to any certainty what would content them; but daily declared everything unsatisfactory, till at last, being pressed to declare what they would have, they put the whole upon an impossibility, as to the King of France obliging his grandson to evacuate Spain; refusing the least equivalent for peaceably giving up such vast dominions above eight year in possession &c.

Many more particulars might be objected here against the methods and measures taken with the enemy, in the last treaty which was managed at Gertruydenberg. But this may suffice to include the whole, (viz.) that we treated them as if the King of Spain had been prisoner of war, and the King of France fled from Versailles; or rather, as if a certain general had put them both into his coach; and as if not only Spain, but France itself, had been lost. And that this may not pass for the words of this pamphlet only, it may not be amiss to note, that when the Marquis of Uxelles complained of the ill success of their negotiation, and that they treated as if they had France in possession, he was answered, that *his master ought to reckon it his good fortune, that he had the honour to save the Kingdom of France upon such easy terms.* Whether it was due to the situation of our affairs at that time, to push matters to such a height, the process of another campaign may better argue than any other kind of demonstration, since another whole summer is passed over, another glorious campaign in Flanders ended. The great, and so much boasted impression the D. of Savoy was to make, is ended, and that Prince retired, and France is not yet won; no, not a foot set in its dominions, and but a very few inches of ground gained, which we have paid dear for, (viz.) many thousands of our best troops killed and wounded; many millions of treasure expended, and near twenty thousand of our men run away and deserted to the enemy. Nay, so great is the desertion of the soldiers for fear of another siege, that even at the writing these sheets, the publick printed news says, *The desertion of the infantry is great to astonishment.* Vide the *Post-Boy*, No. 2532, September the 20th, 1711.

These serve us for so many convictions of the imprudence of our late conduct in treating with the French; which either proceeded from a misgrounded elevation in the Allies, upon the success of the former campaigns, and strange notions that the French were in no condition to carry on the war, no not one campaign more; or else from selfish principles in some of the persons concerned, who for reasons of their own, were unwilling the war should end, and would choose rather to sacrifice their country, and the interest of their Queen, than make use of any opportunity, how advantageous soever, to make a peace with the enemy. It is not the business of this tract to enquire, which of these principles were the fatal overthrow of the treaty; or what has prompted us to carry on the war for this last year, when so good conditions of peace were then offered, and so little gain by the war was in view.

But it is worthy our notice here, and not improper to the purpose, to observe, how very much we have all along deceived ourselves with hopes from the weakness of the French, having so blinded our eyes with the accounts of their bad condition, that we have entirely overlooked the decay of our own. Every autumn we have represented the broken condition of their troops; and through the whole season for recruiting the forces, we have been amused with fictitious accounts of their cavalry being in no condition to take the field, their recruits for the foot not being arrived; the difficulty the intendants of the provinces found to raise men; the men when raised, being forced against their wills, taking all opportunities to desert; the quality of the recruits; their being most made up of boys and youths unfit for service. Yet has it been always observed, that towards the marching of the armies into the field, the accounts have been changed, and we have account, that their cavalry make a fine appearance; that their infantry are new clothed; and every year, to enhance the value of every advantage we gain over them, we forget not to own their superiority in number.

Seeing therefore that these hopes have not yet appeared well grounded, and that, notwithstanding all our expectations, the enemy lets us see, that he is still able to hold out, and that he dares to carry on the war, notwithstanding our threats, and the menaces of our deputies, it seems that it is not now the business of the Allies to amuse themselves with the expectation of reducing him every campaign, as we have done; the vain fruit of which has supported the nation so long.

It seems rather the work of the considering heads now employed, to rectify these errors; and, if it be to be retrieved, make some amends to the nation of Britain for the past mistake. *Peace is the thing we want*; if it should be our misfortune to have any number of men among us, who are of a differing opinion, they are calmly entreated to consider some heads; (1) of our own circumstances; and (2) of our enemies; from both which, if impartially and without prejudice searched into, they may find reason to yield up to this point, (viz.) that it is absolutely necessary to us to put an end to this war.

Nor has it been denied, even by the wisest and best men concerned in the last ministry, that we were in so much necessity of peace; the error lay in this part of it (whether it was a delusion or no, time may discover), that they persuaded us, and perhaps themselves also, that the King of France was in a greater exigence, and that peace was more necessary to him than to the Allies. We shall consider the circumstances of both, and perhaps the inferences may decide the controversies on both sides at the same time.

The questions are very material, and admit of some enlargement; but this may be received as the abstract of the whole.

I. What occasion we have for peace.
II. What condition the French are in to carry on the war.

The occasion we have for peace, it is too harsh to say, the necessity we are in for it, proceeds from:

1. The great loss and hindrance the carrying on this war is to our commerce; to the exportation of our manufactures and home-growth; to the employment of our poor; and to the consumption of the produce of this island in foreign parts. It is an unpleasant work for any writer to expose the weakness of his country, and the decay of trade among our people.

But let any of our general calculators in these matters determine this case. Let it be enquired, whether the rates of our manufactures are held up to the former price; whether our wool is consumed; or whether there is three years' growth of wool now in the hands of the farmers, and graziers, and sheep-masters, in this island unsold. Together with this they may enquire, whether the price of English wool is not, by this great interruption of our trade, fallen near 40 percent. in value; and if this does not yet affect the landed men, no doubt it must affect them in a little time.

Discourses of trade are not the particular talent of the author of this, and therefore farther enlargement on this head is avoided; but if it may be allowed to weigh anything in this case, the reader is desired to observe the number of shops and houses now shut up, and to be let between Cheapside and Charing-Cross; which, as it has been observed, are now more than ever were known. And the like proportion is, as we are credibly informed, in most of the great and trading towns in England.

The author has been told that above 50 shops are shut up, or to be let, between Ludgate and Temple-Bar; that 10 houses, which were formerly of considerable wholesale tradesmen, are shut up about Holbourn-Bridge; and the number of bankrupts in every *Gazette* is an astonishment.

Come we in the next place to consider the taxes and anticipations which are yearly paid, and lie as a dead weight upon the ages to come. That every article of the revenues is mortgaged and anticipated, and that, generally speaking, for an hundred years to come. It is unpleasant to enumerate the funds lodged in the offices of the Exchequer, for payment of annuities, tickets, Exchequer bills and tallies; they are too well known to make it needful in this case. The heads of the projectors have been racked for new-invented taxes, and the number of those taxes exceeds all that ever were practised in the late rebellion. All duties and customs are stretched to the extremity that they can bear, and beyond what it was believed in former times could be practicable. Every necessary import or produce, our corn and cattle excepted, are taxed to the highest pitch they are capable of; such as coals, salt, malt, leather, candles, beer, ale, cyder, perry, spirits, vinegar, glass-windows, hackney coaches, chairs, apprentices, fees, hops; and whatever can be thought capable of paying, or worth collecting duties and customs on importation, are doubled and trebled to such a degree, that is is hard to find out one clause of foreign trade which is able to bear a heavier tax than is already laid; not to mention some, which, by the greatness of the duty, are either not imported at all, or are run in by the arts and vigilance of clandestine traders, the greatness of the duty encouraging them to run the hazard.

By these things the nation appears so entirely exhausted of means to raise more money, that nothing remains but the choice of two ruinous extremes, (viz.) the taxing our food and clothes, which is called a general excise, and which is such a burthen as the nation ought not to be loaded with, if it be possible to avoid it, the number and condition of our poor considered; and is a thing which our Parliament, in all ages, have avoided, and will avoid, till they are brought to the last extremity; which extremity is the ground of the present argument for a peace with France; or (2.) putting a stop to the payment of the interest of the funds already charged and established.

From what has been said, the truth of which may easily be proved, this single question seems to be offered to the consideration of the people of this island: whether ought we, on the one hand, to lay a general excise or tax upon all clothes, household stuff, and food, or stop the payment of the funds; or, on the other hand, put an end to the war.

If any objector will put in his protest against the alternative, and alledge that we are not brought to the necessity of this choice, he must at the same time let us see what door of escape he has found out, and by what other method he can propose to raise money for carrying on the war. The writer of these sheets owns to have seen the schemes of taxes offered by most of the projectors of this town the last year, and does think he may affirm, there is not one which contains not, either some branches of a *general excise*, as above, or something equivalent to it, and equally oppressive; so that the nation either would not, or could not bear them; and he is the bolder therefore to say, there are no other ways but the two abovesaid. We will not say, the stopping the payment of the funds has been projected by either the present or past ministry, though it has been reported of both; but especially was it thrown upon one, perhaps to conceal its being the real design of the other. But it is left to any unprejudiced judgement to consider, what would be the effects of either of these things to the nation.

Nevertheless, one use may not be improperly made of this, which, by way of remark, is laid here before the reader for his consideration; *and it is this*, that the weakness of a topick much made use of among a dissatisfied party of men among us, (viz.) that the way to overthrow the present ministry is to plunge them in the matter of funds, ruin the publick credit, and bring them to such exigencies, that they cannot carry on the war; that then the Queen must change her ministry again; and these people, not being able to support the government, or carry on the war, Her Majesty must, of necessity, have recourse to those who are able to do both. The weakness of which argument appears very conspicuous; for that all the difficulties the present ministry are driven unto by the people who thus endeavour to plunge them, are really no difficulties at all, any other than as the ministry are backward and unwilling to bring hardships and severe things upon the country; that they are loth to lay those heavy taxes upon the people, which must necessarily follow, if they are obliged to raise the whole money, necessary for the service of every year, in that year wherein it is to be wanted; or loth to put a stop to the payment of interest, which falls annually due upon the publick funds for money already borrowed, and which they know would fall heavy upon innumerable families, though it is not doubted, ten parts of twelve of the landed men in England would come into such a proposal. If the ministry would come in to either of these proposals, it is obvious, they may carry on the war as long as they please, without being obliged any more to court those people for upholding the publick credit, who make that advantage a plan for the destruction of the ministry. Either of the two articles aforesaid, (viz.) of general excises, or stopping the payment of the funds, would be sufficient every year for the service of that respective year. This one of their own writers told them plainly enough; for which, I hear him frequently cursed among them, though it seems the man has more penetration in those matters than most of them; for nothing is more certain, than that the endeavours of the Whigs to destroy the publick credit, has exposed them more than any other of their conduct; as if they were a party willing to ruin the nation, rather than not keep the reins in their own hands; and as if they were resolved that the new ministry should fall, though themselves were to fall with them. This, the aforesaid writer, though of their own party, very well indeed, and with pungent reasons, warned them of, under the apposite simily of sinking the ship; but when envy blinds men's eyes, they are rendered deaf to the counsel of their friends, much more are they so to that of their enemies; for they cast stones at the advice, and, as I am informed, at the adviser too.

And now their mistake appears plain, and nothing exposes them more; for it is obvious to every eye, that the government have THREE ways to avoid the mischief; and that snare which the party thought could not fail, is three ways to be broken, and brought to nought.

I. *By general excises*, which will raise sufficient every year for the whole demand of the war for that year.

II. *By stop of the funds*, which would cause the customs, the excise, the duties on salt, leather, coals, candles, hops, windows, stamps, paper, post office, and all other appropriated taxes, to be paid directly into the publick treasury, for carrying on the war.

III. OR, if either of these were not thought fit to be done, then was it in the power of the government, according to Her Majesty's prerogative, to put an end to the war; which, if it were not then so advantageously concluded as it ought to be, or as once it might have been; yet the people might see who had compelled them to it, and on whom all the blame of it ought to be laid.

This leads us to the enquiry, which, as appears by the title, is the main end and design of these sheets, (viz.) What are the reasons why we should put a speedy end to this war? And though there are many more, yet some of them may be understood by these that follow.

1. Because it does not seem to be *easy* for us to carry on the war.

It is with respect to the two former heads, (viz.) the general excises, and the stop of the funds, that the word *possible* is not put here instead of the word *easy*.

It is confessed as aforesaid, that the war might still be continued if the government would so far abandon all concern for the miseries and diseases of the poor, as to load them with the insupportable taxes which are practised in foreign countries; and such as other governments do tax their people with, such as gabels upon cows, as in Italy and Switzerland; polls upon their sheep and black cattle, as in Prussia and Brandenburgh; tailles upon their shops and trades, as in France; or general excise upon their eatables to the very turnips, carrets and cabbage, as in Holland. The war may be continued, though this is not any objection against the reason above, for this will not be called carrying it on *easily*, and therefore the government finding the war cannot *easily* be continued, i.e. without heavy, insupportable and oppressive burthens on the people, and especially on the poor; it must be acknowledged, that to a Queen filled with compassion and moved with the pressures of her subjects, who as a true nursing mother is affected with the sufferings and distresses of her people; this is a good reason why Her Majesty should be willing to put an end to this war.

2. Because by a treaty of peace, it is probable the true ends and designs of this war, and for which it was at first undertaken, may be obtained.

The first pretence of and which for a long time was the introduction to all publick acts relating to this war, was the reducing the exorbitant power of France; by degrees this title to the war was dropped, perhaps by some that found the end obtained sooner than they desired it should be. And then we had it changed for these words: for the obtaining a lasting, safe, and honourable peace. These words were thought so extensive that they might afford the parties room to shift at, and constantly furnish them with matter, to object, and with pretences to keep the rupture on foot, and to keep the wound open on pretence that the cure was not perfect, that the peace was not lasting and safe.

But foreseeing afterwards, that the King of France really made such offers that contained all the three terms which the peace was to have: thus it was honourable, for that the King of France sought it and yielded to many great demands, such as fully confessed his being over-matched in the war; that it was safe, because the King of France restored such strengths, and put into their hands such countries, as might forever enable the Confederates to overpower him; and that both these assisted to make it durable and lasting; foreseeing this, I say, the people who still were unwilling to bring the war to a period, they changed the title a second time, and called it a war for recovering the whole monarchy of Spain. ... Nay, when they come by a treaty to see a probability of obtaining this also, they changed their demands a third time into ... the security for evacuation, refusing the King of France's offer of money to be contributed for his quota of the war, to compel his grandson to evacuate Spain, if he should refuse it.

These things having made it appear that the true ends of the war may be obtained by a treaty of peace, and that there has been some nameless error in all former treaties, which have rendered them abortive; it must be allowed, by reasonable and indifferent people, that if Her Majesty can obtain by a peace what this war was at first undertaken for, this joined to the former, is a good reason why a speedy end should be put to the war.

3. Because that though it were to be allowed, that by continuing the war, some greater advantage in the terms of a peace might be obtained; yet that those advantages do not seem adequate and proportioned to the expense and loss, the effusion of blood, the expense of treasure, and the hardships suffered by the nation in their trade, and in their taxes, which must be the necessary consequences of continuing the war.

This relates to the evacuation of Spain, and putting it into the hands of the House of Austria, which though necessary to be done in the view of things at the beginning of the war, seem not to be either so necessary, or indeed of that consequence to the Allies, as the face of affairs in Europe are now changed as they were before. *First*, with respect to the exorbitant power of France, which is so broken and reduced by this long war, as that 'tis believed France has gotten a full surfeit of the ambitious gust to universal monarchy, and is in no condition to turn his thought that way for a hundred years to come. And *secondly*, with respect to the death of the late Emperour, by which it becomes a question on the other hand, whether it is not every way more safe for Europe, *trade being secured*, to leave Spain in the hands of King Philip, rather than join it undivided to the House of Austria, a thing which was once so fatal to Christendom before.

This alteration of the face of affairs in Europe, making it not altogether so needful to insist upon the entire evacuation of Spain to the House of Austria. . . .; and that article being the only point upon which the last treaty was broken off; the reason must be good why that treaty should now be renewed, and why an end should be put to the war …

The advantages which might be farther obtained by carrying on the war, seem all to be made doubtful by this article, since it remains evident, those advantages will all fall to the share of the Emperour. Whereas it may no more be our real advantage to procure additions to the Emperour, than to France, as things may issue.

* * *

Nothing hath been more the subject of some people's discourse relating to this matter, than the destructive condition of this peace; as if, because those who they desire to be employed therein are not likely to have any hand in it, that therefore those who are employed will betray and give us up to the French, and break in upon the treaty of alliance which we stand engaged in, and ruin the Confederacy. These are hard sayings, and ought to be very well grounded before we take up with them. For those people who speak evil of others ought to be well assured that the evil which they speak carry some evidence with it; otherwise they incur the odious name of slanderers to themselves.

This remark is occasioned by the clamours of some people, who ever since the suggestions of a peace, have spread any breadths among us, have taken hold of that report, to add what nothing but their own prejudices could possibly make rational to them, (viz.) that this peace shall be dishonourable; that it shall be a separate treaty, without the assent of our allies ... that we shall give up Spain to the French, quit the interests of King Charles, and make what they call an unsafe peace; as if it was a necessary consequence, that because the peace is not managed by the Dutch, therefore it must not be a safe peace; that we are not to be trusted with the peace, though we have born the burthen of the war; and that London was not as fit a place to treat with the French in as Gertruydenberg. We cannot be of this mind in the least; and we must needs think that since the weight of the war has lain chiefly upon us, and Her Majesty is essentially the head of the Confederacy, it as much belongs to us to treat of the peace as to the Dutch, and it is all out as reasonable that the Dutch should send their ministers and plenipotentiaries hither, to meet the French, as it is, that we should send our plenipotentiaries thither ... not to mention our ministers standing still to hear and see with Dutch ears and Dutch eyes, and know nothing of the treaty, but what the Dutch deputies pleased to communicate.

We see no necessity of this consequence, that because we desire to have the management of the treaty, that therefore the Dutch are left out of it. Her Majesty has never yet done anything but in concert with her allies; and possibly the Allies may as readily consent to a treaty at London, as a treaty at the Hague. Why then should any person be so chagrin at a treaty at London? As if because the Dutch do not manage the treaty, they were to be left out of it. Nor do we find that the Dutch themselves are in the least manner jealous or uneasy at our measures, though the endeavours of some people to make them so may not have been wanting; but on the other hand, are no doubt, by mutual concert with our Court, sending over two plenipotentiaries to be present here at any conferences that may be held on this occasion ... Where then the grounds are for the suspicions and uneasinesses that are spread among us, upon this appearance of a treaty, supposing it was true, we cannot see, unless some advances were made, and some postulata entered into, which were inconsistent with our obligations to the Allies; if any such did really appear, the Allies themselves, the Dutch in an especial manner, whose penetration is not the least of their character, would take umbrage at it immediately, and by memorials and representations endeavour to put a stop to such private negotiations, that might be to their prejudice. But the Dutch are a wiser people than to amuse themselves with such reports. And indeed how can they have any pretence so to do, when as there is an entire confidence between Her Majesty and her allies, so no measures in these things are entered into on either hand, but by concert and agreement of all parties, and to mutual satisfaction? It seems very unaccountable, that our people here should make objections at the reality and sincerity of the treaty, when entered into, because of our being the more immediate treaters; or suggest that we shall make meaner concessions to the French than our allies, since it does not at all appear that our confederates are made uneasy by the advances yet made, which no man will pretend to say are without the previous concert and agreement of our allies.

The reasons of re-assuming the management of a treaty into Her Majesty's hands may be many, and the King of France's having resented the treatment of his ambassadours at Gertruydenberg by the Dutch may be one; of which more might be said it it were convenient. But it no ways can be inferred, that because there may be less resentment and animosity on this side, that therefore we must yield to dishonourable conditions, and make a peace upon worse terms.

Nay, though all the conditions which were insisted upon at Gertruydenberg should not be now dwelt upon with the same warmth, and the stiffness and vigour which some people acted, with which perhaps they might not now be well pleased themselves, should be something abated, it may not follow that this may not be consistent with a safe and honourable treaty, or that we may not act in it with a perfect harmony and agreement between us and our allies ... So that we see nothing of any ground for jealousies and uneasinesses among us; except that the persons who object, will have it be that Britain is not fit to be trusted with making the conditions of her own peace, without the assistance of the Dutch, or rather without committing it to the Dutch, though at the same time they will allow Britain to bear the principal burthen of the war. Nay, as if Britain was under the tutelage of the Dutch, these people would have all the articles of peace concerted and determined by them, not intrusting us with any share in them, as people not of age, and uncapable of acting for ourselves ... What impositions, what severities, what niceties were the occasion of the breaking off of the last treaty, they take upon them to justify; and make those things, which were even then accounted to be but as circumstances of the treaty, pass for essential. As if no method of treating can be found out but that which was then entered upon, no expedient for this or that difficulty be voted safe for us, but just what was then thought of ... And that the Dutch were the mint in which every article of peace must be coined, or that it could not be current in the Confederacy; or that their politicks were the standard, by which every step we took was to be tried. This is making such an idol of the Dutch, as the Dutch themselves do not desire, or can have any reason to expect.

If we take any step here prejudicial to the Dutch, as our allies, or to any other of the Confederates, let the Dutch alone to complain for themselves, there is no question but they will be forward enough to object; but it must have some other signification, that we should have people here that should complain for the Dutch, before the Dutch complain for themselves, as if they did not understand their own interest, or did not know what was doing among us, as well as those complaining people, who, we have some reason to believe, know little or nothing of the matter neither.

But this is not all; these party politicians not only charge us with the manner of treating, (viz.) without the concurrence of our allies, but with the very terms we are to conclude, and the concessions we are to make to France, before any such terms are treated upon, or such concessions made, or perhaps thought upon, or intended to be made. Though this be an unreasonable and unjust way of judging, yet seeing it is become popular, and they run away with it as fact, it may be useful to take them in their own way, and giving their pretences the full latitude, inquire a little into the fact; as if it were true, whether it be so or no, that such a peace is determined to be made as they suggest. We need not run into many particulars here; the grand supposition is, that the present negotiations on foot, though we do not grant that there are any negotiations of any kind whatever now on foot, or treating of at all, or proposed in order to be treated of; but to grant the question so begged by common fame, (viz.) that we were to give up Spain to the French; which some gentlemen have written of as a thing so fatal, that it was all one with giving up Britain; and the *Review* has had the modesty to say, that no Minister of State dares sign a treaty of peace for the delivery of Spain. However, upon this supposition let us expostulate a little with the *Review*, or his party, upon the point, at the same time protesting that there is not, to our knowledge, any such concession made, or designed to be made, or that France is under any expectation of it.

But upon the foot of this protestation we may grant, for the sake of the argument only, that Spain was to be given up to the possession of Philip V.

Q. 1. Is there no difference between Spain in the possession of the present Philip V and his successours (for he has heirs), and Spain in the possession of the King of France?
2. Will not the heirs of the present K. Philip be as much Spaniards in one age more, as the heirs of King Lewis will be French, and *vice versa*?
3. Will the interests, either politick or trading, of France and Spain be ever capable of any union?
4. Can no treaty of commerce be so stipulated between the Allies and King Philip, so as that our trade may be kept free and secure, whether from embargoes, prohibitions, or impositions, under the general guarantees of the whole Confederacy?
5. Is Spain of any consequence to us, but as our trade to it is, or is not secured?
6. Is Spain, in the hands of King Philip, with a considerable possession freely given us in Peru and Chili, a trade to the rest of America, and a tariff of trade to Old Spain, better for us than Spain, in the hands of King Charles, entirely resigned, without any of those advantages?
7. Whether as to power and the ballance of Europe, may it not be as fatal to have Spain and the Indies, i.e. the whole undivided monarchy of Spain come to the House of Austria, and be annexed to the Empire, as to have part of

it only, in a branch of the House of Bourbon, and that branch not at all annexed to the Kingdom of France?

8. Whether the death of the late Emperour has not altered the case, and changed the face of Europe, so that a partition of the Spanish monarchy, which was not reasonable, the estates of the House of Austria being in two branches, is now become necessary, when they are all united in one?
9. Whether, had the Grand Alliance been now to be made, it would not have been probable, that the Confederates would have stipulated, that the crown of Spain should no more be in the person of the Emperour than of the King of France?
10. Whether, so many expedients offering themselves in this case, it may be worth all the blood that may yet be expended, before France can be compelled to yield up the whole Spanish monarchy, and King Philip be driven entirely out of it; and whether a reasonable partition be not better than such a conquest?
11. Whether we are sure that we shall ever be able to complete the conquest of it, and force them to the evacuation we pretend to; and if not, whether the partition may not at last be made upon worse terms then, than it may now?

These queries are capable of great enlargements; and much may be said to every head ... But as these sheets can by no means contain the full of the argument, it is proposed rather by way of query, in which the judicious reader will see the following things: 1. That there does not seem the same reasons now, which were good reasons then for resolving to make no peace, till the whole undivided monarchy of Spain shall be restored to the House of Austria ... This difference arising from the death of the late Emperour Joseph, by which means an exorbitant power and greatness will accrue to King Charles, who is now likely to be chosen Emperour; and in the nature of the Grand Alliance ought not also to enjoy the whole Spanish dominions both in Europe and America, which would be a power far too great for the rest of Europe, and as K. William said (when Prince of Orange) would give us reason to be as much Frenchmen as we are now Spaniards. *Vide* Sr. Wm. Temple's *Memoirs*, p. 82.

Seeing then that the circumstances of things are altered, the same necessities, and the same conveniences, do not subsist as inferences. 2. Here also we may observe, the same destructive prospect of our commerce does not appear, under an expedient never before thought of, (viz.) of putting the Queen of Great Britain in possession of a part of the Spanish dominions in America, to wit, in the kingdoms of Chili and Peru, with a tariff of trade secured to us in both Old Spain and New. These things destroy the necessity that has all along been upon us to reduce Old Spain into the obedience of the House of Austria; which was made necessary as to Britain, meerly for the security of our commerce, the export and consumption of our manufactures, and the employment of our poor; all which will be effectually provided by entirely putting into our hands such a branch of trade, as is much more than equivalent to all the trade we can expect to lose by France breaking in upon our Spanish trade. So that leaving Spain now in the hands of Philip V is not altogether so fatal a thing as some have suggested, or as it appeared to be before the death of the late Emperour.

Upon the whole, the author of this believing, that everyone will grant a partition of the Spanish monarchy, appears much more reasonable than ever it did before, and the only medium or expedient to put a end to the calamities of Europe, humbly offers two schemes, in which matters stand so fairly, and so equally divided, that if it stands as an alternative to either side, it may perhaps be a difficulty to either party which part to take, and which part to refuse, and the advantage be so little on either side, as that Europe itself cannot find reason to complain in general of any unjust breach upon the ballance of power, so as to enslave one side to the other.

Here follow two several schemes of a partition of the Spanish monarchy, which may either way be the ground of a safe and lasting peace in Europe, and in which division the exorbitant power of either the House of Bourbon, or the House of Austria, are provided against.

* * *

5. A Letter from a Gentleman at the Court of St. Germains

A Letter from a Gentleman at the Court of St. Germains was advertised on 5 September 1710. According to the *Cambridge Bibliography of English Literature*, it is either by Arthur Maynwaring, supervisor of the Whig press from 1710–1712, or by Defoe. According to John Robert Moore, it is "one of Defoe's best and most characteristic writings. ..."[1] On the basis of the style, of the idiosyncratic attitude toward the Dissenters, and of the genre—like his ill-fated *Shortest Way* (1702) and successful Mesnager *Minutes* (1717), the *Letter* is a hoax, in this case a mock-Jacobite tract—I am convinced it was written or carefully rewritten by Defoe.[2] The pamphlet demonstrates an easy mastery of English political and religious history and an acceptance of the principles of the Revolution Settlement: a constitutional monarchy limited by traditional rights of the English people, a guaranteed Protestant succession settled by Parliament, an established Church along with guaranteed religious toleration for Dissenters. Both the historical knowledge and the acceptance of Revolution principles were common to Defoe and Maynwaring. But the tract is notable for embodying, in the publisher who introduces the *Letter* and in the Jacobite gentleman who has authored it, the two important voices that resound and echo through all of Defoe's writings: the honest, plain-speaking plain dealer and the devious, feverishly plotting, double-talking, double-dealer. Marshalling all his intellectual resources in the service of moderation, Defoe shaped this closely-argued 47-page pamphlet as a clever onslaught against the extremist political emotion sweeping England in 1710.

The *Letter* purports to be written by a member of the Pretender's inner circle in France. It contains detailed instructions to Jacobites about how to make use of an advantageous period to work for the establishment of England's "lawful Prince" on the throne. Although the pamphlet pretends to speak of long-term policies, referring only indirectly to the hysteria that rampaged throughout England in 1710 over the Sacheverell Affair ("Our friends never gave us stronger proofs of their zeal and affection than at present"), its publication in September is clearly timed to influence the imminent Parliamentary election.[3] Defoe calculates his argument to frighten moderates of all factions with the danger of a restoration of Roman Catholicism in England if Tory and High-Church extremists are swept into office.

The Machiavellian tactics proposed in the *Letter*, a concerted attack upon the constitutional principles of the Revolution and an unremitting effort to foment divisions among Dissenters, Low-Churchmen, and High-Churchmen, cannot be understood without knowing something about the Sacheverell Affair and its implications.

Dr. Henry Sacheverell had been, throughout the reign of Queen Anne, the principal mouthpiece of the Oxford high-flying clergy. The storm into which all of England was thrown in 1710 was precipitated by the decision of Godolphin's ministry to prosecute the demagogic parson for his sermon of 5 November 1709 in St. Paul's, before the Lord Mayor of London. In that sermon Sacheverell, harping as ever on his favourite theme of hanging out "the bloody flag of defiance" to Whigs and Dissenters, reasserted an extreme form of the doctrines of non-resistance and passive obedience to the monarchy. His choice of 5 November, the anniversary of King William III's landing in England, "seemed an attack on the Revolution, intended to undermine its corollaries, the Act of Settlement and the prospective Hanoverian Succession".[4]

The Godolphin ministry decided to impeach Sacheverell in the House of Lords in spite of the danger of losing its majority in Parliament as a result of the emotions such a legally dubious course might arouse.[5] An important consideration in this decision was the increasing stress of High-Churchmen, especially after the failure of the Jacobite invasion of 1708, on the political theory of a divinely ordained hereditary monarchy with its corollaries of passive obedience and non-resistance to illegal acts of the king. As Geoffrey Holmes writes, "Highflying preachers seemed increasingly bent on convincing the Whigs that they were out to play the Pretender's game by casting doubt on the validity of the whole post-1688 Establishment".[6] A second consideration was that the pulpit was being widely used by High-Church clergy to promulgate the view that the Church was in danger from political moderates, from Dissenters, from latitudinarian clergymen, but above all, from Whigs.

High-Church advocacy of divine right was connected with opposition to moderate religious groups and to the Whig party that favoured them. Both positions were reactions to a decline in power of the Church as a result of the spread of rationalism among the educated and of apathy among the uneducated. Whereas Low-Churchmen and Latitudinarians, envisioning active Christians as a semi-voluntary community, wished to collaborate with Dissenters and Anglican laymen "to make the Christian presence felt in society",[7] High Anglicans preferred to combat the decline in power of the Church by enlisting the arm of the secular government. For this reason they longed for a return to an idealized Stuart past, where Church and state would again be partners, and they bitterly opposed the religious Toleration of 1689 granted to Dissenters. They attempted successfully to prevent religious toleration from being extended to political toleration and unsuccessfully to limit full religious toleration to "indulgence" or "exemption" from Church of England ritual for "tender consciences".

The impeachment proceedings lasted from 27 February to 20 March 1710, amidst an unexpected storm of public passion in favour of Sacheverell and against Whigs and Dissenters. Despite political and personal divisions among the Whigs, they were generally united in their legal interpretation of the Revolutionary Settlement. On the other hand, the Tories, many of them Hanoverians, were embarrassed by the illogicality of a position requiring them to reconcile professions of non-resistance and passive obedience with their own lack of support for the

Stuart James II and welcome for William of Orange in the Glorious Revolution, and by the necessity of supporting a man like Sacheverell, so distasteful to everybody but rabid extremists.[8] Although even the failure of the Jacobite rebellion of 1715 did not deal the death blow to theories of divine right, non-resistance, and passive obedience,[9] the Sacheverell impeachment provided the rationale for their complete discrediting later in the century.

The immediate result of the impeachment proceedings was a disaster for the Whigs. The verdict of guilty was delivered on 20 March, but when the question of punishment was debated, the majority which had supported that verdict began to melt away. Sacheverell was finally condemned to abstain from preaching for three years, and his sermon was burnt by the public hangman. This mildest of possible punishments was interpreted by the Tories as a moral victory. After his trial was over, Sacheverell travelled throughout the country in a regal triumphal procession. By inadvertently making a martyr of the turbulent preacher, the Junto had precipitated its own defeat. Whigs never forgot the lesson they had learned in the Sacheverell Affair; after they returned to power in 1714, they were very careful not to meddle directly with the power of the clergy.

Immediately after Sacheverell's hand had thus been lightly slapped, and it was apparent that the Whigs had lost the confidence of the nation, Queen Anne, on the advice of Harley, Shrewsbury, and Abigail Masham, began dismissing her Whig ministers, replacing them with moderate Tories. In August, after five months, the dismissals were completed when she ordered Godolphin to break the White Staff of his office as Lord Treasurer, and Harley became the effective head of the new ministry. Both the Queen and Harley desired a "ministry above party", but it proved impossible for a new ministry to work with the old Parliament, and dissolution was formally announced in September.

Moderates of both factions felt it was unfortunate that an election could not be postponed, for the country was in a state of hysteria, and "the heat of a man's zeal for Sacheverell was made the test of his suitability as a candidate".[10] The clergy was vociferous in vilifying Dissenters and Low-Churchmen. Dissenting chapels were burned, and the influence of extremists in a particularly violent and drunken election campaign was alarming. Tories were swept into power in the new Parliament, outnumbering Whigs by more than two to one. There were few independents, party fervour having created a rigid division between the two parties.

Only against this complex but exciting historical background can the rhetorical brilliance of the *Letter* be understood and appreciated. Defoe had continued writing in support of the Godolphin ministry, with Robert Harley's approval, after Harley himself had been forced out in 1708. As the moderate Godolphin and Marlborough had been driven further into the arms of the extremist Whig Junto, Robert Harley had seen his chance to make a political comeback. He rode back into power on the wave of the Tory hysteria launched by the Sacheverell impeachment. But Harley himself was a moderate, with no desire to be driven into dependence upon extremist Tories. The politically moderate Defoe, now working for Harley, had to direct his *Letter* to the goal of securing the election of moderates of both parties, Tory and Whig.

For this purpose, therefore, he avoids issues that might exacerbate party divisions at so crucial a moment. Cleverly backdating his letter to 12 January (the pamphlet was actually published in September), Defoe is able to compliment Godolphin's ministry while appearing ignorant that a new ministry of moderate Tories has by now replaced it. He proceeds to a matter certain to unite moderates of both parties: a complicated scheme by Jacobites for reinstating Roman Catholicism in England by placing the Pretender on the throne. Every extremist position detested by Defoe is woven by the ingenuity of his Jacobite persona into the service of his diabolic master plan. The implication to electors is clear: candidates who take any one of these many diverse positions are sinister Jacobites.

The Jacobite gentleman abjures violent methods, for fear of uniting the English against the Pretender, inciting a new civil war, and precipitating an invasion by the Dutch and the Princes of Hanover and Brandenberg; instead he suggests an insidious campaign of propaganda. The two major ends of the Jacobite propaganda campaign should be the discrediting of the Revolution and the creation of conflicts among High-Churchmen, Low-Churchmen, Latitudinarians, and Dissenters. To achieve the first end, the memory of "the Prince of Orange, ... the great cause of all our misfortunes", should be blackened, for "if we can once make the Revolution odious and black, all that is built upon it will fall of course; and we cannot begin better than by giving the people bad impressions of him who was the author of it".

The doctrines of passive obedience and non-resistance to divinely-ordained kings should be forcefully presented, for these doctrines prove that James III, a Stuart, is the only rightful heir to the crown of England. It would be very unwise to mention at this time, however, that according to these doctrines Queen Anne (also a Stuart, but a woman), has no right to sit upon the throne in preference to her half-brother: "We must not touch on that string, till the people's minds be better disposed for 't" (not reproduced). Any logical inconsistency between professions of belief in divine right and what actually happened at the Revolution, when the Act of Succession was "founded only on the pretended rights of the people, to whom it expressly ascribes a power to chuse for King, whom they please; and to despoil them of the royalty whenever they think good, without the least regard to proximity of blood or birth" (not reproduced), can easily be resolved by clerical denials of such inconsistency. Any absurdity will be swallowed by ordinary people, as long as it is advanced by those in authority.[11] The Jacobite author of this tract advances such an absurdity, as he repeats what Defoe regards as the legalistic jargon by which Sacheverell and his defenders had attempted to prove before the House of Lords that the Revolution had not actually been a case of resistance by the people of England, but a voluntary desertion of the throne by James II, so that "having by doing so in a manner abandoned his dominions, they thought it better to chuse another King than to throw themselves into a frightful anarchy, or at least to fall under tyranny" (not reproduced).[12]

The second object of Jacobite propaganda should be to set at odds High-Churchmen, Low-Churchmen, Latitudinarians, and Dissenters. The writer of the *Letter* is fertile in suggestions for this design. For instance, High-Churchmen feel guilty because they now realize that their professions of non-resistance to monarchical power unintentionally misled James II into overstepping the limits which they had assumed he would respect. Persecuting Nonconformists was within these limits, but removing High-Churchmen from their posts in order to replace them with Roman Catholics was not. Thus they had been forced by James's persecution into taking a leading role in the Revolution, and this they now regret in 1710, especially since the Act of Toleration was one of the major results of that Revolution. For this reason, because they are eager now to expiate their disobedience, High-Churchmen will easily be prevailed upon to attack Low-Churchmen and Nonconformists, in order to bring the son of James II to the throne. The eagerness of High-Church zealots can be whetted even further by assuring them that the Pretender will restore to them all their former prerogatives, for instance, former powers of Church Convocation, including that of excommunication, and especially by putting them "in hopes of a restitution of all the church-lands" (not reproduced)!

The *Letter* is particularly noteworthy for the diabolically clever ways of disposing of Nonconformists suggested by the pretended author. First, charge them with the authorship of books really written by Atheists, Deists, and Socinians. Second, represent them as "furious schismaticks", as "senseless and ridiculous fanaticks, who persist in their error out of mere obstinacy, to flatter the corruption of their mind, and to gratify their criminal passions". Third, and most clever of all, "clog the Toleration Act with so many restrictions and limitations, as you may do with it as you please". If you consider the Act as one of indulgence for tender and scrupulous consciences, rather than as one of unconditional approval of Nonconformity, Dissenters will be forced to prove in ecclesiastical courts that their "tender and scrupulous" consciences entitle them to protection of the Act. In this way, you succeed in forcing them to justify their scruples, which they cannot do without proclaiming that the Church of England "entertains fundamental errors and doctrines which can't be embraced without mortal sin".

The last section of this intricately argued tract deals with the heart of the matter as Defoe chose to present it: the return of Roman Catholicism to England in the wake of the events of 1710. Jacobites are advised, first of all, to insinuate that the Pretender will turn Protestant. For a time, says the Jacobite author, James will outwardly profess himself such, but there is no need for Papists to despair: "After his Majesty has reigned peaceably for some years, he may have the happiness to bring back the English to the bosom of the Church of Rome".

In a stinging and coldly logical attack on the rationale of the Church of England, the Jacobite gentleman proves that there is no sect of Protestants "whose principles [are] less consistent than those of the Church of England", which by relying to some extent on church tradition, is forced to "make use of a double weight and a double measure". Other Protestant sects, rejecting tradition more completely, are much more consistent in their principles. After this he concludes, "Who can but admire, at the proud and insulting airs of your divines ... [who] call those who differ from them schismaticks, hereticks, and innovators ...".

Having proved the illogicality of the doctrine of the Church of England, itself heretical in the eyes of the Roman Catholic Church, he proceeds to a historical account of the "scandalous manner by which your Reformation was introduced," beginning with Henry VIII, who "only left the Church of Rome, and opposed the authority of the Pope, because he would not suffer him to divorce his wife and marry another".[13]

He points out the attraction of Roman Catholic practices for High-Church advocates by listing those practices reinstituted by the Church of

England at the time of Charles I (then only in externals), and again in the current period (now in doctrine also), when "according to all the advices we received, they make great advances towards the Catholick Church". By these affinities of taste, concludes the writer, "You see ... how easy a reunion may be effected between the two Churches, were His Majesty restored to the throne of his ancestors".

The intricate logic of the argument Defoe constructs for his sinister Jacobite gentleman cannot be understood without some knowledge about the political issues of the early eighteenth century. Defoe avails himself of the very points made in the course of the Sacheverell trial to turn the theory of divine right with its corollaries against the High-Church advocates, who claimed a monopoly on patriotism. Thus he contributed to the tarring of the whole party with the brush of Jacobitism that was eventually to discredit its theories completely in the eyes of the nation.

Unlike much of Swift's writing, which relies upon exaggeration and therefore requires only a vague recollection of history, Defoe's writing is embedded in the ideas and events of his day. The central metaphor of Defoe's *Letter* is not flamboyant, like the cannibalism in Swift's *Modest Proposal*. More ambiguous, less dramatic, closer to reality, and therefore characteristic of Defoe's writing, it is the "use of a double weight and a double measure". This metaphor can be regarded as the paradigm of Defoe's sense of irony, continuously weighing and measuring discrepancies between principle and practice, theory and fact, intention and execution, ends and means. The metaphor epitomizes the sensibility that stands behind Defoe's habitual castigations of enemies as devious equivocators, in contrast to the plain-speaking and simple men whom Defoe, like his contemporaries, posited as heroes.

Such a hero is the publisher who introduces the *Letter*. His tone is strikingly different from that of the subtle, cynical and devious, author—the Jacobite gentleman. Though a foreigner, the publisher openly professes his concern for the English nation and his affection for the Protestant religion. He has nothing to gain from his warning to the English that concealed Jacobites are systematically playing upon religious divisions to advance the interests of the Pretender; he wishes only to open the eyes of Englishmen whose ill-considered actions make them easy tools of such Jacobite exploitation. The publisher wishes to persuade people who "do not see the consequences of what they are put upon" to act differently, for once the truth, naturally a self-evident one, is exposed to them, they will of course act more reasonably, that is, more moderately. The voice of this publisher is remarkably similar to Defoe's public voice as we hear it in the *Review* or in *Robinson Crusoe*,[14] the voice of an uncomplicated man, the voice which provoked Swift into categorizing him as a "grave, sententious, dogmatical rogue".[15]

The publisher's writing style is characterized by a casual syntax: clauses are not necessarily put in logical sequence, and the loosest and least precise of connectives, "and", serves to link them together. Here are two examples, in which I have italicized the loose connectives and phrases out of logical sequence: "He sent it [the letter] me from Doway, *and* informed me at the same time, that perceiving a sort of valise or portmanteau in his chamber, which he came to after the siege, he desired his landlord to remove it; *and* asked him smiling, if his strong box were not in it." "The concern I have for the English nation, *though a stranger*, and my affection to the Protestant religion, have induced me to publish this letter. ..."

One of the few stage directions Defoe later used for dialogues in his fictions appears in the first example. In this pamphlet, as in the fictions, a smile is inappropriate to the situation, which is much more complex and even dangerous than the smiler imagines. Like many hallmarks of Defoe's writing, this too when analyzed demonstrates the essentially intellectual cast of his mind. His characters smile only partly because Defoe wishes to convey their good nature; more important, they smile because he perceives they have underestimated and oversimplified a situation; a smile is Defoe's shorthand for a certain mental state: an endearing dullness of mind.[16]

Opposed to the voice of the honest publisher is the voice of the Jacobite author of the *Letter*, a man who has access to secret information, who advises concealing meaning by using ambiguous language, a man who relies upon complex logic rather than the common sense natural to honest and good-natured people, and above all, a man who goes about in disguise.

The Jacobite's writing style is characterized by a formal syntax underlined by heavy parallelism. Individual clauses are closely articulated. Almost any sentence in the letter can serve as example. Here are some from the very opening:

> Though for some time I have not had the honour of a letter from you, yet I have been informed by other hands of all that has passed in England with relation to our affairs …
>
> That you may the better understand me, I must pray you to consider that though our countrymen do at first view appear to be fierce, untractable, and savage; yet there are two very different ways to soften and tame them … The second way to become masters of the English, is to make use of mildness, insinuations, and arguments from interest and self-love, *i.e.* to persuade them by plausible reasons, to gain them by submissions and commendations, to satisfy their avarice, and flatter their ambition; to serve ourselves dextrously of one party to destroy another, to foment the hatred and animosities that are betwixt them, and to furnish them with methods to avenge themselves on one another by turns, or at least to free both of 'em from their restraints.

Parallelism is so emphasized in the Jacobite section of the tract that most nouns and some adjectives automatically come in twos even when there is little necessity for a pair. The doubling reflex extends even to verbs and to participial phrases, as a glance at pages 136–7 indicates: "to augment the power of the Dutch our mortal enemies, and to raise them on the ruins of our country"; "if we can once make the Revolution odious and black"; "for they are supported by the Nonconformists whom they caress and maintain"; "the High Churchmen commonly treat them with haughtiness and contempt".

Defoe's mannerism of reminding his readers of the syntax over which he has lost momentary control (because all the parenthetical reservations introduced by a lively mind interfere with the grammatical skeleton of his sentence) appears on pages 139 and 144: "'Twould be proper also dextrously to insinuate, that the House of Hanover, being bred up in principles, which come very near those of the Presbyterians ...", etc.; "In effect, if the assurance which Jesus Christ has given to His Church ... and if the promise which he has made to his ministers ... *I say*, if this assurance and this promise had place for 400 years, let them show us that they have been annulled since ..." (my italics).

The diction of the Jacobite gentleman, who is discussing complex political and religious ideas, is precise and relatively formal. It is not individualized enough to distinguish him from the highly educated group to which he belongs. The diction of the publisher is necessarily simple in that part of his short account consisting of narrative about an army officer, a rented chamber, a landlord, and a valise. The diction associated with the plain-speaking Defoe appears very rarely in the letter itself. Some examples are: "So that there are three powers ready to *rush in*"; "*seized with fury*, *cried out* that all was lost"; "*clog* the Toleration Act"; "*push on things* with too much ardour and precipitation"; "*the meanest cobler* must have as great a prerogative, as your whole Convocation" (my italics). An amusing example of the combination of diction of the Jacobite gentleman and of the plain-speaking Defoe occurs in the following sentence: "You see, Sir, into what a chaos of absurdities, contradictions, and impieties, your *so much boasted* principles of the Church of England *throw you*" (my italics).

A final illustration of the polite and polished tone of Defoe's Jacobite persona can be heard in his reference to Dissenters who practise the occasional conformity of which Defoe disapproved: "I am of the mind that they will find few Dissenters of that sort; 'tis certain at least, that those will not be accounted such who for the sake of a good post are willing to communicate according to the Church of England". In his less polished voice, Defoe described this practice in 1703 as "playing bo-peep with God Almighty", and in the voice of the High-Church bigot of *The Shortest Way* in even blunter terms: "They that will go to Church to be chosen Sheriffs and Mayors, would go to forty Churches rather than be Hang'd" (see page 42, note 5 above).

The Jacobite writer of the *Letter* has a sinister quality associated frequently in Defoe's writings with the diabolic. He is the "subtle, smiling, fawning, wheedling, cautious enemy ... the dangerous enemy", contrasted by Defoe in his *Letter to Mr. Bisset* (1709) with Sacheverell, the furious and open enemy, whose precipitation always causes him to split "himself upon the rocks of his own passion, and throw his cause down the precipice of his own rage." Defoe warns Bisset:

> This, Sir, is an age of plot and deceit, of contradiction and paradox, and the nation can hardly know her friends from her enemies; men swearing to the government, and wishing it overturned; abjuring the pretender, yet earnestly endeavouring to bring him in; eating the Queen's bread, and cursing the donor; owning the succession, and wishing the successors at the devil; making the marriage (UNION) yet endeavouring the divorce; fawning upon the toleration, yet railing at the liberty—It is very hard, under all these masks, to see the true countenance of any man—there are more kinds

of hypocrisie, than that of *Occasional Conformity*—and the whole town seems to look one way, and now another …

Jacobites always loom menacingly on Defoe's political horizon. In a 1705 tract entitled *The Ballance: Or a New Test of Hi-Fliers on All Sides*, he is explicit about his political mythology. The reign of King William was an Eden into which Jacobites looked with an invidious eye on the "unanimity of counsels between Church and Dissenters". Their envy caused them to throw in the apple of division which lost England its Paradise.

Jesuits are equated with Jacobites in Defoe's political demonology. His *Instructions from Rome, in Favour of the Pretender* (1710) contains careful instructions from the wily Pope to his somewhat stupid and very violent English adherents (like Sacheverell):

Study profoundly humours and interests; to the poor magnify *popish charity*, and to the noble, house-keeping of old; to young scholars, the learning of the *Jesuits*, and the excellent method and discipline of their schools beyond the seas; to the debauched, represent the moderation of our Church in voting the *wanton sallies of nature* (as *whoredom*, *adultery*, *incest*, and *sodomy*) but venial peccadilloes, and granting indulgencies at easy rates, for greater crimes …

In the meantime let your emissaries alter their shapes; be one thing today, another tomorrow, now a courtier, by and by a formal cit., or a soldier; sometimes a taylor, othertimes a shoe-maker, or valet-de-chambre; a beau among the ladies; and atheists among wits; or any other variation or transposition, agreeable to our interest.

In an amusing reference to Defoe, substantiating the argument I have been making for a division between two main voices in Defoe's writing, the Pope concludes the above passage by saying, "Endeavour to suppress that damned Review, that's a plaguey fellow. …" Mr. Review represents in this context the diametric opposite of the character advocated by the Pope.

In contrast to Swift, Defoe never took much interest in exposing in his political tracts the arguments of violent and irrational men. For the most part, his observation of them was limited to mimicking bits of their conversation, irresistible to Defoe's acute ear for dialogue because of their energy and drama. But their arguments usually passed into one ear and out the other, never engaging for long the circuits of his brain. On the other hand, he was very much attracted by subtlety, logically complex argument, indirect ways, and disguise. His services to the government were largely secret, he adopted a variety of pseudonyms in those services and in his writings, he used the disguise motif prominently in his fiction, and he was personally attracted by the labyrinthian Harley. The letter to Harley quoted in the introduction (p. 18) reveals a great deal about Defoe's own psychological make-up.

His public behaviour in the Sacheverell case, open and honourable, was in striking contrast to his behind-the-scenes attempt to harm Sacheverell. At first Defoe shrewdly advised treating the matter by ridiculing the preacher, rather than by impeaching him and thus creating a High Tory martyr. In the *Review* he uses homely comparisons for Sacheverell: the parson is like a chained and furious dog, or like an untamed and violent horse, who is given free rein so that he will run himself into exhaustion. Making certain to remind his readers that Sacheverell's sermon contained in plain words the formal propositions of extermination of Dissenters he himself had mimicked in his *Shortest Way*, Defoe came to Godolphin's aid in the *Review* once impeachment proceedings had been decided upon by the ministry. Nevertheless, his defence of the proceedings was conducted in a spirit of moderation, and he urged his readers to condemn the principles rather than the offender. In his *Review* of 9 March 1710, he takes credit for his reticence, asserting that although he knows much to Sacheverell's personal discredit, he has refrained from personal attacks "on account of his troubles".

But the day before this issue was published, Defoe had written a private letter to Stanhope, one of the managers of the impeachment, in which he listed, and offered to have certified by witnesses, discreditable facts about Sacheverell's personal morals and political loyalties. As James Sutherland observes, "There is a frequent discrepancy between Defoe's behaviour in public and in private".[17]

How did Defoe reconcile his dislike and fear of indirect ways, characteristics he usually associates with Satan, with his own predilection for, and even exuberance about, this kind of activity? Perhaps a reconciliation may be inferred from his definition of the concept of lying. In advising Harley to steer a middle course between the parties, so as to obtain general esteem from both sides, Defoe says:

> Though this part of conduct is called dissimulation, I am content it shall be called what they will, but as a lie does not consist in the indirect position of words, but in the design by false speaking, to deceive and injure my neighbour, so dissembling does not consist in putting a different face upon our actions, but in the further applying that concealment to the prejudice of the person. ...[18]

If the principles are good, then deceptive means are justifiable. The deviousness of Defoe's nature inferred from his design in writing *The Shortest Way* reveals itself when he is encouraging some political act, and is justified in his own eyes by his belief that his motives are constructive and that he is serving the cause of some principle: "I am never, sir, you know, for searching an evil to be amazed at it, but to apply the remedies", he writes to Robert Harley on 7 August 1707. To Defoe, government above parties, constitutional monarchy, religious toleration, balance of power in favour of Protestant nations in Europe, are sacrosanct political principles.

The man whose disaster it was "first to be set apart for, and then to be set apart from, the honour of that sacred employ [the pulpit]",[19] had discovered that in the world of men and their daily affairs, honourable ends had often to be sought by dishonourable and clandestine practices. Like Milton Defoe could not praise a fugitive and cloistered virtue; unlike Milton, however, his conscience was sometimes troubled by the compromises he perceived were necessary in order to be effective in the secular world of politics. As a pilloried Nonconformist, it was of course impossible in his day for Defoe to club with Establishment wits, but it is curious that some of his private social life seems to have consisted in tête-à-têtes with Dissenting ministers, almost as if he were seeking in his relaxations some purifying influence lacking in his professional life. The most striking indication that his conscience was troubled is supplied by the split in his personality dramatized in his political writings by his two personae, the plain dealer and the disguised manipulator, and in his fictions, by the Doppelgänger.

He chose to represent himself to his public as a simple, direct man of common sense, and in this role he exercised a great deal of influence. "Short of originality in theory", writes A. L. Smith, "Defoe contributed to political progress in almost every direction". If Addison polished the manners of an uncouth public, it was Defoe who educated "a nation into political sense and morality".[20] Yet at the same time as he appeared in public as the spokesman for principles of common sense, moderation, simplicity, and directness, his practice behind the scenes qualified him for the title of *eminence grise* of English political writers.

Notes

1 John Robert Moore, *A Checklist of the Writings of Daniel Defoe* (Bloomington: Indiana University Press, 1960), p. 77. In his review of Moore's *Checklist*, James Sutherland mentions that this is the first attribution of the Letter to Defoe (*Library*, 17, 1962). But the Lilly Library of Indiana University owns the Defoe collection of William Trent, the foremost Defoe scholar and bibliographer of the late nineteenth and early twentieth century. The Lilly copy of the *Letter* bears a light inscription, which appears to be in Trent's handwriting, at the top of the title page; it says, "Not improbably by Defoe". Possibly Trent's sensitivity to Defoe's style aroused his suspicion, but he never got around to verifying the authorship. Moore, who taught at the University of Indiana, may have been inspired by Trent's remark to search for references to the *Letter* in other of Defoe's writings.

Professor Sutherland also points out in his review of Moore's *Checklist* that it is reasonable to base an attribution on Defoe's reference to the *Letter* in other of his works, since the writer did have the habit of advertising his anonymous writings in this way. The two pamphlets Moore had in mind are mentioned in his *Checklist*: *Queries to the New Hereditary Right Men* (7 October 1710) and *A Supplement to the Faults on Both Sides* (21 October 1710). The first contains a two-page summary of the *Letter*, the second alludes to it. In addition, the *Review* of 31 October 1710 is a summary of the tract, and the issue of 4 January 1711 alludes to it.

Although John Oldmixon admired the pamphlet enough to claim it for his superior, Arthur Maynwaring, and Pierre Des Maizeaux admired it enough to claim it for himself, the modern historians W. T. Laprade and Mary Ransome do not even mention it in their discussions of election pamphlets of 1710. It must be inferred, therefore, that enthusiasm for the *Letter* was confined to the cognoscenti—it was a pamphleteer's pamphlet. If so, Defoe's reference to it as late as January of 1711 suggests the lingering affection of an author for his unappreciated work.

The idea that Maynwaring may have been the author comes from a list of Maynwaring's works in Oldmixon's 1715 biography (p. 324). But Oldmixon's assertions about Maynwaring's work, although usually, are not invariably accurate; Frances Marjorie Harris points out one instance when Oldmixon exaggerated Maynwaring's contribution to a pamphlet by Francis Hare, in her doctoral dissertation, "A Study of the Paper War Relating to the Career of the First Duke of Marlborough, 1710–1712", University of London, 1975, p. 112.

Pierre Des Maizeaux, who claimed authorship in 1732, was a French emigré, a Huguenot best known for his translations, especially of Bayle. Des Maizeaux's self- proclaimed connection with the *Letter* is puzzling; to my knowledge, he wrote no political pamphlets, and according to Disraeli, he wrote "without genius, or even taste, without vivacity or force ..." (*Curiosities of Literature*, New York: Sheldon and Company, 1863, III, 333). It is possible that he translated the tract into French, for he was an intermediary in English and continental translating, publishing, and distributing. It is also possible that he contributed some information on religious history to the author of the *Letter*.

2 See pages 123–5 above for a discussion of Defoe's style in this pamphlet. Maynwaring's

style bears no resemblance at all to that of the publisher who introduces the *Letter* but has some similarities to that of the Jacobite "author". For purposes of comparison, Maynwaring's closely-argued *Four Letters to a Friend in North Britain* should be read in connection with the "Douay letter", as it was called by Defoe, Des Maizeaux, and Oldmixon. Maynwaring's syntax is similar to the Jacobite's, especially in the excessive use of parallel nouns and adjectives discussed on page 124 above. But Maynwaring's diction does not include words like "cobbler", and his illustrations are furnished by Greek drama and English and Roman history; homely examples of army scouts are characteristic of Defoe. Whereas Defoe manifests a tendency to lapse in his syntax (and there are two such lapses in the *Letter*), Maynwaring's tendency is to lapse into heavy sarcasm and indignant exclamation (and there are no such lapses in the *Letter*).

Although Maynwaring seems never to have engaged in literary hoaxes (his broadside of August 1710, *Letter from Monsieur Pett(ecu)m to Monsieur B(u)ys*, discussed below, is a simple forgery, not a banter or hoax as defined by Miriam Leranbaum ("An *Irony Not Unusual*: Defoe's *Shortest Way with the Dissenters*", *HLQ*, 37 (May 1974), 227–250), Defoe frequently did so. His *Shortest Way* of 1702 backfired, but his *Mesnager Minutes* of 1717 were a grand success. He occasionally advocated accomodating political tactics to the passions of the opposition, in the faith that people who succumbed to rage would eventually overreach themselves. Such was his clever advice in the case of the abortive High Church attempt in 1704 to tack a bill against occasional conformity onto a bill of supply. He likewise advised the Earl of Oxford, in a letter of 19 April 1713, to permit the Whigs to proceed in their prosecution against him for his three pamphlets of 1713 (see page 79 above), instead of admitting Defoe's connection with the ministry by instructing the Attorney General not to prosecute.

A spate of pseudo-Jacobite tracts and letters in the fall of 1710 led Defoe to protest to Harley in his September letters about the malicious foisting off of accusations on innocent individuals and about the circulation of Jacobite tracts. He devoted his *Review* of 19 October 1710 to a discussion of Jacobite libels, offering observations to his readers about the absence of significant details about plots in such writing and assuring them that the Jacobites must first poison men's minds before they could make a genuine attempt at a coup d'etat. The *Letter* itself is notable for lacking the detail Defoe advised his readers to seek in determining authenticity; furthermore, it prepares minds about the very issues Defoe mentions in his 19 October *Review*.

In the *Letter* is a combination of ideas about Dissenters that seems unique to Defoe. On the one hand, the Jacobite author compliments Dissenting ministers, attributing the increase of Dissenting sects to the fact that "their preachers are more regular in their conversation than your clergy". On the other hand, he makes an unpleasant remark about the practice of occasional conformity. The compliment to Dissenting ministers is likely to have come from a Dissenter, which eliminates Maynwaring. And of Des Maizeaux and Defoe, only the latter is known to have disapproved loudly of Dissenters practicing occasional conformity.

Finally, the *Letter* is not even a Whig tract. None of the accusations current in Whig circles during August and September 1710 appears, neither those of Maynwaring's August *Pettecum Letter*—that the French refused to make peace because their English friends advised them to buy time while awaiting better terms from a Tory ministry, that the Godolphin ministry is to be discarded, Parliament dissolved, public credit ruined, Marlborough disgraced—nor of his July *Four Letters*, which contains all of these accusations in addition to an attack on Harley, who is referred to as "Harlequin."

The *Letter*, therefore, falls into that category of tracts referred to by Mary Ransome as "Harleyite" pamphlets, tracts "in favour of 'moderation' and against the High Fliers" (pp. 215–216, "The Press in the General Election of 1710," *Cambridge Historical Journal*, 6, 1939). It seems possible that Defoe got hold of some notes or even a pamphlet written by Maynwaring, while he was still in the latter's confidence, and that he revised it to follow the Harleyite line of appealing for the election of moderates of both parties. (If Defoe *had* outwitted Maynwaring, this would account for the rage with which the latter, according to Oldmixon, in *The Life and Posthumous Works of Arthur Maynwaring*, Esq., London, 1715, pp. 167–68, spoke about Defoe. Oldmixon claims that Maynwaring had nothing but contempt for Defoe—as well as for Swift, another "hireling"—but he neglects to mention Maynwaring's very high praise for Defoe's *Review* in his *Four Letters to a Friend in North Britain*, dated July, 1710.) Des Maizeaux's role was to translate what Defoe produced, for the French translation is faithful to the finished pamphlet. It should be noted that Defoe's *A Supplement to the Faults on Both Sides*, one of the tracts listed by Ransome as Harleyite, advertises the *Letter*. As J. A. Downie writes in "Robert Harley and the Press", unpublished Ph.D. dissertation, University of Newcastle upon Tyne, 1976, "Defoe vainly tried to reconcile the new ministry with the old, and he continued to follow this theme in the *Review* until well into 1711, but he was a lone Harleyite skirmisher" (p. 271).

3 Queen Anne announced the dissolution of Parliament only in mid-September, but her

announcement had been anticipated by intense electioneering all through the summer of 1710, and the election actually took place in October.

4 G. M. Trevelyan, *England under Queen Anne: The Peace and the Protestant Succession* (London, 1934), p. 48. The fact that 5 November was also Guy Fawkes Day may have inspired Defoe with the idea of presenting his pamphlet as the written evidence of a Jacobite design to reintroduce Roman Catholicism into England.

5 Geoffrey Holmes, *The Trial of Doctor Sacheverell* (London: Eyre Methuen, 1973), pp. 76–89.

6 *Ibid.*, p. 33.

7 *Ibid.*, Chapter II ("The Church"), and p. 34.

8 Even Queen Anne, who had detested his sermon, was "drawn into the strong Tory current" by the contagion of party spirit, reports Trevelyan, p. 51.

9 Henry L. Snyder believes that acceptance of the implications of the Glorious Revolution was much slower in becoming general than modern historians have recognized. Because the most influential contemporary histories of the period were written by Whigs or by Whig sympathizers, scholars have not realized the extent to which the permanency of the Hanover succession was in doubt, at least until 1745. ("The Politics of the Histories of the Reign of Queen Anne", a paper delivered at the eighth annual meeting of the American Society for Eighteenth-Century Studies, at the University of Victoria, in Victoria, B.C., 5 May 1977.)

10 Trevelyan, p. 59.

11 The Jacobite gentleman cynically observes that success in gaining control of the Parliament will be interpreted by most people as proof of the Jacobite legal interpretation of the Revolution: "For as the people do not see the secret spring, but always judge of things by the event, they look upon the party who gain the victory as the strongest and most numerous, and afterwards side with them accordingly" (not reproduced).

A plain-dealing Defoe describes in homelier terms the same political phenomenon in his 1711 tract, *Rogues on Both Sides*: "The violence of parties are [*sic*] now come to that extravagant bigotry to men and not principle; that if any demagogue cries out in a shower of rain that it rains buttered turnips, the whole party ... will bring out their pewter platters and earthen dishes, and copper and brass vessels, to catch them; and eat whatever these receive with a perfect Israelitish faith."

12 The denial that the Glorious Revolution had resulted from the English people's assertion of their rights was not, as Defoe implies, confined to Jacobites. J. P. Kenyon describes how James II's abdication was used as a convenient rationale for the Revolution by the very men who had engineered William's accession to the throne ("The Revolution of 1688: Resistance and Contract", in *Historical Perspectives*, ed. Neil McKendrick, London: Europa, 1974). This was because the "issue of violent overthrow of legitimate authority" was to eighteenth-century Englishmen, who "remained uneasy over the brazen methods employed to unseat a king", very troublesome. (Gerald Straka, "Sixteen Eighty-eight as the Year One: Eighteenth-Century Attitudes towards the Glorious Revolution", in *Studies in Eighteenth Century Culture*, Cleveland and London: Case Western Reserve University, 1971, p. 150.)

Geoffrey Holmes's summaries of the arguments for the prosecution and defence in Sacheverell's trial make clear how embarrassing the question of resistance was, to Whigs as well as Tories (pp. 138–43 and 179–91 in *The Trial of Doctor Sacheverell*).

13 Note that when Defoe summarized the history of the Reformation (*Review*, 12–26April 1707), he pointed out that Jesuits always claimed Henry VIII was motivated solely by his desire to remarry when he renounced Papal authority.

I have omitted pages 39–45, a detailed account of English church history, in which the Jacobite author observes that the monarchy continuously increased its power over the established Church.

14 In *A Good Peace*, written in 1711, Defoe makes sure to include his byline: "By the *Author of the Review*." "My name on this", he proclaims, "is to show my principle". There are to be no allegories, no similes, "*for I hate disguises*!" After 1710 few of his many writings are signed, but they are often identifiable to readers of his day by several hints, including references to the *Review*, to *The Shortest Way* and to *The True-Born Englishman*.

15 Jonathan Swift, "A Letter ... concerning the Sacramental Test", in *The Prose Works of Jonathan Swift*, ed. Herbert Davis (Oxford, 1939), II, 113.

16 When the guilt-ridden Roxana tells her trusting Dutch admirer how a stormy sea voyage has frightened her, Defoe writes: "... then indeed, he acknowledg'd I had reason to be alarm'd; but smiling, he added, But you, Madam ... are so good a Lady and so pious, you wou'd but have gone to Heaven a little the sooner, the Difference had not been much to you." Roxana confesses, "when he said this, it made all the Blood turn in my Veins, and I thought I shou'd have fainted; poor Gentleman! thought I, you know little of me; what wou'd I give to be really what you really think me to be!" (*Roxana*, ed. Jane Jack, London: Oxford University Press, 1964, p. 137.)

Many readers will recall Robinson Crusoe's smile, as he deludes himself momentarily about not taking money he finds on his wrecked ship: "I smil'd to my self at the Sight of this Money, O Drug! Said I aloud, what art thou good for, Thou art not worth to me, no not the taking off of the Ground, one of those Knives is worth all this Heap, I have no Manner of use for thee, e'en remain where thou art, and go to the Bottom as a Creature whose Life is not worth saving. However, upon Second Thoughts, I took it away. ..." (*Robinson Crusoe*, ed. J. Donald Crowley, London: Oxford University Press, 1972), p. 57.

17 James Sutherland, *Defoe* (London, 1950), p. 172.

18 George Harris Healey, ed., *The Letters of Daniel Defoe* (Oxford, 1955), p. 42.

19 *Review*, VII, 341.

20 A. L. Smith, "English Political Philosophy in the Seventeenth and Eighteenth Centuries", in *The Cambridge Modern History*, ed. A. W. Ward, G. W. Prothero, and Stanley Leathes (Cambridge, 1909), VI, 817.

A Letter from a Gentleman at the Court of St. Germains (1710)

Advertisement from the Publisher at Cologne

The piece which I give here to the publick, is so considerable in itself, that you will certainly be willing to know how it fell into my hands. I owe it to an officer, one of my friends, who has a considerable post in the Confederate army. He sent it me from Doway, and informed me at the same time, that perceiving a sort of a valise or portmanteau in his chamber, which he came to after the siege, he desired his landlord to remove it; and asked him smiling, if his strong box were not in it. His landlord replied, that it did not belong to him, but to a stranger who came from Paris, and called himself an Irishman. He hired that chamber, and having fallen sick, died there of a languishing distemper; and his landlord had kept that valise ever since, till somebody came to demand it. Upon this the officer thought the right of conquest, and some other circumstances which his landlord told him, gave him a title to make use of it. Accordingly he opened it; and finding among other things several papers in English and French, he immediately communicated them to his superiors; and looking upon this memorial as a remarkable piece, he obtained leave to take a copy, on condition that he should leave out the proper names, and certain passages, according to direction.

This is all that my friend informs me. The concern I have for the English nation, though a stranger, and my affection to the Protestant religion, have induced me to publish this letter, that those to whom it belongs may make such use of it as they shall think fit.

The publick news make frequent mention of the different

parties in England: we see that they mutually charge one another with pernicious designs. Many people alledge that there's no foundation for those reciprocal invectives, and that the heads of the parties make use of 'em only to impose on the people, and to possess themselves of the most gainful employments. We can't doubt however that there are concealed Jacobites in that kingdom, who make use of those divisions to advance the interest of the pretended Prince of Wales. Here you have all the springs they make use of; and without penetrating into the hearts of each party we may boldly conclude, that those who follow the instructions of the Court of St. Germains are not the best affected to the religion and liberty of their country; not that I would suggest, that all those who seem to follow them are in the design to bring in the Pretender: God forbid! I believe on the contrary, that many of those people do not see the consequences of what they are put upon, and that they would act quite otherwise than they do, were they persuaded that those measures are designed to overturn their laws and religion. I should think myself very happy if the publication of this piece may open the eyes of that sort of people, and make them return to their duty. Be that how it will, I hope all good Englishmen will take this present in good part; for since I have nothing either to fear or to hope from them, I am induced to this only by my own inclinations, and the passion I have to contribute anything that lies in my power to the happiness of that illustrious nation.

A letter from a Gentleman of the Court of St. Germains, to one of his friends in England: containing a Memorial about the methods to be used for setting the Pretender on the throne of Great Britain. Found at Douay after the taking of that town.

St Germains, Jan. 12. 1710.

Sir,

Though for some time I have not had the honour of a letter from you, yet I have been informed by other hands of all that has passed in England with relation to our affairs. It must be owned that our friends never gave us stronger proofs of their zeal and affection than at present; and provided they don't slacken, we have reason to hope for everything from the happy disposition of the soundest part of the Church of England towards restoring their lawful Prince. I congratulate you upon it with all my heart by this letter in the beginning of the new year, till I can have an opportunity to do it by word of mouth, which perhaps may be sooner than you imagine.

* * *

That you may the better understand me, I must pray you to consider that though our countrymen do at first view appear to be fierce, untractable and savage; yet there are two very different ways to soften and tame them. The first is to treat them with a high hand and authority, and to strike boldly home. This stuns the English at first; and being naturally fearful, their courage abates, and they easily submit, and comply. The reign of the late King gives us several instances of it: 'tis certain that if the Prince of Orange had not crossed the sea to inspire the malecontents with courage, K. James II might easily have accomplished all that he desired. The second way to become masters of the English is to make use of mildness, insinuations, and arguments from interest and self-love, i.e. to persuade them by plausible reasons, to gain them by submissions and commendations, to satisfy their avarice, and flatter their ambition; to serve ourselves dextrously of one party to destroy another, to foment the hatred and animosities that are betwixt them, and to furnish them with methods to avenge themselves on one another by turns, or at least to free both of 'em from their restraints. This method is no less sure than the other; and considering the present disposition of their minds, I take it to be the only method that's practicable.

For to make use of power or force, we must be actually possessed of them, or at least clothed with sufficient authority to impose them. But you know we have no force within the kingdom, and we can't promise ourselves any from abroad. But though we could rely on foreign assistance, I know not whether we should venture to make use of it, till we be well assured of the greatest part of the nation; since otherwise that would tend to a civil war, the consequences of which must certainly be fatal. For in the first place, if His Majesty should endeavour to restore himself by a foreign power, he would by that means lose a great part of his friends. Many people, especially those who possess church-lands, would be afraid that the King, having once subdued his rebellious subjects, would improve his victory, and in that case order all things according to his own will and pleasure. There are others who carry their speculations still further, and are persuaded that if

France have once the power of imposing a king upon them, she will govern him afterwards as she pleases; and by obliging him to follow her directions, will certainly impoverish England, and enrich herself with our spoils; that's to say, by our commerce, which she will by degrees reduce to nothing.

Those people continually remember the easiness of K. Charles II, who, notwithstanding all the mortifications he received from France, went so far into her interest, that he taught her king to build ships, and put him in a condition to have merchant-fleets, which have enlarged her commerce in all parts to the prejudice of ours, and to equip navies that have made England tremble.

There's another thing to be considered, which makes this affair still more nice. The Revolution has transferred the crown from the family of Great Britain to the families of Hanover and Brandenburg; so that we are not to doubt but they will do their utmost to hinder our Prince from coming to the throne. Besides, Holland will always be afraid that a King of England in friendship with France will favour the projects of the Most Christian King, and enter into a league with him to destroy their republick. Moreover, the Dutch have made strict alliances with the Princes of Hanover and Brandenburg; and we may be sure that they have not forgot to make the succession of England one of the articles. So that there are three powers ready to rush in upon our country with a formidable army, as soon as ever they hear that His Majesty is gone to take possession of the throne. You can't but know, Sir, that our enemies in the kingdom would join them; and that by consequence, unless we have destroyed them beforehand, or be sure of most part of the nation, 'twill not be possible for us to resist them. May God preserve us from such a desolation, as so bloody a war would bring upon us! By this you may see, that we must think no more of the King's being restored by a foreign power: we must carefully abandon all those ideas, or at least make use of 'em with a great deal of art, lest we provoke those to turn our enemies who are now well-affected to our cause.

But you and your friends, Sir, have no need of any such advice, since the measures you have taken, and have already been so successful in, are quite different from them. Their Majesties are very well informed of it, and have ordered me to acquaint you with their satisfaction in it, and to return you their thanks for it.

In the meantime, as in occasions of this nature, there are

certain maxims which 'tis good to have always in readiness, and necessary to be practised as the juncture will allow it, I am ordered to impart our reflections to you, that you may make use of 'em from time to time as the case requires. The pleasure with which you have formerly received memorials of this nature, puts us in hope that you will entertain this with the like regard.

Since the Prince of Orange, as I have already observed, was the great cause of all our misfortunes; and that the Revolution was brought about by I know not what affection the infatuated people had for him, and which makes them still adhere to it, 'twill always be a great point gained to lessen their esteem of him, and to blacken his memory as much as possible. 'Twill be very useful to suggest that nothing but his ambition, and desire of a crown, induced him to invade England; nor must you forget to insinuate that the thing he had chiefly in view was to augment the power of the Dutch our mortal enemies, and to raise them on the ruins of our country. In effect, Sir, this ambitious prince perceiving the strict alliance betwixt James II and Lewis XIV, whom he always hated extremely, was sensible that if that union lasted, 'twas in the power of France to humble the Dutch when she pleased, and to reduce them to such a condition as to make no more a figure in Europe by their commerce or their arms; and that by this means he himself should be reduced to a very low state. To ward off this blow, he knew there was nothing else to be done but to invade England, where he did not want his creatures. The Dutch, to whom he imparted his fears, came immediately into his measures, and thought the matter of such importance, that they lent him all their forces, and left their own country naked to go where they thought there was most occasion for them, in order to bring so potent a nation as ours into their own interest. These things, Sir, must be well explained; and it ought to be insisted upon, that religion and liberty were only false pretexts which the Prince of Orange made use of to cover his ambitious designs. This article is so much the more essential, because if we can once make the Revolution odious and black, all that is built upon it will fall of course; and we cannot begin better than by giving the people bad impressions of him who was the author of it.

You must not forget those who were the chief instruments of it in England, and are still its most violent patrons. But what is most perplexing in this affair is that most of 'em are of the Church of England, as least as to profession; which gains them admittance into Parliament, and the chief posts of the State. But if you consider what I said, 'twill not be difficult to represent them as republicans, enemies to royal authority and monarchy, traitors to their country, and men of no religion; who only profess to be of the Church of England for the sake of their interest, but are secretly conspiring her ruin. When once you can possess the people with these maxims, the restoration of our Prince is not far off; for those Low-Churchmen are almost the only and chief obstacle in our way at present. It must be owned, however, that their strength does not lie wholly in their own party, for they are supported by the Nonconformists whom they caress and maintain on all occasions; and as they have procured them a Toleration, and endeavoured to annul or weaken those laws which still restrain the sectaries, they maintain and support the Low Church by way of requital.

But let not that discourage you, it may not be so difficult as you imagine to break that confederacy. Though the Nonconformists can't be ignorant that the High-Churchmen do not love them, yet they are not so untractable as they seem to be; caresses and civilities well managed easily gain them; and they are so much the more sensible of 'em, because the High-Churchmen commonly treat them with haughtiness and contempt, and we have seen them oftener than once vote at elections for such persons to be Members of Parliament as would willingly have voted their extermination in the House; therefore 'tis not impossible to gain them, and break them off from their great patrons.

But though this method should not succeed, there are others remaining which may be more efficacious to destroy those Low-Churchmen, particularly one which is worth all the rest, and that is, Sir, to bring the clergy into your interest, and get them entirely devoted to you. You are not ignorant of the power they have over the minds of the people, who are naturally superstitious; and you know as well as I that, the gown excepted, the clergy are altogether like other men: nay, 'twould seem that they are more addicted to revenge, ambition and avarice than laymen. I speak with the more freedom of your clergy, because you know, Sir, 'twas they, who by their pretended maxims of non-resistance and absolute submission, and by their fair protestations of loyalty and inviolable affection, threw the late King James into a fatal and pernicious security. As long at that Prince treated the Nonconformists according to the rigor of the law, the clergy heaped their eulogiums and blessings upon him; but as soon as he allowed them to have their meetings, and stopped the course of the penal laws, and when he desired that two or three persons might be admitted on his recommendation into the universities, the clergy immediately seized with fury, cried out that all was lost: then all their maxims of passive obedience and absolute submission to the will of their princes, which they had so much preached up, vanished at once. They aim at our patrimony, said the clergy among themselves, therefore we are no more obliged by any duty or oath; let's sound the alarm through all the kingdom, let's cry out that all's lost, and go over to the Prince of Orange, who will do us justice, and not suffer one farthing of our revenue to be touched. They were not wanting to cover those false pretexts with a cloak of religion and liberty; all the discourse was then popery and tyranny; the bishops ordered it so as to be put in the Tower, after they had braved the King in his own palace. What was singular in this matter was that the same persons who had always favoured the Catholicks, did then rail against them with inconceivable fury; as if a handful of people, who had always been their friends, and had so frequently assisted them against the Nonconformists, could have been capable of doing them any hurt. In short, the Church of England clergy did so much animate the people, and possess them with such a fury, that their lawful Prince, and all that was dear to him, not finding themselves safe in their own palace, nor among their own domesticks, could not think themselves secure by any other method than a shameful and precipitate flight.

You may judge by this, Sir, of the power of your ministers, and of the advantage we may make of that order of men, if willing to expiate the crime they have committed; they declare themselves boldly for us, and do as much in our favour as they formerly did to destroy us. 'Twill be so much the more easy to gain them, that they have been a long time sensible they were only made tools of at the Revolution; and no doubt most of 'em have repented of the steps which they then took. In effect, the Nonconformists, whom they dread much more than the Catholicks, and whom the late King designed only to exempt for a time from the severities of the law, have obtained an Act of Parliament, which establishes their sects forever, and by consequence sets them on an equal foot with the Church of England. Their number is by this means extraordinarily increased; and as their preachers are more regular in their conversation than your clergy, they easily impose upon the people, and make proselytes every day. Your ministers are not ignorant of this, but make bitter complaints of it. You must therefore keep up their resentments, increase their jealousy, promise to restore them to their ancient lustre, and to put them in a condition to reduce their enemies.

You must then maintain with them, that the Church of England is in imminent danger, and on the brink of ruin, not only from the Nonconformists, as I just now hinted, but from the Low-Churchmen and Latitudinarians. You must add that the latter are so much the more dangerous, that being got into the Church, and professing a great zeal for the Protestant religion, they easily insinuate themselves, and have a great influence among the common people. But above all you must insist upon this, that the Low-Churchmen do all they can to keep the clergy in servitude, and to bring them lower than they are at present. 'Twould be proper also dextrously to insinuate, that the House of Hanover, being bred up in principles, which come very near those of the Presbyterians, or rather which at bottom are the same; since part of the Lutherans have no bishops, and where they have any, they are only the shadows of bishops, who have no regard to a successive and uninterrupted ordination, upon which your clergy value themselves so much: you must, I say, insinuate that princes educated in that manner may very probably make alterations in the Church of England, either by establishing Presbytery, or endeavouring a Comprehension,* which will be no less pernicious. You must not fail to improve this thought.

In short, as 'tis lawful in so just a cause to make use of all advantages, 'twill be proper to insist on the danger of the Church from the books of controversy which the Nonconformists write against the Church of England. This must be represented as an unheard of piece of insolence and boldness, which is not only contrary to the Act of Toleration, wherein no such thing is specified; but directly tends to the ruin of the Church, by perverting her members and filling her

* *Comprehension:* attempts made since the 1660s by Anglicans of good-will to reconcile Presbyterians and the more moderate Congregationalists and Independents to the Church of England. The Toleration bill of 1689 was originally intended to apply only to the more uncompromising Dissenters; the 1689 failure of Comprehension was a severe blow to the hopes of those who deplored the weakening of the Church of England. It placed an unanticipated strain on the Toleration Act by stretching a hastily drafted measure to cover "perhaps four times as many people as the Baptists, Quakers, and other 'scrupulous consciences' envisaged in the bill's preamble". (Geoffrey Holmes, *The Trial of Doctor Sacheverell* [London: Eyre Methuen, 1973], p. 24). [Ed.]

with trouble and confusion. You may also charge the whole body of the Nonconformists and Latitudinarians* with certain pieces that some Atheists, Deists or Socinians* have published in England since the Revolution. You must aggravate the number of 'em, and declare boldly that unless the authors and favourers of those abominable libels be destroyed, nothing less is to be expected than the judgments of God upon the whole nation, and that the Church should be entirely ruined. There's nothing which strikes or animates the people more than such suggestions.

And as we can't make those persons too odious whom we resolve to destroy, you must draw the Dissenters in such colours as are most like to produce that effect: and in this you will find the clergy naturally disposed to second you. You will always find them ready to make use of the harshest expressions, and the most choaking epithets that can be thought on. Represent them as furious schismaticks, who have rent the bowels of the Church; as senseless and ridiculous fanaticks, who persist in their error out of mere obstinacy, to flatter the corruption of their mind, and to gratify their criminal passions; that they have neither virtue nor honour, which are qualities absolutely incompatible with schism and heresy; that 'tis nothing but worldly interest and unsupportable presumption that keeps them from conforming to the Church; that they are so far from being satisfied with the advantages they enjoy, that they aspire to greater things, and to be masters of all at last; that they do not content themselves to plot against the Church and contrive her ruin, but their design is also laid against the monarchy, to which they have always been enemies; and that they wait only a favourable opportunity to overturn the government, and to set up a republick. On this occasion you must call to mind what they did in the reign of Charles I, and represent them as ready to act the same part over again.

There's still another way to attack them, which comes nothing short of this, and may be more effectual. As all their power is founded on the mischievous Act of Toleration, you must endeavour to undermine it insensibly, for I do not believe that we can easily get it repealed by another act; therefore you must endeavour to clog the Toleration Act with so many restrictions and limitations as you may do with it

* *Latitudinarians:* adherents of the Church of England who, while not sceptics, were tolerant of differences about particular forms of church government and worship.
* *Socinians:* those who denied the divinity of Christ. [Ed.]

what you please. I mean that you must represent it as a provisional act, and not as a fundamental law of the state. You must alledge that 'twas in a manner extorted by the confusion of the times and necessity of affairs: that the Prince of Orange having made himself master of England, and being supported by Holland, and almost all the rest of Europe, the nation was not in a condition to oppose an act formed by a Parliament that was entirely devoted to him. It may be added that this act is rather positive than negative; that it does not establish Nonconformity, but only exempts Dissenters from the fines and penalties the laws had decreed against them; that 'tis merely an act of indulgence and respite, which only suspends the laws, and stops the course of 'em; in short, that this act relates only to consciences that are truly tender and scrupulous, i.e. such persons who, after having examined both religions without bigotry, passion and prejudice, are convinced that they can't conform to the Church of England without wounding their consciences, i.e. without committing a mortal and unpardonable crime.

Now if once you can bring it about to get the act explained in this manner, you may quickly do with those people what you please. In the first place you will bring them into an odious and ridiculous contradiction, since they have hitherto always confessed that the Church of England teaches all the articles necessary to salvation; and that they have nothing to object against her but some matters of discipline, and a few ceremonies of small importance: but then they must be obliged to maintain that she entertains fundamental errors and doctrines which can't be embraced without mortal sin; so that they must either miserably contradict themselves or speak a new language. I need not add, that nothing is capable to render them more odious than such a confession, if they dare be so bold as to make it, or more proper to hasten their destruction; for nobody will endure people who alledge that the Church of England maintains damnable doctrines. But this is not all the advantage which will result from such an explication of the Toleration Act; for by this means, Sir, you will become judges of the consciences of Dissenters. You will then have a power to determine whether those who claim the protection of that act have the qualities it requires; they are not to be trusted upon their own word, this is founded on the nature of all laws. When a law grants a favour to certain persons on condition that they be so and so qualified, 'tis certain that this favour is not conferred upon everyone that claims it; that must be done juridically by magistrates appointed for the execution of the laws; 'tis their part to determine whether the persons who claim it have the qualities prescribed by the law, and whether they are to enjoy the advantages of it. By this means you may exclude whom you please, and at the same time make the act of no effect. If the secular judges find any difficulty in it, you need only erect an ecclesiastical tribunal, which by obliging people to give the reasons of their scruples, and by consequence of their faith, will speedily see whether their consciences be truly tender, and whether their scruples be really and effectually such as they can't change their opinion without incurring eternal damnation. I am of the mind that they will find few Dissenters of that sort; 'tis certain at least, that those will not be accounted such who for the sake of a good post are willing to communicate according to the Church of England. In this case you will have no occasion to revive the Act against Occasional Communion, which unhappily miscarried by being pushed on with too much violence; but it may perhaps be dangerous to propose it again. After all, you need not be so much concerned at the Act of Toleration. The Huguenots had one called the Edict of Nants, because Henry IV, their good friend, gave it them in that city. Their chief ministers drew it up according to their own mind, and 'twas much more favourable to them than this is to the Dissenters; yet Lewis XIV found means to weaken that party by degrees, and in such a manner as gave him afterwards an opportunity to revoke that edict with all the necessary formalities. There will be no great difficulty to follow the same methods as far as they shall be judged necessary.

* * *

These are the methods, Sir, which we think will be most effectual to restore His Majesty of Great Britain. For my own part, I look upon them as infallible, if they be made use of with the discretion and prudence which are necessary on all such occasions. You must not discover yourself too much at first, nor push on things with too much ardour and precipitation. But you may from time to time detach, as from any army, hardy and bold fellows, to sound the fords, to view the enemy, and skirmish with them. Such people as these being well sustained, and supported in due time, do sometimes draw the enemy into defiles, from whence they can't get out without being beat.

As to what remains, you must always speak of the Revolution with applause, and approve the Toleration in a sense duly limited and rightly understood; and since what concerns religion is always the most tender and difficult point, you must appear entirely devoted to the Protestant Succession. At the same time it may be privately insinuated, that the King will turn Protestant; and if that be the only obstacle in the way, however zealous His Majesty is for the Catholick religion, I make no doubt, but with the consent of His Holiness, he will outwardly, for a time, profess himself a Protestant.

I say, *for a time*, because I don't despair, but that after His Majesty has reigned peaceably for some years, he may have the happiness to bring back the English to the bosom of the Church of Rome. For my own part, I could not but return to it, after having compared the books of the most famous Doctors of the Church of England with those of the Catholicks, and discoursed some points with the late Bishop of Meaux. That learned and judicious prelate could not enough admire that our English divines did not see that their own principles convicted them of being schismaticks, and did necessarily lead them back to the Catholick Church. This he could not forbear saying to M. ——, when he thanked him for Dr. Bull's book against the Antitrinitarians, which he presented him with. This great man told me often that of all the sects of Protestants there was none whose principles were less consistent than those of the Church of England, and that their divines have no reason to look upon other Protestants with so much contempt, since they argue more consequentially, and with greater advantage than themselves. The reason of this is, says he, because the Church of England having preserved the ecclesiastical hierarchy, and several ceremonies of the Church, they are obliged to have recourse to tradition, to the authority of the Fathers, and to Councils, to defend themselves against other Protestants who reject all those things and will admit nothing but Scripture. But when they find themselves pressed by the Catholicks, they have recourse to the hypothesis of the same Protestants, abandon their first principle, and entrench themselves within the authority of the Scripture alone. Thus, Sir, you see them reduced to make use of a double weight and a double measure. Allow me to give you an instance.

You may perceive with the least attention that when once men admit, as your divines do, tradition, and the Councils of the six, or if you will, of the four first centuries of the Church (for on this occasion six is the same thing with four, and four with two) and that during this interval Councils were looked upon as infallible, they must also admit tradition and the infallibility of Councils from that time to this, the reasons are perfectly equal on both sides; for if the first be good, the rest must be so likewise. In effect, if the assurance which Jesus Christ has given to His Church, *that the gates of Hell shall never prevail against her*; and if the promise which He has made to His ministers that He will be with them to the end of the world, *and that every time they assemble in His name, He will be in the midst of them*; I say, if this assurance and this promise had place for 400 years, let them show us that they have been annulled since, and tell us the motives which could induce Jesus Christ to act in a manner that appears so strange, and so unworthy of the Saviour of Mankind. Will they say 'tis because the doctrine is corrupted, the discipline become too loose, and that superstition is crept into the Church, and by consequence into the Councils? But besides that this is directly opposite to the promises of Jesus Christ, and that it belongs to no particular person or assembly to judge the Catholick Church, by what marks and characters shall we know this pretended corruption? How shall we prove it? They will say no doubt, because the late Councils have not decreed according to the Word of God. Very well. The first Councils were not then infallible; but because their decisions were agreeable to the Scripture, their infallibility then was not their proper, or what we call an inherent quality; 'twas not from the assistance of the Spirit of God, or an effect of the promise of Jesus Christ, but a meer accident and casual thing, they might have as well decided wrong as right. Then any assembly which determined matters 200 years ago, or shall determine them now according to the Scripture, will be as infallible as any of the first Councils. But what's that I pray to be conformable to the Scripture, who shall be judge? For since by this principle you destroy all absolute and visible authority, every particular person must set up for a judge of controversies, and clothe themselves with that infallibility of which you have so freely dispoiled the Councils. An Independent, a Quaker, a Brownist;* in a word, the first fanatick that offers himself,

* *Brownist*: follower of Robert Brown, sixteenth-century English Puritan and Nonconformist, whose modified principles became those of the Independents. [Ed.]

must have a full right to judge of all the decisions of the Church of England, and the meanest cobler must have as great a prerogative as your whole Convocation. He will compare your decisions with the Scripture, and if he find them not agreeable to it, must have a right to separate from your Church. Now as this principle sets all Christians upon the same foot, and grants 'em equal privileges, your cobler, after having formed a religion of his own, will make his family a church, to which he is to be father, priest, bishop, pope and council. After this, who can but admire, at the proud and insulting airs of your divines; mayn't they be ashamed to call those who differ from them schismaticks, hereticks and innovators; as if those people had not the Scriptures as well as they, and as if they could not judge your Church after their manner, and separate from it when they think good, with as much right and authority as you have judged and separated yourselves from the Catholick Church? You are henceforward as much hereticks, with respect to them, as you can pretend they are with respect to you. The ballance cannot be more just. You see, Sir, into what a chaos of absurdities, contradictions and impieties your so much boasted principles of the Church of England throw you.

* * *

You see, Sir, the advantages we have over you, if we consider things only in general; what must it be then, if by descending to the particulars I set before your eyes the scandalous manner by which your Reformation was introduced. There to make use of the expressions of a great princess of our nation, whom God was pleased to convert, you will see that Henry the Eight only left the Church of Rome, and opposed the authority of the Pope, because he would not suffer him to divorce his wife and marry another. That Edward the Sixth being an infant, his unkle, who governed in his name, abusing the royal authority, enriched himself by appropriating to his family the lands and possessions of the Church. That Queen Elizabeth not being the lawful heiress of the crown, could not be able to maintain herself in her unjust possession but by renouncing the true Church, the purity of whose doctrine was inconsistent with her usurpation. You will perceive that this Queen set herself up as a Papess and head of the Church; that the Parliament assumed to themselves the infallibility of Councils, determined points of religion, and made one after their own fashion, without listening to the remonstrances of the bishops, or the humble requests of the clergy assembled in Convocation.

* * *

The Church of England clergy perceiving that the Revolution had ascertained the Nonconformists a toleration of a larger extent than the late King designed to have granted them, they grew afraid that one day or other they might seize their revenues and possess themselves of their benefices, nor did they dissemble their fear. This, joined to the exhortations and writings of persons who have never violated the submission and fealty which they owed to their lawful Prince, has produced a very good effect. The clergy have renewed the plan of Archbishop Laud; and according to all the advices we received, they make great advances towards the Catholick Church.

We have likewise been informed with extreme satisfaction, that they have already pushed things farther than was designed in the reign of K. Charles the First. There was nothing almost intended at that time, but the externals of religion; they contented themselves, for instance, to separate the chancel from the body of the church, and to place an altar there. But now that this external part is established, they endeavour to introduce the doctrine of the Church. We know very well that in universities and elsewhere they speak of the Eucharist as a real sacrifice, and propitiary oblation, expressions as unknown to Protestants as they are common to Catholicks. 'Tis also certain they can mean nothing else but the doctrine of the Church, as to the real presence of the body and blood of Jesus Christ in the holy sacrament of the altar. 'Tis without doubt, that in this sense your doctors take it, since we understand there are those among them who practise the Elevation. Otherwise 'twould be an impious piece of mockery, and a complication of absurdities, of which I can't believe them capable. They do likewise defend, with success, the prerogatives of the priesthood, the necessity of absolution, and the power of the priest to forgive sins. They do still a great deal more; for they attack the Reformation in its foundations and principles. In short, the most eminent of the clergy write against the pretended supremacy of the Kings of England, and claim it to themselves as their proper right; and that they can't, without sacrilege, be deprived of an authority in matters of religion, distinct and independent from the temporal power, yet 'tis upon the authority of the secular power, as I have shewed you, that the Reformation is founded and solely depends; so that the maxims of those gentlemen being once established, it must necessarily follow that the pretended Reformation is a sacrilegious usurpation, a frightful schism, and a manifest rebellion against the Church of God, and the successors of the apostles; but 'tis the character and spirit of heresy to raise itself upon the ruins of all that is holy and sacred.

You see by this, Sir, how easy a reunion may be effected between the two Churches, were His Majesty restored to the throne of his ancestors.

He will readily grant the clergy that authority and independency for which they wish so ardently. 'Tis their part then to use their utmost efforts to accomplish so good a work, and to hasten the return of a Prince who ought to be so dear and precious to them.

But 'tis time to conclude. You will be pleased to communicate this memorial to all our best friends, and you may let them take copies of it, if you please, except what relates to the matter of religion: for as this is a very nice point, I should be sorry 'twere known; and pray you to communicate it to none but those you are well assured of.

We are very much troubled that we have no news from —— ———. Pray give my service to all our friends, particularly to ——— ———. Adieu, dear Sir. Remember always the duty you owe to your Prince and your country. I am,

&c.

CHAPTER TWO

ECONOMICS AND COMMERCE

Published according to Act of Parliament March 7, 1757, by John Bowles, at the Black Horse in Cornhill, London.   Price Sixpence

THE IMPORTS OF GREAT BRITAIN FROM FRANCE

HUMBLY ADDRESS'D TO THE LAUDABLE ASSOCIATIONS OF ANTI-GALLICANS, AND THE GENEROUS PROMOTERS OF THE BRITISH ARTS AND MANUFACTORIES;

1. Some Thoughts upon the Subject of Commerce with France

Some Thoughts upon the Subject of Commerce with France was published just after Defoe had discontinued his *Review* with the issue of 11 June 1713. As the only one of his publications on the controversy over the commercial articles of the Treaty of Utrecht he acknowledged as his own, this pamphlet should be read as the official pronouncement in the personal style of "The Author of the Review" on the issue of trade between England and France. It is an important contribution to a "pamphlet controversy... which has great interest in the history of economic thought".[1] Illustrating Defoe's intermediate position between the extremes of free trade and mercantilist protectionism, the pamphlet is also interesting as an example of how Defoe's pragmatism about methods of serving England's national interest often earned him the unmerited epithet of turncoat. In *Commerce with France*, arguing in favour of trade with England's great economic rival, Defoe defends himself against Whig accusations that he is a hireling of Harley's Tory ministry; the *Review*, charged the Whigs, had formerly opposed the opening up of Anglo-French trade.

The controversy arose over one of the agreements Bolingbroke had made with France in the Treaty of Utrecht that ended the War of the Spanish Succession. His aim, as Trevelyan explains, "was to dish the Whigs by winning such great commercial advantages for England at the expense of Holland and other countries, that the Tories would appear as the true benefactors not only of the landed interest but of the mercantile community also."[2] The major concessions he secured for England in its Spanish trade were in the main highly popular, but the treaty he proposed with France, opening trade between the two countries (which had been engaged in economic war since 1667), ran into difficulties. Bolingbroke had judged well that England was weary of the Whig policy of continuing the war,[3] but he had miscalculated the economic temper of the country and the extent of popular aversion to Jacobitism, which became linked in the minds even of many Hanoverian Tories with the question of trade with France.

The ensuing pamphlet controversy was based upon a concept of economic theory central to mercantilism, the concept of a favourable balance of trade. Because of the chronic shortage of bullion in seventeenth-century Europe and the absence of a well established paper currency, mercantilist thinkers were led to stress the importance of an adequate supply of gold and silver for national prosperity. This wealth was necessary as a medium of exchange for goods and also for stimulating the national economy by encouraging consumption, thus enlarging the market for goods. The resulting increase in production would contribute to a viable economy with a good tax base. In addition, gold and silver were needed to supply governmental need for revenue to pay for an expanding bureaucracy, and to provide adequate manpower and properly equipped ships for armies and navies. A country lacking gold- and silver-mines, thought mercantilists, had to accumulate specie by selling more to other countries than it bought from them. The debtor countries would then pay to the creditor the difference between purchases and sales in gold and silver. National advantage, therefore, consisted of grabbing a larger slice of a limited international economic loaf than one's neighbour could grab.

Free traders (of whom there were few in 1713) believed that international trade altered the internal economic organization of trading nations, encouraging them to specialize in products with which they were naturally endowed and which they could therefore produce at the lowest possible cost. If every nation were to produce and to export cheaper products, the cost of living would be decreased for everybody, and wealth, measured not in gold and silver, but in widely-distributed and low-cost articles of consumption, would therefore be increased. The international economic loaf was not limited; addition of the yeast of specialization and free trade would result in more bread for all.

Many of the arguments in the economic controversy over the commercial articles of the Treaty of Utrecht emanated from the government-subsidized *Mercator*, which began its career on 26 May 1713, and was written mainly by Defoe,[4] and from the protectionist Whig journal, the *British Merchant*, which won its battle against the Treaty. In *Commerce with France*, the author of the *Review* makes it clear that he is no free trader; like his Whig rivals, he believes in the concept of the favourable balance of trade, but reading the statistics differently from others, he advocates a different implementation of the economic theory they hold in common. Neither practical extreme—no trade at all, or completely free trade with France—appears appropriate to Defoe, who favours a regulated trade between England and France.

Defoe devotes the first part of *Commerce with France* to defending his consistency in advocating trade with France, using supporting quotations from back issues of the *Review*. He proposes the following paradox: whereas during the war years a writer could advocate trade with France yet still be considered a Whig, in 1713, when England and France are at peace, a man is considered a Tory for the same opinion. He solves his own paradox by asserting that the dispute is really a matter of name-calling between those in and out of public office, in which the labels Tory or Whig are irrelevant. In a highly effective paragraph, he decries the incursion of political partisanship into the essentially neutral field of trade, referring to the absurd notion of Whig-walks and Tory-walks on the Exchange.

He explains that he advocates trading with France only because he believes such trade will bring a favourable balance to England and supplies statistical reasons for his belief, adding to the export account of England's own manufactures (principally woollen goods and lead) previously underrated items of England's rapidly growing re-export trade (tobacco, sugar, and so forth), and invisible exports (England's carrying trade). The controversy over statistics on these matters is central to Defoe's argument; as he admits, he himself had at one time been less sanguine about Anglo-French trade relations, believing that the balance of trade stood in France's favour because of English "gust to their wines, brandy, silks, and fashions high". On page 163 Defoe cites as the source of his previous opinions the "paper which passed for current truth in those times, called, *A Scheme, etc.*", declaring that he now believes this Scheme of Trade (which had been drawn up in 1674), to be wholly false.

He disarms potential opponents by reminding them cleverly that the English are not in the position of dictating terms to an enemy who has surrendered unconditionally; rather, the situation calls for shrewd negotiations between two independent nations. He professes to believe that the ministry *has* negotiated shrewdly (in his anonymous writings on the Treaty of Commerce he urged strongly that the bargain be improved, suggesting specific methods to do so and thus resorting to his habitual method of retaining his independence while supporting the ministry), and that the French wool manufacturers will be ruined by the treaty.

Returning to his subject after a brief digression (not reproduced) on the effect of the projected Anglo-French treaty on the existing Anglo-Portuguese Methuen treaty, Defoe considers in detail why future trade between England and France must result in advantage to England: (1) because England herself now manufactures certain essential articles, expecially silks and linens, which she formerly imported from France; and (2) because the proposed treaty will lay duties on popular French goods such as wine and brandy, making them too expensive to be imported in quantities injurious to England's favourable balance of trade. His detailed discussion of these points (not reproduced) demonstrates his comprehensive grasp of the many industries in England and their relation to industries in France.

Defoe's argument is designed to lead up to the central question of the debate: how the treaty will affect England's woollen industry, regarded incorrectly by most economists, including Defoe, as the mainstay of future English foreign trade.[5] Defoe asserts that the treaty "must let in our manufactures into France in a full stream, and open a door for a greater consumption of them in France than ever was before". He scoffs at the notion advanced by many protectionists that the French are now able to compete with the English in manufacturing wool cloth, displaying his national pride to the point of chauvinism in the invidious comparison he makes between the clothing of the French ambassador and that of an English servant.

The remainder of the pamphlet consists of a eulogy on the incomparable qualities of English wool, the inimitable skill of English weavers, the superior efficiency of English to French labourers, interesting as a demonstration of Defoe's national pride in its most full-blown expression, his intimate knowledge of the process of wool manufacture, and his ability to make details about the production of commodities interesting to the general reader. This ability, familiar to all readers of *Robinson Crusoe*, includes among the many plain-dealing devices discussed below, the equating of manufacturing processes with natural forces, as on page 168, where Defoe describes how the spinning of wool is taught by mother to daughter, "as birds learn to sing, cocks to crow, and little children to speak ..."

In addition to its interest as an example of Defoe's ability to express himself clearly and forcefully in so technical a field as economics, *Commerce with France* is significant for three other reasons. First of all, it demonstrates that Defoe was no original theorist in economics: his argument is clearly based upon the premise central to mercantilism, that of a favourable balance of trade. Defoe was familiar with the free trade arguments advanced long before Adam Smith's time by men such as William Paterson, founder of the Bank of England, and one of Defoe's acquaintances. But he preferred the more conservative mercantilistic notion.

Secondly, the pamphlet demonstrates that as a practical economist and statistician, Defoe was ahead of most of the experts of his time, in a controversy that "was the first of its kind in which commercial statistics played a part".[7] Although, like his contemporaries, he overestimated the importance of the export of woollen cloth in relation to re-exports in England's foreign trade, his judgement that England was in 1713 economically more advanced than France was proved correct by the course of eighteenth-century history.[8]

Thirdly, the pamphlet demonstrates how Defoe's flexibility and perspicacity, so superior to most of his contemporaries', earned him often unmerited accusations of being a turncoat and a government hireling. In his 1962 *Economics and the Fiction of Daniel Defoe*, Maximillian E. Novak asserts, "Defoe preferred falsifying statistics to retreating from mercantilist principles".[9] And in his 1976 *The World of Defoe*, Peter Earle, pointing out while "Defoe's attitude to France ... was rather different from that of many of his contemporaries" (he believed it absurd to continue the seventeenth-century prohibition of Anglo-French trade into the eighteenth century, even though England and France were at war, for England now stood to gain by the trade), asserts that in defending the Treaty of Commerce Defoe "had now to prove that even before the wars England had gained from her trade with France, despite having often stated the opposite in earlier numbers of the *Review*. The result was some quite incredible statistical juggling."[10] Yet, as his contemporary critics were quick to point out, Defoe had access to all the public papers in the Customs House. With the aid of these figures, economists have only recently demonstrated that the Scheme of Trade Defoe derides, whose statistics were widely quoted in 1713 by opponents of the Anglo-French commercial treaty, was erroneous in its gloomy conclusions about the unfavourable balance of trade to England.[11] Ralph Davis points out that "a whole series of distinguished writers up to our own time", including Charles King of the *British Merchant*, fall into the statistical trap, "producing absurdly distorted and exaggerated pictures of the development of English trade".[12]

Defoe's occasional lapses into self-pity have been regarded by some scholars, including his biographer, James Sutherland, as the least attractive feature of his personality. In *Commerce with France*, he compares himself with Job, inscribing on his title page, "Suffer me that I may speak, and after that I have spoken, Mock on." If we recall that Mr. Review is clearly signalled as the author of the pamphlet and we examine its prose style, we will understand why self-dramatization is so important in this tract.

Defoe's plain-dealing, plain-speaking voice rings out in its quintessence in *Commerce with France*. It is the voice of common sense embodied in a sturdy, independent-minded crackerbarrel philosopher. This voice was and is frequently identified with that of Defoe himself,[13] both by his contemporaries and by modern readers who resent its self-assurance about its owner's reasoning ability and about the non-existence of intangibles like emotion. Readers and writers like Swift or Joyce,[14] who dislike emotional simplicity and are less deeply interested in ideas as one of the elements in writing, perceive the reasoning of Defoe's plain speaker as rudimentary and the persona as coarse. The vigour and directness of this persona offends their sensibilities.

Defoe makes the vigorous speaker of *Commerce with France* appear larger than life by using very rapid language rhythms of spoken discourse, colloquial, hard-hitting diction, homely imagery, and simple, common sense logic, clear even to the uneducated. In addition, he projects himself as a plain man, much misunderstood and wronged by others. It is for this last reason that the Job imagery is important in *Commerce with France*.

Here are several examples of these literary devices: (1) *language rhythms of rapid spoken discourse*—"What, Gentlemen! have you transferred your reason and judgement of things to the Tories! Are the Tories come down to make the right judgement of trade, and are the Whigs gone from it! You will not allow this sure! What then can be the matter! I'll tell you plainly the matter, and prove it when I have told it ..." (p. 160); (2) *colloquial, hard-hitting diction*— "How coarse, how rusty the black, how spongy, how nappy and rough the clothes ..." (p. 167): (3) *homely imagery*—"... to prohibit our own goods because if we did not the French would, is dying for fear of death, and like a man hanging himself, because he is in danger of being condemned to be hanged" (p. 165); (4) *simple, commom sense logic*—"... I always was of the opinion that we ought to have kept open our trade with France, (viz.) because we could get by the trade; and that we ought to trade with every nation we can get money by. I think I need spend no time to prove the latter, (viz.) that we ought to trade with every nation we can get money by" (p. 165).

Defoe's projection of his persona as a simple and honest man, loudly protesting that he is much misunderstood by others, is reiterated throughout *Commerce with France*. Here are two examples: "I say, if we take the treaty thus, as really it ought to be taken, I must confess, and I must speak my mind freely and plainly, whoever it offends, I do not see how the treaty could be made between the two nations upon more equal terms than it is; if I did, I should not be backward to speak it" (p. 164); and "I appeal to Spittlefields for the truth of this ..." (p. 170).

Another excerpt illustrating how Defoe dramatizes his speaker as a plain dealer is significant because it catches the author in action, setting up as straw man the opposite of the honest man, the devious manipulator. Defoe did the same thing at length in his *Letter from a Gentleman at the Court of St. Germains* and in passing in other of his writings like *Instructions from Rome, in Favour of the Pretender* (See page 126 above), where the devious speaker mentions Mr. Review as his antitype. Here is the quotation from *Commerce in France*: "I am bold to say, such discourse is enough to convince any man that understands manufacturing, that the people who speak it either say it without knowledge, *or against knowledge, I am afraid it is the latter*" (p. 169, my italics).

Commerce with France contains very few slips into the more formal and balanced syntax, educated diction, close reasoning, and clever imagery of the devious manipulator, but one should be noted to emphasize the contrast between Defoe's two most important personae: "The consequence of the thing, *unhappily for the nation*, is this, that whatsoever part the publick managers take, the private party managers oppose. It has happened, that the ministry have made a treaty of commerce: immediately a loud cry is raised against trading with France, as if we were to continue the interdiction of commerce after the war was over, and were still to have a war of trade, though the war of state was at an end" (p. 160).

The Job allusion in the pamphlet, as I mentioned above, is less a simple lapse into self-pity than Defoe's heightening of real life into drama, his characteristic technique of shaping subtly actual events and situations into a literary pattern, in this case the plain-dealing character known as the author of the *Review*. (See pages 123–124 above for a description of a literary relative of Mr. Review, the plain-dealing publisher of *A Letter from a Gentleman at the Court of St. Germains*.) In real life, however, Defoe had indeed been misunderstood on the issue of commerce with France. He admits in his pamphlet that he does not expect justification in his own times from accusations of being a turncoat; he must wait patiently for more impartial judgment from posterity. This proved a realistic evaluation of his own situation, for the statistics of the protectionist Whig *British Merchant* were accepted in England for forty years after its publication, even though Defoe spoke out against them repeatedly.[15] In his advocacy of trade with France Defoe was not denying his previous mercantilist principles; he was being accused falsely of being a turncoat and hireling because other economists could not see that his statistics were more accurate than those of his rivals, that the trade to France, if properly negotiated, could be defended even in mercantilist terms. Only now do Defoe's final words in *Commerce with France* sound prophetic:

> ... I have here given my reasons for my present opinion relating to the trade with France, which I have done rather as a testimony to future times of the foundations upon which my said opinion is grounded, and to answer the calumnies of those people who malign, and, without provocation, insult me, than from any prospect I have, that the soundest reasoning will allay the ferment which the parties among us have unhappily put the nation into.

Notes

1 Sir George Clark, *The Later Stuarts, 1660–1714* (Oxford, 1955), p. 237.

2 G. M. Trevelyan, *England under Queen Anne: The Peace and the Protestant Succession* (London, 1934), p. 254.

3 P. G. M. Dickson reveals, in *The Financial Revolution in England: A Study in the Development of Public Credit, 1688–1756* (London, 1967), p. 23, that "Bolingbroke argued later that the Peace of Utrecht left France 'too powerful, no matter by whose fault, as I am ready to admit that she was'." Dickson gives as his source Bolingbroke's *Works* (1754), III, 146, 153, 155.

4 Defoe also produced several unsigned polemical pamphlets in 1713, as well as his *General History of Trade*, in four monthly installments. The September issue of the *History* deals in relatively impartial terms with the question of trade between England and France and contains a masterly 3-page abridgment of the whole complicated matter.

5 His mention of electors wearing wool in their hats as they go to vote, refers to the opposition of the English wool industry to the Anglo-French treaty.

6 It is for this reason that Schumpeter characterizes the controversy over the commercial clauses of the Treaty of Utrecht as sterile from the point of view of analytic progress in economics, in his *History of Economic Analysis*, ed. E. B. Schumpeter (New York, 1968), p. 372.

7 G. N. Clark, *Guide to English Commercial Statistics 1696–1782* (London, 1938), p. 18. Defoe's ability as statistician was recognized by the committees of the Scottish Parliament, who in 1706 "relied upon him to supply minute details regarding trade and excises and equivalents

and drawbacks under the proposed Union", writes Moore. Moore also reports, in his *Daniel Defoe, Citizen of the Modern World* (Chicago, 1958), pp. 311, 308, that in the 1690 s "while Defoe was accountant to the commissioners of the Glass Duty, who collected the tax on windows," Charles Davenant (a leading economist who in 1705 was appointed Inspector-General of Exports and Imports by Queen Anne), "complained that he could not perfect his own accounts because Defoe would not let him see the ledgers."

8 According to Jacob Viner, the French government was relieved when Parliament rejected the Treaty of Commerce; the French had had second thoughts about disadvantages to themselves. (*Studies in the Theory of International Trade*, New York: Harper and Bros., 1937, footnote 9, p. 117.)

9 Maximillian E. Novak, *Economics and the Fiction of Daniel Defoe* (Berkeley and Los Angeles, 1962), p. 27.

10 Peter Earle, *The World of Defoe* (London: Weidenfeld and Nicholson, 1976), pp. 137, 139.

11 Margaret Priestly, "Anglo-French Trade and the 'Unfavourable Balance' Controversy, 1660–1685," *Economic History Review*, 4 (1951), pp. 40, 48. It should be noted that Defoe's name is frequently linked with that of Charles Davenant, who was highly respected as a statistician. In his *Financial Revolution in England*, P. G. M. Dickson cites Defoe's opinion along with Davenant's that inadequate statistics accounted for false optimism in the House of Commons about forthcoming tax yields. Dickson says, (p. 349), "Davenant writes in 1698 that 'the Projectors of most new Funds, have hitherto been generally mistaken two parts in three', an opinion later confirmed by Defoe [in his *Essay upon Public Credit* of 1710]."

12 Ralph Davis, "English Foreign Trade, 1660–1700," in *Essays in Economic History*, ed. E. M. Carus-Wilson (London, 1962), II, 267.

13 James Sutherland refers to the "plain-spoken, down-to-earth, unpedantic and colloquial style of the *Review*" as "the staple" of Defoe's style, in *Daniel Defoe, A Critical Study* (Cambridge, Mass.: Harvard University Press, 1971), p. 74. In his *Daniel Defoe's Many Voices: A Rhetorical Study of Prose Style and Literary Method* (Amsterdam: Rodopi NV, 1972), E. Anthony James calls this style Defoe's own voice.

14 Swift was contemptuous of Defoe, dismissing his plain-dealing Mr. Review as a "grave, sententious, dogmatical rogue", a "stupid illiterate Scribbler" with a "mock authoritative manner" (*Examiner* no. 15, November 16, 1710 and *A Letter concerning the Sacramental Test.*) Joyce was a great admirer of Defoe's prose style but was repulsed by his authoritative manner, which the Irishman regarded as the voice of English colonialism (*Daniel Defoe*, trans. Joseph Prescott, *Buffalo Studies*, I, p. 24.)

15 Defoe later disavowed his support of the Treaty of Commerce, saying he had made the best of a bad argument, but his disavowal sounds very much like a sportsman-like acceptance of a fait accompli. John Robert Moore says that when Defoe insisted in 1714 and 1717 that the Bill of Commerce would have been a disaster if Parliament had passed it, and that the Earl of Oxford had had nothing to do with it, he was disavowing it in order to muster support for Oxford, accused of treason: "Defoe did not believe this in 1714 any more than he did in 1713, and he did not say it in his own person; but as the anonymous pamphleteer he was not trying to defend the temporarily discredited bill but to save the life of Harley from a vindictive Whig majority. The Whig readers of his defense of Harley would not have been satisfied with less, and Defoe was writing only to make an effective appeal to those Whig readers." *Daniel Defoe: Citizen of the Modern World* (Chicago: University of Chicago Press, 1958), p. 313.

Some Thoughts upon the Subject of Commerce with France (1713)

I could by no means foresee when I formerly published my thoughts about TRADE, that it should come to be so popular a controversy as it is now.

I am very glad, however, as things have since happened, that as my opinion of the trade with France was always the same, and for the same reasons that it is now; so that I did put that opinion in print so many times, and so long ago, that I have left no room for malice itself, without shameful prevarication, to charge me with having changed my hand or my heart in the matters of trade. The time will come when I shall make it appear as plain in other matters also.

Six year and nine year ago, and when the ministry who then governed affairs had locked and barred all the doors of trade against France, I ventured to tell them in so many words, that *if they had been in their trading senses, they would have traded with France all the while they fought with France.* I told them *then* plainly, that we cheated the nation of the profits of an advantageous trade, by prohibiting our lead and our corn going to France, under the weak and foolish pretence of not supplying the enemy with bullets to shoot at us; and not supplying the enemy with corn for their magazines; when at the same time we sold both our lead and our corn to the neuteral powers, who at a double price sold them to France; so that the enemy got our lead and our corn for bullets and magazines, and we only cheated ourselves of the profit.

I complained *then* that the Dutch had the wit to have an open trade with France all the time of the war, and became thereby able to carry on that war, while at the same time they got from the French in trade part of that money they spent upon them in the field; whereas we shut ourselves out of the trade and the profits too, though we were able to get by it as well as they, and wanted the gain as much as they.

I published *then* in print an account of a calculation of the gain we made from France after the Peace of Ryswick, when, by the opinion of some eminent merchants then, and still, flourishing in London, and who can witness if they please on what foot this calculation was made, this nation cleared 90,000 pounds per month by the trade to France; from whence came that wonderful flux of French pistoles among us, which surprised our people and raised that ridiculous clamour of the oyster-barrel,* and of their being sent over to bribe our Parliament men. The truth of which was nothing but this, that our prodigious export of goods to France so much over-ballanced their import upon us, that they were obliged to supply the ballance in gold; the Parliament was obliged to reduce the said pistoles from 17s 6d to 17s, and the quantity was so great, that if our accounts at that time did not err, above eleven hundred thousand of them were melted down at the Tower, and coined into guineas.

All these things, gentlemen, I printed in the *Review*; there they stand as witnesses for or against me; if I have gone from my opinion, changed my sentiments of things, or written against myself, let it appear; if I have not, why am I causelessly bullied and insulted by vile mercenaries and ignorant journey-men scribblers, whose fathers, as Job says, were not fit to be set with dogs of the flock; and who do it only because they think they please you in filling your mouths with scandal and reproach. But further yet, these things, though written against the late measures, and in the time of a Whig government, they could hear then, and not dislike, nor quarrel at, or insult me for writing. If the ministry themselves found it clashed with their proceedings, yet they were always so generous and so just to me, as to allow me a freedom of speech when I spoke my real sentiments of things: believing that I spoke what I thought I had good ground to support; and if they had not allowed me that liberty, I should have ventured their displeasure and have taken it, the day being yet to come that I ever withheld speaking what I thought was needful to say, and what I knew I could defend the truth of,

* *oyster-barrel*: Defoe refers in his "Review" of 17 June 1707 to England's favourable balance of trade with France in that brief period of peace between the signing of the Treaty of Ryswick (1697) and the beginning of the War of the Spanish Succession (1702). The specie earned by England, paid in French pistoles, was so considerable that Defoe says there was a rumour that the French coins had been "brought over in casks full to bribe our Parliament". Some of the casks, presumably, were oyster-barrels. [Ed.]

for fear of any man's face or power in the world. Upon which principle I still act, as appears by my standing fast to my said opinion, in a time when it procures me such a tumult of popular rage, even among those who, I thought, had some reason to have used me better.

But how comes it to pass that what I might say then with so much freedom, I must not speak a word of now? Whence comes this change of your taste? I affirm, and dare tell you, I can prove to your faces, *trade is the same*, there is not one addition or alteration to any part of the trade, which does not more and more confirm what I said then, and make it just to be said now. How comes it to pass that a man could be a Whig and say this four, five and six year ago, and must be a Tory if he says it *now*! What, gentlemen! have you transferred your reason and judgement of things to the Tories! Are the Tories come down to make the right judgement of trade, and are the Whigs gone from it! You will not allow this sure! What then can be the matter!

I'll tell you plainly the matter, and prove it when I have told it: the party strife between the gentlemen out of power and the gentlemen in power has, *cursed be the misfortune*, hooked in the affair of trade into the quarrel, and your commerce is now become a part of your politicks.

The consequence of the thing, *unhappily for the nation*, is this, that whatsoever part the publick managers take, the private party managers oppose. It has happened, that the ministry have made a treaty of commerce: immediately a loud cry is raised against trading with France, as if we were to continue the interdiction of commerce after the war was over, and were still to have a war of trade, though the war of state was at an end. Now, if you please, let the tables be turned, take it the other way. Had the ministry chosen the other part, and made no treaty of commerce, I undertake to prove that it had been the same thing; and the same loud cry had been raised, and that by the very same people, about neglecting the matters of trade, and taking no care, when they had made a peace, to open the trade again, as other of the Confederates had done for themselves.

* * *

What has trade to do with your politick squabbles, and what business have party men with the commerce of the nation? Trade is neither *Whig* nor *Tory*, *Church* or *Dissenter*,

High-Church or *Low-Church.* In all the broils and tumults that have exercised these unhappy nations about *putting in* and *putting out*, trade has stood always neuter till now. There may have been parties in the parishes, in the wardmotes, common-councils and common-halls of the City, and so upward to the Privy Council, Convocation and Parliament; but we never till now brought them upon the *Exchange;* there was never any *Whig-walk* and *Tory-walk*, *High-Church-walk* and *Low-Church-walk* upon *Change*, that ever I knew of till now.

Certainly it is the interest of the whole nation to lay aside this part of the strife. Parties have ruined our peace, our charity, our society already, and almost our religion too. If we let them ruin our trade also, what have we left? Well may the poor people wear wool in their hats when they go to vote for Parliament men; I wish it may direct them to chuse such men as may put a speedy end to this breach; for if parties come to govern our trade, all our commerce will be at an end, and by consequence our woollen manufactures.

* * *

This is the present case, and when it will be otherwise God only knows. But run to what extremes you please, and push your own disasters as far as you please: I am resolved, in all I shall say on the subject of trade, to speak of it as it ought to be spoken of, (viz.) as a thing entirely unconcerned with parties, or with any of our divisions; whether it be *with* or *against* popular opinion, *with* or *against* those people who I hope mean well, or *with* or *against* the government or ministry is not the question to me. What I say now, I said before, I always said, and say again: *if we are in our trading senses, we ought to open the trade to France;* and my reason is the same as it was before, neither the trade, or the reason of the trade, has suffered the least alteration, *we ought to carry on the French trade, because we are able to do it to our advantage;* and we who are a nation depending upon trade, ought *to trade with every nation we can get money by.*

I hope nobody will think so grossly as to suppose that I should mean by this, that we ought to trade to France whether it be to our advantage or no.

It remains to me therefore to examine next, upon what foot of trade we now stand with France, and how it appears that the trade may now be carried on to our advantage?

I have nothing to do here with the question so much canvassed lately in print between the writers of both sides, (viz.) whether the trade to France was always to our advantage or no. I acknowledge I was always of opinion that it was not: I mean as to the ballance of trade. I was bred to the French trade from a youth, and have known my share of the particulars of it, and I know their import was always very heavy when our duties upon them were low, our gust to their wines, brandy, silks, and fashions high, and the number of sorts of goods great, which we dealt with them in.

Yet I must own, since I have seen what has been alledged on both sides, I am more inclined to think that what has been said on that side as to our former advantage by the trade, is more probable than I thought it before; and I crave leave for a small digression, to shew what has so inclined me: not that I design to enter into the dispute about it at all; but meerly hint at what I have observed in it, which I had not considered before.

It must be allowed that our exportations to France in woollen manufactures were very great; I will not enter into particulars here, they are published on both sides many times over. Besides the woollen goods, our allom, corn, fish, lead, shot, cast iron, wrought iron and brass, block-tin, pewter, skins, drugs, coal, but especially leather, rise up to very great sums.

Our foreign trade, or what is called exports by certificate, were likewise very great, and oftentimes much greater than any of the accounts I have yet seen printed; (viz.) our plantation goods, such as sugars, cottons, indico, ginger, pimento, tobacco, etc; our East-India, Turkey, and Spanish West-India goods, as cochenele, indico, gauls, dyers' woods, cotton-yarn, grograms,* oil, Spanish wool; as also elephants' teeth, bees'-wax, drugs and the like.

But if these are not allowed to ballance the imports from France, as I say again, I thought always they did not; yet the two following circumstances which I borrow from another publick hand, do incline me to believe they might; and this is all I shall say to what is past.

These circumstances are, (1) the carrying on the whole trade in our own shipping, the advantage of which I must acknowledge. (2) The advance of the price of the goods sent from hence to France, which are for the most part sold upon the account of the English stocks.

* * *

* *cochenele*: cochineal, a scarlet dye made from the dried bodies of insects.
grograms: coarse fabrics of silk, mohair and wool, frequently stiffened with gum. [Ed.]

But I am not disputing with anybody; I am neither to defend the *Mercator*, or confute the *British Merchant*, let them fight on their own way; I am giving my own thoughts only, which I shall do as impartially as I can.

I must ingeniously acknowledge, that I formerly received my opinion of the ballance of the French trade being 800,000 1. per an. to our loss, from the accounts given then about town, and into Parliament, when I myself was in trade; which made it be received at that time as a common opinion, and as such I printed it in the *Review*, which some people are mighty well pleased to quote upon me now; and this common opinion was derived from the paper which passed for current truth in those times, called *A Scheme, &c.*.

But I have really been amazed to see that scheme detected of such manifest fraud, proved to be wholly false, and designedly to be imposed upon the nation, even to stripping it stark naked from all manner of covering, and not one word said in its defence; so that the authors on that side are careful to publish that they had no hand in it. Vide *British Merchant*, N. 14. Upon these things, can any man blame me then that I acknowledge the error which I, among other people, fell into by taking that account for true? And that I am not now of the opinion that the trade to France was so much to our loss as I then printed it to be?

These are the circumstances which, I say, have inclined me to believe that our trade to France fully ballanced our trade from France in former times.

* * *

I cannot but think, if men were inclined to do me any justice, either in this or anything else; that my having printed this as my opinion several times, and several years ago, before any parties concerned themselves about it, ought to defend me against the malice of those who suggest my doing it now upon the influence of others. But reason and justice are not loud enough to be heard in the noise and clamour of this day; time will make men cooler, and I must wait till then.

The question therefore now before us is very short and plain, (viz.) whether it is our interest to open a trade to France; and whether we shall be gainers by it, if we do it on the terms of the Treaty of Commerce which is now proposed to us. I shall speak only my own thoughts of it.

I have examined as nicely as I can the whole treaty; I will

not say that several things might not have been added to it to make it more to our advantage than it is; but the question then will be, whether it was rational to expect greater advantages could be submitted to by the French. If, indeed, we had been masters of France, and had only one side of a treaty to make, viz. to set down what terms the French king should be obliged to yield to, without conceding anything to them on our part; then it should not have been a treaty, but an Act of Parliament, enacting in what manner the French should trade with us; as we do with Ireland; which had it been our case, I should have taxed the ministry with great indolence and neglect of our interest, that they had not forbid the French making any kind of woollen manufacture at all, and taken off all duties on the importation of ours. They should have caused all woollen manufactures from Holland, Flanders, Germany, Swisserland, &c. to have been prohibited, &c. They should have caused the French to send no more ships to the East-Indies, Turkey, or Canada, and have caused Martinico and Quebec to have been surrendered to us, as they did Newfoundland and St. Christopher's.

I do acknowledge these are all articles, in which the Treaty of Commerce might have been made better than it is.

They might also have continued all the high duties on French goods in England as they now stand, and which are in the nature of prohibitions, and made the whole coast of France a free port to the English, and many other things might have been done.

But take the treaty as a convention between two nations, in which we were to provide for the equity and justice of trade, to settle the equalities of commerce between them, with due regard to the proportions of things, and the circumstances of the respective nations, for the accomodation of the subjects of both; and either nation being free, and without dependence upon the other; I say, if we take the treaty thus, as really it ought to be taken, I must confess, and I must speak my mind freely and plainly, whoever it offends, I do not see how the treaty could be made between the two nations upon more equal terms than it is; if I did, I should not be backward to speak it.

Nay, on the contrary, I do think that the French King has struck such a blow by this treaty to the manufacturers of wool among his own people, that if he stands long to the conditions of it, all the undertakers of woollen manufactures in France must be ruined and undone.

* * *

I come back to the main subject, and to my reasons as above, why I always was of the opinion that we ought to have kept open our trade with France, (viz.) because we could get by the trade; and that we ought to trade with every nation we can get money by.

I think I need spend no time to prove the latter, (viz.) that we ought to trade with every nation we can get money by. We are a nation which depends upon our commerce, and our whole prosperity, wealth and subsistance depends upon it, the landed interest not excepted, whose rents would soon be reduced to such a condition as to starve the landlords as well as the tennants, a few of higher dimensions than ordinary excepted, if our commerce should fail. This commerce is supported and maintained principally by our woollen manufacture, which is so considerable and essential to it, that should we have no more a free export, or a vent abroad for our manufactures, the import we make from abroad would so overballance us from all parts of the world, that we should immediately be exhausted of all our specie, and the other produce of our country would scarce feed us. For this reason nothing but a blindness, which no nation but ours was ever possessed with, would have led us to be accessary to the stopping the exportation of our own manufactures, as has been done by prohibitions of trade, whether to France or to any other part of the world.

I know it has been objected, that if we had not, the French would: to which I answer, then the French should, it was not our business to have done it first; to prohibit our own goods because if we did not the French would, is dying for fear of death, and like a man hanging himself because he is in danger of being condemned to be hanged.

Our business had been to have loaded the French goods here with such duties as might have secured their importations from hurting us, and to have left our woollen manufacture free to be carried to France, or anywhere else, as long as ever they would have bought a piece of them; and if they must have been prohibited, it had been the King of France's business to have prohibited them, not ours. It is our business to sell our woollen manufactures to everybody in the world that would buy them; because the produce of our land, the labour of the poor, the consumption of foreign imported goods which are the returns of them, is all carried on by it, and depends upon it. In short, we ought to trade with every nation we can gain by, because the gain of our trade is the essential article on which the wealth of the nation depends.

Having laid down this foundation, it follows to prove that we can and may gain by the trade to France. This must be proved, by proving that the value of our exportation to France, with its appendices, and additional circumstances, shall exceed the value of our imports from France; and this is proved by two circumstances which attend our trade now, which did not attend it before the war.

1. The several kinds of manufactures which we are now masters of, and make either wholly or in part among ourselves, which we formerly imported from France.

2. The loading the other goods which we shall import from France, with such heavy duties as must necessarily lessen their consumption.

There are other reasons to be given of less moment; but these are the two main reasons which will prove our imports to be very considerably abated.

* * *

This must let in our manufactures into France in a full stream, and open a door for a greater consumption of them in France than ever was before; and this, I say, is the reason on the other side, why I pretend to prove we shall now be gainers by the French trade. For if the only exception against the trade is that of their overballancing our export, if then I prove that their export to us shall now lessen, and our export to them shall now increase, so that we shall for the future overballance them, then my argument must be good, (viz.) that we ought to trade with them.

It is brought as an objection, and it is all the objection that can be brought in the case, (viz.) that the French make all our manufactures now as well as we do, and therefore will not want ours any more. Nay, so warm are some people to have this believed, that they affirm, though I doubt without evidence, that they make as good cloth in France as we do; and as good serges and perpets,* &c. and in such quantities too, as that they can supply all the world; nay, and supply us too, if we will give them leave.

These gentlemen beg the question very peremptorily, and demand that we should strangely take them upon trust. But the matter of fact has never yet been proved, and this is not an

* *perpet*: an abbreviation of perpetuana, a durable fabric of English manufactured wool, to be compared with high quality fabrics like serge or say. [Ed.]

age to believe men on their words, in things of such a nature, when parties byass men so much to strain their principles, as we see is the case every day.

It has been asked in publick by one paper, and I must ask it here; it is so natural, it cannot be strange if every man we talk with should ask it—Where is this fine cloth and woollen manufacture that the French make? Where do they hide it? How comes it to pass that none of the gentlemen who come over hither have any of it ON? Let the French ambassador be a test of this; or any other Frenchman that comes over: look on their clothes, their liveries, their coaches. The French ambassador cannot take it for an affront that we say, an English servant to a private gentleman would have thought himself very ill used to have been clothed in such trappings. How coarse, how rusty the black, how spongy, how nappy and rough the clothes, how ill made, how worse dressed, and how worst of all the wool of the clothes they appeared at first in! The English Colchester bays* would have looked better than some of them looked. If these are the manufactures they boast of, I shall never fear, but when our woollen clothes, stuffs, serges and other goods come among them at reasonable rates for the customs and duties, they will make their own way, and shew the French that they are not able to make our manufacture to any perfection.

* * *

But I shall undertake to prove two things here, that shall confound all this notion: (1.) That neither the workmen, or the wool, will effectually answer for making our woollen manufacture. (2.) That neither the French, or any nation in the world do, or can, work cheaper than the English both can and do.

* * *

The next article is the spinning, and give me leave to say this: as it is the essential, so it is the inimitable part of our manufacture, and the French are utterly unable to do this, and we are unable to teach them; they are so far from being able to imitate the various sorts of spinning which is now

* *bays*: Colchester was famous for its bays, originally a fine wool fabric used for clothing, the manufacture of which was introduced into England in the sixteenth century by refugees from France and the Netherlands. The modern corruption of the plural form of bay, "baize", is a coarse wool fabric used for linings. [Ed.]

practised in England, that really we cannot imitate ourselves. There is so much evidence in this truth, and it is so well known, and so proved by experience, that I freely appeal to all the manufactures of Great Britain for the proof of it.

The spinning, generally speaking, is the work of the women and children, it is learned from mother to daughter, as birds learn to sing, cocks to crow, and little children to speak, (viz.) by immediate imitation. The manner is carried from one to another by that aptness which is in the young of every creature to follow the old, and becomes a natural habit, like a tone in the speech, which is peculiar to this or that county, which they who use it, know not how to alter, and they that do not, know not how to imitate.

Thus you may know the people who are born and bred in the several parts of this kingdom by the shibboleth of the place they come from, they cannot conceal it; nor can a man born in another part of the country mimick them so but that he will easily be known to be a counterfeit. This is plain in the people of Norfolk and north-west; Yorkshire, Durham and Northumberland, north; Scotland, Wales and several other parts.

In like manner every way the same in its kind, and introduced the same way, (viz.) by a meer habit, and that not to be altered by themselves, or imitated by others, is the manufacture of spinning naturalized to the people of the several parts of England, according to the several countries they have been taught to work in. Nay, even in the same countries the spinning differs, as the several manufactures which this or that part of the country are employed in differs.

The consequence of this is essential to the manufacture, whence proceeds the variety of our sorts of goods, which appears not at all according to the nature of the wool, but according to the different places where it is wrought; the reason of which is the spinning, and nothing else.

* * *

How many attempts of this kind have been made in England, (viz.) to transplant the manufacture of one county into another, and we have very rarely found it practicable; if then one county cannot imitate another, if one town cannot imitate another, nay, in some goods one manufacturer cannot imitate another, though they have all the same materials too, how should another nation imitate us?

* * *

I am so near the close of this tract that I cannot enlarge; but I come to another case in our manufacture, wherein I find we are run down by a vulgar error, which however at this time is made mighty use of, and makes more noise that is for our reputation, especially as it comes out of our own mouths, and this is: that the French people work cheaper than we; nay, so great is the assurance which our people speak it with, that they are not slack to say that they can work cheaper by four-pence in a shilling.

I am bold to say, such discourse is enough to convince any man that understands manufacturing, that the people who speak it either say it without knowledge, or against knowledge, I am afraid it is the latter.

Could the poor in France work cheaper than the English by a groat in a shilling, could the spinner, the weaver, the carder, the dresser, the dyer, &c. perform all those works which are at the beginning of the manufacture four-pence in a shilling cheaper than the English, the clothier that finishes it would be able to sell it eight-pence in the shilling cheaper when it was finished; for that difference in the first work would double in the price of the whole cloth, and so the clothes which the English could not sell under twelve shillings per yard at market, the French would sell at four shillings per yard, and of consequence must of necessity have long ago had all the trade of the world.

As this, though but a short hint, is sufficient to expose the falsehood of that suggestion, so I shall lay one thing down as a certain truth, which I know to be true of my own certain knowledge in many cases, and offer to prove by good evidence in others, and I shall leave it to farther enlargement, if I am called to speak to it again; the assertion is this in short:

That set the goodness and quantity of their work against their wages, and no nation in the world works cheaper than the English.

Let no man suggest that this cannot be made out, my name is to this book, I'll make it good, and at any reasonable hazard, I offer to prove it beyond the power of all the cavils of the world. Take it in any, or all the branches or parts of the woollen manufacture, I repeat it again in other words, *set the goodness of the performance, and the quantity of work done, against the wages,* no manufacturers in the world have their work done cheaper, or for less wages, than the English.

I do not deny but in diligence they may out-do us, I know the English poor are not so forward to work as the French, and perhaps when the English have earned their money hardly, they may spend it lightlier than others, and be as poor as any of them. I know that if you hire a Frenchman by the day, he shall come at less wages. I know if the Frenchman works for himself, he shall sit to it more hours. But then the English day man shall do more work in less time. Or the English day man shall make better work. And the Englishman that works for himself shall perform as much in less time than the Frenchman, or make his work deserve more wages. I appeal to Spittlefields for the truth of this in part, and even to the French manufacturers there themselves.

* * *

It is my satisfaction that I am hitherto pursuing no end but what I firmly believe to be the true interest of my country; and I am fully persuaded, that even the people who are at this time so warm, will in a few years be convinced they are in the wrong; and be ashamed of those men who now endeavour to inflame and exasperate us one against another; in the meantime I have here given my reasons for my present opinion relating to the trade with France, which I have done rather as a testimony to future times of the foundation upon which my said opinion is grounded, and to answer the calumnies of those people who malign and, without provocation, insult me, than from any prospect I have, that the soundest reasoning will allay the ferment which the parties among us have unhappily put the nation into.

* * *

2. A Brief Deduction of the Original, Progress, and Immense Greatness of the British Woollen Manufacture

A Brief Deduction of the Original, Progress, and Immense Greatness of the British Woollen Manufacture was published on 15 March 1727. It deals with the history, contemporary condition, and possible future of an industry that for centuries enjoyed the prestige of being the most important in England. Wool, the staple article of the country's export trade in the Middle Ages, remained until the nineteenth century the indisputable basis of her greatest industry, the cloth manufacture. "Every class in the community", writes Peter Bowden, "whether landlord, farmer, merchant, industrial capitalist or artisan, had an interest in wool, and it was the subject of endless economic controversy."[1] The influence of the wool industry on the English imagination is indicated by the remarkable extent to which the English language in popular literature and speech has been "enriched by words and phrases connected in their origin with the manufacture of cloth".[2]

A Brief Deduction . . . of the British Woollen Manufacture is Defoe's major contribution to a solution of the problem of overproduction in England's favoured industry, an industry upon which an army of workers depended for earnings. Running to over 52 closely-printed pages, it bears evidence of careful research and writing, and, like his 368-page *Plan of the English Commerce* (23 March 1728), should be considered as a major contribution to his economic work, referring to issues beyond the scope of the English wool industry alone, and taking a long-range view of economic development. In addition to demonstrating Defoe's rich and comprehensive grasp of English history, world geography, the technical details of manufacturing, and his alertness as an observer of contemporary changes in London, *A Brief Deduction* reveals some of his ideas about political and economic theory. The pamphlet is important for understanding Defoe's version of mercantilism, which differs from the version most familiar to us today, with its overwhelming emphasis upon a favourable balance of trade as the key to national power, by putting equal stress upon another of mercantilism's aspects, that of a system of social welfare.[3]

Defoe's historical account of the rise of the wool industry is surprising for two reasons. First, he categorically refuses to give Edward III any credit for fostering domestic manufacture of wool, in spite of the facts, known to Defoe's contemporaries, that Edward had invited Flemish weavers to settle in England, had forbidden the importation of manufactured cloth, and had prohibited the export of English wool. Second, he ignores the many conflicts in Tudor and Stuart times which arose because of divergent interests among the various classes involved with wool, and presents the period as one of uninterrupted expansion of the cloth industry, directed by benevolent and far-sighted monarchs.

His condemnation of Edward III has been deplored by several scholars who have written about Defoe, one of whom attributes it to a careless use of historical sources which he believes to be typical of Defoe's writing.[4] It is apparent from *A Brief Deduction* that Defoe had only a very sketchy idea of the development of the British wool industry from its origins in the twelfth century until the end of the fifteenth century, although he is correct in asserting that the manufacture of wool into cloth began on a large scale only under the Tudors. (Previously, England's exports had consisted mainly of wool, rather than of finished cloth.) But his disparagement of Edward III is a conscious attack, arising from certain of his theories about politics and economics. An attentive reader will observe that Defoe organizes his history of early woollen manufacture between two poles: Edward III and Queen Elizabeth. Under Edward the Court was splendid, England was "the terror of the world", but the poor were neglected (see pages 182–185). Under Queen Elizabeth rich and poor were clothed, and wool manufactures were exported "into almost all parts of the known world" (page 189).

Underlying his descriptions of the two regimes are two important economic assumptions characteristic of mercantilism. First, mercantilists believed that a large population, fully employed, was the source of national wealth. The Dutch (whose economy Defoe describes admiringly on page 183) were regarded as an example of the correct working out of mercantilist principles. "The wealth of the Dutch", reports E. S. Furniss, "was ascribed to the continuous favorable balance of their foreign trade and this to the industry and parsimony of her laboring population."[5] Second, a favourable balance of trade was best attained by applying skilled labour to a domestic raw material (wool). The labourers' skill increased the value of the wool, so that higher prices could be commanded from other countries for the finished manufacture than for the wool in its original raw state.

Most mercantilists, interested primarily in the national wealth and power accruing from a favourable balance of trade with foreign nations, believed that labour costs, or wages, must be kept at a minimum, so that finished products could compete successfully in the international market. Defoe, however, was in favour of high wages and high prices. His attitude was influenced by humanitarian concern for the poor, pride that English labourers were better fed and clothed than their European counterparts, and empirical observation during his many tours through England that the country appeared more and more prosperous, as trade spread internally. (Indeed, Defoe seemed to regard home and colonial trade as the principal source of English wealth in his *Complete English Tradesman* of 1725, and in his *Plan of the English Commerce* of 1728.) Defoe firmly believed that the source of a nation's power lay in the wealth of its inhabitants.

The combination of pragmatic observation and humanitarianism that led Defoe to this conclusion about the source of national wealth accounts for his denigration of absolutist monarchies and his preference for Queen Elizabeth, and for the constitutional monarchs who reigned in England after the Revolution of 1688. Defoe seizes the opportunity to prove his point when he envisions the consternation of Louis XIV (see page 196), a contemporary example of the absolute monarch, whose power is gained at the expense of his subjects, at the evidences of English national wealth shown in the ability to raise revenue for the War of the Spanish Succession.

In his historical account of the rise of the woollen industry in England, Defoe simplifies greatly the variegated fortunes of wool manufacture during the Tudor and Stuart period up until the end of Charles II's reign, presenting the period as one of uninterrupted expansion.[6] Conceiving of the development of the wool industry in organic terms—birth, growth, maturity, decay—Defoe prefers to express his vision of its growing period as one of continued expansion. Instead of dwelling on the details of painful local readjustments in wool manufacture from one article to another (in a passage not reproduced he indicates that he is aware of those dislocations), he discusses the expansion of cloth production in terms of the dispersion of English exports abroad. For this purpose he uses a spatial image, a map created by great richness of geographical detail. On this map he traces the routes on which English goods moved in all directions, permeating Europe, and travelling to exotic and far distant Africa and Asia (see pages 191–3). Although his image is constructed with place names, it has essentially a literary and rhetorical effect, conveying the love of adventure and exploration that was so important a facet of Defoe's personality. (In his anonymous 1719 *Historical Account of the Voyages and Adventures of Sir Walter Raleigh*, Defoe claimed to be "related to his blood".)[7] Modern readers may perhaps recognize the emotional impact of Defoe's map image when they recall Marlow's words in Joseph Conrad's *Heart of Darkness*:

> Now when I was a little chap I had a passion for maps. I would look for hours at South America, or Africa, or Australia, and lose myself in all the glories of exploration. At that time there were many blank spaces on the earth, and when I saw one that looked particularly inviting on a map ... I would put my finger on it and say, "When I grow up I will go there."

Defoe's presentation of the wool industry in terms of the growth of an organism arises spontaneously from the economic context within which he was writing. The image of England as a national family, so often invoked by Defoe, was the common property of economic and political writers of his time. Indeed, mercantilism, a confusing and often contradictory amalgam of beliefs which predate the development of economics as a social science, was in reality a system of domestic economy writ large. In this system of an ordered national community, every person and each group and class performed its function and received its due reward in a share of the general welfare.[8]

Defoe describes the English wool industry in organic imagery, as a Jew in bondage in Egypt (page 180), a child, born in the time of Edward IV (page 188), an oak tree at its full glory and perfection from 1580–1680 (page 193), a body now too big for its legs (page 195), a swollen body, suffering from dropsy (page 197), and finally as a beautiful and agreeable wife, despised only because her husband is tired of his own family (page 205). Principles of family economy projected on to a national level suggest that the point has come at which English production of cloth has outstripped the international market, which is not only a limited one, but must from now on be divided with other nations currently producing their own cheap woollen cloth (page 203). Principles of family economy also suggest that new towns which "thrust themselves into that trade" (page 201) cause a deplorable anarchy which results in the adulteration of quality. Buyers can no longer distinguish among all the new local products, and the credit of all the traditional manufactures is thereby damaged.

Defoe's prescription for curing the dropsical condition of the English cloth industry is as conservative economically as is his analysis of the causes of the malady, concentrating mainly on production, and viewing the influence of consumer demand as undesirable. First of all, he advocates putting a stop to further increase of production at home (page 198), presumably by governmental action. Secondly, deploring throughout his pamphlet the past readjustment of English production to consumer demand through imitation of cheap French fashions (page 200), he advocates a return to high quality, and to warm English broadcloth and kersey. Because he wishes to reserve for English producers alone the international market for expensive and fine quality cloth (they cannot hope to compete with lower labour and transportation costs on the Continent), he does not advocate one obvious solution to the problem of England's wool growers: return to the export of raw wool. Like his contemporaries, he was falsely convinced of the superiority of English and Irish wool, and its indispensability for continental textile industries,[9] and believed that its export would enable European industries to compete in the fine cloth market he wished to reserve for England. Thirdly, Defoe implores his countrymen to wear their own manufactures; not only is it contemptible to go whoring after foreign trash when native products are so superior, but it is a patriotic duty to support English industry so that poor labourers do not go unemployed, farmers are not left with unbought wool, and manufacturers are not starved.

In this moving appeal (see pages 205–207), we sense a weariness and pessimism about the future of England's greatest industry, which Defoe describes as if it were a beautiful and faithful wife, deserted by a philandering husband. It is apparent to Defoe that government prohibitions against the importation of dyed silks and printed or painted calicoes (1700), and the wearing of even domestically printed calicoes (1721), have been ineffectual in stemming the tide of popular fashion, and if laws and penalties are insufficient, what hope can be expected from mere exhortation based on moral and patriotic grounds?

In the light of the technical knowledge of wool production available to him in 1727, the pessimism expressed by Defoe in this pamphlet is only too well founded.[10] From the mercantilist view-point, the decline of a favourite industry, an industry which not only accounted for the lion's share of England's export trade, but manufactured its products from raw materials grown within its own shores, thus entailing no expenditure at all of national treasure, and employing the maximum number of English men, women, and children in the process of production, could only be catastrophic. Domestic demand could not compensate for the falling off of foreign demand, for English consumers seemed determined to dress in printed calicoes. The idea that domestic cotton textile production might be stimulated by government prohibitions against foreign fabrics,[11] that cotton exports would one day far outstrip woollen manufactures, that an industry relying upon imported raw materials, and a labour force far more highly paid than Indian or Chinese peasants, could by the use of newly-invented machinery supply the world with cheap and attractive goods and set the whole nation to work in this endeavour, would have been incredible to Defoe. The Industrial Revolution, which was to inaugurate a new era, was beyond the horizon in 1727.

The prose style of *A Brief Deduction* can best be appreciated by contrasting it with that of the previous pamphlet, *Commerce with France*. The earlier tract (1713) is by the plain-dealing "author of the *Review*"; accordingly, its speaker is a strongly projected persona with an appropriately hard-hitting style. The speaker of the 1727 tract, on the other hand, is scarcely individualized, and his style, while informal, is politer than that of Mr. Review; indeed, it resembles most closely the style of the Defoe who wrote letters to Robert Harley from 1704 to 1714. The most colloquial passage in the whole pamphlet (and it is not as colloquial as Mr. Review's style), is the following:

> Perhaps a manufacturer did, or suppose he had seated himself at any particular town or place in the country, had brought together some people, and had instructed them in the work, viz. some women to spin, some men to comb, to weave, to dress the cloth, and had built a fulling mill to thicken the cloths, and the like. Then come the two armies into the field, and they march over the country where the poor manufacturer is settled. If it be a friendly army, and they are of the same side, then the kindest thing that could be expected was to call all the poor workmen away, especially the young able-bodied fellows, with their bows and arrows to increase the army. If it were the enemy, then they all run away for fear of being forced. (page 186).

But that is an exception; the average level is this:

> By this the people were distracted and separated, the nobility murthered, the towns ruined, the country plundered, the United Provinces (now called the States-General) entirely broken off from the King of Spain's government; thousands of the people fled over to England, where they were kindly received, hospitably relieved, courteously entertained, and (which was above all the rest) encouraged to set up their manufactures in the towns and corporations, wherever they pleased; and this increased and completed the manufacturing trade in *England*. (page 189).

The same stylistic difference can be seen between the explanations offered by Mr. Review ("I always was of the opinion that we ought to have kept open our trade with France, (viz.) because we could get by the trade, and that we ought to trade with every nation we can get money by"—see page 165) and those offered by the author of *A Brief Deduction*:

In speaking of the manufactures as declined, we are not speaking of the quantity made, but of the quantity sold; or if you will, we must change the terms, and distinguish betwixt the woollen manufacture as a work of fabricature, and as a trade. There may be as many goods made in *England* as ever, but if there are not as many sold as ever, the trade will be allowed to decline; nay, the more there is made, the more the manufacture is declined if they cannot be sold, because the quantity becomes a grievance to itself. (page 197)

The stylistic difference between these two tracts, both of which are devoted to explaining an economic issue, is chiefly a matter of a higher level of diction, a more balanced syntax typical of written language, and an inconspicuous speaker. Even though *A Brief Deduction* is less dramatic than *Commerce with France,* it makes good reading nevertheless because of certain literary devices. First of all, Defoe unifies his long discussion of the history of English wool manufacture by means of a carefully worked out organic image of birth, maturity, and decline. In addition to thus translating a chronological treatment into literary terms, he conveys a sense of excitement about his economic subject by emphasizing its expansion in spatial terms, all over Europe, Asia, and North Africa, into the colonies, and throughout England from one town to another. Secondly, he entertains his readers with rich bits of background information supplied in the form of digressions about the derivation of English names from foreign names, about the Hanseatic League, about D'Oyly, the London warehouse keeper who "got an estate in one summer's trade" (page 200), and so forth. Lastly, he animates *A Brief Deduction* with the enterprising spirit of modernity itself, the systematic effort to improve upon nature for the purpose of ameliorating man's living conditions (see discussion on pages 7–8 above).

The stylistic difference between *Commerce with France* and *A Brief Deduction* is due less to the development of Defoe's prose between 1713 and 1727 or to the different subject or aim of each tract, than to the difference between the audiences for whom Defoe was writing. Whereas the author of the *Review* was addressing himself to men to his own social class and his inferiors,[12] the author of *A Brief Deduction*, like the writer of the letters to Harley, was addressing himself to men of a superior social class and higher educational level, apparently the oligarchy that consolidated its power during the administration of Robert Walpole.[13]

The interest of *A Brief Deduction* to literary scholars, then, is its demonstration that even at the end of his life, Defoe was master of many prose styles. The style of *Robinson Crusoe* or of *The Complete English Tradesman*, akin to that of Mr. Review, was by no means synonymous with the style of the elusive Defoe himself.

Notes

1 Peter J. Bowden, *The Wool Trade in Tudor and Stuart England* (London, 1962), p. xv.

2 E. Lipson, in his *History of the Woollen and Worsted Industries* (London, 1965), pp. 6–7, goes on to list some examples: "to spin a yarn", "weavers of long tales", "the thread of a discourse", "a web of sophistry", "unravelling a mystery", "tangled skein", "fine-drawn theories", "homespun youths", "web of life", "weave in faith, and God will find thread", "to have tow

on one's distaff", "he goes far to warp and the mill so near", "to have neither reed nor gears, shuttle nor shears", personal names such as Dyer, Fuller, Lister, Tailor, Tucker, Walker, Weaver, and Webster, "spinster" (suggesting the close identification of women with the spinning industry).

3 Charles Wilson describes this version of mercantilism as "balance-of-trade mercantilism modified by considerations of employment", or "social mercantilism". Although the body of mercantilist thought included a doctrine of low wages, writers like Josiah Child and John Cary preceded Defoe in associating "mercantilist principles with the idea of social reform". Charles Wilson, "The Other Face of Mercantilism", in *Revisions in Mercantilism*, ed. D. C. Coleman (London, 1969), pp. 135–136.

4 One of them is Karl D. Bülbring, editor of Defoe's posthumously published *Of Royall Education* (London, 1895). Bülbring, obviously a disciple of William Minto's "Defoe was a liar" school, declares, "I need only say that nobody will expect a very sound historical criticism from the author of the *Journal of the Plague* [*sic*]" (p. xvii). Bülbring's apparent authoritativeness on the matter of Edward III's importance to trade in general, and the wool industry in particular, is due to his reliance upon the works of the economic historian, W. Cunningham. But Cunningham's school was refuted by a series of studies carried out by George Unwin and his students. In his edition, *Finance and Trade under Edward III*, Unwin demonstrated that Edward had no far-sighted economic plans; his export policy was in reality based upon his need to extort money for his interminable wars. The findings of Unwin and his students were substantiated by Eli Heckscher in his monumental work, *Mercantilism*, trans. Mendel Shapiro (London and New York, 1955), II, 80, 96.

5 Edgar S. Furniss, *The Position of the Laborer in a System of Nationalism: A Study in the Labor Theories of the Later English Mercantilists* (Boston and New York, 1920), p. 23.

6 Actually, during that period there were innumerable conflicts among the many groups involved with wool. The wool supply itself changed in character and England was forced to import wool from Spain. Adjustment of production to a different wool supply and a changing market demand entailed painful declines for broad-cloth areas, which had experienced a boom during the first part of the sixteenth century, but were in continual depression thereafter, and rapidly increasing prosperity for worsted production centres. Most serious of all, in view of the mercantilist faith that population growth bred prosperity, unemployment continued to plague the industry. Defoe could hardly have been unaware of these facts, for there was a great deal of contemporary literature on the problems of the wool industry, including literature on the continual conflicts between English merchants and the Hanseatic League, whose trade routes Defoe so carefully traces in *A Brief Deduction.*

7 Defoe was attacking the notion that Sir Walter Raleigh's interest in adventure dated from his being banished from Queen Elizabeth's presence because of his romance with one of her Maids of Honour. He said, "It is evident, his martial genius, his vast conceptions, and his aims at new discoveries, for the glory of his country, the fame of his Mistress (the Queen) and the encouragement of other great minds like his own, were originals, founded in the extensiveness of his parts, and the depth of his learning; and he was full of them when he was but a youth at the university, while he read books only, and not men; and as I have the honour to be related to his blood, I can assure the world, that the discoveries of the great Columbus, the conquests of Ferdinand Cortez, Marq. Del Val, the famous Pizarro, and the other leaders of the Spaniards who aggrandized the name of the Emperor V and his son Philip II Kings of Spain, with making the greatest and most surprising addition to their empire, that ever prince received or subject wrought; I say, I can assure the world by family tradition, that these were the favorite histories that took up his early reading, and that on all occasions were the subject of his ordinary discourses while he was but a young man, and before he could have any views of the great things that afterwards presented." (*A Historical Account of the Voyages and Adventures of Sir Walter Raleigh*, 1719, pp. 8–9)

8 Philip Buck describes the general idea succinctly in his *Politics of Mercantilism* (New York, 1942), pp. 190–191: "Though national strength was the most clearly recognizable purpose, mercantilism cannot be regarded as purely and simply a system of power. It was also a system of welfare. The economic activity of the commonwealth was *mobilized* for international rivalry; but at the same time it was *ordered* and *balanced* for the prosperity, employment, and security of its members and classes of members. The poor were many and their living was scant, but it was imperative that they should have employment, and some of the mercantilists even favoured high wages. The rich were to accept responsibility in their spending, if sumptuary laws could be enforced. The merchant, the manufacturer, the lender, and the landlord were subject to state supervision which ran the whole gamut from standardization of goods to control of prices. Invention and enterprise were encouraged by subsidies, tariffs, and monopolies. The interests of the state fortunately coincided with the welfare of its citizens; the Prince and his subjects were to be a strong and disciplined, united and happy family".

9 Bowden, *Wool Trade*, pp. 212–214.

10 In the course of the eighteenth century "the woollen industry probably increased its output by something like 150 per cent", report Deane and Cole. But they also point out that the rate of growth of export trade was very uneven; the century as a whole witnessed "five fairly distinct periods of alternating growth and decline". Fifteen years of "uncertainty and stagnation" followed the War of the Spanish Succession, and although recovery started about 1730, "it was not until the mid-forties that growth again became rapid". (Defoe's pamphlet was written in 1727, in the midst of a decline in foreign trade.) Phyllis Deane and W. A. Cole, *British Economic Growth 1688–1959, Trends and Structure* (Cambridge, 1969), pp. 61, 47, 48.

11 E. Lipson reports, in his *Economic History of England* (London, 1961), III, 42, that "the effect of the Act of 1700 was to give a stimulus to the native printing of foreign calicoes as well as to the native cotton and linen industries".

12 James Sutherland quotes from several issues of the *Review* to explain Defoe's attitude to his audience: "This paper is writ to enlighten the stupid understandings of the meaner and more thoughtless of the freeholders and electors" (24 May 1705), and "I have hitherto preach'd to my inferiors and equals, men of the same class with my self; I hope I have slip'd into no indecencies, and have studied nothing more than to suit my language to the case, and to the persons" (13 October 1705). *Daniel Defoe, A Critical Study* (Cambridge, Mass.: Harvard University Press, 1971), p. 73.

13 See J. H. Plumb, *The Origins of Political Stability: England 1675–1725* (Boston: Houghton Mifflin Co., 1967), *passim.*

A Brief Deduction of the Original, Progress, and Immense Greatness of the British Woollen Manufacture (1727)

Before I enter into the substance of the question now before me, and that I may make as little preamble as possible in a thing of such importance, it is necessary to lay down in plain and direct terms, so as may admit of no cavils or disputes, what I mean, and how I would be understood by the words, *the manufactures of Great Britain.*

By the manufactures of Great Britain (and of which I suggest, that they are now in a declining and decaying condition) I mean the woollen manufactures, such as broad and narrow cloths, serges, kersies, druggets, bays, sayes,* perpets, stuffs, stockings, hats, flannels, and all those woollen goods generally used for wearing-apparel, furniture of houses, and such-like necessary purposes; and as are made by the labour of our people, for use or sale at home (that is to say, in Great Britain) or for exportation abroad, of whatever kind, and by whatever names; for they bear so great a variety of names (especially the Norwich and Spittlefields goods) that it would be as endless as it is needless to enter into the particulars.

That this manufacture is a thing of great importance, of a vast magnitude, and a value beyond all possible calculation, I suppose I need not spend time to prove; 'tis described in the best manner to be understood, by taking notice, that it not only uses and works up all the wool which grows in England, but a very great quantity both from Spain and Ireland,

* *kersey*: a coarse woollen narrow cloth, usually ribbed. Used for petticoats and stockings. Its narrow dimensions, established by laws of 1465, 1552 and 1618, were what distinguished it from broad-cloth.
drugget: formerly used for clothing, and made either all of wool or of combinations of wool and silk or wool and linen. Now a coarse woollen material used for floor coverings, etc.
say: cloth of fine texture, resembling serge. In the sixteenth century it was made partly of silk, but subsequently, entirely of wool. [Ed.]

Barbary, Turkey, and other places wherever it can be had, and of which I shall have occasion to take notice again in its place.

That this manufacture was once in a flourishing condition, vastly extended abroad, and prodigiously consumed at home; was carried on to the employment and enriching of innumerable multitudes of people, and families of people, 'till it had made England (where its centre is fixed) the most opulent, populous, wealthy, and powerful nation in the world; all this I not acknowledge only, but if it should be disputed, am ready to make appear at large upon all occasions.

It is likewise evident, that this flourishing manufacture has risen from small beginnings, and was at first rescued (as it were) out of captivity in a strange land, where (like Israel in Egypt) it suffered bondage, and was engrossed by foreigners who had no title to it, having none of its principles, no materials for carrying it on *de jure*, in their own right, no, not *de facto*, in their possession; but fetched them from us, and then arbitrarily sold back the goods made of them to us at their own price, enriching their people with the profits of the manufacture, while (Spaniard-like) we starved with the mines of gold in our own keeping.

From this captive state, this miserable abandoned condition, it was rescued, by the policy and wisdom of our government, and the impolitick and foolish management of the Spaniards, who by their religious tyranny, and their civil fury, drove their own people over to us to seek bread and liberty, in return for which they gave us wealth and trade, taught our women to spin, and our men to weave; ever since this we have made the manufacture our own, and are now able to teach our teachers, having infinitely improved the kinds, as well as increased the quantity; have made not only innumerable new-invented sorts, but have also made those sorts or kinds of goods much better than ever the Flemings were able to make them before, especially the broad cloths, which are improved to such a degree, and brought to such perfection, as they were never capable of before, or so much as to believe possible.

That by this very article, England, though not an inch of land larger, either in length or breadth, the soil not an ounce richer than it was capable of being made before, the climate not one degree warmer, and without any one advantage of nature, more than it had before; yet by a moderate, and I believe a just and reasonable calculation, between the year

1490, in the beginning of King Henry VII, when we began to manufacture our own wool, and the year 1726, has increased her people from under two millions, to above seven millions, raised the value of lands so, that what was then worth 50 l. per annum, is now worth 1000 l. per annum, as may be seen by the rate of subsidies, and by other rules of calculation, and which has raised the value of personal wealth to such a degree, as admits no comparison, no calculation, and hardly any imagination; insomuch that some are of opinion that taking the wealth of this nation at the medium of time, between the Conquest and the reign of Queen Elizabeth, that is to say, about the reign of Edward II, and excepting only the wealth of churches and monasteries, which indeed was great, there is now more silver in England than there was then block tin, more gold than they had copper, and more diamonds and pearl than they had Bristol-stones.

This increase of people, and of the real and personal wealth of England, may be said to be all owing to the woollen manufacture; and to bring it all to the point, viz. that this woollen manufacture has gone on increasing ever since, even to this time, or (as I may more properly say) to *our* time, 'till its magnitude is such that we may say it is too great, and that not too great for the country only, but too great for the whole world.

It is a strange advance made in this argument, and at the beginning of it too, to say the manufacture of England is too great for the world; but I cannot go back from it; and upon a serious reflexion on its real magnitude, as it now is; and yet how much greater it is possible to make it, that is to say, how many countries, and, as I may say, millions of people are yet unconcerned in it, and unemployed by it, I do insist, that were the wool of Great Britain and Ireland kept entirely at home, the quantity increased as it might be, and all that quantity manufactured at home, as it also might be, if those other countries were set to work, the people of Great Britain and Ireland are able to make more woollen manufactures than all the known inhabitants of the world would wear. To such a perfection of working are the people arrived; to such an immense quantity is the wool brought to amount; to such a prodigious number are the people multiplied; and the last article indeed is the most essential of all the rest, for notwithstanding the increase of the wool, which is a prodigy in itself, yet to such a degree are the people also increased, that all the wool of England, however (as I say) increased, and all the wool of Ireland, from whence no wool was had in those days, and all the wool of Scotland, which was not used at all in England in those times, is now manufactured in England, by less than one quarter part of our people.

* * *

As I have observed in the introduction that the woollen manufacture was (like the Children of Israel) rescued from a state of captivity, and from a strange land, we must make that out a little plainer. The case was thus:

In the reign of Edward III of glorious fame, though England was thought to be at that time in the most flourishing condition that history gives us any account of: the glory of her arms, the vigour of her monarch, and of his eldest son, the gaiety and splendour of the Court were such as never were known before; the last was the resort of all the nobility, youth and gentry of Europe; the second was the admiration and wonder of the world; the greatest princes made their court to them, and kings were captives in their possession. England was the terror of the world; the battles of Cressy and Poictiers, and the re-instating the King of Spain, deposed by his rival, were actions that brought all the powers of Europe to stand at gaze, and as it were to dread the turning of the arms of England so much as towards their dominions. History will confirm all the particulars; I have no room for long quotations:

Yet all this while trade shared no advantages among the conquests of the day; nor do we find the least concern in any of the councils of that glorious prince, or of his ministers of state, for the propagation of commerce, at home or abroad.

Building publick and sumptuous edifices, great churches and monasteries; making feasts, balls, tournaments; adorning Windsor Castle; instituting the famous Order of Knighthood; making leagues and alliances; expensive interviews with foreign princes, such as the Emperor and the Duke of Burgundy, and keeping a magnificent English court at Cologne, for almost a year and a half at a time: these things took up the Court, and turned the eyes (I had almost said turned the heads) of the nation during that whole reign. Things which tended to the glory of the kingdom, and the honour of the majesty of the King, as Nebuchadnezzar said of his great Babel that he had built; but, as we may add, these glorious things gutted England of its wealth, made the monarch powerful and his people poor.

In all his parliaments we see not one Act for the encouragement of trade, for the enlarging commerce, for employment of the poor, for setting up manufactures; to speak the truth, I question if the word manufacture or manufacturer were known in the country; and, for aught I see, as the taylors were the only merchants, so the shoemakers were the greatest manufacturers in the kingdom.

The bountiful hand of heaven had then, and from the beginning, given England the greatest gift of nature that the whole world could be said to enjoy, viz. the wool. The diligent and sensible nations round us understood it, and how to value it; and, which was more, understood how to improve it; and for that end, thronged to the very outmost bounds of the continent of Europe (this way) to be near it, and that they might bring it over as cheap as possible.

By this I mean the Netherlands, where the industrious people, by the help of the wool from England, fell to work in such a manner as that there they made then, as we have since done in England, cloths for all the known parts of the world.

This brought the many thousands and millions of people to inhabit those drowned, overflowed bogs and marshes, which before that were scarce thought fit for human creatures to dwell in, and which were dwelt in only as retreats and fastnesses to secure the fugitive nations from the incursions of the Gauls, and afterwards of the Romans.

This very trade brought people, and built cities and castles, even where the sea allowed no footing, and the land no foundation; from hence, I say, the numberless throngs of people came to dwell in that country, and by degrees, by the increase of their wealth, and by their indefatigable industry (all the effects of trade and manufacture) have brought it to be the richest soil, the fullest of people and of great cities and towns, of any country in the world.

All this while England lay neglected to the last degree; her sons knocking their heads against stone walls, and ranging the field of war in foreign countries, pursued their own poverty, and sought misery, for the glory of their monarch.

But at home it was all a miscellany of sorrow: villainage and vassalage comprised the poor; knighthood and esquireship took up the middle gentry; and glory dwelt only among the barons and princes.

All the trade we read of, was carrying their wool abroad, to give employment to the poor of foreign countries, viz. the Dutch and the Flemings; and this wool, we may say, was the grand fund of the wealth, both of king and people.

If the King made any wars, and demanded subsidies of his Parliament, as was too frequently the case in the time of Edward III, the grand article of *ways and means* was to grant the King ten shillings a pack upon wool, or twenty shillings a pack upon wool, like our two shillings and four shillings per pound upon land; and once they came to such a height, (God forbid we should see the like of our lands) that the Parliament gave the King one half part of all the wool itself for his wars in France; by the same token that (as King Charles II did too often) all the money was spent, and no war with France begun neither; nor did the war break out 'till three years after; so that when it came, they were fain to give the King new subsidies again; that is to say, another tax upon the exportation of wool, and so over and over again several times.

In this state of indolence, or rather horrid ignorance and blindness, was this whole nation, as it were, philtred and bewitched, notwithstanding all the glory, the wisdom, the policy and good government which King Edward III was so famed for.

Like people buried alive in sloth and idleness they sat still, ploughed and sowed as much corn as served just to feed them, sheered their sheep every year, and, as it may be said, threw away their wool; went to the wars, were knocked on the head for the honour of Old England, and the glory of their great kings; and this was the round of life, even from the nobleman to the meanest vassal, peasant or labourer in the nation.

As to the poor women and children, they sat at home, fared hard, lived poor and idle: the women drudged at the husbandry, and the children sat still, blowed their fingers, picked straws; and both might be said not to live, but to starve out a wretched time, then die, and go, *where*——who knows!

As to manufacture or employment, we do not see room so much as to believe that they knew anything of it; any farther than it may be to make some very ordinary things which nature and necessity put them upon for their own covering, and hardly that.

In this miserable condition lay the ancestry of this diligent nation; who being but once let into the method of working the wool, and some authority supporting as well as encouraging them by stopping the stream of its exportation, soon tasted the sweets of it, soon fell heartily upon it, presently became masters of the performance, and in time supplanted the encroachers; engrossed the wool, for it was their own before; redeemed the captives, and at last brought not only the manufactures, but the manufacturers too, over to England; for thousands of the people followed the manufacture for bread, and that they might get employment; and this began the multiplying of the people too, as well as of their wealth; for as trade brings wealth, so work brings the workmen together.

It is just thus still in England: wherever we see the manufactures seated, there we see multitudes of people collected; the labour gathers the hands. And this was the first occasion of making those strict exclusive laws for parish settlements, that the particular parishes where such manufactures were set up might not be oppressed with the numbers of poor flocking in from other parishes.

* * *

But to go back to the introduction of this change: it was in the reign of King Henry VII, and not before, when the English began the bold adventure of manufacturing their own wool, (I mean began it in quantity.) There had some attempt been made before, and we are told of some adventurers in trade who, having been over in Flanders and learned the manner of it, but especially having seen the advantage of it, had brought over with them so much knowledge as to learn the people to spin (so many of them at least as their stocks could compass to employ), and others to comb and card the wool, and so on, through all the other parts of the work; which went a little way, and was promising to go farther in time.

But it is to be observed, that from the first part of the reign of Henry VI, and through all that long reign, and through the reign of Edward IV, and Richard III, the whole nation was miserably embroiled in the civil confusions, such as the wars between the White Rose and the Red; the Houses of Lancaster and York; and the several insurrections and revolutions of affairs which naturally attended those quarrels.

Everyone knows that war is no friend to trade. Arts and improvements, much less manufacture, and the employment of the poor, never plant, or at least never thrive, in the flame and heat of war, especially to the worst of the kind, an intestine, civil, or to speak justly of it, an unnatural war.

Times of feud and faction, rebellion, insurrection, killing and plundering are no times for improvement; and this may be a just reason why the beginnings of the manufacture, which I have mentioned as above, took no considerable root during the confusions of war, both civil and foreign wars, but especially civil wars, which for sixty years almost without intermission vexed this nation.

Perhaps a manufacturer did, or suppose he had seated himself at any particular town or place in the country, had brought together some people, and had instructed them in the work, viz. some women to spin, some men to comb, to weave, to dress the cloth, and had built a fulling mill to thicken the cloths, and the like. Then come the two armies into the field, and they march over the country where the poor manufacturer is settled. If it be a friendly army, and they are of the same side, then the kindest thing that could be expected was to call all the poor workmen away, especially the young able-bodied fellows, with their bows and arrows to increase the army. If it were the enemy, then they all run away for fear of being forced. As for the women and children, they are nobody without the men, for they cannot spin the wool 'till the men comb it, and when they have spun the yarn, 'tis of no use when the men are gone that should weave it; and perhaps the loom which it should be wrought in, burnt by the plunderings and ravagings of the soldiers.

By this means (and I cannot doubt but this was often the case) the beginning of the manufacture was checked and put back, the poor undertaker ruined and undone; and so you heard no more of the attempt for some years.

This is as good an account as I believe can be given why the woollen manufacture began among us no sooner; why it had no encouragement in England, at least no considerable encouragement, 'till the time of King Henry VII, and about the year 1480 to 1490.

* * *

It was some time after these private persons undertook the manufacturing of wool that King Henry, finding his subjects begin to improve, and that the goods they made were able to supply the ordinary demand, or near it, caused the exportation of wool to be prohibited, and foreign-made manufactures also to be excluded, encouraging his people thereby to make larger quantities of those goods at home.

Nor did there need any greater encouragement to the manufacture, than thus shutting out the foreign manufactures; for this increasing the demand at home, the price increased of course, which sufficiently rewarded the labours of the workmen, and increased their wages.

I need not bring any vouchers to prove that this increase of wages improved the manufacture, or increased the number of the workmen; for now, not only the English fell into the trade with courage, and with multitudes, but (as above) multitudes followed the manufacture out of Flanders, encouraged by the gain, and wanting employment at home.

Nor were these of the labouring poor only, but abundance of the master manufacturers, and of those the most skilful in the workmanship; by whom the people here were soon instructed and perfected in the knowledge, not of the art only in general, such as in the sorting, combing, carding, and otherwise managing the wool, in spinning, weaving, knitting, &c., but also in the several kinds of goods fitted for the markets, and demanded as well abroad as at home.

Thus the English secured the trade to themselves, and became first masters of the woollen manufacture; and the very Flemings themselves, who had for so many ages eat the bread out of their mouths, were now their assistants and intructors, in completing them in the knowledge of dressing, sheering, perfecting and finishing the working part; thousands of the said Flemings, and their families, coming over hither for work, and settling among them, and whose posterity became English, immediately after them, scarcely reserving their foreign names, or changing them, to conceal their original.

For it is to be observed, that it was not so easy a matter for foreigners to be naturalized among the English in those times, as it is now, which made those that found means to settle here, and turn their hands to the manufacture, take what care they could to conceal themselves, and so to change their sir-names, or at least shorten and abridge them into differing sounds, that they might be made to speak English as much as possible, that is to say, to sound like English. For example, Jean de Somieres would be called John Sommers; Guillaume de Tournay, William Turner; Estienne D'Anvers, Stephen Danvers; Jaques de Franquemont, James Franks; and so of the rest; by which all the Flemish, Dutch and Walloon names were presently turned into English. And thus of those who had two or three Christian names (as is common among foreigners) they turned the second Christian name into a sir-name, and from thence 'tis said we have so many families of such sir-names among us to this day; for example, Jean

Jaques de Buromeir, leaving out the sir-name, was called John James; Guillaume Jacob Van Platten, William Jacobs; Guillaume Henry de Villangen, William Henry; and many more of this kind, as we find the French refugees of the last age are doing at this very time; Jean de Morlaix is now John Morley; and but the other day, Jaques de Guilote called himself James Gill, and the like is done every day, so that the families are no more known to be foreign. But this is a digression.

We find very little upon record, relating to the wool being carried into Flanders after this; or of the Flemings making broadcloth and stuffs, nor indeed are our laws much concerned about those affairs, except that King Henry VII towards the end of his reign, had some laws made to regulate the lengths and breadths of the cloths made here, in order to bring the clothiers into a regularity of working, and that the several sorts of goods should be all alike, equal to one another, and as near as possible of an equal goodness and value; so to establish the price of every kind at market, and prevent frauds.

Hence came the fixing of marks and seals to the cloths; at first, every maker striving to add a reputation to his own manufacture, and pretending it to be superiour in its fineness or goodness, to his neighbours, set his mark at the end, wrought into the cloth, in some different colour, or (as after some time was practised) leaden seals, with the maker's name, and the weight of the cloth stamped upon them; and hence after some time the several towns and corporations, denominating the manufacture from the place, obtained privileges and immunities, powers and authority to regulate the length and breadth and goodness of the several manufactures made in those towns respectively, stamping the leaden seals with the town marks or arms, as at Colchester, at Norwich, at Leeds, and several other places.

* * *

Thus you see the infant state of the woollen manufacture; from what rational measures it received its first encouragement in England, and how gradually it came on; for we must also observe, that as it was a thing of vast magnitude, as well as of the utmost importance to this nation, so it was not easily, much less suddenly, brought to perfection; the stream or channel of so great a commerce was not soon changed, though our people came into it with chearfulness, and made wonderful progress for the time; yet this Rome was not built in a day, it was many years, nay ages, before it came to perfection.

The first beginnings of it I take to have been in the reign of Edward IV, that is to say, of its being attempted by private hands. The first publick countenance it received, was at nearest about the year 1480, in the time of Henry VII, and it was from thence to the year 1560, (viz.) under Queen Elizabeth, before it came to its perfection; so that it was above an hundred and twenty years, as we may call it, in its state of nonage, though all the while increasing and growing, and in a promising view of a prosperous magnitude, the same which we have since seen it arrive to.

It had indeed a most glorious patron (or patroness) and protector in Queen Elizabeth; who not only promoted and encouraged it at home, but also extended the trade for the consumption of it abroad; for in her time, the several branches of the English commerce were extended into almost all parts of the known world; the Turkey trade, and the Muscovy trade established; the colonies in America discovered and planted, by all which the woollen manufacture obtained a vent in foreign markets, and those great branches of its consumption, which have since been so large, and are still the most considerable, were first established in her time, particularly (I say) that of Turkey and Muscovy.

But nothing contributed so effectually to the prosperity of the woollen manufacture in this nation, and which may be said (under the wise conduct of that glorious Queen) to complete the whole fabrick, giving the mortal stroke to, unhinging the whole trade in, and shutting it forever out from, the Low-Countries, as the long and bloody war between the King of Spain and his subjects in those countries, on account of the liberties and religion of the people.

By this the people were distracted and separated, the nobility murthered, the towns ruined, the country plundered, the United Provinces (now called the States-General) entirely broken off from the King of Spain's government; thousands of the people fled over to England, where they were kindly received, hospitably relieved, courteously entertained, and (which was above all the rest) encouraged to set up their manufactures in the towns and corporations, wherever they pleased; and this increased and completed the manufacturing trade in England. And thus we have brought it within view (at least) of its present state.

CHAPTER II

Of the flourishing circumstances of the English manufactures in the ages past, both abroad and at home; with a summary account of its gradations.

It was not to be reckoned a small part of the increase of the woollen manufacture in England (considering its original was from abroad), that it was made capable of supplying the demands of the home trade, and was considerable enough to clothe its own people. Nor was it under above an hundred years' improvement from its beginning, that this could be attained to, as is noted above.

The manufacturers abroad not only out-worked us, but under-worked us; they made their goods both better and cheaper; the English had great advantages, but no experience, so that still some of the nicer and better manufactures were made in Flanders and Holland, nor was there any avoiding it at first.

But when the Flemings (persecuted and terrified by the cruelty and persecution of the Duke d'Alva) fled over hither, and Queen Elizabeth gave them protection and encouragement here, the English then became absolute masters of the manufactures, and from thence we may date the perfection of their skill; then all foreign importation might be said to cease, and the carrying abroad of the wool was made criminal.

But let us see how its consumption went on.

1 At home, the whole country was clothed, poor and rich; nothing so fine, but it was to be had in Gloucestershire and Wiltshire, Worcestershire and Berkshire. Jack of Newbury was a clothier superior to any that are to be found among us at this time, by many thousands, as money went then; and Mr. Kenrick's will, of St. Christopher's (who was originally a clothier, and then a cloth merchant, dealing to Dort) testifies how considerable the trade was by that time (viz. King James I) when he left above 40,000 l. in gifts and charities, besides the bulk of his estate.

2 But let us also take a view of its increase abroad, from Queen Elizabeth's time, besides its being able fully to supply all the people at home.

1 That Queen established a flourishing company, called the Levant Merchants (the same we now call the Turkey Company), by which she extended the trade of the English, for their fine broad-cloths, into the several courts of Persia, Turkey and Egypt; for either the Queen or the Turkey Company (I am not sure which) making some presents to the Grand Seignior of fine English cloth, of such exquisite workmanship for the fineness of the cloth, and of such beautiful colours, being dyed scarlet and crimson, the said Grand Seignior, and the Grand Vizier, caused fine robes or gowns to be made of the said cloths; and also fine vests, after their manner, which being furred with sables and rich furs, presented them much about the same time from the Great Duke (so the Russian Emperor was then called) of Muscovy, made a most magnificent appearance; the Grand Seignior and his courtiers were so pleased with them, that they soon became the mode or wear of all the great officers, and of the Grand Seignior himself, and so again of the viziers or viceroys of their remotest provinces, and the same at the court of Persia.

Thus in a few years the fine English cloth became the robes of majesty, and (as it were) the badge of greatness and glory, at Constantinople, and at Ispahan, at Alexandria in Egypt, and at Aleppo in Asia, and everywhere else among the Mahometans, where they had money sufficient to purchase them; and thus it continues to this day, which is still more strange than all the rest.

2 The same Levant Company included the trade to Alexandria in the mouth of the great River Nile, by which all the country of Egypt was supplied; and not only the great court of the Vizier of Grand Cairo (who, though a subject or slave of the Grand Seignior, yet keeps a court almost as great and as magnificent as the Emperor his master), but also the same cloths were convoyed to Suez, a seaport of the Turks in the Red Sea, and thence by water to Judde, or Ieddo, the seaport to the city of Medina, the great center of the Mahometan superstition, where the riches and magnificence of their priests is not to be described; and where they are still clothed in the same manner, especially on their days of ceremony.

3 The same Levant Company extended the trade for English cloth to the city of Venice, at the bottom of the Adriatick Gulph, where they drove a very great and advantagious trade; for I suppose that the trade of Smyrna and Scanderoon, and

the caravans by Aleppo to Persia, were not at that time found out by the English, but were carried on (if at all) by the merchants of Venice; who at that time engrossed indeed all the commerce of the East, imported the spices and all the rich goods of the Indies, by the Gulph of Persia, and by the caravans of Bassora and Bagdat to Aleppo, and sent back by the same conveyance such European goods as those countries demanded; among which the fine broad-cloths of England, soon after that time, began to be the most acceptable, and were indeed of the greatest value of anything of that kind in the world.

4 Likewise in this Queen's reign, the passage to Arch-Angel, or the White Sea, being discovered, the English merchants found means to carry on a trade from that port, by water-carriage, to the great city of Muscow, a little way excepted, where their goods were carried by land about sixty miles only.

Here they also found a market for their rich cloths, in the Great Duke's court; and upon this a new society for commerce was erected, and were called the Muscovy Company; who brought back a very gainful return in sables, ermins and other rich furs, the produce of the wild and barren deserts of Siberia and the North.

N.B. These Muscovy merchants found the way, some time after this, to pass by the great River Wolga, to Astracan, and thence into the Caspian Sea, an inland navigation (reckoning from Jerowslaw, where they first embarked their goods) of very near 2,000 miles on one river, viz. the Wolga; hence (unwearied in their search after new worlds of trade) they passed the Caspian, landed in Georgia, passed over the mountains of Armenia, and reached into the heart of the Kingdom of Persia, where they found an extraordinary reception, sold their fine cloths at an extravagant price, such as was even surprising to themselves; and brought back bales of raw silk to a very great advantage also; so that notwithstanding the extraordinary charges of so exceeding long a travel, they made a very profitable voyage.

These two new trades gave a very great encouragement to the English merchants, and particularly to the manufacture of English cloth, which now obtained such a reputation over the whole trading world, that nothing was equally valuable in any, or perhaps in all the courts of Europe and Asia.

5 In the latter end of this Queen's reign, the same manufactures were demanded in an exceeding manner in the

Northern parts of the Empire, and the countries bordering on the Baltick; and this trade naturally fell into the hands of the *Hans*, that is to say, the society of merchants who called themselves the Hans, a word signifying a brotherhood, or an united company; and because there were so many (for there was once no less than seventy-two cities of them), they were called the Hans Towns; these carried on the trade of the North, as the Venetians did that of the South and East, mentioned above.

By these towns the English manufacture was indeed wonderfully extended, that is to say, into all the countries in the Baltick, the Kingdoms of Denmark and Norway, the coasts of Mecklemberg, both the Pomerens, Prussia, Courland, Livonia, Easthonia, &c. and up the great rivers of those countries, into the very heart of the Empire, and of all the Northern countries.

* * *

In this flourishing condition Queen Elizabeth left the woollen manufacture of England; being at that time not the greatest manufacture in Europe only (for so it may be called still, though sinking and declining apace), but the most increasing, thriving and rising trade (at that time) in the world.

As the woollen manufacture had thus been about an hundred and fifty years in its growing and increasing condition, like a young oak in the woods; so now being grown major, or as we say *of age*, and out of its nonage, we may allow it to have continued above another century in its flourishing and prosperous state; that is to say, it held its own, and continued in its full glory, extended to an infinite length and breadth, triumphing over the whole world of commerce, not rivalled, not imitated, I will not say not envied, but really not rivalled by any people or in any country in the world; no, not so much as pretended to be rivalled anywhere. And this last hundred years which I reckon to be the state of its full glory and perfection, I take to be from the middle of Queen Elizabeth's reign to the end of the reign of King Charles II, that is to say, near the end of it, viz. from the year 1580, twenty years before Queen Elizabeth died, to the year 1680, being the latter end of the reign of King Charles II.

During this time the manufactures were so far from receiving any blow, any mortal wound or sensible disaster, either from abroad or at home, that the several circumstances relating to the vent and consumption of them concurred to enlarge them and render their condition yet more flourishing and prosperous, if that could be, than they were before. For example,

First, during that interval of time, many flourishing and now famous colonies of English had been settled in America, and in other remote parts of the world; the discoveries of the indefatigable adventurers of that age, such as Sir Francis Drake, Sir Walter Raleigh, the famous Earl of Cumberland, Captain Smith and others, too many to name, by whom the commerce of the English was extended in a prodigious manner, and their dominions also; as in the following countries in particular:

1.	Virginia	1.	Barbadoes
2.	New England	2.	Bermudas
3.	Newfoundland	3.	Nevis
4.	Hudson's-Bay	4.	Antegoa
5.	New-York	5.	Montserrat
6.	New-Jersey	6.	St. Christopher's
7.	Pensilvania	7.	Jamaica, &c.
8.	Carolina		

In all these, the succeeding generations have so improved, the plantations have been so spread, so well managed, and the numbers of people are so surprisingly increased, that whereas in the beginning of King James's reign it is creditably affirmed there were not five thousand people in all of them, Negroes excepted, and not abundance of them, 'tis now as creditably insisted upon, that there are not less then a million of British subjects, slaves included; which monstrous increase is not only an addition to the greatness and glory of the British dominion and to their commerce, by the immense return of their product to England, such as from the continent in tobacco, rice, pitch, tar, turpentine, train-oil, fish, whale-fins, furs, drugs, &c., and to the other colonies on the islands in corn, meal, peas, pork, beer, horses, &c., and from the islands to England in sugar, rum, molasses, ginger, cotton, indico, pimento, cocoa, and many other valuable things; I say, this increase of people is not only an increase of commerce, in the returns above-named, but it adds to the consumption of the British manufactures in an extraordinary manner; not only all that million of people being to be clothed from hence, but that they have in all places upon the said continent taught the natives of the country to go clothed also; and who are supplied with manufactures from England; all which is a meer addition to the trade, as well as to the navigation of England, since the time above-named; nothing of those countries being then known, much less any trade to them.

* * *

Hitherto then we have seen the bright side of the subject, and have brought the manufacture to its meridian height. It is only to be observed as an addition to what has been said, that as the consumption of the manufacture increased abroad, so the quantity made increased at home. The manufactures increasing, the manufacturers increased also; the trade spread at home in proportion as it spread abroad; and that which was at first the work of a few counties and cities, became now the employment of whole provinces or divisions of the country, being a kind of district consisting of several counties or parts of counties together.

Thus the manufacture, first erected at Norwich, spread in a little after the said time over the whole counties of Norfolk and Suffolk, as the bay trade of Colchester, first confined to that town and the adjacent country, is now extended through the whole county, one of the largest and most populous in England. The clothing trade erected first at the towns of Oakingham, Reading, Newbery and Andover, in the counties of Wiltshire and Berkshire, is now spread farther into Wiltshire and Somersetshire, extending along a vast tract of ground from the edge of Gloucestershire to the side of Dorsetshire, for near an hundred miles, through the richest and most fruitful vale in all the west part of England, called the Vale of White-Horse, and including the populous towns of Malmsbury, Tedbury, Cirencester, Stroud, Marshfield, Caln, Chipenham, Devizes, Bradford, Trowbridge, Froom, Warminster, Westbury, and many more, with innumerable populous villages.

The like in the clothing of Worcestershire, extended into the counties of Salop, Hereford, Gloucester, and the counties adjacent.

Thus, I say, the manufacture flourishing abroad, spread in proportion at home, till at length it arrived to the magnitude which we see it in at this time, when its body is said to be too big for its legs; and the multitudes employed in it are such, that at the same time that the markets are decayed abroad, the extent of it not being limited at home, the laws of proportion have been broken; and though the sale has been lessened, the people have still gone on making, till according to some the quantity has been superior to what the whole world could, or at least in the ordinary course of trade would consume. And this brings us to the present state of the manufacture, as it stands abroad just now with respect to the sale, and as it stands at home with respect to the production, by which it will be easily seen, whether the manufacture as a trade or as a business is in a thriving or a declining condition.

* * *

That Great Britain grew immensely rich in those ages of trade is not to be denied, or indeed disputed; we might give a long account of the increase of her wealth and riches, her greatness and glory, and how it was all raised by, and the effect of, her increased commerce; but it is too long for a tract of this nature, it will be seen in its consequences, and in nothing more than in the prodigious efferts made by the whole nation, in the late double war, from the Revolution to the Peace of Utrecht; in which, let but the immense sums of money which were raised upon trade only be taken account of, and they will give us a fair sketch of the improvement itself.

Nay, let the vast sums raised annually, to this day, by the customs upon trade, speak something of the increase of it since those days. I need not enter into the detail of those productions, such as the duties on wines, tobacco, brandies; East-India, and Italian, and Turkey importations; the excises on beer, ale, malt, spirits, coffee, tea, &c., which at this time raise such sums as no nation in the world can show the like of, and as this nation never came up to before.

I shall close the abstract of it with this short return of the late King Lewis XIV, to the account of the last year's state of the war in England; when he saw the establishment of the South-Sea Company, and the provision made by the Parliament for the old, unprovided-for debts, and for the service of the growing year, both which amounted to near eleven millions sterling, a sum so frightful, put into French money, that the King upon sight of it spread out his hands, and said, "I see 'tis time to put an end to the war! I never believed that England could have made such efforts as these; let us make peace upon the best terms we can."

* * *

But I need not enlarge upon these things; for were the increase of these foreign consumptions much greater than it is, and were the places, where that increase has been, five times larger than they are, the declining state of the manufacture would still be made out, from other opposite circumstances, too evident to be denied, and too strong to be balanced by those advances.

First, the unreasonable increase of the quantity made is to be considered, the growing condition of the manufacture itself, in which we may venture to say there are some circumstances that not only will not be equalled by any addition of commerce either abroad or at home; but, to speak boldly to it, would not be equalled, if all the nations to whom our manufacture is exported, were to increase the consumption of it in proportion to that of Portugal or Leghorn, as above.

It is evident our manufacture is increased to a degree almost inexplicable, insomuch that it is in itself too great for the consumption of all Europe. Now it seems a little of a paradox that I should bring the increase of the quantity as an argument to prove the declining of the manufacture that is increased. But a little reflection will set that part to rights in your thoughts, and the difficulty will immediately vanish.

In speaking of the manufactures as declined, we are not speaking of the quantity made, but of the quantity sold; or if you will, we must change the terms, and distinguish betwixt the woollen manufacture as a work or fabricature, and as a trade. There may be as many goods made in England as ever, but if there are not as many sold as ever, the trade will be allowed to decline; nay, the more there is made, the more the manufacture is declined if they cannot be sold, because the quantity becomes a grievance to itself.

If it be apparent that the quantity made increases faster than the quantity sold off, or that there is more made than can be sold, the manufacture is under evident discouragement. On the other hand, if there are more made and less sold, that discouragement increases to a distraction; the manufacture languishes, and is in a kind of dropsy, where the repletion exceeding the evacuation, the body swells in bulk, but declines in strength, and dies of the worst kind of consumption.

There is no question but that upon the apparent increase of the manufactures in England, during those many years mentioned in particular as above, the great advantage made by that trade, and the vast estates acquired even by the manufacturers themselves in their ordinary business, encouraged others to fall into it, and even encouraged those that were in it to enlarge their business, to launch out as their stocks increased, farther and farther, into that trade.

This humour continues to this day, and is now become the great grievance of the manufacture in general; and will, if not timely prevented, be ruinous to the trade in the end, as I shall make appear in its place.

While the manufacture was in its full extent abroad, while it was the mistress of the world in trade, had no rivals, and no attempts were made to mimick it, or imitate it, but that it had an uninterrupted sale abroad; the increase of the quantity at home was far from being a grievance, either to the country or to the trade; and during the happy years of its thus currently going off, vast additions to the quantity were made at home, such as, if you will give credit to some people, would in a few years have glutted the whole world with our goods, though there had been no check given to the vent of it abroad.

I could give a long history of the increase of the manufacture in England, I mean as a work or fabrick; even whole towns, nay, parts of counties, have, within the memory of some still alive, been employed in it, who were never employed before.

I could likewise enter into the detail of the changes and turns which the manufacture itself has suffered by changing the kinds, as particularly the changing the clothing or cloth-making into the making narrow and lighter kinds of cloth, such as we call druggets and kersies, instead of broad-cloth, in the western parts of England, such as the counties of Wilts, Berks and Devon; and sagathies and duroys,* a thin and light sort of stuff, instead of thick cloth-serges, at Taunton in Somersetshire, and other parts adjoining; by which exchange of kinds, it is the opinion of many men of judgment, the English manufacture in general has suffered extremely, and a door opened to the attempts of foreigners, who encroached upon us by those imitations and delusions, but were not able to come up to us in the essential part of the manufacture, (viz.) the clothing part. The case was thus:

The French were the first who, as I have said, set up to rival our manufactures, and having gotten workmen as well

* *sagathies*: woollen fabrics of good quality, like serges.
duroys: coarse woollen fabrics manufactured in the west of England. [Ed.]

materials from England, they set up a clothing manufacture as well at Rouen and Caen and other places in Normandy, as at Nismes and the adjacent cities in Languedoc and Provence.

But the French (according to the known superficial humour of the nation) contenting themselves with keeping up to the standard of broad-cloth in Languedoc only, because they were obliged to follow the pattern of the English there, for the Turkey trade; in other places made it light, loose and spongy, thinner in substance, and slighter in workmanship; and this not being able to carry the breadth of the broad-cloth, they altered to the usual stuff breadth of half ell, or half yard, as their ordinary stuffs were made.

These they called cloths at first; but seeing they would not keep up the credit of that name, as the English cloth did, they gave them several names from the towns or counties where they were made, such as *drap de Normandy*, *drap de Berry*, *drap de Lorrain*, and so of the rest.

Had we let the French go on their own way, and kept up at home to the old English manufacture of broad-cloth, the French to this day had been distanced in their new attempt; but with a weakness never to be defended, while they with difficulty followed us, we faced about, and simply followed them.

They brought their silk stuffs, and Spanish druggets, and light, thin French serges, into wear, and into fashion; and they were in the right, because they could make no better. We, to ape them in their mode, fall into the same sorts of stuffs, and so made that, which was their necessity, be our mischief.

By this means, not only we wore their sorry slight manufactures and even brought them privately from France itself, but (fond of our own mischiefs) we quit the broad-cloth, the ancient glory of England (as to manufacture), and fall into the making of light stuffs for men's wear, to the ruin of our own manufactures, as much as in us lay; for these new foolish things neither employed an equal number of hands, or consumed an equal quantity of the wool, in both which they accomodated the French, who neither had at first a number of skilful workmen to make them, or a quantity of wool to make them with; but in both we weakened our own country, for this at once caused the wool to lie on hand unwrought, and thousands of poor to go unemployed.

The great promoter of this debauchery in trade (for such it might be called) was one D'Oyly, a warehouse-keeper in

London, who, valuing himself upon that for which he ought (according to the laws of Persia) to have his name be made infamous, and his house be made a dunghill, boasted of his merit, and called his new French mimickry of a manufacture, Doyly's stuffs, and such was the vanity of the day, that we saw the whole town, nay, we might say the whole nation, run into them, and the ancient manufacture of broad-cloth lay by the walls; the substantial woollen-drapers had nothing to do, no trade at their shops; and the new stuff-merchant D'Oyly had his great warehouse near Exeter-Exchange in the Strand thronged with buyers from morning to night, and the man got an estate in one summer's trade.

It is true, God, and a hard winter, should have the thanks of the poor manufacturers, while they live; the severity of the great frost (falling in immediately upon it) brought the good warm clothing trade into mode again, and set the poor at work in some tolerable degree, so at least as to relieve them for that time.

But this unhappy humour revived so far, as brought our manufacturers into the way of making a middle kind, between cloth and stuff, so as on one side to suit the climate, and yet (as near as might be) on the other, to follow the French folly also, and this introduced the making druggets, sagathies, chamlets,* duroys, and the several kinds of men's stuffs, with which we have (as it were) made war with our own manufacture, and jostled the broad-cloth as much as we could out of the world; so that in short, if those light things which the French made, because they could make no better, did not become the universal mode of our country, and the better and more important clothing, on which the whole nation depended, go quite out of use, it was none of our fault.

The truth is, though the first madness wore off, and the D'Oyly stuffs in a little time did sicken and glut the town, yet this is certain, that the wearing of drugget and stuffs, chamlets and duroys, and such-like slight things, was a terrible blow to the ancient clothing manufacture; to this day it has not recovered it, and perhaps never will.

Thus far the manufacture declined by our own folly. It is true indeed that these slight thin stuffs, though they did not consume so much wool, or employ so many hands as the clothing, yet, as they sent the people oftener to market, the quantity made seemed to be some amends to the

* *chamlets*: obsolete form of camlet, meaning any cloth marked or variegated with wavy veins. [Ed.]

manufacture, and to the poor. But then they opened a door to the French to sell their slight, half-made goods at foreign markets; for the fashion also took root, whereas (if the manufacture of broad-cloth had been kept up) the French would never have been able to have hurt us, at home or abroad.

But this is not all; I shall give you a farther account of the declining of the manufacture in its sale abroad, and of the reasons of it in particular, more ruinous than this. But here I must take notice too, as I have said above, how the making increased, whether the sale increased or no ...

* * *

It is evident while this trade was contained within the particular towns of Colchester and Bocking in Essex, where the making of bays was first begun, and was at least principally established, the trade flourished, the goods were current abroad, commanded ready money at home, and were seldom or never without a market, nor was there a manufacture in Europe which better maintained the credit of its make; insomuch that a merchant at Cadiz or Lisbon coming to an English merchant's warehouse to buy bays, had no more to do but to open one corner of the bale, and look upon the seals of the town of Colchester, and by that they were sure to know of what value the goods were, and were certain to find them answer both in lengths and goodness.

But the neighbouring towns finding the Colchester and Bocking bay-makers grow rich, thrust themselves into that trade, and now the bays are made at Coggeshal, at Witham, at Kelvedon, at Braintre, at Halsted, and in a word, at almost all the most considerable towns in Essex beyond Chelmsford.

Nor is this all, but even the bay-makers themselves, upon the least start of the trade, and upon any sudden quick demand from abroad, push in with such eagerness, and increase their quantity to such a degree, that they bring more to the market than all the world can take off.

This has, I may say, ruined the trade; and the consequence is, that as soon as ever that small run is over, and the demand from abroad ceases, the market is immediately thronged with goods, they are pawned and pledged to every monied man in the place, 'till they can be put off; the price sinks, the labour of the poor stops and the bay-makers are often broke and undone.

Nor is the credit or real value of the goods supported, for the bay-makers being now extended over the whole country, and working out of the jurisdiction of the Bay-hall at Colchester, they put what goods they please upon the market, and what marks or seals they please upon the goods; so that the credit of the manufacture is sunk, and no man trusts to the seals of the goods any more, but takes care to look into the goods himself, and see with his own eyes that he is not cheated.

I cannot but esteem this last to be one eminent degree of the declining of that manufacture; for if once a manufacture declines in its credit, I shall always conclude it is declined in its sale, or will soon be so; *but that by the way*. The present article I am upon, and which I lay the whole stress of the question now upon, is the increase of the quantity beyond the demand; that more are made than are or can be consumed, which I think is apparent in many other particulars.

I sum the whole observation up in this one head, (viz.) that this very increase is a grievance, which in the end may be ruinous to the whole woollen manufacture of England, if some new doors of commerce are not opened abroad to raise a consumption equal to that increase, or some method be not taken to put a stop to the farther increase of the fabrick at home, so as not to make the manufacture be too great for the sale, whether it be at home or abroad.

CHAPTER V

Of the real causes of the decay of our manufacture; arising partly from prohibitions abroad, but chiefly from our refusing the wear of it at home; and something offered for the remedy.

But 'tis needful now to enquire into the state of our manufacture abroad, as to the consumption of the several species in those countries where our trade used to be settled. If we find the sale or demand increasing abroad, the increasing of the quantity at home would certainly be so far from a grievance, that it would be the glory and prosperity of our commerce and of our country; and if every county in England were as fully employed in manufacturing as Wiltshire, Devonshire, Norfolk and Essex, every city as Norwich and Exeter, and every market town as Froom, Taunton, Leeds or Colchester, it would be the wealth of the whole, and the greatest felicity that this world ever produced to a nation.

But the case is not so, but far otherwise; instead of the

consumption increasing abroad, instead of a larger demand, we see all parts of the world envying us, most parts endeavouring to imitate us, and as many as can encouraging their own upstart manufactures in the room of the British; and too many totally prohibiting the sale or the wearing our manufactures, that their own, however mean and ordinary, may take place.

And not to dwell upon some late prohibitions of the English woollen goods in Spain and in the island of Sicily, at Lintz, Passau, Vienna, and other places in the Emperor's dominions, done rather by way of insult to our nation at this crisis of their affairs, than that they are able to carry on any equivalent manufactures of their own; I say, not to lay any stress upon these, yet it must be said, that other places have of late years attempted our manufacture, and some but with too much success, and prohibitions rather natural and consequential, than political, increase upon us every day.

It is the general opinion (and I have joined with it in part, in the beginning of this discourse) that there is no wool to be found in any part of the world, or at least not in Europe, capable of working into such manufactures, and of making such several sorts of goods, as we at present furnish the world with; and upon this very principle we carry our boasts of the British manufacture so high. Now in some particular things we are right; I mean, right in our judgment, namely, that the world has not the wool, that is, has not any wool capable of working into such manufactures as we make; though as to boasting, as we do, I shall never come into that part, because boasting of our superiority is but firing the rest of the world with an unwearied application to supply the defect.

But let us distinguish here with a little more temper than we usually do. There is a manifest difference between having no wool fit for any manufacture at all, and not having the best and the finest wool, of the longest staple, the firmest body, and the finest and softest quality. There is a manifest difference between the wool being good for nothing, and being not so good as the English or Irish wool. To descend to particulars: it is true, Europe, take it by and large (as we express it) from end to end, does not produce a wool capable of making our fine broad-cloths of Warminster, Trowbridge, Bradford and Froom; or our fine Gloucester and Worcester whites; no, nor perhaps such as our Wakefield and Leeds cloth, though what we call coarse, yet of substance and weight inimitable; nor of many several manufactures of other kinds, such as Devonshire kersies, Exeter and Taunton serges, Devizes and Bristol druggets, Andover and Newberry shaloons,* and the like.

But to say therefore that there are no other of our manufactures that can be made abroad, and that even where they have no English wool, that I cannot and must not grant, because experience teaches us the contrary every day, to our great disadvantage in trade.

* * *

It is true our finer cloths gain still an admittance into those countries, because the wool (even of Saxony) is not fine enough for such a manufacture; and this may shew us, that we have certainly been in the wrong of it, and have weakened the interest of our manufactures abroad exceedingly, by leaving our clothing trade to sink upon our hands, and turn our workmen to the lighter manufactures, which other countries with their coarse wool are so much easier able to supply.

* * *

However, it may be well worth considering, whether if this general humour of manufacturing should spread far in Europe, as we are just now told it begins to do in Poland, and in Muscovy, and is threatened in Spain, what the impression it may make upon our manufactures in England may be in a few years.

As these invasions are increasing, so our manufacture must be declining in proportion, unless it could be said that some yet farther branch of foreign commerce can be found out for the consumption of our manufacture, which it is time enough to speak of when we see it in prospect, and which I should be glad to say was probable.

I must acknowledge if the present war should proceed to extremities, so as to lay open the trade from England to the Spanish West-Indies directly, I should venture to say it would give our manufactures a new turn, and they would feel a spring of prosperity for some time, and that considerably too; expecially if some bounds were set to the manufacturers at home, else (if they launched out in quantity, according to custom, as is mentioned above) they would glut the market,

* *shaloon*: a closely woven woollen material, used for linings. [Ed.]

though they were to have a new America opened to them for the trade once in every five years.

However, I see no room to argue upon this remote prospect. They that are sanguine enough upon the war to run on making, and lay up a stock of goods in expectation of a market the next fair at Porto-Belo, or when La Vera Cruz shall be turned English, may go on their own way, I am for sharing no bear-skins.*

But I must come nearer home still, and must take the freedom to insist, that our manufacture is in a state of decay too from our conduct at home, much more than from all prohibitions and interruptions abroad. I am not disposed to make this work a satyr upon my own country, but certainly we are the first, if not the only nation in the world, who having the best and most profitable product, and the best and most agreeable manufacture of our own, of any nation in Europe, if not in the world, are the most backward to our own improvement.

A manufacture valuable in itself, infinitely profitable to the poor, unexceptionably pleasant to the rich; not too hot for the summer, not too cold for the winter; light enough for July, warm enough for December; beautiful as the finest silks, suiting with laces, embroidery, and all manner of ornaments, better than even silk itself, and yet ornamental and rich in its own lustre.

A manufacture receptive of the brightest and deepest colours; gay enough for the bridegroom, solemn enough for the widow; rich enough for a coronation, grave enough for the deepest mourning.

A manufacture that has not one exception to be made against it, or one reason to be given for disliking it; except the weakest of all reasons, the love of change and variety; or that wicked reason which a man gave why he did not love his beautiful and agreeable wife, viz. only because she was his own.

A manufacture that all the world covets, envies us for, strives to imitate, nay, are vain of but thinking they can imitate it.

A manufacture which those other nations (when they have faintly imitated it) are obliged to prohibit by the severest laws,

* *bear-skins*: the phrase "to sell the bearskin" probably comes from the proverb about selling the bearskin before one has caught the bear. The term, which became popular at the time of the South Sea Bubble, referred to the practice of speculators who sold stock for delivery at a future date, expecting prices to fall, and thus to buy back at a lower price what they had so contracted to sell at a higher price. [Ed.]

or else all their people would run into them, and which they do strive to come at and purchase, notwithstanding the strictest prohibitions.

A manufacture which is apparently declining for want of a consumption equal to its bulk, and because of the too successful attempts of other people to set it up among themselves; and because of the improvements that the industry of strangers, and the indolence of the British manufacturers assists them in.

And yet with such a manufacture as this, we cannot persuade ourselves to wear our own produce, to propagate our own industry, or employ our own people; but we are no sooner prohibited the use of one foreign bauble, but we fly to another; first we turned our backs upon our own wrought silks, and run to India and China for all the slightest and foolishest trash in the world, such as their chints,* slight silks, painted cottons, herba,† silk and no silks, as if anything but our own was to be thought beautiful, and anything but what was best for us, was to be encouraged by us.

When this extravagance was also checked by a law, we run then into another extreme, and still turning our fancy against our own manufactures, on a sudden we saw all our women, rich and poor, clothed in callico, printed and painted; the gayer and the more tawdry, the better; and though ordinary, mean, low-prized, and soon in rags, the gayest ladies appeared in them on the greatest occasions.

Thus the ancient manufactures of Great Britain were despised by our own people, and the bread taken out of the mouths of the poor; the hands that would have laboured could get no work; the trade sunk; the manufacturers starved, and the wool lay by in heaps unwrought, and unsold, to the general impoverishing of the people, and the ruin of the manufacture itself.

We are now by another law of prohibition restrained from the wearing of painted callicoes; and what follows? The temper is not at all reclaimed, nor do they so much as incline to return to the use of their own manufactures, which is the main and best end of the prohibition. But, as if we were resolved to run down our whole country, and ruin our poor with our own hands, we run to the remotest corners for some

* *chints*: plural of chint. Like "bays", which became "baize", this material is now referred to in the singular as "chintz". Chint was the name of a painted or stained calico imported from India. Chintz now means a flowered cloth of many colours, often glazed. [Ed.]

† *herba*: a grass cloth, formerly imported from India. [Ed.]

shift or other to cheat ourselves; and now we see the general clothing (of the meaner people especially) runs into the meanest, tawdriest colours, stamped upon the most ordinary linnen, fetched from Scotland, Ireland, or indeed anywhere; as if anything but our own was to be our choice, and as if we had forsworn our own manufactures, and were ashamed to be dressed in our own cloths.

How shall we expect our own manufactures should grow and increase, while this is the case? And if we will not encourage our own growth, and the labour of our own people, how should we expect foreigners should do it?

In short, as I said of the woollen manufactures of Saxony, that they are an effectual prohibition of the English, so I may say of our people's running into the wear of printed linnens, callicoes, &c., they are a tacit prohibition of the manufactures; for what is a rejecting the manufacture by a kind of general consent, but a prohibition in effect? And how should the manufacture be supported, when our own people turn their backs upon it, and when even the people that make it will hardly be persuaded to wear it?

I believe no man will ask me, after this, how I will prove the manufacture to be in a declining state, or what is the reason of it; no more can they ask what remedy is proper to apply to this evil. 'Tis an unaccountable thing in a manufacturing nation like this, that men should ask what will restore the trade, when they see so evidently what has been the ruin of it.

The answer is short, and (according to my title) the only way to restore our manufactures, is to WEAR THEM. The consumption at home is infinitely great: if our whole populous nation were obliged to clothe only in their own manufacture, we should neither complain of ourselves, or value the prohibition of others.

If you will not do this (and the next direction is as short as that), you must abate the quantity; and, as you consume less, make less. What will increasing the work do for us, while we decrease the consumption? It will in the end not only ruin the trading people, but ruin the trade itself. But I have no room to enlarge upon that part here.

3. A Brief State of the Inland or Home Trade, of England

A Brief State of the Inland or Home Trade, of England was published between 18 February and mid-April in 1730. It is an appeal to Parliament to suppress hawkers (street sellers who cried their wares in a town), pedlars (house-to-house retailers who travelled either on foot or with a pack-horse about the countryside, buying or selling for cash), and other retailers who falsely claimed they were selling the products of their own manufacture. The pamphlet is part of a well-organized pressure campaign by shopkeepers and follows their usual line of argument, but Defoe places the controversy in the context of general economic theory. He thus demonstrates that what seems to be the complaint of a special interest group is in actuality a problem affecting the welfare of the entire nation. *A Brief State of the Home Trade* is very well written. Contemporary recognition of its literary merit is suggested by an old manuscript note on a British Museum copy: "This is one of the clearest and most masterly History [sic] ... of the Home Trade I ever read".[1]

Because there were more goods available for sale, trade of all kinds increased throughout the seventeenth century, and pedlars took their share in the general increase. Unimpeded by the liabilities of settled shopkeepers—the practice of giving generous credit terms to customers (pedlars sold only for cash), and the difficulty of acquiring sufficient stock for a store (stock was not plentiful, and a shopkeeper had to have good connections and good credit to acquire it, whereas a pedlar, needing relatively little, could easily replenish and diversify what he had by constant travelling—pedlars increased in numbers. "In 1698", writes Dorothy Davis, "it was thought financially worth while to resume the taxing of pedlars that had lapsed since Commonwealth days. Four pounds a year was the cost of a licence and as much again for a horse, though sellers of their own or their employers' products were exempt."[12]

Obviously shopkeepers resented the competition, and their complaints grew more and more frequent. In the seventeenth century they had accused pedlars, not without some cause, of selling contraband items. All these complaints are echoed in Defoe's pamphlet, but he broadens the issue by considering it in its relationship to the whole system of production and distribution in England.

Contrary to most of his educated contemporaries, "who seemed to think that export expansion was almost the only object of an economy", Defoe "thought that home demand was even more important" in maintaining national prosperity.[3] High wages, deplored by most ecomonic commentators of the period, were to Defoe the key to English welfare. "Far more interested in distribution than in the means of production",[4] Defoe gave little attention to the role superior productivity played in creating higher wages for English workers than for their continental counterparts. Instead, he believed high wages to be an automatic result of interdependence stimulated by high density of population in certain areas. Since the wage structure was not related to productivity, any alteration in a favourable economic status quo—introduction of labour-saving equipment, innovation in selling methods or distribution, changes in methods of circulation—could have only an adverse effect, eliminating jobs, therefore increasing the number of unemployed, therefore decreasing the demand for goods, therefore leaving the farmer and manufacturer with no outlet for their production, therefore throwing the entire economy ever deeper into a downward economic spiral.

Presupposing high wages and thus the ability to purchase high-priced goods, Defoe believed that the more hands through which goods passed, the more employment would be created. Consequently, he deplored the disastrous effect of pedlars' activities on the general level of employment (see page 218). His concept of the origin and importance of high wages enabled him to honour the mercantilist premise that "Numbers of people are without question, the strength and wealth of a nation" (p. 227), for numbers of unemployed people are obviously no such thing. Granted the English blessing of high wages, however, Defoe could proceed to stipulate, "But then it must be numbers of legally settled inhabitants, not numbers of vagrants and wandering people" (p. 227). Settled inhabitants are the source of England's wealth, for they provide the manpower needed to produce "the exigences of the whole body" of the nation, and they furnish through the taxes they pay revenue needed by local and national government for public works and social services (see page 227).

In the pamphlet, then, Defoe reveals his conservatism about distribution, the result of his lack of insight about production and the effect of increased productivity upon wages. Like most mercantilists he looks with suspicion and distaste at consumer demand for cheaper goods, objects to the deterioration of quality such cheapness entails (in a pre-industrial economy, there was no way of cutting costs without cutting the amount of human labour invested in a product, thus diminishing its quality), and fails to perceive that increase in consumer demand resulting from low distribution costs eventually stimulates production and therefore employs more people than the system he is advocating. Furthermore, he does not indicate in his pamphlet that he is aware of the shortage of shop distribution services in his time that encouraged the increase in the number of itinerant retailers, who were particularly useful to isolated country customers.

Some of the reasons for his position are explained by Peter Earle: Defoe's travels in England brought him into contact with distributors rather than producers, who were not as visible in their small workshops as merchants or carters dining out at inns; his historical approach to economics led him to overemphasize past developments like the cloth industry and to underestimate present technological change; and the stable level of world trade during the period in which he lived led him to fear change that would lead in the short run to over-production and unemployment.[5]

The pamphlet itself, which appears to have had little effect upon Parliament (no new legislation on pedlars was passed until the 1780s), makes delightful reading. Clearly the author of *Robinson Crusoe* is responsible for the interesting descriptions of the number of operations and hands an item passes through before it reaches its ultimate consumer. Defoe's ability to simplify and to select only essential details from production and distribution makes the reader as interested and as convinced as he is of the importance of even a pin: "from the brass cannon of 50 to 60 hundred weight, to half an inch of brass wire, called a pin, all equally useful in their place and proportions" (page 213). (Note how the balanced phrases of the comparison between brass in the forms of cannon and of wire emphasize the order and proportion that make tiny pins as useful as huge cannon.) Equally interesting is his simplified picture of the distribution of products all over England, made clear and compelling by his use of concrete examples: the farmer who needs salt from the shopkeeper to preserve his home-raised beef (page 216), the tailor who must "send to the shop for silk and thread" (see page 217) to produce a coat from cloth.

Not only is distribution interesting; Defoe makes it actually exciting as he gradually intensifies the image of trade as a gentle stream—"Unhappy creatures must they be, whose station in life, by the fate of their own ill policy, is placed in the midst of this stream, to intercept the course of the trade in its natural channels, and where it circulates so aptly for the good of the whole ..."—by emphasizing the bustling activity of distribution taking place on the surface of this stream: the opening of shops in "every village and hamlet" as "business is extended into the remotest parts of the kingdom"; the constant traffic between London and the country as "all the manufactures of England in whatsoever part of the country they are made, are sent up to London for sale, and from London circulated again as above, into all the remotest parts among the shopkeepers ..."; and the spread of exotic foreign products throughout England: "By this means the tea of China, the coffee of Arabia, the chocolate of America, the spices of the Moluccas, the sugars of the Caribees, and the fruit of the Mediterranean Islands, are all to be found in the remotest Corners of England, Scotland, Wales, and Ireland".

Trade and distribution are envisioned as a stream and also as the circulation of the body, uniting in wholesome activity country and city in England:

> No more (on the other hand) could the citizens of *London* supply the country chapmen with foreign goods, without a double charge for carriage, which would make the price so much the dearer to the buyer; so that this circulation is an alternative to trade, the country is a help to the city, and the city is a help to the country; as a French proverb expresses it, *One hand washes t'other hand, and both hands wash the face* (page 215).

The shopkeeper whose trade is interrupted by the clandestine trader "has the gleanings of the trade, while the pedlar and the hawker have the harvest; the shopkeeper has the milk, and the pedlar the cream" (page 227). As in his other writings on economics, like *A Brief Deduction*, Defoe makes use of natural images to explain and to humanize economic processes.

His fictionalizing imagination, awakened by the effort to explain an economic phenomenon, is stimulated to look at this phenomenon from a metaphysical point of view. The clandestine trader who interrupts the healthy natural circulation of domestic distribution becomes a diabolic figure in this pamphlet. (In Defoe's political writings Jacobites play the role of Satan; in his economic writings, the role is usually reserved for stock jobbers.) Ensnared by one of the seven deadly sins, "Avarice masked with a pretence of frugality", he looks on "this beautiful order of the trade *with an evil eye*, he projects to cut off the progress of things from their natural course". The clandestine trader insinuates himself into the opinion of the ignorant with "notorious falsehoods and suggestions", as he "comes at them [his goods] in the dark, so he disperses them in the dark," he abuses the "judgment" of his buyers by "possessing the fancy", he carries his goods "in small parcels not to be discovered ... selling them to the ladies even in their bed-chambers". Above all, Defoe objects to the clandestine element in the trade of these dealers, "the hawking and peddling in all its various forms and shapes, however disguised and concealed".

The speaker of *A Brief State of the Home Trader* is not individualized. Of a higher social and educational class than the Mr. Review of *Commerce with France*, he addresses himself politely to Members of Parliament. The terms in which he proposes to explain his argument should be contrasted with those in terms in which Mr. Review reasons with his readers (see page 155 above):

> If then in the process of this work we show, as we doubt not to do, that they neither buy at the best hand, are furnished with the best goods, nor are able to sell the best cheap; we hope there will be no difficulty to convince the honourable persons to whom we address these sheets, that they are a people pernicious in themselves, and that they ought to be suppressed (page 220).

The speaker of *A Brief State of the Home Trade* is not, like the speaker of *The Complete English Tradesman*, a shopkeeper speaking to other shopkeepers. Of the same general class as the speaker of *A Brief Deduction*, he addresses his social superiors with a modesty tempered by self-confidence based upon the awareness of his own intelligence and expertise. The tone that results from this combination of social inferiority and intellectual superiority is more dignified than Mr. Review's robust bonhomie, so frequently equated with Defoe's. It is a delightful balance between condescension and excessive humility toward readers, manly yet urbane.

Notes

1 Quoted by John Robert Moore in his *Checklist of the Writings of Daniel Defoe* (Bloomington, Indiana, 1960), p. 224.

2 Dorothy Davis, *Fairs, Shops, and Supermarkets: A History of English Shopping* (Toronto, 1966), p. 241.

3 Peter Earle, *The World of Defoe* (London: Weidenfeld and Nicolson, 1976), p. 108.

4 *Ibid.*, pp. 126–127.

5 *Ibid.*, pp. 126–127. My discussion in the preceding three paragraphs relies heavily upon Earle's analysis in his chapter, "The Economics of Stability", pp. 107–157.

A Brief State of the Inland or Home Trade, of England
(1730)

* * *

Almost everything that is sold, whether it be the product of nature or art, passes through a great variety of hands, and some variety of operations also, before it becomes (what we call) fit for sale.

Even our very provisions, which may be said to make the least stop, and pass through the fewest hands, yet are traced through several, before they come to the consumer: for example,

1. Our *flesh-meat*; the cattle are first bred, then fed, then driven to one fair or market, then to another, then sold to the butcher, and then to the eater. In every one of those circulating removes, the breeder, feeder, drover, butcher, with their cattle, horses, servants, and families, are severally maintained by, and get a small share of profits from the creature sold; and which is at last charged upon, and returned from the price of the meat when killed, and bought by the consumer.

2. The *corn*, as suppose the wheat; here is first the farmer, who raises the crop, (not to mention the landed man): the plough, the seed, the harvesting, and the carrying it to market, is the business of the farmer; but under him it passes all the operations of the horses, the servants, the carriages, and several other things included in that part called husbandry; and for the support of which several other tradesmen are concerned; such as the smith, the wheelwright, the collar- and harness-maker, the tanner, and many others; all whose families find their subsistance out of the meer husbandry (so it is very properly called) of the corn. But when all that is over, it passes another whole class of operators, before it comes to the end of its circulating race:

1. It is carried to the mill to be ground; under that head comes in the mill-wright, several tradesmen furnishing the timber, the iron-work and brass-work for the mill; the millstones out of Derbyshire, or from France. The carriage of those heavy articles and all the etceteras depending thereon.

Then the dressing, the grinding for fine or coarse; then it passes one sale at least to the baker, then 'tis baked into bread its last operation, and passes many depending hands upon that account.

2. The second branch of corn is the *barley*; this is first sold to the maltster; then malted, then sold again (perhaps more than once), then brewed, pays excise, and is doubly gauged in the malt and in the liquor; then sold to the victualler and innholder, and then to the consumer; in all which motions necessary to their sale, the several tradesmen through whose hands they pass, with their servants, horses, and families, and many others depending upon them, especially in the brewing and malting, gain a maintenance out of the increasing value, and live by the profits of their trade; and the like of other sorts of provisions, some of which come from the growth to the mouth with a shorter, some with a larger circulation.

* * *

To bring this all to the same point: with what admirable skill and dexterity do the proper artists apply to the differing shares or tasks allotted to them, by the nature of their several employments, in forming all the beautiful things which are produced from those differing principles? Through how many hands does every species pass? What a variety of figures do they form? In how many shapes do they appear?—from the brass cannon of 50 to 60 hundred weight, to half an inch of brass wire, called a pin, all equally useful in their place and proportions.

On the other hand, how does even the least pin contribute its nameless proportion to the maintenance, profit, and support of every hand and every family concerned in those operations, from the copper mine in Africa to the retailer's shop in the country village, however remote? And this brings us down to the circulation of the manufactures, in that we call the buying and selling part, as well wholesale as retail; which I refer to a chapter by itself.

* * *

Nature and the course of business has made London the chief or principal market, for all these things called manufactures, not those above specified only, but all the rest. And it is easy to shew, 1. That there must be such a chief or principal market; and 2. That it is also necessary that London should be the place.

1. It is necessary there should be such a chief market, because as the manufacturers and tradesmen in the country have much to sell; that is to say, more than lesser and meaner towns can take off, so they have by themselves, and their correspondents in the country much to buy; that is to say, more than any less capital port and market, or a place of less general correspondence could supply; nothing less than London could answer the ends of a wholesale trade.

2. This proves also that London must be the place. The merchants of London carrying on a general correspondence with all the world, are able to vend the quantity of manufactures which the clothiers send up, be it never so great, and this they do by the bulk of their exportation. They are also able to supply the carriers with back-carriage, from the bulk of their importations, and thus they spread and circulate the growth of foreign countries in return for our own.

* * *

By this sending up the finished manufactures in bulk to the City of London, and the country shopkeepers buying their goods from thence in return, the following advantages follow to the general body of the people of England, (viz.):

1. All that innumerable number of carriages, horses, and servants, with all the necessary appendices of land carriage which such a trade calls for, are maintained. It is not the business of this work to make calculations of numbers, but it is our business to give the reader a clear view of the benefit and gain of the several branches of our circulating trade; that he may have a like clear view of the injurious consequence of those new methods of trade which would destroy it.

2. As the carriage is prodigious great, as well by land as water (for it is the first we are now speaking of), so the number of inns and publick-houses are incredible, which are now to be seen, not only in the towns and cities, but everywhere on the roads, where those carriers and travellers pass. All these are chiefly maintained by those carriages, and by the men and

horses which travel continually for the carrying on the general correspondence to and from London. Their number is really prodigious.

3. The increase of trade among those inns, &c. and by their means the consumption of fodder, hay, corn, &c. with provisions of all sorts is unaccountably great, and the benefit of it to the landed interest is a speculation worth the notice of all gentlemen of estates throughout England. They feel most sensibly the benefit of this circulation; they are easily made sensible what the benefit to trade is, that London is able to furnish a back-carriage by shopkeepers' goods (as they are called) such as grocery, oil, wine, fruit, and in a word all goods of foreign importation; without this, how would the Sheffield and Birmingham carriers bring up their wrought iron, things of a heavy carriage? How would the Warwickshire people bring up their cheese? The Yorkshire men their coarse cloths? The manufacturers of Exeter, Taunton, Norwich, Wilts, Gloucester and Worcester their fine goods? They must all come the dearer to market.

No more (on the other hand) could the citizens of London supply the country chapmen with foreign goods, without a double charge for carriage, which would make the price so much the dearer to the buyer; so that this circulation is an alternative to trade, the country is a help to the city, and the city is a help to the country; as a French proverb expresses it, *One hand washes t'other hand, and both hands wash the face.*

Unhappy creatures must they be, whose station in life, by the fate of their own ill policy, is placed in the midst of this stream, to intercept the course of the trade in its natural channels, and where it circulates so aptly for the good of the whole, and who would cut short the means of its doing good to the whole community.

* * *

By this admirable oeconomy of trade, business is extended into the remotest parts of the kingdom; shops are opened in every parish, nay, in every village and hamlet. These smaller shops diffuse and spread not the manufactures of the remotest part of the country only, but the product and imported growth of foreign countries and kingdoms, into every corner of the island; where they are all sold by retail, to the particular families and inhabitants of their neighbourhood.

By this means the tea of China, the coffee of Arabia, the

chocolate of America, the spices of the Moluccas, the sugars of the Caribees, and the fruit of the Mediterranean Islands, are all to be found in the remotest corners of England, Scotland, Wales and Ireland. By this method also, all the several manufactures of England, though made in the most different and the remotest counties, are to be bought in every place, all being supplied from the great center of the nation's commerce, the City of London. The reason of mentioning this shall appear presently; let us look a little first into the consequences of it.

Those little retailing shops are the life of all our trade; by those the bulk of the business is carried on to the last consumer, and here all the wholesale trade, as well of home manufactures as foreign importations is terminated and finished.

The people that keep these shops are supplied at the like tradesmen's shops, in the larger towns or cities, according as situation directs; the keepers of those shops being supposed to have larger stocks, and so are able to give these lesser dealers some credit. Again, the shopkeepers in those greater towns are furnished by the wholesale men (who are such as we call country dealers in London), who likewise give credit to those chapmen in the principal towns in the country.

These wholesale men in London are indeed the support of the whole trade, they give credit to the country tradesmen (chapmen) and even to the merchants themselves; so that both home trade and foreign trade is in a great measure carried on upon their stocks.

To these men, or to the factors and warehouse men, of whom these dealers buy, all the manufactures of England, in whatsoever part of the country they are made, are sent up to London for sale, and from London circulated again as above, into all the remotest parts among the shopkeepers; and by them in retail trade to the wearers and consumers.

It is on these retailers that all the people of England depend for the supply of common necessaries, whether for food, cloths, household-stuff, ornament, or whatever else they think fit to lay their money out in; even the clothier himself cannot clothe himself, or the farmer feed himself or family without them.

The farmer may have corn sufficient, and cattle sufficient for the supply of his family. But when he comes to kill them for food, he sends to the shopkeeper for salt, or the beef will spoil before he can use it; he must send to the shop for fruit, for spice, for sugar, to supply his wife in her kitchen; he must send to another shop for pewter and brass for his kitchen utensils, to the smith for spits and jack, iron pots, and the like of other things; and all this, though the iron, tin, copper, and the salt are the growth of his own country, for they do not grow at his own door, and the mines are not in his farm; nor are the manufacturers of hard-ware, the smiths of Sheffield and Birmingham at his door; the casters of iron, tin, or lead do not live in his town; so he must send to the shopkeepers for all those things, as he wants them. The shopkeeper, for the same reason, must have them from London; for if he would send to Sheffield or to Birmingham for them, he could find no carriers to bring them; and if they did, he had nothing to load them back with, so that the goods would cost him double carriage. Of this also we shall have occasion to speak again.

Come we next to the clothiers, they are most important men in their way; speaking of them in general terms, we say they are able to clothe the whole world. But it must be taken with a due latitude, for them and their neighbours; for there is not a clothier in England that can clothe himself; nay, he cannot make himself a coat, take him in what country you will; he can indeed make the outside, and he can call for a taylor, who is everywhere at hand to make it up.

But even the taylor himself must send to the shop for silk and thread to sew it together; and for even needles and a thimble, or he will make but poor work; he must send to another shop for sheers and sissars to cut out with, and the like.

Then for the clothier himself when he has made the cloth, he must buy shalloon, or perhaps some other manufacture made 150 miles off, for a lining; he must have buttons out of Cheshire, about Macclesfield; dimity to line the wastcoat out of Manchester; linen to line the breeches, out of Ireland; and a hundred little nameless things; some out of one county, some out of another, before the clothier can be clothed; his hat comes from one place, stockings from another, gloves from a third, and so on; all those he sends to the shopkeeper for, and the shopkeeper to the London wholesale man, and he to the several counties, where those several things are, the proper business of the place; and thus we see the City must of necessity be the center of the trade; for the London dealer has every sort of goods brought up by the proper carriers, and he enables those carriers to bring them up cheap; because he or the dealers in other goods which the shopkeepers in that country call for, can load them back and so get the carrier a double freight.

We might enquire here into the probable number of these shopkeepers in the several countries all over this island, thereby farther to illustrate this argument, and judge of the importance of this circulation of trade. But the thing is impracticable, it is out of the reach of all calculation, it is enough to say they are in their particulars innumerable, and may only be talked of by thousands and hundreds of thousands; for taking them with their real dependencies, they include almost the whole body of our people.

This will serve to stop the mouths of all those who having no other plea to bring in favour of the *hawkers* and *private traders*, those enemies to all fair trade, would move us to pity and compassion for them on account of their great numbers. Whereas they do not reflect how infinitely more numerous the families of the shopkeepers, manufacturers and wholesale dealers are, who they injure, and may be said to starve and reduce; and how numerous the poor are who depend on those fair traders for employment and subsistence, and who all cry to them for their bread. Here compassion ought to work, these we should turn our eyes to, and not to the other who eat them up and devour them, and who either for their numbers or significance are not to be named with them.

* * *

Avarice masked with a pretence of frugality is the most fatal snare of a tradesman; it leads him not into mischiefs only which are personal, and which wound himself, but it pushes him upon measures ruinous to trade in general, and so he becomes an enemy to his country, and envies the prosperity of all about him.

He sees trade run on in a happy round of buying and selling, importing and exporting, carrying up and carrying down, and that all the way as it passes, though through a multitude of hands, it leaves something of gain everywhere behind it, and yet lessens not the value of what it carries on; and looking on this beautiful order of the trade *with an evil eye*, he projects to cut off the progress of things from their natural course; shorten the length of the circulation, which is indeed the life of the whole, and thinking to put all the gain of five or six stages of the trade into his own pocket, he contrives or at least pretends to carry the goods a shorter way to the last consumer; so bringing things to an immediate period, making himself the carrier, factor, wholesale dealer, chapman, and retailer all in one hand, putting the gain of all those trades into the single purse of a pedlar; and this is the man we are now to speak of.

His original as above is founded in avarice and envy, and the measures he pursues tell us that it is his trade to be a supplanter. He acts like a man that maliciously turns the stream of a mill-river to his own private use, perhaps trifling and mean; valuing not the starving twenty mills which lie on the same stream and must get their bread, and the subsistence of their families, by the fair produce of their labour.

In this he acts like a thief and destroyer, not only to the trade in general, an invader and pirate to the fair trader in particular, but at the same time is a cheat to the buyers and consumers of the goods he sells; and in the whole to himself; for he defeats his own expectations, and generally dies a beggar, all which we doubt not to make appear to the meanest understanding in the process of these sheets.

At an unhappy juncture of time, when funds for raising money to the government were wretchedly wanting, and at a time when the fair traders stood in need of all possible encouragement, to enable them to pay the great taxes which they then began to feel the weight of; at that very time, and we may say, *in an evil hour*, a project to licence these pernicious people was proposed, and for a trifling payment, compared to the fatal effects of it to trade, was closed with, and the said licences granted. We call it a trifling payment, because it seems to be so, not only by comparison as above, but by the small sums it brings in to the publick.

Ever since that time they have been like moths in trade, and have eaten into the very vitals of our commerce, in a fatal and most injurious manner, encroaching upon the *fair traders*, almost in every branch of business, where the goods they sell are light and portable; spreading themselves into all parts of the country as well as city; insinuating into the opinion of the ignorant, by notorious falsehoods and suggestions; particularly that they have their goods from the makers, buy them at the best hand, have the best of everything of its kind, and to sum up all, that they sell everything at a cheaper rate, than they (the buyer) can be supplied at by the shops; all which in every particular we take upon us to prove are downright falsehoods, calculated on purpose to deceive and impose upon the ignorant buyer. And in a word, that their whole trade is a stated and premeditated fraud, that it is so in the very nature and method of it, as well as in the design.

If then in the process of this work we show, as we doubt not to do, that they neither buy at the best hand, are furnished with the best goods, nor are able to sell the best cheap; we hope there will be no difficulty to convince the honourable persons to whom we address these sheets, that they are a people pernicious in themselves, and that they ought to be suppressed.

It may look like making room for an objection here, to say that these men do not buy, and cannot sell cheaper than the fair trading shopkeepers; for then it may be said, what hurt can they do to trade?

The answer is very plain and direct, (viz.)

1. That they pretend to, and loudly affirm the contrary, and so abuse the ignorant buyers; they intercept the trade, they turn the stream from the mill, as was observed above, they invert the due order and course of business; for instead of the customers going to the shop, they carry the shop to the customers; instead of the country inhabitants frequenting the markets, which are the proper places of trade, they make the markets walk about to the inhabitants, calling upon them at their doors; where if the people get nothing else, they are gratified by saving them the trouble of going out of doors to the shops, or to the market towns; (which in some cases is to them a thing of consequence, as distance and situation of places may be); and if it were no more than this, the shopkeeper is supplanted and cut out of the trade, and all the chapmen and dealers between him and the London wholesale men are likewise cut out of their business in their proportion.

We might enlarge here upon the fatal consequences of thus cutting off the country shopkeepers from their business, intercepting trade, and obstructing its regular course, the necessity of which for the publick prosperity we have so largely insisted upon above, how by that means so many thousands of families are supplanted in their trades, open their shops in vain, and are left destitute. But we leave that to its proper place.

It is needful first to take these people in their own way, and lay open a little the fraud which they use in their ordinary course of business: how the people in the countries (ay, and in the city too) are imposed upon by them; and when we have detected them in their known cheats, we shall have the clearer view of the fatal consequences of those cheats in trade.

FAIR DEALING is the honour of trade, and the credit of the tradesman; a shopkeeper may perhaps run out sometimes in words, for the setting out his goods (and the buyer in running him down, and not believing truth in the most solemn manner expressed, is really the principal cause of all those excursions of words, which the shopkeeper is as it were under a necessity of making); but these people can speak no other dialect; truth is out of their way; their business will not bear it; their trade is a fraud in itself, and must be supported by falsehood, and if they should at any time deviate into sincerity, they would be kicked out of doors; they can trade no longer than they can l——e, for the very beginning and end of their business is to deceive. Let us look a little into the particulars.

1. That they buy their goods at the best hand. This even in itself is false, and known to be so; for we see them every day in the shops and warehouses of the wholesale dealers, in all places where the country chapmen deal, and where they buy indeed what the others leave, which leads of course to the next pretence, (viz.)

2. That they buy the best goods, which is as false as the other; for it is well known that they buy the worst and meanest goods of the several kinds they deal in, and particularly that which the country chapmen refuse; nor indeed will the wholesale dealers, where they are men of honesty, and have the sense of their own interest, as well as of justice in trade, sell to such people as those the best of their goods, which are laid in to supply their constant chapmen, who buy large quantities, and merit to be used well; nor does the pedlar's bringing his ready money weigh in this case; for the country chapman who, as above, deals largely and constantly, and pays well, merits to be used as well, and indeed better, than a hawking clandestine trader, who brings his money because he has no credit; and pays down, because he cannot buy without it; who runs about from warehouse to warehouse to pick out anything for the sake of cheapness, and is fixed nowhere. The warehouse men will never show these their best goods. They know also, 1. they are not for their turn; and 2. they will not give a price for them; and in this manner the pedlars stock themselves with goods.

Let us view them next upon their circuits in the country, for selling them off. It is true they travel as we call it cheap, that they feed their horse upon the waste, and themselves upon the spoil, that they lodge at the meanest houses and in the meanest places, where they live like themselves, that is, wretchedly and at little or no expense, and this indeed is one just article against their being suffered in trade; for at the same time that they supplant the established settled shopkeepers, who as above are the supports of the whole body, maintain both Church and State, the civil and religious government, feed the poor, and clothe the rich; these people do nothing in civil government, pay for nothing, bear no offices, raise no taxes, and which is still more, pay no rent, for they have no houses nor legal settlement. They pay neither Scot or Lot, Church or poor, but in short, are complete vagrants; and ought, their late unhappy advantage excepted, to be treated as such.

Yet notwithstanding, take them with all these advantages, it is not true in fact that they can carry their goods cheaper in bulk than the shopkeeper can have them carried, and the reason is very plain, because the carriers by having constant business backward, shall deliver goods one kind with another, at a cheaper rate, than even the pedlar can carry them; and if we allow for carriage by water, whether by sea or river navigation, much cheaper.

The same argument is against him in his selling for less profit than the shopkeeper, which is also a mistake; because the shopkeeper outdoes him in quantity, which makes up the profit in the whole to him, though in the particulars he may not gain so much. It is a maxim in trade, that light gain makes a heavy purse, and the meaning is, that a small profit on a large return makes the tradesman rich; now 'tis a mistake to say the pedlar or private trader can live on less profit than the shopkeeper, because where the one returns one hundred pound, the other returns a thousand, perhaps much more, and can by consequence lay up more by an advance of two or three per cent on his goods, than the other can by an advance of ten per cent.

This makes the mischievous consequence of the pedlar more and more evident; for if by intercepting the shopkeeper's trade, as above, he prevents the said shopkeeper making so large a return; he by the same rule prevents his selling his goods at all to profit, and so the poor retailer is ruined of course.

* * *

If then he neither buys the best goods nor sells best cheap, as is plain above, what can be said for a set of men who supplant the fair seller, and do the buyer no good? They must be taken as they really are, for pirates in trade, thieves to their country; for though they may not be said to rob and break open houses (though they stand pretty fair for a charge of that kind too sometimes), yet they rob their country in a most egregious manner, supplanting the tradesmen, and confounding the course of trade, by which the whole country is maintained; and in this they are enemies to the publick prosperity, they starve the poor, impoverish the diligent industrious tradesmen, and by consequence the manufacturers also who depend upon the trade, as it is carried on in its due course, and would be brought to starve and sink in the sinking of the shopkeepers, and that in a most deplorable manner.

* * *

As the retailer is the life of all trade, so the pedlar is the essence of all clandestine trade; as the receiver is the support of all thieving, so the hawker is the life of all smuggling; he hands on the goods to the consumer; as he comes at them in the dark, so he disperses them in the dark; into innumerable hands, and into small parcels where it is not possible to the officers to discover or detect them; for when uncustomed goods are divided into innumerable parts, like the blood in the capillary vessels, it is impossible to come at them in the form of a legal prosecution.

* * *

Thieves, they say, sell good pennyworths; they must do so, else nobody would buy; what they buy in the dark they must sell in the dark ...

* * *

We might observe from this particular part of their management, how fond they are to be thought worse knaves than they are, and to make the buyers believe those goods are run, which really are not; at the same time being very rarely without others that are; nor would it be an unprofitable thing to argue upon, in representing these people to the Parliament, since it would be well worth the consideration of that honourable House, whether a set of people should be any longer continued in trade, whose greatest advantage it is to have their customers believe them to be knaves and thieves, and who are chiefly traded with upon that foot; a set of men who if they were really just and honest, could not live by their business, and if their customers did not think them rogues (that is smugglers), would have no business at all.

* * *

The complaint in general lies indeed against the licenced hawker or pedlar, and in order to have those licences taken away; and it seems by that part, as if these were the only people against whom the charge lies; but we are to observe that there are of late a great number of other people crept into the same business; who also may be called hawkers and pedlars as well as any of the rest; and who merit as much to be suppressed; these have no licences, and yet, taking the hazard of the penalty, run up and down in all the great towns and cities in Britain, but especially in London, to private houses with their goods. Here they get into the favour of the ladies, and especially of their maidservants; pretending that having goods immediately from on board a ship, or from particular interests with other persons that have them so, they are able to sell cheaper than the shops.

These are a set of people who, as we have observed before, value themselves upon being guilty of more sins than they can commit; and pretend to have run and uncustomed goods to sell when they have not, as well as when they have.

These have their arts however to delude and impose upon the buyers, and particularly by selling some goods to loss, rather than not suit the fancy of the lady they are dealing with; that so the person may boast of the pennyworth, and recommend the private trader; in which case they forget not, and seldom fail to make up their loss with advantage at the next occasion.

By thus insinuating themselves into the opinion of the buyers, they have infinite advantages to deceive and impose upon them; nor need we argue here upon the power of the imagination, which acts so much in their favour, or how easy it is to abuse the judgement by possessing the fancy; it is too well known in many like cases, that where the buyer is previously possessed with a belief, that the person *can* sell cheaper than others, 'tis next to impossible to persuade them that he *does not*, and harder still to persuade them that they are cheated and abused.

This charge particularly relates to such private traders as go from house to house, but would not be called hawkers or pedlars, nor do they take any licences, so that they defraud the publick both ways. These apparently carry no goods, for what they have to sell being in small bulk they easily conceal it; or if not, they have servants to carry for them at some distance, so as to be called on any occasion.

That they are really hawkers in the sense of the Act, is out of the question, and they ought by the Act to take licences; that they really do sell uncustomed and prohibited goods is equally certain, and that they frequently abuse those they sell to, by pretending their goods are such, is as certain; and they have been frequently detected, and made to confess the fraud.

* * *

It comes now of course to observe, that though it is true that the licencing these people is a manifest grievance to trade, and by which they are encouraged to insult the tradesmen, even in those towns and cities where they have no legal right, no, not by their licences to trade, yet the bare taking off or repealing the Acts of Parliament for granting such licences, is not the only subject of this humble application.

It is true that the licenced hawkers have been the original of all, or most part of the mischief suffered, and that those licences have in a great measure taken off the edge of the people's just aversion to them, believing that the laws would not have allowed them, if they had been really injurious to trade in general, or to the shopkeepers in particular.

But this is not all; from this abatement of the people's disgust at the pedlars and hawkers, throngs of private traders have broke in upon even the hawkers and pedlars themselves; who would not be called by the name, but do equal mischief, in plying as it were at people's doors, and that even in the greatest cities and best governed corporations; carrying their goods in small parcels not to be discovered, and selling them to the ladies even in their bed-chambers; as effectually and fatally circumventing and anticipating the fair traders, as it is possible for any pedlar or hawker to do.

So that though it is true that we complain of the licencing and permitting the hawkers and pedlars as such, and under the several denominations and descriptions given of them above, and humbly hope for relief against them, by the repeal of the several laws granting those licencing, yet we must insist also, that it is absolutely necessary to have some proper clauses, granted in such new law as shall be made, as may effectually suppress all those private clandestine traders also, otherwise the rest will be of no effect.

It is not the men that we so earnestly move against, as they are men, but as they are injurious and destructive by their foul practice in trade; 'tis the hawking and peddling in all its various forms and shapes, however disguised and concealed, whether with or without a licence, and indeed of the two, those without a licence seem to be the most mischievous in great towns and cities; those with the licence are so in country towns and villages, and especially at *lone houses* as we call them, houses standing single and scattered about the country.

Those who ply or practice (call it as you will) in cities and populous towns, and especially in London, are supposed to be more in number than those that are licenced, and consequently may do most mischief; besides they have the chance to deal among the richer sort of people, and with those who have most money to lay out; so that they not only take more ready money than the other, but as they can sooner supply themselves with quantities of the like goods, than they can who travel farther off, so they make quicker returns, and require less stock.

Every one of these articles are injurious to the fair trader, for all these sums of ready money if not thus intercepted would circulate in a regular manner, in the ordinary way of trade, and give life and spirit to the shopkeeper, of whatever trades the buyer was formerly used to deal with; and the goods pass, through all the circulating meanders of trade, which are known so much to support the body of our tradesmen.

This is a reason well worthy the consideration of the legislature, and which if duly weighed would shew the necessity of suppressing these people; namely, that by this they will restore trade to its ancient state, such as it was, when the wealth and oppulence of this nation was first raised; for we must insist that the greatness of our country has been chiefly, if we may not say wholly raised by our trade.

The increase of our people, the raising the value of lands, the infinite improvements, in cultivation, in navigation, in arts, in manufactures, and in a word, in every valuable thing, has been all (under Providence) owing to our trade; and of all trade, our home trade is the life, the soul, and the support of all the rest.

This home trade is wounded, weakened, we may almost say murthered by these pirates, and by their depredations; it languishes like children without the breast; the stream, as is said above, is turned away from the mill; the buyers or customers are turned away from the shops; the money which was the life of their trade, runs into other hands. If any trade is left to the shopkeeper it is the trusting part, where the money comes slow, where losses often fall heavy; so that the shopkeeper has the gleanings of the trade, while the pedlar and the hawker have the harvest; the shopkeeper has the milk, and the pedlar the cream.

With these disadvantages in the trade, the poor decaying shopkeeper has a large rent to pay, and family to support; he maintains not his own children only, but all the poor orphans and widows in his parish; nay, sometimes the widows and orphans of the very pedlar or hawker, who has thus fatally laboured to starve him....

Were these people removed, trade would soon return and revive; when once trade came to flow in its right channel, it would recover its former magnitude and glory, and the shopkeepers would thrive again as they formerly did.

* * *

Numbers of people are without question the strength and wealth of a nation; we most readily grant the general. But then it must be numbers of legally settled inhabitants, not numbers of vagrants and wandering people. Settled inhabitants are industrious, laborious, and lend their helping hands to all the exigences of the whole body, whether publick or private. They pay their just proportions in all rates, assessments and taxes, as well to the government and to the Church as to the maintenance of the poor, to the repair of highways, bridges, publick edifices, and whatever the community calls for.

These are the inhabitants whose numbers are of import in a government; and if we had two millions or three millions of such more than we have, the kingdom would be still so much the richer and stronger. These all live by honest means, carry on lawful employments, and support their families by industry and application in their respective callings; and if they have not estates beforehand, oftentimes raise estates by their own genius and inclination to business.

* * *

4. An Essay upon Loans

An Essay upon Loans was published in October 1710. It was a sequel to Defoe's highly successful pamphlet of the previous August, *An Essay upon Publick Credit*, in which he had demonstrated an idea very novel in 1710, that national credit depended upon "just and honourable" dealing of Parliament and the Crown, rather than upon the particular ministers who managed government finances.[1] Because the first pamphlet had quickly reached a third edition, Defoe makes sure to indicate that the *Essay upon Loans* is the work of the "Author of the *Essay upon Credit*". (Both pamphlets were originally thought to be the work of Robert Harley, probably because their author was so well informed about national finance,[2] and spoke in the tone of someone accustomed to command.) At the end of his *Essay upon Loans* Defoe suggests that he may write another pamphlet on the subject of funds (long-term capital loaned to the government and secured by Parliamentary guarantee to pay interest on it),[3] but unfortunately no such work is known to have ensued.

In the *Essay upon Loans*, which deals in general terms with all kinds of government borrowing, Defoe is attempting to remedy the financial crisis that had come to a head when Queen Anne dismissed the brilliant financial expert Godolphin, in favour of a new Tory ministry headed by Robert Harley. Increasingly heavy war debts, a bitter winter, poor harvests, high prices, failure of the 1709 peace negotiations, and the bloody battle of Malplaquet, had all contributed to this crisis. The City rated Godolphin's abilities so highly, and was so incensed by Queen Anne's appointment of the Tories, that Whigs began threatening to discontinue investing in loans to the financially-pressed government.

Defoe sets out to help Robert Harley find alternative sources of credit by proving that: (1) in times of crisis the government can always attract loans by offering especially advantageous terms to lenders; (2) investors are now so accustomed to placing their extra money gainfully with the government, that the investment market is as dependent upon government securities as the government is dependent upon investments; (3) investment in government securities is so widespread that no group of individuals can monopolize the practice.

Defoe's history of the details of public financing from 1690 to 1710 (not reproduced) is so concise that it is somewhat confusing. All that is necessary for the non-specialist to know is that when William III declared war against Louis XIV in 1689, supplies were at first raised by indirect taxes on commodities and direct taxes on land and foreign trade. Soon it became necessary to borrow money in anticipation of receipt of taxes. Such loans were temporary, and were wiped out once taxes had been collected. As war expenses increased, however, the government found it increasingly difficult to meet its bills, and the size of the debt in arrears became alarming.

In the 1690s various schemes and projects for raising money on credit, rather than by simple anticipation of shortly forthcoming revenue, were advanced and tested. They included projects for both short- and long-term borrowing: the issuing of life annuities, including an unpopular tontine scheme, government lotteries with special prizes, the issuing of Exchequer Bills (government paper money notes), increased issuing of tallies (originally notched wooden receipts for money or supplies advanced to the Exchequer), the abortive attempt to establish a Land Bank, and the financially revolutionary Act founding the Bank of England in 1694.

The so-called Financial Revolution,[4] or the system of public borrowing developed by England in the early eighteenth century, was devised to compensate for the inadequacies of taxation in a country relatively unsophisticated economically, and it served to keep taxes lower than they would otherwise have been. It created "a whole range of securities in which mercantile and financial houses could safely invest, and from which they could easily disinvest", writes Dickson.[5] It caused the City of London to emerge as a financial centre, capable of "financing the capture of empire, and [of] stimulating the growth of the internal capital market".[6] The City, therefore, was enabled to marshal capital needed for future economic growth in England.

Only the most dire financial difficulties, however, could have forced Parliament to pass the Act founding the Bank of England, for the idea of a National Debt (a debt never to be paid off, but to be secured by perpetual payments of interest to stock subscribers, the interest to be financed by ship tonnage duties and taxes on beer, spirits, and ale), seemed novel and unsound to many people in 1694. They could not perceive that "a nation can, so to speak, be regarded as a public corporation in which the population as a whole can be invited to invest".[7] In addition, certain special interests felt threatened by the existence of a National Bank. Most of all, many feared that the Crown might use the Bank to become financially independent of Parliament. Clauses were added to the Statute of 1694 to meet the objections of the special interests, and, most important of all, to keep the Bank under parliamentary control by forbidding it to lend to the Crown or to purchase Crown lands without parliamentary consent.

The most virulent attacks upon the new system of public borrowing came from those with special political and economic interests, Tories, landed men, goldsmiths, money-lenders, merchant bankers, and trading men. Only a minority, to which Defoe belonged, believed it was advantageous to England. Political criticism alleged that the National Debt had been created to secure support for the Revolutionary Settlement of 1689 from powerful moneyed groups concerned in government loans; it was not economic need, the need for greater revenue, they said, but political trickery instituted by King William, that had created the National Debt. Swift and Bolingbroke lent their pens to this standard Tory myth.

Social and economic criticism came from landed and trading interests.

The former believed that diversion of money into government loans lowered the price of land, and therefore the social position of the landholders. Spokesmen for the landed interests, including Swift and Bolingbroke, made serious attacks, based on incipient class hatred, "owing to the implicit eighteenth-century assumption that it [the landed interest] had special virtues denied to other members of society".[8] Trading interests opposed the National Debt on economic grounds: they at first believed that loans to the government were starving trade of capital.[9] When this belief was disproved, as government stock dividends began to fall by 1713, trading interests replied that if they were not being starved, their capital was being intolerably burdened with taxes to service the National Debt.

Defoe takes an advanced economic position, arguing in favour of the National Debt in his *Essay upon Loans*, and thus speaking for the national, rather than for any special, interest. In this he is of one mind with Robert Harley, who resisted extremist Whigs and Tories "while allaying the fears of moderates in both Parliament and City". As B. W. Hill writes, Harley "was able to convince a nation still unused to national debt both that public credit was dependent on government as such, rather than a particular party, and that government, even a government composed of Tories, depended on the specialist abilities of the great financial interests."[10]

Defoe's judgement of the increased financial strength of the government and its improved credit position by 1710 was a good one, as his pragmatic judgements usually were. The credit crisis that began in 1710 lasted only until 1711 and was much less severe than previous financial crises, precisely because the English system of public finance had been on the whole well administered by Godolphin and the Bank of England and continued to be well administered by Harley. Yet, in contrast to his economic ideas, Defoe's feelings about the new system, like most of his personal feelings, were ambivalent. The metaphors and similes that appear in the *Essay upon Loans* suggest this ambivalence.

One literary device he uses to explain the economics of public finance is unambiguous. This is his use of Biblical allusion. He cites Solomon's description of the borrower as servant (page 238), contrasting Biblical economics to current English state economics. He perceives that primitive concepts of borrowers and lenders are no longer appropriate to a more advanced stage of economic development. In 1710, the government "is no more servant to the lender than the lender is servant to him; having an unquestioned security to give, he scorns to ask you twice. ..." The Biblical reference serves as an excellent device to explain a modern economic concept to Defoe's eighteenth-century audience, still well versed in the Bible: "The whole nation ... depends so much upon the publick credit, that they can no more do without the funds, than the funds can do without the loan" (see page 237). Defoe's contrast between Solomon's servant-borrower and the government as an independent borrower, implies satisfaction with the latter condition; freedom is infinitely preferable to bondage in the eyes of the independence-loving Defoe.

Defoe's modernization of a Biblical lesson would seem to place him in the ranks of the avant-garde in economics, an avant-garde versed in, though critical of its literary and religious heritage. Yet elsewhere in *An Essay upon Loans* he expresses conservative economic notions that go back to medieval suspicions about the borrowing and lending of money. "As late as the seventeenth century", explains Dickson, "borrowing tended to be regarded as an index of necessity, and lenders as those who took advantage of necessity."[11] Because monarchs had often acted irresponsibly in contracting and paying for debts, loans to the Crown naturally commanded high interest rates. These rates "seemed shocking to contemporaries, who thought that the state was being drained by leeches".[12] Financial difficulties of the English government in the 1690s are described by Defoe in a simile that rests upon this medieval notion: "The government appeared like a distressed debtor, who was every day squeezed to death by the exorbitant greediness of the lender" (page 235).

Defoe's explanation of economic events in terms of individual greed, or desire for gain, is what Dickson refers to as "the time-honoured but futile identification of economic pressures with human wickedness. ..."[13] Defoe expresses indignation about ungrateful moneyed men[14] who have grown wealthy as the result of their previous speculation in debased government tallies and Exchequer Bills, and who now assert that they will refuse to invest in government securities. His pamphlet is designed to demonstrate to such men that they cannot now stay out of the stream of economic activity, or construct towers or dams against such a stream:

> It may not be improper here for some people to reflect, that in the advantages granted by the government upon these loans ... were founded the great stocks of money, banks, and powerful credit; *with which some people are grown to such a height, especially in their own opinion*, as to talk of influencing the publick affairs, and as it were menacing the government with apprehensions of their lending or not lending, as they are, or are not pleased with the management of, or managers in the publick oeconomy ... (page 235, my italics)

If great wealth, which has contributed to the pride of these men, is insufficient as a bulwark against the stream of economic determinism, why then was the amassing of their estates the result of greedy and selfish free will, and not of economic determinism? In his eagerness to convince Whigs that their dislike of the Tory ministry is futile, as well as immoral—they are powerless to divert the flow of investment capital from government securities—Defoe seems to have trapped himself into an economic variation on the paradox of Adam's fall.

The concept of economic man, powerless to resist the greed implanted in him by original sin, yet responsible morally because of his free will for having made his private fortune at the expense of a financially distressed government, is paradoxical. The economic stream Defoe describes in the metaphor pervading his entire pamphlet, is equally paradoxical. The stream, which cannot be resisted, expresses the notion of economic determinism, a notion that grates unpleasantly on the ears of many modern readers. Yet Defoe envisions this stream as fresh and flowing. (He often spoke with distaste of landed estates as stagnant ponds.) He describes credit and loans without credit in organic and agrarian terms: credit is a flower, loans without credit are "like the labouring plowman upon a barren soil, who works, cultivates, sweats, and toils, but to no purpose, all the fruit of his labour ends in sterility and abortion" (page 234).[15]

Metaphors garnered thus from nature do not suggest unpleasant mechanical forces.

Defoe reconciles the ambivalent connotations of the economic stream by using the image finally as a unifying force for the harmony he is always seeking in politics. Reluctant to admit that political or economic conflicts of interest are irreconcilable, Defoe merges his metaphor of the economic stream with an image of the ocean, mighty, irresistible, and eternal, and thus dignifies England's great system of public finance:

> Keep up but the credit of Parliament, and let that Parliament find funds, it is not in the power of any party of men to stop the current of loans, any more than they can stop the tide at London-Bridge, in its constant course of flux and re-flux from and to the sea.[16]

Notes

1 The originality of this idea is explained in P. G. M. Dickson's excellent book, *The Financial Revolution in England: A Study in the Development of Public Credit 1688–1756* (London and New York, 1967), especially in Chapter I. Other expedients for finding money for governmental needs were those of currency inflation and writing off accumulated debts. Resort to these expedients proved self-defeating to eighteenth-century France, in that it damaged the public credit irretrievably, making it impossible for that nation, so superior to England in resources of population, natural wealth, and military organization, to tap its wealth for purposes of war with England.

2 In Defoe's *Memoirs of Public Transactions in the Life and Ministry of his Grace the Duke of Shrewsbury* (1718), he suggests that it was on Shrewsbury's direction that the *Essay upon Publick Credit*, and therefore presumably also *An Essay upon Loans*, was written.

The easy authority of the speaker in this pamphlet is that of a leader accustomed to addressing his inferiors. Strikingly different from the informality and easy egalitarianism of Defoe's voice in the *Review*, it must have sounded to contemporaries like the voice of a prominent statesman.

3 "The fact that Parliament guaranteed all these loans made them 'debts of the nation' or 'national debts', and both Englishmen and foreigners were quick to realize that this change from merely royal security was extremely important", explains Dickson (p. 50).

4 Dickson, Chapters I and II.

5 *Ibid.* p. 11.

6 *Ibid.* p. 12.

7 John Giuseppi, *The Bank of England* (London, 1966), p. 11.

8 Dickson, p. 24.

9 Since the period from 1680–1750 was one of slow population growth and an increased national output both in manufactures and in agriculture, the standard of living improved during these years, according to A. H. John in his essay, "Aspects of English Economic Growth in the First Half of the Eighteenth Century", to be found in *Essays in Economic History*, ed. E. M. Carus-Wilson (London, 1962), II, 360–373.

Capital was therefore available for investment, but trade and manufacturing organizations were in so rudimentary a state of organization that they could not provide investment opportunities for people interested in safe investments. "In consequence", says Dickson, "investors tended to put their money into land or government securities. The development of provincial capital resources, and the further growth of financial specialization and expertise in London, were to be needed before funds could be raised on a sufficient scale to finance the Industrial Revolution and the concurrent revolutions in transport, lighting, and housing" (Dickson, p. 489).

10 B. W. Hill, "The Change of Government and the 'Loss of the City', 1710–1711". *Economic History Review*, 24 (February 1971), 411.

11 Dickson, p. 39.

12 *Ibid.*, p. 39.

13 *Ibid.*, p. 516.

14 Defoe is referring to men like Gilbert Heathcote, who had bought up debased

government tallies at a 40 per cent or greater discount while he was a Bank Director, and had made a great deal of money when in 1697 the Bank agreed to accept these tallies at par value, succeeding in paying them all off by 1707. It was Sir Gilbert who went personally to Queen Anne to protest her dismissal of Godolphin in 1710, an act resented as highly impertinent by Tories.

15 Defoe is thinking of the financial difficulties of the government during the 1690s. Lacking credit, the government was forced to pay so much interest to raise loans, that it found itself sinking deeper and deeper into debt.

16 Cf. Joseph Conrad's description of the sea-reach of the Thames in *Heart of Darkness*; he evokes

"... the great spirit of the past upon the lower reaches of the Thames. The tidal current runs to and fro in its unceasing service, crowded with memories of men and ships it has borne to the rest of home or to the battles of the sea. ... It had known the ships and the men. They had sailed from Deptford, from Greenwich, from Erith—the adventurers and the settlers; kings' ships and the ships of men on Change; captains, admirals, the dark 'interlopers' of the Eastern trade, and the commissioned 'generals' of East India fleets."

An Essay upon Loans
(1710)

Having treated in brief upon the difficult subject of credit, and that, if the town is not a deceiver, with some success; it seems necessary to speak a word or two upon the great object upon which that credit operates, viz. *loans of money* upon the publick demands.

The Author, *an enemy to long prefaces*, presents his thoughts to the world upon this head, without any other apology than this, that he thinks it a service at this time, to remove the mistakes which some make, and others improve to our disadvantage, while they think it is to the disadvantage of somebody else. While they aim at an object they would hurt, they wound themselves; and in prosecuting private or party prejudices, injure, weaken, and assault the publick good; which every man has a property in, and therefore is in duty bound to defend.

A discourse upon credit is naturally an introduction to a discourse upon loan; credit without loan is a beautiful flower, fair to the eye, fragrant to the smell, ornamental to the plot of ground it grows in; but yielding neither fruit nor seed, neither profit to the possessor of it, by making due advantage of its produce, or benefit to posterity, by propagation of its species. On the other hand, loans without credit are like the labouring plowman upon a barren soil, who works, cultivates, sweats and toils, but to no purpose; all the fruit of his labour ends in sterility and abortion.

Loans are the consequences of credit, and the evidence of that particular quality, which in the preceding discourse of credit I laid down as its foundation; I mean general probity, punctual, just and honourable management.

To explain things as I go, though this needs but little: by

loans, I am now to be understood to mean *lending money to the present government*. The thing will extend to private affairs, and I might take up a great deal of your time in speaking of the effects of credit in trade, such as delivering goods by tradesmen to one another, paper credit in affairs of cash; pledging, pawning, and all the articles of security for money practised in general commerce; but these things are not to the present purpose.

The author of this confines his discourse to the government borrowing money of the subject, whether upon securities established by Parliament, equivalent in value delivered, publick faith, general credit, or otherwise.

The nature of these securities, the reason, the usefulness, and the foundation they stand on, are no part of the present subject; they are reserved by the author to a head by themselves, if leisure and the publick service make it proper to present you a discourse upon *funds*.

* * *

By this method has the greatest part of our yearly taxes, since that time, been raised; the Parliament establishing funds for payment of interest, and the people advancing money, by way of loan, on those interests.

It may not be improper here for some people to reflect, that in the advantages granted by the government upon these loans, and the great discounts upon tallies on the deficient aids, mentioned above, were founded the great stocks of money, banks and powerful credit; with which some people are grown to such a height, especially in their own opinion, as to talk of influencing the publick affairs, and as it were menacing the government with apprehensions of their lending or not lending, as they are, or are not pleased with the management of, or managers in the publick oeconomy; and this is the subject I am a little to speak to.

Loans to the government, by the gradations aforesaid, having been found essentially necessary, the first steps to that new method were found fatally incumbering; the high premios given, the great advantages proposed, and the large interests paid to the lender. The government appeared like a distressed debtor, who was every day squeezed to death by the exorbitant greediness of the lender; the citizens began to decline trade and turn usurers; foreign commerce attended with the hazards of war had infinite discouragements, and the people in general drew home their effects, to embrace the advantage of lending their money to the government. Then grew up the Bank, whose second subscription being founded upon a parliamentary security, for making good the deficient tallies, was formed by receiving in those tallies at par, which cost the subscribers but 55 to 65 per cent; by which the greatest estates were raised in the least time, and the most of them, that has been known in any age, or in any part of the world.

This, I say, turned the whole City into a corporation of usury, and they appeared not as a bank, but rather one general society of bankers; all men that could draw any money out of their trades, run with it to Exchange Alley, to buy stocks and tallies, subscribe to banks or companies; or to the Exchequer with it to put into loans, and lend it upon the advantageous funds settled by Parliament.

It is meet to mention these things, for the sake of the people who have gotten such great estates by the government, to let them know from whence the advantages they have made, did proceed; and also for some other reasons which will appear in the sequel of this discourse.

The government, to preserve to themselves the advantage of these loans, and yet to avoid being imposed upon and oppressed by those exorbitant interests and encouragements, about the year 1698, entered into measures to secure the loan of money, and yet lower the advantages given to the lenders.

The first was done by the Parliament, applying themselves to restore credit, by a vote to make good all deficiencies, and erecting a punctual, just and fair management of the payments; by which every several engagement being honourably complied with, the credit of the publick affairs revived, and the exorbitances the former years were exposed to; wore off of course.

This tedious recapitulation of things will appear less trouble to the reader, when he sees the use I shall make of it. Here may be seen several things, which, if well considered, tend to the lowering the high and extravagant imaginations of some people, with respect to *loans*, *credit*, *borrowing* and *lending* of money to the government; such as these:

I. Large interest, advantages, premios for advance of money, and the like, will bring in loans in spite of parties, in spite of deficiencies, in spite of all the conspiracies in the world to the contrary; while a just, honourable, and punctual performance on the part of the government does but maintain the credit of the nation.

II. As the affairs of the government have made loans necessary, and they cannot go on without borrowing; so the stream of trade and cash is so universally turned into publick funds, the whole nation feels so much of, gains so much by, and depends so much upon the publick credit, that they can no more do without the funds, than the funds can do without the loan.

III. These borrowings and lendings are become so much a trade, so many families have their employment from, and get so great estates by the negotiating these things, that it is impossible for any set of men to put a stop to it; or to get any such power into their hands, as to give the government just grounds of apprehension, that this or that party of men can put a cheque to the publick affairs, be they *Whigs*, *Tories*, *City*, *court*, *banks*, *company* or what they please to call themselves.

I shall not tie myself to speak to these apart, *the liberty of this tract will not admit of it*, but in a summary way you will find the fact demonstrated, and the consequence evident.

Men in trade, more especially than the rest of mankind, are bound by their interest; gain is the end of commerce: where that gain visibly attends the adventurer, as no hazard can discourage, so no other obligation can prevent the application. *Impiger extremos currit Mercator ad Indos.*

To pretend after this, that parties shall govern mankind against their gain, is to philosophize wisely upon what may be, and what would be politick to bring to pass; but what no man can say was ever put in practice to any perfection; or can be so by the common principles that govern mankind in the world.

There have been combinations in trade, and people have seemed to act counter to their present interests; nay, have gone on in apparent loss, in pursuance of such combinations; but they have always been made in order to secure a return of greater gain; and therefore the laws made against such combinations are not made to prevent people's going on to their loss, but to prevent the end of that appearing loss; viz. the engrossment or monopolizing of trade, to come at some advantage over others, and thereby make an exorbitant gain.

But it was never yet heard, that the zeal of any party got the better so much of their interest, as to put a general stop to the current and natural stream of their interest; that a people should reject the fair and just advantages which have raised so many estates, and are the due supplies to the breaches made by the war upon general commerce. To talk, that we will not lend money to the government, while the Parliament settles funds, allows interests, gives premios and advantages, is to say nature will cease, men of money will abstain from being men loving to get money. That tradesmen should cease to seek gain, and usurers to love large interests; that men that have gained money should leave off desiring to get more; and that zeal to a party should prevail over zeal to their families; that men should forfeit their interest for their humour, and serve their politicks at the price of their interest.

Let those that promise themselves these things enquire among the merchants, and see if parties govern anything in trade; if there is either *Whig* or *Tory* in a good bargain; Churchman or Dissenter in a good freight; High Church or Low Church in a good adventure; if a shopkeeper sees a good pennyworth, a scrivener a good mortgage, a moneyed man a good purchase; do they ever ask what party he is of that parts with it? Nay, rather in spite of party aversions, do we not buy, sell, lend, borrow, enter into companies, partnerships, and the closest engagements with one another, nay, marry with one another without any questions of the matter?

Let us come to the general body of people as fate has unhappily divided us; where are the men? (supposing a party conspiracy against the government in this matter of loan); where are the men who would hold together, and refuse making seven per cent of their money to preserve the engagement? Where the men who would stay their hands, and lose the probability of gaining a thousand pounds a year by a lottery? No, no, it is not to be done; the stream of desire after gain runs too strong in mankind, to bring anything of that kind to perfection in this age. The thing is so impracticable in its nature, that it seems a token of great ignorance in the humour of the age to suggest it; and a man would be tempted to think those people that do suggest it, do not themselves believe what they say about it.

* * *

This leads me to examine the difference between *loan* and *fund* in this case. Examining which, something may perhaps come to light for our instruction, which has not been much thought of before.

Solomon tells us, *the borrower is servant to the lender*; but with the wise man's leave, in this case it is not so. Solomon is there to be understood speaking of the poor borrowing wretch, who borrowed upon the foot of charity and compassion, and therefore he just before says, *the poor uses many entreaties, but the rich answer roughly*. The poor man that borrows on his single promise to supply his urgent necessity, *uses entreaties*, as we may say, *he begs to borrow*; but the *rich lender* is surly, hardly consents, *answers roughly*, and is with difficulty brought to lend.

But we are to distinguish here between Solomon's borrower described as above, and he that borrows on a sufficient current security. He is no more servant to the lender than the lender is servant to him; having an unquestioned security to give, he scorns to ask you twice; but if you do not think fit to lend your money, he goes to another.

This is apparent in the publick securities, as well as in private; and will make it out, if ever put to the test, that the people of England stand in as much need of the funds to lend their money upon, as the government stands in need of their money *upon those funds*. I prove this by a matter of fact, fresh in your memories, and undeniable in all its circumstances. In the beginning of the war, when the money lay abroad in trade, the knowledge of affairs young, and the people not apprized of the thing; the anticipations upon taxes and loans came heavy, and were small. *What drew them on?* Large premios, high interests, chances of prizes, survivorship, and the like.

Thus when the necessities of the government were great, and their credit young to borrow, the lenders made their market. But when the government found themselves rich in funds, their demands, though great, yet not pressing; credit established, the Parliament, *the great fund of funds*, and centre of credit, ready to make good deficiences, and leaving no room for jealousies in the minds of the people, *what was the case*? You took off your premios, you drew no more lotteries for 16 years, you lowered your interest, you brought your annuities from 14 to 7 per cent, and your interest on tallies from 7 to 6 per cent per ann. From 7 per cent upon Exchequer bills, you came down to 4 per cent. And what was the consequence? The necessity of the lenders being more to lodge their money for improvement, than the necessity of the borrowers was to ask, they came always down to your price; and had you brought the general interest of loans to 4 per cent, they must have come down, for money is no longer money than it can be improved. Nay, it is to be observed, the eagerness of the people to bring in their money increased, as the advantages of lending decreased. Having no way to improve it better, they were under an absolute necessity of bringing it in, for the sake of the improvement.

Are these any of the people, who can be supposed to say to the Parliament, they will not lend their money? It would almost provoke a man to laugh at them. You won't lend your money! Why, what will you do with it?

Perhaps you won't lend it to the government, well, you will then lend it upon private security, upon land, and the like; why then, those you lend it to, will lend it to the government, and so the malice of the affair will be lost, and the advantage too. Will you run it into trade? Do so by all means. Some of those hands it will circulate through, will lend it to the government. Your very export and import is a loan to the government. In short, the government shall have your money *first or last*, do what you will with it.

Suppose it were possible to divide this nation into two parts, the landed men and the moneyed men, and the government were to be put into the hands of the first against the consent of the last; and the moneyed men, knowing the landed men could not carry on the war without money, resolved to lend them none, I mean as a government, what course should the landed men take?

In my opinion, they should pass an Act, that none of those people should be admitted to lend any money to the government at all; what then would be the consequence? They would be immediately distressed with the weight of money without improvement; they would eagerly lend it to the landed men at 4 per cent upon their land; and they again lending it to the government at 6 and 7 per cent, the government would be supplied, and the landed men would get 3 per cent, by the other men's money.

I am not making application; but let any of the present parties, who boast of their having the gross of the money, reflect what they would say, if an Act were to pass, that no Whig's money, or no Dissenter's money, or no High-Churchman's money should be accepted upon loan; that they should not be allowed a transfer upon any stock, or to buy any annuity; the complaint would be very loud of their being excluded the common advantages of their fellow subjects; and that paying their share of taxes, they ought to have room for equal improvements, and ought not to be excluded; *and this is true too*, it would be hard. Then they would run about to their friends among the contrary party, shelter their money under their names, and perhaps give ½ per cent or 1 per cent commission to others to lend, buy and transfer for them. And what would the government feel in all this?

The case is this, no party can be so foolish to think they can be able to stop the loan of money to the government; nor need the government think of putting the laws in execution against such combination (*though if any such appeared, no doubt, they might be prosecuted*). Keep up but the credit of Parliament, and let that Parliament find funds, it is not in the power of any party of men to stop the current of loans, any more than they can stop the tide at London-Bridge, in its constant course of flux and reflux from and to the sea.

There is no doubt but the French have agents among us, who would be glad to weaken our hands in the war, and prevent our supplies for that purpose. From them it must be that these notions creep into people's heads; Englishmen cannot in their common senses be so weak; telling us that we shall have no loans, is much at one to telling us we shall have no recruits to our army; as, while you can pay armies, you shall never want men; so while you can pay interest, you shall never want loans.

The estates that some men boast of, by which they are enabled to lend, and made bold enough to threaten a stop of it, were gained by lending. Those that have them are too eager to increase them, those that want them too eager to gain them, by the same method, and all too covetous and too selfish not to come into any good proposal.

The worst these men can do, is, by making things appear backward, to raise the rate of interests, and move the Parliament to add something to the usual encouragements for lending; and if the nation pays this, who have they to blame for it? Yet neither will they be able to do this, the present credit of the British Parliament putting it out of their power; for as the necessity of lending will prompt on one hand, the undoubted security of parliamentary credit removes all the jealousies our party men would raise on the other.

The zeal some men shew for their country, as well as justice to the government, is nevertheless very conspicuous in this; who (first) to glorify their party prejudices would have the war miscarry, rather than money should be lent, while such men manage as they pretend not to like; (secondly) reproach some people with designs to make peace with France, and yet endeavour by discouraging loans to render it impossible for them to carry on the war.

But both these will be disappointed. While the Parliament supports credit, and good funds support the Parliament, money will come in as naturally, as fire will ascend, or water flow; nor will it be in the power of our worst enemies to prevent it.

If the author of this appears again in publick, it may be upon the subject of FUNDS.

5. The Freeholder's Plea against Stock-Jobbing Elections of Parliament Men; The Villainy of Stock-Jobbers Detected, and the Causes of the Late Run upon the Bank and Bankers, Discovered and Considered; The Anatomy of Exchange Alley: or a System of Stock-Jobbing

The following section contains writings on the evils of stock speculation excerpted from three of Defoe's pamphlets: *The Freeholder's Plea* (23 January 1701), *The Villainy of Stock-Jobbers* (11 February 1701), and *The Anatomy of Exchange Alley* (July 1719). Economic historians rely upon the descriptions and statistics Defoe supplies in these pamphlets, and Defoe thought so highly of the literary merits of the first two pamphlets that he included them in collected editions of his works, and referred to them in the later pamphlet, *The Anatomy of Exchange Alley*.

The three pamphlets deal with different aspects of stock speculation: the first with corrupt electoral practices engaged in by stock manipulators or "jobbers", the second with the effect of stock speculation on the credit and trade of the entire English nation, and the third with specific methods by which speculators manipulate the prices of stock.

Defoe was not alone in his opposition to stock-jobbing. Although the development of a securities market in London proved to be of great political and economic utility to eighteenth-century England, contemporary opinion was united in its opposition to this feature of the new system of public finance. A recent historian of the English financial revolution writes of the stock market, "It was denounced as inherently wicked and against the public interest. The phrase 'stock-jobbing', freely used to denote every kind of activity in the market, had clear overtones of self-interest and corruption."[1] Both landed and trading interests opposed stock-jobbing, the former largely on social, the latter on economic grounds. All groups believed that national interests were endangered when, in pre-war or war periods, jobbers capitalized on public anxiety, selling large blocks of government securities ("bear" sales) to drive down prices even further, so that they could then repurchase surreptitiously even larger blocks of the same stock at reduced prices.

Defoe's "hatred of stock-jobbers was such", remarks James Sutherland, "that he appears to have put them considerably lower in his moral scale than pirates like Captain Singleton or thieves like Moll Flanders."[2] Just as the Jacobite plays the role of Satan in Defoe's political world, the speculator in stocks performs this function in Defoe's economic world. A concealed enemy, and therefore a dangerous enemy, he corrupts with his blighting touch a complex and bustling world, metamorphosing it into a sterile and static hell of weights and measures, of slave-owning tyrants and slavish human property. Not only does he transform England's "green and pleasant Land" into an early eighteenth-century version of Blake's landscape of "dark Satanic Mills"; his activities portend the destruction of religious liberty and constitutional government in England, the victory of the Jacobites, and the hegemony of France. Charged with a weight of emotion not easily discernible in his best-known fictions, Defoe's passionate denunciations of speculators in his economic writings are accordingly of particular interest to students of literature.

The Freeholder's Plea concentrates upon the practice of bribery in Parliamentary elections, a practice that had existed before 1701, and indeed had been the subject of previous Parliamentary restriction. Defoe perceives that corruption is inherent in an antiquated electoral system that over-represents municipal corporations and old, decayed towns, at the expense of propertied county voters, of flourishing new towns, and of London itself. This inherent potential for corruption has been seized on in the 1701 election by stockholders of the competing Old and New East India Companies, bidding for the votes of small and corrupt boroughs in order to secure the controlling interest in Parliament that will enable them to wipe out their competitors in the lucrative trade to the East Indies.

Faced by the threat of another war with France (the War of the Spanish Succession did, in fact, break out in May 1702), the English nation is particularly unfortunate in its parliamentary election at such a time of crisis. Defoe resents strongly the impertinent intrusion, into the process of selecting well-qualified members of Parliament, of an issue distinctly inferior to those of war and peace and the Protestant succession to the English throne. His indignation was indeed justified, for economic historians substantiate the accuracy of his description of vote purchasing by stockholders of the two competing East India Companies.

Defoe presents the case against stock manipulators in terms of simple and idealistic principles of national interest opposed to complex and self-serving economic practice. Very shrewdly, he chooses the most appropriate spokesman for this point of view, with which he agrees; his persona is one of the humbler county freeholders, opposed to corrupt moneyed interests and puzzled by their machinations. The plain-dealing propensity of the semi-illiterate speaker (see footnote 12, page 178), is emphasized by his confused syntax, scrambled pronouns, and striking colloquial expressions, all exemplified by the following passage:

> Only we find we are swingingly taxed; and they tell us 'tis done by the Parliament; but we never understood they had any of the money themselves, we always thought the money was for the King, though they had the giving of it, then we see in the King's Proclamation for calling a Parliament, that it was to advise with them, about affairs of the highest importance to the kingdom.

The speaker's mock naïveté quickly gives way to an attack upon stock-jobbers couched mainly in terms of the scorn of the landed classes for "mechanicks, tradesmen, stock-jobbers", who understand nothing but their own petty trade interests, and who lack sense, not to mention honesty. Such men are unfit by occupation to deal with weighty matters of international politics like the dreaded "union of France and Spain" (page 257). Only once (on page 256) does Defoe hint at a more sinister evil in stock-jobbers, a correspondence between the French Court and Jonathan's Coffee House (like Garraway's, a favourite Exchange Alley meeting-place of brokers,) when he says, "Some, and not a few, of our stock-jobbing brokers, are Frenchmen ..." (In the two later pamphlets he develops his indictment of stock-jobbing by identifying it more closely with Jacobite, treasonable interests.) *The Freeholder's Plea* concludes with an impassioned appeal to reasonable and patriotic readers of all classes: "But when you come to talk of Parliament men, gentlemen, pray consider 'tis the whole nation lies at stake" (page 258). Social snobbery is replaced by rhetoric designed to unite all Englishmen in the interest of the nation as a whole.

The Villainy of Stock-Jobbers describes in detail the practices by which members of the Old East India Company in 1701 artificially engrossed current cash and Bank notes and then created a run on the Bank of England and the Exchequer, in order to damage public credit. Their purpose was to hurt the Bank, which had extended financial support to their rivals, and to remind the Whig government of their economic power. (The Old East India Company, under its director, Sir Josiah Child, a friend of King James II, was identified after the Revolution with the Court, anti-Whig interest.) Defoe's account of the devices used by the Old Company is substantiated by economic historians.

Defoe believes that the Old Company wishes to gain control of the New Company in order to manipulate its rival's stock, regardless of its intrinsic value. Such manipulation, he states (see page 259), caused the wild fluctuations of East India stock that took place in the 1690s. This conclusion has been rejected by modern economists,[3] who regard excessive stock manipulation not as cause, but as the result of more basic factors. Fear of war with France, coupled with the deadly rivalry between the Old and New East India Companies, was the underlying cause of the financial crisis of 1701.[4]

Defoe suggests that rivalry between the companies be terminated by amalgamating the two groups (an agreement leading to eventual amalgamation was signed in 1702), and that the trade of the new body be regulated by the government to prevent importation of goods competitive with English manufactures (trade of the East India Company had always been, and continued to be, regulated by the government.) His third suggestion, that Parliament pass measures limiting the transfer of stocks between individuals, was short-sighted. Such measures had already been passed in 1697 and had proven futile. Godolphin allowed them to be renewed in 1708 more as "a sop to public opinion ... than a serious attempt to regulate prices".[5] External factors, not human vice or wickedness, cause sustained sharp plunges of the market, and it proved impossible to eliminate the external factors by coercing jobbers.[6]

I have reproduced a passage from *The Villainy of Stock-Jobbers* in which Defoe tells an anecdote, inviting the reader to take it either as parable or history (see page 259). His anecdote illustrates why it would have been wiser for the Bank of England to "have stood their ground boldly" in 1701, instead of "offering double interest at a time, when a storm threatened them" (page 261). The story is notable as an example of Defoe's ability to explain complicated economics in a simple and interesting manner. It is also significant because it suggests that Defoe recognized the role psychology plays in the matter of credit and was recommending the use of game psychology to control the financial environment. Without the anecdote, one might easily be misled into concluding that Defoe believed solely in the "intrinsic value" of stock, or the concrete resources of a company, and had therefore very primitive notions about the nature of credit, ignoring the effect of psychological factors on demand.

In view of the unlimited and mysterious powers economic writers of his period attributed to the then uninvestigated phenomenon of "funds of credit",[7] Defoe's comment about the difference between the credit of the stock or principal of the Bank of England, and the credit of Bank bills, or the Bank's cash, is significant. It suggests that he had analysed the concept of a fund of credit, and had some ideas about the economic limits to the expansion of credit which were in advance of his time: "To ask the world to stay for their money and take interest, is to weaken the credit of their cash, and transfer themselves to the credit of their stock which nobody doubts to be good".[8] It is unfortunate that Defoe never wrote the *Essay upon Funds* he mentioned in his *Essay upon Loans*. He would probably have dealt with the problem of limitation of credit in such an essay, and his ideas would undoubtedly have been interesting. His insight into the complex subject of credit was far more profound than has yet been appreciated; it is unfortunate that no economist has investigated thoroughly Defoe's ideas on the matter.

Another passage I have reproduced from *The Villainy of Stock-Jobbers* (see page 262) is interesting for its literary and psychological, rather than for its economic implications. The metaphor of a war conducted by speculators through artifice, undermining, and poison that works at a distance, demonstrates why Defoe preferred even pirates or thieves to stock-jobbers: it was for the same reason that he preferred an open and confessed enemy to a concealed one, as he explains in his *Letter to Mr. Bisset* (1709). A furious and open enemy destroys himself by his own impetuosity, whereas a subtle enemy is more dangerous. Stock-jobbers in *The Freeholder's Plea* were abhorrent because they were too stupid and insensitive to appreciate the qualitative values inherent in the Protestant religion, the English form of representative government, and the danger to these values represented by a too powerful France; no matter what the issue, stock-jobbers were interested only in quantitative values, or the price of stocks.[9] Stock-jobbers appear in *The Villainy of Stock-Jobbers* in a more sinister light; they are engaged in clandestine warfare against their own nation. In economics, as in politics (see essay on *A Letter from a Gentleman at the Court of St. Germains*), the metaphor of the diabolic hidden enemy and concealed warfare occurs to Defoe when he wished to describe an ultimate evil.

The Anatomy of Exchange Alley is a long pamphlet of 64 pages, supposedly by an insider, "a jobber", able to describe with authority the particular methods used by speculators over a period of some thirty years up to 1719, to manipulate stock prices to their advantage. The aim of the pamphlet is to prove that in recent years stock-jobbers' practices have become a more serious danger to the English nation than ever before. Their activities consist no longer merely of cheating unsuspecting individuals, other stock-jobbers, poor widows or orphans, or even the entire tax-paying public; they have now acquired the "capacity of intermeddling with the publick, assisting rebellion, encouraging invasion", and, asserts Defoe, "if I do not bring the stock-jobbers, even the Whigs among them, to be guilty of treason against their King and country, and that of the worst kind too, then I do nothing" (page 269).

Stock speculation in the face of the only too real danger of Jacobite uprisings and invasions,[10] combined with flagrant complicity in dubious financial activities by many Court, Parliament, and ministry members[11] breaks down Defoe's habitual mask of moderation, and perhaps accounts in part for the disjointedness of the pamphlet. Defoe's excitement is revealed in his challenge to battle of unnamed but influential potential enemies. To those who have cautioned him to avoid offending powerful Whigs, he replies:

> My first answer is, *so I will*. I will have a care of them, and in the next place let them have a care of me; for if I should speak the whole truth of some of them, they might be Whigs, but I dare say, they would be neither P—— [Parliament] men, or friends to the Government very long ... (pp. 269–70)

John Robert Moore has demonstrated in his essay, "Defoe in the Pillory", how Defoe's detestation of financial or moral misbehaviour in public officials drove him beyond the bounds of discretion in some of his early writings. The powerful enemies he had antagonized were responsible for his being pilloried in 1703 for an offence that did not habitually earn such severe punishment.[12] Similarly, his brief imprisonment in 1713 was less the result of any misunderstanding of the irony in his pamphlets about the Protestant succession than of personal animosity against the outspoken author. In the *Anatomy* the fifty-nine-year-old writer demonstrates that age has not mellowed his fighting spirit; he is willing once more to risk his liberty and the fortunes of his family by speaking out against financial corruption in statesmen.

The *Anatomy* is not a well organized essay, but it is a goldmine of inspired individual passages. Two sections on the methods of speculators are particularly lively because of Defoe's use of colloquial speech. One (on pages 263–4) describes the gulling of a young tradesman who has a little money to invest, in a manner that suggests the influence of Restoration comedy. (Defoe specifically compares on page 274 the mulcting of young tradesmen on the Exchange with that of young country gentlemen visiting London.) The other is a short description of the 1690s practices of Sir Josiah Child of the Old East India Company, as he outwitted other experienced stock speculators (pages 266–7).

After his description of Sir Josiah's invention of false rumours of unfavourable foreign news in the 1690s in order to drive down stock prices ("bear selling", considered highly unpatriotic), Defoe discusses increased manipulation of foreign news by stock-jobbers in the early years of the eighteeth century. He objects to what he regards as the dissemination of false news, invented by members of Exchange Alley. Since financial crises are caused by a concurrence of unfavourable objective factors with a loss of confidence in buyers (subjective factor), Scott believes, "The improvement of the press appears at first to have had the effect of making crises somewhat more frequent, since the increase of information came quickly, and businessmen of the time were inclined to exaggerate the unfavourable news which was supplied to them copiously."[13] Like his contemporaries, Defoe failed to recognize the increased scope of foreign news coverage, attributing the new flood of information affecting finance to the operation of a self-interested rumour mill in Exchange Alley. Only with the perspective of time is it now possible to observe that "the daily valuation of the government's credit on the floor of Jonathan's was, like the popular press, one of the features of England's 'open' form of government in the eighteenth century; and that this form despite the risks it involved, was to prove more secure in the long run, because more firmly based on public discussion and evaluation, than the closed and supposedly more efficient bureaucratic governments of France and other European Powers."[14]

Defoe proceeds from his discussion of Sir Josiah Child and the bad news mongers of Exchange Alley to an attack upon statesmen corrupted by the temptations of stock speculation. He describes the collusion of statesmen in mulcting the general public by speculation on government lottery tickets (probably in 1711 or 1712). His description demonstrates how he could make clear in succinct terms a rather complex economic transaction, driving his point home tersely with the maxim: " 'Tis very hard when our statesmen come into a confederacy to bite the people, and when dukes turn stock-jobbers" (page 268).

He attempts to prove that stock-jobbing in times of national crisis is equivalent to high treason, in an argument that demonstrates his rhetorical ability to marshal moral indignation in support of a legally dubious equation. His own common sense rebels, however, against his extremist position, for he admits (see page 270) that speculators are not really traitors according to the letter of the law: "If they were, I should not satyrize them, but impeach them."

His description of the topography and population of Exchange Alley (pages 272–3) serves as a protest against the presence of statesmen in such an environment. The topographical description should remind readers of the relish evident in *Moll Flanders* and *Journal of the Plague Year* for details of London's geography.

Pages 274–5 are devoted to Defoe's impassioned warnings about the dangerous political consequences to England of unchecked economic power in the hands of speculators, and of the even more alarming prospect of corrupt ministries capturing this economic power in order to rule the country by bypassing Parliament.[15] The imagery of this passage deserves close examination, for it proceeds from an equation of stock-jobbers with terrifying midnight fire (the concealed enemy theme mentioned on page 244 above), avoids the equation of stock-jobbers with traitors (he senses that his argument has been unconvincing), and culminates with an apocalyptic evocation of the state of slavery that will ensue once prices (quantities) have triumphed over private emotions and concern for the welfare of England (qualities), and once emotions and moral values have been reduced to mere fertilizer for a petrified forest of stock prices (see page 274). Defoe's hell is not, like Pope's, the triumph of Dullness and Night over civilized wit and intelligence. It is—a fact that should be noted by readers who still insist upon regarding the exceedingly complex Defoe as merely a spokesman for shopkeepers[16]—the transformation of all of England into a stock exchange, a mere piece of property, owned by government ministers and populated by automatons.

If Defoe's myopia about the relationship of the stock market and stock speculation to the financial revolution taking place in England united him in one way with his contemporaries, in another way he was unlike most writers of his day. He was not a special pleader for land-owning or trading classes; he was concerned with the effect of stock speculation upon the quality and strength of the whole English nation, especially as it affected England's struggle for power with France. French victory to Defoe spelled the triumph of the Stuart dynasty and the end of constitutional government and religious liberty in England.

In the early 1800s only an economic genius could have discerned the laws underlying the fluctuations of the stock market. Wholesale lapses in financial probity by statesmen were much more salient in the feverish years of 1719 and 1720, before the South Sea crash, than were general economic laws.[17] In one essential way, Defoe's objection to stock speculation by statesmen was as impeccable economically as it was ethically, for corruption in statesmen responsible for administering public finance is as damaging to national credit as are false economic notions about the infinite expansibility of public credit. As Scott observes, the South Sea episode of 1719–1720 "exhibited the inevitable outcome of an economic fallacy, developed in an atmosphere of political corruption".[18]

Notes

1 P. G. M. Dickson, *The Financial Revolution in England: A Study in the Development of Public Credit, 1688–1756* (London, 1967), pp 32–33.

2 James Sutherland, *Daniel Defoe: A Critical Study* (Cambridge, Mass., 1971), p. 33.

3 "East India stock was liable to marked variations in its price, owing to a number of different factors: the political battles preceding the union in 1709 of the English Company of 1698 and the Old Company; the return or loss of Indian cargoes; the issues of native wars; the smiles or frowns of princes. Basically it was a speculator's stock." (Dickson, p. 495.)

4 W. R. Scott, *The Constitution and Finance of English, Scottish and Irish Joint-Stock Companies to 1720* (Cambridge, 1912), I, 366.

5 Dickson, p. 517.

6 *Ibid*., p. 519.

7 A "fund of credit" meant that government debt to a company could be used as collateral for raising loans for the company's commercial activities. Since the government paid interest on the debt, assigning in advance revenues from specific taxes for such payment, the company was assured of a steady income.

8 Had John Law in France and the promoters of the English South Sea Company in 1719 been more careful about using the same basic stock or principle over and over again to reduce the national debt by "juggling obligations of the State from one fund to another", (Scott, I, 437), perhaps the acute financial crisis of 1720 would not have occurred.

9 In *The Compleat English Tradesman* (Vol. II, 1727), Defoe describes with disgust a scene that took place between King James II and a "purse-proud Tradesman" after James had abdicated and attempted to escape to France. Threatened by a crowd in which a certain man appeared to be the leader, James asked to have him brought in, attempting, in an eloquent speech, to persuade the man to behave with more restraint. The tradesman remained tongue-tied while James himself spoke but then responded insolently to one of the king's gentlemen:

Don't talk to me, says he, *about it; what can I do?* and so goes on to the stairs. As soon as he was got fairly to the stair-head, and saw his way open, he turns short about to the gentleman, and raising his voice so that the King, who was but in the next room, should be sure to hear him, says he, I have a bag of money as long as my Arm, HOLLOW, boys, HOLLOW. (pp. 253–254)

10 Rumours about invasions and rebellions in favour of the Pretender had been rife throughout 1718, as the tension between England and Spain grew, culminating in open hostilities later in the year. In 1719, during the course of the short Anglo-Spanish war, the Duke of Ormond, financed by Cardinal Alberoni of Spain, had attempted unsuccessfully to land a squadron in England, and a Jacobite uprising took place in Scotland but was crushed at Glenshiel.

11 During the Parliamentary investigations of the South Sea crash, it was apparent that many members of both houses of Parliament had interests in South Sea stock, and that the company had engaged in extensive bribery of legislators, women favourites of George I, and

members of the ministry, including the Chancellor of the Exchequer and one of the Secretaries of the Treasury. Since the South Sea fever started in 1719, it is probable that Defoe's indignation is based upon inside knowledge of some of the shady business taking place at the time he wrote *The Anatomy of Exchange Alley*.

12 John Robert Moore, "Defoe in the Pillory: A New Interpretation" in *Defoe in the Pillory and Other Studies* (Bloomington, Indiana, 1939), pp. 2–32.

13 Scott, I, 476.

14 Dickson, pp. 515–516.

15 Scott points out that there was at one time a real possibility of the South Sea Company's coming to control the entire country. "In the corrupt state of domestic politics, it was feared at the time that the company would be able to control the ministry in power at any given period, and that therefore it could secure parliamentary sanction of its schemes.... If such a trust had been formed in Britain, its power could only have been curbed by a revolution against the new plutocracy." (III, 352–353.)

16 Ian Watt, Dorothy Van Ghent, and Mark Schorer, to mention only a few brilliant and influential critics who have convinced a whole generation of teachers and readers that the original and erratic Defoe can be understood by confining him within a stereotype of the middle-class man, seem not to have read widely enough in his writings to realize that he could laugh in one context at the same thing he despised and feared in another context. Moll Flanders illustrates this characteristic, for Defoe presented her tendency to value everything in monetary terms in tones of amusement; he considered her outlook appropriate to her position in society and her profession as thief. In a letter of 1722 printed in *Applebee's Journal* and signed "Betty Blueskin", niece to "the *famous Moll Flanders*", Defoe has Betty write:

I never went to Salter's lecture, or St. Lawrence's Church, and came away without a gold watch, or a tweeser, or some other valuable prize, in my life. I rarely came empty-handed from the theatre, especially if the play was anything popular. I assure you *Cato* was worth above 100 guineas to me, and yet I reckon the things taken, as we generally sell such things; namely at half value.... *Harlequin* has been tolerably beneficial to me; but the auditories were a little too much French. There were not so many gold watches there, as on other occasions; however, I don't complain.

Reprinted in William Lee, *Daniel Defoe, His Life and Recently Discovered Writings* (London, 1869), III, 334.

In this passage Defoe's amusement is obvious. He delights in reducing Addison's fashionable play *Cato* to the dimension it would assume in the eyes of a pickpocket, and in making a malicious little joke about the poverty of the French.

What was appropriate and even amusing in Moll and in Betty, however, was anathema to Defoe in a statesman.

17 Walpole himself, the outstanding financial expert of his time, believed without qualification in the fund of credit idea and considered that excessive stock speculation had caused the crash of 1720. He did not perceive that "insofar as the ministry had betrayed its trust, the creditors were forced into wild speculation, where the dice were loaded against them". (Scott, I, 431.)

18 Scott, I, 436.

The Freeholder's Plea against Stock-Jobbing Elections of Parliament Men (1701)

* * *

The grand work which the whole nation is now intent upon, is chusing their representatives in Parliament, chusing men to meet, and advise with the King about the most important affairs of the kingdom.

And while all men ought to be fixing their eyes upon such men as are best qualified to sit in that place of honour, and to examine who are fittest to be entrusted with the religion and peace of England, and perhaps of all Europe.

Here we are plagued with the impertinence of two East India Companies, as if the interest of either company were to be named in the day with the *Protestant religion and the publick peace*, or as if they, who are fit to be representatives of the people in the great matters of peace and war, leagues, and alliances of neighbours, succession of crowns, and protection of the Protestant religion, should not be capable of deciding the petty controversy in trade between two rival companies.

The grand question asked now, when your vote is required for a Parliament man, is not as it ought to be, "Is he a man of sense, of religion, of honesty and estate?" but, "What company is he for, the new, or the old?"

If Mr. A. M. set up as a candidate in a neighbouring borough, who set him up? 'Tis known he is no inhabitant there, nor ever was, has no freehold, or copyhold, or leasehold estate there, nor is not known there, and of himself possibly was not acquainted with twenty people there.

But enquire what company he is for; and then see if all the rest of that company were not found running over the water, to make their interest with their friends for his election.

And the time would fail us, and the paper too, to give you a list of the shopkeepers, merchants, and pedlars, and the stock-jobbers, who, with their hired liveries, in coaches, and six horses, who, God knows, never had coach or livery of their own, are come down into the countries, being detached from London, by either company to get themselves chosen Parliament men, by those boroughs who are easy to be imposed upon, and who, like well-meaning men, that know nothing of the matter, choose them upon the recommendation of the country gentlemen that have interest in the towns, which country gentlemen are prevailed upon to quit their own pretensions, to advance theirs; but by what arguments we cannot pretend to determine.

We have formerly been told that spending money upon the inhabitants of towns, was a pernicious practice; and no doubt it was, and an Act of Parliament has been wisely made to prevent it.

What any man could propose to himself by spending 2,000 (nay, 11,000 pound was spent at the town of Winchelsea) to be chosen to sit in a House, where there is not one farthing to be gotten honestly, was a mystery everyone did not understand.

But here is a new way of getting money: for if a country gentleman has so much interest in a town, that he can be chosen a Member of Parliament, if he will decline it, here is a sort of folks they call *stock-jobbers*, help him to a 1,000 g——s for his interest.

This is Parliament-jobbing, and a new trade, which, as we thought it the duty of English freeholders thus to expose, we hope an English Parliament will think it their duty to prevent.

For as this stock-jobbing in its own nature is only a new invented sort of *deceptio visus*, a legerde-main in trade; so mixed with trick and cheat, that 'twould puzzle a good logician to make it out by syllogism; so nothing can be more fatal in England to our present constitution, and which in time may be so to our liberty and religion, than to have the interests of elections jobbed upon exchange for money, and transferred like East India stock to those who bid most.

By this method, the country gentlemen may sit at home; and only corresponding with the brokers at Jonathan's and Garraway's, as the prizes rise or fall, they may dispose of their interests in the towns they can govern, at as good a rate as they can.

The citizens, or such who have their several companies and interest to serve, will ease themselves of the expense of travelling, with the fine borrowed equipages before mentioned; and only go to market in Exchange Alley, and buy an election, as the stock-jobber and they shall agree, which election shall be managed by the country gentleman, who is to have his bargain, no purchase, no pay, and is to go through with it, or else he gets none of the money.

Elections of Parliament men are in a hopeful way; and Parliaments themselves are in a hopeful way, by this concise method of practice, to come under the absolute management of a few hands, and no doubt things will go on accordingly.

Banks and stocks may be laid up, and employed in a short time, for the purchasing the interest of gentlemen, and our gentry being willing to get a penny *in an honest way*, as we say, will but too often sell their interests and their country too, especially such gentlemen whose estates are reduced to an occasion for it.

The truth of it is, 'tis a paradox, a riddle, that we countrymen cannot understand, nor never could, what makes our gentlemen so fond of being Parliament men, we do not very well understand what the business is at the Parliament. Only we find that we are swingingly taxed; and they tell us 'tis done by the Parliament; but we never understood they had any of the money themselves, we always thought the money was for the King, though they had the giving of it, then we see in the King's proclamation for calling a Parliament, that it was to advise with them, about affairs of the highest importance to the kingdom. Now we cannot see they can get anything by coming together to be advised with, and our knights of the shire tell us they get nothing by it. And here lies the difficulty, we can never reconcile their spending so much money to be chosen, going up 200 miles to London, and spending six months sometimes there in attending the House, and all for nothing; we have often been thinking there must be something else in the case, and we are afraid there is.

Nor did ever anything explain this riddle so much, as the struggling of these two companies to make Members of Parliament; for the meaning to us seems thus: that they suppose which company so ever gets most friends in the House, will be most likely to be farther established, to the ruin of the other, and therefore they make such a stir to get friends there.

Whence first it must be supposed that the matter shall not stand or fall by true merit, and that company be suppressed that deserves it; for if so, it might be probable they would both be suppressed; for we apprehend they are both destructive to our English trade in general and manufactures in particular.

* * *

Wherefore we think it very needful to publish our resentments at such a practice, and to protest against it in this our honest plea, as an indirect, wicked and pernicious practice, and which may be of very ill consequence to the nation, on these following accounts:

1. A hundred, or an hundred and fifty such Members in the House, would make a dead weight, as it used to be called, to carry any vote they are for, or against, either in the negative or affirmative, as they shall agree, and if so, it will be almost in their power to dispose of our estates, persons, liberties and religion, as they think fit.

2. If it be true, as is very rational to suppose, that they who will buy will sell; or if it be true, which seems still more rational, that they who have bought must sell, must make a penny of it, or else they lose their purchase, and some their fortunes, which they expected to raise by these mercenary elections; then the influence such a number of Members, gotten into the House by the method we are speaking of, will be capable of selling our trade, our religion, our peace, our effects, our King, our crown, and everything that is valuable or dear to the nation.

If stock-jobbing elections be the first step, in all probability stock-jobbing of votes will be the second; for he that will give a thousand pounds, or more, only for a power to vote, expects to get something by voting, or gives away his money for nothing.

* * *

This inequality, we humbly conceive opens the door to the fraudulent practices, which have all along been made use of in elections, buying of voices, giving freedoms in corporations, to people living out of corporations, on purpose to make votes, debauching the electors, making whole towns drunk, and feasting them to excess for a month, sometimes two, or more, in order to engage their voices.

These things were so notorious, and withal so ruinous to the gentry themselves, of whom several men of plentiful estates have been miserably beggared and undone, that the

Parliament wisely took notice of it, and have prohibited the practice.

But as if the Devil owed the nation a grudge, and was rummaging his invention to find it out; here is a new project found out, to succeed the other, which is tenfold more the child of hell than that.

Elections were obtained by those clandestine vicious ways, only to sit in the House in general; but here the design seems to be formed beforehand, what they would be chosen for, and the measures concerted, nay we have heard that it may be known already, and wagers have been laid in, or near, Exchange Alley, which company has most friends in the ensuing Parliament, and how many of the members of each company stand fairest to be chosen.

Those gentlemen who have intelligence suitable to such nice calculations, are equally capable of jobbing the whole nation; and as is already noted, have gotten the way of buying and selling, that is jobbing elections, will soon influence such persons to act, as the money they are able to bid shall direct. 'Twould be but a melancholy thought, to reflect that the matter of our Succession should come to be debated before a Parliament, that had a governing number of such Members, who could imagine but that the settlement of our crown would attend the highest bidder, and our future liberty, religion, and all that's dear to us, be mortgaged to the bribes of foreigners.

The French King need not keep great armies on foot, build ships, and strengthen himself at sea to ruin us, if the great affairs of the kingdom concerted in Parliament should come to be prepared, managed, and byassed at Garraway's and Jonathan's Coffee-House, and exposed to sale by a parcel of stock-jobbers.

And how shall it be otherwise, they that can make members, will always govern members; creation supposes a right of disposing, the gentlemen who buy are obliged to stand in good terms with the broker, lest they should find a better chapman, and leave him in the lurch the next election, so that by the nature of the thing, they are always subject to this mercenary, scandalous thing, called a broker, and he keeps them under his girdle, if he bids them vote for, or against, they do it, the mischiefs are endless and innumerable that may attend it.

To all men whose eyes are to be opened with reason and argument, it should be enough to fill them with abhorrence, to think that the scandalous mechanick upstart mystery of job-broking should grow upon the nation; that ever the English nation should suffer themselves to be imposed upon by the new invented ways of a few needy mercenaries, who can turn all trade into a lottery, and make the Exchange a gaming table: a thing, which like the imaginary coins of foreign nations, have no reality in themselves; but are placed as things which stand to be calculated, and reduced into value, a trade made up of sharp and trick, and managed with impudence and banter.

That six or eight men shall combine together, and by pretended buying or selling among themselves, raise or sink the stock of the East India Company, to what extravagant pitch of price they will, so to wheedle others sometimes to buy, sometimes to sell, as their occasions require; and with so little regard to intrinsick value, or the circumstances of the company, that when the company has a loss, stock shall rise; when a great sale, or a rich ship arrived, it shall fall; sometimes run the stock down to 35 l., other times up to 150 l., and by this method buy and sell so much, that 'tis thought there are few of the noted stock-jobbers, but what have bought and sold more stock than both the companies possess.

Thus let them job, trick and cheat one another; and let them be bubbled by them that know no better; but for God's sake, gentlemen, do not let the important affairs of the state come under their wicked clutches.

Don't let them prepare our Acts of Parliament, and then chuse Members to vote for them. If fate and popish confederacies, and union of popish powers abroad threaten us, let us alone to struggle with them, and have fair law, and honourable conditions for it; but to be bought and sold, to have our elections of Members, and our laws, liberties and estates stock-jobbed away, is intolerable.

Some, and not a few, of our stock-jobbing brokers are Frenchmen; a little correspondance between the French Court and Jonathan's Coffee-House, with a currency of louis d'ors, will make strange alterations here, if this method of buying and jobbing elections should go on.

The Parliament of England is the governing council; their breath is our law, and on their breath under the direction of God's Providence we all depend, the greatest nicety that is possible should be used in chusing men of untainted principles, and unquestioned wisdom, to compose a body so eminent in their power and influence.

But to attempt to fill the House with mechanicks, tradesmen, stock-jobbers, and men neither of sense nor honesty, is tricking at the root, and undermining the nation's felicity at once; and 'tis a wonder the impudence of this attempt has not made them stink in the nostrils of the whole nation.

How can the King be encouraged to place that confidence in his people, which he mentions in the late proclamation, by which people, His Majesty understands, the true representative body assembled in Parliament, if instead of a true representative, the House is filled with elections clandestinely procured by tricks and shams imposed upon the people?

How can the King depend upon his Parliament, to carry him through anything he shall undertake by their advice, if mercenary men fill the House, whose suffrages shall be guided by the bribes and private procurations of his, and the nation's enemies?

How shall the Protestant religion be espoused and defended, which wise men say is in great danger?

How shall trade be encouraged and protected, and the niceties of it disputed and defended?

How shall reformation of manners, which is so much wanted, and which the King has so often recommended, be promoted?

Are stock-jobbers, agents of regiments, taylors, and East India Companies, qualified for these works? Or will any sort of men, who purchase elections with money, to bring to pass private interests and parties, espouse these general cases on which the welfare of the nation depends?

Tell a stock-jobber of the union of France and Spain; of the Muscovites breaking the peace; of the difference between the Danes and the Duke of Holstein; tell him of a good barrier in Flanders against the French, or of assisting the Emperor on the Rhine (talk Gospel to a kettle drum), 'tis all excentrick and foreign to him. But talk of the great Mogul, and the pirates of Madagascar; of Fort St. George, and St. Helena, there you'll hit him, and he turns statesman presently.

It was a famous stock-jobber, and one who is very likely to be a Parliament man, who when somebody was talking lately of the election of the new Pope, and having heard the particulars very attentively, brought out this very grave question at the end on't: "Well", says he, "I am glad 'tis over, and don't you think that stock will rise upon't?"

A learned question upon the case, truly; upon which, pray give us leave to ask another:
"And is't not pity,
But such a one should represent the City?"

You Londoners may make them sheriffs, aldermen, and deputies, and common-council men, and welcome; you know them, and they can hurt nobody but themselves.

But when you come to talk of Parliament men, gentlemen, pray consider, 'tis the whole nation lies at stake; a man may set his own house on fire, and welcome, provided it stands by itself, and neither hurts nor endangers nobody's else, and the law has nothing to say to him; but if it stands in a town, or a city, he deserves to be hanged, for he may burn out, and undo his neighbours.

Nor are you chusing men to sit in Parliament, as persons to act for you only whom they represent; but they are representatives in a double capacity: separately considered, every Member represents the people who chuse him, and all together represent the whole nation. Their right to sit is separately devolved; but their right in act, is conjunctively inherent, every man represents the whole, and acts for the whole, thought he is sent but from part.

The fate of Bristol, or New Castle, may be decided by a Member of London, or Canterbury, whose vote on an equality of voices carries it which way he pleases.

Therefore London cannot say to Bristol, or New Castle, "What have you to do with our election?" or they to London, "What have you to do with ours?" Why one bad Member may ruin a city, a town, or family, a person, or perhaps all together; and if any town, or city, or borough, or private person, is pleased to give a friendly admonition or caution to another, especially if they seem to be proceeding against their own, or the nation's interest, they ought to accept the hint, and reflect upon what they are doing with honesty, and reform it.

Upon this, we hope it shall be justified, that we have ventured to lay open the villainous practices of some people to corrupt and procure elections, in order to get Members into the ensuing Parliament, who shall serve a turn, and a party, without considering whether they are men qualified for the other great affairs which are to be considered there, and which His Majesty has assured us, are of the highest importance to the kingdom.

The Villainy of Stock-Jobbers Detected (1701)

* * *

The old East India stock, by the arts of these unaccountable people, has within 10 years or thereabouts, without any material difference in the intrinsick value, been sold from 300 l. per cent to 37 l. per cent; from thence with fluxes and refluxes, as frequent as the tide, it has been up at 150 l. per cent again; during all which differences, it would puzzle a very good artist to prove, that their real stock (if they have any), set loss and gain together, can have varied above 10 per cent upon the whole; nor can any reasons for the rise and fall of it be shewn, but the politick management of the stock-jobbing brokers; whereby, according to the number of buyers and sellers, which 'tis also in their power to make and manage at will, the price shall dance attendance on their designs, and rise and fall as they please, without any regard to the intrinsick worth of stock.

The New Company, the Bank of England, the Exchequer, the whole nation, as has been lately well observed by the author of "The Freeholder's Plea against Stock-Jobbing Elections of Parliament Men", is, or is in a fair way to be subjected to the same management.

* * *

I cannot however forbear to blame the Bank of England, for publishing at such a juncture as this, their willingness to allow an interest on their sealed notes; which seems too plain to discover their fears of the party, and is a downright begging of credit. I shall ask leave here to tell a short story, something allusive to this, and which will explain what I mean. Whether the reader please to take it for a parable or a history, 'tis all one to me, and will serve my turn as well one way as another.

A certain tradesman in London had borrowed a thousand pounds of a scrivener at 6 per cent interest, and had kept it in his hands some time; but losses coming upon him, and particularly one which strook his foundation, he began to apprehend that if it came to the ears of that creditor, the scrivener, he would call in his money, and at that juncture such a demand would entirely ruin him.

To go to the scrivener and give him a bribe, to promise the continuing the money, though he knew that sort of people willing enough to take money, yet he thought it looked like lessening himself, and would injure his reputation, and possibly only serve to make that certain, which yet was but doubtful, and put him upon calling for the money sooner than otherwise; upon which he resolved on a quite contrary method.

He goes to the scrivener, and tells him he had borrowed such a sum of money on him, and paid him interest for it; but he found the interest of money run high, and 'twas a hard thing for a tradesman to pay it, that 'twas but working for other folks; for he found trade was dull, and he gave long credit and the like, and therefore in short, he desired him to take in the money again, for he was uneasy to be so deeply in debt.

The scrivener asked him when he would pay it, he told him that afternoon, if he would send the bond to his house, he had ordered his man to tell up the money.

The scrivener told him, it was hard to put the money on them without warning, and would be a loss to his client to oblige him to take it in before he was provided to put it out again; that if he had called it in, he would ha' given him three months' time to pay it in, and so much notice he expected.

"Aye, but", says the tradesman, "that will be a loss to me too, for I must keep it by me, or else it may not be ready at the time." But, "Pray Sir", said the scrivener, "keep the money, trade may mend; a man that has a thousand pound by him, meets with opportunities that he did not think on."

The tradesman finding his design take, answers coldly "No", and so they parted; at next meeting, the scrivener still pressing him to keep the money, he tells him: "Look ye Sir, you desire me to keep this money; if your client will abate me 1 per cent of interest, I'll keep it longer." The scrivener agrees, and the tradesman answered his end, whereas had he gone and offered him 1 per cent more for interest or continuance, 'tis ten to one but they had called for their money.

I leave anybody to apply this story to the Bank of England, offering double interest at a time, when a storm threatened them; they indeed are the best judges of their own affairs, but if they had stood their ground boldly without it, I am of opinion with submission, their credit had stood clearer.

The credit of the Bank of England does not immediately consist in the reality of their foundation. Sir, sure it does originally depend upon the goodness of their bottom, but the more immediate credit of their proceeding depends upon the currency of their bills, and the currency of their bills depends upon their immediate pay; *the Bank has no advantage of the meanest goldsmith as to their current bills*, for no longer than their payments continue punctual and free, no longer will any man take their bills, or give them credit for money.

All the credit which remains to the Bank after their payment comes to stop, *if ever such time shall be*, is that people have a satisfaction; that at long run their principle is safe, and their bottom will pay their debts. This is the credit of their stock, but the credit of their cash ends, if ever they baulk but one bill.

To ask the world to stay for their money and take interest, is to weaken the credit of their cash, and transfer themselves to the credit of their stock, which nobody doubts to be good.

I know therefore nothing the Bank could have done more to injure the credit of their running cash, than to make such a proposal of interest upon their bills, which formerly they publickly refused.

* * *

On the whole matter, [the financial crisis of 1701—see page 245] Whether we consider the injury to the publick credit by the villainy of stock-jobbers,

The exposing the essentials of the nation's prosperity, to the management of mercenary brokers and parties; who upon every occasion they are pleased to take, when such as they think fit to approve of, are not chosen Lord Mayors or Parliament men, shall take the liberty to shew their resentments by affronting the government, ruining banks and goldsmiths, and sinking the stocks of all the companies in the town.

Or, the powerful influence they have by their money on the current cash of the nation.

Whether any of these things are considered, I leave it to the wise heads of the nation, now concerned to reflect and examine, whether it be consistent with the safety of the English nation, with the honour of the English government, or with the nature of the English trade, to suffer such a sort of people to go on unprescribed and unlimited, or indeed unpunished.

What safety can we have at home, while our peace is at the mercy of such men, and 'tis in their power to *job* the nation into feuds among ourselves, and to declare a new sort of civil war among us when they please?

Nay, the war they manage is carried on with worse weapons than swords and musquets; bombs may fire our towns, and troops overrun and plunder us. But these people can ruin man silently, undermine and impoverish by a sort of impenetrable artifice, like poison that works at a distance, can wheedle men to ruin themselves, and *fiddle them out of their money*, by the strange and unheard-of engines of *interests, discounts, transfers, tallies, debentures, shares, projects*, and the *devil and all* of figures and hard names. They can draw up their armies and levy troops, set stock against stock, company against company, alderman against alderman; and the poor passive tradesmen, like the peasant in Flanders, are plundered by both sides, and hardly know who hurts them.

What will become of the honour of the English nation, if the principal affairs relating to the credit both of the publick and private funds is dependent upon such vile people, who care not who they ruin, nor who they advance, though one be the nation's friends, and the other its enemies, and exposed to their particular resentments?

He is a worthy patriot, and fitly qualified for a representative, who would join his strength to overthrow the credit of the City, and ruin trade only to shew his private resentment for not being chosen as he thought fit to expect.

Lastly, what condition must the trade of England be soon reduced to, when banks and paper credit, which must be owned to be a material part of its subsistance, are become so precarious as to be liable to a general interruption from the breath of mercenary, malicious and revengeful men?

* * *

The Anatomy of Exchange Alley (1719)

* * *

But before I come to the needful ways for restraining those people, I think 'twill be of some service to expose their practices to common view, that the people may see a little what kind of dealers they are.

And first, they have this peculiar to them, and in which they outdo all the particular pieces of publick knavery that ever I met with in the world, viz. that they have nothing to say for it themselves; they have indeed a particular stock of hard ware, as the braziers call it, in their faces, to bear them out in it; but if you talk to them of their occupation, there is not a man but will own, 'tis a complete system of knavery; that 'tis a trade founded in fraud, born of deceit, and nourished by trick, cheat, wheedle, forgeries, falsehoods, and all sorts of delusions; coining false news, this way good, that way bad; whispering imaginary terrors, frights, hopes, expectations and then preying upon the weakness of those whose imaginations they have wrought upon, whom they have either elevated or depressed. If they meet with a cull, a young dealer that has money to lay out, they catch him at the door, whisper to him, "Sir, here is a great piece of news, it is not yet publick, it is worth a thousand guineas but to mention it. I am heartily glad I met you, but it must be as secret as the black side of your soul, for they know nothing of it yet in the coffee-house; if they should, stock would rise 10 per cent in a moment, and I warrant you South-Sea will be 130 in a week's time, after it is known." "Well", says the weak creature, "prethee, dear Tom, what is it?" "Why, really Sir, I will let you into the secret, upon your honour to keep it till you hear it from other hands; why 'tis this, the Pretender is certainly taken and is carried prisoner to the castle of Millan, there they have him fast; I assure you, the government had an express of it from my lord St——s within this hour." "Are you sure of it?" says the fish, who jumps eagerly into the net. "Sure of it! Why if you will take your coach and go up to the Secretary's office, you may be satisfied of it yourself, and be down again in two hours, and in the meantime I will be doing something, though it is but a little, till you return."

Away goes the gudgeon with his head full of wildfire, and a squib in his brain, and coming to the place, meets a croney at the door, who ignorantly confirms the report, and so sets fire to the mine; for indeed the cheat came too far to be baulked at home. So that without giving himself time to consider, he hurries back full of the delusions, dreaming of nothing but of getting a hundred thousand pounds, or purchase two;* and even this money was to be gotten only upon the views of his being beforehand with other people.

In this elevation, he meets his broker, who throws more fireworks into the mine, and blows him up to so fierce an inflamation, that he employs him instantly to take guineas to accept stock of any kind, and almost at any price; for the news being now publick, the artists made their price upon him. In a word, having accepted them for fifty thousand pounds more than he is able to pay, the jobber has got an estate, the broker 200 or 300 guineas, and the esquire remains at leisure to sell his coach and horses, his fine seat and rich furniture, to make good the deficiency of his bear-skins, and at last, when all will not go through it, he must give them a brush for the rest.

* * *

But now, that I may make good the charge, (viz.) that the whole art and mystery is a meer original system of cheat and delusion; I must let you see too, that this part of the comedy may very well be called "A Bite for the Biter"; for which I must go back to the broker and his gudgeon. The moneyed gentleman, finding himself let into the secret indeed, and that he was bitten to the tune of 30,000 l. worse than nothing, after he had unhappily paid as far as his ready money would go, of which piece of honesty they say he has heartily repented, *and is in hopes all that come after him will forgive him for the*

* *or purchase two*: an obsolete noun, *purchase* refers to the hunting or catching of prey, hence violence, plunder, robbery. In his *New Voyage Round the World*, Defoe contrasts "traffic", or trade, with "purchase", or piracy. Thus the sentence here might mean: "dreaming of getting [by luck] a hundred thousand pounds", or [by] "purchase", or robbery, two hundred thousand. [Ed.]

sake of what followed, stopped short, as he might well, you'll say, when his money was all gone, and bethinks himself, "What am I a doing! I have paid away all this money like a fool; I was drawn in like an ass, by the eager desire of biting my neighbours to a vast sum, and I have been fool enough in that, but I have been ten thousand times a worse fool to pay a groat of the money, especially since I knew I could not pay it all. Besides, who but I would have forgot the nature of the thing I was dealing in, and of the people I was dealing with? Why, is it not all a meer body of knavery? Is not the whole doctrine of stock-jobbing a science of fraud? And are not all the dealers meer original thieves and pick-pockets? Nay, do they not own it themselves? Have not I heard T. W. B. O. and J. S. a thousand times say they know their employment was a branch of highway robbing, and only differed in two things, *first in degree*, (viz.) that it was ten thousand times worse, more remorseless, more void of humanity, done without necessity, and committed upon fathers, brothers, widows, orphans and intimate friends; in all which cases, highwaymen, generally touched with remorse, and affected with principles of humanity and generosity, stop short and choose to prey upon strangers only. *Secondly in danger*, (viz.) that these rob securely; the other, with the utmost risque that the highwaymen run, at the hazard of their lives, being sure to be hanged first or last, whereas these rob only at the hazard of their reputation, which is generally lost before they begin, and of their souls, which trifle is not worth the mentioning. Have I not, I say, heard my broker, Mr. ——, say all this, and much more? And have I not also heard him say, that no man was obliged to make good any of their Exchange Alley bargains, unless he pleased, and unless he was in haste to part with his money, which indeed I am not. And has not all the brokers and jobbers, when they have been bitten too hard, said the same thing, and refused to pay?

"Pray, how much did old Cudworth, Ph. C——p——m, and Mr. Goo——g, eminent jobbers, monarchs in their days of Exchange Alley, break for? And how much did they ever pay? One, if I mistake not, compounded at last for one penny per pound, and the other two for something less.

"In a word, they are all a gang of rogues and cheats, and I'll pay none of them. Besides, my lawyer, Sir Thomas Subtle, tells me, there's not a man of them dares sue me; *no, though I had no protection to fly to*, and he states the case thus:

" 'You have, Sir' (says Subtle) 'contracted to accept of stock at a high price: East India at 220, Bank at 160, South Sea 120, and the like. Very well, they come to put it upon you, the stock being since fallen; tell them you cannot take it yet. If they urge your contract, and demand when you will take it, tell them you will take it when you think fit.

" 'If they swagger, call names, as rogue, cheat, and the like, tell them, as to that, you are all of a fraternity; there is no great matter in it, whether you cheat them, or they cheat you; 'tis as it happens in the way of trade, that it all belongs to the craft; and as the Devil's broker, Whiston, said to Parson Giffard, tell them you are all of a trade. If they rage, and tell you the Devil will have you, and such as that, tell them they should let the Devil and you alone to agree about that, 'tis none of their business; but when he comes for you, tell them you would advise them to keep out of the way, or get a protection, as you have got against them.

" 'After this, it is supposed they will sue you at law; then leave it to me, I'll hang them up for a year or two in our courts; and if ever in that time the stock comes up to the price, we will tender the money in court, demand the stock, and saddle the charges of the suit upon them; let them avoid it if they can.'

"This is my lawyer's opinion," says he to himself, "and I'll follow it to a tittle"; and so we are told he has, and I do not hear that one stock-jobber has begun to sue him yet, or intends it, nor indeed dare they do it.

This experiment indeed may teach understanding to every honest man that falls into the clutches of these merciless men, called stock-jobbers; and I give the world this notice, that in short, not one of their Exchange Alley bargains need be otherwise than thus complied with; and let these buyers of bear-skins remember it; not a man of them dare go to Common Law to recover the conditions; nor is any man obliged, further than he thinks himself obliged in principle, to make good one of his bargains with them; how far principle will carry any man to be just to a common cheat, that has drawn him into a snare, I do not indeed know; but I cannot suppose 'twill go a very great length, where there is so clear, so plain, and so legal a door to get out at.

* * *

——— if we may believe the report of those who remember the machines and contrivances of that original of stock-jobbing, Sir Josiah Child, there are those who tell us, letters have been ordered, by private management, to be written from the East-Indies, with an account of the loss of ships which have been arrived there, and the arrival of ships lost; of war [with] the great Mogul, when they have been in perfect tranquility, and of peace with the great Mogul, when he has come down against the factory of Bengale with one hundred thousand men: just as it was thought proper to calculate those rumours for the raising and falling of the stock, and when it was for his purpose to buy cheap, or sell dear.

It would be endless to give an account of the subtilties of that capital che——t, when he had a design to bite the whole Exchange. As he was the leading hand to the market, so he kept it in his power to set the price to all the dealers. The subject then was chiefly the East India stock, though there were other stocks on foot too, though since sunk to nothing; such as the Hudson's Bay Company, the linnen manufacture stock, paper stock, salt-petre stock and others, all at this day worse than nothing, though some of them then jobbed up to 350 per cent, as the two first in particular.

But the East India stock was the main point, every man's eye, when he came to market, was upon the brokers who acted for Sir Josiah. Does Sir Josiah sell or buy? If Sir Josiah had a mind to buy, the first thing he did was to commission his brokers to look sower, shake their heads, suggest bad news from India; and at the bottom it followed, "I have commission from Sir Josiah to sell out whatever I can", and perhaps they would actually sell ten, perhaps twenty thousand pound. Immediately the Exchange (for they were not then come to the Alley) was full of sellers; nobody would buy a shilling, 'till perhaps the stock would fall six, seven, eight, ten per cent, sometimes more; then the cunning jobber had another set of men employed on purpose to buy, but with privacy and caution, all the stock they could lay their hands on, 'till by selling ten thousand pound, at four or five per cent lost, he would buy a hundred thousand pound stock at ten or twelve per cent under price; and in a few weeks by just the contrary method, set them all a buying, and then sell them their own stock again at ten or twelve per cent profit.

These honest methods laid the foundation, we will not say of a fine great stone house, on a certain forest, but it certainly laid the foundation of an opulent family, and initiated the crowd of jobbers into that dexterity in tricking and cheating one another, which to this day they are the greatest proficients in that this part of the world ever saw.

* * *

Hitherto craft and knavery appears to be their method, but we shall trace them now a little further; and like true hussars that plunder not the enemy only, but their own army, as the opportunity presents, so these men are now come to prey upon the government itself.

Let us look into the late lotteries; had not a piercing eye detected the roguery, and not the fall of other things taken off the edge of the people's fancy for venturing, these artists had brought up the tickets to 16 s. apiece advance, even before the Act was passed. That this could not be but by securing the possession of all the tickets in their own hands, except such select tickets as were not to come to market; I say, that this could not be but by connivance, and this everyone knows; and that this connivance again could not be but by some higher people than those that were named to it, this also everyone may know; who they were is none of my business to enquire, though 'tis easy to guess. 'Tis very hard when our statesmen come into a confederacy to bite the people, and when dukes turn stock-jobbers. Yet that this was done is most certain, and what was this but making a property of the power that might be in their hands, the better to bite the people? For if the Parliament appointed 500,000 l. in tickets to be given out at a certain rate that was low and reasonable, was it not to encourage the people on whom the rest of the national burthen lies? And if by the craft and knavery of jobbers the people are made to pay 600,000 l. for them, which is much about the case, pray why not pay the hundred thousand pounds to the publick, either to pay off a hundred thousand pounds of debt, or to make the burthen of the current year a hundred thousand pounds lighter, of which I am sure there is need enough?

It has been indeed our happiness, that a worthy Member being informed of this abominable cheat, detected it, and laid it before the House; upon which a vote was passed to make void all bargains made for tickets before the Act was passed; so the biters were bitten, and a certain Sir George ——— was obliged to refund; but the roguery of the design was never a jot the less for that.

But the fatal influences of this growing evil does not end

here, and I must trace stock-jobbing now to its new acquired capacity of intermeddling with the publick, assisting rebellion, encouraging invasion; and if I do not bring the stock-jobbers, even the Whigs among them, to be guilty of treason against their King and country, and that of the worst kind too, then I do nothing.

Had the stock-jobbers been all Jacobites by profession, or had the employment led them, by the necessity of their business to put King and nation, and particularly their own, to bargain and sale; and had the selling of news been their property, and they had an Act of Parliament, or patent, to entitle them to the sole privilege of imposing what false things they pleased on the people, I should have had much the less reason to have complained of their roguery, and have rather turned myself to the rest of the people, who are the subject they work upon, and only have stood at Exchange Alley end, and cried out, "Gentlemen, have a care of your pockets".

Again, had it been a private club, or society of men, acting one among another, had the cheats, the frauds, and the tricks they daily make use of, *in which the English rogue was a fool to them*, been practised upon themselves only; and like gamesters at a publick board, they had only played with those that came there to play with them; in this case also I should have held my tongue, and only put them in mind of an old song; every stanza of which chimed in with *Tantararara*, Rogues all, Rogues all.

But when we find this trade become a political vice, a publick crime, and that as it is now carried on, it appears dangerous to the publick, that whenever any wickedness is in hand, any mischief by the worst of the nation's enemies upon the wheel, the stock-jobbers are naturally made assistant to it, that they become abettors of treason, assistant to rebellion and invasion, then it is certainly time to speak, for the very employment becomes a crime, and we are obliged to expose a sort of men who are more dangerous than a whole nation of enemies abroad, an evil more formidable than the pestilence, and in their practise more fatal to the publick than an invasion of Spaniards.

It is said by some, that the principal leaders in the jobbing trade at that time, and at whom most part of the satyr in this work ought to be pointed, are Whigs, Members of Parliament, and friends to the Government; and that therefore I had best have a care of what I say of them.

My first answer is, *so I will*. I will have a care of them, and in the next place let them have a care of me; for if I should speak the whole truth of some of them, they might be Whigs, but I dare say they would be neither P—— men or friends to the Government very long, and it is very hard His Majesty should not be told what kind of friends to him such men are.

Besides, I deny the fact; these men friends to the Government! *Jesu Maria!* The Government may be friendly to them in a manner they do not deserve; but as to their being friends to the Government, that is no more possible than the Cardinal Alberoni or the Chevalier de St. George are friends to the Government; and therefore, without reflecting upon persons, naming names, or the like; *there will be no need of names, the dress will describe them*; I lay down this new-fashioned proposition, or *postulatum*, take it which way you please, that I will make it out by the consequences of what I am going to say.

1. That stock-jobbing, as it is now practised, and as is generally understood by the word stock-jobbing, is neither less or more than high treason in its very nature, and in its consequences.

2. That the stock-jobbers who are guilty of the practices I am going to detect, are eventually traytors to King George, and to his Government, family and interest, and to their country, and deserve to be used at least as confederates with traytors, whenever there are any alarms of invasions, rebellions, or any secret practices against the government, of what kind soever.

This is a black charge, and boldly laid, and ought therefore to be effectually made out, which shall be the work of a few pages in the following sheets.

First, I lay down this as a rule, which I appeal to the laws of reason to support, that all those people, who at a time of publick danger, whether of treasonable invasion from abroad, or trayterous attempts to raise insurrections at home, shall willingly and wittingly abet, assist, or encourage the traytors, invading or rebelling, are equally guilty of treason.

Secondly, All those who shall endeavour to weaken, disappoint and disable the government in their preparations, or discourage the people in their assisting the government to oppose the rebels or invaders, are guilty of treason.

All that can be alledged in contradiction to this, and perhaps that could not be made out neither, is that they are not traytors within the letter of the law; to which I answer, if they were, I should not satyrize them, but impeach them. But if it appears that they are as effectually destructive to the peace and safety of the government, and of the King's person and family, as if they were in open war with his power, I do the same thing, and fully answer the end proposed.

As there are many thieves besides house-breakers, highwaymen, lifters and pick-pockets, so there are many traytors besides rebels and invaders, and perhaps of a much worse kind; for as in a dispute between a certain Lord and a woman of pleasure in the town, about the different virtue of the sexes, the lady insisted that the men were aggressors in the vice, and that in plain English, if there were no whore-masters, there would be no whores; so, in a word, if there were no parties at home, no disaffection, no traytors among ourselves, there would be no invasions from abroad.

Now I will suppose for the purpose only, that the people I am speaking of were not disaffected to the government; I mean, not originally, and intentionally pointing their design at the government; nay, that they are hearty Whigs, call them as we please; yet if it appear they are hearty knaves too, will do anything for money, and are by the necessity of their business obliged, or by the vehement pursuit of their interest, that is to say, of their profits, pushed upon things as effectually ruinous and destructive to the government, as the very buying arms and ammunition by a professed Jacobite, in order to rebellion could be; are they not traytors even in spite of principle, in spite of the name of Whig; nay, in spite of a thousand meritorious things that might otherwise be said of them, or done by them?

A gun-smith makes ten thousand firelocks in the Minories, the honest man may be a Whig, he designs to sell them to the government to lay up in the Tower, or to kill Spaniards, or any of the rest of the King's enemies; a merchant comes and buys some of them, and says they are for the West Indies, or to sell into France. But upon enquiry it appears they are bought for rebellion; the undesigning gun-smith comes into trouble of course, and it will be very hard for him to prove the negative, (viz.) that when he has furnished the rebels with arms, he had no share in the rebellion.

To bring this home to the case in view, who were the men, who in the late hurry of an expected invasion, sunk the price of stocks 14 to 15 per cent? Who were the men that made a run upon the Bank of England, and pushed at them with some particular pique too, if possible, to have run them down, and brought them to a stop of payment? And what was the consequences of these things? Will they tell us that running upon the Bank, and lowering the stocks, was no treason? We know that, literally speaking, those things are no treason; but is there not a plain constructive treason in the consequences of it? Is not a wilful running down the publick credit, at a time when the nation is threatened with an invasion from abroad, and rebellion at home; is not this adding to the terror of the people? Is not this disabling the government, discouraging the King's friends, and a visible encouragement of the King's enemies? Is not all that is taken from the credit of the publick, on such an occasion, added to the credit of the invasion? Does not everything that weakens the government, strengthen its enemies? And is not every step that is taken in prejudice of the King's interest, a step taken in aid of the designed rebellion?

* * *

But it is needful, after having said thus much of the crime, to say something of the place, and then a little of the persons too. The center of the jobbing is in the kingdom of Exchange Alley, and its adjacencies; the limits are easily surrounded in about a minute and a half, (viz.) stepping out of Jonathan's into the Alley, you turn your face full south, moving on a few paces, and then turning due east, you advance to Garraway's; from thence going out at the other door, you go on still east into Birchin-Lane, and then halting a little at the Sword-Blade Bank to do much mischief in fewest words, you immediately face to the north, enter Cornhill, visit two or three petty provinces there in your way west. And thus having boxed your compass, and sailed round the whole stock-jobbing globe, you turn into Jonathan's again; and so, as most of the great follies of life oblige us to do, you end just where you began.

But this is by way of digression; and even still, before I come to the main case, I am obliged to tell you; that though this is the sphere of the jobbers' motion, the orbe to which they are confined, and out of which they cannot well act in their way; yet it does not follow, but that men of foreign situation (I mean foreign as to them, I do not mean foreign by nation) and of different figure are seen among them; nay, some whose lustre is said to be too bright for the hemisphere of a coffee-house, have yet their influence there, and act by substitutes and representatives.

* * *

Having thus given the blazing characters of three capital sharpers of Great Britain, knaves of lesser magnitude can have no room to shine; the Alley throngs with Jews, jobbers and brokers, their names are needless, their characters dirty as their employment, and the best thing that I can yet find out to say of them, is that there happens to be two honest men among them, Heavens preserve their integrity; for the place is a snare, the employment in itself fatal to principle, and hitherto the same observation which I think was very aptly made upon the Mint, will justly turn upon them, (viz.) that many an honest man has gone in to them, but [I] cannot say that I ever knew one come an honest man out from them.

But to leave them a little, and turn our eyes another way; is it not surprising to find new faces among these scandalous people, and persons even too big for our reproof? Is it possible that stars of another latitude should appear in our hemisphere? Had it been Sims or Bowcher, or gamesters of the drawing room and masquerades, there had been little to be said; or had the Groom-Porter's* been transposed to Garraway's and Jonathan's, it had been nothing new; true gamesters being always ready to turn their hand to any play. But to see statesmen turn dealers, and men of honour stoop to the chicanry of jobbing; to see men at the offices in the morning, at the P—— House about noon, at the Cabinet at night, and at Exchange Alley in the proper intervals, what new *phenomina* are these? What fatal things may these shining planets (like the late great light) foretell to the state, and to the publick? For when statesmen turn jobbers the state may be jobbed.

* * *

Stock-jobbing is play; a box and dice may be less dangerous, the nature of them are alike, a hazard; and if they venture at either what is not their own, the knavery is the same. It is not necessary, any more than it is safe, to mention the persons I may think of in this remark; they who are the men will easily understand me.

In a word, I appeal to all the world, whether any man that is entrusted with other men's money (whether publick or private is not the question), ought to be seen in Exchange

* *Groom Porter*: an officer of the English royal household. From the sixteenth century onwards his principle functions were to regulate all gaming within the Court, furnish cards, dice and other materials, and to settle disputes. The office was abolished under George III. [Ed.]

Alley. Would it not be a sufficient objection to any gentleman or merchant, not to employ any man to keep his cash, or look after his estate, to say of him, *he plays*, *he is a gamester*, or *he is given to gaming*? and *stock-jobbing*, which is still worse, gives the same, or a stronger ground of objection in the like cases.

Again, are there fewer sharpers and setters in Exchange Alley than at the Groom-Porter's? Is there less cheating in stock-jobbing than at play, or rather is there not fifty times more? An unentered youth coming to deal in Exchange Alley, is immediately surrounded with bites, setters, pointers, and the worst sort of cheats, just as a young country gentleman is with bawds, pimps, and spongers, when he first comes to town. It is ten thousand to one, when a forward young tradesman steps out of his shop into Exchange Alley, I say 'tis ten thousand to one but he is undone; if you see him once but enter the fatal door, never discount his bills afterwards, never trust him with goods at six months' pay any more.

If it be thus dangerous to *the mean*, what is it to *the great*? I see only this difference, that in the first the danger is private, in the latter publick.

* * *

Even this way it appears that these stock-jobbers are dangerous to the peace, since 'tis in their power to set a rate whenever they please, not only upon private estates, but even upon the whole nation, and in that capacity it is to be hoped the Parliament, who have hitherto redressed the publick grievances, will take care of these people in particular, and deliver the publick from such a set of men as are more fatal to them than a midnight fire, more dangerous than an enemy embarked, nay, I had almost said, than an enemy landed.

For in a word, these men take upon them to put a standard upon our fears; and we are to ask them, when intelligence comes from abroad, whether anything be to be slighted or apprehended; every publick piece of news, every menace of the nation's enemies is to receive its weight from them; and the price of stocks is the rule by which we are to guide our judgement in publick affairs, by which we are either to hope or to fear when anything amiss present itself to our view.

Is this an advantage fit to be put into the hand of a subject? Are the King's affairs to go up and down as they please, and the credit of His Majesty's councils rise and fall as these men shall please to value them? This would be making them kings, and making the King subject to the caprice of their private interest, his affairs be liable to be rated in Exchange Alley, and to be run down as they pleased; an article which, as the Roman Pontiff, in the first politicks of the Church, made all the kings of the earth become pensioners to the priests, so it would make all the Kings of Britain pensioners to Exchange Alley.

It must be confessed, it looks as if this were the present view in the manner which stock-jobbing now goes on; and there are more mischiefs in it than perhaps we are aware of; the extremes either way seem dangerous enough, for example:

If one way the stock-jobbers manage the publick, they scandalously subject the government, the ministers of state, the publick credit, nay, even the elections of Parliament to their orders. So if a government should come absolutely to get the management of the stock-jobbers, it might be many ways fatal to the people's interest, and indeed put the purse-strings of the nation so much into the hands of a ministry, that if they did not at any time command the general treasure, and be able to raise what money they pleased without a Parliament, they would be able to add what value they pleased to the funds given, raise them when they pleased to draw money in, and sink them when they pleased to issue money out. That in a word, the rate of stocks should be settled every day in the Exchequer; and though they might not be said to stand no more in need of Parliaments, it would be most certain, that they would not stand in so much need of Parliaments as they used to do, and as it is convenient for us they should do.

I must run out a great length in the enumeration of the mischief to the liberty of Great Britain, which might attend such a thing as this; and though at present it may be objected, that it is unreasonable, and entirely needless, because we are under a King that stands in need of no artifices, and is too just to attempt any encroachment on the liberties of his people, and a ministry who we have reason to hope are above taking any such mean steps; yet if ever a time shall come again, when every politick step shall be enquired after to bring grist to the publick mill, and every way that can be found practicable, shall be thought justifiable; then let you citizens of London have a care of a bear-skin Court, and a stock-jobbing ministry, when Exchange Alley shall be transposed to the Exchequer, and the statesmen shall make a property of the brokers.

* * *

CHAPTER THREE

HISTORY AND MEMOIRS

GREAT STORM IN THE DOWNS, 1703,

1. The Storm: or a Collection of the Most Remarkable Casualties and Disasters which Happened in the Late Dreadful Tempest, Both by Sea and Land

The Storm was published on 17 July 1704. Defoe was now over forty, his thriving business of pantile manufacture ruined and his reputation as a promising writer damaged by his pillorying and imprisonment in Newgate as a result of having written his *Shortest Way with the Dissenters* (Dec. 1702). With *The Storm* he launched his career as a reporter and historian of contemporary events, and provided for the first time in English literary history "an elaborate factual account of a recent natural phenomenon—solely as recorded by reliable eyewitnesses".[1]

The great storm of 26–7 November 1703 was "without rival in the recorded history of our island", writes G. M. Trevelyan. A squadron of English fighting ships lying in the Downs and off the Gunfleet, and another squadron off the coast of Holland, were forced to run out to sea to avoid being dashed to pieces on the shore, along with thousands of merchantmen of all sizes. "For a week to come the North Sea was covered with English shipping, in every variety of peril", continues Trevelyan. When the damages were calculated, "the Royal Navy had lost Admiral Beaumont, 1,500 seamen and 15 warships varying from second to sixth rate, besides smaller craft. The total losses of the merchant service were never estimated, but amounted to several hundred craft of all sorts."[2]

On land, the hurricane hit hardest in the south-west. "Starting from Cornwall, the Great Storm traversed England in an eastern direction with a touch of north. Trees went down in battalions; the lead roofs on cathedrals and parish churches were all rolled up like carpets; in many places scarce a chimney remained standing, not a roof uninjured. Boats were flung out of river beds, carriages thrown over hedges into the fields."[3]

Defoe hit upon the idea of recording his own observations of the effects of the storm in London and outlying areas, and combining these observations with first-hand accounts from eyewitnesses in the countryside and on board ships. He solicited the accounts from outside London through an advertisement which he ran in the *London Gazette* and in other newspapers only five days after the storm was over. John Robert

Moore observes that this was "the first time in his life he attempted to organize a systematic plan of news-gathering from correspondents".[4]

Defoe's solicitation was addressed mainly to "Gentlemen of the Clergy", presumably because they were the single most reliably literate group in a generally uneducated population. In addition, a great natural calamity like the storm provided an admirable opportunity for clerical observations upon Divine retribution for mankind's sins, and Divine Providence in preserving the lives of survivors of the calamity. One section of the *Storm* is devoted to accounts of "Remarkable Providences and Deliverances", and it is significant that most of Defoe's clerical correspondents were members of the Church of England, "no doubt", as Moore observes, "some of them High Churchmen who had accepted *The Shortest Way* as a reasonable proposal for rooting out the Dissenters and who had rejoiced when its author had been set in the pillory."[5]

The result of Defoe's enterprise is not only a remarkable first-hand account of a natural disaster; it is also an interesting forerunner of some of his later historical works, most notably his *History of the Union of Great Britain* (1709), which is intercalated with the texts of various proclamations, minutes of legislative debates, and other material which make it an important source of data for historians. Most significantly for students of literature, the *Storm* adumbrates in its documentation, its use of a narrator, and its interest in the effect upon human behaviour and the religious implications of a great natural disaster, Defoe's sombre and moving fiction of 1722, *A Journal of the Plague Year*.

Early biographers of Defoe were puzzled by his own descriptions of the effects of the storm in and around London, which he claimed were eyewitness accounts. In the preface, which he signs "The Age's Humble Servant", he sets forth a highly scrupulous conception of the awesome responsibility of the historian, accountable to posterity for the accuracy of his data, and therefore inexcusably derelict in his duty if he "forget[s] a story". Every anecdote or account must be presented to the world with "the special testimonial of its proper voucher and where it comes without such sufficient authority, he [the historian] ought to say so". Such a solemn declaration of responsibility seemed extraordinary, since until the twentieth century it was believed that Defoe had remained inside the walls of Newgate until July of the summer following the storm. (Actually, he was released in November 1703.) Defoe's vivid first-hand descriptions were seen, therefore, as evidence of the amazing ability to lie convincingly for which his contemporary and posthumous adversaries have always censured him.

Evidence of the careful research he believes indispensable for a historian appears in his fresh and charming first and second chapters (not reproduced), "Of the Natural Causes and Original of Winds", and "Of the Opinion of the Ancients, that this Island was more subject to Storms than other Parts of the World". In the first chapter he discusses the question of primary and secondary causes, the opinions of ancients amd moderns on the phenomenon of wind, concluding that although it is permissible to study natural causes, and that many "philosophers" have been good Christians (with the regrettable exception of "Mr. Hobbs"), "'Tis apparent, that God Almighty seems to have reserved this, as one of those secrets in Nature which should more directly guide them [scientists] to himself". Defoe ventures to disagree on grounds of common sense with the opinion about the origin of wind advanced by a contemporary scientist, while admitting candidly that he himself is "a meer junior" in "philosophical study".

In the second chapter Defoe ridicules the "horrid apprehensions" of ancient navigators about storms and tempests in the British Isles. That England must have been damper in ancient times, before the fencing off and drying up of many of its interior lakes, Defoe is prepared to admit: "This seems demonstrated from *Ireland*, where the multitude of loughs, lakes, bogs, and moist Places, serve the air with exhalations, which give themselves back again in showers, and make it be called the *piss-pot of the world.*" Nevertheless, rainy and misty climate does not necessarily mean tempests and prodigious storms, and Defoe explains that ancient sailors were "fairweather seamen: the chief of their navigation was coasting; and if they were driven out of their knowledge, had work enough to find their way home, and sometimes never found it at all; but one sea conveyed them directly into the last ocean, from whence no navigation could return them." With the advance of the art of navigation in modern times, though,

Our shores are sounded, the sands and flats are discovered which they knew little or nothing of, and in which more real danger lies, than in all the frightful stories they told us; useful sea marks and land figures are placed on the shore, buoys on the water, lighthouses on the highest rocks; and all these dreadful parts of the world are become the seat of trade, and the centre of navigation. Art has reconciled all the difficulties, and use made all the *horribles* and *terribles* of those ages become as natural and familiar as daylight. (page 20, not reproduced)

Having thus established that the great tempest of 26–7 November was unprecedented, Defoe proceeds to describe the storm and its after-effects, in his own eyewitness accounts from London, and in letters from other areas. His own descriptions are significant for visual details of the storm and its damages; such visualization is usually absent in his writing, but apparently was at his command in those rare instances when he considered it necessary. Noteworthy in the letters from outlying areas are certain contrasts of style, social class, and subject matter which Defoe attempts to bring out by selection and arrangement of his material.[6] The letter from Edward Shipton, Vicar from Fairford, Gloucestershire (see pages 290–2), is formal and ceremonious in tone, describing in precise detail the damage to his parish church, and declining to enter into detail about the houses of the poor or the fall of trees. Following Shipton's letter is a compilation of letters written by "very honest plain and observant persons" in "a homely stile," and dealing with damage to homes of humble people, to apple trees, retribution to a drunk and foul-mouthed "company of wicked people" (page 293), loss of a "woman's pair of bodice" (page 294), the discontinuation of witchcraft in the town of Butly, presumably as a result of the tempest (page 294). In one of the humbler letters I have not reproduced, a "plain, but honest account", the correspondent remarks dolefully, "Our loss in the apple-trees is the greatest; because we shall want liquor to make our hearts merry; the farmer's sate them up again but the wind has blown them down since the storm".

Letters from seamen include one from Miles Norcliffe, which Defoe characterizes as "course and sailor like", but explains, "I have inserted this letter, because it seems to describe the horror and consternation the poor sailors were in at that time... though every circumstance in this letter is not litterally true, as to the number of ships, or lives lost." Norcliffe's is a moving account of the drowning of Admiral Beaumont and hundreds of sailors (see pages 294–5), after which Defoe inserts one "better expressed" by R.P. (not reproduced). In his own redaction of reports from Deal (see pages 295–6), Defoe contrasts the "great barbarity" of the townspeople, scavengers of the pitiful possessions of sailors stranded at low tide on the deadly Goodwin Sands, with the charity of Mayor Thomas Powell of the same town, who valiantly saved the lives of over 200 of the stranded sailors (not reproduced).

One of the letters I have reproduced from the chapter on "Remarkable Providences and Deliverances" is from Reverend John Gipps (see pages 297–9), who thanks Defoe for a personal visit the author apparently made to the minister, and recounts the terror of himself and his "infantry", huddled into one bed during the tempest, recalling the "shrieks and cries" of his "dear babes", that still ring in his ears.

The Storm is linked together loosely by the running commentary of its anonymous narrator. In an open and informal manner, "The Age's Humble Servant" alludes to various problems he encountered in compiling the book, comments on the letters he has included, refers to his own actions and those of his family at the time of the storm, and offers his individual opinions on scientific matters, on the effects of the tempest on the prices of tiles, thatch, and grain, and on moral and religious questions. The hints he thereby provides about his own personality suggest that he is good-natured, informal, ingenuous, extremely alert, and indefatigably inquisitive.

Indefatigable inquisitiveness in particular is a characteristic highly appropriate for the reporter of such an event as the great storm. Defoe produces impeccable credentials for a reporter's profession when he tells us:

> Nor shall I often trouble the reader with the multitude or magnitude of trees blown down, whole parks ruined, fine walks defaced, and orchards laid flat, and the like. And though I had, myself, the curiosity to count the number of trees, in a circuit I rode over most part of Kent, *in which being tired with the number, I left off reckoning after I had gone on to 17,000* ... yet in some parts of England ... they had much more mischief. (page 70, not reproduced, my italics)

Only those characteristics which establish his credibility for the task he has undertaken are mentioned by the narrator, who is not otherwise sharply individualized. When we compare him with H. F. of *A Journal of the Plague Year*, the latter appears to have a much more definite personality. H. F. is as observant as the anonymous narrator of the *Storm*, but he is a worried man, troubled by doubt about whether his religious duty requires him to remain in London or to flee the stricken city. As scrupulous about detail as "The Age's Humble Servant", he uses his details, the increase and decrease in numbers on the mortality bills of different sections of London, to structure his account of the rise, spread, and decline of the plague. He appears to embrace the whole of suffering London as he carefully records the increasingly ineffectual efforts of magistrates to care for the inhabitants of the city and to cope with the supernatural visitation of a dreaded disease. When the fires built to fumigate the city are finally left to die, London seems to face final extinction, and H. F., with his steady concern for the metropolis, his sober and continuing search for remedies for human suffering, combined with his genuine piety and awe in face of God's dreadful chastisement, provides the only point of stability and reassurance in the entire story.[7]

Such a comparison reveals the enormous distance Defoe travelled from his earlier historical work to the later fiction, which also deals with a great natural disaster and is structured around facts, but in which every detail is suffused with a sombre and religious atmosphere that appears only intermittently in the first work.

Strict fidelity to fact is what Defoe stresses in his preface to the *Storm*, and such fidelity he seems to have observed scrupulously in those of his works he considered formal histories, memoirs, and contemporary reports, like his 1709 *History of the Union*, his 1716 and 1717 *Annals of King George*, his 1718 *Memoirs of ... the Duke of Shrewsbury*, and his 1724–6 *Tour thro' the Whole Island of Great Britain*. His "historical writings established him among his contemporaries as a significant minor historian", writes a recent student of Defoe's writing, and "he has retained that stature in the eyes of modern historical scholars".[8]

But it is as a writer of fictional histories that Defoe is known to a wider public than specialists. *A Journal of the Plague Year* is the most impressive fiction that developed from the simple notion of truth expressed by the narrator of the *Storm*. But behind H. F., the conscientious historian narrating this fiction, stands Daniel Defoe, whose truth is more complex than that of strict fidelity to fact: it is the rendition of the mood and exploration of the significance of a particular moment in history. At the opposite pole stands the *Minutes of the Negotiation of Monsr. Mesnager* (the last excerpt in this chapter), a work in which historical facts are distorted and obscured for the purpose of constructing a scenario in which Robert Harley can star in the role of saviour of the Protestant succession in England.

Belonging to the genre of "secret history", the *Minutes* are almost fiction. For his secret histories of Harley's ministry, Defoe accused himself, probably repeating the words of his enemies, of raising a dust so that Harley might be lost in the cloud. His attitude toward truth in these writings seems to have been that justice takes precedence over historical accuracy: Harley was innocent of treason and should be defended by all possible means.

Although Defoe presumably felt justified about the liberties he took with historical facts when defending Harley, the sinister tone pervading the Mesnager *Minutes* resembles that of no other of Defoe's works so much as his 1724 fiction, *Roxana*. Both the Mesnager *Minutes* and *Roxana* are notable for an unnerving discrepancy between polite and ceremonious talk and equivocal motives and actions. In both works the narrators eventually undergo a failure of understanding and a loss of control over events. And these characteristics are emphasized in both works by a significant dearth of concrete objects and an obscurity about dates.

It appears, therefore, that too much freedom from the anchor of historical fact and physical object was frightening to Defoe, in spite of his profession of faith in a higher truth than that of fact. The Mesnager *Minutes* had a laudable political aim—and yet it is deeply tinged with the sinister. The nightmarish *Roxana*, which had only the aim of truth to a psychological insight to anchor it in rectitude, was the last of Defoe's fictions to be so free of historical, physical, and geographical fact.[9]

After 1724 Defoe concentrated upon non-fiction—social reform and economics—returning to fiction only occasionally, and principally in a genre with which he had already experimented profitably, travel narrative. As indicated in the section on economics, facts about manufacture and trade were associated in Defoe's mind with geographical facts (see the essays on wool manufacture and the home trade above). Economics seems to have stimulated his domestic, home-making imagination, travel and geography his adventure-loving imagination. Whereas allusions to *Moll Flanders* occurred naturally in the discussion of Defoe's political writings, allusions to *Robinson Crusoe* arose as naturally in the discussion of his economic writings. Much as I would like to propose one solution to the complex and frequently debated question of the imaginative genesis of Defoe's great fictions, my own careful reading of his non-fiction convinces me that Defoe's interest in history accounts for only a few of his major fictions, and these do not include *Robinson Crusoe*.

The fictions that emanated from Defoe's historical imagination include, at one pole, *A Journal of the Plague Year*, and at the other, obliquely refracted from the Mesnager *Minutes*, *Roxana*. Situated somewhere between the two is a series of military memoirs, the most successful of which is the 1720 *Memoirs of a Cavalier*. Fidelity to fact is important in these fictions, indeed was intended to attract readers, but it is subservient to other aims. In *Memoirs of a Cavalier* the aim is fictional, exploration of the problem of what constitutes true courage in battle; in the histories of Charles XII of Sweden and in the Ramkins and Carleton memoirs (still not definitively attributed to Defoe), the aim is polemical. In spite of the qualified importance of factual accuracy in these fictions, they should still be regarded as products of Defoe's historical imagination, for facts take precedence over character; with the exception of Ramkins, their narrators are relatively colourless and insignificant.

Although *Memoirs of a Cavalier* is regarded highly, Defoe's real triumph in historical fiction remains his *Journal of the Plague Year*. Only in that work did he fully succeed in balancing historical with fictional demands—accuracy of fact with imaginative characterization—and in fusing the two with an appropriate style. Only in the *Journal* did fictional truth coincide perfectly with historical truth.

Notes

1 John Robert Moore, *Daniel Defoe, Citizen of the Modern World* (Chicago, 1958), p. 153.
2 G. M. Trevelyan, *England under Queen Anne: Blenheim* (London, 1930), p. 308.
3 *Ibid.*, p. 310.
4 Moore, p. 152.
5 *Ibid.*, p. 154.
6 It is not inconceivable that Defoe may have touched up a word here and there to heighten contrasts in style. See pages 19 and 22–3 above (Introduction) for a description of his editorial activity.

Although he was a very effective editor and secret censor, he could not have done a great deal of revising in the *Storm*, because many of his correspondents must have been waiting eagerly for publication of the book in which their own letters would appear in print, and heavy-handed redaction would have aroused a storm of a different nature from the one described in the book.

7 I owe this observation to Professor Thomas Conley of the Speech and Rhetoric Department of S.U.N.Y., Albany.

8 Raymond Albert Klopsch, "Daniel Defoe as a Historian", unpublished Ph.D. dissertation, University of Illinois, 1962, p. 164.

9 Michael Shinagel pointed out that in *Roxana* "Defoe no longer was able to control his imagination or his material, and being a good Puritan he decided not to tempt the devil any longer. He ceased writing imaginative biographies in which he identified with his creations not wisely but too well." (*Daniel Defoe and Middle-Class Gentility*, Cambridge, Mass.: Harvard University Press, 1968, p. 194.)

The Storm: or a Collection of the Most Remarkable Casualties and Disasters which Happened in the Late Dreadful Tempest, Both by Sea and Land (1704)

* * *

It did not blow so hard till twelve a clock at night, but that most families went to bed; though many of them not without some concern at the terrible wind, which then blew. But about one, or at least by two a clock, 'tis supposed, few people, that were capable of any sense of danger, were so hardy as to lie in bed. And the fury of the tempest encreased to such a degree, that as the editor of this account being in London, and conversing with the people the next days, understood, most people expected the fall of their houses.

And yet in this general apprehension, nobody durst quit their tottering habitations; for whatever the danger was within doors, 'twas worse without; the bricks, tiles, and stones, from the tops of the houses, flew with such force, and so thick in the streets, that no one thought fit to venture out, though their houses were near demolished within.

The author of this relation was in a well-built brick house in the skirts of the City; and a stack of chimneys falling in upon the next houses, gave the house such a shock, that they thought it was just coming down upon their heads. But opening the door to attempt an escape into a garden, the danger was so apparent, that they all thought fit to surrender to the disposal of almighty Providence, and expect their graves in the ruins of the house, rather than to meet most certain destruction in the open garden; for unless they could have gone above two hundred yards from any building, there had been no security. For the force of the wind blew the tiles point blank, though their weight inclines them downward; and in several very broad streets, we saw the windows broken by the flying of tile sherds* from the other side; and where

* *tile sherds*: fragments, or shards, of tiles. [Ed.]

there was room for them to fly, the author of this has seen tiles blown from a house above thirty or forty yards, and stuck from five to eight inches into the solid earth. Pieces of timber, iron, and sheets of lead, have from higher buildings been blown much farther; as in the particulars hereafter will appear.

It is the received opinion of abundance of people, that they felt, during the impetuous fury of the wind, several movements of the earth; and we have several letters which affirm it. But as an earthquake must have been so general, that everybody must have discerned it; and as the people were in their houses when they imagined they felt it, the shaking and terror of which might deceive their imagination, and impose upon their judgment; I shall not venture to affirm it was so. And being resolved to use so much caution in this relation as to transmit nothing to posterity without authentick vouchers, and such testimony as no reasonable man will dispute; so if any relation come in our way, which may afford us a probability, though it may be related for the sake of its strangeness or novelty, it shall nevertheless come in the company of all its uncertainties, and the reader left to judge of its truth. For this account had not been undertaken, but with design to undeceive the world in false relations, and to give an account backed with such authorities, as that the credit of it should admit of no disputes.

For this reason I cannot venture to affirm that there was any such thing as an earthquake; but the concern and consternation of all people was so great, that I cannot wonder at their imagining several things which were not, any more than their enlarging on things that were, since nothing is more frequent, than for fear to double every object, and impose upon understanding, strong apprehensions being apt very often to persuade us of the reality of such things which we have no other reasons to shew for the probability of, than what are grounded in those fears which prevail at that juncture.

Others thought they heard it thunder. 'Tis confessed, the wind by its unusual violence made such a noise in the air as had a resemblance to thunder; and 'twas observed, the roaring had a voice as much louder than usual, as the fury of the wind was greater than was ever known. The noise had also something in it more formidable; it sounded aloft, and roared not very much unlike remote thunder.

And yet though I cannot remember to have heard it

thunder, or that I saw any lightning, or heard of any that did in or near London; yet in the countries the air was seen full of meteors and vaporous fires, and in some places both thunderings and unusual flashes of lightning, to the great terror of the inhabitants.

And yet I cannot but observe here, how fearless such people as are addicted to wickedness, are both of God's judgments and uncommon prodigies; which is visible in this particular, that a gang of hardened rogues assaulted a family at Poplar, in the very height of the storm, broke into the house, and robbed them. It is observable, that the people cried "Thieves!" and after that cried "Fire!" in hopes to raise the neighbourhood, and to get some assistance; but such is the power of self-preservation, and such was the fear, the minds of the people were possessed with, that nobody would venture out to the assistance of the distressed family, who were rifled and plundered in the middle of all the extremity of the tempest.

It would admit of a large comment here, and perhaps not very unprofitable, to examine from what sad defect in principle it must be that men can be so destitute of all manner of regard to invisible and superior power, to be acting one of the vilest parts of a villain, while infinite power was threatening the whole world with disolation, and multitudes of people expected the Last Day was at hand.

Several women in the City of London who were in travail, or who fell into travail by the fright of the storm, were obliged to run the risque of being delivered with such help as they had; and midwives found their own lives in such danger, that few of them thought themselves obliged to shew any concern for the lives of others.

Fire was the only mischief that did not happen to make the night completely dreadful; and yet that was not so everywhere, for in Norfolk the town of ——— was almost ruined by a furious fire, which burnt with such vehemence, and was so fanned by the tempest, that the inhabitants had no power to concern themselves in the extinguishing it; the wind blew the flames, together with the ruins, so about, that there was no standing near it; for if the people came to windward they were in danger to be blown into the flames; and if to leeward the flames were so blown up in their faces, they could not bear to come near it.

If this disaster had happened in London, it must have been very fatal; for as no regular application could have been made for the extinguishing it, so the very people in danger would have had no opportunity to have saved their goods, and hardly their lives. For though a man will run any risque to avoid being burnt, yet it must have been next to a miracle, if any person so obliged to escape from the flames had escaped being knocked on the head in the streets; for the bricks and tiles flew about like small shot; and 'twas a miserable sight, in the morning after the storm, to see the streets covered with tile sherds, and heaps of rubbish, from the tops of the houses, lying almost at every door.

From two of the clock the storm continued, and increased till five in the morning; and from five, to half an hour after six, it blew with the greatest violence. The fury of it was so exceeding great for that particular hour and half, that if it had not abated as it did, nothing could have stood its violence much longer.

At this rate it held blowing till Wednesday about one a clock in the afternoon, which was that day seven-night on which it began; so that it might be called one continued storm from Wednesday noon to Wednesday noon, in all which time, there was not one interval of time in which a sailor would not have acknowledged it blew a storm; and in that time two such terrible nights as I have described.

And this I particularly noted as to time, Wednesday, Nov. the 24th was a calm fine day as at that time of year shall be seen; till above four a clock, when it began to be cloudy, and the wind rose of a sudden, and in half an hour's time it blew a storm. Wednesday, Dec. the 2d., it was very tempestuous all the morning; at one a clock the wind abated, the sky cleared, and by four a clock there was not a breath of wind.

* * *

Indeed the City was a strange spectacle, the morning after the storm, as soon as the people could put their heads out of doors. Though I believe, everybody expected the destruction was bad enough; yet I question very much, if anybody believed the hundredth part of what they saw.

The streets lay so covered with tiles and slates, from the tops of the houses, especially in the out-parts, that the quantity is incredible; and the houses were so universally stripped, that all the tiles in fifty miles round would be able to repair but a small part of it.

Something may be guessed at on this head, from the sudden rise of the price of tiles; which rise from a 21 s. per thousand to 6 l. for plain tiles; and from 50 s. per thousand for pantiles, to 10 l. and bricklayers' labour to 5 s. per day. And though after the first hurry the prices fell again, it was not that the quantity was supplied, but because:

1st, The charge was so extravagant, that an universal neglect of themselves, appeared both in landlord and tenant; an incredible number of houses remained all the winter uncovered, and exposed to all the inconveniences of wet and cold; and are so even at the writing of this chapter.

2nd, Those people who found it absolutely necessary to cover their houses, but were unwilling to go to the extravagant price of tiles; changed their covering to that of wood, as a present expedient, till the season for making of tiles should come on; and the first hurry being over, the prices abate. And 'tis on this score, that we see, to this day, whole ranks of buildings, as in Christ-Church Hospital, the Temple, Asks-Hospital, Old-Street, Hogsden-Squares, and infinite other places, covered entirely with deal boards; and are like to continue so, perhaps a year or two longer, for want of tiles.

These two reasons reduced the tile merchants to sell at a more moderate price. But 'tis not an irrational suggestion, that all the tiles which shall be made this whole summer, will not repair the damage in the covering of houses within the circumference of the City, and ten miles round.

* * *

Honoured Sir,

In obedience to your request I have here sent you a particular account of the damages sustained in our parish by the late violent storm; and because that of our church is the most material which I have to impart to you, I shall therefore begin with it. It is the fineness of our church which magnifies our present loss, for in the whole it is a large and noble structure, composed within and without of ashler* curiously wrought, and consisting of a stately roof in the middle, and two aisles running a considerable length from one end of it to the other, makes a very beautiful figure. It is also adorned with 28 admired and celebrated windows, which, for the variety and fineness of the painted glass that was in them, do justly attract the eyes of all curious travellers to inspect and behold them; nor is it more famous for its glass, than newly renowned for

* *ashler*: a square hewn stone for building purposes or pavements; sometimes cut in thin slabs and used for facing buildings. [Ed.]

the beauty of its seats and paving, both being chiefly the noble gift of that pious and worthy gentleman Andrew Barker, Esq., the late deceased lord of the manor. So that all things considered, it does equal, at least, if not exceed, any parochial church in England. Now that part of it which most of all felt the fury of the winds, was, a large middle west window, in dimension about 15 foot wide, and 25 foot high; it represents the general Judgment, and is so fine a piece of art, that 1,500 l. has formerly been bidden for it, a price, though very tempting, yet were the parishoners so just and honest as to refuse it. The upper part of this window, just above the place where our Saviour's picture is drawn sitting on a rainbow, and the earth his footstool, is entirely ruined, and both sides are so shattered and torn, especially the left, that upon a general computation, a fourth part, at least, is blown down and destroyed. The like fate has another west window on the left side of the former, in dimension about 10 foot broad, and 15 foot high, sustained; the upper half of which is totally broke, excepting one stone munnel.* Now if this were but ordinary glass, we might quickly compute what our repairs would cost, but we the more lament our misfortune herein, because the paint of these two, as of all the other windows in our church, is stained through the body of the glass; so that if that be true which is generally said, that this art is lost, then have we an irretrievable loss. There are other damages about our church, which, though not so great as the former, do yet as much testify how strong and boisterous the winds were, for they unbedded 3 sheets of lead upon the uppermost roof, and rolled them up like so much paper. Over the church porch, a large pinnacle and two battlements were blown down upon the leads of it, but resting there, and their fall being short, these will be repaired with little cost. This is all I have to say concerning our church. Our houses come next to be considered, and here I may tell you, that (thanks be to God) the effects of the storm were not so great as they have been in many other places; several chimneys, and tiles, and slats, were thrown down, but nobody killed or wounded. Some of the poor, because their houses were thatched, were the greatest sufferers; but to be particular herein, would be very frivolous, as well as vexatious. One instance of note ought not to [be] omitted; on Saturday the 26th, being the day after the storm, about 2 a clock in the afternoon, without any previous

* *munnel*: probably an error, or a local variation on "mullion", a vertical bar dividing the lights in a window. [Ed.]

warning, a sudden flash of lightning, with a short, but violent clap of thunder, immediately following it like the discharge of ordnance, fell upon a new and strong-built house in the middle of our town, and at the same time disjointed two chimneys, melted some of the lead of an upper window, and struck the mistress of the house into a swoon, but this, as appeared afterwards, proved the effect more of fear, than of any real considerable hurt to be found about her. I have nothing more to add, unless it be the fall of several trees and ricks of hay amongst us, but these being so common everywhere, and not very many in number here, I shall conclude this tedious scrible, and subscribe myself.

Sir
Your most obedient and humble servant,
Fairford, Gloucest. Edw. Shipton, Vic.
January 170¾

The following letters, though in a homely style, are written by very honest, plain and observing persons, to whom entire credit may be given.

BREWTON

Sir,

Some time since I received a letter from you, to give you an account of the most particular things that happened in the late dreadful tempest of wind, and in the first place is the copy of a letter from a brother of mine, that was an exciseman of Axbridge, in the west of our county of Somerset; these are his words:

What I know of the winds in these parts, are, that it broke down many trees, and that the house of one Richard Henden, of Charter-House on Mendip, called Piney, was almost blown down, and in saving their house, they, and the servants, and others, heard grievous cries and scrieches in the air. The tower of Compton Bishop was much shattered, and the leads that covered it were taken clean away, and laid flat in the churchyard. The house of John Cray of that place, received much and strange damages, which together with his part in the sea wall, amounted to 500 l. Near the saltworks in the parish of Burnham, was driven five trading vessels, as colliers and corn dealers, betwixt Wales and Bridgwater, at least 100 yards on pasture ground. In the North Marsh, on the sides of Bristol river, near Ken at Walton Woodspring, the waters broke with such violence, that it came six miles into the country, drowning much cattel, carrying away several hay ricks and stacks of corn. And at a farm at Churchill near Wrington, it blew down 150 elms that grew most in rows, and were laid as uniform as soldiers lodge their arms.

At Cheddar near Axbridge, was much harm done in apple trees, houses, and such like; but what's worth remark, though not the very night of the tempest, a company of wicked people being at a wedding of one Thomas Marshall, John, the father of the said Thomas, being as most of the company was very drunk, after much filthy discourse while he was eating, a strange cat pulling something from his trenchard, he cursing her, stoopt to take it up, and died immediately.

At Brewton what was most remarkable was this, that one John Dicer of that town, lay the night as the tempest was, in the barn of one John Seller, the violence of the wind broke down the roof of the barn, but fortunately for him there was a ladder which staid up a rafter, which would have fell upon the said John Dicer; but he narrowly escaping being killed, did slide himself through the broken roof, and so got over the wall without any great hurt.

* * *

What was about Wincanton, was, that one Mrs. Gapper had 36 elm trees growing together in a row, 35 of them was blown down; and one Edgehill of the same town, and his family being abed did arise, hearing the house begin to crak, and got out of the doors with his whole family, and as soon as they were out the roof of the house fell in, and the violence of the wind took off the children's head cloaths, that they never saw them afterwards.

At Evercreech, three miles from Brewton, there were a poor woman begged for lodging in the barn of one Edmond Peny that same night that the storm was, she was wet the day before in travelling, so she hung up her cloaths in the barn, and lay in the straw; but when the storm came it blew down the roof of the barn where she lay, and she narrowly escaped with her life, being much bruised, and got out almost naked through the roof where it was broken most, and went to the dwelling house of the said Edmond Peny, and they did arise, and did help her to something to cover her, till they could get out her cloaths; that place of Evercreech received a great deal of hurt in their houses, which is too large to put here.

At Batcomb easterly of Evercreech, they had a great deal of

damage done as I said before, it lay exactly with the wind from Evercreech, and both places received a great deal of damage; there was one Widow Walter lived in a house by itself, the wind carried away the roof, and the woman's pair of bodice, that was never heard of again, and the whole family escaped narrowly with their lives; all the battlements of the church on that side of the tower next to the wind was blown in, and a great deal of damage done to the church.

* * *

There has been a strange thing at Butly, eight miles from Brewton, which was thought to be witchcraft, where a great many unusual things happened to one Pope, and his family, especially to a boy, that was his son, that having lain several hours dead, when he came to himself, he told his father, and several of his neighbours, strange stories of his being carried away by some of his neighbours that have been counted wicked persons; the things have been so strangely related that thousands of people have gone to see and hear it; it lasted about a year or more. But since the storm I have inquired of the neighbours how it was, and they tell me, that since the late tempest of wind the house and people have been quiet; for its generally said, that there was some conjuration in quieting of that house. If you have a desire to hear any farther account of it, I will make it my business to inquire farther of it, for there were such things happened in that time which is seldom heard of,

Your humble servant,
Hu. Ash.

Our town of Butly lyes in such a place, that no post house is in a great many miles of it, or you should hear oftener.

* * *

Sir,
These lines I hope in God will find you in good health, we are all left here in a dismal condition, expecting every moment to be all drowned. For here is a great storm, and is very likely to continue; we have here the Rear Admiral of the Blew in the ship, called the Mary, a third rate, the very next ship to ours, sunk, with Admiral Beaumont, and above 500 men drowned; the ship called the Northumberland, a third rate, about 500 men all sunk and drowned; the ship called the Sterling Castle,

a third rate, all sunk and drowned above 500 souls; and the ship called the Restoration, a third rate, all sunk and drowned. These ships were all close by us which I saw; these ships fired their guns all night and day long, poor souls, for help, but the storm being so fierce and raging, could have none to save them. The ship called the Shrewsberry that we are in, broke two anchors, and did run mighty fierce backwards, within 60 or 80 yards of the sands, and as God Almighty would have it, we flung our sheet anchor down, which is the biggest, and so stopt. Here we all prayed to God to forgive us our sins, and to save us, or else to receive us into his heavenly kingdom. If our sheet anchor had given way, we had all been drowned. But I humbly thank God, it was his gracious mercy that saved us. There's one Captain Fanel's ship, three hospital ships, all split, some sunk, and most of the men drowned.

There are above 40 merchant ships cast away and sunk. To see Admiral Beaumont, that was next us, and all the rest of his men, how they climed up the mainmast, hundreds at a time crying out for help, and thinking to save their lives, and in the twinkling of an eye were drowned. I can give you no account, but of these four men of war aforesaid, which I saw with my own eyes, and those hospital ships, at present, by reason the storm hath drove us far distant from one another. Captain Crow, of our ship, believes we have lost several more ships of war, by reason we see so few; we lye here in great danger, and waiting for a northeasterly wind to bring us to Portsmouth, and it is our prayers to God for it; for we know not how soon this storm may arise, and cut us all off, for it is a dismal place to anchor in. I have not had my cloaths off, nor a wink of sleep these four nights, and have got my death with cold almost.

Yours to command,
Miles Norcliffe

* * *

And here I cannot omit that great notice has been taken of the townspeople of Deal, who are blamed, and I doubt not with too much reason for their great barbarity in neglecting to save the lives of abundance of poor wretches; who having hung upon the masts and rigging of the ships, or floated upon the broken pieces of wrecks, had gotten ashore upon the Goodwin Sands when the tide was out.

It was, without doubt, a sad spectacle to behold the poor

seamen walking to and fro upon the sands, to view their postures, and the signals they made for help, which, by the assistance of glasses was easily seen from the shore.

Here they had a few hours' reprieve, but had neither present refreshment, nor any hopes of life, for they were sure to be all washed into another world at the reflux of the tide. Some boats are said to come very near them in quest of booty, and in search of plunder, and to carry off what they could get, but nobody concerned themselves for the lives of these miserable creatures.

* * *

Nor can the damage suffered in the river of Thames be forgot. It was a strange sight to see all the ships in the river blown away, the pool was so clear, that, as I remember, not above 4 ships were left between the upper part of Wapping, and Ratcliff Cross, for the tide being up at the time when the storm blew with the greatest violence. No anchors or landfast, no cables or moorings would hold them, the chains which lay cross the river for the mooring of ships, all gave way.

The ships breaking loose thus, it must be a strange sight to see the hurry and confusion of it, and as some ships had nobody at all on board, and a great many had none but a man or boy left on board just to look after the vessel, there was nothing to be done, but to let every vessel drive whither and how she would.

Those who know the reaches of the river, and how they lie, know well enough, that the wind being at southwest westerly, the vessels would naturally drive into the bite or bay from Ratcliff Cross to Limehouse Hole, for that the river winding about again from thence towards the new dock at Deptford, runs almost due southwest, so that the wind blew down one reach, and up another, and the ships must of necessity drive into the bottom of the angle between both.

This was the case, and as the place is not large, and the number of ships very great, the force of the wind had driven them so into one another, and laid them so upon one another as it were in heaps, that I think a man may safely defy all the world to do the like.

The author of this collection had the curiosity the next day to view the place, and to observe the posture they lay in, which nevertheless 'tis impossible to describe; there lay, by the best account he could take, few less than 700 sail of ships, some very great ones between Shadwel and Limehouse inclusive, the posture is not to be imagined, but by them that saw it, some vessels lay heeling off with the bow of another ship over her waste, and the stem of another upon her forecastle, the boltsprits of some drove into the cabin windows of others; some lay with their sterns tossed up so high, that the tide flowed into their forecastles before they could come to rights; some lay so leaning upon others, that the undermost vessels would sink before the other could float; the numbers of masts, boltsprits and yards split and broke, the staving the heads, and sterns and carved work, the tearing and destruction of rigging, and the squeezing of boats to pieces between the ships, is not to be reckoned; but there was hardly a vessel to be seen that had not suffered some damage or other in one or all of these articles.

There was several vessels sunk in this hurry, but as they were generally light ships, the damage was chiefly to the vessels; but there were two ships sunk with great quantity of goods on board, the Russel galley was sunk at Limehouse, being a great part laden with bale goods for the Streights, and the Sarah galley lading for Leghorn, sunk at an anchor at Blackwall; and though she was afterwards weighed and brought on shore, yet her back was broke, or so otherwise disabled, as she was never fit for the sea; there were several men drowned in these last two vessels, but we could never come to have the particular number.

Near Gravesend several ships drove on shore below Tilbury Fort, and among them five bound for the West Indies, but as the shore is ouzy and soft, the vessels sat upright and easy, and here the high tides which followed, and which were the ruin of so many in other places, were the deliverance of all these ships whose lading and value was very great, for the tide rising to an unusual height, floated them all off, and the damage was not so great as was expected.

If it be expected I should give an account of the loss, and the particulars relating to small craft, as the sailors call it, in the river, it is to look for what is impossible, other than by generals.

* * *

Sir,
I thank you for your charitable visit not long since; I could have heartily wished your business would have permitted you

to have made a little longer stay at the parsonage, and then you might have taken a stricter view of the ruins by the late terrible wind. Seeing you are pleased to desire from me a more particular account of that sad disaster; I have for your fuller satisfaction sent you the best I am able to give; and if it be not so perfect, and so exact a one, as you may expect, you may rely upon me it is a true, and a faithful one, and that I do not impose upon you, or the world in the least in any part of the following relation. I shall not trouble you with the uneasiness the family was under all the fore part of the evening, even to a fault, as I thought, and told them, I did not then apprehend the wind to be much higher than it had been often on other times; but went to bed, hoping we were more afraid than we needed to have been. When in bed, we began to be more sensible of it, and lay most of the night awake, dreading every blast till about four of the clock in the morning, when to our thinking it seemed a little to abate; and then we fell asleep, and slept till about six of the clock, at which time my wife waking, and calling one of her maids to rise, and come to the children, the maid rose, and hastened to her; she had not been up above half an hour, but all on the sudden we heard a prodigious noise, as if part of the house had been fallen down. I need not tell you the consternation we were all in upon this alarm; in a minute's time, I am sure, I was surrounded with all my infantry, that I thought I should have been overlayed; I had not even power to stir one limb of me, much less to rise, though I could not tell how to lie in bed. The shrieks and the cries of my dear babes perfectly stunned me; I think I hear them still in my ears, I shall not easily, I am confident, if ever, forget them. There I lay preaching patience to those little innocent creatures, till the day began to appear.

Preces & Lachrimae Prayers and tears, the primitive Christians' weapons, we had great plenty of to defend us withal; but had the house all fallen upon our heads, we were in that fright as we could scarce have had power to rise for the present, or do anything for our security. Upon our rising, and sending a servant to view what she could discover, we soon understood that the chimney was fallen down, and that with its fall it had beaten down a great part of that end of the house, *viz.* the upper chamber, and the room under it, which was the room I chose for my study. The chimney was thought as strong, and as well built as most in the neighbourhood; and it surprized the mason (whom I immediately sent for to view it) to see it down. But that which was most surprizing to me, was the manner of its falling; had it fallen almost any other way than it did, it must in all likelihood have killed the much greater part of my family, for no less than nine of us lay at that end of the house, my wife and self, and five children, and two servants, a maid, and a man then in my pay, and so a servant, though not by the year. The bed my eldest daughter and the maid lay in joined as near as possible to the chimney, and it was within a very few yards of the bed that we lay in; so that as David said to Jonathan, there seemed to be but one single step between death and us, to all outward appearance. One thing I cannot omit, which was very remarkable and surprizing. It pleased God so to order it, that in the fall of the house two great spars seemed to fall so as to pitch themselves on an end, and by that means to support that other part of the house which adjoined to the upper chamber; or else in all likelihood, that must also have fallen too at the same time. The carpenter (whom we sent for forthwith) when he came, asked who placed those two supporters, supposing somebody had been there before him; and when he was told, those two spars in the fall so placed themselves, he could scarce believe it possible; it was done so artificially, that he declared, they scarce needed to have been removed.

In short, Sir, it is impossible to describe the danger we were in; you yourself was an eyewitness of some part of what is here related; and I once more assure you, the whole account I have here given you is true, and what can be attested by the whole family. None of all the unfortunate persons who are said to have been killed with the fall of a chimney, could well be much more exposed to danger than we were; it is owing wholly to that watchful Providence to whom we are all indebted for every minute of our lives, that any of us escaped; none but he who never sleeps nor slumbers could have secured us. I beseech Almighty God to give us all that due sense as we ought to have of so great and so general calamity; that we truly repent us of those sins that have so long provoked his wrath against us, and brought down so heavy a judgment as this upon us. O that we were so wise as to consider it, and to *sin no more lest a worse thing come upon us!* That it may have this happy effect upon all the sinful inhabitants of this land is, and shall be, the daily prayer of Dear Sir,

Your real friend and servant,

John Gipps

* * *

2. The Military Memoirs of Captain George Carleton

The Memoirs of an English Officer (retitled on 27 May *The Military Memoirs of Capt. George Carleton*) were published on 16 May 1728, but, for reasons I will discuss below, were not associated with Defoe until the nineteenth century. The book, which runs to over 350 pages, falls into three sections: the first begins in 1672 with Carleton's military adventures during the Anglo-Dutch war, proceeds to his service on the Continent under William of Orange, and follows his career under King William in England, Scotland, and on the Continent until 1705; the second covers the years 1705 to 1707, and deals with the exploits of the Earl of Peterborough during his tenure as English military and naval commander of the Spanish war theatre during the War of the Spanish Succession; the third covers the years 1708 to 1713, when Carleton, then a prisoner of war, did some sightseeing in Spain. It is the second section, devoted to Peterborough's exploits, that is the raison d'être of the *Memoirs*; as such, it contains some of the best writing in the book.

The Earl of Peterborough was an eccentric, brilliant, but irascible and volatile individual, a highly contentious figure. His popularity was as unstable as his personality. One of the greatest peers of England, consistent only in his adherence to constitutional government, hatred of royal tyranny, and dislike for all organized religion, he found England too dangerous for him during the reign of James II, retiring to Holland for safety in 1686, where he became an intimate adviser of William of Orange, and formed a lasting friendship with John Locke. He accompanied William in his invasion of England of November 1688, and upon the accession of the new king became one of his leading statesmen, entrusted with many posts of honour in the ministry. By his irresponsible plots in the 1690s against his colleagues and his disrespect to the king himself for not supporting his intrigues, he lost William's confidence. In January 1697 he was actually committed to the Tower of London by the House of Commons, but by his petition to the House of Lords, he was discharged on 30 March. From 1698 he was active among the Lords as an associate of Marlborough and Godolphin, forming a faction with Tories who had disliked James II and Whigs who were discontented with William. He voted in 1701 with those Tory peers who wished to impeach Whig ministers for their participation in William's negotiation with Louis XIV of a Treaty of Partition of the Spanish Empire.

Because of his intimacy with the Marlboroughs, Peterborough received new state offices upon the accession of Queen Anne. In April and May 1705, he was appointed General and Commander-in-Chief of the Allied Forces in Spain, and Joint-Admiral and Commander-in-Chief of the Fleet with Sir Cloudesley Shovell. Thus began the military career in Spain that later aroused such controversy. Recalled to England by the exasperated Godolphin and Marlborough in March 1707 to explain his erratic conduct, he took his time obeying, arriving in England only at the end of August. The 1708 Parliamentary inquiry about his conduct was inconclusive, the Tories hotly upholding "the heroism of as great a Whig as could be found in the kingdom"[1] in order to embarrass the Whig ministry. The House of Commons adopted none of the accusations against Peterborough, but also refused to vote thanks to him. Perhaps on the advice of Harley, whose "opinion was that it was better to find him work to defend himself than to leave him at leisure to do mischief",[2] the Government, temporarily attaching his estates, continued to keep him busy trying to render an account of the monies he had received and disbursed in Spain. (His book-keeping had, characteristically, been extremely lax.)

With the Court Revolution of 1710, new vistas again opened before him. The new Tory ministry saw how to use this staunch Whig to discredit the previous Whig administration, and to facilitate their secret negotiations to end the war. Galway's defeat at Almanza in 1707 and Stanhope's capture at Brihuega in December 1710, marking the last phase of Allied defeat in the Peninsula, provided perfect ammunition for the Tories. G. M. Trevelyan describes succinctly how partisan politics in 1710 influenced evaluations of the prowess of England's military heroes:[3]

> An examination into "the late ill success in Spain" was, therefore, staged in the Upper House. Party capital must be made out of it and the blame put upon Marlborough, the late Ministers, and the Whig generals in the Peninsula, Galway and Stanhope. Peterborough, whom Marlborough and the Junto had recalled, must be magnified at their expense. ... At the end of these debates the only thanks the late Ministry received for winning the war against France in Europe and on the sea, was to be censured by Lords and Commons for having lost it in Spain. Peterborough was acclaimed by resolutions of both Houses as the national hero, less from any real gratitude to him than out of spite to the victor of Blenheim and Ramillies.[3]

The new Tory ministry was careful not to employ Peterborough again in military operations. Instead, flattering him by taking him into its inner social coterie, it devised various diplomatic missions for him in Europe, trying to render as innocuous as possible his dashing about from statesmen in one country to those in another. All agreed it was unwise to make an enemy of the fiery, impetuous, and superhumanly energetic Earl of Peterborough.

Peterborough's daring and imaginative capture of Barcelona in

September–October of 1705 is one of the best descriptions in the *Memoirs*. In order to discuss other of the exploits "Carleton" describes, such as Peterborough's capture of the province of Valencia through a series of elaborate stratagems, his relief of Barcelona, besieged by French forces, his advice to "Charles III" (the Allied candidate for the throne of Spain) to proceed to the capital city of Madrid, his unwillingness to aid General Galway during the latter's advance on Madrid, one would have to do a great deal of sorting out of historical fact from Peterborough fantasy. Fortunately, "Carleton's" account of the capture of Barcelona has been verified by independent sources, and so the reader has only to grasp several details in order to understand this excerpt from the *Memoirs*.

The Allied forces at Barcelona were composed of the English, led by Lord Peterborough, who was both chief commander of the army, and, with Sir Cloudesley Shovell, joint commander of the navy; by Prince George of Hesse Darmstadt, hero of the defence of Gibraltar, (Hesse was acquainted with Catalonia, where he had been a popular governor under the late king of Spain); and by the young "Charles III" and his German advisers. Hesse wished to land in Valencia and advance with Charles to Madrid. Peterborough's plans changed daily; sometimes he favoured Hesse's plan, sometimes he favoured proceeding to the Spanish possessions in Italy and aiding the Prince of Savoy. Naval officers, resenting Peterborough's joint command with Shovell, wished to attack Barcelona. The Catalans, hating the Spanish and the French, were reputed ready to welcome the Allied royal candidate, and the English home government and Charles were equally eager to capture Barcelona, the key city of Catalonia. But when some army battalions were landed near Barcelona in August, the Miquelets, or Catalonian patriots, revealed that they had only their enthusiasm to offer the Allies; regrettably, they lacked weapons and organization. For three weeks Councils of War failed to come to any conclusion about what to do. Finally, in September, it was decided, upon Peterborough's urging, to march on two minor Catalonian cities, Tarragona and Tortosa, a mere face-saving device to conceal failure to reach accord on any other plan.

At the last moment Peterborough saw a way to attack Barcelona with some chance of success, despite the facts that its defences were stronger than those of any other city in Spain, its Governor, Count Francisco de Velasco, certain to fight doggedly in its defence, and the north-east side of Barcelona, the only place where the Allies could disembark without opposition, was unsuitable as the site of a gun battery, for the ground was a marsh. Hearing from deserters about the lack of defences at the Citadel, a fortress at Monjuic, (south of Barcelona) "crowning a steep hill that rose 575 feet straight out of the sea",[4] Peterborough decided to capture Monjuic and attack Barcelona from the south-eastern, least protected side. He informed Prince George of his plans, and they agreed to co-operate in the surprise attack. "At six on Sunday evening [13 September 1705]", reports Trevelyan, "a thousand picked infantry of whom eight hundred were English, started off under Peterborough and Hesse, as though they were marching to Tarragona. ..."[5]

Defoe's account takes up the attack at this point. Based upon Dr. John Freind's lengthy defence of Peterborough composed for the 1707–1708 Parliamentary inquiry into the Earl's conduct, Abel Boyer's *Life of Queen Anne*, and contemporary newspaper accounts,[6] the description is accurate in its general outlines, but reveals by its arrangement of details the shaping hand of a writer of fiction and an apologist for Peterborough. What was essentially a scramble for Monjuic is presented as if it were an orderly plan to capture bastions of the fort consecutively, a plan interrupted occasionally by misfortunes of war. For instance, the attack took place by daylight, not because Peterborough designed it that way, but because his company had become lost and scattered during its night march.[7] Prince George received his death wound not because he had been tricked into exposing himself and his men, but because in his attempt to cut the communications between the fort and Barcelona, he unwisely led his men through a path exposed to enemy fire instead of through a protected one. Peterborough was not present at the moment, having gone out to issue a call for Brigadier Stanhope to bring up his reserve troops.[8] After Prince George fell, Charlemont, next in command, attempted to withdraw his men, but was demoralized during the retreat by the pretended surrender of the enemy, who then opened fire upon his forces. At this juncture Peterborough returned, warned of the panic of the soldiers, not by Carleton (see pages 312–3), but by a Colonel Rieutort.[9] True enough, Peterborough courageously led the men back to their dangerous posts, but his bravery was the result of one of his temper tantrums, not of the considered courage described by Carleton (see page 313).[10]

Peterborough and Stanhope did act admirably in quelling the uprising in Barcelona which occurred as soon as the Miquelets and townspeople perceived that the hated Velasco was in difficulty; Stanhope later maintained that restraining plunderers and protecting the lives of Velasco and his men had been more dangerous than the siege itself, but, as Trevelyan points out, if Carleton's anecdote about Peterborough's protracted rescue of the beautiful Duchess of Popoli were strictly accurate, (see page 318), "more credit would be due to his officers and men than to himself for averting a general massacre".[11]

Obviously, if such a rescue occurred at all,[12] "Carleton" embroidered it, inspired by the traditional association between Mars and Venus. In real life, even in his sixties, Peterborough carefully cultivated his reputation for gallantry; by 1728, at the age of about seventy, an anecdote emphasizing his magnetic effect upon aristocratic ladies would hardly have been unwelcome to him. The anecdote about Brigadier Stanhope and the Catalonian gentleman whose son's head is struck off in his presence by a cannon shot (see page 319), highly unlikely, but typical of Defoe's practice of embellishing his histories, is inserted for literary variety; the gentleman's rapid recovery of self-possession because of his profound Catholicism is not only dramatic, it is unbelievable, and expresses succinctly the ghostwriter's irony about that religion. "Carleton's" graceful compliment to Stanhope (see page 319), who had died in 1721, is perhaps a significant acknowledgement of gratitude, for Stanhope's ministry employed Defoe after George I succeeded Queen Anne. "Carleton" terminates his account of the siege of Barcelona with a description (not reproduced) of the public ceremonies that followed Peterborough's capture of the city. The description serves as coda to the military operations, and is replete with picturesque gestures such as the Earl of Peterborough scattering silver coins to the populace from his balcony, and a float releasing clouds of birds from a cage to symbolize the liberation of Barcelona.

Although Carleton himself was a real person whose military career paralleled that of the fictional Carleton, and who, according to Secord, "insisted on attempting to condense and to amplify Defoe's work while it was going through the press",[13] little of his personality colours the book; for, as Secord demonstrates, events are seen, not through the eyes of a participant in limited actions, but through those of someone with a broad, inclusive view of the Peninsular war.[14] The traces of Carleton's personality which appear occasionally are a querulous tone and a pretentious literary style. An example of the former occurs on page 315, where Carleton objects to the ingratitude of an English public official who refuses to reward him for the important service he performed during the Peninsular campaign. Ironically, as Defoe himself, who supported a policy of partition of the Spanish empire, must have realized long before 1728, the "*Minister petite*" was correct in his observation; as Trevelyan remarks:

It is in keeping with the fantastic character of Peterborough's career that his one great achievement as a soldier probably did more harm than good to his country and to the world. Had he failed in the attempt on Barcelona, the Allies must have abandoned all serious intention of placing "Charles III" on the throne; in that case the men and money that England so long continued to lavish in Spain could have been profitably used elsewhere, in Flanders, Toulon, or Canada; or else peace might have been arranged years earlier on terms at least as good as those of Utrecht.[15]

The ghostwriter relied upon different sources for the three sections of this book, but it is surely Carleton himself who not only inserted "four wildly irrelevant concluding paragraphs",[16] but whose language occasionally appears in other passages he must have inserted, as in the following pretentious explanation designed to conceal the real reason he did not in 1702 proceed to the West Indies with his regiment:

Yet as little as I admire a life of inactivity, there are some sorts of activity, to which a wise man might almost give supineness the preference; such is that of barely encountering elements, and waging war with nature; and such, in my opinion, would have been the spending of my commission, and very probably my life with it, in the West Indies. For though the climate (as some would urge) may afford a chance for a very speedy advance in honour, yet, upon resolving to my mind, that those rotations of the wheel of fortune are often so very quick, as well as uncertain, that I myself might as well be the first as the last; the whole of the debate ended in somewhat like that couplet of the excellent Hudibras:

Then he, that ran away and fled,
Must lie in Honour's truckle-bed.

However, my better planets soon disannulled those melancholy ideas, which a rumour of our being sent into the

West Indies had crowded my head and heart with. For being called over into England, upon the very affairs of the regiment, I arrived there just after the orders for their transportation went over; by which means the choice of going was put out of my power, and the danger of refusing, which was the case of many, was very luckily avoided. (Pages 70–71, not reproduced)

Carleton had been cashiered in 1700 for duelling with an inferior officer and had been living miserably from hand to mouth with his wife and three children until 1705, when he went to Spain as a volunteer, not as a regular member of any officer's regiment. Consequently, he existed on the charity of the soldiers and officers he followed. His own language was not that of a plain and honest soldier; that language was a literary counterfeit created by a writer of historical fiction purporting to be the memoirs of plain and honest soldiers. (See footnotes 7, 8, 9, and 11 for examples of the scrambled and telegraphic language characteristic of a real soldier, a plain and honest eyewitness of the Barcelona siege.)

The *Memoirs* have had a curious history. Hardly noticed for years after their publication, they were first acclaimed by Samuel Johnson in 1784, "who told Sir Joshua Reynolds that he was going to bed when it [the book] came, but was so much pleased with it, that he sat up till he had read it through, and found in it such an air of truth, that he could not doubt of its authenticity."[17] Sir Walter Scott took up the cause, in 1809 issuing the *Memoirs* as authentic history. But Defoe scholars, beginning with Walter Wilson in 1830, began including them in his canon. Previous to Colonel Arthur Parnell's publication of his *History of the War of the Spanish Succession in Spain* in 1888, "practically every nineteenth century history of the Peninsular campaigns used the 'Memoirs' as authentic ... and at the same time practically all the nineteenth century editions of Defoe's works included the 'Memoirs'."[18] Historians believed that since Carleton had been a real person, it was irrelevant to name Defoe in connection with the *Memoirs*. Parnell demonstrated that the account had not been written by Carleton and argued that it must have been written by Swift, an intimate friend of Peterborough's. Arthur Secord in 1724 made a powerful case for the *Memoirs* having been written by Defoe, but objections have been raised in the 1970s by Rodney Baine and by Stieg Hargevik.[19]

It is difficult to know why, if Peterborough wished to be commemorated for his military prowess, he did not turn to his friend Swift, who was to demonstrate his abilities in the genre with his 1731 *Memoirs of Captain John Creichton*. The most probable explanation is that Swift was in 1727 and 1728 preoccupied with the imminent death of Stella and in no condition to undertake such a work. How contact was made between Peterborough and Defoe remains a mystery. Possibly Peterborough, who had in 1707 forced himself upon Charles XII of Sweden, and was highly interested in his career,[20] read one of Defoe's three anonymous works of 1715, 1717, and 1720 glorifying the military exploits of that irresponsible king, made inquiries about the author, and discovered his identity. The same pride that caused Peterborough to conceal for thirteen years his marriage to a lady vastly inferior to him in rank would have prevented his revealing to Swift or Pope any association with Defoe. But an association with some ghostwriter is a fact, revealed by an annotation on a copy of the first edition of the *Memoirs* at a point where the narrative breaks off abruptly: "Here is much omitted that Lord Peterbor had approved."[21]

Defoe, only a humble hack writer in the eyes of such celebrities as Pope and Swift, may have performed a remarkable service for Peterborough, a service for which his talents as political hoaxter and pseudo-historian were better suited than theirs. Although the Carleton *Memoirs* are inferior to *Memoirs of a Cavalier* (1720), for the latter is given thematic unity by the question of what constitutes true courage in military campaigns, the ghostwriter succeeded in the former work in establishing for Peterborough in English imaginations and among English historians an unfounded reputation of military genius that endured "for more than a century and a half".[22] Challenged vigorously in 1888 by Colonel Arthur Parnell, Peterborough's bloated military reputation has only in the twentieth century been deflated to something closer to its true proportions by historians no longer seduced by the Carleton *Memoirs*.

Notes

1 William Stebbing, *Peterborough* (London, 1890), p. 167.

2 Stebbing, p. 165.

3 G. M. Trevelyan, *England under Queen Anne: The Peace and the Protestant Succession* (London, 1934), pp. 112–113.

4 G. M. Trevelyan, *England under Queen Anne: Ramillies and the Union with Scotland* (London, 1932), p. 68.

5 *Ibid.*, p. 72.

6 Arthur W. Secord, *Studies in the Narrative Method of Defoe* (Urbana, Illinois, 1924), pp. 199–200. Rodney Baine discounts the importance of these borrowings in his article "Daniel Defoe and Captain Carleton's *Memoirs of an English Officer*" (*TSLL*, 13, 1972, 624), but Stieg Hargevik reluctantly concludes in his full-length study of the authorship of the *Memoirs*, "As can be seen in this chapter it is impossible to refute the accusation that the author of Captain Carleton's *Memoirs* borrowed somewhat indiscriminately from certain contemporary works, but mainly from Freind's book on Peterborough" (*The Disputed Assignment of* "Memoirs of an English Officer" *to Daniel Defoe*, Stockholm, Almquist & Wiksell, 1974, p. 46).

7 G. M. Trevelyan, "Peterborough and Barcelona, 1705; *Narrative* and *Diary* of Col. John Richards," *Cambridge Historical Journal*, III (1931), 255, 258. Richards says in his *Narrative*: "It is needles to repeat all the particulars of this tidious and fateguing march. Our Guides mistook the way, so that we arriv'd an hower later than we Intended, for it was almost sun rising when we came up wth the fort. Consequently we were discover'd by the Enemy's out Guards who fir'd upon us and allarm'd the rest, and they again fired their Great Guns wch allarrm'd the Town." In his *Diary*, written at the time of the siege, he says: "The getting up the Hill was Verry painful to us that were allready tyr'd by the Length of the March, and what was Worse Our Guides Mistook the Way. The Granadears Went one way, The Musquetears an Other, the Prince and My Lord a 3d and all wrong it was therefore break of Day before we Came in Sight of the Cittadel, so that we were discovered by the Ennemys Micaletes who fyr'd upon us and gave the Alarme...."

8 *Ibid.*, p. 256. Richards says:

"In this juncture the Pr. Hess and my Ld. Peterborrow came up, misled as well as many others by their Guides. The Pr. propos'd the Cutting of the Communication between them and the Citty, wch indead was absolutely necessary, but to my great amazement (as it afterwards appear'd) absolutely mistook the way, wch a body would think scarcely possible for a man of his Caracter, and that had Commanded 6 years in this Town; he attempted this by way of the Grand ffosse of the Cittadel where we were all seen from head to foot, whilst we saw nothing more of the Enemy than their Hatts, whereas had we on the outside of the Glaci, or to speak more properly of the Rubbish wch was thrown out of the Ditch, and not as yet finnished, we had done the Busines Effectually, and had bin as well cover'd as if we had bin a league of. But his Glass being runne out, ffate Cut the thred of Life of the bravest man in the world, and that by a very slight wound in appearance, it being a shott in the small of his right Thigh near unto an other wound wch he receiv'd at the Seage of Bonne, but this having cut the grand artury he blead to death in les than half an howers Time.

My Ld. Peterborrow who see how matters were likely to go, was just before stept on one syde to give the Necessary Orders for the advancing of more Troops to support us, and perticularly a Reserve Commanded by Brigadeir Stanhope. It was during his abscence yt the Pr. was kill'd."

9 Secord, *Narrative Method of Defoe*, p. 201.

10 Trevelyan, "Peterborough and Barcelona, 1705", pp. 256–257. Richards says: "In this juncture my Ld. Peterborrow return'd, who seeing what was done fell into the Horriblest Passion yt ever man was seen in, with a great deal of bravery and Resolution led us back again, to the Posts wch we had quitted. I must confess I then thought it very rash, for the Enemy was plainly seen to sally from the Town in Order to cut between us and home; and the reason yt they did not was yt they learnt yt the Pr. of Hess was Kill'd, and yt my Ld. Peterborrow was there in Person wch made them turne back, for they never would beleave yt such persons would come so slightly accompany'd. So yt this action of my Ld. Peterborrows had all the good success Immaginable, and without any flattery Intitled us to all yt afterwards follow'd."

11 Trevelyan, *Ramillies and the Union with Scotland*, pp. 75–76.

12 The Duke and Duchess of Popoli had arrived shortly before the siege at Barcelona, on a Neapolitan ship carrying reinforcements to Velasco. On the evidence of Richards' diary, Trevelyan reports that both the Duke and his Duchess "were accomodated together in Peterborough's quarters". (*Ramillies and the Union with Scotland*, p. 76.)

13 John Robert Moore, Daniel Defoe, *Citizen of the Modern World* (Chicago, 1958), p. 263.

14 Secord, *Narrative Method of Defoe*, p. 180.

15 Trevelyan, *Ramillies and the Union with Scotland*, p. 63.

16 Moore, *Defoe*, p. 263.

17 *Boswell's Life of Johnson*, ed. G. B. Hill and L. F. Powell (Oxford, 1934), IV, 334.

18 Secord, *Narrative Method of Defoe*, p. 168.

19 The studies by Rodney M. Baine and Stieg Hargevik cited in footnote 6 above are the most recent contributions to the debate about authorship of Carleton's *Memoirs*. Both scholars admit that a ghostwriter was involved; but Baine, while suggesting Aaron Hill, Peterborough's secretary from 1707 to 1710, concludes that "the identity of Carleton's ghostwriter may never be discovered" (619), whereas Hargevik minimizes the importance of the ghostwriter and maximizes that of Carleton.

A full-length book being necessarily more detailed than an article, Hargevik's arguments against Defoe's editorship of the *Memoirs* merit point by point attention.

Although Hargevik's stylo-statistical method is carefully designed and impressively documented, to my mind it is vitiated by both his general premise, "Any writer's creation is by itself unique, but surely this uniqueness must be in form or idea" (p. 15), and his specific premise about Defoe's style: "At once I was struck by the idea that this book [Carleton's *Memoirs*] with its unusual freshness and vivacity could not be the product of the repetitive Daniel Defoe" (p. 1).

In addition, Hargevik assumes that Defoe had only one style, which developed "noticeably in the period 1700–1730, and the change consisted in an increase in favourite words and stock phrases" (p. 110). But Defoe had many styles, as the difficulty of attribution should suggest, as his contemporaries knew, and as he prided himself upon (see pages 17–18 and 22–3 above, as well as my discussion of voice and audience in individual essays on Defoe's political and economic writings). The increased prominence of his Crusoe-Mr. Review style in the 1720's is as much the result of his being forced to rely upon a market of less educated readers for his writing because he was no longer employed by the ministry, as it is the result of a natural development of his style. And his economic writing of the 1720s is in a different style from his popular self-instruction manuals of the same period (see *A Brief Deduction*, pp. 171–207 above). Furthermore, the favourite words and phrases isolated by Hargevik do not in separation from their context convey any definite impression even of Defoe's plain style. Finally, Hargevik ignores entirely the effect of the material Defoe is editing upon his style, assuming that Defoe is writing, not rewriting, someone else's work. (See pages 22–23 above for a reference to Defoe's sensitivity and expertise in editing.)

In tracing consistent ideas in Defoe and contrasting them to those of Carleton, Hargevik ignores the question of rhetorical purpose in Defoe's individual works, treating him as if he were an amateur who wrote solely to express his own ideas rather than a professional, frequently a hack, writer. That Defoe extolled General Galway in the *Review* when he was writing for Godolphin's pro-Galway ministry before 1710, for instance, does not preclude his having ghostwritten 1728 memoirs minimizing Galway's achievements in order to maximize those of his rival Peterborough.

The whole problem of ideas in Defoe must be handled very carefully, not only with due regard to differences dictated by different rhetorical purposes, but also with due care not to rely upon adverse comments by writers and critics whose prejudices and incomplete acquaintance with Defoe's works influenced their judgments. No writer except Swift, who also admired intelligent women, could have treated women with more respect than Defoe, as any reader of *Moll Flanders* and *Roxana*, not to mention the *Essay on Projects*, can testify—to quote Charles Dickens, the propagandist of the angel in the home sentimentality, is misleading. And since the scandalous Rochester, along with the righteous Milton, was Defoe's favourite author, Defoe's puritanism about sex is not to be accepted at face value.

Finally, in contrasting figures from Carleton's *Memoirs* to figures on the same battles in Defoe's writing, Hargevik ignores Defoe's practice and the whole question of the genre of the fictionalized history as he established it. Defoe altered numbers slightly in order to imitate the carelessness or incomplete knowledge of his narrators and also to conceal his own sources.

20 Stebbing reports that Peterborough fancied he might be more successful than Marlborough had been several months before in persuading Charles XII to direct his forces against France instead of Russia, "through the sympathy perhaps of mixed heroism and craziness". (*Peterborough*, p. 159.)

21 Moore's transcription from "marginal notes in a copy of the first edition owned by Sir Harold Williams. These contemporary notes were entered by someone who had compared the manuscript with the printed copy—someone who knew Peterborough and Carleton, but whose handwriting was unlike Defoe's." (*Defoe*, p. 263.)

22 Stebbing, *Peterborough*, p. 139.

The Military Memoirs Of Captain George Carleton
(1728)

* * *

But I now proceed to give an exact account of this great action; of which no person, that I have heard of, ever yet took upon him to deliver to posterity the glorious particulars; and yet the consequences and events, by what follows, will appear so great, and so very extraordinary, that few, if any, had they it in their power, would have denied themselves the pleasure or the world the satisfaction of knowing it.

The troops, which marched all night along the foot of the mountains, arrived two hours before day under the hill of Monjouick, not a quarter of a mile from the outward works. For this reason it was taken for granted, whatever the design was which the General had proposed to himself, that it would be put in execution before daylight; but the Earl of Peterborow was now pleased to inform the officers of the reasons why he chose to stay till the light appeared. He was of opinion that any success would be impossible, unless the enemy came into the outward ditch under the bastions of the second enclosure; but that if they had time allowed them to come thither, there being no palisadoes, our men, by leaping in upon them, after receipt of their first fire, might drive 'em into the upper works; and following them close, with some probability, might force them, under that confusion, into the inward fortifications.

Such were the General's reasons then and there given; after which, having promised ample rewards to such as discharged their duty well, a lieutenant, with thirty men, was ordered to advance towards the bastion nearest the town; and a captain, with fifty men, to support him. After the enemy's fire they were to leap into the ditch, and their orders were to follow 'em close, if they retired into the upper works. Nevertheless, not to pursue 'em farther, if they made into the inner fort; but to endeavour to cover themselves within the gorge of the bastion.

A lieutenant and a captain, with the like number of men and the same orders, were commanded to a demi-bastion at the extremity of the fort towards the west, which was above musket shot from the inward fortification. Towards this place the wall, which was cut into the rock, was not faced for about twenty yards; and here our own men got up; where they found three pieces of cannon upon a platform, without any men to defend them.

Those appointed to the bastion towards the town were sustained by two hundred men; with which the General and Prince went in person. The like number, under the directions of Colonel Southwell, were to sustain the attack towards the west; and about five hundred men were left under the command of a Dutch colonel, whose orders were to assist, where, in his own judgment, he should think most proper; and these were drawn up between the two parties appointed to begin the assault. My lot was on the side where the Prince and Earl were in person; and where we sustained the only loss from the first fire of the enemy.

Our men, though quite exposed, and though the glacis* was all escarped upon the live rock, went on with an undaunted courage; and immediately after the first fire of the enemy, all, that were not killed or wounded, leaped in, *pel-mel*, amongst the enemy; who, being thus boldly attacked, and seeing others pouring in upon 'em, retired in great confusion; and some one way, some another, ran into the inward works.

There was a large port in the flank of the principal bastion, towards the northeast, and a covered way, through which the General and the Prince of Hesse followed the flying forces; and by that means became possessed of it. Luckily enough here lay a number of great stones in the gorge of the bastion, for the use of the fortification; with which we made a sort of breastwork, before the enemy recovered of their amaze, or made any considerable fire upon us from their inward fort, which commanded the upper part of that bastion.

We were afterwards informed, that the commander of the citadel, expecting but one attack, had called off the men from the most distant and western part of the fort, to that side

* *glacis*: a sloping bank, landscaped in such a way that every part of it can be swept by the fire from the ramparts. [Ed.]

which was next the town; upon which our men got into a demi-bastion in the most extreme part of the fortification. Here they got possession of three pieces of cannon, with hardly any opposition; and had leisure to cast up a little retrenchment, and to make use of the guns they had taken to defend it. Under this situation, the enemy, when drove into the inward fort, were exposed to our fire from those places we were possessed of, in case they offered to make any sally, or other attempt against us. Thus we every moment became better and better prepared against any effort of the garrison. And as they could not pretend to assail us without evident hazard; so nothing remained for us to do, till we could bring up our artillery and mortars. Now it was that the General sent for the thousand men under Brigadier Stanhope's command, which he had posted at a convent, halfway between the town and Monjouick.

There was almost a total cessation of fire, the men on both sides being under cover. The General was in the upper part of the bastion; the Prince of Hesse below, behind a little work at the point of the bastion, whence he could only see the heads of the enemy over the parapet of the inward fort. Soon after an accident happened which cost that gallant Prince his life.

The enemy had lines of communication between Barcelona and Monjouick. The governor of the former, upon hearing the firing from the latter, immediately sent four hundred dragoons on horseback, under orders, that two hundred dismounting should reinforce the garrison, and the other two hundred should return with their horses back to the town.

When those two hundred dragoons were accordingly got into the inward fort, unseen by any of our men, the Spaniards, waving their hats over their heads, repeated over and over, "Viva el Rey! Viva!" This the Prince of Hesse unfortunately took for a signal of their desire to surrender. Upon which, with too much warmth and precipitancy, calling to the soldiers following, "They surrender! They surrender!" he advanced with near three hundred men (who followed him without any orders from their General) along the curtain which led to the ditch of the inward fort. The enemy suffered them to come into the ditch, and there surrounding 'em took two hundred of them prisoners, at the same time making a discharge upon the rest, who were running back the way they came. This firing brought the Earl of Peterborow down from the upper part of the bastion, to see what was doing below. When he had just turned the point of the bastion, he saw the

Prince of Hesse retiring, with the men that had so rashly advanced. The Earl had exchanged a very few words with him, when, from a second fire, that Prince received a shot in the great artery of the thigh, of which he died immediately, falling down at the General's feet, who instantly gave orders to carry off the body to the next convent.

Almost the same moment an officer came to acquaint the Earl of Peterborow, that a great body of horse and foot, at least three thousand, were on their march from Barcelona towards the fort. The distance is near a mile, all uneven ground; so that the enemy was either discoverable, or not to be seen, just as they were marching on the hills or in the vallies. However, the General directly got on horseback, to take a view of those forces from the rising ground without the fort, having left all the posts, which were already taken, well secured with the allotted numbers of officers and soldiers.

But the event will demonstrate of what consequence the absence or presence of one man may prove on great occasions. No sooner was the Earl out of the fort, the care of which he had left under the command of the Lord Charlemont (a person of known merit and undoubted courage, but somewhat too flexible in his temper) when a panick fear (though the Earl, as I have said, was only gone to take a view of the enemy) seized upon the soldiery, which was a little too easily complied with by the Lord Charlemont, then commanding officer. True it is; for I heard an officer, ready enough to take such advantages, urge to him, that none of all those posts we were become masters of, were tenable; that to offer at it would be no better than wilfully sacrificing human lives to caprice and humour; and just like a man's knocking his head against stone walls, to try which was hardest. Having overheard this piece of lip oratory, and finding by the answer that it was too likely to prevail, and that all I was like to say would avail nothing, I slipped away as fast as I could, to acquaint the General with the danger impending.

As I passed along, I took notice that the panick was upon the increase, the general rumor affirming, that we should be all cut off by the troops that were come out of Barcelona, if we did not immediately gain the hills, or the houses possessed by the Miquelets. Officers and soldiers, under this prevailing terror, quitted their posts; and in one united body (the Lord Charlemont at the head of them) marched, or rather hurried out of the fort; and were come halfway down the hill before the Earl of Peterborow came up to them. Though on my acquainting him with the shameful and surprising accident he made no stay; but answering, with a good deal of vehemence, "Good God, is it possible?" hastened back as fast as he could.

I never thought myself happier than in this piece of service to my country. I confess I could not but value it, as having been therein more than a little instrumental in the glorious successes which succeeded; since immediately upon this notice from me, the Earl galloped up the hill, and lighting when he came to Lord Charlemont, he took his half-pike out of his hand; and turning to the officers and soldiers, told them, if they would not face about and follow him, they should have the scandal and eternal infamy upon them of having deserted their posts, and abandoned their general.

It was surprising to see with what alacrity and new courage they faced about and followed the Earl of Peterborow. In a moment they had forgot their apprehensions; and, without doubt, had they met with any opposition, they would have behaved themselves with the greatest bravery. But as these motions were unperceived by the enemy, all the posts were regained, and anew possessed in less than half an hour, without any loss. Though, had our forces marched half musket shot farther, their retreat would have been perceived, and all the success attendant on this glorious attempt must have been entirely blasted.

Another incident which attended this happy enterprise was this: the two hundred men which fell into the hands of the enemy, by the unhappy mistake of the Prince of Hesse, were carried directly into the town. The Marquis of Risburg, a Lieutenant-General, who commanded the three thousand men which were marching from the town to the relief of the fort, examined the prisoners, as they passed by; and they all agreeing that the General and the Prince of Hesse were in person with the troops that made the attack on Monjouick, the Marquis gave immediate orders to retire to the town, taking it for granted, that the main body of the troops attended the Prince and General; and that some design therefore was on foot to intercept his return, in case he should venture too far. Thus the unfortunate loss of our two hundred men turned to our advantage, in preventing the advance of the enemy, which must have put the Earl of Peterborow to inconceivable difficulties.

The body of one thousand, under Brigadier Stanhope, being come up to Monjouick, and no interruption given us by the enemy, our affairs were put into very good order on this side; while the camp on the other side was so fortified, that the enemy, during the siege, never made one effort against it. In the meantime, the communication between the two camps was secure enough; although our troops were obliged to a tedious march along the foot of the hills whenever the General thought fit to relieve those on duty on the side of the attack, from those regiments encamped on the west side of Barcelona.

The next day, after the Earl of Peterborow had taken care to secure the first camp to the eastward of the town, he gave orders to the officers of the fleet to land the artillery and ammunition behind the fortress to the westward. Immediately upon the landing whereof, two mortars were fixed; from both which we plied the fort of Monjouick furiously with our bombs. But the third or fourth day, one of our shells fortunately lighting on their magazine of powder, blew it up; and with it the governor, and many principal officers who were at dinner with him. The blast, at the same instant, threw down a face of one of the smaller bastions; which the vigilant Miquelets, ready enough to take all advantages, no sooner saw (for they were under the hill, very near the place) but they readily entered, while the enemy were under the utmost confusion. If the Earl, no less watchful than they, had not at the same moment thrown himself in with some regular troops, and appeased the general disorder, in all probability the garrison had been put to the sword. However, the General's presence not only allayed the fury of the Miquelets; but kept his own troops under strictest discipline. So that in a happy hour for the frighted garrison, the General gave officers and soldiers quarters, making them prisoners of war.

How critical was that minute wherein the General met his retreating Commander! A very few steps farther had excluded us our own conquests, to the utter loss of all those greater glories which ensued. Nor would that have been the worst; for besides the shame attending such an ill-concerted retreat from our acquests on Monjouick, we must have felt the accumulative disgrace of infamously retiring aboard the ships that brought us; but Heaven reserved for our General amazing scenes both of glory and mortification.

I cannot here omit one singularity of life, which will demonstrate men's different way of thinking, if not somewhat worse; when many years after, to one in office, who seemed a little too deaf to my complaints, and by that means irritating my human passions, in justice to myself, as well as cause, I urged this piece of service, by which I not only preserved the place, but the honour of my country; that *Minister petite*, to mortify my expectations and baffle my plea, with a grimace as odd as his logick, returned, that, in his opinion, the service pretended was a disservice to the nation; since perseverance had cost the government more money than all our conquests were worth, could we have kept 'em. So irregular are the conceptions of man, when even great actions thwart the bent of an interested will!

The fort of Monjouick being thus surprisingly reduced, furnished a strange vivacity to men's expectations, and as extravagantly flattered their hopes; for as success never fails to excite weaker minds to pursue their good fortune, though many times to their own loss; so is it often too apt to push on more elevated spirits to renew the encounter for achieving new conquests, by hazarding too rashly all their former glory. Accordingly, everybody now began to make his utmost efforts; and looked upon himself as a drone, if he was not employed in doing something or other towards pushing forward the siege of Barcelona itself, and raising proper batteries for that purpose. But, after all, it must in justice be acknowledged, that notwithstanding this prodigious success that attended this bold enterprise, the land forces of themselves, without the assistance of the sailors, could never have reduced the town. The commanders and officers of the fleet had always evinced themselves favourers of this project upon Barcelona. A new undertaking so late in the year, as I have said before, was their utter aversion, and what they hated to hear of. Elated therefore with a beginning so auspicious, they gave a more willing assistance than could have been asked, or judiciously expected. The admirals forgot their element, and acted as general officers at land. They came every day from their ships, with a body of men formed into companies, and regularly marshalled and commanded by captains and lieutenants of their own. Captain Littleton in particular, one of the most advanced captains in the whole fleet, offered of himself to take care of the landing and conveyance of the artillery to the camp. And answerable to that his first zeal was his vigour all along; for finding it next to an impossibility to draw the cannon and mortars up such vast precipices by horses, if the country had afforded them, he caused harnesses to be made for two hundred men; and by that means, after a prodigious fatigue and labour, brought the cannon and mortars necessary for the siege up to the very batteries.

In this manner was the siege begun; nor was it carried on with any less application; the approaches being made by an army of besiegers, that very little, if at all, exceeded the number of the besieged; not altogether in a regular manner, our few forces would not admit it; but yet with regularity enough to secure our two little camps, and preserve a communication between both, not to be interrupted or incommoded by the enemy. We had soon erected three several batteries against the place, all on the west side of the town, *viz.* one of nine guns, another of twelve, and the last of upwards of thirty. From all which we plied the town incessantly, and with all imaginable fury; and very often in whole vollies.

Nevertheless it was thought not only advisable, but necessary, to erect another battery, upon a lower piece of ground under a small hill; which lying more within reach, and opposite to those places where the walls were imagined weakest, would annoy the town the more; and being designed for six guns only, might soon be perfected. A French engineer had the direction; and indeed very quickly perfected it. But when it came to be considered which way to get the cannon to it, most were of opinion that it would be absolutely impracticable, by reason of the vast descent; though I believe they might have added a stronger reason, and perhaps more intrinsick, that it was extremely exposed to the fire of the enemy.

Having gained some little reputation in the attack of Monjouick, this difficulty was at last to be put upon me; and as some, not my enemies, supposed, more out of envy than good will. However, when I came to the place, and had carefully taken a view of it, though I was sensible enough of the difficulty, I made my main objection as to the time for accomplishing it; for it was then between nine and ten, and the guns were to be mounted by daylight. Neither could I at present see any other way to answer their expectations, than by casting the cannon down the precipice, at all hazards, to the place below, where that fourth battery was erected.

This wanted not objections to; and therefore to answer my purpose, as to point of time, sixty men more were ordered me, as much as possible to facilitate the work by numbers; and accordingly I set about it. Just as I was setting all hands to work, and had given orders to my men to begin some paces back, to make the descent more gradual, and thereby render the task a little more feasible, Major Collier, who commanded the train, came to me; and perceiving the difficulties of the undertaking, in a fret told me, I was imposed upon; and vowed he would go and find out Brigadier Petit, and let him know the impossibility, as well as the unreasonableness of the task I was put upon. He had scarce uttered those words, and turned himself round to perform his promise, when an unlucky shot with a musket ball wounded him through the shoulder; upon which he was carried off, and I saw him not till some considerable time after.

By the painful diligence, and the additional compliment of men, however, I so well succeeded (such was my great good fortune) that the way was made, and the guns, by the help of fascines,* and other lesser preparations below, safely let down and mounted; so that that fourth battery began to play upon the town before break of day; and with all the success that was proposed.

In short, the breach in a very few days after was found wholly practicable; and all things were got ready for a general storm. Which Don Valasco, the Governor, being sensible of, immediately beat a parley, upon which it was, among other articles, concluded, that the town should be surrendered in three days; and the better to ensure it, the bastion, which commanded the Port St. Angelo, was directly put into our possession.

But before the expiration of the limited three days, a very unexpected accident fell out, which hastened the surrender. Don Valasco, during his government, had behaved himself very arbitrarily, and thereby procured, as the consequence of it, a large proportion of ill will, not only among the townsmen, but among the Miquelets, who had, in their zeal to King Charles, flocked from all parts of Catalonia to the siege of their capital; and who, on the signing of the articles of surrender, had found various ways, being well acquainted with the most private avenues, to get by night into the town. So that early in the morning they began to plunder all that they knew enemies to King Charles, or thought friends to the Prince, his competitor.

Their main design was upon Valasco the Governor, whom, if they could have got into their hands, it was not to be questioned, but as far as his life and limbs would have served, they would have sufficiently satiated their vengeance upon.

* *fascines*: long cylindrical faggots of brush, bound together and used to fill up ditches. [Ed.]

He expected no less; and therefore concealed himself, till the Earl of Peterborow could give orders for his more safe and private conveyance by sea to Alicant.

Nevertheless, in the town all was in the utmost confusion; which the Earl of Peterborow, at the very first hearing, hastened to appease; with his usual alacrity he rid all alone to Port St. Angelo, where at that time myself happened to be; and demanding to be admitted, the officer of the guard, under fear and surprise, opened the wicket, through which the Earl entered, and I after him.

Scarce had we gone a hundred paces, when we saw a lady of apparent quality, and indisputable beauty, in a strange, but most affecting agony, flying from the apprehended fury of the Miquelets; her lovely hair was all flowing about her shoulders, which, and the consternation she was in, rather added to, than anything diminished from the charms of an excess of beauty. She, as is very natural to people in distress, made up directly to the Earl, her eyes satisfying her he was a person likely to give her all the protection she wanted. And as soon as ever she came near enough, in a manner that declared her quality before she spoke, she craved that protection, telling him, the better to secure it, who it was that asked it. But the generous Earl presently convinced her, he wanted no intreaties, having, before he knew her to be the Dutchess of Popoli, taken her by the hand, in order to convey her through the wicket which he entered at, to a place of safety without the town.

I stayed behind, while the Earl conveyed the distressed Dutchess to her requested asylum; and I believe it was much the longest part of an hour before he returned. But as soon as ever he came back, he, and myself, at his command, repaired to the place of most confusion, which the extraordinary noise full readily directed us to; and which happened to be on the parade before the palace. There it was that the Miquelets were making their utmost efforts to get into their hands the almost sole occasion of the tumult, and the object of their raging fury, the person of Don Valasco, the late Governor.

It was here that the Earl preserved that governor from the violent, but perhaps too just resentments of the Miquelets; and, as I said before, conveyed him by sea to Alicant. ... Valasco, before his embarkment, had given orders, in gratitude to his preserver, for all the gates to be delivered up, though short of the stipulated term; and they were accordingly so delivered, and our troops took possession so soon as ever that governor was aboard the ship that was to convey him to Alicant.

During the siege of Barcelona, Brigadier Stanhope ordered a tent to be pitched as near the trenches as possibly could be with safety; where he not only entertained the chief officers who were upon duty, but likewise the Catalonian gentlemen who brought Miquelets to our assistance. I remember I saw an old cavalier, having his only son with him, who appeared a fine young gentleman, about twenty years of age, go into the tent, in order to dine with the Brigadier. But whilst they were at dinner, an unfortunate shot came from the bastion of St. Antonio, and entirely struck off the head of the son. The father immediately rose up, first looking down upon his headless child, and then lifting up his eyes to heaven, whilst the tears ran down his cheeks, he crossed himself, and only said, "Fiat voluntas tua," and bore it with a wonderful patience. 'Twas a sad spectacle and truly it affects me now whilst I am writing.

The Earl of Peterborow, though for some time after the Revolution he had been employed in civil affairs, returned to the military life with great satisfaction, which was ever his inclination. Brigadier Stanhope, who was justly afterwards created an earl, did well deserve this motto, "Tam Marte quam Mercurio"; for truly he behaved, all the time he continued in Spain, as if he had been inspired with conduct; for the victory at Almanar was entirely owing to him; and likewise at the battle of Saragosa he distinguished himself with great bravery. That he had not success at Bruhega was not his fault; for no man can resist fate; for 'twas decreed by Heaven that Philip should remain King of Spain, and Charles to be Emperor of Germany. Yet each of these monarchs have been ungrateful to the instruments which the Almighty made use of to preserve them upon their thrones; for one had not been King of Spain but for France; and the other had not been Emperor but for England.

Barcelona, the chief place in Catalonia, being thus in our hands, as soon as the garrison, little inferior to our army, had marched out with drums beating, colours flying, etc., according to the articles, Charles the Third made his publick entry, and was proclaimed king, and received with the general acclamations, and all other demonstrations of joy suitable to that great occasion.

*   *   *

3. A True Account of the Proceedings at Perth

According to an old manuscript note on the British Museum copy of the 76-page pamphlet, *A True Account of the Proceedings at Perth* was published on 12 May 1716. It deals with the petering out of the Jacobite rebellion of 1715, when the only substantial rebel force still in arms decided to retreat from its last enclave, rather than to stand and fight the advancing government forces led by the Duke of Argyll. Supposedly "written by a rebel", it purports to record the speeches that took place during a great council called to debate the question of whether to fight or to retreat.

"So essentially true to fact were Defoe's 'councils', and so lifelike in their narrative style", writes John Robert Moore, "that ... *A True Account* was assigned to the Master of Sinclair [one of the rebel leaders]. At least one Jacobite owner of the original tract scratched out the title-page ascription to 'a Rebel' and wrote in his own attribution to 'an old Royalist'."[1] It has been widely accepted as a primary source by historians, and even in the most up-to-date history of the rebellion, *The Jacobite Rising of 1715* (published in 1970), John Baynes draws several times upon details from *A True Account*, although he knows it was actually written by Defoe.

The uprising of 1715 was supposed to have its centre in the southwest of England, where there was a great deal of sympathy for the Jacobite cause, especially in Oxford and Bath, but the government, fully aware in advance of the rebel design, acted quickly to stamp out incipient opposition, arresting the principal leaders at the end of September. "With roughly a dozen peers and Members of Parliament out of the way", reports Baynes, "the uprising simply fizzled out."[2] But little of this depressing information got back to the Pretender, and he sent the Duke of Ormonde (who had fled to France on 21 July 1715) to land an invasion force near Plymouth. Ormonde arrived on 28 October , and finding the situation hopeless, went down the coast to Cornwall, discovered that it was impossible to land there either, "returned to Saint-Malo, where James was waiting, and reported that any idea of landing in the west of England was out of the question. The Pretender was left with no alternative but to switch his attention to those who had come out in his cause in the north."[3]

In Scotland the Earl of Mar, whose professions of devotion had been rejected by King George I, took charge of the Jacobite uprising, which proved much more formidable than that in the southwest of England. Mar was at his peak of strength in men and arms by the beginning of October.

In less than two months he had made himself master of the Highlands, controlled Inverness, thus assuring friendly territory to his rear, captured Perth, and was in position to attack Edinburgh, the Scottish capital. It appeared that nothing could stop him from controlling all of Scotland by the end of October. The Duke of Argyll, positioned with his little army at Stirling (near Edinburgh), anxiously and repeatedly urged the government to hurry with reinforcements.

With everything in his favour, the Earl of Mar, who was more of an administrator than a general, allowed his pace to slacken. Instead of attacking during the temporary period when most government forces were concentrated in England, he frittered away his superior position, divided his forces to muster more men, arms and money, and failed to demolish Argyll's army while the latter was at a disadvantage. 13 November 1715 was a black day for the northern rebels. A major section of their army, sent to pick up support in Lancashire, was surprised at Preston and decided to surrender after twenty-four hours. On the same day, Mar fought Argyll at Sheriffmuir (near Dunblane), a moor above Stirling, where Mar had intended to attack Argyll. The battle was in one sense indecisive, but by failing to annihilate Argyll's army at Sheriffmuir, when the Jacobites outnumbered government forces by about three to one, Mar lost his last chance to win Scotland for the Pretender before the inevitable reinforcements reached Argyll in December and January.

When the Pretender, "James III", after wasting precious time waiting to join Ormonde in England, finally arrived at the real centre of the rebellion on 22 December, the Jacobites were in dire straits. Mar's men were deserting and clans withdrawing every day, and his army had dwindled to about 4,000 horse and foot, only 2,500 of whom could be relied upon as fighting men.[4] James arrived at last in a small boat, with only about six attendants, and it soon became clear that no troops and supplies from France were following him.[5]

By January 1716 the attention of the Jacobite force in Perth was riveted on the military build-up of Argyll's force in Stirling, rather than upon such ceremonial events as James's coronation at Scone on 23 January. Terrified by Argyll's reconnaissances of the roads leading to Perth on 21 and 24 January, the Jacobites decided to put into operation a scorched earth policy to impede his eventual advance. Between 25 and 29 January, six villages were burnt to the ground, and their poor inhabitants left without food or shelter in the middle of a particularly cold and snowy winter. On 29 January Argyll's army marched out of Stirling toward Perth. On 31 January the rebel army retreated from Perth, and on 1 February Argyll's army entered the city.

The great council described in *A True Account* supposedly records the arguments in favour of fighting or retreating advanced by various members of the Jacobite army. On the veracity of these arguments Moore offers a salutary warning:

> Only a very bold or a very wise man could say with assurance just when Defoe really knew what his adversaries had said, when as a strategist he assigned certain speeches to them, and when (in the grand tradition of the speeches of Thucydides) he offered essential truth in place of demonstrable fact. For some of the ablest dialogue the reader feels constrained to ask not

how Defoe could know that it was actually spoken but how anyone else could know that it was not actually spoken.[6]

Tiptoeing in where angels fear to tread, I must venture to express the belief that Defoe's account is closer to fiction than to history. My judgment is based on both external and internal evidence.

John Baynes points out, while discussing Defoe's *True Account*, that "There is a remarkable similarity between the course of events at the end of the Battle of Preston and the last days in Perth as feeling began to run high between the supporters of the different courses of action. The ones who wished to fight began to taunt the others for their lack of courage."[7] The Battle of Preston had been fought in November 1715; the more socially important prisoners had been brought to London by December and tried amid great publicity in December, January, and February. Defoe must surely have known about the real disputes, mainly between Highlanders and English, that took place before the Preston Jacobites had agreed to surrender. On the other hand, information from Jacobite sources in Scotland could not have been easily accessible to him by 12 May 1716, when his *True Account* was published. A large number of the Jacobite prisoners in Scotland were released in June 1716, when the Habeas Corpus Act came back into force after a year's suspension. Most of the rest of the unreleased prisoners were tried in Carlisle, England, in November 1716.[8] Although it is possible that correspondents in Scotland or the ministry itself, by which he was employed, supplied Defoe with secret information about the Perth withdrawal, it is more probable that the inspiration for his great council came to him at the time of public excitement over the Preston trials.

Another piece of external evidence comes from the *Annals of King George*, Vol. II (published in October 1717), Defoe's official history of the Jacobite uprising, which he promises at the beginning of his *True Account* will shortly be forthcoming. In the *Annals* Defoe says:

We meet with very little transacted, either the Pretender or his party, after this, till the motions of the D. of Argyle began to put them upon serious reflections on the state of their affairs; and, upon considering closely whether to stand the attack of the royal army, or to provide in time for their own safety. *Some have said these things took up long debates; but I have been assured, that from the first of the Pretender's landing*, when they found the French declined him, and would not venture an open declaration in his favour; and he saw how divided, how naked of defence, and how uncapable of engaging the royal army they were at home, *it was no more a difficulty with them, whether they should retreat or no*. ... (pages 190–91; my italics)

Later on in the same paragraph he mentions Jacobite attempts to suggest they were preparing for a vigorous defence, including "the holding a great Council", but if such a council ever took place, it must have been as perfunctory as the other actions Defoe lists, because in spite of frenetic last minute activity, Perth was in fact never highly fortified against Argyll's expected attack.

Internal evidence suggesting that *A True Account* is mainly fictional is Defoe's imprecision about exact dates. As an official historian he was exceedingly careful about his facts and dates. His *History of the Union of Great Britain* (1709), and his account of the rebellion in Vol. II of the *Annals of King George* amply demonstrate his scrupulosity. In *A True Account*, however, events which actually occurred before the days on which the great council is supposed to have debated are telescoped into 29 and 30 January. One of the misdated events that occurs during the course of the debate is Argyll's reconnaissance mission of 21 or 24 January. The debate itself seems longer than the two days Defoe actually assigns it, and its outcome more dramatic and uncertain than real events proved it could have been. The most important chronological change occurs when Defoe obscures the relationship between the opening of the debate and the Jacobite burning of the six Scottish villages on Argyll's route. The narrator says (page 21 of the pamphlet, not reproduced) that spies informed the Jacobites on 28 January that Argyll intended to begin his march on the 29th. The council of chief officers sat continuously on the 28th to deliberate what should be done. The Jacobite soldiers were eager for battle. "In the mean time", states the narrator, "all the villages between that [Tullibardine] and Perth were ordered to be burnt, and all the corn and forrage to be destroyed, that the enemy might not find either shelter or provisions" (page 23, not reproduced).

Actually, the villages were burnt between 25 and 28 January, before the exact date of Argyll's advance was known, and before the supposed general council. Defoe deliberately confuses the dates in order to make the general council seem plausible; it would have been incredible to have committed an atrocity on the grounds of its necessity for a battle that still had to be decided upon in council. As an official historian, in his *Annals of King George*, it is clear to Defoe that this barbarity was occasioned by the need of the Jacobite leaders to make "their own people believe that they resolved to fight the royal army, and it was not words that would do this..." (p. 191). But in a secret history devoted to an account of a full-scale debate on whether to fight or to retreat, accurate chronology was not artistically compatible with verisimilitude or drama.

The deliberate blurring and misplacing of dates in *A True Account* is a technique Defoe used in other of his secret histories, which were partially factual, partially fictional, and largely polemical. His most ingenious use of this technique occurs in his *Mesnager Minutes*, the last excerpt in this history section.

Another internal suggestion that *A True Account* is largely fictional, and has a polemical purpose, is Defoe's patterning of the debate itself, which resembles a standard Augustan literary device described by Moore,[9] the Miltonic Infernal Council. The Pretender (described as the "Chevalier") is chosen to play the role of a comically gloomy and inept version of Satan. He is the leader who opens the great debate—in characteristically few words. Poor James makes a very unimpressive Satan indeed; the narrator finds him decidedly unprepossessing, certainly more depressing as a leader than a convinced Jacobite would have been prepared to admit in print.

It is the Earl of Mar who steals the limelight from his nominal leader, not only in a major speech reproduced on pages 330–2, but also in his secret speeches after the debate of 30 January (not reproduced) to a few selected leaders. Mar's physical appearance (he was a hunchback) is, significantly, not mentioned by the narrator (though he is careful to describe the physiognomy of the Pretender); his speech, graceful and convincing to those not in possession of the facts, suggests that Defoe has appointed him to the role of Milton's Belial. The Jacobite narrator recognizes that Mar's allusion to the battle of Dunblane (Sheriffmuir) as a "victory" is a distortion of the facts, as is his assertion that the Chevalier has brought supplies, money, arms and ammunition with him, but he cannot know that the French preparations for a new descent upon England led by Ormonde are sheer fantasy, nor that strategy for the Jacobite uprising was not concerted between Ormonde and Mar—indeed, lack of an overall strategy was the major reason for the Jacobite fiasco of 1715. The narrator perceives the drift of Mar's speech, however: "It was easy to see that his Lordship was very well prepared to join with those who should think we were in no condition to fight the national troops" (page 332), and even accuses Mar of manipulating the figures of the opposing forces in order to make the Jacobites appear more vulnerable than they are. In sum, Mar, like Belial, counsels ignoble ease.

Moloch, the fierce spirit who is all for open war, even at the cost of certain death, is suitably represented by a Highland officer—the fiercest and most savage of all fighting men. It is probable that Defoe chooses to reproduce his words directly instead of in the third person because they are more passionate, offering only two extreme choices, and therefore more dramatic, than the reasoned discourses: "How much less terrible is death in the field than in a ditch? And how much rather had all our people die with swords in their hands, than starve in the mountains?"

The arguments of those who seek to make the best of their disadvantageous position by human ingenuity, the "ways and means" speakers, interest Defoe as much as the hypocrisy of Mar (Belial). In this category we can place the Lowland gentleman (page 332), the French engineer (page 334) who advises destroying the country around them, forgetting that by the time of the great debate this has already been done, the sensible general officer (pages 335–6) who suggests, on the basis of his experience in the Swedish army, that a good retreat requires a plan of where to place themselves at better advantage, not a downright running away and shifting for themselves, and the man of years (pages 336–8), who wants to decide for battle or retreat on the basis of whether the Jacobites are a match for Argyll in the open field. His speech, like that of the Highland Officer (Moloch), is presented in the first person, certainly not for its intrinsic dramatic appeal, but probably because Defoe approved of his reasoning and wished to stress his contribution to the debate. The arguments of this group of speakers illustrate Defoe's interest in different points of view on the same issue. These moderate voices are not inspired by Book II of *Paradise Lost*. Although their suggestions differ, they all emanate from the same type, not Milton's Mammon, but brave men who wish to fight according to some rational plan, and who are admired by the narrator, who resembles Defoe in admiring constructive ingenuity. As the narrator says after learning that Mar, the Chevalier, and his retinue have abandoned their men, "Well, there was now no remedy, complaining and exclaiming was to no purpose, we had a powerful army at our heels, our business was to consider what was before us" (page 339).

The supreme irony of this Infernal Council is the Chevalier's rapid recovery of spirit once he finds himself safely on board ship, bound for

France (page 328), so contrary to the attitude of Milton's Satan, who accepts with his elevated position "as great a share/Of hazard as of honour". The Chevalier's despondency lifts when he is relieved of the necessity of being "a meer state VICTIM, appointed for a sacrifice to expiate the sins of other men", of acting in accordance with the theory of divine right under which he claimed the throne of England—that of being God's anointed, or Christ on earth, to men.

Moore explains why Milton's Infernal Council was so attractive to Augustan writers:

> To start with, there was the conception of political leaders hopelessly in the wrong through rebellion against Church or State or any other allegiance. ... There was the dramatic crisis of a conclave at which some decision was to be reached, and in which the characters revealed themselves through speeches, much as in the familiar debates in the English House of Lords. ...[10]

He goes on to list some of the works in which Defoe relied upon this device. Defoe himself suggests the presence of a diabolic element in the Jacobite uprising in the introduction to his redaction of the Earl of Mar's *Journal* (Summer 1716):

> ... it was an attempt, not without probability only, but even without possibility of success; and therefore can be called neither more nor less than an undertaking of madmen and fools. *Unless I should break in upon charity, and suggest, that it was a hellish plot, to draw in two or three thousand gentlemen of quality and estates, on purpose that they might be ruined and undone*. (Page v, my italics)

A True Account is obviously a polemical piece directed against the Jacobite leadership and aiming to win back to the fold disillusioned Jacobite followers. As such, it is unfair to the Pretender, not only in its description of James, but in its failure to mention that the Chevalier left Scotland with reluctance, persuaded that his remaining would incite the government to hunt down Jacobites more assiduously than otherwise. James left behind him almost all of his money, "with instructions that it should be used to pay off all the troops, after which anything left over was to be passed on to the inhabitants of the burnt villages in Perthshire."[11] Furthermore, General Gordon's conduct of the retreat was such as to insure that very few involved in the Perth retreat were ever captured by government forces.

Defoe's use of the Infernal Council in *A True Account* is more than mere imitation of a fashionable Augustan literary device. He adapts Milton's invention to his own point of view, following his original in offering different arguments on one issue, and in suggesting a serious Satanic counterpart for the Earl of Mar. But his comic deflation of Satan himself does not originate from Book II of *Paradise Lost*; humour is always important in Defoe's writing, and in this case it serves his polemical purpose of attracting reasonable Jacobites back to the Hanoverian fold. The esteem Defoe displays for human ingenuity, in this case knowledge of military strategy and engineering, is another constant element in his writing. Although the debate in *A True Account* is consequently less Satanic in these respects, the element of diabolism in the pamphlet is not simply a residue evoked automatically by derivation from a Miltonic original. As we have already seen in many of the preceding excerpts, certain evils consistently appeared sinister to Defoe; one of these evils was the breach of loyalty combined with treachery and the attempt to pervert others, developed most fully in his novel *Roxana*.

Notes

1 John Robert Moore, *Daniel Defoe, Citizen of the Modern World* (Chicago, 1958), p. 271.

2 John Baynes, *The Jacobite Rising of 1715* (London, 1970), p. 23.

3 *Ibid.*, p. 24.

4 *Ibid.*, p. 163.

5 Louis XIV had died in September 1714, and the Duke of Orléans, Regent for the young Louis XV, was not anxious to antagonize the English while he had domestic strife and financial problems to settle at home. For this reason, the Duke of Berwick, illegitimate son of James II and older sister of the Duke of Marlborough, an outstanding general and Marshall of France, was not permitted to take charge of the Scottish military operations.

6 John Robert Moore, "Milton among the Augustans: The Infernal Council," *SP*, XLVIII (1951), 25.

7 Baynes, p. 174.

8 *Ibid.*, pp. 195–198.

9 John Robert Moore, "Milton among the Augustans", pp. 15–25.

10 *Ibid.*, p. 22.

11 Baynes, p. 178.

A True Account of the Proceedings at Perth
(1716)

*   *   *

Having looked thus far back, come we next to the time of the Ch——'s arrival; at the first news whereof, it is impossible to express the joy and vigour of our men. Now we hoped the day was come when we should live more like soldiers, and should be led on to face our enemies, and not lie mouldering away into nothing, attending the idle determinations of a disconcerted council; but our joy was very much abated, when we came to hear that there was no troops arrived, only about eighty officers, which in truth, there was not by above half the number.

We were indeed buoyed up with the account spread abroad, that the troops were shipping off, and might be expected in a very few days; that the Ch—— being willing to encourage his friends with his presence, and eager to be at the head of his armies, could not be easy in staying any longer for the shipping the troops, but resolved, though with the extreme hazard of his person, to venture alone, and came away before. This tale took pretty well, and we being willing to hope for the best, acquiesced, though we professed ourselves to be very much disappointed.

On the other hand, the Ch——, as soon as he came to Perth, and had some leisure to look about him, began to enquire into the state of the army, and desired to see some of the troops, which when he had done, it was easy to perceive by his countenance that he was under a very great disappointment, and that he thought himself betrayed, which we heard more of in a few days.

He enquired after our men, and desired to see the little kings with their armies, so he was pleased to call the clans; we appeared, and he saw our exercise and manner of fighting, and the goodness of our arms, all which he appeared exceedingly pleased with, and was very inquisitive to know how many such as we were in arms for him; but when he was told how few, he gave tokens again of a disagreeable surprise.

* * *

I had thought here to have set down my observations at large, of the person who was then called King, and in whose quarrel we were now in arms; but I will not take that freedom here as was intended, because I know not whether it may turn to good or ill, according as into whose hands these memoirs may happen to fall. However, in brief his person is tall and thin, seeming to incline to be lean rather than to fill as he grows in years. His countenance is pale, and perhaps he looked more pale, by reason he had three fits of an ague, which took him two days after his coming on shore; yet he seems to be sanguine in his constitution, and has something of a vivacity in his eye, that perhaps would have been more visible, if he had not been under dejected circumstances, and surrounded with discouragement, which it must be acknowledged were sufficient to alter the complexion even of his soul as well as of his body; and I was told, that as soon as he was on board the ship which carried him away, he spoke with a different spirit, and discovered such a satisfaction as might well signify, that he looked upon himself before as a meer state VICTIM, appointed for a sacrifice to expiate the sins of other men, and that he was escaped as from certain destruction. His speech was grave, and not very clearly expressing his thoughts, nor overmuch to the purpose; but his words were few, his behaviour and temper seemed always composed; what he was in his diversions we knew nothing of, for here was no room for those things, it was no time for mirth, neither can I say that I ever saw him smile. Those who speak so positively of his being like King James VII, must excuse me for saying, that it seems to tell me they either never saw this, or never saw King James VII, and yet I must not conceal, that when we saw the person who they called our King, we found ourselves not at all animated by his presence, and if he was disappointed in us, we were tenfold more so in him; we saw nothing in him that looked like spirit; he never appeared with chearfulness and vigour to animate us. Our men began to despise him, some asked if he could speak; his countenance looked extremely heavy; he cared not to come abroad among us soldiers, or to see us handle our arms or do our exercise; some said the circumstances he found us in dejected him; I am sure the figure he made dejected us, and had he sent us but 5,000 men of good troops and never come among us, we had done other things than we have now done.

* * *

The great men were up all night, and nothing was seen but posting to and fro between Schone and Perth. The case as we afterwards learned was this, *viz.* that all the military men were positive in the resolutions for fighting; the Earl of Mar, two or three clergymen who kept with him, and some others, who for the sake of the times I do not name, were resolved not to put it to the hazard, their pretence was the safety of the Ch——'s person; whether that were the true and only reason, I shall say more of by and by; but nothing is more true, than that we who were soldiers and voluntiers did not believe them; we told them we had as much concern for the safety of the Ch——'s person as they had, and if we were for putting it to hazard, it was not without the hazard of our lives; and to show the sincerity of our resolutions, we were willing the Ch—— should retreat to some place of security, and let all that had a value for his cause, fight for it like men, and not bring things this length, to turn our backs like scoundrels and poltrons, and not strike a stroke for him when he was come so far to put himself and his fortunes upon our services and fidelity. We carried this so high, that some of our number ruffled the great men in the open streets, called them cowards, and told them they betrayed the Ch—— instead of advising him. One of them, an intimate of the Earl of Mar, stopped and talked some time with our people, who indeed began to threaten them if they offered to decline fighting. "Why, what would you have us do?" said he. "Do", says the Highland man, "What did you call us to take arms for? Was it to run away? What did the Ch—— come hither for? Was it to see his people butchered by hangmen, and not strike a stroke for their lives? Let us die like men, and not like dogs." "What can we do?" says the other. "Let us have a council of war," says the soldier, " and let all the general officers speak their minds freely, the Ch—— being present, and if it be agreed there not to fight, we must submit."

This was not the only ruffle, they met with a bold Norlander of Aberdeenshire, who threatened them in so many words, that the loyal clans should take the Ch—— from them; and that "if he was willing to die like a prince, he should find there were ten thousand gentlemen in Scotland that were not afraid to die with him."

Things began that night to be very disorderly and tumultuous, and I know not what it might have ended in, if some more discreet than the rest had not interposed, who satisfied the soldiery, by telling them there would be a great council in the evening; that the Ch—— desired all that were his friends would acquiesce in such measures as should be resolved on there; that if it was advisable to put it to the hazard, the Ch—— would take his fate, with his faithful friends; if it was otherwise advised, he would do as they should direct, or to this purpose. And accordingly a great council was held in the evening of the 29th, and the most weighty and ultimate debates taking up so much time, that it could not be concluded that night, it was renewed the 30th, when the fatal resolutions of giving up their cause were taken, on the same unhappy day that the grandfather of the Ch—— was beheaded at the gate of his palace, by the English usurper; a day unlucky to the family, and which as it dethroned them before for almost twelve years, so it seems to have extirpated the very name of Stuart at last, and left the race to God's mercy, and a state of pilgrimage without hope of recovery.

* * *

When the council was set, the Ch—— spoke a few words, and they were but few indeed, to let them know that they were met to consider of the present situation of their affairs, and to give their opinions in what was to be done; that their enemies were preparing to attack them; and that it was necessary to consider of the properest measures to defend themselves; and that he had ordered everything to be laid before them, and desired that every man would freely speak their opinion; that whatever was resolved on, it might be with their general agreement and consent, and might be executed immediately, for no time was to be lost.

The Ch—— having spoken, the Earl of M—— took the word, as was appointed, and opened the case in a long speech to the purpose following:

He told them, that ever since the battle of Dumblane (I think he said the *victory* of Dumblane), he had endeavoured to keep the army together, and to put them in as good a posture for service as possible, having two expectations on which they all knew their whole affair depended upon, (*viz.*) the coming of the Ch——, and the rising or landing of the D—— of O——d in England, as had been concerted and agreed between him and the said D—— of O——d, as well before his going from England, as since; that the first of these had answered their expectation, and the Ch—— was happily arrived, having also caused to be brought to them powerful supplies of money, arms, ammunition, and other necessaries, as well before as since his arrival, all which had come safe to their hands, not one vessel having fallen into the enemy's hands; but that their friends in England had met with many disappointments, and their designs having been betrayed, the chief gentlemen on whom the D—— of O——d relied for assistance, had been taken up, so that their measures had been entirely broken, and that when the D——, not satisfied with the advices he received, had sailed even to the very coast of England, and had actually gone on shore there, yet he found their friends so dispersed and discouraged, that it was impossible to bring them together without a sufficient force to be landed from abroad to make a stand, and give time for those who were well affected in England to come together with safety; that upon this disappointment, his Grace was gone back to France, where preparations were making for his descent upon England, with such a power as should protect their friends, and give them opportunity to shew themselves in a proper manner and place.

That these things, however, have brought the weight of the war upon them in Scotland, and not only so, but had caused those succours which they expected from abroad, to be stopped and reserved for the said expedition of the D—— of O——d which was now in a great forwardness in the western parts of France. But as by this means the national army was encreased, by the addition of foreigners brought over to fall upon them; and that according to certain intelligence, they were resolved to march, notwithstanding the violence of the season, in order to attack them, as they gave out, in the city of Perth; it was to be now considered of, whether they were in a condition to maintain themselves in their present situation or not, and that if the affirmative were resolved on, the army might be disposed in such manner as it might act with the greatest vigour, and most to their advantage; and if not, that the retreat might be appointed in such manner, and to such parts as the enemy might be least able to annoy them; and that they might prevent the hurry and disorder that such things are usually attended with, and that the person of the Ch—— might be secured, and the troops kept so together as not to be insulted by any parties, or obliged to halt by the enemy's horse, so as to be brought to the necessity of a general battle, whether they thought fit or not; in all which cases they would be obliged to fight with disadvantage, and the enemy obtain a cheaper victory, than it would be possible for them to get, if they were obliged to attack them where they now were.

After his Lordship had finished his discourse, he threw down several copies of the intelligence he had received from Sterling, of the forces of the Duke of Argyle's army, and likewise lists of his own troops, in which copies it was easy to see that his Lordship was very well prepared to join with those who should think we were in no condition to fight the national troops; the lists, as we all afterwards believed, being calculated by themselves for the purpose, having so far magnified the enemy's forces, and diminished our own, as that we appeared much inferior.

* * *

These things being thus laid before them, the debates began. A Lowland gentleman speaking first, told them, as we were informed, that he had seriously weighed everything, that as a gentleman, and as a soldier, and especially as one concerned for the person of him who they had in trust to defend, he ought to do; and it was his opinion, that they had it perfectly in their choice, either to make a stand, or to retreat, which they would, and that either might be done without any great hazard of loss or disorder. That however the Duke of Argyle seemed superior in his numbers, and, perhaps, had some advantage in the experience of his troops, yet he thought he had so much disadvantage by the severity of the season, that he made no doubt but they might defend the town of Perth, till the enemy's foot should perish in the lying before it. He then went on to tell them, that true it was, the national army had with them a train of artillery, etc., for a siege, but that they could not break ground, the frost being so severe; that they could raise no batteries, nor open any trenches, and he believed it was never heard of, that ten thousand men within the town, were attacked by but ten thousand men without the town, and taken sword in hand.

On the other hand, as he said, supposing they thought it advisable to retreat, they might do it with all the leisure imaginable, leaving about 2,000 men in the town, and before those men could be obliged to surrender, the army might be posted in what advantageous part of the kingdom they thought fit.

A Highland officer stood up next. "I am ashamed," says he, "to repeat what I hear in the streets, and what the town is full of, (*viz.*) that we are met here to resolve to run away like cowards, from an enemy who we have once already seen in the field like men. I hope none here will doubt, whether we dare see them again or no; I am persuaded there is not a man in the troops I have the honour to be at the head of, but had rather fight and be killed, than turn their backs and escape. I beseech your Lordships to consider, whither shall we retreat? I should have called it *flee*; if for we turn our backs on the Bank of Tay, we shall turn our faces nowhere else; if we flee to the coast, have we ships to carry us to sea? If we turn to the hills, can we subsist? How much less terrible is death in the field than in a ditch? And how much rather had all our people die with their swords in their hands, than starve in the mountains? But what need we speak of it in such a melancholy tone, let us enquire of the engineers and men of judgment, whether our situation is such as that we ought not to dispute it; and that we shall be forced out, though our men do their duty. For my own part, I am not a professed engineer, yet I am of opinion, as our few cannon may be placed, and as some of our men may be posted, we may not only defend the town, but post the rest of our army so, as that they shall not be able to attack the one or the other, without the greatest disadvantage possible, and evident hazard of being ruined; and if they cannot attack us and storm us sword in hand, we know very well they cannot lie before the place, the severity of the weather will make it unsufferable, and they will not pretend to it; so that for my share, I do not see the least reason for retreating."

Upon this speech, it was said the Ch—— appeared a little terrified, for as we understood afterward, he was so possessed with secret apprehensions of his being to be betrayed, that if the impetuosity of the common soldiers had obliged them to resolve on a stand, as it was much feared it would, he would certainly have retired in the night before with Lord Mar and others. In this consternation, as soon as the officer had done speaking, the Ch—— looked at a French officer, who was also an engineer, and who had formerly advised the fortifying the town of Perth with a complete rampart with five bastions, courtins, ravelins,* and a double counterscarp, and offered to have made it tenable in five weeks' time.

This gentleman reminding them of what he had offered, and how much better it had been if those measures had been taken, told them, shaking his head, that he did not think the town was to be defended against a regular siege, nor that it could hold out five days' open trenches; but as it was observed, that the enemy could neither raise batteries or dig trenches, nor lie before it 24 hours without ruining their infantry, it was his opinion they might very easily maintain the place if they thought fit, at least so long, as to put the enemy to the necessity of going into quarters, and turning it into a blockade; in which case he told them it would be their business to destroy the country round, and secure all the provisions, so as that the army should find no subsistance, it being known already that they had but five days' provisions with them, and that the forrage for the horses might easily be destroyed.

This gentleman told them, however, that it would be needful that they should come to a speedy resolution in this case; for that if he had order to prepare for a defence, he must desire as much leisure as possible, and must have as many workmen pressed in from the country, as could be had, in which case he would do his endeavour to find them some difficulty before they should be able to attack the town itself.

He was desired then to give in some plan of his design, and by what method he would make the place defensible in so short a time, and how he would have the army posted. He answered with modesty, that the marshalling the army was not his part, but belonged to the general officers, who he knew understood their business. It was true, it was usual for engineers to give in an account how many men were required to garrison a town after they had fortified it; but that he thought the case differed here, and he supposed this was rather to be a battle than an attack of a place; and that as the national army seemed to resolve to attack them immediately, or perhaps with a little random battery, as they may suppose, only to clear the way, and then to fall in sword in hand, and by the desperate courage of their men, to carry the place; and,

* *courtins*: the wall of a fortified place, or the part of it connecting two bastions, towers, gates, etc. [Ed.]
ravelin: "a work that consists of two faces that makes a salient angle, commonly called half moon by the soldiers; it is raised before the courtines. ..." (Samuel Johnson)

in this case, his business was, as he conceived, to give them a warm reception, and upon such an occasion, the whole army, except the horse, would be necessary to be posted in the town, and to be so drawn up, as, from the main body, to relieve every part as the generals saw occasion; as to the horse, the generals were to be consulted in what manner to post them, and where, and what service to appoint them.

It was evident, the questions put to this gentleman, were rather to get room to raise objections against it, and make it a matter of long debate, for it was certainly concluded beforehand, not to stand or defend the place at all. However, it seems there were several general officers who were not let into that part of the secret, of which number one of them having heard this French gentleman with patience, yet discovering that he had something to offer, desired leave to give his opinion; whereupon he told them, that when he was an officer in the Swedish army, it was counted a dishonour for any general to mention a retreat in any case whatsoever, and that as he always thought a soldier and a man of honour, could with much more satisfaction, fight, though at a manifest disadvantage, than turn his back; yet since, of late years, it has been thought a part of generalship to make a good retreat with an army, and not to be forced to fight at the pleasure of the enemy, which he would not deny required great skill and experience, so he wanted much to hear what manner of retreating it was that was proposed here, whether a retreat, in order to post themselves with more advantage, or a downright running away, separating and shifting for themselves, and giving up the cause they were engaged to; and that till this was determined, no man knew what to offer; for if they retreated, only to post themselves where they might receive the enemy with more advantage, then he told them he was to ask where that was, and that it was his opinion, that no general would, in such a case, decamp from one advantageous situation, without knowing where they should post themselves next, and whether it was more to their satisfaction or not. On the other hand, if by retreating, was meant giving up the design, and shifting for themselves, he desired to know if they had considered what the consequence of such a manner of retreating would be, and how much better to the soldiery it would be to be overthrown in battle, and after they had done their duty like men of honour, to die fighting, or accept of quarter from the enemy.

To retreat in this manner, he told them, was to abandon,

not only the cause, but the Ch——, who had ventured his person to put himself at the head of the army, and not at the head of an army of runaways and poltrons, but an army of gentlemen ready to die in his service. He told them, he believed the Ch—— had been imposed upon abroad, and made believe that his army here was stronger than it was; yet it was not so weak, but that they were ready to do their duty, and to let him see, that if he was deluded, they were not the men that had done it, or had any hand in it. He concluded, that he depended upon the engineer's opinion, *viz.* that the place might give them an opportunity to fight with advantage, and he thought that was all could be desired, and therefore he declared he was for fighting.

In a word, all the generals or other officers who came over with the Ch——, and all those who belonged to the clans of Highland men, were unanimously for fighting.

The arguments for fighting were the subject of many hours' debate, for many more spoke their opinions than those above-mentioned; it came then to the turn of those who were in the secret, to act the part they had agreed on.

A young nobleman, but a warm forward man, who gave many proofs that he wanted not courage, was yet the first man that broke the ice in favour of a retreat; but he told them plainly he did it, not that he believed they were not strong enough to maintain their ground, and to give the D—— of A—— his hands full, "but", said he, "because I see no concert of measures among us; they that are not for fighting, will certainly fight but very indifferently when they are forced to it; and if we are not all faithful and resolved to do our duty as we ought to do it, let us never suffer ourselves to be brought to it."

Another eminent person, a man of years, and in good credit with the army, then entered on a serious discourse concerning the circumstances of their forces, and directing his speech to the lord M——, seemed to discover that he was not yet in the main secret. "My Lord", said he, "these gentlemen who are for fighting, shew a great deal of gallantry and resolution worthy of themselves and to the honour of our nation; but I fear neither they or the engineers have discovered some part of our present condition, in which I foresee we may, as our present situation is, be worsted without much fighting, and fall an easier prey into the enemy's hands than they are aware of. I observe", said he, directing himself then to the French gentleman, who they called an engineer, "that it is this gentleman's opinion, that we are able to defend ourselves in this town, and in case of an attack, may make the enemy sensible of their mistake by their loss, and by the ruin of their infantry, and I am fully of his mind; and if they will ensure us that the Duke of Argyle shall add that mistake to the rest of his conduct, and attack us in this advantageous post, I shall be willing to give my vote for fighting, not questioning to make them repent the rashness of so hazardous an attempt.

"But because I think that attempt so hazardous, therefore I cannot believe the Duke will be so weak as to undertake it, especially when there will be so many several ways to ruin us without it, and therefore I desire to ask a few questions of these gentlemen, which when they have answered to your satisfaction, I shall give my vote for fighting with all my heart.

"My observation", continued he, "has been in all your discourses, that you are of opinion we are able to fight them in the town, posted to advantage, and covered with barricadoes and some regular works; but I have not heard one of these gentlemen say yet, that we are in a condition to fight them in the open field; not, my Lords, that I am for quitting any advantage, and so chuse to fight in the field when we may fight upon better terms; but let me first ask, whether we are able to fight them fairly in open field or not?

"If we can, then I am for standing firm in the town, to see if they will venture to attack us there; which if they decline, we may be able to prevent them doing us any other mischief, by marching out after them if they offer to go to any other part, and perhaps cutting off their retreat. But on the other hand, if we are not a match for them, but under the shelter of the city, and that we dare not march out after them though they should proceed into our side of the country, leaving us behind them; then the consequence will be, that they will hold us blocked up, and in the meantime ruin the country, consume the forrage, surround our quarters, and at length, oblige us to surrender for want of provisions; in the meantime all our friends will be ruined by their cavalry, and all those countries, from whence our supplies come, will be eaten up and destroyed. So that the question is not, whether we can maintain this post, but, whether we can at the same time protect the country behind us, and keep the enemy from quartering there at discretion, and so destroying the country and us too. If this cannot be done, we must consider of quitting this place, and posting ourselves somewhere else to more advantage."

They began now to be weary of these debates, they found the arguments for fighting grew popular, and they were terribly afraid that the soldiery should get a scent of the design, so the grand council was adjourned to next morning; but notice being given to a certain number selected for the purpose, to meet in an hour or two after, they had a private meeting accordingly, and here the Lord Mar opened to them the whole mystery, telling them, *in a few words*, that the present debates did not answer their circumstances; that the question was not concerning their ability just now of maintaining that post, which perhaps they might all be of opinion, as he also was, might be done well enough, but they were to consider the situation *of their affairs in general*; that there were many reasons which made it inconvenient to make publick all the circumstances of their affairs, and those especially which made it necessary to retreat; but that it was evident they were come now to a crisis in which it was advisable not to retreat only, but to put an end to the design in general *for a time*, and that measures might be taken to do it so now, as that the enemy might make less advantage of their retreat than at another time when the country was more easily to be passed. However, as this design was not to be communicated to the army, lest it should too much discourage their troops, so all those who heard it would be less surprised when they should hear the reasons for it, which should be communicated in form to them by the Ch——'s order. He told them also, that they must agree to give the Ch—— assurances of their keeping private the present debate, in return for which, they should all be assured, that their personal safety should be taken care of equally with the Ch——'s own life; that true it is, the enemy would make great advantages of their retreat, and some of their friends would be in danger of falling into their hands; but they were also to observe, that measures were taken for such a retreat, as that many thousands of their men should always keep together, and that so many could not fall this way as would necessarily fall in so hot an action as fighting the present army must of necessity be; that the gentlemen should all be furnished with shipping to carry them over to France, where they should all be taken care of, have the half pay of officers allowed them, and be soon satisfied that they should return strong enough to retrieve all that should be lost by this retreat, and to make their enemies pay dear for all the spoil they should commit, and all the blood they should shed of their friends who might fall into their hands.

*   *   *

We made but small stay at Dundee, and kept on to Montrose; all this while we knew nothing of the real design, but were told, that by this march we should harrass the enemy's army, render them unfit for service, and have them cheap when we came by North Spay, and the Brays of Mar, where their horse would be useless. The thing was rational enough had it been really in their design, nor did they suspect what followed in the least; if they had, I would not have answered for the heads of all those that were in the secret.

But had you seen the confusion we were in the next morning, when we were told that the Ch——, my Lord Mar, and all the generals and officers, with several lords of his council, the French engineers, etc., were gone, it is impossible to express the rage of the soldiers, and especially of some of the noblemen and general officers, how they exclaimed against the Earl of Mar in particular; how they cried out they were betrayed from the beginning; brought into a snare, and abandoned in the basest and most cowardly manner imaginable.

Well, there was now no remedy, complaining and exclaiming was to no purpose, we had a powerful army at our heels, our business was to consider what was before us; General Gordon, Ecclin, Buckley, and several other very good officers were with us still, with seven or eight noblemen, and they called a council of war. The Ch—— had left a letter directed to Gordon to continue his march to Aberdeen. It was told us that there was also a letter of instructions which he was not to open till he arrived there; but others said there was a private order to him to provide shipping at Aberdeen for all the gentlemen, if possible, and to follow him. However, they gave it out in the army, that they would live and die together, and that they expected a supply of men and money at Aberdeen.

All this while the Duke of Argyle followed with his whole army, and we lost a day's march in the confusions and distractions, which anyone might suppose these things put us in; but we were easy in that part, for we knew we could gain that again at pleasure. We arrived at Aberdeen, and making no great stay there, General Gordon drew us out in a line, and caused us to be acquainted, that we were to separate, and make the best of our way to the hills; that the Ch—— had assured us we should speedily hear from him again; that he was sorry he was obliged to quit his enterprise for the present, but that we should soon see his affairs settled upon a better foot, and that he would not fail to remember the faithful services of his friends.

This was heavy news to us; however, necessity obliging, we had nothing to do but to comply and to shift for ourselves.

* * *

4. Minutes of the Negotiation of Monsr. Mesnager at the Court of England during the Four Last Years of the Reign of Her Late Majesty Queen Anne

The Mesnager *Minutes* were published on 17 June 1717, during the week set for the treason trial of Robert Harley, Earl of Oxford, in the House of Lords. Purporting to be the writing of an insider, the French negotiator of the treaties ending the War of the Spanish Succession, the book caused a sensation. James Sutherland reports, "It soon became clear to those who had read the *Minutes*—whether they wanted to believe it or not—that Harley had played a more honourable part in the peace negotiations than was generally supposed. If the *Minutes* were to be trusted, he had stood firmly for the Protestant Succession, and had resolutely opposed the insertion of any clause [in the Preliminaries of October 1711 and Treaties of 1713] in favour of the exiled Stuarts."[1]

But were the *Minutes* to be trusted? Contemporary writers immediately deduced that the book was a forgery and attributed the work to Defoe, some even claiming it had been written by direction of Harley himself, who had supplied the inside information it contained.[2] Sutherland still seems uncertain, in his 1950 biography of Defoe, how much of the *Minutes* was actually translated from Mesnager, and how much created by Defoe.[3] In 1960 John Robert Moore, Defoe bibliographer and biographer, included the book unconditionally in the Defoe canon. My close examination of the distortion of historical facts in the *Minutes* and of the treatment of some of Defoe's favourite themes, marks the book in its entirety for me as the legitimate offspring of Defoe's pen.[4]

Like his many other secret histories of 1714–15 by supposedly privileged insiders, the best-known of which was Defoe's three-part *Secret History of the White Staff*,[5] the *Minutes* "were almost certainly published with the intention of assisting Harley," writes Sutherland, "and they certainly appear to have had that effect. On 1 July [1717], amidst prolonged applause from his peers, he was acquitted of the charge of high treason and immediately set at liberty."[6]

The *Minutes* are fascinating reading for those with some knowledge of the turbulent last four years of Queen Anne's reign, during which a furious battle raged between the Tory ministry and its Whig opposition over the issue of peace with France, while fierce dissension among Tory ministers resulted in mixing into the peace negotiations the question of the Protestant Succession to the throne of England. As exciting as a modern spy thriller, the *Minutes* provide accounts of prominent personalities involved in the peace campaign and descriptions of the complex manoeuvring always present in delicate diplomatic negotiations, and particularly salient in 1710–1713, when the Tory ministers had to keep their eyes on each other, the Whigs, the Jacobites, and the Allies, as well as on England's supposedly principal enemy, the French. Defoe's abiding interest in the contrast between the monolithic politics of a country ruled by an absolute monarch, and those of a country ruled by a constitutional monarch and divided by party controversies, is revealed in Mesnager's many comparisons between English and French politics.[7]

Above all, the *Minutes* are interesting as literature: the formal and ceremonious conversations between Mesnager and the Duke of Shrewsbury, treating on behalf of the Oxford Ministry, the manoeuvring for position veiled by polite language, appear again in *Roxana*, Defoe's 1724 novel of life led in aristocratic circles. The subtlety and cynicism of Mesnager and Louis XIV, watching and waiting for their opportunity to exploit English domestic strife, the caution and punctilious correctness of Shrewsbury in evading possible embarrassment for himself and for the ministry, the secret counterplot of the labyrinthian Harley, working unnoticed behind the scenes to frustrate a plot in favour of the Pretender, suggest again the devious and indirect facet of Defoe's nature, so clearly displayed in his *Letter from a Gentleman at the Court of St. Germains*. Lastly, the *Minutes* (1717), conceived by Defoe as secret history, provide a significant contrast with the *Storm* (1704), his first historical writing, revealing how far the ingenuous recorder of historical fact, "The Age's Humble Servant", had travelled along the path leading to the creation of history, or what is in essence a fictional account of some of the political events of contemporary history, inspired by the polemical purpose of protecting Harley.

The *Minutes* are divided into two major parts. The first part deals with the Anglo-French discussions leading up to the Preliminary Agreements of October 1711, the second with the affair of the Pretender. Defoe's strategy in the first part is to keep Harley completely off the stage. His choice of English negotiators falls upon the Duke of Shrewsbury, nowhere mentioned by name in the *Minutes*, but recognizable to his contemporaries by his characteristic behaviour, very cautious and correct. (In Defoe's 1718 biography of Shrewsbury, he names the Duke as the Lord referred to in Mesnager's *Minutes*.) Defoe's choice of Shrewsbury as the major figure in the negotiations leading to the Preliminaries is very clever; of the four English leaders actually involved in these dealings, not entirely unjustly characterized by eighteenth-century Whigs and by twentieth-century historians as treacherous to England's allies, Shrewsbury was the least controversial. The Earl of Jersey, who died in 1711, was a Jacobite, Bolingbroke had fled to France in 1715 and joined the entourage of the Pretender, and Harley was in 1717 on trial for his life. The Whig Duke of Shrewsbury, on the other hand, was generally respected, considered honourable, and had truly desired to end the war without betraying England's allies. Throughout his political career he had always been courted both by Whigs and Tories. By making Shrewsbury (actually the least active of the four) his central figure in negotiations considered disreputable in 1717, Defoe is associating Harley with the most respectable of his colleagues.

In addition to constructing his scenario of the Preliminary negotiations around Shrewsbury, Defoe does his best to throw up a smokescreen around the actual dates involved. He places Mesnager's arrival in England at several different dates, on one occasion declaring that Mesnager arrived shortly after the death of the Earl of Rochester (which occurred in May 1711), but most of the time implying that the French negotiator arrived sometime in the fall of 1710, conveniently early enough to be witness to the street battles that took place during the Parliamentary election period of October 1710. Mesnager did not really arrive in England until August 1711, when he was sent with Matthew Prior to conduct some hard last-minute bargaining on commercial affairs, and to sign the Preliminaries of October 1711.

Why did Defoe choose to have Mesnager present through all the Whig-Tory battles over the peace negotiations from October 1710 to October 1711? There are two possible reasons for his choice. One is that he suspected something not known definitely until much later, when French Foreign Office papers revealed to posterity what the Whigs would have been very happy to have had proof of in 1715, at the time they brought the ex-Tory ministers to account: the French minister Torcy's official request of April 1711 that the two countries should treat, had not actually initiated the whole negotiation: it had, in fact, begun back in August 1710, at the request of the Tory ministers.[8] The other reason Defoe prolongs Mesnager's sojourn in England is that he wished to make use of a theme we have seen running throughout his political and economic writings: party divisions between Whigs and Tories weakened England so that it became susceptible to the influence of the French and of Jacobites, who watched like Satan for any signs of vulnerability in their intended victim. At several points in the *Minutes* Mesnager is advised by Louis XIV to watch and wait for the best opportunity before approaching any of the English ministers. The street battles engendered by the 1710 Parliamentary election, the English method of rigging elections, and the activities of English political pamphleteers and journalists, including Defoe himself, provide excellent opportunities for Frenchmen seeking to fish in troubled waters. The cynical Mesnager is quick to observe that in practice the political liberty enjoyed by Englishmen is a good deal more circumscribed than English theories of constitutional monarchies, accompanied by invidious contrasts with French despotism, would admit.

Defoe is very imprecise and indeed contradictory about dates in the *Minutes*, a deliberate imprecision in a practised journalist and historian, whose accurate and fully documented *History of the Union of Great Britain* (1709) is an indispensable source document for Scottish historians. His memory could not have failed him in the two years since he had produced an elaborately documented pamphlet on the same subject as the *Minutes*, a pamphlet in which he attempted to prove that every one of Harley's peace efforts had been dictated by Queen Anne and approved by votes (numbers specified by Defoe) in both Houses of Parliament (*Memoirs of the Conduct of her Late Majesty and her Last Ministry, Relating to the Separate Peace with France*, by the Right Honourable the Countess of ———, 6 January 1715). Defoe's confusion of dates is designed to "raise a dust that he [Harley] may be lost in the cloud", as the fictitious author of another of Defoe's defences of Harley points out on a different occasion.[9]

In addition to obscuring the date of Mesnager's arrival in England, Defoe places the beginning of the Shrewsbury-Mesnager conversations at several vague and different points in the 1710 and 1711, seeming to hover around April 1711, when the formal proposal was actually received from France, and when—something Defoe does not reveal in the *Minutes*—

Shrewsbury insisted that Queen Anne read the proposal to her Cabinet, thus insuring that the whole ministry was informed frankly about the peace negotiations. Defoe also insists, inaccurately, that discussions were broken off for a while because of Tory fear of Whig reprisals, and recommenced only when protocol had been decided upon: Matthew Prior, "a private gentleman", would go to France, whereupon he would be asked by the French foreign minister to carry back to Queen Anne the message that Louis XIV desired to make proposals for ending the war. The Queen would then extend entry permission for persons designated by Louis to carry these proposals. Mesnager, who had in the meantime returned to France, was of course the person designated by the King to carry the proposals. It is obvious that Defoe has here scrambled together the April proposal with the October Preliminaries, which had in reality been preceded by Prior's August visit to France, and his return with Mesnager in September, when the French negotiator arrived in England for the first time.[10]

In order to prepare the English public for this whole charade (Defoe asserts that negotiations with Mesnager had reached their conclusion before Prior's visit; indeed, he maintains, Prior was unaware that Mesnager had been in England before the former's mission to France), Defoe reports that a flurry of rumours was first deliberately set off by the Tory ministry to confuse the Dutch and the Whigs (see pages 357–9). In fact the newspaper excitement to which he refers occurred *after* the October 1711 publication of the Anglo-French Preliminary agreement to convene all the Allies for peace talks. Indeed, Defoe prints as the text of the Preliminaries only one of the two documents signed by Mesnager, " 'the paper for Holland', as St. John called it"[11] contemptuously, which was couched in ambiguous, general, and honourable-sounding terms, not the first document, which, because it detailed many special advantages promised by the French to the English at the expense of England's allies, occasioned most of the contemporary controversy.[12] In 1717 Defoe was not anxious to remind those of his readers whose memories of the first document might have become a little hazy in the almost six years that had elapsed since the signing of the 1711 Preliminaries, about the actual terms of that document. Defoe wished to argue in the *Minutes* that French support was indispensable in 1711 to Harley's ministry because the Whigs so adamantly opposed any peace at all. He had therefore to present the outcome of Anglo-French collusion in terms of the more honourable and less controversial of the two Preliminary documents.[13]

The second part of the *Minutes* deals with the affair of the Pretender. Here Defoe is obliged to prolong the English sojourn of Mesnager until January 1712, when the formal peace conference of all the belligerent nations opened in Utrecht, even though Mesnager had in fact departed shortly after 13 November 1711, after the Preliminaries had been signed, and he had paid a visit to Queen Anne.[14] The period of most intensive effort to place "James III" on the throne as successor to Queen Anne began in March 1713, right after the Treaties of Utrecht were signed, and continued until shortly before her death on 1 August 1714. The reason "Mesnager" discusses this Jacobite activity as if it had occurred between October 1711 and January 1712, is that there was only one tangible proof Defoe could offer in order to demonstrate that Harley had not been treasonably involved in the affair of the Pretender:[15] by the Treaty of Utrecht Louis XIV recognized Queen Anne as the legitimate ruler of Great Britain, acknowledged the Protestant Succession after her, and promised not to aid the Pretender. Defoe had therefore to construct the second part of the *Minutes* as if the Jacobite scheme had centred upon keeping those clauses out of the Treaty. (Actually, Torcy's *Mémoires* are devoted mainly to details of the haggling that went on over rapacious English demands for territorial and commercial advantages; Louis's recognition of Queen Anne's legitimacy was indicated by his entering into peace negotiations with her ministers, and the question of the Pretender was broached unexpectedly on 30 September by Bolingbroke, who was prevailed upon to raise the issue, at the very last minute, by Shrewsbury's fears about future Whig prosecutions.[16]

According to Defoe's rendition of the events, the omniscient and ever-alert Harley managed to checkmate the Jacobite scheme at a dramatic moment, thus outwitting the subtle Mesnager, who was acting in collusion with Queen Anne's Jacobite confidante, Abigail Masham. Mesnager's initial description of Harley, the Treasurer, (page 350), and his comments on Queen Anne's pliability, which he contrasts with the firmness of Louis XIV (page 360), sketch the dramatis personae for this scenario, which is played out in many interesting scenes, several of which I have reproduced. As in early French psychological novels, physical objects are strikingly absent from these scenes. On the momentous occasion when "Mesnager" first meets Abigail Masham in the Queen's apartments (see pages 365–8), Defoe feels compelled to provide a perfunctory list of a few physical props, but the sketchiness of his description is startling to readers accustomed to more physical detail. Relying entirely on dialogue, Defoe manages to convey all the cautiousness of Shrewsbury, the perplexity of the well-meaning Queen Anne, the suaveness of Mesnager, and the feather-headed intrepidity of the meddlesome Masham. The dramatic last-minute failure of the Jacobite intrigue is acted out strikingly in the Masham-Mesnager letters (see pages 369–73), as the two plotters suddenly recognize the fine hand of Harley directing their discomfiture.

Many Jacobite intrigues were conducted during the last years of Queen Anne's reign. In the *Minutes* Defoe selects as scapegoats for all these intrigues the Abbé Gaultier (the permanent French correspondent in England) and agents from St. Germains (the Pretender's Court). He condenses the many intrigues into one design, inventing a master Jacobite plot to restore the Stuarts by means of the Treaty of Utrecht. The clumsy intervention of Gaultier and St. Germains in so delicate a matter, until then well handled by the astute Mesnager, playing upon the eager Abigail Masham, allows Harley to get wind of the plot which the official French negotiator was too clever to trust him with, and to foil all Jacobite schemes at once, in a last-minute anticlimax.

The events of both the first and second parts of the *Minutes*, the negotiations leading up to the Preliminaries of October 1711, and the affair of the Pretender, have been transformed by Defoe's imagination from history to fiction: (1) the fiction of the ever-alert enemy waiting secretly for the moment of maximum vulnerability in order to make tempting offers to Harley's ministry, and (2) the fiction of the secretive and subtle Harley, watching behind the scenes for his opportunity to foil the carefully laid plot with his clever counterplot. In fact, Harley sank more and more into indecisiveness and lethargy toward the end of his ministry, taking refuge in drink,[17] and both he and Bolingbroke were deeply implicated in the Jacobite schemes of 1713–14.[18] Most historians, however, believe that Harley was merely keeping his habitual second string on his bow, and really favoured the Hanoverian succession, while the extremist Bolingbroke, having burnt all his bridges behind him, was in earnest.

Whether or not Defoe accurately deduced the extent of Harley's double-dealing with Hanoverians and Jacobites will never be certain. It would have been more consistent with his own profound personal loyalty to the man who had in 1703 rescued him from what then seemed to be a life-time of imprisonment, and whom he knew to be persecuted by political enemies, that he convinced himself, and did his best to convince moderate Englishmen, that Jacobite intrigues in the Tory ministry originated from sources other than Harley. He devoted many works of 1714 and 1715 to defending his former protector from different perspectives: at times he argued that the Treasurer had been reduced to inaction by virulent Whig opposition, by opposition from extremists within his own party, and by Queen Anne herself, who dictated policy to him which he was forced to obey; at other times, as in the *Minutes*, he argued that Harley had acted as an energetic Prime Minister, and had succeeded in forcing the enactment of the measures he most cherished.

Although Defoe was undoubtedly committed to defending Harley, with whom he was never again in contact after September 1714, and who may really have disapproved of the efforts of his devious defender, it would be short-sighted to ignore how much Defoe enjoyed the process of raising "dust that he [Harley] may be lost in the cloud". "It was the pleasantest thing in the world, to see how all the Confederates were alarmed at those rumours [about peace negotiations]," he writes in the *Minutes* about the flurry of rumours set off by the Tory ministry to confuse the Whigs and the Allies. When Harley denounced from the Tower the first and second parts of Defoe's *Secret History of the White Staff*, Defoe hastened to issue his *Secret History of the Secret History of the White Staff, Purse and Mitre* (4 January 1715). Then he wrote part III of his *Secret History of the White Staff* (29 January 1715), subsequently issuing the three parts together as one pamphlet. Obviously he believed his secret histories were helping Harley, but realized that it must not look as if the former Treasurer believed his actions required any self-defence.[19] In the *Secret History of the Secret History*, Defoe asserted that all secret histories were romances and fables, the product of Grub Street writers, not of Harley, Defoe, or any other hireling of the former minister. The publishers of these works, he pointed out, "laugh at mankind":

On the one hand, they hire a man, or men, to write a secret history, pretending to vindicate and defend the character of the person of him whom they call the White Staff——— On the other hand, the same men hire another man, perhaps the same man, to mimmick the opposite party——— and when all this is said and done, and when the world has been amused with this *ambodexter* scuffle thus long, it appears, that neither the white Staff abusing, or the Mitre and Purse abused, have the least knowledge of the matter; the person who is charged with writing for them is sick in his bed, and knows little or nothing of it; and the secret history of these secret histories, is, that they were coined in one mint, all formed by one and the same set of men, and with the same truly mercenary design, *viz.* to get a penny. ...

"Getting a penny" by writing was not an activity despised by Defoe, but his engagement in Harley's defence was based upon motives more complex than those of simply earning a living. Loyalty and a commitment to fair play were two other motives. And the "ambodexter scuffle" very obviously amused and excited him, calling forth his literary talents.

The penchant for the indirect, the devious and the concealed, which I have attempted to demonstrate in Defoe's political writing is associated in his mind with the intelligent but also with the diabolic and sinister, is in addition associated with a sense of fun. It is this combination of the sinister and the playful that is particularly evident in the Mesnager *Minutes*. Huizinga describes in *Homo Ludens* the competitiveness manifested by a desire to outwit rivals and even audiences of initiates, and the combination of seriousness and playfulness, as characteristic of the spirit of play that gives rise to culture. In the Mesnager *Minutes*, as in his novels, Defoe created a work of fiction for which his era provided no aesthetic theory; forced to vacillate between calling his writings non-fiction and fiction, history or romance and fable, Defoe was unable to supply a theory of literary criticism for those of his works in which, as *homo ludens*, he believed and disbelieved at the same time.

Notes

1 James Sutherland, *Defoe* (London, 1950), p. 219.

2 William Lee, *Daniel Defoe, His Life and Recently Discovered Writings* (London, 1869), I, 269. If any such directions reached Defoe from Harley, they would have had to travel along very devious paths. As Sutherland points out, Harley spent the last seven years of his life in retirement, engaging, among other activities, in "a dignified correspondence with Swift, Pope, Arbuthnot, and the other celebrated wits who had known him in the days of his greatness. He kept their letters, and one may reasonably assume that if he had received any from Defoe he would have kept these too. But there is nothing to indicate that the two men ever met or corresponded after the year 1715. To have done so would have been highly imprudent on Defoe's part. He had formed other loyalties, and his new masters would have looked with grave suspicion upon any attempt on his part to renew his old intimacy with their political enemy." (Sutherland, pp. 220–221).

3 Sutherland, p. 220.

4 It is interesting to compare the instructions Louis XIV gives to Mesnager in the *Minutes* upon the latter's departure for the Hague upon the eve of the Gertruydenberg negotiations of 1710 with those Defoe supposed he had received from Harley in 1706 before his departure for Scotland. Louis's instructions are those of a peremptory master to his efficient servant:

> Place yourself at the Hague incognito.
> Acquaint yourself with persons as you see occasion.
> Correspond with nobody but myself.
> You know your business. (*Minutes*, p. 17)

Defoe's letter of 13 September, 1706, sets down the instructions he supposes he has received from his employer, who was notorious for never completing a conversation. Defoe wished to make sure that he understood his business correctly:

1 To inform myself of the measures taking or parties forming against the Union and apply myself to prevent them.
2 In conversation and by all reasonable methods to dispose peoples minds to the Union.
3 By writing or discourse, to answer any objections, libels or reflections on the Union, the English or the Court, relating to the Union.
4 To remove the jealousies and uneasiness of people about secret designs here against the Kirk &c.

The above appears in *The Letters of Daniel Defoe*, ed. George Harris Healey (Oxford, 1955), p. 126.

5 *The Secret History of the White Staff* was published in three parts. Four editions of Part I appeared before 27 October 1714, Part II was published on 27 October 1714, and Part III on 29 January 1715. Subsequently the three parts were issued together.

6 Sutherland, p. 220. Sutherland points out in a footnote to this page that the immediate cause of Harley's acquittal was due "in large measure to the skillful work of his friends in the House of Lords, who out-manoeuvred the much less friendly Commons." It was also due to the co-operation of Walpole, Townshend, and their followers, who were determined to obstruct the programme of the Stanhope-Sunderland ministry, by whom they had been ousted from power.

7 Defoe was always interested in the contrasts between the domestic and international politics of authoritarian monarchies and constitutional monarchies. Many of the issues in the first volume of the facsimile edition of his *Review* discuss these contrasts between France and England in terms of how the theoretical constitutional differences actually affect the practices of both nations. Here we see another illustration of Defoe's continuing interest in the contrast between principle and practice.

8 The French proposals had been "collusively arranged between Jersey, Harley, and Shrewsbury on the one side and Louis's minister Torcy, on the other", writes Trevelyan. Negotiations had actually begun in August 1710 between the Earl of Jersey and the Abbé Gaultier, Torcy's secret agent in England. Bolingbroke introduced himself into the affair only in March, 1711, when Harley was indisposed as the result of the illness he suffered after an unsuccessful attempt on his life by an assassin. Once Bolingbroke became involved, his driving energy resulted in his taking over the whole affair.

Only in 1757, upon the publication of the *Mémoires* of Torcy, did it become known that the Tory ministry had been in contact with the French as early as 1710. In 1870 Lord Stanhope revealed much of the background of these negotiations in his history of Queen Anne's reign. G. M. Trevelyan, *England under Queen Anne: The Peace and the Protestant Succession* (London, 1934), pp. 176–177.

9 Daniel Defoe, *The Secret History of the Secret History of the White Staff, Purse and Mitre* (London, 1715), p. 5. (Supposedly written "by a Person of Honour".)

10 It is possible that Defoe, who was of course not privy to the negotiations at all, but who was always alert, was really somewhat confused about the sequence of events, about which he had learned something indirectly, and in garbled form. He may even have suspected that Anglo-French contacts predated 1711. By 1718 he seems to have grasped the fact that secret conferences before the Congress of Utrecht (1712) were held with the Abbé Gaultier, not with Mesnager, although he was reluctant to dispense with Mesnager altogether (*Memoirs of ... the Duke of Shrewsbury*, p. 103), and speaks of an account he has seen in manuscript "in some things differing from those printed under the title of Memoirs of Monsieur *Mesnager*" (*Shrewsbury*, p.119). But he still seems convinced in 1718 that "some private Persons sent hither at the same time with Monsieur *Mesnager*" were involved in plotting with certain English gentlemen on behalf of the Pretender, and perhaps he knew some details that have not yet been discovered by historians.

On the real Mesnager's supposed comings and goings between London and Paris Defoe was probably confused, because there actually was at one time a possibility of his having to return to France during September 1711 for more detailed instructions from Louis XIV. Gaultier was sent instead of Mesnager, however, and according to Torcy's *Mémoires* (Vol. III, 67), arrived again in London on 23 September. Mesnager never left London, therefore, and negotiations proceeded without interruption during Gaultier's absence.

11 Douglas Coombs, *The Conduct of the Dutch: British Opinion and the Dutch Alliance during the War of the Spanish Succession* (The Hague and Achimota, 1958), p. 275.

12 The ministry had expected to announce Dutch agreement to the Preliminaries at the same time as it released the text of its document, but, unable to force the Dutch to concur before the second, general paper was leaked to the newpapers, and finding public reaction even of English Tories unfavourable to treating of peace on the basis of such generalities, it was then forced to release to the papers the first document. This Preliminary detailed the special advantages England had been promised, at the expense of its Allies, by the French. "The ministry had been forced to risk the wrath of its allies in an attempt to retain its support at home", concludes Coombs (p. 261).

13 The only reference Defoe makes in the *Minutes* to England's betrayal of the Dutch is Mesnager's cynical observation that French demands for compensation for giving Dunkirk to the English did not matter much to Shrewsbury, "so long as the *Dutch* were to give it [compensation]" (Mesnager *Minutes*, p. 150).

14 Monsieur de Torcy, *Mémoires* (London and Amsterdam, 1757), III, 88, 92.

15 Defoe offers the same proof in other of his writings in Harley's defence: *Some Reasons Offered by the Late Ministry in Defence of their Administration* (3 March 1715), and *An Account of the Conduct of Robert Earl of Oxford* (July 1715), reissued under a different title, *Memoirs of Some Transactions during the Late Ministry of Robert E. of Oxford*, on 22 June 1717.

16 Torcy, III, 69. "Les Ministres d'Angleterre paroissoient toujours également agités, surtout Schrewbury. Ménager ne pouvoit en deviner la cause, encore moins quelle en seroit la fin.

Cette cause étoit en partie la timidité naturelle du Duc de Schrewbury. Il connoissoit son pays, & le péril où sont exposés les Ministres du Souverain, soit que le règne change, soit que le crédit & l'autorité passent d'un parti à l'autre. Plus il étoit éclairé, plus la prévoyance craintive de l'avenir faisoit d'impression sur son esprit; elle l'entraîna même, malgré la douceur de son caractère, à parler durement à Ménager dans une des conférences. Schrewbury désiroit cependant la paix autant qu'aucun des autres Ministres. Tous étoient frappés de la crainte d'un tems qui peut-être ne seroit pas éloigné, & nonobstant leurs bonnes intentions, la réflexion les retenoit, à l'exception de Saint Jean."

17 It comes as a surprise to learn that Defoe was actually aware of Harley's torpid condition, for he does not breathe a hint of this recognition in any of his pamphlets written in defence of the former Treasurer. Only in 1718, in his *Memoirs* of the Duke of Shrewsbury (Harley had been acquitted of treason in 1717), does Defoe acknowledge Harley's lethargy of spirit during his last years in office.

18 "Louis undertook by the terms of the Treaty of Utrecht not any longer to aid the Pretender, but in fact the activities of his Minister at Versailles and of his Ambassador and agents in London were redoubled on James's behalf as a result of the signing of peace. Nor can this be wondered at, since both Oxford and Bolingbroke entered into the plot. English Ministers wrote nothing direct to the Pretender, but they sent him continual messages and promises and received his answers through the agency of Gaultier and Torcy. The degree of their sincerity, especially in the case of Oxford, is open to endless question, but the facts of this intrigue are to be found in the French Foreign Office Archives———
For the important negotiations of Oxford and Bolingbroke with James in January–March 1714, and their unsuccessful attempt, aided by the Abbé Gaultier, to persuade him to declare himself a Protestant, see *E.H.R.*, July 1915..." (Trevelyan, *England under Queen Anne*, pp. 336–337).

19 In addition to trying to exonerate Harley of having written, or caused to be written, *The Secret History of the White Staff*, Defoe reissued in 1717, at the time of Harley's trial, his pamphlet *An Account of the Conduct of Robert Earl of Oxford* under the new title, *Memoirs of Some Transactions during the Late Ministry of Robert E. of Oxford*. Harley had denounced the first issue of the pamphlet from the Tower in July 1715.

Minutes of the Negotiation of Monsr. Mesnager at the Court of England during the Four Last Years of the Reign of Her Late Majesty Queen Anne (1717)

* * *

Having mentioned this person, who, as above, I rank as a private gentleman, but at my coming, I found to be Prime Minister in the British Court; I must stop a little to speak of him, who has made so much stir in the world, and whose fate is not yet determined.

He is a person of real great capacities, general knowledge, and polite learning, a taking and very engaging way of conversation, and when one discourses with him on indifferent affairs, he speaks most readily and clearly to everything, having a vast memory, and a very happy elocution; he is affable and courteous, easy of access, and prevents all ceremony by a familiarity that is extremely obliging.

In publick business only, he differs from himself; for there his discourse is always reserved, communicating nothing, and allowing none to know the whole event of what they are employed to do; his excess of caution makes business hang on his hands, and his dispatches were thereby always both slow and imperfect; and it is said, he scarce ever sent any person abroad, though on matters of the greatest importance, but that he left some of their business to be sent after them. The fame of his parts brought him into the greatest employments, but *when he was in*, it never failed to render him uneasy to all that were either above or below him. He knew too much to take his measures from any man, and it was said, that it was the hardest thing in the world for any man to take measures from him; he has been thought by most people to design well in the main, but has taken such exotick measures to bring his good designs to pass, that his good would be as fatal as other people's evil; his being so absolute in his own measures, as to enter into no freedoms with any, has been the cause that he has broke with everybody first or last. When I came to England, his character was very strangely compounded of a mixture of good and evil, no man spoke well of him in the general, all applauded him in particular; he had many virtues, and few personal vices attended him; he had less avarice than ambition, a complete government of his passions, and seemed to be perfectly void of pride. As to money, he strove even to a fault, to merit that character given by a famous author to his predecessor, (*viz.*) *to be frugal of the Queen's money, and lavish of his own.* He had a genius for the greatest undertakings, and a courage equal to the boldest attempts; an instance of which was the establishing the funds for the debts unprovided for, and settling the South Sea Company, the first, even against the wills of most of the persons to whom those debts were due, the last, against the universal dislike of the whole nation; both which he reduced; and erected such a scheme both for ascertaining a precarious debt, and appointing an unpracticable commerce, that in less than one year, those who were the greatest opposers of the first steps in it, were the men who bought up all the stock; insomuch that it was thought by some, that they opposed it at first rather because they envied him the success of it, than that they did not think it the best scheme of its kind that ever was laid in that nation. But his courage has appeared in one particular, which his worst enemies must acknowledge, *viz.* his making twelve peers at once, when he was in some exigence in the administration of affairs; a step, hardly ever ventured upon by any man before him. And now what is yet more than all the rest, his intrepidity in standing his ground, and hazarding himself and his cause to any trial, rather than give his adversaries any advantage over him by an ignominious flight; when at the same time, others, who acted under him, have done it, and not dared to stand the trial; for there is, as I have heard in England, one thing in the trials of the nobility, which, were it to be in any other nation, would render their case very unhappy, (*viz.*) that when they are obliged to submit to publick justice, and appear to plead for their lives, it may happen that many of those men who give their votes for their life or death, may be their professed, declared enemies; as also others, who may be depending upon the Court for their fortunes, by places and trusts. This would be a just objection, and is even allowed in England itself, in the case of any but peers; for if a juryman is charged by the criminal, for having declared himself his enemy, the exception shall be allowed; but, on the contrary, here, the whole body of peers are jurors, and are to give their vote. Nor have the prisoners the liberty to object, or challenge any of them; likewise the sovereign has a power to make lords, even out of the prisoner's worst enemies, to add to the number of those who shall try him, and may occasion his being found guilty.

* * *

Nor were we deceived in these measures at all; for as the new elections came forward, the animosities increased, and it was with an inexpressible pleasure that we, who were *incognito* in every corner, saw the rabbles and tumults among the common people, *which England, above all other nations, is eminently known by*, carried on with all the violence and brutality that could be desired, even to the insulting one another upon the most ordinary occasions.

The English common people, among the many good qualities which some of them may possess, are a furious and brutal people, especially in their private quarrels; and it would be the strangest thing in the world, among polite nations, to see such things practised as are frequent among them in Britain. In their discourses of publick affairs, 'tis next to impossible to have any mixed company agree; and as they differ, they fail not to give all the abusive, unsufferable words to one another that are to be thought of, and yet they do not call this a quarrel; there would be more bloodshed in London in a year, than was at the Battle of Malplaquet, were any other nation in the world to quarrel as the English do: Frenchmen would draw their swords and pass through one another's souls, at half the ill treatment these give, even before they are said to begin to be angry; were it in Holland, how many faces full of scars would appear on the Exchange? How many slit noses, fingers cut off, and the like scarrifying work, would there be with their knives on these occasions? But here, a foul tongue has a full liberty to abuse every man absent or present; the language of rogue, villain, rascal, etc., is reciprocal, and is both given and received without resentments; the highest quality is not free from the raillery and insults of the coffee-houses, and the streets; and when I came to understand a little of the English tongue, I was amazed to hear the great lords of the Court, the ministers of state, and especially Mr. H——, then High Treasurer, called rogues, villains, thieves, etc., and the friends of the government, as well as those of the former Treasurer, damned and cursed to hell, by the several parties in their ordinary discourse, and in the common companies in every coffee-house; and yet no quarrel all the while among the people who did so.

As this was the way in conversation, it made the society of such men very odious, and we that were Frenchmen blessed ourselves that we were of a nation accustomed to better breeding, and where the laws of reason and good manners had more prevailed to civilize the people and restrain their passions. But if this was indeed strange to us, who had been used to converse among a nation of politer manners, the behaviour of the canaille was yet more brutal and even terrible. It is impossible to describe the fury and terror of their rabbles; were you to see two armies of them march against one another in the night, and in the streets of London, armed with clubs and sticks, you would expect nothing less when they meet, than the killing of several hundreds at the shock; instead of which, you find it all issue in roaring and foul language, shouting out the names of the heads of their parties, throwing dirt, and perhaps a few broken heads, so they call it when anyone bleeds; and then they part and go down other streets, or return back shouting as if they had gained the most important victory. If on these occasions they came to real fighting, it seldom or never amounted to more than several single fellows grappling together after the savage way of that island; in which they do not use weapons as other nations always have done, since the creation of the world; but fall upon one another, tearing, bruising, and battering one another with their hands, heads, and feet, as wild beasts do with their claws and teeth, now standing on their feet, anon rouling in the dirt; till covered with blood and mire, and rather wearied than wounded, they give over by consent, or are parted by their fellows; and then perhaps, other couples taking up the same quarrels, and beginning always with a shower of vile and provoking language, fall on one another in the same manner.

This was the frequent practice in that country, the most part of the time that I was among them; and though they are a nation otherwise agreeable enough, and who by their wealth and luxury are arrived to a way of living easy, and are in many things a happy people; yet those exercises greatly expose them, and made their very name my aversion; so that

I thought myself more happy than ever, when I was returned to France, where men live in a manner much more agreeable to the ends of life, and the temper and constitution of reasonable creatures, enjoying a perfect tranquillity of soul, in the most courteous, affable conversation, and the undistinguished practice of mutual civility.

But to return to my story: the elections of their Members, or Deputies of Parliament, were in their height soon after my arrival there; and as the names of the persons chosen came to be known, the Court appeared a little chagrin, for that the number of the Whigs, who were first chosen, seemed to be very much beyond their expectation; especially in that the Whigs boasted that their chief strength lay in the western or northern part of the island, particularly the provinces or shires of Cornwall, Devon, Somerset, Dorset, Wilts, etc., places needless to name here, but which are generally called among them the West Country, though in truth, they are situated in the south-west part of the island; here they depended much on the interest of the former Treasurer, the Earl of Godolphin, and some of his dependencies, who had formerly secured that part of the country, much in his interest, being himself a native of the province of Cornwall, from whence they sent up no less than 44 Deputies to the Parliament.

But I must do this justice to Mr. H——, (*viz.*) that if he was not so resolved at first in the measures taken, *that is to say*, for the dissolving the Parliament, yet he left no stone unturned in the managing the elections, after he was come into it; and that he did this so effectually, and with so much judgment and success, that even the Earl of Godolphin lost almost all the elections in that, which was called *his own country*. There was not a town where his interest was strong, but he saw himself supplanted, and an interest formed to oppose and overthrow him; *the like success* was seen in other parts; and in a word, it appeared that he had laid his measures so true, and was served so punctually, that at the summing up of the numbers, the Whigs saw themselves distanced, and outnumbered in a surprising manner, as to the Deputies of their lower Parliament. As to the upper Parliament, or upper House, as they term it, he had his eye so intent upon that also, was so vigilant in taking his advantages, and so dexterous in improving them, that he carried his point there also; as I shall note in its place.

It is significant to observe, how little these people differ from us in France, in the effect of an absolute monarchy, after all the boasts they make of their liberty, the subordination of their kings to the sovereignty of the laws, the ancient rights of the people, which they call their birth-right, etc., seeing by the power of Court artifice, the influence of money, and the management of subtle statesmen, the people are always made tools to operate in their own bondage; and to enthral themselves, either to this, or that party, or prince, as effectually, as if the said prince had them under his absolute direction; nay, in this also, the prince has the advantage, (*viz.*) that this is done so by the agency of the ministers, that the tyranny is always charged upon them, and the prince is not blamed; and if ever the power of the law gets an interval to exert itself, it is the minister who bears the resentment, not the sovereign; of whom no more is desired, but to change hands, and all things are quiet in a moment. It's true that it has been otherwise, as in the example of King James; but the reason of all that difference lay in the impolitick measures of the prince, who espoused his ministers to his own ruin, and took the whole upon himself. But wise princes in that country have no more to do, but to let their ministers subject the constitution to the absolute will of the sovereign, by the insensible degrees abovementioned, and the English are as easily made slaves as other nations. Nay, they will make themselves slaves, for they will sell and betray their own liberties and rights for money; as they effectually do, who sell their votes in the choice of the Deputies of Parliament. And it is most certain, that such is the blindness and unconcernedness of the people of that obstinate nation, and so far are they from having any notion of the circumstances of their constitution, that whatever ministry comes in play, and will wisely dispose such sums of money as are necessary for the work, they shall not want a Parliament to their minds; who may give up to them all those valuable rights that a nation can possess, who have the best constitution in the world.

Upon the whole, the English are a nation, who talk high of their liberty, and of the government being qualified to make the monarch great and the people happy; but are in truth as easily enslaved, and reduced to irretrievable bondage, were they politickly managed, as any nation in the world; and it is evident, had King James proceeded by due gradations, and with moderate management of that power, which he had assumed, and left the article of the Catholick religion out of his first schemes; he might in a few years have reversed the whole constitution of that country, and have made himself, even by their own consent, as absolute a monarch, not as the King of France only, but as the Grand Seignior, or the Czar of Muscovy; and by this method he might at last have planted the Catholick religion there also, and have transplanted the hereticks to what part of the world he had pleased; but he precipitated himself into ruin by that weakness, which our august monarch was never in danger of: I mean, by being guided by the clergy, rather than by the soldiery; and setting up the interest of the Church, before he had secured that of the state. This observation is foreign to my minutes of fact, but is left here for my own improvement on other occasions.

* * *

Those writers of pamphlets in England, are the best people of the kind that are anywhere to be found; for they have so many turns to impose upon their people, that nothing I have met with was ever like it; and the people of England, of all the people I have met with, are the fondest of such writings. My writer had an excellent talent, and words enough, and was as well qualified to prove nonentities to contain substance, and substance to be entirely spirituous, as anyone I have met with; I was no judge of his style, having but little of the tongue; but as I kept him entirely private, I found the people always eager to read what he wrote, and frequently his books were said to be written by one great lord, or one eminent author or other; and this made them be more called for at the booksellers than ordinary, and the man gained by the sale, besides what I allowed to him, which was not inconsiderable. It was a great disappointment to me, in some other views I had at that time, that this man fell sick and died. I attempted once or twice to furnish myself with another, but could never get one like him, except a certain person, who the Swedish resident, Monsieur Lyencroon, recommended, and who wrote an excellent tract in our interest, entituled, *Reasons why this Nation* (meaning England) *ought to put an end to this expensive war*, etc. I was extremely pleased with that piece, though I could not read it distinctly, and for that reason had it translated into French, and caused it to be printed at St. Omer in Flanders, and dispersed through the Low Countries, and at Paris, for the publick information of our own people. Monsieur Lyencroon used his endeavour to bring this author into my measures; and to facilitate the thing, I caused an hundred pistols to be conveyed to him, as a compliment for that book, and let him know, it came from a hand that was as able to treat him honourably, as he was sensible of his service. But I missed my aim in the person, though perhaps the money was not wholly lost; for I afterwards understood that the man was in the service of the state, and that he had let the Queen know of the hundred pistols he had received; so I was obliged to sit still, and be very well satisfied that I had not discovered myself to him, for it was not our season yet.

This kind of secret negotiation was now the most of our employ in London, where, with myself, there was now no less than five secret agents of France employed, as well to listen into everything that was doing in publick, as to infuse proper notions into the minds of the people who we were among, as we had occasion; and so faithfully was the King served in these things, that although we did not all correspond with one another, yet being all guided by the same hand, we took the most regular measures; and as there was nothing passed without our observation, so the King was sure to have an exact account of everything that was done or doing, either in the City or the Court.

* * *

That for this reason, they were afraid of everybody, though they could charge nobody, and being very uneasy at the rumour of a treaty, they were obliged to give it over for awhile; but that now they had resolved to have the rumour spread on their side, while there was really nothing doing, that the Whigs might be amused with generals, and be able to dive into no particulars.

I cannot say, but as they were stated in England at this time, this was a good thought enough, and they pursued it as well; for they caused reports to be spread in Holland, of a negotiation privately set on foot in England, and that it was avowedly carried on by the ministry, though they concealed the persons they treated with. That there were two French agents come to London, who appeared publickly, though without any character, and as these rumours were continually cultivated, they came at length to report, that the said negotiations went very well on, that the peace advanced apace, and that it was expected, in a few days, the ministry would declare themselves upon it. Nor was this all; but they went on to give about privately, *schemes of the peace itself*, and heads of the Preliminary Articles, quite remote from the real things of which we had discoursed, and yet calculated to employ the speculations of the people, and prompt them to discourse frequently of the thing.

Nor was this all, but as all publick news flies from shore to shore, letters were written every post of it from Holland, and the Dutch were made uneasy to the last degree; nay, so perfectly was the true design covered, that an agent the Court of France had at the Hague, wrote to the Court about it, as of a thing certain, and the King himself seemed a little amused about it, knowing what order I had, and how constantly I had acquainted him with the full stop we had been at for some time, and how I had received his Majesty's order to let it continue in that posture for awhile. But it was not many days before I gave his Majesty the eclairicissement in that affair, and the King was exceedingly pleased with the stratagem, and indeed his Majesty had reason.

It was the pleasantest thing in the world, to see how all the Confederates were alarmed at those rumours. The envoys and residents at London, were tormented with the reproaches of their masters, who complained, that having sent them to reside at the British Court, to take care of their interest, they should sit still, and let a negotiation of that consequence go on in so publick and open a manner, and give them no notice of any of the particulars, nor so much as write for further instructions, how to act on such an occasion. Upon this they came buzzing about the Court, were inquisitive, uneasy, and so importuning, that had it not been diverting to the ministry on another account, it would have made them very uneasy.

I should have mentioned, that not only these rumours were raised in Holland; but letters written, as if coming from the Hague, were secretly sent to the writers of the publick *Gazette*, and of newsprints in the City of London, who printed openly in their articles from the Hague, the account given there of the progress made in England, in the secret negotiations of peace, and sometimes a sketch of the Articles they were upon.

This being printed in England, and no enquiry made of the writer, to punish him for such an open publication, or to demand his authority for it, left the people abroad, no room to doubt of the truth of fact. It is impossible to describe the confusion the Whig Party were in; the great ones, and those of the most penetration, could make nothing of it, the ministry denied it with all possible seriousness, as well they might; all the vigilance, all the observation, and conjectures, all the spies and secret attempts for a discovery in this matter came to nothing. The Court was still and quiet, the ministry appeared busied upon other things; nor was there the least appearance of anything of this kind; *for the truth was*, that not one step was all this while taken in the matter.

When this had wearied the world some time, and as they thought long enough, my old correspondent gave me notice, that he would meet me again. When we were together, he began merrily with this part: "Well, Monsieur," says he, "How do you like this last push?" "My Lord," says I, "I think it is a masterpiece, and has done more than all that ever you have said or done before; all the Confederates think you have made the peace, I know nothing to do now, but to be so kind to them, as to convince them, that they are not mistaken." "Let that be as it will," says my Lord, "we have yet the pleasure of reproaching them with injuriously charging us, when we have no hand in any such thing, and if we bring their predictions to pass, we only do that which they abused us for, and we cannot, I think, do them a greater piece of justice, than to make good what they have with so much confidence, charged us with doing."

I told his lordship he knew the disposition of those people better than I; that as to the temper of parties in England, I thanked God, it was new to me, that we knew no such thing in France; that I had heard much in France, of the happiness of the people of Great Britain, on account of the liberty they enjoyed; but that I could not be persuaded to be of the opinion, that to have the people above government, or without government, was to be called liberty, or was capable of being thought happiness; that it was true, our kings were absolute, and in that respect, might in their language be called tyrants; but that I had rather be under any tyranny, than that of parties; that however, this was nothing to our purpose; that his Lordship knew what part I had to act, and that I was ready to take my measures from his directions.

* * *

But to return to the history of the affair in hand, which will illustrate these observations; I found the peace or treaty now proposed was doubtless of the utmost weight to the English nation, and on the management whereof, depended the whole ballance of power in Europe; and yet how easily did they give it up to the conduct of a woman; and a woman through the goodness of her disposition, not the least easy of all the women in the world, to be imposed upon by her servants.

In the conduct of Her Majesty's particular, I also found reason to make one observation, which may be of use to us in France (*viz.*) that goodness of disposition is not always a virtue, or at least, is not the safest virtue in a prince; our august monarch is a most happy example of this; who by the inimitable fire of his temper, governed at the same time by an unexampled sagacity, wisdom, and prudence, has maintained such an authority in all his administrations, that his ministers of state have been entirely kept within the bounds of their duty; though they have been capable of advising, yet have they never been capable of imposing upon their sovereign.

* * *

We had no meeting after this for five or six days, except once, when company prevented any private discourse, only my Lord took an opportunity just at taking his leave, to say, he had *thought much* of what we discoursed last, and that he believed something would be done in it. But two days after, he sent a servant to tell me, that if I pleased to sup with him in private, he should be glad to see me at eight a clock. I went accordingly; and we were in private indeed, not a servant being admitted to us, but one that waited while we eat. After supper, my Lord told me, he had met with an unexpected opportunity of mentioning to the Queen what I had recommended to him about the Chevalier, and that the manner was diverting. He told me, he had the honour to be drinking tea in the apartment of a certain lady, very near the Queen, and that as the discourse everywhere was upon these new Preliminaries, so much more was it so there, and that the lady began very freely with him upon that head. "And sir," says he to me, "I think you should have had a conference with her on this subject, for by my faith, the women dare say anything."

I was mighty earnest to hear the particulars, and begged his Lordship would be pleased to let me into the introduction, as well as into the story itself. He told me he would do so at large, and then went on thus.

"Why," says he, "she began with me, thus. 'My Lord,' says she, 'I cannot make out these dark things you call Preliminaries for my life, I wish you would read me a lecture of politicks upon them.'

" 'Lord Madam,' said I, 'you are a better politician than I.' 'Not I,' says she, 'I cannot understand them, I am all in the dark about them.'

" 'Well Madam,' said I, 'but cannot your Ladyship be content to stay a little till they explain themselves?' She returned, laughing, 'We women, you know, my Lord, love to come to the eclairicissement.'

" 'Well Madam,' said I, 'but what is it that you are so much in the dark about, where is your difficulty?'

"Here she spoke softly, 'Why, what', says she, 'do you intend to do with the *Pretender*? So, Sir, you know he is called among our people, and sometimes by those who are not his worst enemies, especially if company presents.'

"I was surprised, you may be sure, to hear her put such a bold question, and so publickly too, for there was three ladies more at the tea table, but they were all friends, 'tis true, and all of the family.

" 'Madam,' says I, 'what can we do with him?'

" 'Well, but', says she, 'I see no article about him in the Preliminaries, I hope you have secured things there.'

"This looked very oddly, for I knew that lady was none of his enemy, and therefore I answered her accordingly: 'Madam,' said I, 'you see the succession is to be acknowledged as by the present settlement.' She found I spoke ambiguously, and she put it home to me: 'I know,' says she, 'how you would have the people understand it, but I hope you understand it as I do.'

" 'Madam,' said I, 'you cannot think, but that by the present settlement, the whole world understands the settlement of the succession in the House of Hanover.'

" 'Does the whole world understand it so?' said she.

" 'We are to suppose they do,' said I.

" 'Come, come, my Lord,' said she again, 'neither you nor I understand it so, besides many honest people that you and I know.' She went on then and told me, she thought I need not have been so shy of what I said, by which I knew my company and replied, that I was far from being shy, but that whatever was our desire, or whatever thoughts we had of that person and of his affairs, I did not see it possible, *as things stood*, to do anything for him, or to introduce any clause in the treaty in his favour. I told her, she knew how we were stated, and how vigilent the Whigs were to lay hold of every opportunity to charge us with favouring his interests, and I did not see it possible to avoid articling against him in the strongest terms. She confessed we had reason for that part, and she was of my mind, but she thought there might be some private agreement made to serve his interest *in petto*; and that as all agreements were to be made between the Queen and the King of France, they might by mutual consent dissolve the obligation of those agreements whenever they pleased, declaring them now to be so understood, as that they should bind no longer than SO or SO. 'This', she said, 'was taking away all reproach of breaking articles on either side.'

"This was so near what you, Sir, had proposed to me," said he, "that I began to think whether you had been confering notes with her or not, though I believe you had not.

"I told her, I thought that was straining some points, which princes that regard their parole of honour could not pass over, and that it was no more than a mental reservation in discourse. She insisted that I was wrong, that the agreement was just, because mutual and not concealed from one another.

"I replied, I would not dispute a thing which I had so much inclination to have true; but I did not see how this would answer his end. She said, it might not *just then*, but that hereafter it might.

" 'But what will you do in the meantime,' says she warmly, 'will ye drive him about the world like a vagabond, will you oblige the King of France to abandon him and do nothing for him, and you at the same time ruin him here too, what, must he perish, will you have the Queen starve her own brother?'

"I began to be a little in earnest with her at this. I told her, I did not think she was so serious as I found she was, that I believed she was satisfied I was for starving nobody, but she also knew on what ticklish terms we stood in England, and that our enemies wanted nothing to bring the mob about us, but to be able to say, we were now bringing in the Pretender, or acting for the Pretender; that she could not but see they said so already at all adventures, whether true or false; but if they were able to prove it, all was undone.

" 'Lord,' says she, half merrily, half seriously, 'What a parcel of statesmen Her Majesty has here! Why, 'tis no wonder the Queen is so frighted, every now and then at the Whigs, when you are all so faint hearted.'

" 'Madam,' said I, 'you don't know what it is to fall into the hands of the Whigs, you know they are people that *never forgive*.'

" 'Well, my Lord, I see you are all afraid of being called to account by the Whigs. If ever the young gentleman does come here, as I don't question but he will, I hope he will call you all to account for a parcel of ———.'

"I took this for a jest, though I found she was in earnest enough, and therefore I added, laughing, 'Cowards and defecters, you were going to say, Madam, you had as good have spoken it out, perhaps we should not be such cowards, if the Queen would be advised.'

"Here she turned her jesting way immediately into a serious and warm discourse, which was really very pertinent to the subject, but is too long to repeat."

Here my Lord made as if he would have broken off the discourse, but I begged him to go on; I told him, this discourse was essential to what I had in commission, that I could not but insist upon it, that his Lordship would be so free with me as to communicate it.

"Why," says he, "it is impossible to repeat her discourse, besides the Queen came in and interrupted us."

This made me more eager to know the particulars of their discourse, and I pressed him as much as good manners would permit, when on a sudden he turned about. "I think", says he, "I must bring you and my Lady ——— together, and see what you can make of it; she will talk as freely of it as you can desire, for my part, I am afraid so much as to talk to myself of it."

I answered, I would be infinitely obliged to him to introduce me to such a lady, as by his character of her, I found she was, and especially being one near the Queen too; but I begged of him, nevertheless, to go on a little further with the story, especially because he had mentioned that the Queen came into the conversation. He told me he would oblige me as far as he could, but that he could not remember it all; but that when he spoke of the Queen's being advised, she reflected seriously on their not advising the Queen, that they might be sure the Queen expected they should make that matter easy to her as well as other things. That the Queen saw them all so frightened about the Whigs calling them to an account, that it made her change the ministry. They represented the Whigs to the Queen as a most contemptible party, who they were able to overthrow in everything; and now on a sudden they were afraid of the very shadow of them; that there was not a man among the whole ministry but my Lord Treasurer, that ever spoke a chearful word to the Queen, that they ought to know she was a woman as well as a sovereign, and that if they were not able to support what they had undertaken, they ought to tell her so honestly, that she might find other hands that understood their business better.

That in the new articles there seemed nothing digested, and they seemed to have left things so much to the plenipotentiaries, that they had not found so much as a scheme for them to act upon, for example in this case of the Chevalier. Whenever the Queen enquired about it, all the answer she could get was, that they put it off from one to another, one knew nothing of it, and another knew nothing of it; and if ever their opinion was separately asked, everyone always answered for himself, that he did not know what to advise; that he durst not talk of it, that it was a dangerous point to speak of, and such stuff, as that she wondered what men of council and state wisdom as they all pretended to be, could answer a Queen in such a manner, that by the Preliminaries she found he was to be forgotten, and not so much as named, but we might depend upon it he should be named in the treaty; and if the plenipotentiaries were not instructed how to act, he would be left at the mercy of the Dutch, or indeed of his worst enemies, be starved, or murthered, or worse. "And," she added aloud, "can you think, my Lord, but that the Queen has many thoughts of this kind, can she be easy to have you murther her brother?"

"Just as she had named the word *brother*, the Queen came into the place. 'What,' says the Queen, 'are you always talking politicks?'

" 'Lord, Madam,' says she merrily, 'here's my Lord ———,' naming me to the Queen, 'turned Whig.' 'I cannot think that,' says the Queen. 'He is turned cruel and barbarous,' replies she, 'and that I think is to be a Whig.'

" 'What is the matter?' says the Queen.

" 'Nay, Madam, it is all before your Majesty,' says she, 'their new Preliminaries here have been the dispute. I tell my Lord, they are so worded, that they will neither let your Majesty do anything for a certain person, or do it themselves. I suppose they would be rid on him at any price; I wish they would tell your Majesty what you are to do with him.'

"Says the Queen, 'I can never get one of them so much as to speak of him, or to answer me a question about him, and I don't press them, but I hope they will do as becomes them.'

"I replied presently to my Lady, not mentioning anything of what the Queen had said: 'Madam, you complain of the ministry's doing nothing in that affair, perhaps you do not know what is offered at by some persons at this very time.'

" 'Not I, indeed,' says she, 'all things are so locked up with my Lord Treasurer, that we hear nothing; my Lord is incommunicable, all the Queen herself knows from him, amounts to little more, than that in general all things go well, and be easy, Madam, be easy.'

" 'Madam,' says I, turning to the Queen, 'your Majesty knows Monsieur M—— is still in town, he desires nothing more than to talk freely of this matter; and it is true, as my Lady ——— says, that the ministry are all afraid of meddling with it; he says, he has something of very great importance to offer about it, and thinks it hard, that after the Preliminaries are settled with him, nobody will give him audience on the rest. I think if your Majesty pleases to hear it, my Lady ——— would be the best plenipotentiary in such an affair; I'll bring Mons. ——— to wait on her.' 'With all my heart,' says my Lady ———, 'if the Queen will give me leave I won't be so much afraid, as all your politicians are, that you dare neither speak nor hear.'

" 'I think,' says the Queen, 'there can be no harm in this, any more than in the Preliminaries, to hear what they offer.'

* * *

It was not long after this, that he carried me to Court, where I followed him through several apartments; at last we were stopped, by the Queen's happening to be passing out of her withdrawing room into her closet, we paid our complements, and passed on; at length we came into a room where was a table by the fire, and a large easy chair, and a table at another side of the room with two candles and some loose cards. I found afterwards this was the lady's apartment that I was to meet, that there had been some ladies at play, but that the Queen had come in, and the ladies were all fled; that the Queen had sat by the fire some time after, and was just come away when we met her.

The lady I was to meet with, it seems, was with the Queen; but both the Queen and she too, seeing my Lord ——— and another person with him going on, she came back to us and found us in her chamber.

When her Ladyship was come into the room, my Lord ——— I found, paid her great respect, which though it gave me no light into her name or quality, yet it imported that she was a person fit for me to talk with. After some discourse between them, he presented me to her, and told her, this was the gentleman he had told her Ladyship of, and that I was in commission from the King of France, so that she might put confidence in all that I should say; that she knew what subject we were to talk upon; that the Court of St. Germains were very anxious about the share they should have in negotiations that were on foot as to the Chevalier.

He was going to say more when she interrupted him. "Pray, my Lord, do not call him by that barbarous name, call him anything but that, and Pretender."

"Well, Madam," said he, "I'll call him by no name that shall offend you; but I cannot talk of him at all, I refer it all to this honourable person and yourself."

With that she turned to me, and told me she should be very glad of a little discourse upon that head. "Lord," said she, "these politick people are so shy one of another, they are frighted at shadows, for my part I fear nothing," says she, "I'll hear whatever you can say, Sir, and do whatever I can for him. Call him what you will," added she, "is he not the Queen's brother? I know him by that name, and no other." And with this she made me sit down.

Being thus entered upon discourse, my Lord withdrew among some ladies who were playing at cards in the next room, and I found myself alone with my Lady ———.

Here I was at some loss how to break my design, but she let me soon know that she expected no ceremony. "Sir," said she, "I know your character, what you have been doing here, and have been always with the Queen when my Lord ——— has given her Majesty an account of the private discourses you two have had, for this is the room where the Queen always retired to hear it." With this she related several branches of our discourse, which convinced me, that what she said was true.

Whereupon rising up and making her a very low bow, I told her I had had the honour of a great deal of discourse in confidence with my Lord, as I perceived she knew, that he always told me, that what I communicated to him, he always laid before the Queen, as I on the other hand had done the like to the King; that it was the true end of our confidence mutually to serve our respective sovereigns, and to bring them to those terms of peace and friendship, which they both desired, and that I hoped we should have the success we desired; but that I had a secret commission which I was very loth to communicate to any but such as his Lordship should think proper, and that it was for this end I was introduced to her Ladyship, and desired to know if she required me to shew my credentials.

"No, by no means, Sir," said she, "I am no plenipotentiary, but I know the meaning is, that we should talk of that poor distressed branch of the royal blood that is in exile in your country, we are very anxious about him."

"Madam," said I, "the sum of what I have in commission is this, that the King my master would be glad to know, what is her Majesty's pleasure to have done in this case."

"Lord," said she, "we are at the greatest loss imaginable, we must not appear to have the least concern about him, we know the Whigs will oblige us to push at his destruction, if possible."

"But Madam," says I, "the King hopes you won't go such a length."

Upon this she drew a little table which stood by her nearer to me, and desired me to sit down, and with an air of most obliging freedom told me, that she was very glad to have an opportunity to converse with me upon this affair, that indeed it was a tender subject, and the ministers were afraid to speak of it, even to the Queen herself; but that if I thought fit to communicate to her what I had in charge upon that head, she would assure me she would not be so shy of it.

I told her that I had no instructions to propose, because the King was now to receive his measures from Her Majesty, being resolved to act as the Queen should direct.

She answered, that was putting hard upon Her Majesty, that the Queen could do nothing in his favour, as things stood; but that it was hoped the King of France might find out some way to act in his behalf, if not now, at least hereafter.

I told her, that must be according as they bound him, or left him free, by the treaty; and therefore as the King was sincerely willing to serve the Chevalier to his uttermost, as occasion should present, so the business for her Ladyship and I to negotiate, was to see if possible, that the King might sit loose in that article, or at least that no obligation might be laid upon him, but what Her Majesty might hereafter acquit him of.

She told me I must not ask anything of the Queen that her Majesty could not grant.

I answered, that I would not willingly do so, but that I thought as all the articles which concerned the succession to Her Majesty's dominions, were properly a capitulation with herself only; it was in Her Majesty of right to limit the extent of the obligation, and to declare how far they should or should not be binding upon France after her death.

She told me, she was fully of my mind, but that she feared the Queen would not be brought to give any such explanation to that article, or to sign any such declaration under her hand by any means.

I told her, there appeared to me no other way than one of these two, either that the articles which should oblige the King to acknowledge the present settlement, should be made so, as not to bind the King beyond Her Majesty's person, and the term of her life, or that some secret explanatory article should be entered into, to settle the matter, so as that at Her Majesty's decease, France might be at liberty to act as should be convenient. She replied, these were difficult points; however she would take a little time to think of them, and that we might meet again in a day or two upon them, which I submitted to, and took my leave, the lady calling my Lord ——— who was *l'introducteur d'ambassadeurs* for that time, to go out with me.

About three days after, my Lord ——— sent to me again; and when I came to him, he told me the lady desired to speak with me again upon the old affair; so I went directly with him, and found her all alone waiting on purpose for me; we sat down to discourse with very little ceremony, my L——— withdrawing as before. She began very frankly with telling me, that she knew I had but very little time here, that the affair we had to discourse of was, in her opinion, brought into a very narrow compass; and that our debate related to two things, which she summed up thus:

1. That a treaty being absolutely necessary to be set on foot to restore peace to the two kingdoms, whose interests were not now esteemed so remote, as they were formerly thought to be: it would follow, that for the satisfaction of the people, and of the Allies abroad, the King should be required in the Queen's name to abandon her brother and his interest, on pretence of adhering to the succession as it was now established.

2. That nevertheless this seeming to abandon the said interest, was to be so understood, that the King should not be obliged, in case of her Majesty's decease, not to use his endeavours for the placing the said prince on his father's throne, to which he had an undoubted right.

We joined immediately in granting that this was the case, but how this interpretation of the said clause of abandoning the Chevalier should be made authentick, remained a difficulty. I said it must be referred to the treaty, and that if possible the clause for abandoning should be made so safe, that his Majesty might not be obliged to harder terms of that kind than need must, and that the plenipotentiaries should be instructed accordingly.

I then asked her if I should have the honour to hear how things went on here, what might be the resolutions taken in that case, and what conditions might be granted, which I told her would be of great use to me, because the King had done me the honour to name me to be one of his plenipotentiaries at the treaty.

She complemented me upon the honour I had received, and said some very fine things to me upon that head, which I received with a due acknowledgment of her goodness, and asked her if she would do me the honour, to give me leave to communicate to her Ladyship what should pass on this occasion, and receive her instructions. She told me, with all her heart, she should be glad to correspond, and that she would give me a key to write to her by, and that her letters should be enclosed to Monsieur, who belonged to the embassy, and would not fail to be there.

* * *

Accordingly I waited on her the next evening, without any introductor, when she received me with all the civility, and in the most obliging manner imaginable; she told me she had it in charge to let me know how well I was with the Queen, and how agreeable it was to Her Majesty to hear that I was to be at Utrecht; and going to her cabinet, she called me to her, and presented me in a purse of crimson velvet, made up like a case, and fastened with a gold clasp, Her Majesty's picture set round with diamonds. I started back a little, and offered to receive it on my knee, which she understood immediately, but would not suffer me. "For, Sir," says she, "I do not tell you that the Queen presents you, but you may be assured *by it*," says she, "how satisfactory your visits here have been, and how much I think it my honour to hand this present to you."

* * *

Sir,
I am not surprised at all, at the news you send me, that no

private instructions are sent to our ministers at Utrecht, seeing your Court have thought fit to make it the subject of a particular negotiation *here*; who their agents are, I depend on it, I need not inform you, and who their instrument here, I *cannot* inform you; but you may be assured it has put that which took a good train before, into a condition not easily to be recovered. You will judge the better what a concern this is to the *Chevalier's* friends here, by reflecting how agreeable all you had done before of another kind, was to

Yours, etc.

I had nothing to do, after I had received this letter, but to reflect how unfortunate the Court of St. Germains was, and as I believe will ever be, in precipitating their own affairs, and by their following the rash counsels of those about them, who are impatient of their exile, though the King had done all that could be desired of him to make it easy to them; for it presently occurred to me, that this was some private negotiation, which they had set on foot to engage some of the ministry in England, and perhaps *the Treasurer*; many of whom, they vainly thought, would befriend them; whereas I saw clearly when I was in England, that the ministry there would give them promises in plenty; but not run the least hazard for them to do anything effectual; and that if any dependance was upon them, they would certainly be deceived, after the greatest expectations, nay, and engagements too.

* * *

Madam,
I could not be more surprised at your letter, than I am just now with an express from the King my master, complaining of the measures taken by some of his servants in your Court. The unhappy Chevalier, a person fated to be undone, has often before now had the fairest prospect of his affairs clouded and eclipsed, but never so effectually as by the hasty council of St. Germains, where they are never easy, but when they have agents at work to perplex their own measures. I find, Madam, all you say is right; with this addition, that the King has been ill served in England, and resents it accordingly. His Majesty is now told, that a person is to be sent over to Utrecht to negotiate with me, and the British ministers, the measures to be taken in the Chevalier's affair. I confess, I neither relish nor

understand it; and beg your Ladyship to let me so soon into the secret of it, as you shall think proper for the service of the Chevalier, and for the King my master's satisfaction. I know, if a proper person were sent hither, fully instructed, this affair might be settled here with more secresy, and by consequence with more safety than any other way. But then I must add, that I shall despair of any effect by it, unless your Ladyship would do me the honour to let me know, that such person comes instructed from one no less interested in the Queen, and zealous for the Chevalier, than yourself; and whoever brings credentials from your hand, I shall gladly enter into a confidence with, in this case; and then I should have the assurance to let the King my master know, he might expect something from the negotiations which should follow.

Utrecht, Feb 12th, 1711

I am with the profoundest respect,
May it please, etc.

* * *

Sir,
Were it not that I am exceedingly concerned for the miscarriages of an affair which I had so much hope from, and which I thought was, by your good management, entirely out of danger, I should be very merry with the Court of St. Germains, on account of their new secret negotiations here. I take it for granted, that they are fallen into the hands of my Lord T——; he loves a secret, and is famous for making intricacies, where there is a sterility of intrigues; and no less renowned for causing everything of such a nature to miscarry; if their assurances are from him, I doubt not he values himself upon having deceived them; and if the person to be sent to Utrecht comes from him, I dare promise you that when he comes there, he wants his instructions. In the meantime, assure yourself, the people to whom all this ought to have been communicated, have not so much as known that a word has been spoken of it; and are wondering much that they are not applied to. 'Tis true, the T—— dares not mention it now, because, as he knows, he would not be trusted in such an affair; so some here who owe him an ill turn, would not fail to pay the debt, and turn such a secret negotiation to his entire ruin.

If he is not your man, it must be my Lord ———; he has more probity; but I cannot see upon what foot he could make such promises, as your last implies; for I am persuaded he never mentioned it to the Queen. The truth is, those things are of so nice a nature, that, as you may remember, I told you when you were here, there is not any two among our ministry, that dare make a confidence about it, nor any one of them that would venture to mention it to the Queen. And I undertake to assure you, that whatever your agents have informed the King your master of, or given His Majesty reason to expect, 'tis all in the clouds here, and the Queen has not so much as heard a word of it; and this makes me suppose their great secret remains with my Lord T—— where secrets often sleep and die.

We know nothing less or more of a person to be sent to Utrecht, neither are there any private instructions can be sent with any authority. And by these omissions I foresee the thing will miscarry. Who are to be blamed, you best know. But depend upon it, this matter can never be brought to any head, but by the method you and I concerted; they who have taken other steps, give me reason to know their intelligence is bad, and that they do not miscarry for want of ignorance. If anything occurs, favour me with a line as usual.

St. James's, March 2, 1711–12 — I am, etc.

As I have observed, the the fifth of March new style, and before I received the above letter, the British ministers delivered in their specifick demands; and if I lost all patience at the rigid demands that appeared in them relating to the Chevalier, it was, because I had, as I thought, laid so good a plan for the preventing it. However, to give vent to my concern, and let them know in England what was done; the following letter was hurried away a little faster than I used to do things of such consequence.

Madam,
Your Ladyship will have the satisfaction, by the papers I enclose you, containing the specifick demands of the British ministers, to see to how little purpose I have given you all this trouble, and how easily the weakness of friends may serve the enemy, as well, nay perhaps better, than the treachery of persons intrusted. I know it would have been much easier to have prevented this blow, than it is to retrieve it. Nor can I expect that any instructions can now be given to the ministers to recede, which would not alarm your enemies, and ours also. I have the satisfaction, however, to have discharged

punctually the part I had in this affair, and the honour of your knowing where the fault lies. It is my felicity that this was not the essential part of my commission in England, but rather what by accident offered. Meantime, Madam, I am infinitely bound to your Ladyship, for the honour done me in England, and must leave the Chevalier to his bad fortune.

Utrecht, Ma. 7, 1712

* * *

CHAPTER FOUR

SOCIOLOGY AND PSYCHOLOGY

The Complete English Tradesman

The Complete English Tradesman, published in September 1725, "went through a bewildering series of modifications" during Defoe's lifetime,[1] so that John Robert Moore specifies its publication date as 1725–7.[2] The modifications were designed both to expand the work and to direct it to experienced tradesmen as well as to the beginners for whom it was first written. Moore links it with the 1724 *Tour thro' the Whole Island of Great Britain* as one of the "two ... miscellaneous didactic works which had the greatest sale and the most enduring appeal".[3]

In a sense, *Defoe's Complete English Tradesman* is a controversial work; sampled by the wrong readers, its message is misinterpreted and its author condemned for his supposed narrowness of vision. Even its remarkably good style is accounted a debit in the assessments of Defoe's sensibility by genteel literati. The reaction of Charles Lamb in 1822 furnishes an illustration of these assertions:

> The pompous detail, the studied analysis of every little mean art, every sneaking address, every trick and subterfuge (short of larceny) that is necessary to the tradesman's occupation, with the hundreds of anecdotes, dialogues (in Defoe's liveliest manner) interspersed ... if you read it in an *ironical sense*, and as a piece of *covered satire*, make it one of the most amusing books which Defoe ever wrote, as much so as any of his best novels. It is difficult to say what his intention was in writing it. It is almost impossible to suppose him in earnest. Yet such is the bent of the book to narrow and degrade the heart, that ... had I been living at that time, I certainly should have recommended to the Grand Jury of Middlesex, who presented the *Fable of the Bees* [by Mandeville] to have presented this book of Defoe's in preference, as of a far more vile and debasing tendency.[4]

Yet the economic precepts of *The Complete English Tradesman* were old-fashioned even in 1725, and the standard of conduct prescribed for tradesmen impossibly idealistic. Defoe's faith in intrinsic values, and his concept of an ordered national economic community in which every person and class performed its function and received its due reward in a share of the general welfare, both characteristic of mercantilism, are expressed repeatedly throughout the work. A few examples among many are his distaste for flashy displays of merchandise, his castigations of exaggeration by shopkeepers and customers in their praise or criticism of merchandise, his strictures against shopkeepers' overexpansion and engrossment of too large a share of the stream of trade, his advice to retire in good time in order to make room for newcomers, and his warnings to tradesmen against diverting too large a stock of ready money from inventory to investment in stocks and shares. The behaviour he prescribes for tradesmen includes only two examples that could uncharitably be classified under Lamb's rubric of "trick and subterfuge": the quoting of one price with the intention of coming down in bargaining, and the promise to pay bills without the explicit proviso that payment is contingent upon such facters as being paid oneself by others. These exceptions to a generally high rule of probity Defoe sensibly permits in the light of conventional trading practices.

The main content of *The Complete English Tradesman* is its information for beginners about practical matters such as learning about one's merchandise, keeping books, writing business letters, and taking partners. In addition, Defoe prescribes an entire way of life for the lower-middle-class readers he is addressing in the section designed for new tradesmen. Central to this manner of living is self-restraint: the new shopkeeper must not marry before he is financially able; he must refrain from pleasures and diversions that demand too many of his working hours[5] (such diversions include over-frequent prayers, a stricture presumably addressed to Dissenters); he must avoid luxurious living above his income; he must not cheat others because he has been cheated himself; he must be careful not to injure the credit of fellow tradesmen with malicious slander; he must remain silent and self-controlled, must continue to conduct himself with dignity in spite of the impertinence of customers (which Defoe describes graphically in dialogue form), and so forth.

Defoe's admiration for trade is apparent throughout the book. Although he frequently expressed his delight in the movement and activity suggested by the circulation of goods throughout England, Defoe apparently appreciated trade most because it seemed to offer a kind of basic stability. The stability it suggested to him was perhaps inherent in the plainness and intrinsic values of the concrete objects that made up its stock, and in the numbers and figures with which it could be described. Perhaps too, it was associated in his mind with values absorbed in the course of his childhood. Whatever the reason, as images of stately buildings were used by Augustans like Swift and Pope to suggest stability,[6] so images of trade were used by Defoe:

> Trade is not a ball, where people appear in masque, and act a part to make sport; where they strive to seem what they really are not, and to think themselves best dressed when they are least known. But tis a plain visible scene of honest life, shewn best in its native appearance, without disguise; supported by

prudence and frugality; and like strong, stiff, clay land, grows fruitful only by good husbandry, culture and manuring (p. 117).

His esteem for trade is partly the result of his experience in the slippery soil of politics: the world is juster, he observes, in evaluating a man in trade than in other fields such as politics, for there is less caprice, less fashion in this evaluation.

This admiration of the trading life, however, is tempered by a recognition of its limitations. He cautions his readers, "Now in order to have a man apply heartily, and pursue earnestly the business he is engaged in, there is yet another thing necessary, namely, that he should delight in it. To follow a trade, and not to love and delight in it, is a slavery, a bondage, not a business. The shop is a Bridewell, and the warehouse a house of correction to the tradesman, if he does not delight in his trade" (p. 56). Indeed, this writer of convincing military memoirs and admirer of great generals exaggerates the contrast between the timid tradesman and the enterprising soldier in order to drive home to his readers the limitations of a life of trade: "Bold adventures are for men of desperate fortunes, not for men whose fortunes are made ... when you mount the man, you dismount his courage; when he is upon the pinacle of his fortunes, he is past the pinacle of his enterprising spirit; he has nothing to do then, but to keep himself where he is. Now, though this is a scoundrel spirit in a hero, 'tis yet a noble spirit in a tradesman. 'Tis a meanness hardly honest in a general; but 'tis a wisdom and a prudence never enough to be commended in a tradesman" (vol. II, part 2, p. 177).

Defoe is very clear about the social level of the person for whom shopkeeping is appropriate. In the first excerpt from *The Complete English Tradesman* reproduced below, he defines the word tradesman in several currently accepted senses, explaining that he is addressing retail shopkeepers and wholesalers (the latter being of a slightly higher social level),[7] not labourers, of a lower social level, nor merchants, of a higher one: "These by whatever particular circumstances distinguished, are the people understood by the word *tradesman* in this work, and for whose service these sheets are made publick." In the second excerpt, where he supplies homely illustrations of how necessary it is for a tradesman to know the vocabulary of his trade, Defoe apologizes, "I mention these lower things, because I would suit my writing to the understandings of the meanest people, and speak of frauds used in the most ordinary trades, to the capacity of the tradesmen for whom I write."

In spite of his own clarity about the meaning of the term *tradesman*, the social level, the manner of life, and the writing style appropriate to that occupation, in spite of his addressing tradesmen as an outsider with inside information, Defoe himself is continuously identified with the class. The sneer of his contemporary enemies has been mindlessly accepted by many nineteenth-and twentieth-century scholars and men and women of letters, American as well as English, even though neither *tradesman* nor *shopkeeper* is idiomatic: the American pejorative equivalent is *salesman*.

Knowledge about Defoe's private life and business ventures has probably been largely responsible for the misclassification of this versatile writer as a tradesman; otherwise, one might equally regard him as a powerful spokesman for military officers or even for criminals. In addition, the language of *The Complete English Tradesman* is so compelling in its freshness and charm that it is difficult to conceive of the writer as other than a shopkeeper, at home among equals. The work deserves to be reprinted in full. The lively excerpt that follows, concerned with business writing and business vocabularies, does not include examples of the delightful dialogues in which the book abounds. It is significant, however, for expressing Defoe's theory of style and his instinctive grasp of decorum, or appropriateness of style to subject. In addition, the excerpt demonstrates that although Defoe is advocating restraint in language, he is so interested in the aberrations of style he is ostensibly decrying, that he takes great pleasure in describing them at length. This tendency to be attracted to the very things he deplored was a general and enduring characteristic of Defoe's make-up, and is perhaps the key to his versatility and to his peculiar elusiveness.

Notes

1 John Robert Moore, *A Checklist of the Writings of Daniel Defoe* (Bloomington: Indiana Univ. Press, 1960), p. 199. This is the only instance in this collection where I have not used a first edition; the text used, obviously corrected by Defoe himself, is the so-called second edition, 2 volumes, printed for C. Rivington in 1727. I have used excerpts from volume I, sold for Caldwell. Moore reports that this edition, actually the third, was published on September 1726 but dated 1727.

2 John Robert Moore, *Daniel Defoe, Citizen of the Modern World* (Chicago: Univ. of Chicago Press, 1958), p. 220.

3 *Ibid.*, p. 220.

4 Letter of 16 Dec., 1822 to Walter Wilson, the Defoe biographer. Quoted by Pat Rogers in *Defoe: The Critical Heritage* (London: Routledge and Kegan Paul, 1972), p. 86.

5 Defoe was not on principle adverse to pleasure and diversion. Even while recommending self-restraint to tradesmen, he points out, "There are very few things in the world that are simply evil, but things are made circumstantially evil when they are not so in themselves. ..." Innocent pleasures are acceptable, except when a man should be tending his shop, "for it cannot be supposed I should insist that all pleasure is forbidden him, that he must have no diversion, no spare hours, no intervals from hurry and fatigue ..." (pp. 97, 103).

6 Paul Fussell, *The Rhetorical World of Augustan Humanism* (Oxford: Clarendon Press, 1965), p. 264.

7 Those business activities of Defoe that aroused his enemies to sneer at him as a hosier seem rather to belong to the category of wholesaler or warehousekeeper than of shopkeeper. J. H. Plumb distinguishes between the upper classes of society, involved in politics, and the lower classes. The upper levels include aristocracy, gentry, merchants, and middling merchants. The lower levels begin with shopkeepers. (*Sir Robert Walpole: The Making of a Statesman*, London: Cresset Press, 1956, chapter I: "The Classes of Men.") Since Defoe dabbled in politics even in the seventeenth century, while he was still primarily a businessman, even his early career would put him outside the ranks of shopkeepers.

The Complete English Tradesman

INTRODUCTION

Being to direct this discourse to the tradesmen of this nation, 'tis needful, in order to make the substance of this work and the subject of it agree together, that I should in a few words explain the terms, and tell the reader who it is we are to understand by the word *tradesman*, and how he is to be qualified in order to merit the title of *complete*.

This is necessary because the said term *tradesman* is understood by several people, and in several places, in a different manner. For example, in the north of Britain, and likewise in Ireland, when you speak of a tradesman, you are understood to mean a mechanick, such as a smith, a carpenter, a shoemaker, and the like, who we call here a *handicraftsman*. In like manner, abroad they call a tradesman such only as carry goods about from town to town, and from market to market, or from house to house to sell; these in England we call *petty chapmen*, in the North *pethers*, and in our ordinary speech *pedlars*.

But in England, and especially in London, and the south part of Britain, we take it in another sense; and in general, all sorts of warehousekeepers, shopkeepers, whether wholesale dealers, or retailers of goods, are called *tradesmen*; or to explain it by another word, *trading men*. Such are, whether wholesale or retail, our grocers, mercers, linen and woollen drapers, Blackwell-hall factors, tobacconists, haberdashers, whether of hats or small wares, glovers, hosiers, milleners, booksellers, stationers, and all other shopkeepers, who do not actually work upon, make, or manufacture the goods they sell.

On the other hand, those who make the goods they sell, though they do keep shops to sell them, are not called tradesmen, but *handicrafts*, such as smiths, shoemakers, founders, joiners, carpenters, carvers, turners, and the like; others, who only make, or cause to be made, goods for other people to sell, are called *manufacturers* and *artists*, etc. Thus distinguished, I shall speak of them all as occasion requires, taking this general explication to be sufficient; and I thus mention it to prevent being obliged to frequent and further particular descriptions as I go on.

As there are several degrees of people employed in trade below these, such as workmen, labourers, and servants; so there is a degree of traders above them, which we call *merchants*; where 'tis needful to observe, that in other countries, and even in the north of Britain, and Ireland, as the handicraftsmen and artists are called *tradesmen*, so the shopkeepers, who we here call tradesmen, are all called *merchants*; nay even the very pedlars are called *travelling merchants*. But in England the word *merchant* is understood of none but such as carry on foreign correspondences, importing the goods and growth of other countries, and exporting the growth and manufacture of England to other countries; or to use a vulgar expression, because I am speaking to and of those who use that expression, *such as trade beyond sea*. These, in England, and these only, are called *merchants*, by way of honourable distinction. These I am not concerned with in this work, nor is any part of it directed to them.

As the tradesmen are thus distinguished, and their several occupations divided into proper classes; so are the trades. The general commerce of England, as it is the most considerable of any nation in the world, so that part of it, which we call the *home* or *inland trade*, is equal, if not superior to that of any other nation; though some of those nations are infinitely greater than England, and more populous also, as France and Germany in particular.

I insist that the trade of England is greater and more considerable than that of any other nation, for these reasons: (1.) Because England produces more goods as well for home consumption as for foreign exportation (and those goods all made of its own produce or manufactured by its own inhabitants), than any other nation in the world. (2.) Because England consumes within itself more goods of foreign growth, imported from several countries where they are produced or wrought, than any other nation in the world. And (3.), Because for the doing this England employs more shipping and more seamen, than any other nation (and some think than all the other nations) of Europe.

Hence, besides the great number of wealthy merchants who carry on this great foreign negoce, and who by their corresponding with all parts of the world, import the growth of all countries hither; I say, besides these, we have a very great number of considerable dealers, whom we call *tradesmen*, who are properly called *warehousekeepers*, who supply the merchants with all the several kinds of manufactures, and other goods of the produce of England, for exportation; and also others who are called *wholesalemen*, who buy and take off from the merchants all the foreign goods which they import; these, by their corresponding with a like sort of tradesmen in the country, convey and hand forward those goods, and our own also, among those country tradesmen, into every corner of the kingdom, however remote; and by them to the retailers; and by the retailer to the last consumer, which is the last article of all trade. These by whatever particular circumstances distinguished, are the people understood by the word *tradesmen* in this work, and for whose service these sheets are made publick.

Having thus described the person, who I understand by the English *tradesman*, 'tis then needful to enquire into his qualifications, and what it is that renders him a finished or *complete* man in his business.

1. That he has a general knowledge of not his own particular trade and business only; that part indeed well denominates a handicraftsman to be a *complete artist*; but our *complete tradesman* ought to understand all the inland trade of England; so as to be able to turn his hand to anything, or deal in anything, or everything, of the growth and product of his own country, or the manufacture of the people, as his circumstances in trade or other occasions may require; and may, if he sees occasion, lay down one trade, and take up another, when he pleases, without serving a new apprenticeship to learn it.

2. That he not only has a knowledge of the species or kinds of goods, but of the places and peculiar countries where those goods, whether product or manufacture, are to be found; that is to say, where produced, or where made, and how to come at them, or deal in them, at the first hand, and to his best advantage.

3. That he understands perfectly well all the methods of correspondence, returning money or goods for goods, to and from every county in England; in what manner to be done,

and in what manner most to advantage; what goods are generally bought by barter and exchange, and what by payment of money; what for present money, and what for time; what are sold by commission from the makers, what bought by factors, or by giving commission to buyers in the country, and what bought by orders to the maker, and the like; what markets are the most proper to buy everything at, and where and when; what fairs are proper to go to, in order to buy or sell, or to meet the country dealers at; such as Sturbridge, Bristol, Chester, Exeter; or what marts, such as Beverly, Lyn, Boston, Gainsborough, and the like.

In order to complete the English tradesman in this manner, the first thing to be done is to lay down such general maxims of trade as are fit for his instruction, and then to describe the English or British product, being the fund of its inland trade, whether we mean its *produce* as the growth of the country, or its *manufactures*, as the labour of her people; then to acquaint the tradesman with the manner of the circulation where those things are found, how and by what methods all those goods are brought to London, and from London again conveyed into the country; where they are principally bought at best hand, and most to the advantage of the buyer, and where the proper markets are to dispose of them again when bought.

These are the degrees by which the *complete tradesman* is brought up, and by which he is instructed in the principles and methods of his commerce, by which he is made acquainted with business, and is capable of carrying it on with success, after which there is not a man in the universe deserves the title of a *complete tradesman*, like the English shopkeeper.

* * *

LETTER II
Of the Tradesman's Writing Letters

Sir,

I have mentioned already the necessity of a young tradesman being acquainted with the goods he is to trade in, the customers he is to sell to, and the merchant he is to buy of; and especially of the manner and method of keeping his books, and the necessity of being very exact and regular in his entering, ballancing, and posting his accounts; I hope I need add nothing to those heads.

I come next to mention what some think of small value, but which indeed I think is very material, *viz.* his learning how to write good tradesman's language, how to indite his letters in a tradesman's stile, and to correspond in short like a man of business.

As plainness and a free unconstrained way of speaking is the beauty and excellence of speech, so an easy free concise way of writing is the best stile for a tradesman. He that affects a rumbling and bombast stile, and fills his letters with long harangues, compliments, and flourishes, should turn poet instead of tradesman, and set up for a wit, not a shopkeeper. Hark how such a young tradesman writes out of the country to his wholesale man at London upon his first setting up.

"Sir, the destinies having so appointed it, and my dark stars concurring, that I, who by nature was framed for better things, should be put out to a trade, and the gods having been so propitious to me in the time of my servitude, that at length the days are expired; I am now launched forth into the great ocean of business, I thought fit to acquaint you, that last month I received my fortune, which by my father's will had been my due two years past, at which time I arrived to man's estate, and became major; whereupon I have taken a house in one of the principal streets of the town of ——— where I am entered upon my business, and hereby let you know that I shall have occasion for the goods hereafter mentioned, which you may send to me by the carrier."

This fine flourish, and which no doubt the young fellow dressed up with much application, and thought was very well done, put his correspondent in London into a fit of laughter, and instead of sending him the goods he wrote for, put him either first upon writing down into the country to enquire after his character, and whether he was worth dealing with, or else it obtained to be filed up among such letters as deserved no answer.

The same tradesman at London received by the next post another letter from a young shopkeeper in the country to the purpose following.

"Being obliged, Sir, by my late master's decease to enter immediately upon his business, and consequently open my shop without coming up to London to furnish myself with such goods as at present I want, I have here sent you a small order, as underwritten; I hope you will think yourself obliged to use me well, and particularly that the goods may be good of the sorts, though I cannot be at London to look them out myself. I have enclosed a bill of exchange for 75 l. on Messrs. A—— and B—— and company, payable to you or your order at one and twenty days' sight; be pleased to get it accepted, and if the goods amount to more than that sum, I shall, when I have your bill of parcels, send you the remainder. I repeat my desire, that you will send me the goods well sorted, and well chosen, and as cheap as possible, that I may be encouraged to a farther correspondence.

I am

Your humble servant,

C. K."

This was writing like a man that understood what he was doing; and his correspondent in London would presently say, this young man writes like a man of business; pray let us take care to use him well, for in all probability he will be a very good chapman.

The sum of the matter is this: a tradesman's letters should be plain, concise, and to the purpose; no quaint expressions, no book-phrases, no flourishes; and yet they must be full and sufficient to express what he means, so as not to be doubtful, much less unintelligible. I can by no means approve of studied abbreviations, and leaving out the needful copulatives of speech in trading letters; they are *to an extreme* affected, no beauty to the stile, but on the contrary, a deformity of the grossest nature. They are affected to the last degree, and with this aggravation, that it is an affectation of the grossest nature; for in a word, 'tis affecting to be thought a man of more than ordinary sense, by writing extraordinary nonsense; affecting to be a man of business by giving orders and expressing your meaning in terms which a man of business may not think himself bound by: for example, a tradesman at Hull writes to his correspondent at London the following letter.

"Sir, yours received, have at present little to reply. Last post you had bills of loading with invoice of what had loaden for your account in Hambro factor bound for said port. What have farther orders for shall be dispatched with expedition. Markets slacken much on this side, cannot sell the iron for more than 37 s. wish had your orders if shall part with it at that rate. No ships since the 11th. London fleet may be in the roads before the late storm, so hope they are safe. If have not ensured, please omit the same till hear farther; the weather proving good, hope the danger is over.

My last transmitted three bills exchange, import l. 315 please signify if are come to hand, and accepted, and give credit in account current to

Your humble servant."

I pretend to say there is nothing in all this letter, though appearing to have the face of a considerable dealer, but what may be taken any way *pro* or *con*. The Hambro factor may be a ship, or a horse, be bound to Hambro, or London. What shall be dispatched may be one thing, or anything, or everything in a former letter. No ships since the 11th may be, no ships come in, or no ships gone out. The London fleet being in the roads, it may be London fleet from Hull to London or from London to Hull, both being often at sea together. The roads may be Yarmouth roads or Grimsby, or indeed anywhere.

By such a way of writing, no orders can be binding to him that gives them, or to him they are given to. A merchant writes to his factor at Lisbon:

"Please to send *per* first ship 150 chests best Seville, and 200 pipes best Lisbon white. May value yourself *per* exchange 1,250 l. sterling for the account of above orders. Suppose you can send the sloop to Seville for the ordered chests, etc.

I am"

Here is the order to send a cargo, with a *please to send*, so the factor may let it alone if he does not please. The order is 150 chest *Seville*; 'tis supposed he means oranges, but it may be 150 chests orange trees as well, or chests of oil, or anything. *Lisbon white* may be wine, or anything else, though 'tis supposed to be wine. He may draw 1,250 l. but he may refuse to accept it if he pleases, for anything such an order as that obliges him.

On the contrary, orders ought to be plain and explicit, and he ought to have assured him, that on his drawing on him his bills should be honoured, that is, accepted and paid.

I know this affectation of stile is accounted very grand, looks modish, and has a kind of majestick greatness in it; but the best merchants in the world are come off from it, and now choose to write plain and intelligibly; much less should it be practised by country tradesmen, citizens and shopkeepers, whose business is plainness and meer trade.

I have mentioned this in the beginning of this work, because indeed it is the beginning of a tradesman's business. When a tradesman takes an apprentice, the first thing he does for him, after he takes him from behind his counter, after he lets him into his compting house and his books, and after trusting him with his more private business, I say, the first thing is to let him write letters to his dealers, and correspond with his friends; and this he does in his master's name, subscribing his letters thus:

I am,
for my master A.B. and company,
your humble servant,
C. D.

And beginning thus:
Sir, I am ordered by my master A.B. to advise you that ——
Or thus:
Sir, By my master's order, I am to signify to you that ——
Or thus:
Sir, These are by my master's order to give you notice ——

Orders for goods ought to be very explicit and particular, that the dealer may not mistake, especially if it be orders from a tradesman to a manufacturer, to make goods, or to buy goods, either of such a quality, or to such a pattern; in which if the goods are made to the colours, and of a marketable goodness, and within the time limited, the person ordering them cannot refuse to receive them, and make himself debtor to the maker. On the contrary, if the goods are not of a marketable goodness, or not to the patterns, or are not sent within the time, the maker ought not to expect they should be received. For example:

The tradesman, or warehouseman, or what else we may call him, writes to his correspondent at the Devize in Wiltshire, thus:

"Sir, the goods you sent me last are not at all for my purpose, being of a sort which I am at present full of. However, if you are willing they should lie here, I will take all opportunities to sell them for your account; otherwise, on your first orders they shall be delivered to whoever you shall direct; and as you had no orders from me for such sorts of goods, you cannot take this ill. But I have here enclosed sent you five patterns as under marked, 1 to 5; if you think fit to make me fifty pieces of druggets of the same weight and goodness with the fifty pieces, No. A.B. which I had from you last October, and mixed as exactly as you can to the enclosed patterns, ten to each pattern, and can have the same to be delivered here anytime in February next, I shall take them at the same price which I gave you for the last; and one month after the delivery you may draw upon me for the money, which shall be paid to your content.

Your friend and servant.

P.S. Let me have your return *per* next post, intimating that you can or cannot answer this order, that I may govern myself accordingly.

To Mr. H.G. clothier in the Devize."

The clothier accordingly gives him an answer the next post, as follows:

"Sir, I have the favour of yours of the 22d past, with your order for fifty fine druggets, to be made of the like weight and goodness with the two packs, No. A.B. which I made for you and sent last October, as also the five patterns enclosed, marked 1 to 5, for my direction in the mixture. I give you this trouble, according to your order, to let you know, I have already put the said fifty pieces in hand, and as I am always willing to serve you to the best of my power, and am thankful for your favours, you may depend upon them within the time, that is to say, sometime in February next, and that they shall be of the like fineness and substance with the other, and as near to the patterns as possible. But in regard our poor are very craving, and money at this time very scarce, I beg you will give me leave (twenty or thirty pieces of them being finished and delivered to you at any time before the remainder), to draw fifty pounds on you for present occasion; for which I shall think myself greatly obliged, and shall give you any security you please that the rest shall follow within the time.

As to the pack of goods in your hands, which were sent up without your order, I am content they remain in your hands for sale on my account, and desire you will sell them as soon as you can, for my best advantage.

I am, etc."

Here is a harmony of business, and everything exact; the order is given plain and express; the clothier answers directly to every point. Here can be no defect in the correspondence; the diligent clothier applies immediately to the work, sorts and dyes his wool, mixes his colours to the patterns, puts the wool to the spinners, sends his yarn to the weavers, has the pieces brought home, then has them to the thicking or fulling mill, dresses them in his own workhouse, and sends them up punctually by the time, perhaps by the middle of the month. Having sent up twenty pieces five weeks before, the warehousekeeper to oblige him, pays his bill of 50 l. and a month after the rest are sent in, he draws for the rest of the money, and his bills are punctually paid. The consequence of this exact writing and answering is this.

The warehousekeeper having the order from his merchant, is furnished in time, and obliges his customer; then says he to his servant, "Well, this H.G. of the Devize is a clever workman, understands his business, and may be depended on. I see if I have an order to give which requires any exactness and honest usage, he is my man; he understands orders when they are sent, goes to work immediately, and answers them punctually."

Again, the clothier at Devize says to his head man, or perhaps his son, "This Mr. H. is a very good employer, he is worth obliging; his orders are so plain and so direct a man cannot mistake, and if the goods are made honestly and to his time, there's one's money; bills are chearfully accepted, and punctually paid; I'll never disappoint him, whoever goes without goods, he shall not."

On the contrary, when orders are darkly given, they are doubtfully observed; and when the goods come to town, the merchant dislikes them, the warehouseman shuffles 'em back upon the clothier, to lie for his account, pretending they are not made to his order; the clothier is discouraged, and for want of his money discredited, and all their correspondence is confusion, and ends in loss both of money and credit.

I am, etc.

LETTER III

Of the Trading Stile

Sir,

In my last I gave you my thoughts for the instruction of young tradesmen in writing letters, with orders, and answering orders, and especially about the proper stile of a tradesman's letters, which I hinted should be plain and easy, free in language, and direct to the purpose intended; give me leave to go on with the subject a little farther, as I think 'tis useful in another part of the tradesman's correspondence.

I might have made some apology to you for urging tradesmen to write a plain and easy stile; let me add to you, that the tradesman need not be offended at my condemning him *as it were* to a plain and homely stile; easy, plain, and familiar language is the beauty of speech in general, and is the excellency of all writing, on whatever subject, or to whatever persons they are that we write or speak. The end of speech is that men might understand one another's meaning; certainly that speech, or that way of speaking which is most easily understood, is the best. If any man was to ask me, what I would suppose to be a perfect stile or language, I would answer, that in which a man speaking to five hundred people, of all common and various capacities, idiots and lunaticks excepted, should be understood by them all, in the same manner with one another, and in the same sense which the speaker intended to be understood, this would certainly be a most perfect stile.

All exotic sayings, dark and ambiguous speakings, affected words, and as I said in my last, abridgments of words, or words cut off, as they are foolish and improper in business, so indeed are they in any other things; hard words and affectation of stile in business, like bombast in verse, is a kind of rumbling nonsense, and nothing of the kind can be more ridiculous.

The nicety of writing in business, consists chiefly in giving every species of goods their trading names; for there are certain peculiarities in the trading language, which are to be observed as the greatest proprieties, and without which the language your letters are written in would be obscure, and the tradesmen you write to would not understand you. For example, if you write to your factor at Lisbon, or at Cadiz, to make your returns in *hard ware*, he understands you, and sends you so many bags of pieces of eight. So if a merchant comes to me to hire a small ship of me, and tells me 'tis for the pipin trade; or to buy a vessel, and tells me he intends to make a *pipiner* of her, the meaning is, that she is to run to Seville for oranges, or to Malaga for lemons. If he says he intends to send her for a lading of fruit, the meaning is, she is to go to Alicant, Denia, or Xevia, on the coast of Spain, for raisins of the sun, or to Malaga for Malaga raisins. Thus in the home trade in England, if in Kent a man tells me he is to go among the *night riders*, his meaning is, he is to go a carrying wool to the seashore; the people that usually run the wool off in boats, are called *owlers*; those that steal customs, smugglers, and the like. In a word, there is a kind of a cant in trade, which a tradesman ought to know, as the beggars and strollers know the gypsy cant, which none can speak but themselves; and this in letters of business is allowable, and indeed they cannot understand one another without it. Take an example to the purpose, for explaining this.

A brickmaker being hired by a brewer to make some bricks for him at his country-house, wrote to the brewer that he could not go forward unless he had two or three load of *Spanish*; that otherwise his brick would cost him six or seven chaldron of coals extraordinary, and the bricks would not be so good and hard neither by a great deal when they were burnt.

The brewer sends him an answer, that he should go on as well as he could for three or four days, and then the *Spanish* should be sent him. Accordingly, the following week the brewer sends him down two carts loaded with about twelve hogsheads or casks of *molasses*, which frighted the brickmaker almost out of his senses. The case was this: the brewers formerly mixed molasses with their ale, to sweeten it, and abate the quantity of malt, molasses being at that time much cheaper in proportion; and this they called *Spanish*, not being willing their customers should know it. Again, the brickmakers all about London, do mix seacoal ashes, and laystall stuff, as we call it, with their clay of which they make brick, and by that shift save eight chaldron of coals out of eleven, to the burning an hundred thousand of bricks, in proportion to what other people use to burn them with; and these ashes they call *Spanish*. But this neither the brewer on one hand, or the brickmaker on the other, understood any other of than as it related to their separate business.

Thus the received terms of art in every particular business are always to be observed; of which I shall speak to you in its turn; I name them here to intimate, that when I am speaking of plain writing in matters of business, it must be understood with an allowance for all these things. And a tradesman must be not only allowed to use them in his own stile, but cannot write proper without them; it is a particular excellence in a tradesman to be able to know all the terms of art in every separate business, so as to be able to speak or write to any particular handicraft or manufacturer in his own dialect; and it is as necessary as it is for a seaman to understand the names of all the several things belonging to a ship.

This therefore is not to be understood as an error, when I say that a tradesman should write plain and explicit, for these things belong to, and are part of the language of trade.

But even these terms of art or customary expressions, are not to be used with affectation, and with a needless repetition, were they not called for.

Nor should a tradesman write those *out of the way* words, though 'tis in the way of the business he writes about, to any other person, who he knows, or has reason to believe does not understand them; I say, he ought not to write in those terms to such, because it shews a kind of ostentation, and a triumph over the ignorance of the person they are written to, unless at the very same time you add an explanation of the terms, so as to make them assuredly intelligible at the place, and to the person to whom they are sent.

A tradesman, in such cases, like a parson, should suit his language to his auditory; and it would be as ridiculous for a tradesman to write a letter filled with the peculiarities of this or that particular trade, which trade he knows the person he writes to is ignorant of, and the terms whereof he is unacquainted with, as it would be for a minister to quote St. Chrysostome and St. Austin, and repeat at large all their sayings in the Greek and the Latin, in a country church among a parcel of ploughmen and farmers. Thus a sailor writing a letter to a surgeon, told him he had a swelling on the northeast side of his face, that his windward leg being hurt by a bruise, it so put him out of trim that he always heeled to starboard when he made fresh way, and so run to leeward till he was often forced aground; then he desired him to give him some directions how to put himself into a sailing posture again. Of all which the surgeon understood little more, than that he had a swelling on his face, and a bruise in his leg.

It would be a very happy thing, if tradesmen had all their *lexicon technicum* at their fingers' ends; I mean (for pray remember that *I observe my own rule*, not to use *a hard word without explaining it*), that every tradesman would study so the terms of art of other trades, that he might be able to speak to every manufacturer or artist in his own language, and understand them when they talked one to another; this would make trade be a kind of universal language, and the particular marks they are obliged to, would be like the notes of music, an universal character, in which all the tradesmen in England might write to one another in the language and characters of their several trades, and be as intelligible to one another as the minister is to his people, *and perhaps much more.*

I therefore recommend it to every young tradesman to take all occasions to converse with mechanicks of every kind, and to learn the particular language of their business; not the names of their tools only, and the way of working with their instruments as well as hands; but the very cant of their trade, for every trade has its *nostrums,* and its little made words, which they often pride themselves in, and which yet are useful to them on some occasion or other.

There are many advantages to a tradesman in thus having a general knowledge of the terms of art, and the cant, as I call it, of every business; and particularly this, that they could not be imposed upon so easily by other tradesmen, when they came to deal with them. If you come to deal with a tradesman or handicraftsman, and talk his own language to him, he presently supposes you understand his business; that you know what you come about; that you have judgment in his goods, or in his art, and cannot easily be imposed upon; accordingly he treats you like a man that is not to be cheated, comes close to the point, and does not crowd you with words, and rattling talk, to set out his wares, and to cover their defects; he finds you know where to look or feel for the defect of things, and how to judge of their worth. For example:

What trade has more hard words and peculiar ways attending it, than that of a jockey or horse-courser, as we call them? They have all the parts of the horse, and all the diseases attending him, necessary to be mentioned in the market upon every occasion of buying or bargaining. A jockey will know you at first sight, when you do but go round a horse, or at the first word you say about him, whether you are a dealer, as they call themselves, or a stranger. If you begin well, if you take up the horse's foot right, if you handle him in the proper places, if you bid his servant open his mouth, or go about it yourself like a workman, if you speak of his shapes, or his goings in the proper words, "O," says the jockey to his fellow, "he understands a horse, he speaks the language." Then he knows you are not to be cheated, or at least not so easily; but if you go aukwardly to work, whisper to your man you bring with you, to ask everything for you, cannot handle the horse yourself, or speak the language of the trade, he falls upon you with his flourishes, and with a flux of horse rhetorick, imposes upon you with oaths and asseverations, and in a word, conquers you with the meer clamour of his trade.

Thus if you go to a garden to buy flowers, plants, trees and greens, if you know what you go about, know the names of flowers, or simples, or greens; know the particular beauties of them, when they are fit to remove, and when to slip and draw, and when not; what colour is common, and what rare; when a flower is good, and when ordinary; the gardener presently talks to you as to a man of art, tells you that you are a lover of art, a friend to a florist, shews you his exotics, his greenhouse, and his stores; what he has set out, and what he has budded or inarched, and the like. But if he finds you have none of the terms of art, know little or nothing of the names of plants, or the nature of planting, he picks your pocket instantly, shews you a fine trimmed furzbush for a juniper, sells you common pinks for painted ladies, an ordinary tulip for a rarity, and the like. Thus I saw a gardener sell a gentleman a large yellow auricula, that is to say, *a runaway*, for a curious flower, and take a great price; it seems the gentleman was a lover of a good yellow, and 'tis known that when nature in the auricula is exhausted, and has spent her strength in shewing a fine flower, perhaps some years upon the same root, she faints at last and then turns into a yellow, which yellow shall be bright and pleasant the first year, and look very well to one that knows nothing of it, though another year it turns pale, and at length almost white. This the gardeners call a run-flower, and this they put upon the gentleman for a rarity, only because he discovered at his coming that he knew nothing of the matter. The same gardener sold another person a root of white painted thyme for the right *Marum Syriacum*, and thus they do every day.

A person goes into a brickmaker's field to view his clamp,* and buy a load of bricks; he resolves to see them loaded because he would have good ones; but not understanding the goods, and seeing the workmen loading them where they were hard and well burnt, but looked white and grey, which to be sure were the best of the bricks, and which perhaps they would not have done if he had not been there to look on them, they supposing he understood which were the best, he in the abundance of his ignorance finds fault with them, because they were not of a good colour, and did not look red; the brickmaker's men took the hint immediately, and telling the buyer they would give him red bricks to oblige him,

* *clamp*: a large quadrangular stack of bricks, left for burning in the open air. [Ed.]

turned their hands from the grey hard well-burnt bricks to the soft *sammell** half-burnt bricks, which they were glad to dispose of, and which nobody that had understood bricks, would have taken off their hands.

I mention these lower things, because I would suit my writing to the understandings of the meanest people, and speak of frauds used in the most ordinary trades, to the capacity of the tradesmen for whom I write; it is the like in almost all the goods a tradesman can deal in. If you go to Warwickshire to buy cheese, you demand the cheese of the first make, because that is the best. If you go to Suffolk to buy butter, you refuse the butter of the first make, because that is not the best, but you bargain for the right rowing butter, which is the butter that is made when the cows are turned into the grounds which have been mowed, where the hay has been carried off, and the grass is grown again, and so in many other cases. These things demonstrate the advantages there are to a tradesman, in his being thoroughly informed of the terms of art, and the peculiarities belonging to every particular business, which therefore I call the language of trade.

As a merchant should understand all languages, at least, the languages of those countries which he trades to, or corresponds with, and the customs and usages of those countries as to their commerce; so an English tradesman ought to understand all the languages of trade, within the circumference of his own country at least, and particularly of such, as he may by any of the consequences of his commerce, come to be any way concerned with.

Especially it is his business to acquaint himself with the terms and trading stile, as I call it, of those trades which he buys of; as to those he sells to, supposing he sells to those who sell again, 'tis their business to understand him, not his to understand them; and if he finds they do not understand him, he will not fail to make their ignorance be his advantage, unless he is honester and more conscientious in his dealings than most of the tradesmen of this age seem to be.

* * *

* *sammell:* imperfectly burnt brick or tile (nowadays spelt "samel"). [Ed.]

Two Andrew Moreton pamphlets:
1. The Protestant Monastery
2. Augusta Triumphans

The Protestant Monastery was first published in November 1726, and *Augusta Triumphans* in March 1728. Both of them, along with *Every-Body's Business is No-Body's Business*, *Parochial Tyranny*, and *Second Thoughts are Best*, were signed, or in later advertisements attributed to, Andrew Moreton, Defoe's favourite pseudonym from 1725 to 1728. All these pamphlets are concerned with social reform, an interest manifested by Defoe in his first full-length work, the *Essay upon Projects* of 1697.

The Restoration of Charles II in 1660 ushered in a period of intense interest in administrative reform and the management of national wealth.[1] The intellectual background of this interest derived ultimately from Francis Bacon's ideas about the value of experimental science for the advancement of learning and for the public good. As R. F. Jones points out, the utilitarian spirit, manifesting itself in "phenomena not obviously scientific" like "the enthusiastic promulgation of projects", is nevertheless part of the Baconian philosophy: "... the desire to organize all possible forces for the practical good of mankind, to introduce what might today be called a scientific method in meeting the everyday needs of men, and to lay a new emphasis upon the active and practical as opposed to the meditative and speculative can hardly be dissociated from the scientific movement of the period."[2] Post-Baconian impetus to the general dissemination of this attitude was provided by contributions from the new sciences of physics and mathematics, from thinkers like Isaac Newton and Robert Boyle, and from members of the Royal Society.[3] Another seminal contribution came from William Petty (1623–1687), the founder of the method of "quantification, or statistical procedure, as a tool of analysis in economic thought and in demography",[4] called "political arithmetic".

Yeast to this intellectual mixture was the energy released by trading and commercial interests as a result of alternating periods of peace and war: first by the termination of England's civil war, next by the separate peace of 1674, which freed England to absorb some of the foreign trade of the warring French and Dutch, and finally by the Anglo-French war of 1689–97, which, by impeding foreign trade, forced investment capital to seek an outlet in armaments and in domestic development of commerce and industry. The most significant outlet for this energy, however, was provided by the financial exigencies of a government seeking to organize necessary administrative services and to conduct an expensive war with

France. The founding of the Bank of England in 1694 was only the most spectacular of many events in the ensuing financial revolution that prepared the ground for the industrial revolution of the end of the eighteenth century.[5]

The result of these intellectual, economic and administrative ingredients was an explosion of proposals for inventions, industrial and agricultural improvements, commercial and financial expedients and institutions, conveniences of domestic and city life, and social reform. The financing of many proposals through the formation of joint-stock companies was encouraged by the boom of 1692–5 in the stock and share market. This boom had been initiated by the astonishing success of William Phipps's 1688 expedition to recover a Spanish treasure ship lost in 1646; the bonanza for investors in the venture had been one hundred times their initial outlay.[6]

The government, preoccupied by the war with France, failed to exert control over the formation of new stock companies—it was not until after the South Sea panic of 1720 that Parliamentary consent was required for the granting of charters.[7] As a result, companies mushroomed, and fraudulent methods began to be practised by some of their promoters. The promoters were known as "projectors", and soon the pejorative connotations of the word "project", which originally meant "a scheme for improvement", but could always imply a rash scheme, became predominant. Jacob Viner believed it had become a derogatory term as early as the beginning of the seventeenth century, but Defoe distinguishes carefully between honest and dishonest projectors in his 1697 *Essay upon Projects*, basing his distinction solely upon the fiscal integrity of the projector.

Viner defines "project" and "projector" as pejoratives "applied indiscriminately to almost any proposal for innovation, whether in government, religion, industrial and financial procedures, or philanthropy. It carried implications of 'jobs', 'schemes', 'bubbles', 'illegitimate profit', or 'innovations', in presumptuous disregard of the sanctity of established traditions and ways of doing things."[8] His definition sounds familiar to modern readers because of Swift's *A Modest Proposal*, and the third voyage of Gulliver to the Academy of Projectors in Lagado.

The distaste of Augustan writers like Swift and Arbuthnot for projects, projectors, and the projecting spirit arises partly from their opposition to what they perceived as mechanical solutions to matters more appropriately dealt with by reason, or common sense.[9] In *A Modest Proposal* the projector, applying the methods of political arithmetic to the solution of poverty in Ireland, reveals himself to be worse than merely impractical in his single-minded concentration upon his scheme. His total insensitivity to aspects of human life other than objective and numerical marks him as a monster of inhumanity. The Augustans' distaste for the projecting spirit also arises partly from their opposition to optimism about human progress; they and many of their opponents did not distinguish clearly between moral and material progress. In addition, the Augustans, believers in the two cultures, were convinced of the incompatibility between the sciences and the humanities; the ridiculous projectors of the Lagado Academy were members of the Royal Society. Finally, they aligned themselves with landed as against commercial interests, subscribing to "the implicit eighteenth-century assumption that [the landed interest] had special virtues denied to other members of society".[10]

To the distaste of the Augustans, one could point out that Defoe's schemes for business, urban, administrative, and social reforms, with the conspicuous exception of projects aimed at eliminating unemployment (a feat no Western economist has yet accomplished), were generally practical and today are even commonplace: marine and fire insurance, a home for disabled seamen, improved laws for debtors, a Foundling Hospital, the University of London, the Royal Academy of Music, improved roads, improved street lighting, etc. But it should be observed that Defoe's optimism about the social benefits of his projects did not extend to wide-eyed optimism about human nature. The *Essay upon Projects* includes safety devices to guard against the natural propensity to cheat of prospective beneficiaries and administrators. Again Defoe emphasizes the omnipresent discrepancy between professed aims and actual practice. In *The Protestant Monastery* and *Augusta Triumphans* he describes the cruelty that gives rise to abuses like wife beating or mistreating the aged. Above all, along with his sympathy for commercial interests went the compassion for the sick, the mentally deficient, the old, and the weak, to be found in Henry Fielding and in Samuel Johnson, but very rare among Defoe's contemporaries, whether Augustans or Addisonians.

The following excerpt from *Augusta Triumphans* will be of interest to modern readers because of the topicality and liveliness of its comments on wife beating and on street crime. Defoe's suggestions about the latter should remind readers of the interest in crime (otherwise unrepresented in this anthology) revealed by his writings of 1720–26, including, in his non-fiction, *A General History of ... the Most Notorious Pyrates*, *A Narrative of All the Robberies, Escapes, etc. of John Sheppard*, *The Life of Jonathan Wild*, and his contributions to *Applebee's Original Weekly Journal*, and, in fiction, *Captain Singleton*, *Moll Flanders*, and *Colonel Jack*.

The excerpt from *The Protestant Monastery* will be particularly intriguing to literary scholars because of Defoe's handling of the persona of Andrew Moreton and because of its demonstration of his talents in two usually incompatible disciplines, the social sciences and literature. The voice of a crotchety old man, deploring modern ways—the indulging of children, the sparing of the rod, the contempt for old people—is clearly heard as he remembers the good old days: let the young ladies who

> toss up their noses at sober matrons and elderly ladies ... consider, that those very persons were once young and beautiful as themselves, if not more beautiful. For to say truth, tea, drams, wine, and late hours, have not a jot added to the beauty of the present generation.

In addition to his querulous tone, the infirmities of age bedevil poor Moreton:

> But as this is only a sketch or rough draught, farther particulars from me would be needless. Besides, I am but a poor calculator, and only give the hint to the publick, as my duty to my fellow Christians. I wish for nothing more than to see it improved, and if I don't properly explain myself, people must be so charitable to think for me. For I write even this

under many bodily infirmities; and am so impatient to have done, that I forget half I have to say.

No doubt Defoe did suffer from illness as he grew older—he was afflicted with gout and kidney stone—but it is improbable that he ever forgot half of what he had to say.

Defoe's versatility, his ability to think either as a writer of fiction or as a social scientist, is demonstrated in *The Protestant Monastery*, of which the introduction is dominated by a long scene dramatizing the Lear-like fate of Moreton's old friend, the retired merchant mistreated by the daughter and son-in-law to whom he has handed over his entire fortune. The fiction-like introduction is longer than the actual project Defoe offers for establishing an old age home for Protestant men; the project itself, influenced by the same method of political arithmetic that inspired Swift to write *A Modest Proposal*, is a proposal typical of a social scientist. Thus Defoe supplies evidence in one pamphlet that a statistical approach to remedying a social evil does not automatically preclude sensitivity to the non-quantifiable elements of human nature.

The natural tendency of students of literary figures is to look for signs of technical development in their authors. Comparing both *Augusta Triumphans* and *The Protestant Monastery* with the *Essay upon Projects*, separated by about thirty years in time, one would be tempted to point to a greater directness in the later works, a more self-confident assertion of personality by the writer, a more assured intimacy with his audience. But that would be overlooking the nature of the audience, an omission so professional a writer as Defoe would never have committed. The *Essay upon Projects* is addressed to the nation as a whole, with one eye fixed upon Parliament, whereas the Moreton pamphlets are addressed primarily to London readers of the middling ranks of the middle class familiar to Defoe.

It would be more accurate in tracing the evolution of Defoe's style to compare his Moreton pamphlets of 1725–28 with an earlier rendition of an old man. But the old man who speaks in the 1715 pamphlet, *An Account ... of James Butler (Late Duke of Ormond)* is of a higher social class than Moreton, more unworldly and much gentler: "Pardon me, Excellent and Reverend, that some warmth naturally attends a thought as this", characterizes the tone of this old country gentleman addressing the University of Oxford. Moreton's vigour is rather to be found in an early work, Defoe's 1698 *Poor Man' Plea*: "Nay, so far has custom prevailed that the top of a gentleman's entertainment has been to make his friend drunk; and the friend is so much reconciled to it that he takes that for the effect of his kindness which he ought as much to be affronted at as if he had kicked him downstairs."

In generalizing about the development of Defoe's style, therefore, the commentator must be particularly alert to the age, temper, and social class of the voice Defoe is mimicking, the composition of his audience, and his object in writing a particular work. Defoe's literary ambition was to "acquire a universal character in writing" (*A Vindication of the Press*, London, 1718), by which he appears to have meant trying his hand at every subject, every point of view on that subject, and every voice arguing that point of view. It is significant that the school course he remembered with greatest delight in his later years was his Newington Academy writing class, where the students had impersonated different characters writing letters on subjects specified by Charles Morton. This early ability was exercised in the political writing Defoe did from the 1690s to the 1720s. That is why broad acquaintance with his works reveals, instead of a straight line of technical development, a bewildering number of facets of a complex and versatile talent: Defoe appears to haver emerged from obscurity around the age of forty, already fully grown as a writer.

Notes

1 P. G. M. Dickson, *The Financial Revolution in England* (London: Macmillan, 1967), p. 3

2 Richard Foster Jones, *Ancients and Moderns: A Study of the Rise of the Scientific Movement in Seventeenth-Century England* (St. Louis: Washington University Press, 1961), p. 148.

3 Dickson, pp. 3–4.

4 Jacob Viner, "Satire and Economics in the Augustan Age of Satire", in *The Augustan Milieu*, ed. H. K. Miller, E. Rothstein, and G. S. Rousseau (Oxford: Clarendon Press, 1970), p. 98. I owe the reminder about Petty's impact upon projectors to Professor Michael Seidel, editor of the scholarly edition of Defoe's *Essay upon Projects* to be published by Southern Illinois University Press.

5 Dickson, p. 12.

6 W. R. Scott, *The Constitution and Finance of English, Scottish and Irish Joint-Stock Companies to 1720* (Cambridge: Univ. Press, 1910–12), I, 326.

7 *Ibid.*, p. 337.

8 Viner, p. 96.

9 Paul Fussell, *The Rhetorical World of Augustan Humanism* (Oxford: Clarendon Press, 1965), p. 22 and *passim*.

10 Dickson, p. 24.

The Protestant Monastery

OR, a Complaint against the Brutality of the Present Age

(1726)

There is nothing on earth more shocking, and withal more common, in but too many families, than to see age and grey hairs derided, and ill used. The Old Man or the Old Woman, can do nothing to please; their words are perverted, their actions misrepresented, and themselves looked upon as a burthen to their issue, and a rent charge upon those who came from their loins.

This treatment, as it is directly opposite to the dignity and decency of human nature, calls aloud for redress; the helpless and innocent ought to be the care of the healthy and able. Shall a man or woman toil and moil to bring up a numerous issue? Shall they rear up, through all the uncertainties and fatigues of childhood, a race who shall spring up but to abandon them? Shall they enfeeble themselves to give strength to those who shall one day thrust them aside, and despise them?

* * *

It is well it has never been in the young ones' power, to bring in a bill for the better trimming of mankind, *i.e.* to knock all ancient people on the head.

But though they are suffered to live, 'tis under many hardships and restrictions, many humps and grumps; and scarce a day, but they are asked, what they do out of their graves. This is a very common, but withal, a most impious and unchristian saying; nay, not only unchristian, but even unmahometan. For the very infidels themselves pay more veneration to old age, than the Christians do; to the shame and scandal of our holy profession.

Far be it from me, to tax all Christians, or all children with so severe a reproach. No, I only blame those who triumph in the strength of their youth, and snuff up their nostrils at *old age*, who laugh at the groanings of the hoary head, and have no bowels of compassion for the bowels that gave them nourishment.

* * *

I am sure I speak by experience, for but very lately I went to see an old schoolfellow and acquaintance of mine, who had lately married his daughter, and settled himself in her family; accordingly he gave me a general invitation to come one day or other and take a dinner with him; he had been a merchant from his youth, and always lived in what we call high life, had travelled much, and was master of the most manners I ever met with.

This gentleman being very weary, and indeed almost incapable of business, thought it best to leave off housekeeping, to marry his daughter, and settle in her family. Accordingly he gave her his all for her portion, made her a fortune of 12,000 pounds, and matched her to an eminent merchant, who used the same trade with himself.

During the honeymoon, and till the portion was paid, the old gentleman lived in clover; nothing was too hot or too heavy for him. 'Twas "Dear Sir! Dear Father!" at every word; the servants were ordered to respect him, and he was in some share master of the family; but alas! he found this but a short-lived dream, the servants began to taunt at him, and he must call twenty times for a thing, before he could have it. If he gently chid 'em, or reasoned with them, they flew to their mistress, and made twenty stories about it; so that his life was in a manner a burthen to him.

I went in my chariot to see him; and had not the little appearance I made, commanded some respect, I had danced attendance, till they should find in their hearts to call him. However, without much ceremony, they directed me up three pair of stairs, into a better sort of a garret; there might be indeed some lodging-rooms overhead for the servants; but I have seen many servants have much better apartments. But the room would not have so much surprised me, had the furniture been anything tolerable. I dare swear it was as old as the house, and had no doubt passed from tenant to tenant half a score times.

This I thought an odd residence for my friend, but he seemed contented; and I saw no reason I had to make him otherwise. He amused me till dinnertime, with shewing me his books, and reading some of his verses to me, as having a pretty knack that way. He would have played me a lesson on his flute, but that he said it would disturb his daughter, who did not love musick. I saw that all his little arts were only to beguile the time, lest a whet before dinner, which I never missed at his house, should be expected; and which I believe was now out of his power to give. At last the bell rang, and he desired me to walk down to dinner, but with an air that seemed chidingly to say, "Ah! why did you not come sooner, when I had more authority?" However, with a long apology to his son and daughter, he introduced me; and by pleading our long and intimate acquaintance, and the obligations he was under to me, he prevailed on them at last to bid me a very ceremonious welcome. Excusing themselves, as indeed they had need, that they had not made a proper provision, and pleading their ignorance of my coming, accordingly down we sate to some cold roast beef, a few herrings, and a plate of fritters. Everything was indeed very clean, and we had attendance enough, but never in my life made I a worse dinner. Herrings are my aversion, I never eat cold meat, judge then what a bellyful I could make of my share of the fritters. I happened by mistake to call for a glass of wine, without which I never dine, when the gentleman told me he had none in the house; but if I pleased he would send for some, recommending at the same time some of his home-brewed ale, which I in complaisance could not but accept in preference to wine. They took me at my word, and with much ado I got down half a glass of the worst potion I ever took in my life. But had the dinner been never so elegant, my indignation would have spoiled my stomach; to hear the daughter at every turn, take up her father in his discourse, as if he had been an idiot or an underling, with, "Oh! fie, Sir!" and "I wonder, Father, you should say so!" But lest the readers, by my recital of the lady's phrases, should think my friend spake ludicrously or indecently, I beg leave to assure them the contrary, and that he is a man of great wit and strict modesty. Even the son, who was the least severe upon him, could not refrain contradicting him every now and then, meerly for contradiction sake, with, "Pray, Sir, give me leave", and "Indeed, Sir, you have forgot yourself"; this was my whole entertainment. For my part I said little, but admired not only at this wondrous frugality, but the surprising impertinence and ingratitude of the young couple. However, I was undeceived at last, as I hope my readers will be when I assure them, that the reason why *Sir* and *Madam*, eat so sparingly with us was, because they had devoured in hugger mugger by themselves, a good handsome fowl, and oyster sauce, and dispensed with a bottle of wine, though they could drink none in our company.

Seeing this penurious management, and the awe my poor friend was in, I thought it best to adjourn to the tavern to smoak a pipe, and withal to take a glass to warm my stomach, which raked prodigiously. I had before learned that the poor old soul had been obliged to leave off smoaking, because forsooth his spitting and spawling turned *Madam*'s stomach; his smoaking, she said, made the house stink, and damaged the furniture. He had been from his youth a great smoaker, and this sudden check, upon a habit of so long standing, had very much impaired his health.

Accordingly to the tavern we went; where a pipe and a bottle gave new life to my old acquaintance; he resumed his native gaiety; and eleven of the clock stole upon us, before we could think of parting, and even then but with great reluctance; so agreeably did the time pass away in recounting our old adventures. Indeed our sweet was intermixed with sour, for his poor heart was so full, he could not contain himself from lodging his sorrows in the bosom of his old friend. With tears in his eyes, he recounted all the indignities he daily met with, not only from his own children, but from the very servants. If he spake to them as to servants, his daughter would take him up, and tell him he domineered too much in her house. If he spake submissively, he was told he had no occasion to make himself so little; insomuch that he knew not what medium to take.

He told me his daughter had lately a chambermaid, who was the daughter of a decayed gentleman, and who having had a tolerable education, had imbibed high notions of virtue; and amongst other things, an abhorrence of undutifulness in children, or indeed any disrespect in old age. This young woman having learned in what fashion my friend had once lived, could not without indignation, see how ill he was treated; and being of a good family herself, scorned to take part with the other servants, to torment a poor old man; but on the contrary, would do him all the Christian offices she could, would constantly get him something warm in a morning, and if he was out of order at any time, would tend him, and do him a thousand little services, for which he in recompence, when her lady was gone a visiting, would read to the girl a whole afternoon together, while she sat at work. And as so many good offices must consequently engage her to him, especially when everybody else had abandoned him, he, with an innocent familiarity, used to call her his *Nanny*. This was taken in great dudgeon, and the spiteful servants improved it into an intrigue, and never left till poor *Nanny* was turned away; and with her all the old man's comfort; for he had no warm breakfast now; if he was sick, there he might lie, for nobody would help him; and as for attendance, they neglected him so much, he was scarce clean, which drew tears from my eyes, as knowing what a neat old man he was used to be. And but for disgracing his children, he wished himself a thousand times in the Charterhouse, or some other place of publick charity. I dissuaded him from such thoughts, and comforted him in the best manner I could; and so we both parted and ended our pleasant evening, with heavy hearts and wet eyes.

* * *

A Project for Erecting a Protestant Monastery

That a joint stock of twenty thousand pounds be raised between 50 persons, by an equal deposite of four hundred pounds each; which stock is to be vested in themselves only. For this being no charity, but rather a co-partnership, there is no need of having any governor, treasurer, director, or other commanding officer, but what may be chosen among themselves; and as the money is their own, they are the fittest persons to keep it.

2. That after they have obtained his Majesty's sanction, and are become a body corporate under what name or title they shall think fit, they may chuse from among themselves, one treasurer, two wardens, and such other officers they shall deem proper; which officers shall have annual rotation, and new ones be chosen every year.

3. That instead of consuming all, or a great part of the stock in building, which would nip the project in the bud, they shall rent a convenient hall or house in town or country, at their

own option; which house must be equally divided into apartments; and to save another great expense, as well as to prevent partiality, or disgust, 'tis fit that every person furnish their own apartment, which furniture they may bequeath to whom they please. For as all the members of the College are to be upon an equal footing, 'tis highly necessary there should not be the least distinction among them in diet, lodging, etc. And if one person dresses or furnishes better than another, there will be no need of complaint, because they do it at their own charge. Though to speak my mind, it would look most lovely, to have a decent equality and uniformity in dress.

4. The kitchin, the infirmary, and other offices, to be furnished at the common expense, but not to be taken out of the joint stock. On the contrary, every person to pay an equal proportion, which cannot amount to above two guineas a head. But in case the joint stock increases, the money to be refunded.

5. That they call a court among themselves as often as they shall think fit; at which every member shall have an equal vote; the treasurer taking the chair. At these courts everything shall be settled, all bargains made, all accounts audited, servants hired or displaced, the diet, and College hours settled; and bye-laws made or amended as occasion, or the general consent shall point out.

6. As all are to share the benefit, it may readily be supposed that the best advantage will be made of the money; but above all they will go on a sure footing, and content themselves with the less interest, upon the greater security. Though I must confess I know of no safer and more profitable method than to lend money on proper deposits; as goods, merchandises, etc., after the manner of the charitable corporation in Fenchurch Street. This, or some such sure method, may bring in twenty per cent on their money, which will considerably increase their capital, better their provisions, etc., and in time make them a very wealthy body. But in case no more than five per cent interest be produced from their capital of twenty thousand pounds, it will amount to one thousand pounds *per annum*; which may be laid out after this, or the like manner:

	l. *per an.*
To a physician	20 00 00
To a clerk for the treasury	20 00 00
To a chaplain	20 00 00
To a cook	10 00 00

To a laundry maid	05 00 00
To a housemaid	05 00 00
To two nurses for the infirmary	20 00 00
	100 00 00

These salaries may be enlarged as the College increases in wealth, or the whole subscription may be doubled at first, and everything in proportion. But as this is only a sketch or rough draught, farther particulars from me would be needless. Besides, I am but a poor calculator, and only give the hint to the publick, as my duty to my fellow Christians. I wish for nothing more than to see it improved, and if I don't properly explain myself, people must be so charitable to think for me. For I write even this under many bodily infirmities; and am so impatient to have done, that I forget half I have to say.

* * *

Augusta Triumphans
OR, the Way to make London the most Flourishing City in the Universe
(1728)

* * *

The lewdest people upon earth, ourselves excepted, are not guilty of such open violations of the laws of decency. Go all the world over, and you'll see no such impudence as in the streets of London, which makes many foreigners give our women in general a bad character, from the vile specimens they meet with from one end of the town to the other. Our sessions-papers are full of the trials of impudent sluts, who first decoy men, and then rob 'em, a meanness the courtesans of Rome and Venice abhor.

How many honest women, those of the inferior sort especially, get loathsome distempers from their husbands' commerce with these creatures, which distempers are often entailed on posterity? Nor have we an hospital separated for that purpose, which does not contain too many instances of honest poor wretches made miserable by villains of husbands.

And now I have mentioned the villainy of some husbands in the lower state of life, give me leave to propose, or at least to wish, that they were restrained from abusing their wives at that barbarous rate, which is now practised by butchers, carmen, and such inferior sort of fellows, who are publick nusances to civil neighbourhoods, and yet nobody cares to interpose, because the riot is between a man and his wife.

I see no reason why every profligate fellow shall have the liberty to disturb a whole neighbourhood, and abuse a poor honest creature at a most inhuman rate, and is not to be called to account because it is his wife; this sort of barbarity was never so notorious and so much encouraged as at present, for every vagabond thinks he may cripple his wife at pleasure, and 'tis enough to pierce a heart of stone to see how barbarously some poor creatures are beaten and abused by merciless dogs of husbands.

It gives an ill example to the growing generation, and this evil will gain ground on us if not prevented. It may be answered, the law has already provided redress, and a woman abused may swear the peace against her husband, but what woman cares to do that? It is revenging herself on herself, and not without considerable charge and trouble.

There ought to be a shorter way, and when a man has beaten his wife (which by the bye is a most unmanly action, and great sign of cowardice), it behoves every neighbour who has the least humanity or compassion, to complain to the next Justice of the Peace, who should be impowered to set him in the stocks for the first offence; to have him well scourged at the whipping-post for the second; and if he persisted in his barbarous abuse of the holy marriage state, to send him to the house of correction till he should learn to use more mercy to his yoke-fellow.

How hard is it for a poor industrious woman to be up early and late, to sit in a cold shop, stall, or market, all weathers, to carry heavy loads from one end of the town to the other, or to work from morning till night, and even then dread going home for fear of being murdered? Some may think this too low a topic for me to expatiate upon, to which I answer, that it is a charitable and a Christian one, and therefore not in the least beneath the consideration of any man who had a woman for his mother.

The mention of this leads me to exclaim against the vile practice now so much in vogue among the better sort, as they are called, but the worst sort in fact, namely, the sending their wives to madhouses at every whim or dislike, that they may be more secure and undisturbed in their debaucheries; which wicked custom is got to such a head, that the number of private madhouses in and about London, are considerably increased within these few years.

This is the heighth of barbarity and injustice in a Christian country, it is a clandestine Inquisition, nay worse.

How many ladies and gentlewomen are hurried away to these houses, which ought to be suppressed, or at least subject to daily examination, as hereafter shall be proposed?

How many, I say, of beauty, virtue, and fortune, are suddenly torn from their dear innocent babes, from the arms of an unworthy man, who they love (perhaps but too well) and who in return for that love, nay probably an ample fortune, and a lovely offspring besides, grows weary of the pure streams of chaste love, and thirsting after the puddles of lawless lust, buries his virtuous wife alive, that he may have the greater freedom with his mistresses?

If they are not mad when they go into these cursed houses, they are soon made so by the barbarous usage they there suffer, and any woman of spirit who has the least love for her husband, or concern for her family, cannot sit down tamely under a confinement and separation the most unaccountable and unreasonable.

Is it not enough to make anyone mad to be suddenly clapped up, stripped, whipped, ill fed, and worse used? To have no reason assigned for such treatment, no crime alledged, or accusers to confront? And what is worse, no soul to appeal to but merciless creatures, who answer but in laughter, surliness, contradiction, and too often stripes?

All conveniences for writing are denied, no messenger to be had to carry a letter to any relation or friend; and if this tyrannical Inquisition, joined with the reasonable reflections a woman of any common understanding must necessarily make, be not sufficient to drive any soul stark staring mad, though before they were never so much in their right senses, I have no more to say.

When by this means a wicked husband has driven a poor creature mad, and robbed an injured wife of her reason, for 'tis much easier to create than to cure madness, then has the villain a handle for his roguery, then perhaps he will admit her distressed relations to see her, when 'tis too late to cure the madness he so artfully and barbarously has procured.

But this is not all, something more dismal effects attend this Inquisition, for death is but too often the cure of their madness and end of their sorrows; some with ill usage, some with grief, and many with both are barbarously cut off in the prime of their years and flower of their health, who otherwise might have been mothers of a numerous issue, and survived many years. This is murder in the deepest sense, and much more cruel than dagger or poison, because more lingering; they die by peacemeal, and in all the agonies and terrors of a distracted mind.

Nay, it is murder upon murder, for the issue that might have been begot, is to be accounted for to God and the publick. Now if this kind of murder is connived at, we shall no doubt have enough, nay too much of it; for if a man is weary of his wife, has spent her fortune, and wants another, 'tis but sending her to a madhouse and the business is done at once.

How many have already been murdered after this manner is best known to just Heaven, and those unjust husbands and their damned accomplices, who, though now secure in their guilt, will one day find 'tis murder of the blackest dye; has the least claim for mercy, and calls aloud for the severest vengeance.

How many are yet to be sacrificed, unless a speedy stop be put to this most accursed practice, I tremble to think; our legislature cannot take this cause too soon in hand. This surely cannot be below their notice, and 'twill be an easy matter at once to suppress all these pretended madhouses. Indulge, gentle reader, for once the doting of an old man, and give him leave to lay down his little system without arraigning him of arrogance or ambition to be a law-giver. In my humble opinion, all private madhouses should be suppressed at once, and it should be no less than felony to confine any person under pretence of madness without due authority.

For the cure of those who are really lunatick, licensed madhouses should be constituted in convenient parts of the town, which houses should be subject to proper visitation and inspection, nor should any person be sent to a madhouse without due reason, inquiry, and authority.

* * *

Most gracious and august Queen Caroline! Ornament of your sex, and pride of the British nation! The best of mothers, the best of wives, the best of women! Begin this auspicious reign with an action worthy your illustrious self, rescue your injured sex from this tyranny, nor let it be in the power of every brutal husband to cage and confine his wife at pleasure, a practice scarce heard of till of late years. Nip it in the bud, most gracious Queen, and draw on yourself the blessings of numberless of the fair sex now groaning under the severest and most unjust bondage. Restore 'em to their families, let 'em by your means enjoy light and liberty, that while they fondly embrace, and with tears of joy weep over their dear children, so long withheld from them, they may invoke accumulated blessings from Heaven upon your royal head!

And you, ye fair illustrious circle! who adorn the British Court! and every day surround our gracious Queen: let generous pity inspire your souls, and move you to intercede with your noble consorts for redress in this injurious affair.

Who can deny when you become suitors? and who knows but at your request a bill may be brought into the House to regulate these abuses? The cause is a noble and a common one, and ought to be espoused by every lady who would claim the least title to virtue or compassion. I am sure no honest Member in either honourable House will be against so reasonable a bill; the business is for some publick-spirited patriot to break the ice, by bringing it into the House, and I dare lay my life it passes.

I must beg my reader's indulgence, being the most immethodical writer imaginable; 'tis true, I lay down a scheme, but fancy is so fertile I often start fresh hints, and cannot but pursue 'em; pardon, therefore, kind reader, my digressive way of writing, and let the subject, not the stile or method, engage thy attention.

* * *

An Effectual Method to Prevent Street Robberies

The principal encouragements, and opportunity given to street robbers is, that our streets are so poorly watched; the watchmen, for the most part, being decrepid, superannuated wretches, with one foot in the grave, and t'other ready to follow; so feeble, that a puff of breath can blow 'em down. Poor crazy mortals! Much fitter for an alms-house than a watch-house. A city watched and guarded by such animals, is wretchedly watched indeed.

Nay, so little terror do our watchmen carry with them, that hardy thieves make a mere jest of 'em, and sometimes oblige even the very watchmen, who should apprehend 'em, to light 'em in their roguery. And what can a poor creature do, in terror of his life, surrounded by a pack of ruffians, and no assistance near?

Add to this, that our rogues are grown more wicked than ever, and vice in all kinds is so much winked at, that robbery is accounted a petty crime. We take pains to puff 'em up in their villainy, and thieves are set out in so amiable a light in the *Beggar's Opera*, that it has taught them to value themselves on their profession, rather than be ashamed of it.

There was some cessation of street robberies, from the time of Bunworth and Blewitt's execution, till the introduction of this pious opera. Now we find the Cartouchian villainies revived, and London, that used to be the most safe and peaceful city in the universe, is now a scene of rapine and danger. If some of Cartouch's gang be not come over to instruct our thieves, and propagate their schemes, we have, doubtless, a Cartouch of our own, and a gang, which, if not suppressed, may be full as pernicious as ever Cartouch's was, and London will be as dangerous as Paris, if due care be not taken.

We ought to begin our endeavours to suppress these villainies; first by heavenly, and then by earthly means.

By heavenly means, in enforcing and encouraging a reformation of manners, by suppressing of vice and immorality, and punishing prophaneness and licentiousness. Our youth are corrupted by filthy, lewd ballads, sung and sold publickly in our streets; nay, unlicensed and unstamped, notwithstanding Acts of Parliament to the contrary.

Coachmen, carmen, etc., are indulged in swearing after the most blasphemous, shocking, and unaccountable rate that ever was known. New oaths and blasphemies are daily uttered and invented, and rather than not exercise this hellish tallent, they will vent their curses on their very horses; and, Oh stupid! damn the blood of a post, rather than want something to curse.

Our common women too have learned this vice; and not only strumpets, but labouring women, who keep our markets, and vend things about street, swear and curse at a most hideous rate. Their children learn it from the parents, and those of the middle, or even the better sort of people, if they pass through the streets to school, or to play, catch the infection, and carry home such words as must consequently be very shocking to sober parents.

Our youth, in general, have too much liberty; the Sabbath is not kept with due solemnity; masters and mistresses of families are too remiss in the care of the souls committed to their charge. Family prayer is neglected; and, to the shame of scoffers be it spoken, too much ridiculed. All ages and sexes, if in health, should be obliged to attend publick worship, according to their respective opinions. Were it only to keep youth out of harm's way, it would do well. But it is to be hoped, if their parents, masters, or mistresses, should oblige their attendance at publick devotion, they would edify by what they should hear, and many wicked acts would be stifled in their infancy, and checked even in the intention, by good and useful doctrine.

Our common people make it a day of debauch, and get so

drunk on a Sunday, they cannot work for a day or two following. Nay, since the use of geneva has become so common, many get so often drunk they cannot work at all, but run from one irregularity to another, till at last they become arrant rogues. And this is the foundation of all our present complaints.

We will suppose a man able to maintain himself and family by his trade, and at the same time to be a geneva drinker. This fellow first makes himself incapable of working, by being continually drunk; this runs him behindhand, and he either pawns or neglects his work, for which reason nobody will employ him. At last, fear of arrests, his own hunger, the cries of his family for bread, his natural desire to support an irregular life, and a propense hatred to labour, turn but too many an honest tradesman into an arrant desperate rogue. And these are commonly the means that furnish us with thieves and villains in general.

Thus is a man, that might be useful in a body politick, rendered obnoxious to the same. And if this trade of wickedness goes on, they will grow and increase upon us, insomuch, that we shall not dare to stir out of our habitations; nay, it will be well if they arrive not to the impudence of plundering our houses at noonday.

Where is the courage of the English nation, that a gentleman with six or seven servants, shall be robbed by one single highwayman? Yet we have lately had instances of this; and for this we may thank our effeminacy, our toupee wigs, and powdered pates, our tea, and other scandalous fopperies; and above all, the disuse of noble and manly sports, so necessary to a brave people, once in vogue, but now totally lost among us.

Let not the reader think I run from my subject, if I search the bottom of the distemper before I propose a cure, which having done, though indeed but slightly, for this is an argument could be carried to a much greater length, I proceed next to propose earthly means in the manner following.

Let the watch be composed of stout, able-bodied men, and of those at least treble the number now subsisting, that is to say, a watchman to every forty houses, twenty on one side of the way, and twenty on the other; for it is observable, that a man cannot well see distinctly beyond the extent of twenty houses in a row; if 'tis a single row, and no opposite houses, the charge must be greater, and their safety less. This man should be elected, and paid by the housekeepers themselves, to prevent misapplication and abuse, so much complained of, in the distribution of publick money.

He should be allowed 10 s. *per annum* by each housekeeper, which at forty houses, as above specified, amounts to 20 l. *per annum*, almost treble to what is at present allowed; and yet most housekeepers are charged at least 2s. 6d. a quarter to the watch, whose beat is, generally speaking, little less than the compass of half a mile.

This salary is something of encouragement, and a pretty settlement to a poor man, who, with frugality, may live decently thereon, and, by due rest, be enabled to give vigilant attendance.

If a housekeeper break, or a house is empty, the poor watchman ought not to suffer, the deficiency should be made up by the housekeepers remaining.

Or, indeed, all housekeepers might be excused, if a tax of only 1 s. *per annum* were levied on every batchelor within the Bills of Mortality, and above the age of one and twenty, who is not a housekeeper; for these young sparks are a kind of unprofitable gentry to the state; they claim publick safety and advantages, and yet pay nothing to the publick, nay indeed, they, in a manner, live upon the publick, for (on a Sunday especially) at least a million of these gentlemen quarter themselves upon the married men, and rob many families of part of a week's provision, more particularly when they play a good knife and fork, and are of the family of the *Tuckers*.

I beg pardon for this whimsical proposal, which, ludicrous as it seems, has something in it; and may be improved. Return we, in the meantime, to our subject.

The watch thus stationed, strengthened, and encouraged, let every watchman be armed with firearms and sword; and let no watchman stand above twenty doors distant from his fellow.

Let each watchman be provided with a bugle-horn, to sound on alarm, or in time of danger; and let it be made penal, if not felony, for any but a watchman to sound a horn in and about the City, from the time of their going on, to that of their going off.

An objection will be here made on account of the post-boys, to obviate which, I had thoughts of a bell, but that would be too ponderous and troublesome for a watchman to carry, besides his arms and lanthorn. As to a fixed bell, if the watchman is at another part of his walk, how can he give notice? Besides, rogues may play tricks with the bell; whereas a horn is portable, always ready, and most alarming.

Let the post-boys, therefore, use some other signal, since this is most convenient to this more material purpose. They may carry a bell in a holster, with ease, and give notice by that, as well as those who collect the letters.

That the watchmen may see from one end of their walks to the other, let a convenient number of lamps be set up, and those not of the convex kind, which blind the eyes, and are of no manner of use; they dazzle, but give no distinct light. And farther, rather than prevent robberies, many, deceived and blinded by these *ignes fatui*, have been run over by coaches, carts, etc. People stumble more upon one another, even under these very lamps, than in the dark. In short, they are most unprofitable lights, and, in my opinion, rather abuses than benefits.

Besides, I see no reason why every ten housekeepers can't find a lamp among themselves, and let their watchman dress it, rather than fatten a crew of directors. But we are so fond of companies, 'tis a wonder we have not our shoes blacked by one, and a set of directors made rich at the expense of our very blackguards. Convenient turnpikes and stoppages may be made to prevent escapes, and it will be proper for a watchman to be placed at one of these, fixed at the end of a lane, court, alley, or other thoroughfare, which may happen in any part of his beat, and so as not to obstruct his view to both ends thereof, or being able to give notice, as aforesaid; for the watch ought to be in view, as well as in the hearing of each other, or they may be overpowered, and much danger may happen.

The streets thus guarded and illuminated, what remains, but that the money allotted by the government be instantly paid on conviction of every offender; for delays in this case are of dangerous consequence, and nobody will venture their lives in hopes of a reward, if it be not duly and timely paid. If there is reason of complaint on this head, it ought to be looked into by those at the helm; for nothing can be more vile than for underlings to abuse the benevolence of the publick, or their superiors, by sinking, abridging, or delaying publick or private benefits. And it is by no means below the dignity, or care, even of the greatest, to see the disposal of their own bounty and charity; for it loses but too often by the carriage. And where a nobleman, or other generous person, has ordered five guineas to be given, 'tis well if the proper object has had even one.

Something allowed by the Chamber of London, to every person apprehending a robber, would have a good effect, especially if it be not told over a gridiron,* but paid without delay, or abatement. And what if the fewer custards are eat, so it augment the publick safety?

* * *

* *gridiron*: a figure apparently invented by Defoe to describe the delay and reluctance in paying in full a reward promised for information leading to the capture of a robber. Telling or counting the coins over a gridiron would reduce their value by melting them down. [Ed.]

The Family Instructor

The Family Instructor, Defoe's first didactic treatise, was published in March 1715. A second volume appeared in 1718, and *A New Family Instructor* in September 1727. The 1718 volume reached a third edition by 1728, but the 1715 volume, the first of Defoe's works to be reprinted in the U.S., went through 10 editions in his lifetime, and "became the most popular book of domestic instruction in a century which took delight in didactic writings."[1]

The basic concepts in Defoe's *Family Instructor*—the sanctification of marriage, with its corollary, a companionate relationship between husband and wife, and the patriarchal family, with moral and religious instruction as its central function—were traditional, dating from the Reformation. It was then that people stopped regarding marriage merely as "an unfortunate necessity to cope with human frailty", and instead endowed it with a virtue of its own, superior to that of celibacy. "The married state", writes Lawrence Stone, "became the ethical norm for the virtuous Christian."[2]

This new ideal, with its emphasis upon companionship between husband and wife, was common to Anglican and Puritan moral theologians. In 1549 Archbishop Cranmer added to the two ancient reasons for marriage, procreation of children and avoidance of fornication, that of "mutual society, help, and comfort, that the one ought to have of the other, both in prosperity and in adversity." The Presbyterian Richard Baxter "reversed the order of marriage motives in the prayer book, and put mutual comfort and support before procreation—an order of priorities first adopted by William Tyndale as far back as 1528."[3]

Like the sanctification of marriage, the patriarchal family was an outgrowth of the Reformation, which saw the emergence of strong, authoritarian state systems and their substitution for feudal community organizations. "The growth of patriarchy", writes Stone, "was deliberately encouraged by the new Renaissance state on the traditional grounds that the subordination of the family to its head is analogous to, and also a direct contributory cause of, subordination of subjects to the sovereign." Accordingly, the Reformation church placed "heavy responsibility ... upon the head of the household to supervise the religious and moral conduct of its members ... The power of the husband and father was greatly enhanced by his inheritance from the pre-Reformation priest of the duty to indoctrinate his family in piety and morality through daily family prayers and Bible reading."[4]

By the time Defoe wrote his 1715 *Family Instructor*, according to modern historians the practice of family prayers was clearly on the decline:[5] the Restoration of Charles II after the reign of the Puritans had been accompanied by an enduring wave of general revulsion against religious enthusiasm, and indifference had spread among the uneducated, deism among the educated classes.[6] Since the book was so very popular throughout the century, either modern historians have underestimated the continuing popularity of family prayers, or the appeal of the book must have come largely from something more modern than its call to family prayers.

Comparing it with its popular predecessor of the early seventeenth century, *A Godly Form of Household Government*, amended by Robert Cleaver and John Dod from Robert Cawdry's book of 1562, one discovers that although the two treatises prescribe the same practices, what Defoe's dialogues actually dramatize are family relations based less on paternalism than on affective individualism. As described by Stone, the affective individualism that characterizes the modern family, distinguishing it from patriarchal predecessors, includes closer, warmer relations between husband and wife, and parents and children: a more equal partnership between spouses and greater freedom for children.[7] A natural development of the companionate marriage prescribed by Anglican and Puritan moral theologians, affective individualism probably displaced patriarchy first "among the more pious, often nonconformist middle-class families of the late seventeenth century. The Presbyterian Richard Baxter and his wife married one another, not with a view to worldly advancement, but for their personal qualities."[8]

These familial values were soon accepted by a wealthy entrepreneurial bourgeoisie whose whole way of life was "based on a strict code of personal behaviour" and whose "high level of literacy" and "sense of moral purpose" made them "avid readers of current didactic literature." More important, the same values were embraced by the English squirarchy, with its "near monopoly of high prestige and status", because there was "a high degree of intermarriage between them and the bourgeoisie"; there was a "congruence of the ideas with the political 'country' ideology of the contract state which had been evolved to justify squirarchy control of the political machine"; and there was a "congruence of ideas about 'holy matrimony' that had been passed on from the moral theologians ... in the first half of the seventeenth century." The acceptance of the new cultural values among this carrier elite—wealthy merchants and landed classes—ensured their eventual spread throughout the population.[9] "As far as there was a public opinion", writes J. H. Plumb, the wealthy merchants, "with the gentry, formed it."[10]

Since Defoe is frequently misperceived as writing primarily for shopkeepers, his best-selling *Family Instructors* are important documents testifying to his appeal to classes like the squirarchy and the urban upper middle class. Defoe's affective individualism would have been attractive to those classes when it could not have been so to shopkeepers, for the familial arrangements of smallholders, shopkeepers and artisans, Stone points out, did not keep pace with those of the squirarchy and upper bourgeoisie. The former groups, "anxious to preserve a precarious economic foothold one rung above the poor", "dependent on capital to get a start in life", "much at the mercy of economic circumstances", "were probably more concerned with capital and property accumulation as a motive for marriage than any other group in society except the highest aristocracy."[11]

Defoe's call to family prayers may have been especially attractive to the squirarchy, which would tend to maintain some conservative social practices after they had become unfashionable in urban settings. Robert Harley for one, the quintessential country gentleman, was very particular about the performance of worship within his family. Although it might be objected that Harley was untypical, for he had originally been Presbyterian, godly Puritan families were not unknown among the Anglican gentry. Stone points out that these families might be "drawn from any level of social class, but in practice mostly from the yeoman, husbandman, artisan and tradesman level, *with some gentry leadership at the top*" (my italics).[12]

The 1715 *Family Instructor* was published anonymously by Defoe, probably because he did not wish his political notoriety as a Tory writer to injure him with potential Whig buyers, and certainly because he did not wish his reputation as a Dissenter to prevent Anglicans from buying the book.[13] Defoe's ecumenical intention is clear from his introduction: "There is no room to inquire here who this tract is directed to, or who it is written by, whether by Church of England man, or Dissenter; it is evident both need it, it may be useful to both, and it is written with charity to, and for the benefit of both".

The 1718 *Family Instructor* begins with the marital difficulties of two friends, one a country gentleman, the other his urban social equivalent, evidently a wealthy merchant of the upper middle class. The superiority of their social rank to that of the comfortable City family described in the 1715 *Family Instructor* is indicated by Defoe's preface:

> The whole scene now presented, is so perfectly new, so entirely differing from all that went before, and so eminently directed to another species of readers, that it seems to be more new than it would have been, if no other part had been published before it; nay, to any considering people that reflect upon the differing scenes of human life, and the several stations we are placed in, and parts we act, while we are passing over this stage; it cannot but be known, that there are follies to be exposed, dangers to be cautioned against, and advices to be given, particularly adapted to the several stages of life.

The excerpt from the 1715 *Family Instructor* demonstrates how Defoe's imagination converted didacticism into fiction, and how the book that should have been offering as new only the setting forth in dramatic dialogues of the patriarchal precepts of *A Godly Form of Household Government*, was actually promulgating new familial values. Although the dialogue between father and son might have been mildly instructive to fathers wishing to play autocrat to their adolescent sons, for the father clearly gets all the best arguments, the significant thing is that the father considers his son important enough to try to convince him by reason. Furthermore, Defoe has conveyed so well the impotent rage and despair of a young man frustrated in what he regards as his legitimate recreation, that many readers cannot fail to come away sympathizing with the underdog.

The excerpt from the 1718 *Family Instructor*, ostensibly designed to demonstrate the proper management of a headstrong wife opposing family prayers by a patient husband, actually dramatizes the extravagant emotions arising from concealed sexual warfare. The husband's intimate passion for his wife, and the wife's struggle not to be mastered by it, underlie her opposition to his conduct of family worship and the excessive and irrational form taken by her rebellion.

The style and tone of this passage are similar to those of the 1724 *Roxana*, in which Defoe described higher social classes than in his other fictions, the urban upper-middle merchant class and even the aristocracy. In *Roxana*, as in this excerpt from the 1718 *Family Instructor*, he seems to be exploring the psychology of obsession (in his terms, diabolic possession). Roxana's inability to escape from the memory of her past gradually leads her to thoughts of murder, just as the wife's inability to free herself from her husband's power leads her to become obsessed by the fashionable phrase, "Poison him!", and to brood about applying it literally to her husband.

Defoe's *Family Instructors* make fascinating reading, not only for social historians interested in the dissemination of new cultural values among specific classes, but also for literary scholars interested in the different styles Defoe used for different readers and in the sources of some of his fictions.

Notes

1 John Robert Moore, *Daniel Defoe, Citizen of the Modern World* (Chicago: Univ. of Chicago Press, 1958), p. 218.

2 Lawrence Stone, *The Family, Sex and Marriage in England 1500–1800* (New York: Harper & Row, 1977), p. 135.

3 *Ibid.*, p. 136.

4 *Ibid.*, pp. 152, 154, 158.

5 *Ibid.*, p. 244.

6 Geoffrey Holmes, *The Trial of Doctor Sacheverell* (London: Eyre Methuen, 1973), pp. 25–28.

7 Stone, p. 221. Stone stresses the cyclical nature of family relationships. The patriarchal family reappeared in Victorian England, again to be replaced by affective individualism in the twentieth century.

8 *Ibid.*, p. 361.

9 *Ibid.*, pp. 260, 261.

10 J. H. Plumb, *Sir Robert Walpole: The Making of a Statesman* (London: Cresset Press, 1956), p. 29.

11 Stone, p. 362.

12 *Ibid.*, pp. 140–41.

13 Dessagene C. Ewing, "The First Printing of Defoe's *Family Instructor*", *Papers of the Bibliographical Society of America*, 65 (1971), 269–72. 269–272. Ewing points out that the first printing, in Newcastle, was arranged to preserve Defoe's anonymity, firstly because he was under indictment for libelling the Earl of Anglesey, one of King George's regents, and secondly because he did not wish to injure the sale of the book to Anglicans by letting it be known a Dissenter had written it. Complaints about the poor quality of the printing, Ewing argues, turn out to be based on problems caused by the last-minute insertion of a new section, the final dialogue of Part II. Defoe was particularly eager to include this section, because it stresses the value of both Dissenting and Anglican positions on the common basis of Christianity. Such a passage "would appeal to a wide audience without revealing that the author himself was a Dissenter" (p. 272).

The Family Instructor (1715)

* * *

The Seventh Dialogue

The father had not been so happily surprised in his discourse with his second son, in the morning, but he is as unhappily mortified with the rencounter he meets with in his eldest son, in the afternoon. The young gentleman was above stairs with his eldest sister, as noted in the Fourth Dialogue, when his father called for him, and being a little ruffled in his humour with the ill usage, as he thought it, that his mother had given his sister, he came down with a grave, discomposed look, and appeared not very respectful in his behaviour. His father, who knew him to be hot and fiery in his disposition, was not willing to have been angry, and designed to treat him, as will appear, very kindly, but he takes up the case first, and began with his father.

Son Sir, did you forbid Thomas letting us have the coach?

Father I ordered *in general*, that none of the servants should stir out today.

Son I thought so, and told the dog that I was sure you had not forbid him; I'll break the rascal's head this minute. (Offers to go out)

Father Hold, George, I must speak with you first.

Son I'll come again, Sir, *immediately*. (Offers to go again)

Father *No, no*, I must speak with you NOW; sit you down, I'll have nobody's heads broke today. Don't you know it is Sabbath day?

Son Better day, better deed, Sir; it's never out of season to correct a rascal. (Offers to go a third time)

Father George, sit down, I say, and be easy; perhaps you may be better satisfied presently, if you can have patience.

Son Sir, I am satisfied from your own mouth that the villain not only refused when I ordered him to get the coach out, but told me a lie, and said you forbid him, which I then told him I did not believe, and promised to cane him if it were not true, and I must be as good as my word.

Father Well, well, but let it alone for the present, I say.

Son I must and will beat the villain, by ——. (Swears softly, yet so that his father overhears him)

Father The coachman's usage is not so rough to you, but I think yours is as rude to your father.

Sir Why sir, what do I say? I don't speak disrespectfully to you, Sir; but I speak of this same fellow.

Father I heard what you said, Sir, and what you might be sure I did not like; and wherever you use such language, if you had any respect to your father, you would not take that freedom where I am.

Son If it had not been in respect to you, Sir, why did I speak softly?

Father That was a *seeming* respect indeed, but you took care I should not be ignorant.

Son I did not design you should have heard; I intended no disrespect.

Father Well, sit down here then, and suspend your foolish passion of the fellow.

Son I suppose you don't keep servants on purpose to affront me at that rate.

Father If my son had as much patience with his father, as he obliges his father to have with him, he might have had an answer to that before now; but you are too hot for your father to talk with you, it seems.

Son No Sir, I am not hot, but it would provoke anybody, to be used so by a servant.

Father Then you must turn your anger this way, and quarrel with your father; for the fellow has done nothing but what I commanded him.

Son Why, you said, Sir, you did not bid him refuse me.

Father You must have everything nicely explained to you, it seems. I tell you, what he said to you was the natural consequence of what I ordered, though perhaps the fellow did not give you the true reason, but in general I had bid him stay at home.

Son He might have said so then.

Father No, perhaps I had commanded him otherwise too.

Son I find I am not to know how it is, nor what it means; nor do I care whether I do or no.

Father In time you may.

Son As you please, Sir.

Father Well, in this it shall be as I please then; but if you had thought fit to have come to talk with me with less heat in your temper, and waited a little till I had spoke what I had to say to you, all your fury at him, and your indecency to me, might have been spared.

Son I did not know what you sent for me for.

Father And did not design to know it, I suppose, for you gave me no time to speak.

Son I only told you of the treatment of the coachman, I have no more to say.

Father Then I may take my turn, I hope. I shall tell you then, that I sent for you, as I purpose to do for all your brothers and sisters, to tell you that whereas we have lived in an open, professed contempt of God's commands, prophanation of the Sabbath day and omission of all religious duties, it is high time to take up a new course; that I was convinced of what was my own duty as a father; and a master of a family; that hitherto the sin lay too much at my door, but for the future I would discharge myself better. That if my children would go on, it should no longer be through my omission, but their own. To this purpose, I began with my servants, who, as soon as I came from church, I commanded to be all at home, and that I would have no going abroad; then I resolved to tell my mind to my children, who I expected would not give me the trouble of commanding, or using the authority of a father, or governor, with them; but that I might with reason and argument persuade, and with affection and tenderness invite them to a thing which must necessarily so far convince their consciences, as to leave them no room to question but it was infinitely for their advantage, and for their general good, both soul and body.

Son I knew nothing of this, Sir.

Father Well, that's true; but, as I said, you might ha' known it before, if you had had patience, or had thought fit to have given me time to speak to you.

Son Nay, I do not understand it, now I do know it.

Father Your ignorance shall serve you but a short while; you can easily understand this part of it, that without troubling you with any more of the reasons of it, I will have none that are under my roof, children or servants, stir out of my doors on the Sabbath day, after church is done.

Son You will take it ill perhaps, if your children should ask you the reason why they must be so confined; and your children will not fail to think it hard to be confined so, and not know the reason of it.

Father I might with much more justice insist upon my undoubted right to govern my own family, without giving an account to my children of what I do; also in a case so plain as this, methinks, they need not seek for a reason for such an order; but since they pretend ignorance, let them read the commands of God to keep holy the Sabbath day.

Son Those commands were as strong before, as they are now, and yet we never were thus confined before.

Father The worst of that is mine, Son, and all that can be said for an answer to that, is, that *before* I was to blame, and neglected my duty, *now* I resolve, God willing, to do my duty, and neglect it no longer, and if it be otherwise, they that are guilty shall be to blame, not I.

Son Everybody may do their own duty for themselves.

Father But is is my unquestioned duty, to make all that are under my command, do their duty.

Son I do not desire to be confined.

Father My desire, or my design, was not to confine you, but to persuade you to confine yourself by the rules of your Christian duty; but you have pushed it farther than I expected, and if you will not do it yourself, I must do it for you.

Son I hate to be confined, or to confine myself.

Father That makes it more my duty to confine you, and since I think your business is to obey, and not to dispute, I desire no more of your arguments, but expect to see my orders observed, since I know they are founded upon both religion and reason.

Son You may oblige us to stay within, but you cannot oblige us to be willing.

Father Then I must be content with as much of your obedience as I can get.

Son And I hope [you] will expect it no longer than while we cannot help it.

Father But [I] will take care that you shall not help it while you call me *Father*, for I will not bear the title without the authority.

Son Liberty is a native right, the brutes seek it; not a bird will be in a cage, if it can be free.

Father Liberty to do evil is an abandoned slavery, the worst of bondage, and confinement from doing evil, is the only true liberty. But to cut this discourse short, I can give liberty no longer to any under my roof to break God's commands, or prophane his Sabbath, it is not in my power; if you will not submit to my government, you must quit my dominions; and as I foresee you will be forward enough to carry it high, you are mistaken if you think I shall wait to be told by you, that you will go abroad, or that you will not stay in the family; for unless you will submit to regulate your life after a different manner than you have done, and to receive advice from your father for your conduct, flatter not yourself with your father's affection, I'll love none that hate God, nor shelter none of his rebels, my doors shall be open to let you out when you please.

Son I care not how soon.

Father That's what I expected from you. My answer shall be very plain: you shall be at liberty to go this hour, Son, before the next; but take this with you whenever you go, that if ever you set your foot without the door on this account, you never get leave to set your foot within it again, but upon your knees, and with the humblest repentance and submission both to God and your father, for I am not in jest with you.

Note: No wise father ought to suffer himself to be threatened by his children with going away from him, but rather to make their being thrust from their parents be the greatest punishment they have to fear. (The father goes out of the room, but returns again immediately)

Father I did not expect this treatment at your hands, Son.

Son I do not know what you would have me do.

Father What I would have you do is very plain, and is nothing but what your duty to God requires, *viz.* to submit to the regulations and orders which I shall give in my family, for the worship of God, and for regulating our morals, and our way of living, and especially, for restoring a general face of religion and virtue upon our conversation, that we may, according to the Scripture, *live soberly, righteously and godly in the present evil world*, and not be eminent in the place we live in for the loosest, and most profligate family in the whole neighbourhood.

Son I think we are religious enough; what should we do more than we do?

Father I think my first work is to let you know what you should *not* do; for if this cannot be obtained, *viz.* to refrain from what we do that is wrong, how shall we come to ascertain what is right; and if we know not what evils to refuse, how shall we know what duties to perform?

Son I know nothing we do, that we ought to leave off.

Father That is the reason why I bewail so much your want of instruction and education, and that I am so willing to retrieve the loss. I can soon tell you what you should leave off, *viz.* you should leave prophaning the Lord's day in sports, diversions, visiting, riding to the park, company, and the like, and spend it, as it was appointed to be spent, in acts of religious worship, in hearing and reading God's Word, and in other duties proper to that purpose. Next, you should leave off the playhouses, and reading plays, as not only introductory to vice, and an extravagant mispender of time; but as they lead to engaging in such society and bad company, as will be destructive to any sober character in the world. Thirdly, that a general sobriety of behaviour be fixed upon the whole scheme of your conversation, free from passion, ill words, swearing, blaspheming God's name, and from drunkenness, and all other excesses. These are the main heads of the negatives which I speak of, and which I desire to be observed; and this is so just, so easy, and so equitable, that I cannot but expect, especially considering how my children are circumstanced, a ready compliance with it; I shall direct you to positive duties afterwards.

Son I know not how we are circumstanced, or what you would have me understand by that word.

Father I find your temper is such, that I am rather to let you know what I expect, than to hope for your observing it, and thay you will put the hardship upon me of doing all with you by force. This is a treatment, I think, very disingenuous, and unlike a dutiful son. I am willing to indulge you in everything that is reasonable and just; but as I am convinced what I desire is not only your duty, but your interest to comply with, I therefore cannot indulge you to your own ruin; and for that reason, if you will oblige me to use violent methods to restore you, and to restore my family, although I shall be sorry for it, yet as it is my duty I must do it, and I let you know therefore very plainly my resolution, and the reason of it; if you can give better reasons why you should not comply with these things, I am ready to hear them.

Son What signifies giving reasons against what you resolve to do?

Father It might take off the scandal of disobedience from you, when you pretend to oppose your practise to my directions.

Son I don't concern myself about scandals, not I.

Father You fortify yourself against everything a wise man ought to be concerned at, and that by a general negligence of God and man, as if you were unconcerned for conscience or reputation; I hope you don't desire to be known by such a character.

Son I don't see that I do anything that deserves reflection.

Father Well, come, examine a little. Is your Lord's day conduct to be justified? Do you think you keep the Sabbath day as you ought to do?

Son Why, Sir, do I not go constantly to church?

Father Where do you find in God's Law, that going to church is the sum of the Sabbath day duties? If you can shew me that in the Scripture, then I am put to silence.

Son I see no harm in taking the air a little after sermon time.

Father If sermon time be the whole of the Sabbath day, you are in the right; but then you must prove that the Fourth Commandment should have been translated thus, *viz. Remember that thou keep holy THE SERMON TIME on the Sabbath day.*

Son I think there is no need of so much strictness.

Father God and your father are of another opinion, or else neither the rules of one, or the discourse of the other are to be credited; I see all your arguments against these things are only *general*, that you do not think *thus*, or you do not see *that*; but have you any just objections against the express commands of God? If you have, let us hear them.

Son I do not object against the commands of God, but I do not see, on the other hand, that I break the commands of God in taking a turn in the park, or visiting a friend on a Sunday, after sermon.

Father I'll lock up all argument on that side against you, thus: if you can prove that taking your pleasure on the Sabbath day is keeping it holy, you may justify yourself; if not, you cannot, and for that read this text, Is. 58. 13: *If thou turn away thy foot from the Sabbath, from doing my pleasure on my holy day*, etc. There is the word of God directly against you; would you have any farther authority?

Son I cannot dispute of these things.

Father They that cannot dispute, should not contradict; however, I think it my duty to let all of you know, that as I have no reason to doubt but the command of God is clear, and that I ought to see it obeyed, I join to it my own command, *viz.* that in my family I will have no more prophaning the Lord's day; no more going to plays; no more swearing, drunkenness, or immorality whatsoever, if I can help it; and I expect to be put to as little trouble as possible in having this order of mine submitted to.

Son I suppose you may find some opposition besides what you think I shall make, you have more children than me.

Father You have the less need to make my task harder, and join with them; however, I am speaking now not of *their* obedience, but *yours*.

Son Perhaps I may obey as much as they, but I suppose I may bear the blame of their standing out.

Father If you do well you are sure to be accepted; if not, sin lies at the door; if you are an encouragement to their disobedience, you take your share of the guilt, whether it be by words, or by example. My business, however, is not with them now, but with you, and I desire to know your mind, having now told you what I expect.

Son I know not what you would have one say; you say you will be obeyed, then I must obey, I think. I know nothing else to be said. If you will make the house a monastery, I must turn monk, I think; but nothing is more certain than that we shall all think it hard, and think we are not used kindly.

Father The commands of God are not grievous, nor are my resolutions hard or unjust; and that makes the opposition which you make, the more unnatural. However, since you are not to be wrought upon to think it reasonable, I must content myself to take your outward compliance, whether willing or unwilling, though I think your behaviour highly disobliging, and shall always let you know I resent it as such.

Son You will find *all* your children will think it hard as well as I.

Father That cannot be true, for I know some of them to whom God has given more grace.

Son I am sure then others have not.

Father Yes, I know your sister has shewn herself, much to the disgrace of her good breeding, as obstinate as yourself, and has been very insolent to her mother, and I hear she talks at a rate of her mother that does not become her; I shall assure her it shall not be born with.

Son I think my mother used her very ill.

Father I find you are too partial to be judge of it, and therefore ought to let it alone. What has her mother done to her?

Son She has taken away all her books of value, and not only ruffled her with hard words, but even struck her with very little provocation.

Father You have a truer account of the fact, I find, than of the provocation; as to striking her, I regret that she had not done it sooner, and repeated it oftener; her sauciness to her mother, and her contempt of God, were unsufferable. It was her good fortune that I was not there; and as to taking her books, I have had the mortification to look them all over, and with a great deal of affliction, to think that any child of mine should spend their time in such foolish, filthy, and abominable books.

Son What, do you mean the plays?

Father Yes, I do mean the plays, songs, novels, and such like, which made up her whole study. Were they fit for a young maid's contemplation?

Son I must own I think them very fit.

Father Then your sin is come up to a maturity very fit for a publick reformation, and it is high time you were begun with; wherefore I tell you very plainly, I shall cause you to pass the same trial with your sister, and if I find any such like books in your custody, you may be sure they shall all go the same way.

Son Then you will put me to the expense of buying more, for I cannot be without my plays; they are the study of the most accomplished gentlemen, and no man of sense is without them.

Father No man of vice (you might say) is without them; but I am positive against plays, as before, and I had rather have you not accomplished than that the other inconveniencies of plays should be your lot; but I can shew you many accomplished young gentlemen who are no ways concerned with them.

Son What, who never see a play?

Father No, never.

Son It is impossible!

Father No, no, far from impossible.

Son I can never promise not to go to the play.

Father Then you and I shall differ to the greatest extremity.

Son (He flies out in a rage) This is intolerable! I had as liev you would turn me out of your door; I'll be content to go to the West Indies, or be a foot soldier, or anything, rather than be made such a recluse. Why was I not bred up a Papist? Then you might ha' sent me to a monastery, and I might have been used to a cloister life, but to breed me up for a gentleman, and then confine me as no gentleman is confined; this is exposing me, and making me look a fool among all company!

Father I had rather see you a foot soldier or anything, than listed in the service of the Devil. But here is no need of these desperate resolutions; here is nothing required of you but what becomes a gentleman very well, and as much a gentleman as anybody. Can you pretend you cannot serve God, and be a gentleman? That you cannot live a virtuous life, and obey the commands of God, and yet be a gentleman? This is a reproach upon the very name of quality, and such a slander on a gentleman, as no one will allow. However, this, in short, is the case, Son, and if confining you from unlawful pleasures, and from ruining your own soul, will make you desperate, and you will be a foot soldier, or run away to the West Indies, you must, I cannot help it, I suppose you will be weary of it quickly.

Son I care not what I do, or whither I go. (He walks about in a great passion)

Father Unhappy foolish youth! Had I extorted obedience to any unreasonable, unjust thing; had I put you to any hardships; had I exposed you to any dangers, or deprived you of your lawful pleasures, these things might ha' been the effect, and you might have had some pretence for talking thus to your father; but all this for laying before you your unquestionable duty, for requiring nothing of you but what your great Master commands, nothing but what is equal, just, and good! This is a deplorable instance of the woful depravity of your judgment, and corruption of your nature. However, though I heartily pity and grieve for you, yet the thing I desire is so just, so reasonable, so necessary, so much my duty to command, and your interest to obey, that I cannot, I will not go from it, or abate one tittle of it; and therefore you may consider of it, and act as you will, you know my desire, and fall back, fall edge, I will have it done; so you may take your choice for God or the Devil. (Father goes out and leaves him)

Son You may be as resolute as you will, you will never bring me to your beck. What, must I forsake all my mirth and good company, and turn hermit in my young days! Not I, I'll go to the gallies rather, I'll seek my fortune anywhere first. Not go to the park! nor see a play! be as demure as a Quaker! and set up for a saint! what shall I look* like? (*swears aloud) I won't be a mountebank convert, not I; I hate hypocrisy and dissimulation, I have too much honour for it.

Well, I'll go up to my sister, she is an honest resolute girl, if she will but stand to me, we will take our fate together. What can my father do? Sure we are too big for his correction; we will never be made fools on at this rate.

The father had sent for his eldest daughter, and she had refused to come, as before, and the servant brought word she would not come. (Father returns)

Father Will not come!

Servant She said she would not, indeed, first, but afterwards she said she could not, Sir.

Father Go to her again, and tell her from me, if she does not come immediately, I'll come and fetch her.

Servant Sir, she was laid upon the bed, and said she was indisposed, and could not come.

Father Well, go back then, and tell her, her mother and I will come to her.

Servant Indeed I told her that I thought you would do so.

Father Well, and what said she?

Servant She said, Sir, she was not fit to speak to you. I believe she is ill, for she has been crying vehemently.

Father I suppose you and she have conferred notes?

Son I told you, Sir, you would have more opposition to your design, than from me.

Father Perhaps by your means.

Son If that could be without my knowledge, something might be, but I said before I should be taxed with it, whether guilty or no.

Father I'll deal with it, let it be where it will.

The son as soon as he could get away from his father, goes up to his sister's apartment; it seems the father, though he had resolved to talk to his daughter, had deferred it for some time, and did not go up to her chamber presently.

Being then in some passion at his son's behaviour, and withal being preparing for the great work which he had resolved to begin that evening, he was unwilling to discompose himself, and make himself unfit for what was before him. The rest of the conduct both of the son and daughter, and also the history of the father's management at his first beginning his family reformation, will all be largely set down in the next dialogue.

THE END OF THE SEVENTH DIALOGUE

The Family Instructor
(1718)

* * *

They had not many more words about it; but taking her brother at his word, she went away the same day in disgust, and not resolving presently whither to go, she stayed at a neighbour's house two or three days; in which time she went once down to her own house. She knew indeed her husband was not at home, but she had a mind to see the children and talk with her nurse, who it seems she heard had been at Sir Richard's.

The old nurse was overjoyed to see her, and treated her with abundance of "God bless you's, Madam", as was the poor woman's way; and it was believed, if her husband had been at home, she might have been prevailed with to stay; but she broke away again, though the poor old nurse fell down of her knees to her, to entreat her to stay.

Being gone thus in a wild humour, enraged that her brother had, as it were, turned her out of doors; she passes by a good sober house in the town, where she might have been welcome, and would have had good advice, and went to the house of one of her old companions, about two miles off; who was indeed ten times more the child of hell than herself.

Here she told her tale, and had a she-devil at her elbow to say *yes* to all she affirmed, and *amen* to all she resolved; that prompted her to be worse than ever the Devil, *for want of an agent*, perhaps, had an opportunity to desire her to be; till at last, she made her so wicked, that she was frighted with her own picture, and was brought to reflect upon herself, and repent, by those very steps the Devil took to ruin her.

It would be a sad, and far from a diverting story, to give an account of all the mad steps these two creatures took together—I do not mean as to common vices; she was too much a gentlewoman to behave herself scandalously; nor was anything of that kind ever suggested, that I have met with. But her disgust at her brother, her aversion to her husband, and her contempt of all that was sober and religious, was carried up by the assistance of this companion of hers, to such a height, that she despised all advice, was deaf to the importunities of her friends, and even of her husband, as shall be farther related presently.

This companion of hers took that common, but foolish way, that many think the method of obliging their friends, (*viz.*) of agreeing, and saying yes to everything, right or wrong; she had been intimate with this gentlewoman from her youth, and bred up just in the same loose untaught manner; as to anything religious, a perfect stranger; as to sense, she was like herself, a toy, gay and vain, empty of all that was good; as foolish and as prophane as her heart could wish. Here she was perfectly easy, for nobody was friendly enough to admonish her, or sincere enough to advise her; and she lived to see, and to acknowledge, how empty and insignificant that friendship is, that is not honest enough to bear, and faithful enough to give reproof.

This she-friend, among the rest of her follies, had accustomed herself to a most abominable looseness of the tongue, and gave herself such a latitude of ill words, that she scarce spoke ten words without intermixing some of them by way of ornament; a custom grown up of late to such a height, that it is become the vice of our conversation; while at the same time it is so fashionable too, that such people think it adorns their speech, and that their language is not polite or genteel without it.

Among the rest of her foolish phrases, she had this in particular: "Poison it"; or if spoken of any person, "Poison him", or "Poison her". This was grown so frequent and so familiar to her tongue, that it became the very catchword of all her discourse; nothing came without it, though in itself an unmusical, course, and odd saying, scarce ever used by any before her. If her coffee or her tea was too hot, or too cold, 'twas always the same: "O poison it, 'tis nasty stuff". If she talked to her servants, 'twas "Poison them" at every word, if she did not like anything. So that in short, it run through all her discourse, and yet the foolish creature had no thoughts of ill, when she said it; meant nothing, would not have hurt anybody, much less poisoned them; but the word had gained upon her fancy, she liked it for a word to be tossed upon her tongue; she thought it sat well upon her speech; and in a word, she had let it grow upon her to a habit, so that it was meerly natural to her. Our unhappy lady being now in the family, they grew intimate to be sure, and in their conversation she failed not to tell this new confident all her grievances; first, about her uncle, the good old minister, and his calling all the house to prayers. "And you know, Madam," says she, "how I hate their priestcraft, and the wheedling ways that these parsons take to make themselves the heads of people's families, and to make us think them all saints; yet as I expect to be the old man's heir, and he has a good estate, what could I do? You know, Madam, a body would not differ with an old fool, and so disoblige him."

"No, poison him," says she, "one would bear anything on that account."

"But then, Madam," says the lady, "he carried it on so long, that my poor fool of a husband, pretends to like it; and when the parson was gone, he pretends to be chaplain himself."

"O poison the old fellow," says she, "what did he stay so long for?"

"Why, Madam," says the other, "he was lame of the gout, and we could not be rid of him sooner. Nor did that trouble me so much, but to see my husband turned parson, and whine out the prayers morning and night; that was such a thing, 'twould have provoked anybody; would not it, Madam?"

"Indeed, Madam, it would," says she again, "Poison me, I should never have born with it."

"Truly, Madam," says the lady, "I did not bear with it long, I tried to break him of it a good while; but when I found 'twas to no purpose, I told him my mind very plainly; and in short, this is the reason of our parting."

"Poison me, Madam," says the companion, "and a good reason too."

Wife And now, my brother, wants to have me to go home again, and beg my husband's pardon; and because I won't do that, he falls upon me like a fury."

Companion Who? Sir Richard, Madam? Poison him, nobody minds what he says.

Wife Yes, and my Lady too, she has been upon my back.

Companion Ay, poison her, she is a mighty wise busy thing too, she knows nothing of the matter; she only says as Sir Richard bids her.

Wife Now, Madam, would you advise me to go back to my

husband, Madam, upon such terms?

Companion Go back, Madam; no, poison him, you ought never to go near him till he gives you satisfaction, Madam.

This was a companion now to her heart's content, and in such conversation you may be sure her separate condition began to be very easy to her, and she began to have a perfect aversion to her husband; nay, so natural was this foolish empty, flattering conversation of her new companion's grown to her, that she began to be infected with her language; and if anybody talked of her husband, or of her going back to her husband, she would frequently answer, he should be poisoned first.

In the middle of this extravagance, and as if she was now brought to a right disposition for affronting the tenderest husband that ever woman had, a messenger brought her word that her husband was come to the house to see her, and was below stairs.

The story of the honest gentleman's being come from London, his resolution to find out his wife, and to use all possible means to persuade her to return to him, is reserved to another place; only it is proper to observe, that he came prepared with all the calmness and affection that he was capable of, to invite her home, and that all things might be forgotten between them; and in a word, to do even more than became him, to win and engage her to him again.

She was surprised very much, when she heard he was below stairs; and had she not had the evil spirit at her elbow in her wicked adviser, she had certainly gone down to him, and home with him; nay, had she done the first, she could not have resisted the last; he had resolved to treat her with so much affection, and such passionate persuasions, that she must have been a tyrant to herself, and a very monster of her sex, if she had refused him.

But in the very juncture this creature comes into her chamber. "O! Madam," says she to her new companion, "who do you think is below?"

Companion I can't imagine; but you look surprised, I warrant 'tis Sir Richard ——; if it be, you shall not see him; let me go down to him.

Wife No, no, it is not Sir Richard, I assure you.

Companion Who is it then, I beseech you?

Wife Nobody but my husband.

Companion Your husband! Poison him, that's impossible, why he's at London, Madam.

Wife Why, I thought so too; but it seems he is come back, and he has sent for me; what shall I do, Madam? I entreat you advise me.

Companion Do! Poison him, you shan't see him.

Wife I think I had not best see him; what would you advise me to?

Companion By no means; he wants to have you go home, he should be poisoned first. No, no, Madam, if you let him have you too cheap, he will make you pay for it too dear. No, poison him, he should go home as wise as he came.

Wife I am of your mind, I won't see him; here, Betty, go down and tell Mr. —— I can't be spoke with. (She calls in the servant)

Betty Madam, have they told you how long he has been here? he has waited above an hour already; and if I say you can't be spoke with, he'll stay longer.

Wife Well, well, do you do as I bid you, or go and call my own maid to me.

Betty Yes, Madam.

(Betty goes and calls her own maid. "Here, Sue," says she, "go to your mistress, I think she's stark mad; your master is come a purpose to her, and she won't be spoke with; for my part, I can't carry the poor gentleman such a message, not I; so your mistress bids me call you."

Says Susan, "I'll go to her, but I won't carry such a message to my master, I'll assure her.")

Susan Madam, did you want me?

Wife Yes, yes; go down and see who that is wants me, and tell them I am indisposed, and can't be spoke with.

Susan Indisposed, Madam, why 'tis my master! I wonder Betty should not tell you who it was all this while; he has stayed this hour, and more, walking all alone.

Wife Your master, you fool; your master is at London.

Susan Madam, I hope you'll believe I know my master when I see him; I'm sure I spoke to him.

Wife Spoke to him! And what did you say?

Susan Why, Madam, he asked me how you did, and I told him you were very well; then he asked me if you were up; and I told him, "Up, Sir, yes, a great while ago", and that you were up and dressed. Then he asked me if you were busy, or had anybody with you. And I told him, you were not busy; you were doing nothing but drinking a dish of tea. You know, Madam, it was all true; what could I say else?

Companion Poison you, for a dull jade, could not you have

run up first, and have asked your mistress what you should have said?

Susan I might have done so indeed, Madam; but my master came in before I was aware; but what could my mistress have bid me say to such questions as those?

Companion Why, you fool, you, poison you, you might have said your mistress was not at home, could not ye? You know she did not desire to see him.

Susan Madam, I'll serve my mistress as faithfully as anybody; but I can't lie for my mistress.

Companion Can't you, hussy, then poison me, if I'd give sixpence a year for such a servant!

Susan Others will Madam; nay, some ladies will give sixpence a year the more for a servant on that very account, than they will for another.

Companion They are fit for nothing, that can't speak their mistress's mind.

Susan Madam, you'll be pleased to remember, that those servants who will tell a lie for you, will tell a lie to you.

Companion 'Tis no matter for that.

Susan Well, Madam, 'tis my misfortune perhaps, but I can't do it; and if I am not fit for your service, I am for the place I'm in, I hope, and I am very easy; I desire no better a mistress.

Wife Well, what must we do? She has said I am well, I am up, I am dressed, I am at leisure; what can I say next?

Companion Say? Poison him, send him word plainly, you have no business with him, and you won't be spoke with.

Wife Well, let it be so then; go, Sue.

(Susan falls a crying)

Companion What ails the fool?

Wife Go, Sue.

(Sue cries, but does not go)

Companion Can't ye go, ye fool, and deliver the message as your mistress orders you?

Susan If I had as little respect for my mistress as you have, Madam, I could; but I can't see my mistress ruined, and be the messenger to help to bring it to pass.

Companion You are a saucy wench, poison you; if you were my servant, I'd turn you out of doors this minute.

Susan I had rather be turned out of doors than deliver such a message to my master; I wish I had been turned out of doors before I came into your house; I am sure you'll be the ruin of my mistress.

Wife Hold your tongue, and go down, and say as I bid you!

Susan Indeed, Madam, I love your service, and will do anything to oblige you; but I beg you would not let me go of such an errand.

Companion Come, Madam, servants will be saucy, I'll go myself, I warrant you I sent him packing; he shall trouble you no more here. (She goes down)

Susan O dear, Madam, how can you use my master so? (Susan cries)

Wife How do I use him?

Susan Why, to let this devil of a woman go down to hector and bully him, when he comes so kindly to see you? Did not you tell me, Madam, that you only wanted him to come after you, and you would go home again?

Wife Well, but my mind is altered now; that's none of your business.

Susan Such power has bad counsel, madam, where it is listened to! Can this wicked woman be sensible of the mischiefs that will follow this, Madam? Have you not two poor, innocent children at home, left without a mother? Han't you disobliged Sir Richard and all your friends already? And will you provoke your husband without the least occasion, by setting a mad creature to insult him? I beseech you, Madam, consider!

Wife All this is no business of yours, Mistress.

Susan It is true, Madam, 'tis none of my business; but as I am come from your house with you, the world will suppose I have had some hand in the breach, which God knows I abhor; and if I beg my bread, I won't live with any mistress upon such terms. I wish, Madam, you may see your mistake before you are quite ruined; if you please to give me the small matter that is due to me, I'll withdraw, and I hope you won't take it ill.

Wife Well, well, I'll give you your wages by and by.

During this little dialogue, the raving creature, her companion, goes downstairs, and enters into the following discourse with her friend's husband.

Woman Who would you speak with, Sir?

Husband My wife, Madam.

Woman Your wife, Sir, who is that pray?

Husband Mrs. ——, Sir Richard ——'s sister; I suppose she is here.

Woman Yes, Sir, she is here, but she is not to be spoken with.

Husband No, Madam, that's very odd; does she know I am here?

Woman I suppose she does.

Husband Is she not to be spoken with by anybody, or not by me only?

Woman I suppose the latter, Sir.

Husband Pray, Madam, let me ask you one question more: do you deliver her words or your own?

Woman Her words, I assure you, Sir.

Husband Can I speak with Susan, her maid?

Woman I believe not, Sir, I do not know where she is.

Husband But, Madam, you can cause her to be called.

Woman It's true, Sir, but I see no occasion for it; I can deliver any message to your lady.

Husband You seem to treat me in a manner very disobliging; but do you know, Madam, that I have authority to command my wife out of your hands, and that you have no authority to detain her?

Woman I value not your authority; I know you are a Justice of Peace, but that signifies nothing in this case.

Husband If it were not in respect to my wife, I should try it, Madam; I have other power, I assure you, than my own.

(Susan comes by the door)

Woman Sir, my answer is short; your wife says in so many words, she has nothing to say to you, nor will not see you; and I won't have anybody seen here by force.

Husband Susan, Susan, come hither.

Susan Yes, Sir.

Husband Go to the door, and bid George and Goodman Page come to me.

(They come in)

Here Page, you are a constable, seize that woman, and keep her safe, I'll make her *Mittimus** instantly; I'll see, Madam, whether I can't teach you manners, whether I do the rest of the business I come about or no.

(The companion offers to go back and run upstairs)

Constable Nay Madam, you must not go away.

Companion What, in mine own house too?

Husband Yes Madam, better in your own house than anywhere.

Companion I don't value this, nor all the rest you can do.

Husband Susan, you can prove your mistress is in the house, can't you?

* *Mittimus*: a warrant signed by a Justice of the Peace, ordering the keeper of a prison to receive and hold the person specified in the warrant until that person is delivered by due course of law. [Ed.]

Susan Yes, Sir, I come this minute from her, and I am sure my mistress would have come to you, Sir, at first word, if that wicked creature had not hindered her.

(It seems he had had an account from somebody how things went, and how he might expect to be treated; and that a warrant from my Lord Chief Justice might be wanted. So he furnished himself accordingly.)

Husband Well Susan, I'll deal with her well enough; but in the meantime do you go up to your mistress, desire her not to be frightened, I am not come to give her any disturbance; if she would have been pleased to let me speak with her, I should have treated her very kindly. But since she is prevailed upon to be so unkind, I will offer her no violence, though I have power to do it, as you see; nor would I have meddled with this firebrand if she had not treated me rudely.

Susan went up, but before she came her mistress had heard what had passed, and was in a terrible fright; there was a pair of back stairs, and a door at the stairhead, at which she might have got away. But the door was locked, and the servants were all so enraged at her, that though she enquired of them for the key, nobody would give it her. So finding no way to escape, she sat trembling, and expecting every minute her husband, or the constable, should come up and take her away by force.

But he had no mind to expose her so much, nor to disorder her at all, his design being to use all the persuasions and entreaties he could, if possible to bring her to a kind and willing compliance; so he went away, and had Susan tell her, he would come again another day when her surprise was over.

Susan delivered her message with all the comforting expressions to her mistress that she was able. But she had thrown herself on the bed, and would not speak a word. So the cavalcade ended; her husband went away, and the constable kept the lady's companion in custody, and carried her away with him.

She was now left alone, her spirits were in a flame, and she seemed to talk wildly and extravagantly, like one discomposed in the highest degree. Poor Susan, though she was dismissed, would not leave her in that condition, but sat by her all the afternoon, and watched her all night; for Susan was afraid she might do herself some mischief.

But alas, her head run upon worse things; the Devil had lost his agent, and was now fain to do his work himself; and indeed, finding his advantage, he laid hold of it. Her passion, the Devil's best handle, and by which he takes the fastest hold of us all, was in a violent ferment; and nothing was so horrid but she was capable to entertain a notion of it and approve it.

The object of her highest aversion now was her husband; the affront offered her was such that nothing could appease her, nothing be a satisfaction to her; the sleep she took in the night gave no assistance to abate her fury, but she meditated revenge with an implacable and an unalterable resolution.

While she was thus playing with the edged tools of her own passions, dangerous weapons they are, the question presents to her thoughts, what should she do, once or twice, as she owned afterwards? The Devil prompted her to go home to him, and in the night to set the house afire. But she had not courage for that. "No," said she to herself, using her companion's wicked word, "no, poison him; I won't do that, I may burn the children too."

The dreadful word which her profligate companion had used without any meaning, or at least without any thought of mischief, continually rung now in her ears; it only dwelt upon the tongue before; but the subtle Deceiver handed it into her enflamed inclination, and placed it in ambuscade there; it was for some days working up to a height, the words followed her like a voice, "Poison him, poison him!" At first she started at the suggestion, and seemed frighted at the thoughts of such a horrid thing; but he that set it at work, plied it so close, that she thought she heard no other sound for some time, but that: "Poison him, poison him!"; and as her wicked companion had made the ugly unsounding horrid word familiar to her; so her new Tempter began by degrees to make the fact familiar to her also; and first she pored upon the practicableness of the thing, her head run night and day upon the methods of doing it, and of concealing it; she found all easy enough; he that prompted her to do it, presented her with a great variety of practicable schemes; so that finding no great difficulty in the thing, and that it would, as she supposed, answer her end, she came to a point, and in a word, she took up the horrid resolution to *poison her husband.*

It was not long after she had resolved upon this horrid fact, but she prepared for the execution. And one morning, she calls her maid Susan, and with a most complete face of hypocrisy tells her, she had considered her circumstances, and found things were run to such a height, that truly she was loth all the fault of ruining the family should lie upon her; and she could find in her heart, if her husband and she could come to any reasonable conditions, that she might be satisfied she should not be ill-used after it, she would go and live at home again.

"O Madam," says Susan, "if God would put it into your heart, I dare say my master would do anything you should desire of him."

"And will you go to him, Susan, and tell him I desire to speak with him?"

"Yes Madam, with all my heart; I am sure he will come."

"Well Susan, tomorrow morning you shall go."

Susan rejoices, and was so elevated with the thoughts of it, that she did nothing but cry for joy all that afternoon; but little did the poor wench imagine that she was to be the instrument of the Devil, to betray an innocent gentleman to be murthered!

At this meeting, and under the colour of this treaty, did this enraged woman wickedly resolve to give her husband poison in a dish of chocolate, and it seems had furnished herself with the materials for that purpose.

It is hardly possible for anyone that has not been engaged in such dreadful work as this, to express, or indeed to conceive of the horror and confusion of her spirits all that day, and all the night; neither her reason, or her affection, not the natural pity of a mother for her children, or the tenderness of her sex as a woman, took any place with her; but she went to bed, nay and to sleep, with the hellish resolution of destroying her husband; and was so far guilty of intentional murther, as it is possible for anyone to be that had not actually made the attempt.

She had not been long asleep but her disturbed imagination working still upon the same subject, she dreamed herself into the very fact.

She dreamed that her husband came to her, according to the message she had sent by Susan; that she entertained him with a shew of tenderness and kindness; that he kissed her, and told her, he was very sorry she would not see him last time he came; that he had resolved to be reconciled to her, and that the terms should be her own, for he could have no comfort or satisfaction without her; that if she was offended, he would ask her pardon, and would abate all acknowledgment on her part.

In her very dream she fancied her conscience reproached her with the reflection upon her wicked resolution; and bade her ask herself how she could be so treacherous to one, that after all she had done, treated her in so obliging a manner.

Yet it seems she got over it all, for though she did not dream of her actually giving him the poison, and his drinking it; yet, at some distance of time, for she awaked between, she dreamed she saw her husband and her two children lie dead upon the floor, and that somebody asked, how it all happened, and a servant that stood by answered, that nobody could tell; when on a suddain, she thought she saw a black cloud, and heard a voice as loud as thunder out of it, which said, "That wicked woman, his wife, has poisoned him and her own children, let her be taken, and let her be burned."

It is not to be wondered at if she waked in a dreadful fright; she shrieked and cried in such a manner that frighted all the house; the servants rise and come to her, and an ancient woman in particular, that lay near her chamber, came in first, and asked her, what was the matter. When they came in she was sitting upright in her bed, but trembling and staring in a dreadful manner. However, it being some time after her crying out, before they could get out of their beds to come to her, she was thoroughly awake, and had recovered herself so far as to know that it was but a dream, before they asked her what was the matter.

This gave her some immediate relief, and particularly it brought her to so much presence of mind as to conceal the particulars; and when they asked her what it was she dreamed, she said, she dreamed her two children were murthered, which was true.

Though she recovered from her first surprise, yet she remained very ill all the night, and all the next day; and particularly was overwhelmed with melancholly, speaking very little, and receiving no manner of sustenance. Susan stayed with her, and endeavoured to divert her; but she was capable of receiving no comfort from her, and often bid her withdraw, and sit in the next room within call.

In those intervals when Susan had left her, she began to reflect upon herself, and would fly out with such words as these: "What a monster am I? What a length has the Devil gone with me! Murther my husband! What, my own flesh and blood! Nay, and murther my two little dear innocent children! Horrid wretch! It's true, I had not intended to murther them. But would it not have been murthering them, to kill their father? It's true also, I have not murthered him; but I had fully resolved it, my soul had consented to it, and I am as guilty as if I had done it. Nay, I have been murthering him these three weeks past, I have murthered that peace and satisfaction which it was my part to preserve and increase to him; I have tormented and grieved his very soul; I have killed all his joy, all his comfort that he was to have had in a wife; I am a murtherer every way, a vile abominable monster, and murtherer."

Then she gave some vent to her passion by crying; after which, throwing herself on the bed, and her fright and disorder having kept her waking most part of the night, she fell asleep, but in so disordered a manner, and with so much confusion upon her thoughts, that she started every now and then, as if she had been terrified with some apparition.

At length she got up again, and walking about the room, but still confused with strange distraction of thoughts; on a sudden a casual storm happening abroad, it lightened, and a terrible clap of thunder followed; she was so frightened at this, considering the relation it had to the other part of her dream, that she swooned and fell down on the floor, without speaking a word.

Susan, who sat in the next room before, but had come in while she was on the bed, run and took her up, and laid her on the bed again; but it was long ere they brought her to herself. When she began to come to herself, she asked Susan if she heard the thunder.

"Yes, Madam," says Susan, "it was a dreadful thunder; and the lightning was so terrible, Madam," said she, "it frighted me out of my wits."

Mistress But did you hear nothing but thunder, Susan?

Susan No, Madam; what should I hear?

Mistress No, did not you hear a voice?

Susan No, Madam, I should have died away, I'm sure, if I had.

Mistress Well, but I did die away you see, for I'm sure I heard it.

Susan You fright me, Madam; pray what did you hear?

Mistress A dreadful voice, Susan! a dreadful voice, Susan!

By this time she was more composed, and Susan being inquisitive, she put her off; "I don't mean now, Susan," said she, "but in my dream." Susan thought she talked a little wild with the fright, and so said no more.

But now the thunder in her dream came into her thoughts. "Well," says she, "if I had been such a horrible monstrous wretch to have murthered my husband, what a fool had I been also to have thought to conceal it, when a voice from Heaven should proclaim it in thunder and lightning, to my certain destruction." She paused, and then breaks out again, thus.

"Well, there is certainly some mighty Power above, something that knows and sees all we think, or act. I have been a dreadful creature; for there is certainly a God that knows all things, and can discover the most secret designs that we form but in our thoughts. And I never acknowledged him. And what if he should by such a voice, discover now that I intended this bloody thing; then I am undone, and should be the very abhorrence and loathing of all mankind."

She went on awhile in private reflections; at length she breaks out again, "And is there a God!" said she. "How can that be, and I yet alive! Why did not that clap of thunder strike me dead! Sure if he is a just God, he could not suffer me to live, I ought to be brought out and burned, as the voice said of me, for I am a murtherer, a blasphemer, a despiser of God, an enemy both to God and man, a monster, not a reasonable creature."

She lived in these agonies two or three days, when calling Susan to her one morning before she was up, "Dear Susan," says she, "carry me out of this dreadful place."

Susan Carry you out, Madam. Ay, with all my heart.

Mistress But whither shall I go?

Susan Go, Madam! to your own house, and to your own family, Madam, where you will be welcome, I am sure, and where my master longs to have you come.

Mistress Home, Susan! How can I go home? If your master did me justice he would never let me come within his doors again.

Susan Dear Madam, do not afflict yourself, and your family, any more; will you give me leave to let my master know you intend to come home?

Mistress Do what you will, Susan. But if I sleep another night in this wicked place, I shall be frighted to death.

Honest Susan sent her master word of all that had happened, and of all the discourse, by a very trusty messenger. But when the messenger came to his house he was not at home. Susan, uneasy, for fear her mistress's mind should alter, packed up all their things they had, and sending to borrow Sir Richard's coach, gets her mistress, who was now wholly in her disposing, and carries her directly home.

It seems Sir Richard and her husband were gone to deliver the wretch out of custody, who they had taken up, she having humbled herself, and promised to use her endeavour to persuade the other lady to return home; and it seems she came home to her house just as Susan was helping her mistress down stairs. She sent Susan word, she would speak with her mistress before she went. But Susan bad the servant tell her, that her mistress had nothing to say to her. So she came away, brought her mistress home, carried her upstairs in her arms, for she was very ill, and put her to bed.

When she had done thus, she sent far and near for her master, but he could not be found a good while, which perplexed Susan very much. But at last her master came home, and Sir Richard with him.

Her master had but just patience to hear Susan tell part of her story, and then run upstairs to his wife. She was so weak she could hardly raise herself upon the bed; but she took him in her arms, asked him pardon in the most passionate terms, till he could bear it no longer; and till he obliged her to say not a word more of it. He told her, Sir Richard was below. "My dear," says she, "I am not able to speak to him now; but tell him, I am sensible I have used him very ill; and I will ask him pardon, and my Lady too."

Sir Richard would fain have seen her; but she desired to be excused for that night, for she was very ill and desired a little rest.

She was now brought home to her family; but as this was not done till she was touched from Heaven with a sense of her sins, so it was evident in her, that the first effect of real conviction, is an immediate return to a sense of duty. She had broke over all the obligations and bounds of her conjugal relation, as a consequence of her rebellion against God; and as soon as ever she was struck with a sense of her sin against God, it carried her immediately back into the course of her relative duty.

* * *

Religious Courtship

Religious Courtship was published in 1722, Defoe's annus mirabilis that also produced *Moll Flanders*, *A Journal of the Plague Year*, and *Colonel Jack*. Treating one particular aspect of family relations, *Religious Courtship* belongs in the same general category of didactic work as Defoe's *Family Instructors*. Although it had a slow start, not reaching a second edition until 1729, it was ultimately successful, by 1789 in its twenty-first edition.[1]

Selection of a marriage partner, one of the most important decisions in the private life of an individual, depends upon methods that are closely related to the type of family structure currently prevalent in the social group to which the individual belongs. As Lawrence Stone points out, in England during the sixteenth and seventeenth centuries, when paternal absolutism was the usual type of family structure, particularly among the higher ranks of society, family interest and authoritarian control of parents over the marital choices of their children were taken for granted.[2]

With the spread of the Protestant idea of holy matrimony, however, attitudes about the making of marital arrangements slowly began to change. In order for a couple to develop the mutual affection now believed essential for a good marriage, some prior sympathy between the two was conceded to be necessary. Thus the idea that a child of either sex must be permitted the right of veto over a spouse chosen by parents eventually became accepted by the end of the seventeenth century.[3]

Nevertheless, the dissemination of this idea through English society varied in speed according to social level and class. Among those at the bottom of society, whose parents had little property to leave them, and who in any case usually "left home at the age of ten to fourteen in order to become apprentices, domestic servants, or living-in labourers in other people's houses,"[4] freedom was greatest. As Defoe pointed out, "Persons of a lower station are, generally speaking, much more happy in their marriages than princes and persons of distinction. So I take much of it, if not all, to consist in the advantage they have to choose and refuse."[5] But at the upper levels of society, especially among the highest aristocracy, where a great deal of property and power was involved in the marital choice, the right of veto was only very slowly conceded to children.

According to Stone, the vanguard for the change of consciousness among the upper classes in the late seventeenth century consisted of the wealthy bourgeois and the professional classes, and spokesmen from these groups disseminated their ideas to the gentry and squirarchy in the early eighteenth century.[6] Quoting from fashionable playwrights and writers like Addison, Astell, Behn, Fielding and Richardson, Stone concludes, "This literary evidence shows that there was a prolonged public argument during the late seventeenth and eighteenth centuries about a child's freedom of choice of a marriage partner, with more liberal views slowly but steadily becoming more common among authors catering both to the middling ranks of commercial and professional people, and also to the wealthy landed classes."[7]

Yet economic, occupational, and geographical classifications do not completely account for the rate of dissemination of the new attitude about children's rights in choosing their marital partners. A complicating factor, cutting across the various segments of the urban middle class, professionals and country gentry, was that of religion. As Stone observes, two of the legacies of Puritanism to the secular society that eventually succeeded the collapse of the Puritan experiment of 1640 to 1660 were "respect for the individual conscience directed by God" in an otherwise repressive and authoritarian movement, and the "need for holy matrimony". The first legacy could not but "induce a respect for personal autonomy in other aspects of life", and the second "was ultimately incompatible with patriarchal authority which [Puritans] also extolled". Stone concludes, "The concession of some element of choice was an inevitable by-product of such thinking, and it is no accident that it was the late seventeenth-century nonconformists who led the way in demanding freedom for children in the choice of spouse."[8]

The public interest in these concepts—some freedom of choice for children and the importance of personal affection in marital arrangements—among the urban middle and upper middle classes, professionals, and country gentry, combined with the acceptance of the concepts by nonconformists of all classes, throws a new light on the social character of Defoe's audience. Although the 1715 *Family Instructor*, addressed to the middle ranks of the urban middle class, was more popular than his 1718 *Family Instructor*, addressed to the urban upper middle class and country gentry, the 1718 volume must have been successful enough for Defoe to address the same readership in 1722 with *Religious Courtship*. The father of the marriageable girls in this work is a prosperous retired merchant, a member of the urban upper middle class, yet he is related to the squirarchy. Probably Defoe pictured him as one of the younger sons of the gentry apprenticed for their profession to merchants, for the father's late brother-in-law was a Sir James, a huntsman who kept hounds. One of the suitors of the daughters is a lord of the manor whom Defoe describes conversing not only with a poor tenant but also with a nobleman. The gist of their conversation, similar to conversation in Defoe's posthumous *Compleat English Gentleman*, is that religion, far from demeaning a gentleman, is his ornament.

Since *Religious Courtship* enjoyed a steady popularity in the eighteenth century, it seems significant that the right of the daughters to exercise a veto over their father's choice of suitor is accepted by everyone in the story, including the father himself. The real conflict is over the motives for marriage: that the suitors be attractive to the daughters is as much taken for granted as that they be financially acceptable; but that the quality of attractiveness must include religious compatibility as well as a pleasant personality, good manners, and physical presentability is the point of

Defoe's polemic. The success of *Religious Courtship* argues that certain of its assumptions must have been acceptable to its readers; but since the 1749 *Clarissa Harlowe* of Richardson and *Tom Jones* of Fielding reveal that a battle was still raging about motives and methods of marital arrangements, *Religious Courtship* may well have owed some of its popularity to the conservative attitude toward family religion it expressed. Although Stone points out that by the early eighteenth century the old-fashioned practice of family worship was well on the decline,[9] apparently this was not necessarily so, not only among Dissenters, but also among the socially conservative squirarchy. (See page 421)

The values of *Religious Courtship* are also pertinent to a reassessment of the popular notion that Defoe was primarily a spokesman for the urban lower middle class. As Stone emphasizes, "the lower middle class seems to have accepted one aspect of the new ideas, namely that the choice should lie with the children, but rejected the other, that prior affection rather than financial gain and prudent calculation should be the basis of the choice."[10]

In addition to the questions it raises about the dissemination of new social ideas and old religious values among the squirarchy and about Defoe's contribution as a writer to this class, *Religious Courtship* is of great literary interest. Like the 1718 *Family Instructor*, it anticipates his 1724 fiction, *Roxana*. The excerpt chosen centres on a jewelled cross, which belongs to a small but significant family of sinister objects in Defoe's writing: the necklace stolen by Moll Flanders from the innocent child she contemplates murdering, a diamond necklace fastened around Roxana's neck by her prince in an ambiguously painful gesture of love, the jewelled portrait of Queen Anne in the 1717 Mesnager *Minutes*, and a diamond necklace stolen from a child in a nightmare recounted by Defoe in his 1726 *Political History of the Devil* and his 1727 *Essay on the History and Reality of Apparitions*. In *Religious Courtship*, Defoe's concentration upon the diamond cross serves to magnify the object, suggesting that it has some vitality of its own, greater than that of the human beings associated with it.

The sombre atmosphere of the scenes described in the excerpt is due to the condition of the Protestant wife, who seems to have been trapped in a nightmarish state of paralysis while her husband was living, deprived not only of power over, but even of understanding of the external world. Significantly, she fails to understand what is being said on several important occasions: when her husband places the sinister jewel around her neck he keeps it in his hand so that she cannot see it, "saying something in Italian, which [she] did not understand," and when the Venetians dine at her house, she cannot understand much of their conversation, for it is in Italian.

Vulnerable through her wearing the cross to the "attacks" of her husband, of Catholic passers-by in the street, of the Venetian ambassador and his retinue, she begins to feel that the object to which they all pay homage has some occult power over her, that "the glittering jewel [has] a strange influence" on her. Concern of others about her religious salvation becomes an evil. The attempts of Catholics to convert her are presented as a form of persecution; even her husband's great affection for her is sinister and dangerous: "The more he loves her, the stronger are the bonds by which he draws her."

Her passivity is suggested by the very language of the scene, which is notable for the absence of concrete, homely nouns. The reasoning that takes place is of a different kind from Defoe's usual attempts to analyze and to translate words or abstract concepts. We note, for instance, that the widows's father and older sister attempt to divest the dead husband's gifts to his wife of emotional influence, the father by observing that they belong to an estate whose value can be calculated, the sister by assigning the necklace a monetary value. The widow, however, resists accepting this point of view, which would demystify the gifts by considering them in their material aspect alone. She herself attempts, when reasoning with her husband, to separate the religious from the affective value of the jewelled cross: "I told him, I hoped I should not undervalue it as his present, if he did not overvalue it upon any other account." But her husband's subtlety is "too hard" for her; he replies in an ambiguous and equivocal phrase that "the last is impossible".

The equivocation apparent in the husband's response is typical of the whole scene, in that the polite and ceremonious attentions of the husband, the Catholic passers-by, the Venetian ambassador, serve to disguise their designs on the Protestant's soul, and to make these designs more dangerous than usual because more subtle and difficult to counter: "... the ambassador and all his retinue paid so many bows and homages to me, or to the cross, that I scarce knew what to do with myself, nor was I able to distinguish their good manners from their religion." The combination of equivocal motives—the husband means well by his wife, but conversion to Catholicism, good in his eyes, is evil in hers—and of a discrepancy between the ceremonious talk and the ulterior motives of such talk, is highly sinister.

In this excerpt from *Religious Courtship*, therefore, the undertone in Defoe's works referred to on page 28 above and emphasized at the ends of the politics and history sections is clearly audible. Individual elements contributing to this undertone, as we have seen, are heard most frequently in those of his writings directed at the higher social classes. Personal experience may have contributed to this association in Defoe's mind between indirect ways and the upper classes, for the country gentleman Defoe knew so well was popularly called "Robin the Trickster"; indeed, Robert Harley, the behind-the-scenes hero of the Mesnager *Minutes*, is depicted by Defoe as the King of tricksters.

The Catholic husband of *Religious Courtship* is a devious manipulator, belonging to the same category as that of the Jacobite gentleman of the Court of St. Germains and the Machiavellian M. Mesnager. Smooth, urbane, and intellectually complex, in contrast to the more numerous Defoean class of plain speakers and plain dealers represented in *Religious Courtship* by the father and sisters of the widow, his courtly exterior conceals sinister designs.

The widow, attracted to her husband, but belonging by birth and by nurture to a forthright family, can almost be regarded as a surrogate for Defoe himself—the Defoe originally designated for the Dissenting ministry but lured away by the glittering world; the Defoe whose affection and respect for his upright classmates and co-religionists were tinged with contempt for their intellects; the Defoe who amidst the quicksands of politics longed for the solid verities of numbers in economics and precepts in religion and morals; the Defoe whose plain speakers are in the final analysis no match for his devious manipulators. Viewed in this light, one of the secrets of Defoe's peculiarly elusive personality may well be an unstable sense of self resulting from his inability to reconcile his two very different modes of thought: on the one hand, that of the legitimate son of his family background, his education, and his readers' desire for plain dealers; on the other, that of the illegitimate offspring of his penetrating and wide-ranging powers of empathy and observation.

Notes

1 William Lee, *Daniel Defoe: His Life, and Recently Discovered Writings* (London: John Camden Holten, 1869), I, 357.

2 Lawrence Stone, *The Family, Sex and Marriage in England 1500–1800* (New York: Harper and Row, 1977), pp. 180–193.

3 *Ibid.*, p. 190.

4 *Ibid.*, p. 192.

5 *Complete English Tradesman*, p. 26. Quoted by Stone, p. 326.

6 Stone, pp. 274–7.

7 *Ibid.*, pp. 280–1.

8 *Ibid.*, pp. 262–3.

9 *Ibid.*, p. 244.

10 *Ibid.*, p. 288.

Religious Courtship
Of Husbands and Wives being of the Same Opinions in Religion with One Another
(1722)

* * *

Widow Why you know, Sister, Mr. —— was a very serious grave man; and I assure you, in his way he was very devout; and this made his yielding to me sometimes to be very difficult to him; he had very strong struggles between his principles and his affection.

Elder Sister Dear Sister, it is always so where there are differing opinions between a man and his wife; the more zealous and conscientious they are in their several ways, the more difficult it is for them to yield those points up to one another, which kindness and affection may incline them to give up. But pray give us a little account of your first disputes about these things.

Widow 'Tis a sad story, Sister, and will bring many grievous things to remembrance.

Elder Sister I should be very unwilling to impose so irksome a task upon you; but I think it will be very instructing to us all.

* * *

Elder Sister Did he never go about to bribe you to it?

Widow O Sister! very frequently; and that with all the subtlety of invention in the world; for he was always giving me presents upon that very account.

Father Presents to a wife! what do they signify? 'Tis but taking his money out of one pocket, and putting it into the other; they must all be appraised, Child, in the personal estate.

Widow It has been quite otherwise with him indeed, Sir; for he has made it a clause in his will, that all the presents he gave me shall be my own, to bestow how I please; besides all the rest that he has left me more than he was obliged to do.

Elder Sister Then they seem to be considerable.

Widow He has, first and last, given me above 3,000 l. in presents, and most of them on this very account; but one was very extraordinary, I mean to that purpose.

Elder Sister I suppose that is your diamond cross?

Widow It is so; he brought it home in a little case, and coming into my room one morning before I was dressed, hearing I was alone, he told me smiling and very pleasant, he was come to say his prayers to me. I confess I had been a little out of humour just at that time, having been full of sad thoughts all the morning about the grand point, and I was going to have given him a very unkind answer; but his looks had so much goodness and tenderness always in them, that when I looked up at him, I could retain no more resentment. Indeed, Sister, it was impossible to be angry with him.

Elder Sister You might well be in humour indeed, when he brought you a present worth above six hundred pounds.

Widow But I had not seen the present, when what I am telling you passed between us.

Elder Sister Well, I ask pardon for interrupting you; pray go on where you left off, when he told you he was come to say his prayers to you.

Widow I told him I hoped he would not make an idol of his wife.

Elder Sister Was that the ill-natured answer you were about to give him?

Widow No indeed; I was a going to tell him, he need not worship me, he had idols enough in the house.

Elder Sister That had been bitter and unkind indeed; I hope you did not say so?

Widow Indeed I did not; nor would I have said so for a thousand pound; it would have grieved me every time I had reflected on it afterwards as long as I had lived.

Elder Sister It was so very apt a return, I dare say I should not have brought my prudence to have mastered the pleasure of such a repartee.

Widow Dear Sister, 'tis a sorry pleasure that is taken in grieving a kind husband; besides, Sister, as it was my great mercy that my husband strove constantly to make his difference in religion as little troublesome and offensive to me as possible, it would very ill have become me to make it my jest; it had been a kind of bespeaking the uneasinesses which it was my happiness to avoid.

Elder Sister Well, you had more temper than I should have had, I dare say; but I must own you were in the right. Come, pray how did you go on?

Widow Why, he answered, he hoped he worshipped no idols but me, and if he erred, in that point, whoever reproved him, he hoped I would not.

Elder Sister Why that's true too; besides, 'tis not so often that men make idols of their wives.

Widow Well, while he was saying this, he pulls out the jewel, and opening the case, takes a small crimson string that it hung to, and put it about my neck, but kept the jewel in his hand, so that I could not see it; and then taking me in his arms, "Sit down, my dear", says he, which I did upon a little stool; then he kneeled down just before me, and kissing the jewel, let it go, saying something in Italian, which I did not understand; and then looking up in my face, "Now, my dear," says he, "you are my idol."

Elder Sister Well, Sister, 'tis well he is dead.

Widow Dear Sister, how can you say such words to me?

Elder Sister He would certainly have conquered you at last.

Widow If the tenderest and most engaging temper, the sincerest and warmest affection in nature could have done it, he would have done it, that's certain.

Elder Sister And I make no doubt but they are the most dangerous weapons to attack a woman's principles; I cannot but think them impossible to resist; passion, unkindness, and all sorts of conjugal violence, of which there is a great variety in a married life, are all nothing to them; you remember, Sister, some lines on another occasion, but very much to the case,

Force may indeed the heart invade,
But kindness only can persuade.

Widow I grant that 'tis difficult to resist the influence of so much affection, and everything that came from so sincere a principle, and to a mind prepossessed with all the sentiments of tenderness and kindness possible to be expressed, made a deep impression, but I thank God I stood my ground.

Elder Sister Well, well, you would not have stood it long I am persuaded; and this is one of the great hazards a woman runs in marrying a man of a differing religion, or a differing opinion from herself, *viz.* that her affection to her husband is her worst snare; and so that which is her duty and her greatest happiness, is made the most dangerous gulph she can fall into; well might our dear mother warn us from marrying men of different opinions.

Widow It is very true, I acknowledge it; my love was my temptation; my affection to my husband went always nearest to stagger my resolution; I was in no danger upon any other account.

Younger Sister Well, but pray go on about the jewel; what said you to him?

Widow Truly, Sister, I'll be very plain with you. When he kissed the jewel on his knees, and muttered as I tell you, in Italian, I was rather provoked, than obliged; and I said, "I think you are saying your prayers indeed, my dear; tell me what are you doing? what did you say?"

Younger Sister Indeed I should have been frighted.

Widow Dear Sister, let me confess to you, fine presents, flattering words, and the affectionate looks of so obliging, so dear, and so near a relation are dreadful things, when they assault principles; the glittering jewel had a strange influence, and my affections began to be too partial on his side. O let no woman that values her soul venture into the arms of a husband of a differing religion! The kinder he is, the more likely to undo her; everything that indears him to her doubles her danger; the more she loves him, the more she inclines to yield to him; the more he loves her, the stronger are the bonds, by which he draws her; and her only mercy would be to have him barbarous and unkind to her.

Younger Sister It is indeed a sad case, where to be miserable is the only safety; but so it is no doubt, and such is the case of every woman that is thus unsuitably matched; if her husband is kind, he is a snare to her; if unkind, he is a terror to her; his love, which is his duty, is her ruin, and his slighting her, which is his scandal, is her protection.

Widow It was my case, dear sister; such a jewel! such a husband! How could I speak an unkind word? Everything he did was so engaging, everything he said was so moving, what could I say or do?

Elder Sister Very true; and that makes me say, he would have conquered you at last.

Widow Indeed I can't tell what he might have done if he had lived.

Younger Sister Well, but to the jewel: what said you to him?

Widow I stood up and thanked him, with a kind of ceremony; but told him, I wished it had been rather in any other form. "Why, my dear," says he, "should not the two most valuable forms in the world be placed together?" I told him, that as he placed a religious value upon it, he should have it rather in another place. He told me, my breast should be his altar; and so he might adore with a double delight. I told him, I thought he was a little prophane; and since I did not place the same value upon it, or make the same use of it, as he did, I might give him offence by meer necessity, and make that difference which we had both avoided with so much care, break in upon us in a case not to be resisted. He answered, "No, my dear, I am not going to bribe your principles, much less force them. Put you what value you think fit upon it, and give me the like liberty." I told him, I hoped I should not undervalue it as his present, if he did not overvalue it upon another account. He returned warmly, "My dear, the last is impossible; and for the first 'tis a trifle; give it but leave to hang where I have placed it, that's all the respect I ask you to shew it on my account."

Younger Sister Well, that was a favour you would not deny if a stranger had given it you.

Widow Dear Sister, you are a stranger to the case; if you had seen what was the consequence of it, you would have been frighted, or perhaps have fallen quite out with him.

Younger Sister I cannot imagine what consequences you mean.

Widow Why, first of all, he told me, that now he would be perfectly easy about my salvation, and would cease to pursue me with arguments or intreaties in religious matters.

Younger Sister What could he mean by that?

Widow Why he said, he was sure that blessed form that hung so near my heart, would have a miraculous influence some time or other, and I should be brought home into the bosom of the Catholick Church.

Younger Sister Well, I should have ventured all that, and have slighted the very thoughts of it.

Widow You cannot imagine what stress he laid on it; now, he said, every good Catholick that saw me but pass by them, would pray for me; and every one in particular would exorcise me by the passion of Christ out of the chains of heresy.

Younger Sister What said you to him?

Widow I put it off with a smile, but my heart was full, I scarce knew how to hold; and he perceived it easily, and broke off the talk a little; but he fell to it again, till he saw the tears stood in my eyes, when he took me in his arms, and kissed me again; kissed my neck where the cross hung, and then kissed the jewel, repeating the word *Jesu* two or three times, and left me.

Elder Sister This was all superstition, Sister, I should not have born it, I would have thrown the jewel in his face, or on the ground, and have set my foot upon it.

Widow No, Sister, you would not have done so I am sure; neither was it my business to do so; my business was not to quarrel with my husband about his religion, which it was now too late to help, but to keep him from being uneasy about mine.

Elder Sister I should not have had so much patience; I would not have lived with him; I do not think it had been my duty.

Widow Nay, Sister, that's expressly contrary to the Scripture, where this very case is stated in the plainest manner imaginable; "The woman that hath a husband which believeth not, if he will dwell with her, let her not leave him." I Cor. vii. 13.

Elder Sister That is true indeed; I spoke rashly, Sister, in that; but it was a case, I confess, I do not know what I should have done in it; I would not have wore it then.

Widow That had been very disobliging.

Elder Sister I would have obliged him to have forborn his little idolatrous tricks then, and used them on other occasions.

Widow That had been to desire him not to be a Roman Catholick. Why, in foreign countries, that are Popish, as I understand, they never go by a cross, whether it be on the road, or on any building, but they pull off their hats.

Father So they do, my dear, and often kneel down, though it be in the dirt, and say over their prayers.

Widow It is impossible to tell you how many attacks I had of that kind when I wore this jewel.

Father I do not doubt it; especially if he brought any strangers into the room. How did you do, Child, when the Venetian ambassador dined at your house? Had you it on then?

Widow Yes, Sir, my spouse desired me to put it on, and I could not well deny him. But I did not know how to behave; for the ambassador and all his retinue paid so many bows and homages to me, or to the cross, that I scarce knew what to do with myself, nor was I able to distinguish their good manners from their religion; and it was well I did not then understand Italian, for, as my dear told me afterwards, they said a great many religious things that would have given me offence.

Father Those things are so frequent in Italy, that the

Protestant ladies take no notice of them, and yet they all wear crosses, but sometimes put them out of sight.

Widow I did so afterwards; I lengthened the string it hung to, that it might hang a little lower, but it was too big; if it went within my stays, it would hurt me; nor was it much odds to him; for if he saw the string, he knew the cross was there, and it was all one.

Younger Sister Did he use any ceremony to it after the first time?

Widow Always, when he first came into any room where I was, he was sure to give me his knee with his bow, and kiss the cross as well as his wife.

Elder Sister I should never have born it.

Widow You could never have resisted it any more than I, for I did what I could; but his answer was clear: "My dear," says he, "take no notice of me, let my civilities be to you; take them all to yourself, I cannot shew you too much respect; believe it is all your own, and be easy with me."

Elder Sister How could he bid you believe, what you knew to be otherwise? Why did you not leave it off, and reproach him with the difference?

Widow Dear Sister, I did so for months together. But then he doubled his ceremonies, and told me, I only mortified him then by obliging him to reverence the place where once the blessed figure had been lodged, as the holy pilgrims worshipped the Sepulchre.

Elder Sister He was too hard for you every way, Sister.

Widow Ay, and would have been too hard for you too, if you had had him.

* * *

BIBLIOGRAPHY

PRIMARY SOURCES:

Collections

Aitken, George A., ed. *Romances and Narratives*. 16 vols. London: Dent, 1895.

Maynadier, G. H., ed. *The Works of Daniel Defoe*. 16 vols. New York: George D. Sproul, 1903–4.

Shakespeare Head edition. *Novels and Selected Writings*. 14 vols. Oxford: Basil Blackwell, 1927–28.

Editions: Non-Fiction

Bülbring, Karl, ed. *The Compleat English Gentleman*. London: David Nutt, 1890.

——. *Of Royall Education*. London: David Nutt, 1895.

Cole, G. D. H. and Browning, D. C., eds. *A Tour through the Whole Island of Great Britain*. 2 vols. Everyman's library. London: Dent, 1962.

Healey George Harris, ed. *The Letters of Daniel Defoe*. Oxford: Clarendon Press, 1955.

——. *The Meditations of Daniel Defoe*. Cummington, Mass.: The Cummington Press, 1946.

Secord, Arthur W., ed. *Defoe's Review*. 22 vols. New York: Facsimile Text Society, 1938.

Editions: Fiction (Oxford English Novels Series)

Boulton, James T., ed. *Memoirs of a Cavalier*. London: Oxford University Press, 1972.

Crowley, J. Donald, ed. *Robinson Crusoe*. London: Oxford University Press, 1972.

Jack, Jane, ed. *Roxana*. London: Oxford University Press, 1964.

Kumar, Shiv K., ed. *Captain Singleton*. London: Oxford University Press, 1969.

Landa, Louis, ed. *A Journal of the Plague Year*. London: Oxford University Press, 1969.

Monk, Samuel Holt, ed. *Colonel Jack*. London: Oxford University Press, 1965.

Starr, G. A., ed. *Moll Flanders*. London: Oxford University Press, 1971.

Anthologies

Boulton, James T., ed. *Daniel Defoe*. London: B. T. Batsford, 1965.

Shugrue, Michael F., ed. *Selected Poetry and Prose of Daniel Defoe*. Rinehart

Editions. New York: Holt, Rinehart and Winston, 1968.
Sutherland, James, ed. *Robinson Crusoe and Other Writings*. Riverside Editions. Boston: Houghton-Mifflin, 1968.

Other works by Defoe were read either in their first editions or in microform.

SECONDARY SOURCES: BOOKS

Aitken, George A. *The Life of Richard Steele*. London: William Isbister, 1889.
Ashton, T. S. *An Economic History of England: The Eighteenth Century*. London: Methuen, 1966.
Baine, Rodney M. *Daniel Defoe and the Supernatural*. Athens, Georgia: Univ. of Georgia Press, 1968.
Baynes, John. *The Jacobite Rising of 1715*. London: Cassell, 1970.
Bernbaum, Ernest. *The Mary Carleton Narratives, 1663–1673*. Cambridge, Mass.: Harvard Univ. Press, 1914.
Beyer, Abel. *The History of the Reign of Queen Anne, Digested into Annals*. London: 1703–13.
Biddle, Sheila. *Bolingbroke and Harley*. London: Allen & Unwin, 1974.
Bowden, Peter J. *The Wool Trade in Tudor and Stuart England*. London: Macmillan, 1962.
Buck, Philip W. *The Politics of Mercantilism*. New York: H. Holt, 1942.
Butterfield, H. *The Englishman and His History*. London: Cambridge Univ. Press, 1944.
——. *The Whig Interpretation of History*. London: G. Bell & Sons, 1931.
Clapham, John. *The Bank of England*. Vol. I: *1694–1797*. 2 vols. Cambridge: The University Press, 1945.
Clark, G. N. *Guide to English Commercial Statistics 1696–1782*. London: Office of the Royal Historical Society, 1938.
Clark, George. *The Later Stuarts, 1660–1714*. 2nd ed. Oxford: Clarendon Press, 1955.
Clifford, James L., ed. *Man Versus Society in Eighteenth-Century Britain*. Cambridge: at the Univ. Press, 1968.
Coombs, Douglas. *The Conduct of the Dutch*. The Hague: Martinus Nijhoff, 1958.
Davis, Dorothy. *Fairs, Shops and Supermarkets*. Toronto: Univ. of Toronto Press, 1966.
Deane, Phyllis and Cole, W. A. *British Economic Growth 1688–1959, Trends and Structure*. 2nd ed. First paperback edition. London: Cambridge Univ. Press, 1969.
Dickson, P. G. M. *The Financial Revolution in England*. London: Macmillan, 1967.
Dottin, Paul. *Daniel Defoe et ses Romans*. 3 vols. in 1. Paris: Les presses universitaires de France, 1924.
Downie, J. A. "Daniel Defoe's *Review* and Other Political Writings in the Reign of Queen Anne". Master's Diss. Newcastle upon Tyne, 1973.
——. "Robert Harley and the Press". Ph.D. Diss. Newcastle upon Tyne, 1976.
Earle, Peter. *The World of Defoe*. London: Weidenfeld & Nicolson, 1976.
Ehrenpreis, Irvin. *The Personality of Jonathan Swift*. London: Methuen & Co., 1958.
——. *Swift: The Man, His Works, His Age*. Vol. I. London: Methuen & Co.,

1962. Vol. II. London: Methuen & Co., 1967.
Elliott, Robert C., ed. *Twentieth Century Interpretations of Moll Flanders*. A Spectrum Book. Englewood Cliffs, New Jersey: Prentice-Hall, 1970.
Ellis, Frank H., ed. *Twentieth Century Interpretations of Robinson Crusoe*. A Spectrum Book. Englewood Cliffs, New Jersey: Prentice-Hall, 1969.
Ewald, William Bragg, Jr. *The Masks of Jonathan Swift*. Cambridge, Mass.: Harvard Univ. Press, 1954.
Feiling, Keith. *A History of the Tory Party*. Oxford: Clarendon, 1924.
Furniss, Edgar S. *The Position of the Laborer in a System of Nationalism*. Boston and New York: Houghton Mifflin, 1920.
Fussell, Paul. *The Rhetorical World of Augustan Humanism*. Oxford: Clarendon Press, 1965.
George, M. Dorothy. *London Life in the Eighteenth Century*. London: Kegan Paul & Co., 1925.
Giuseppi, John. *The Bank of England*. London: Evans Bros., 1966.
Goldgar, Bertrand A. *The Curse of Party*. Lincoln: Univ. of Nebraska Press, 1961.
——. *Walpole and the Wits*. Lincoln: Univ. of Nebraska Press, 1976.
Hanson, Laurence. *Government and the Press 1695–1763*. London: Oxford Univ. Press, 1936.
Hargevik, Stieg. *The Disputed Assignment of 'Memoirs of an English Officer' to Daniel Defoe*. Stockholm: Almquist and Wiksell, 1974.
Harris, Frances Marjorie. "A Study of the Paper War Relating to the Career of the 1st Duke of Marlborough, 1710–1712". Ph.D. Diss. London, 1975.
Heckscher, Eli F. *The Continental System*. Ed. Harald Westergaard. Oxford: Clarendon Press, 1922.
——. *Mercantilism*. Trans. Mendel Shapiro. Revised ed. E. F. Söderlund. 2 vols. London: Allen, 1955.
Hill, B. W. *The Growth of Parliamentary Parties, 1689–1742*. London: Allen & Unwin, 1976.
Hill, Christopher. *Reformation to Industrial Revolution*. Vol. II of *The Pelican Economic History of Britain*. Revised ed. Suffolk: Pelican Books, 1969.
Holmes, Geoffrey, ed. *Britain after the Glorious Revolution, 1689–1714*. London: Macmillan, 1969.
Holmes, Geoffrey. *British Politics in the Age of Anne*. London: Macmillan, 1967.
——. *The Trial of Doctor Sacheverell*. London: Eyre Methuen, 1973.
Hoselitz, Bert, ed. *Theories of Economic Growth*. New York: The Free Press, 1960.
Huizinga, J. *Homo Ludens*. Trans. R. F. C. Hull. London: Routledge and Kegan Paul, 1949.
Hunter, J. Paul. *The Reluctant Pilgrim*. Baltimore: Johns Hopkins Press, 1966.
Jeannin, Pierre. *L'Europe du nord-ouest et du nord aux XVIIe et XVIIIe Siècles*. Paris: Presses universitaires de France, 1969.
Johnson, E. A. J. *Predecessors of Adam Smith*. New York: Prentice-Hall, 1937.
——. *Some Origins of the Modern Economic World*. New York: Macmillan, 1936.
Joyce, James. *Daniel Defoe*. Trans. Joseph Prescott. Buffalo: State Univ. of New York, 1964.
Kennett, White. *A Complete History of England*. 3 vols. London: 1706.
Kenyon, J. P. *The Stuarts*. New York: Macmillan, 1959.
Kramnick, Isaac. *Bolingbroke and His Circle*. Cambridge, Mass.: Harvard Univ. Press, 1968.

Laprade, William Thomas. *Public Opinion and Politics in Eighteenth-Century England to the Fall of Walpole*. New York: Macmillan Co., 1936.
Laslett, Peter. *The World We Have lost*. London: Methuen, 1965.
Lee, William. *Daniel Defoe, His Life and Recently Discovered Writings Extending from 1716 to 1729*. 3 vols. London: J. C. Hotten, 1869.
Lipson, E. *The Economic History of England*. Vols. II and III: *The Age of Mercantilism*. 12th ed. 3 vols. London: Black, 1961–62.
——. *The History of the Woollen and Worsted Industries*. London: Cass, 1965.
Londo, Richard J., ed. "Arthur Maynwaring's *Medley* Papers: An Annotated Edition". Ph.D. Diss. Wisconsin, 1974.
Luttrell, Narcissus. *A Brief Historical Relation of State Affairs*. Oxford: Univ. Press, 1857.
Marshall, Dorothy. *English People in the Eighteenth Century*. London: Longmans, Green, 1956.
Maynwaring, Arthur. *Four Letters to a Friend in North Britain*. London: 1710.
McInnes, Angus. *Robert Harley, Puritan Politician*. London: Gollancz, 1970.
Moore, John Robert. *A Checklist of the Writings of Daniel Defoe*. Indiana Univ. Humanities Series No. 47. Bloomington: Indiana Univ. Press, 1960.
——. *A Checklist of the Writings of Daniel Defoe*. 2nd ed. Hamden, Conn.: Archon Books, 1971.
——. *Daniel Defoe: Citizen of the Modern World*. Chicago: Univ. of Chicago Press, 1958.
——. *Daniel Defoe and Modern Economic Theory*. Indiana University Studies, No. 104. Bloomington: Indiana Univ. Press, 1935.
Nicholson, T. C. and Turberville, A. S. *Charles Talbot, Duke of Shrewsbury*. Cambridge: Cambridge Univ. Press, 1930.
Novak, Maximillian E. *Defoe and the Nature of Man*. London: Oxford Univ. Press, 1963.
——. *Economics and the Fiction of Daniel Defoe*. Berkeley: Univ. of California Press, 1962.
Oldmixon, John. *The Life and Posthumous Works of Arthur Maynwaring*. London: 1715.
Peterson, Spiro, ed. *The Counterfeit Lady Unveiled and Other Criminal Fiction of Seventeenth Century England*. Anchor Books. New York: Doubleday, 1961.
Plant, Marjorie. *The English Book Trade*. London: Allen & Unwin, 1974.
Plumb, J. H. *The Death of the Past*. London: Macmillan, 1969.
——. *In the Light of History*. London: Allen Lane, 1972.
——. *Men and Centuries*. Boston: Houghton Mifflin Co., 1963.
——. *The Origins of Political Stability*. Boston: Houghton Mifflin, 1967.
——. *Sir Robert Walpole: The Making of a Statesman*. London: The Cresset Press, 1956.
——. *Sir Robert Walpole, the King's Minister*. Vol. II. Boston: Houghton Mifflin, 1961.
Richetti, John J. *Popular fiction before Richardson*. Oxford: Clarendon Press, 1969.
——. *Defoe's Narratives*. Oxford: Clarendon Press, 1975.
Robbins, Caroline. *The Eighteenth-Century Commonwealthman*. Cambridge, Mass.: Harvard Univ. Press, 1959.
Roberts, Clayton. *The Growth of Responsible Government in Stuart England*. Cambridge: at the Univ. Press, 1966.
Rogers, Pat, ed. *Defoe: The Critical Heritage*. London: Routledge & Kegan Paul, 1972.
——. *Grub Street: Studies in a Subculture*. London: Methuen, 1972.

Roscoe, E. S. *Robert Harley, Earl of Oxford*. London: Methuen, 1902.
Ross, John F. *Swift and Defoe*. Berkeley: Univ. of California Press, 1941.
Schumpeter, Joseph A. *History of Economic Analysis*. Ed. Elizabeth Boody Schumpeter. London: George Allen & Unwin, 1955.
Scott, W. R. *The Constitution and Finance of English, Scottish and Irish Joint-Stock Companies to 1720*. 3 vols. Cambridge: Univ. Press, 1910–12.
Secord, Arthur Wells. *Robert Drury's Journal and Other Studies*. Urbana: Univ of Illinois Press, 1961.
——. *Studies in the Narrative Method of Defoe*. Univ. of Illinois Studies in Language and Literature, Vol. IX, no. 1 (Feb. 1924). Urbana: Univ. of Illinois Press, 1924.
Shinagel, Michael. *Daniel Defoe and Middle-Class Gentility*. Cambridge, Mass.: Harvard Univ. Press, 1968.
Smithers, Peter. *The Life of Joseph Addison*. Oxford: Clarendon Press, 1968.
Somerville, Dorothy H. *The King of Hearts: Charles Talbot, Duke of Shrewsbury*. London: Allen, 1962.
Spearman, Diana. *The Novel and Society*. London: Routledge and Kegan Paul, 1966.
Starr, G. A. *Defoe and Casuistry*. Princeton: Princeton Univ. Press, 1971.
——. *Defoe and Spiritual Autobiography*. Princeton: Princeton Univ. Press, 1965.
Stauffer, Donald A. *The Art of Biography in Eighteenth Century England*. Princeton: Princeton Univ. Press, 1941.
Stebbing, William. *Peterborough*. London: Macmillan, 1890.
Stevens, David Harrison. *Party Politics and English Journalism 1702–1742*, Chicago: Univ of Chicago libraries, private edition, 1916.
Stone, Lawrence. *The Family, Sex and Marriage in England 1500–1800*. London: Weidenfeld & Nicholson, 1977.
Sutherland, James. *Daniel Defoe: A Critical Study*. Cambridge, Mass.: Harvard Univ. Press, 1971.
——. *Defoe*. 2nd ed. London: Methuen, 1950.
——. *On English Prose*. Toronto: Univ. of Toronto Press, 1977.
Tawney, R. H. *Religion and the Rise of Capitalism*. London: John Murray, 1926.
Tillyard, E. M. W. *Epic Strain in the English Novel*. London: Chatto & Windus, 1958.
Torcy, Jean Baptiste Colbert, marquis de. *Mémoires de Monsieur de Torcy*. 3 vols. London: Nourse et Vaillant, 1757.
Trent, William P. *Daniel Defoe, How to Know Him*. Indianapolis: Bobbs-Merrill Co., 1916.
Trevelyan, G. M. *England under Queen Anne*. Vol. I: *Blenheim*; Vol. II: *Ramillies and the Union with Scotland*; Vol. III: *The Peace and the Protestant Succession*. 3 vols. London: Longmans, Green, 1930–34.
——. *The English Revolution 1688–1689*. Galaxy Books. New York: Oxford Univ. Press, 1965.
Unwin, George, ed. *Finance and Trade under Edward III*. New York: Kelley, 1962.
Viner, Jacob. *Studies in the Theory of International Trade*. New York: Harper, 1937.
Watt, Ian. *The Rise of the Novel*. London: Chatto & Windus, 1957.
Williams, Basil. *The Whig Supremacy 1714–1760*. Oxford: Clarendon Press, 1939.
Zimmerman, Everett. *Defoe and the Novel*. Berkeley: Univ. of California Press, 1975.
Zweig, Paul. *The Adventurer*. New York: Basic Books, 1974.

SECONDARY SOURCES: ARTICLES

Alkon, Paul K. "Defoe's Argument in *The Shortest Way with the Dissenters*". *Modern Philology*, 73 (1976), S12–S23.

Baine, Rodney M. "Chalmers' First Bibliography of Daniel Defoe". *Texas Studies in Literature and Language*, 10 (1969), 547–68.

——. "Daniel Defoe and Captain Carleton's *Memoirs of an English Officer*", *Texas Studies in Literature and Language*, 13 (1972), 613–27.

——. "The Evidence from Defoe's Title Pages". *Studies in Bibliography*, 25 (1970), 158–91.

Beckworth, Frank. "Desmaizeaux's 'Lethe' ". *Times Literary Supplement*, 18 April, 1935, p. 257.

Boyce, Benjamin. "The Question of Emotion in Defoe". *Studies in Philology*, 50 (1953), 45–58.

——. "*The Shortest Way*: Characteristic Defoe Fiction". In *Quick Springs of Sense*. Ed. Larry S. Champion. Athens: Univ. of Georgia Press, 1974.

Brown, Homer. "The Displaced Self in the Novels of Daniel Defoe". *Essays in Literary History*, 38 (1971), 562–90.

Cook, Richard I. " 'Mr. *Examiner*' and 'Mr. *Review*': The Tory Apologetics of Swift and Defoe". *Huntington Library Quarterly*, 29 (1966), 127–46.

Davies, K. G. "Joint-Stock Investment in the Later Seventeenth Century". Vol. II of *Essays in Economic History*. Ed. E. M. Carus-Wilson. 3 vols. London: E. Arnold, 1954– 62.

Davis, Ralph. "English Foreign Trade, 1660–1700". Vol. II of *Essays in Economic History*. Ed. E. M. Carus-Wilson. 3 vols. London: E. Arnold, 1954–62.

Everitt, Alan. "Social Mobility in Early Modern England". *Past and Present*, 33 (April 1966), 56–73.

Fisher, F. J. "Commercial Trends and Policy in Sixteenth-Century England". Vol. I of *Essays in Economic History*. Ed. E. M. Carus-Wilson. 3 vols. London: E. Arnold, 1954–62.

——. "The Development of London as a Centre of Conspicuous Consumption in the Sixteenth and Seventeenth Centuries". Vol. II of *Essays in Economic History*. Ed. E. M. Carus-Wilson. 3 vols. London: E. Arnold, 1954–62.

Hill, B. W. "The Change of Government and the 'Loss of the City', 1710–1711." *Economic History Review*. 24 (1971), 395–413.

Hinton, R. W. K. "The Mercantile System in the Time of Thomas Mun". *Economic History Review*, 7 (1955), 277–90.

Holmes, Geoffrey. "The Electorate and the National Will in the First Age of Party". Univ. of Lancaster inaugural lecture. 26 November, 1975.

——. "Gregory King and the Social Structure of Pre-Industrial England". *Transactions of the Royal Historical Society*, 5th ser. (1977), 41–68.

——. "The Sacheverell Riots: The Crowd and the Church in Early Eighteenth-Century London". *Past and Present*, 72 (1976), 55–85.

Howard, William J., C. S. B. "Truth Preserves Her Shape: An Unexplored Influence on Defoe's Prose Style". *Philological Quarterly*, 47 (1968), 193–205.

John, A. H. "Aspects of English Economic Growth in the First Half of the Eighteenth Century". Vol. II of *Essays in Economic History*. Ed. E. M. Carus-Wilson. 3 vols. London: E. Arnold, 1954–62.

Joslin, D. M. "London Private Bankers, 1720–1785". Vol. II of *Essays in Economic History*. Ed. E. M. Carus-Wilson. 3 vols. London: E. Arnold, 1954–62.

Kenyon, J. P. "The Revolution of 1688: Resistance and Contract". In *Historical Perspectives*. Ed. Neil McKendrick. London: Europa, 1974.

Kestner, Joseph. "Defoe and Mme de la Fayette: *Roxana* and *La Princesse de Monpensieur*". *Papers on Language and Literature*, 8 (1972), 297–301.

Leranbaum, Miriam. "An Irony Not Unusual: Defoe's *Shortest Way with the Dissenters*". *Huntington Library Quarterly*, 37 (1974), 227–50.

Levett, A. E. "Daniel Defoe". In *Social and Political Ideas of Some English Thinkers of the Augustan Age*. Ed. F. J. C. Hearnshaw. London: G. G. Harrap, 1928.

MacLeod, Henry Dunning. "Banking in England". Vol. II of *A History of Banking in All the Leading Nations*. Ed. W. Dodsworth. 4 vols. New York: Journal of Commerce and Commercial Bulletin, 1896.

Maxfield, Ezra Kempton. "Daniel Defoe and the Quakers". *Publications of the Modern Language Association*, 47 (1932), 179–90.

McInnes, Angus. "The Political Ideas of Robert Harley". *History*, 50 (1965), 309–22.

Moore, John Robert. "The Canon of Defoe's Writings".

——. "The Character of Daniel Defoe". *Review of English Studies*, 14 (1938), 68–71.

——. "Defoe's Hand in *A Journal of the Earl of Marr's Proceedings* (1716)". *Huntington Library Quarterly*, 17 (1954), 209–28.

——. "Defoe in the Pillory: A New Interpretation". *Defoe in the Pillory and Other Studies*. Indiana Univ. Humanities Series, No. 1. Bloomington: Indiana Univ. 1939.

——. "Defoe's Religious Sect". *Review of English Studies*, 17 (1941), 461–67.

——. "Milton among the Augustans: The Infernal Council". *Studies in Philology*, 48 (1951), 15–25.

Novak, Maximillian E. "Conscious Irony in *Moll Flanders*". *College English*, 26 (1964), 198–204.

——. "Defoe's *Shortest Way with the Dissenters*: Hoax, Parody, Paradox, Fiction, Irony, and Satire". *Modern Language Quarterly*, 27 (1966), 402–17.

——. "Defoe's Theory of Fiction". *Studies in Philology*, 61 (1964), 650–668.

—— and Davis, Herbert J. *The Uses of Irony: Papers on Defoe and Swift Read at a Clark Library Seminar*. William Andrews Clark Memorial Library. Los Angeles: Univ. of California Press, 1966.

Parnell, Arthur. "Dean Swift and the *Memoirs of Captain Carleton*". *English Historical Review*, 6 (1891), 97–151.

Payne, William L. "Defoe in the Pamphlets". *Philological Quarterly*, 52 (1973), 85–96.

Plumb, J. H. "The Growth of the Electorate in England from 1600 to 1715". *Past and Present*, 45 (1969), 90–116.

Postan, M. M. "The Rise of a Money Economy". Vol. I of *Essays in Economic History*. Ed. E. M. Carus-Wilson. 3 vols. London: E. Arnold, 1954–62.

Poston, Lawrence, III. "Defoe and the Peace Campaign, 1710–1713: A Reconsideration". *Huntington Library Quarterly*, 27 (1963), 1–20.

Priestly, Margaret, "Anglo-French Trade and the 'Unfavourable Balance' Controversy, 1660–1685". *Economic History Review*, 4 (1951), 36–52.

Ransome, Mary. "The Press in the General Election of 1710". *Cambridge Historical Journal*, 6 (1939), 209–21.

Rogers, Pat. "The Authorship of *Four Letters to a Friend in North Britain* and Other Pamphlets Attributed to Robert Walpole". *Bulletin of the Institute of Historical Research*, 44 (November 1971), 229–38.

Schonhorn, Manuel. "Defoe: The Literature of Politics and the Politics of

Some Fictions". In *English Literature in the Age of Disguise*. Ed. Maximillian E. Novak. Berkeley: Univ. of California Press, 1978.

Smith, A. L. "English Political Philosophy in the Seventeenth and Eighteenth Centuries". Vol. VI of *The Cambridge Modern History*. Ed. A. W. Ward, G. W. Prothero, and Stanley Leathes. 13 vols. Cambridge: Univ. Press, 1909.

Snyder, Henry L. "Arthur Maynwaring and the Whig Press, 1710–1712". In *Literatur als Kritik des Lebens*. Ed. Rudolf Haas, Heinz-Joachim Müllenbrock, and Claus Uhlig. Heidelberg: Quelle & Meyer, 1977.

——. "The Circulation of Newspapers in the Reign of Queen Anne". *The Library*, 5th ser., 23 (1968), 206–35.

——. "Daniel Defoe, Arthur Maynwaring, Robert Walpole, and Abel Boyer: Some Considerations of Authorship". *Huntington Library Quarterly*, 33 (1970), 133–53.

Speck, W. A. "From Principles to Practice: Swift and Party Politics". In *The World of Jonathan Swift*. Ed. Brian Vickers. Oxford: Blackwell, 1968.

——. "Political Propaganda in Augustan England". *Transactions of the Royal Historical Society*, 5th ser., 22 (1972), 17–32.

Stone, Lawrence. "Literacy and Education in England, 1640–1900". *Past and Present*, 42 (1969), 69–139.

——. "Social Mobility in England, 1500–1700". *Past and Present*, 33 (1966), 16–55.

Straka, Gerald M. "Sixteen Eighty-Eight as the Year One: Eighteenth-Century Attitudes towards the Glorious Revolution". In *Studies in Eighteenth-Century Culture*, vol. I, *The Modernity of the Eighteenth-Century*. Ed. Louis T. Milic. Cleveland: Case Western Reserve Univ., 1971.

Starr, G. A. "Defoe's Prose Style: 1. The Language of Interpretation". *Modern Philology*, 71 (1974), 277–94.

Sutherland James, "The Circulation of Newspapers and Literary Periodicals, 1700–30". *The Library*, 4th Ser., 15 (1934), 110–124.

——. "The Relation of Defoe's Fiction to His Non-Fictional Writings". In *Imagined Worlds*. Ed. Maynard Mack and Ian Gregor. London: Methuen, 1968.

——. Review of Moore's 1960 *Checklist*. *Library*, 17 (1962), 325–25.

——. "Some Aspects of Eighteenth Century Prose". In *Essays on the Eighteenth Century Presented to David Nichol Smith*. Oxford: Clarendon Press, 1945.

Sykes, Norman. "Benjamin Hoadly, Bishop of Bangor". In *Social and Political Ideas of Some English Thinkers of the Augustan Age*. Ed F. J. C. Hearnshaw. London: G. G. Harrap, 1928.

Trevelyan, G. M. "Defoe's England". In *English Social History*. New York: David McKay Company, 1965.

——. "Peterborough and Barcelona, 1705: *Narrative* and *Diary* of Col. John Richards". *Cambridge Historical Journal*, 3 (1931), 253–59.

Van Klaveren. "Fiscalism, Mercantilism and Corruption". *Revisions in Mercantilism*. Ed. D. C. Coleman. London: Methuen, 1969.

Viner, Jacob. "Mercantilist Thought". *International Encyclopaedia of the Social Sciences*. Vol. IV. New York: Macmillan, 1968.

——. "Power Versus Plenty as Objectives of Foreign Policy in the Seventeenth and Eighteenth Centuries". In *The Long View and the Short*. Glencoe: Free Press, 1958.

——. "Satire and Economics in the Augustan Age of Satire". In *The Augustan Milieu*. Ed. H. K. Miller, E. Rothstein, and G. S. Rousseau. Oxford: Clarendon Press, 1970.

Walton, James. "The Romance of Gentility: Defoe's Heroes and Heroines". *Literary Monographs*, 4 (1971), 89–135.
Wilson, Charles. "The Other Face of Mercantilism". In *Revisions in Mercantilism*. Ed. D. C. Coleman. London: Methuen, 1969.